S0-AZX-918

BEYOND THE SAFE ZONE

COLLECTED STORIES OF

ROBERT SILVERBERG

WARNER BOOKS

A Warner Communications Company

For
Henry Kuttner
Cyril Kornbluth
Ted Sturgeon
Phil Dick
Jim Blish

You sure were tough acts to follow, guys.
But I'm doing my best.

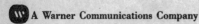

BEYOND THE SAFE ZONE

ROBERT SILVERBERG

Also by Robert Silverberg

Hawksbill Station
To Live Again
A Time of Changes
Tom O'Bedlam
The Stochastic Man*
Tower of Glass*
Son of Man*

Published by
WARNER BOOKS   *forthcoming

CONTENTS

INTRODUCTION

Science fiction is supposed to be about the future, but in fact it has always been deeply rooted in the present, and its nature changes as our perception of the present-day world changes. For example, the science fiction of the dark, gloomy, hopeless 1930s tended to be bright, optimistic stuff, looking forward to a happy world in which technology would lead us out of the economic morass of the Great Depression. The science fiction of the 1940s, when the world was riven by war, was generally built around simple melodramatic conflicts between good and evil, which was the way we were encouraged to perceive the war. In the 1950s, when a period of relative tranquility held sway most of the time and we managed even to keep the fear of atomic doom well under control, a kind of slick, suburban s–f evolved, smoothly written and published in shiny-looking magazines. It dealt with such matters as what it was like to be the hostess at a cocktail party for aliens, and how to program your household robot to serve low-calorie meals.

Then came the 1960s, when that serene suburban world fell apart, and the 1970s, when we were left with the task of putting the lopsided pieces back together. During that crazy time—which began, I think, with the bullet that took John F. Kennedy's life in Dallas in 1963 and is only now beginning to end—science fiction and fantasy reached unparalleled popularity in the United States and most other Western industrial nations. That should not be very surprising. When the world turns incomprehensible, it makes sense to look for answers from some other world. In former times it was sufficient to look no further than the Church: God was there, emanating love and security, offering the hope of passing onward from this vale of tears to the true life beyond. One of the difficulties of twentieth-century life is that most of us have lost the option of using religious faith as a consolation. It may be, that science fiction has evolved into a sort of substitute: a body of texts offering an examination of absolute values and the hypothetical construction of alternative modes of living.

But, as I have already observed, the science fiction of the moment is always rooted in the moment. As the traditional values of society crumbled in the late 1960s, the science fiction written at that time reflected the dislocations and fragmentations that our society was experiencing. New writers, armed with dazzling new techniques, took up the materials of s–f and did strange new things with it. Older writers, formerly content to produce the safe and simple stuff of previous decades, were reborn with sudden experimental zeal. It was a wild and adventurous time, when we were all improvising our way of life from day to day or even from hour to hour, and the science fiction of that period certainly shows it.

These stories were written in those troubled times when there was no longer any safe zone in the world—the years from 1968 to 1974, with a heavy concentration of stories appearing in 1972 and 1973. People wore strange clothes and strange hair, doped themselves with strange drugs, read and wrote strange things. Those manifestations of the times—beginning now to seem quaint to us, and almost unreal to the young—were symptoms, naturally, of deeper malaise and confusion. I have pegged the onset of that time of troubles to the moment of the Kennedy assassination not because Kennedy was himself a peerless leader— he had his flaws, as we now know all too well, and at the time of his death he was finding it almost impossible to find support in Washington for his programs—but because he was a perfect symbol of energy and youth and the promise of the future. When he was struck down, it seemed to me and to a great many others that this shining promise had been forfeited and that the common-wealth itself had been ripped apart. And so it was. I think we would probably have had the troubles that followed even if

Kennedy had lived, just as we would have had World War One eventually even if the archduke Franz Ferdinand had not been assassinated at Sarajevo; but in each case the murder proved to be a historical catalyst.

After Kennedy came new and more foolish leaders who mired us in a dismal and hopeless war against which the nation's young rebelled, and everything fell into chaos. Two consecutive presidents were overthrown and driven from office—the result of popular outcry against their philosophies and methods. On all levels of society, desperate new styles of behavior reflected the desperation within. We slid into a widespread and catastrophic breakdown of society, the effects of which may only now be beginning to subside. The upheaval brought us into blunt confrontation with the future, and what we saw—energy crises, uncontrollable inflation, free-floating terrorism, the unrelenting hostility of the former colonial nations, the threat of atomic destruction from, perhaps, some randomly self-appointed enemy—terrified us into becoming a nation of science fiction fans, seeking for answers in the literature of tomorrow.

Things are quieter now, though no less perilous. The disturbing, fragmented s–f of the last decade has given way to the bland, comforting, predictable fantasies of today, in which benevolent wizards hold out the hope that the Staff of Wisdom will ultimately return to the hands of the High King and all will be right in the world. The stories in this book are, by and large, not like that. The world that they sprang from was the troubled, bewildering, dangerous, and very exciting world of those strange years when the barriers were down and the future was rushing into the present with the force of a river unleashed. But of course I think they speak to our times, too, and that most of them will remain valid as we stagger onward toward the brave new world of the (astonishingly close) twenty-first century. I am not one of those who believes that all is lost and the end is nigh. Like William Faulkner, I do think we will somehow endure and even prevail against increasingly stiff odds.

A great many strange and dizzying things happen to the characters in these twenty-seven stories, and the reader who makes the journey from beginning to end of all twenty-seven will be taken on many a curious trip, as was their author during the years when they were being written. But if there is any underlying message, it is the one that is stated most explicitly at the very end of the story that I have chosen to place at the end of the entire collection:

> "These are darker times than most, Leaf."
> "Perhaps."
> "These are evil times. The end of all things approaches."
> Leaf smiled. "Let it come. These are the times we were meant to live in, and no asking why, and no use longing for easier times. Pain ends when acceptance begins. This is what we have now. We make the best of it. This is the road we travel. Day by day we lose what was never ours, day by day we slip closer to the All-Is-One, and nothing matters, Shadow, nothing except learning to accept what comes."

—Robert Silverberg
Oakland, California
June, 1985

CAPRICORN GAMES

NIKKI STEPPED INTO the conical field of the ultrasonic cleanser, wriggling so that the unheard droning out of the machine's stubby snout could more effectively shear her skin of dead epidermal tissue, globules of dried sweat, dabs of yesterday's scents, and other debris; after three minutes she emerged clean, bouncy, ready for the party. She programmed her party outfit: green buskins, lemon-yellow tunic of gauzy film, pale orange cape soft as a clam's mantle, and nothing underneath but Nikki—smooth, glistening, satiny Nikki. Her body was tuned and fit. The party was in her honor, though she was the only one who knew that. Today was her birthday, the seventh of January, 1999: twenty-four years old, no sign yet of bodily decay. Old Steiner had gathered an extraordinary assortment of guests: he promised to display a reader of minds, a billionaire, an authentic Byzantine duke, an Arab rabbi, a man who had married his own daughter, and other marvels. All of these, of course, subordinate to the true guest of honor, the evening's prize, the real birthday boy, the lion of the season—the celebrated Nicholson, who had lived a thousand years and who said he could help others to do the same. Nikki . . . Nicholson. Happy assonance, portending close harmony. You will show me, dear Nicholson, how I can live forever and never grow old. A cozy soothing idea.

The sky beyond the sleek curve of her window was black, snow-dappled; she imagined she could hear the rusty howl of the wind and feel the sway of the frost-gripped building, ninety stories high. This was the worst winter she had ever known. Snow fell almost every day, a planetary snow, a global shiver, not even sparing the tropics. Ice hard as iron bands bound the streets of New York. Walls were slippery, the air had a cutting edge. Tonight Jupiter gleamed fiercely in the blackness like a diamond in a raven's forehead. Thank God she didn't have to go outside. She could wait out the winter within this tower. The mail came by pneumatic tube. The penthouse restaurant fed her. She had friends on a dozen floors. The building was a world, warm, snug. Let it snow. Let the sour gales come. Nikki checked herself in the all-around mirror: very nice, very very nice. Sweet filmy yellow folds. Hint of thigh, hint of breasts. More than a hint when there's a light-source behind her. She glowed. Fluffed her short glossy black hair. Dab of scent. Everyone loved her. Beauty is a magnet: repels some, attracts many, leaves no one unmoved. It was nine o'clock.

"Upstairs," she said to the elevator. "Steiner's place."

"Eighty-eighth floor," the elevator said.

"I know that. You're so sweet."

Music in the hallway: Mozart, crystalline and sinuous. The door to Steiner's apartment was a half-barrel of chromed steel, like the entrance to a bank vault. Nikki smiled into the scanner. The barrel revolved. Steiner held his hands like cups, centimeters from her chest, by way of greeting. "Beautiful," he murmured.

"So glad you asked me to come."

"Practically everybody's here already. It's a wonderful party, love."

She kissed his shaggy cheek. In October they had met in the elevator. He was past sixty and looked less than forty. When she touched his body she perceived it as an object encased in milky ice, like a mammoth fresh out of the Siberian permafrost. They had been lovers for two weeks. Autumn had given way to winter and Nikki had passed out of his life, but he had kept his word about the parties: here she was, invited.

"Alexius Ducas," said a short, wide man with a dense black beard, parted in the middle. He bowed. A good flourish. Steiner evaporated and she was in the keeping of the Byzantine duke. He maneuvered her at once across the thick white carpet to a place where clusters of spotlights, sprouting like angry fungi from the wall, revealed the contours of her body. Others turned to look. Duke Alexius favored her with a heavy stare. But she felt no excitement. Byzantium had been over for a long time. He brought her a goblet of chilled green wine and said, "Are you ever in the Aegean Sea? My family has its ancestral castle on an island eighteen kilometers east of—"

"Excuse me, but which is the man named Nicholson?"

"Nicholson is merely the name he currently uses. He claims to have had a shop in Constantinople during the reign of my ancestor the Basileus Manuel Comnenus." A patronizing click, tongue on teeth. "Only a shopkeeper." The Byzantine eyes sparkled ferociously. "How beautiful you are!"

"Which one is he?"

"There. By the couch."

Nikki saw only a wall of backs. She tilted to the left and peered. No use. She would get to him later. Alexius Ducas continued to offer her his body with his eyes. She whispered languidly, "Tell me all about Byzantium."

He got as far as Constantine the Great before he bored her. She finished her wine, and, coyly extending the glass, persuaded a smooth young man passing by to refill it for her. The Byzantine looked sad. "The empire then was divided," he said, "among—"

"This is my birthday," she announced.

"Yours also? My congratulations. Are you as old as—"

"Not nearly. Not by half. I won't even be five hundred for some time," she said, and turned to take her glass. The smooth young man did not wait to be captured. The party engulfed him like an avalanche. Sixty, eighty guests, all in motion. The draperies were pulled back, revealing the full fury of the snowstorm. No one was watching it. Steiner's apartment was like a movie set: great porcelain garden stools, Ming or even Sung; walls painted with flat sheets of bronze and scarlet; pre-Columbian artifacts in spotlit niches; sculptures like aluminum spiderwebs; Dürer etchings—the loot of the ages. Squat shaven-headed servants, Mayans or Khmers or perhaps Olmecs, circulated impassively offering trays of delicacies: caviar, sea urchins, bits of roasted meat, tiny sausages, burritos in startling chili sauce. Hands darted unceasingly from trays to lips. This was a gathering of life-eaters, world-swallowers. Duke Alexius was stroking her arm. "I will leave at midnight," he said gently. "It would be a delight if you left with me."

"I have other plans," she told him.

"Even so." He bowed courteously, outwardly undisappointed.

"Possibly another time. My card?" It appeared as if by magic in his hand: a sliver of tawny cardboard, elaborately engraved. She put it in her purse and the room swallowed him. Instantly a big, wild-eyed man took his place before her. "You've never heard of me," he began.

"Is that a boast or an apology?"

"I'm quite ordinary. I work for Steiner. He thought it would be amusing to invite me to one of his parties."

"What do you do?"

"Invoices and debarkations. Isn't this an amazing place?"

"What's your sign?" Nikki asked him.

"Libra."

"I'm Capricorn. Tonight's my birthday as well as *his*. If you're really Libra, you're wasting your time with me. Do you have a name?"

"Martin Bliss."

"Nikki."

"There isn't any Mrs. Bliss, hah-hah."

Nikki licked her lips. "I'm hungry. Would you get me some canapés?"

She was gone as soon as he moved toward the food. Circum-navigating the long room—past the string quintet, past the bartender's throne, past the window—until she had a good view of the man called Nicholson. He didn't disappoint her. He was slender, supple, not tall, strong in the shoulders. A man of presence and authority. She wanted to put her lips to him and suck immortality out. His head was a flat triangle, brutal cheek-bones, thin lips, dark mat of curly hair, no beard, no mustache. His eyes were keen, electric, intolerably wise. He must have seen everything twice, at the very least. Nikki had read his book. Everyone had. He had been a king, a lama, a slave trader, a slave. Always taking pains to conceal his implausible longevity, now offering his terrible secret freely to the members of the Book-of-the-Month Club. Why had he chosen to surface and reveal himself? Because this is the necessary moment of revela-tion, he had said. When he must stand forth as what he is, so that he might impart his gift to others, lest he lose it. Lest he lose it. At the stroke of the new century he must share his prize of life. A dozen people surrounded him, catching his glow. He glanced through a palisade of shoulders and locked his eyes on hers; Nikki felt impaled, exalted, chosen. Warmth spread through her loins like a river of molten tungsten, like a stream of hot honey. She started to go to him. A corpse got in her way. Death's-head, parchment skin, nightmare eyes. A scaly hand brushed her bare biceps. A frightful eroded voice croaked, "How old do you think I am?"

"Oh, God!"

"How old?"

"Two thousand?"

"I'm fifty-eight. I won't live to see fifty-nine. Here, smoke one of these."

With trembling hands he offered her a tiny ivory tube. There was a Gothic monogram near one end—FXB—and a translucent green capsule at the other. She pressed the capsule, and a flickering blue flame sprouted. She inhaled. "What is it?" she asked.

"My own mixture. Soma Number Five. You like it?"

"I'm smeared," she said. "Absolutely smeared. Oh, God!" The walls were flowing. The snow had turned to tinfoil. An instant hit. The corpse had a golden halo. Dollar signs rose into view like stigmata on his furrowed forehead. She heard the crash of the surf, the roar of the waves. The deck was heaving. The masts were cracking. *Woman overboard!* she cried, and heard her inaudible voice disappearing down a tunnel of echoes, boingg boingg boingg. She clutched at his frail wrists. "You bastard, what did you *do* to me?"

"I'm Francis Xavier Byrne."

Oh. The billionaire. Byrne Industries, the great conglomerate. Steiner had promised her a billionaire tonight.

"Are you going to die soon?" she asked.

"No later than Easter. Money can't help me now. I'm a walking metastasis." He opened his ruffled shirt. Something bright and metallic, like chain mail, covered his chest. "Life-support system," he confided. "It operates me. Take it off for half an hour and I'd be finished. Are you a Capricorn?"

"How did you know?"

"I may be dying, but I'm not stupid. You have the Capricorn gleam in your eyes. What am I?"

She hesitated. His eyes were gleaming too. Self-made man, fantastic business sense, energy, arrogance. Capricorn, of course. No, too easy. "Leo," she said.

"No. Try again." He pressed another monogrammed tube into

her hand and strode away. She hadn't yet come down from the last one, although the most flamboyant effects had ebbed. Party guests swirled and flowed around her. She no longer could see Nicholson. The snow seemed to be turning to hail, little hard particles spattering the vast windows and leaving white abraded tracks: or were her perceptions merely sharper? The roar of conversation seemed to rise and fall as if someone were adjusting a volume control. The lights fluctuated in a counterpointed rhythm. She felt dizzy. A tray of golden cocktails went past her and she hissed, "Where's the bathroom?"

Down the hall. Five strangers clustered outside it, talking in scaly whispers. She floated through them, grabbed the sink's cold edge, thrust her face to the oval concave mirror. A death's-head. Parchment skin, nightmare eyes. No! No! She blinked and her own features reappeared. Shivering, she made an effort to pull herself together. The medicine cabinet held a tempting collection of drugs, Steiner's all-purpose remedies. Without looking at labels Nikki seized a handful of vials and gobbled pills at random. A flat red one, a tapering green one, a succulent yellow gelatin capsule. Maybe headache remedies, maybe hallucinogens. Who knows, who cares? We Capricorns are not always as cautious as you think.

Someone knocked at the bathroom door. She answered and found the bland, hopeful face of Martin Bliss hovering near the ceiling. Eyes protruding faintly, cheeks florid. "They said you were sick. Can I do anything for you?" So kind, so sweet. She touched his arm, grazed his cheek with her lips. Beyond him in the hall stood a broad-bodied man with close-cropped blond hair, glacial blue eyes, a plump perfect face. His smile was intense and brilliant. "That's easy," he said. "Capricorn."

"You can guess my—" She stopped, stunned. "Sign?" she finished, voice very small. "How did you do that? Oh."

"Yes. I'm that one."

She felt more than naked, stripped down to the ganglia, to the synapses. "What's the trick?"

"No trick. I listen. I hear."

"You hear people thinking?"

"More or less. Do you think it's a party game?" He was beautiful but terrifying, like a Samurai sword in motion. She wanted him but she didn't dare. He's got my number, she thought. I would never have any secrets from him. He said sadly,

"I don't mind that. I know I frighten a lot of people. Some don't care."

"What's your name?"

"Tom," he said. "Hello, Nikki."

"I feel very sorry for you."

"Not really. You can kid yourself if you need to. But you can't kid me. Anyway, you don't sleep with men you feel sorry for."

"I don't sleep with you."

"You will," he said.

"I thought you were just a mind-reader. They didn't tell me you did prophecies too."

He leaned close and smiled. The smile demolished her. She had to fight to keep from falling. "I've got your number, all right," he said in a low, harsh voice. "I'll call you next Tuesday." As he walked away he said, "You're wrong. I'm a Virgo. Believe it or not."

Nikki returned, numb, to the living room. "... the figure of the mandala," Nicholson was saying. His voice was dark, focused, a pure basso cantante. "The essential thing that every mandala has is a center—the place where everything is born, the eye of God's mind, the heart of darkness and of light, the core of the storm. All right. You must move toward the center, find the vortex at the boundary of Yang and Yin, place yourself right at the mandala's midpoint. *Center yourself.* Do you follow the metaphor? Center yourself at *now,* the eternal *now.* To move off-center is to move forward toward death, backward toward birth, always the fatal polar swings. But if you're capable of positioning yourself constantly at the focus of the mandala, right on center, you have access to the fountain of renewal, you become an organism capable of constant self-healing, constant self-replenishment, constant expansion into regions beyond self. Do you follow? The power of . . ."

Steiner, at her elbow, said tenderly, "How beautiful you are in the first moments of erotic fixation."

"It's a marvelous party."

"Are you meeting interesting people?"

"Is there any other kind?" she asked.

Nicholson abruptly detached himself from the circle of his audience and strode across the room, alone, in a quick decisive knight's move toward the bar. Nikki, hurrying to intercept him, collided with a shaven-headed tray-bearing servant. The tray slid smoothly from the man's thick fingertips and launched itself into the air like a spinning shield; a rainfall of skewered meat in an oily green curry sauce spattered the white carpet. The servant was utterly motionless. He stood frozen like some sort of Mexican stone idol, thick-necked, flat-nosed, for a long painful moment; then he turned his head slowly to the left and regretfully contemplated his rigid outspread hand, shorn of its tray; finally he swung his head toward Nikki, and his normally expressionless granite face took on for a quick flickering instant a look of total hatred, a coruscating emanation of contempt and disgust that faded immediately. He laughed: hu-hu-hu, a neighing snicker. His superiority was overwhelming. Nikki floundered in quicksands of humiliation. Hastily she escaped, a zig and a zag, around the tumbled goodies and across to the bar. Nicholson, still by himself. Her face went crimson. She felt short of breath. Hunting for words, tongue all thumbs. Finally, in a catapulting blurt: "Happy birthday!"

"Thank you," he said solemnly.

"Are you enjoying your birthday?"

"Very much."

"I'm amazed that they don't bore you. I mean, having had so many of them."

"I don't bore easily." He was awesomely calm, drawing on some bottomless reservoir of patience. He gave her a look that was at the same time warm and impersonal. "I find everything interesting," he said.

"That's curious. I said more or less the same thing to Steiner just a few minutes ago. You know, it's my birthday too."

"Really?"

"The seventh of January, 1975 for me."

"Hello, 1975. I'm—" He laughed. "It sounds absolutely absurd, doesn't it?"

"The seventh of January, 982."

"You've been doing your homework."

"I've read your book," she said. "Can I make a silly remark? My God, you don't *look* like you're a thousand and seventeen years old."

"How should I look?"

"More like him," she said, indicating Francis Xavier Byrne.

Nicholson chuckled. She wondered if he liked her. Maybe. Maybe. Nikki risked some eye contact. He was hardly a centimeter taller than she was, which made it a terrifyingly intimate experience. He regarded her steadily, centeredly; she imagined a throbbing mandala surrounding him, luminous turquoise spokes emanating from his heart, radiant red and green spiderweb rings connecting them. Reaching from her loins, she threw a loop of desire around him. Her eyes were explicit. His were veiled. She felt him calmly retreating. Take me inside, she pleaded, take me to one of the back rooms. Pour life into me. She said, "How will you choose the people you're going to instruct in the secret?"

"Intuitively."

"Refusing anybody who asks directly, of course."

"Refusing anybody who asks."

"Did *you* ask?"

"You said you read my book."

"Oh. Yes. I remember—you didn't know what was happening, you didn't understand anything until it was over."

"I was a simple lad," he said. "That was a long time ago." His eyes were alive again. He's drawn to me. He sees that I'm his kind, that I deserve him. Capricorn, Capricorn, Capricorn, you and me, he-goat and she-goat. Play my game, Cap. "How are you named?" he asked.

"Nikki."

"A beautiful name. A beautiful woman."

The emptiness of the compliments devastated her. She realized she had arrived with mysterious suddenness at a necessary point of tactical withdrawal; retreat was obligatory, lest she push too hard and destroy the tenuous contact so tensely established. She thanked him with a glance and gracefully slipped away, pivoting toward Martin Bliss, slipping her arm through his. Bliss quivered at the gesture, glowed, leaped into a higher energy state. She resonated to his vibrations, going up and up. She was at the heart of the party, the center of the mandala: standing flat-footed, legs slightly apart, making her body a polar axis, with lines of force zooming up out of the earth, up through the basement levels of this building, up the eighty-eight stories of it, up through her sex, her heart, her head. This is how it must feel, she thought, when undyingness is conferred on you. A moment of spontaneous grace, the kindling of an inner light. She looked love at poor sappy Bliss. You dear heart, you dumb walking pun. The string quintet made molten sounds. "What is that?" she asked. "Brahms?" Bliss offered to find out. Alone, she was vulnerable to Francis

Xavier Byrne, who brought her down with a single cadaverous glance.

"Have you guessed it yet?" he asked. "The sign."

She stared through his ragged cancerous body, blazing with decomposition. "Scorpio," she told him hoarsely.

"Right! Right!" He pulled a pendant from his breast and draped its golden chain over her head. "For you," he rasped, and fled. She fondled it. A smooth green stone. Jade? Emerald? Lightly engraved on its domed face was the looped cross, the crux ansata. Beautiful. The gift of life, from the dying man. She waved fondly to him across a forest of heads and winked. Bliss returned.

"They're playing something by Schönberg," he reported. "*Verklärte Nacht.*"

"How lovely." She flipped the pendant and let it fall back against her breasts. "Do you like it?"

"I'm sure you didn't have it a moment ago."

"It sprouted," she told him. She felt high, but not as high as she had been just after leaving Nicholson. That sense of herself as focal point had departed. The party seemed chaotic. Couples were forming, dissolving, reforming; shadowy figures were stealing away in twos and threes toward the bedrooms; the servants were more obsessively thrusting their trays of drinks and snacks at the remaining guests; the hail had reverted to snow, and feathery masses silently struck the windows, sticking there, revealing their glistening mandalic structures for painfully brief moments before they deliquesced. Nikki struggled to regain her centered position. She indulged in a cheering fantasy: Nicholson coming to her, formally touching her cheek, telling her, "You will be one of the elect." In less than twelve months the time would come for him to gather with his seven still unnamed disciples to see in the new century, and he would take their hands into his hands, he would pump the vitality of the undying into their bodies, sharing with them the secret that had been shared with him a thousand years ago. Who? Who? Who? Me. Me. Me. But where had Nicholson gone? His aura, his glow, that cone of imaginary light that had appeared to surround him—nowhere.

A man in a lacquered orange wig began furiously to quarrel, almost under Nikki's nose, with a much younger woman wearing festoons of bioluminescent pearls. Man and wife, evidently. They were both sharp-featured, with glossy, protuberant eyes, rigid faces, cheek muscles working intensely. Live together long enough, come to look alike. Their dispute had a stale, ritualistic flavor, as though they had staged it all too many times before. They were explaining to each other the events that had caused the quarrel, interpreting them, recapitulating them, shading them, justifying, attacking, defending—you said this because and that led me to respond that way because . . . no, on the contrary, I said this because you said that—all of it in a quiet screechy tone, sickening, agonizing, pure death.

"He's her biological father," a man next to Nikki said. "She was one of the first of the in vitro babies, and he was the donor, and five years ago he tracked her down and married her. A loophole in the law." Five years? They sounded as if they had been married for fifty. Walls of pain and boredom encased them. Only their eyes were alive. Nikki found it impossible to imagine those two in bed, bodies entwined in the act of love. Act of love, she thought, and laughed. Where was Nicholson? Duke Alexius, flushed and sweat-beaded, bowed to her. "I will leave soon," he announced, and she received the announcement gravely but without reacting, as though he had merely commented on the fluctuations of the storm, or had spoken in Greek. He bowed again and went away. Nicholson? Nicholson? She grew calm again, finding her center. He will come to me when he is ready. There was contact between us, and it was real and good.

Bliss, beside her, gestured and said, "A rabbi of Syrian birth, formerly Muslim, highly regarded among Jewish theologians."

She nodded but didn't look.

"An astronaut just back from Mars. I've never seen anyone's skin tanned quite that color."

The astronaut held no interest for her. She worked at kicking herself back into high. The party was approaching a climactic moment, she felt, a time when commitments were being made and decisions taken. The clink of ice in glasses, the foggy vapors of psychedelic inhalants, the press of warm flesh all about her—she was wired into everything, she was alive and receptive, she was entering into the twitching hour, the hour of galvanic jerks. She grew wild and reckless. Impulsively she kissed Bliss, straining on tiptoes, jabbing her tongue deep into his startled mouth. Then she broke free. Someone was playing with the lights: they grew redder, then gained force and zoomed to blue-white ferocity. Far across the room a crowd was surging and billowing around the fallen figure of Francis Xavier Byrne, slumped loose-jointedly against the base of the bar. His eyes were open but glassy. Nicholson crouched over him, reaching into his shirt, making delicate adjustments of the controls of the chain mail beneath. "It's all right," Steiner was saying. "Give him some air. It's all right!" Confusion. Hubbub. A torrent of tangled input.

"—they say there's been a permanent change in the weather patterns. Colder winters from now on, because of accumulations of dust in the atmosphere that screen the sun's rays. Until we freeze altogether by around the year 2200—"

"—but the carbon dioxide is supposed to start a greenhouse effect that's causing *warmer* weather, I thought, and—"

"—the proposal to generate electric power from—"

"—the San Andreas fault—"

"—financed by debentures convertible into—"

"—capsules of botulism toxin—"

"—to be distributed at a ratio of one per thousand families, throughout Greenland and the Kamchatka Metropolitan Area—"

"—in the sixteenth century, when you could actually hope to found your own empire in some unknown part of the—"

"—unresolved conflicts of Capricorn personality—"

"—intense concentration and meditation upon the completed mandala so that the contents of the work are transferred to and identified with the mind and body of the beholder. I mean, technically what occurs is the reabsorption of cosmic forces. In the process of construction these forces—"

"—butterflies, which are no longer to be found anywhere in—"

"—were projected out from the chaos of the unconscious; in the process of absorption, the powers are drawn back in again—"

"—reflecting transformations of the DNA in the light-collecting organ, which—"

"—the snow—"

"—a thousand years, can you imagine that? And—"

"—her body—"

"—formerly a toad—"

"—just back from Mars, and there's that *look* in his eye—"

"Hold me," Nikki said. "Just hold me. I'm very dizzy."

"Would you like a drink?"

"Just hold me." She pressed against cool sweet-smelling fabric. His chest unyielding beneath it. Steiner. Very male. He steadied her, but only for a moment. Other responsibilities summoned him. When he released her, she swayed. He beckoned to someone else, blond, soft-faced. The mind reader, Tom. Passing her along the chain from man to man.

"You feel better now," the telepath told her.

"Are you positive of that?"

"Very."

"Can you read any mind in the room?" she asked.

He nodded.

"Even *his?*"

Again a nod. "He's the clearest of all. He's been using it so long, all the channels are worn deep."

"Then he really is a thousand years old?"

"You didn't believe it?"

Nikki shrugged. "Sometimes I don't know what I believe."

"He's *old.*"

"You'd be the one to know."

"He's a phenomenon. He's absolutely extraordinary." A pause—quick, stabbing. "Would you like to see into his mind?"

"How can I?"

"I'll patch you right in, if you'd like me to." The glacial eyes flashed sudden mischievous warmth. "Yes?"

"I'm not sure I want to."

"You're very sure. You're curious as hell. Don't kid me. Don't play games, Nikki. You want to see into him."

"Maybe." Grudgingly.

"You do. Believe me, you do. Here. Relax, let your shoulders slump a little, loosen up, make yourself receptive, and I'll establish the link."

"Wait," she said.

But it was too late. The mind reader serenely parted her consciousness like Moses doing the Red Sea and rammed something into her forehead, something thick but insubstantial, a truncheon of fog. She quivered and recoiled. She felt violated. It was like her first time in bed, in that moment when all the fooling around at last was over, the kissing and the nibbling and the stroking, and suddenly there was this object deep inside her body. She had never forgotten that sense of being impaled. But of course it had been not only an intrusion but also a source of

ecstasy. As was this. The object within her was the consciousness
of Nicholson. In wonder she explored its surface, rigid and
weathered, pitted with the myriad ablations of reentry. Ran her
trembling hands over its bronzy roughness. Remained outside it.
Tom, the mind reader, gave her a nudge. Go on, go on. Deeper.
Don't hold back. She folded herself around Nicholson and drifted
into him like ectoplasm seeping into sand. Suddenly she lost her
bearings. The discrete and impermeable boundary marking the
end of her self and the beginning of his became indistinct. It was
impossible to distinguish between her experiences and his, nor
could she separate the pulsations of her nervous system from the
impulses traveling along his. Phantom memories assailed and
engulfed her. She was transformed into a node of pure perception: a steady, cool, isolated eye, surveying and recording.
Images flashed. She was toiling upward along a dazzling snowy
crest, with jagged Himalayan fangs hanging above her in the
white sky and a warm-muzzled yak snuffling wearily at her side.

A platoon of swarthy little men accompanied her, slanty eyes,
heavy coats, thick boots. The stink of rancid butter, the cutting
edge of an impossible wind: and there, gleaming in the sudden
sunlight, a pile of fire-bright yellow plaster with a thousand
winking windows, a building, a lamasery strung along a mountain ridge. The nasal sound of distant horns and trumpets. The
hoarse chanting of lotus-legged monks. What were they chanting?
Om? Om? Om! *Om,* and flies buzzed around her nose, and she
lay hunkered in a flimsy canoe, coursing silently down a midnight river in the heart of Africa, drowning in humidity. Brawny
naked men with purple-black skins crouching close. Sweaty
fronds dangling from flamboyantly excessive shrubbery; the snouts
of crocodiles rising out of the dark water like toothy flowers;
great nauseating orchids blossoming high in the smooth-shanked
trees. And on shore, five white men in Elizabethan costume,
wide-brimmed hats, drooping sweaty collars, lace, fancy buck-
les, curling red beards. Errol Flynn as Sir Francis Drake, blun-
derbuss dangling in crook of arm. The white men laughing,
beckoning, shouting to the men in the canoe. Am I slave or
slavemaster? No answer. Only a blurring and a new vision:
autumn leaves blowing across the open doorways of straw-
thatched huts, shivering oxen crouched in bare stubble-strewn
fields, grim long-mustachioed men with close-cropped hair riding
diagonal courses toward the horizon. Crusaders, are they? Or

warriors of Hungary on their way to meet the dread Mongols? Defenders of the imperiled Anglo-Saxon realm against the Norman invaders? They could be any of these. But always that steady cool eye, always that unmoving consciousness at the center of every scene. *Him*, eternal, all-enduring. And then: the train rolling westward, belching white smoke, the plains unrolling infinityward, the big brown fierce-eyed bison standing in shaggy clumps along the right of way, the man with turbulent shoulder-length hair laughing, slapping a twenty-dollar gold piece on the table. Picking up his rifle—a .50-caliber breech-loading Springfield—he aims casually through the door of the moving train, he squeezes off a shot, another, another. Three shaggy brown corpses beside the tracks, and the train rolls onward, honking raucously.

Her arm and shoulder tingled with the impact of those shots. Then: a fetid waterfront, bales of cloves and peppers and cinnamon, small brown-skinned men in turbans and loincloths arguing under a terrible sun. Tiny irregular silver coins glittering in the palm of her hand. The jabber of some Malabar dialect counterpointed with fluid mocking Portuguese. Do we sail now with Vasco da Gama? Perhaps. And then a gray Teutonic street, windswept, medieval, bleak Lutheran faces scowling from leaded windows. And then the Gobi steppe, with horsemen and campfires and dark tents. And then New York City, unmistakably New York City, with square black automobiles scurrying between the stubby skyscrapers like glossy beetles, a scene out of some silent movie. And then. And then. Everywhere, everything, all times, all places, a discontinuous flow of events but always that clarity of vision, that rock-steady perception, that solid mind at the center, that unshakeable identity, that unchanging self—with whom I am inextricably enmeshed—

There was no "I," there was no "he," there was only the one ever-perceiving point of view. But abruptly she felt a change of focus, a distancing effect, a separation of self and self, so that she was looking at him as he lived his many lives, seeing him from the outside, seeing him plainly changing identities as others might change clothing, growing beards and mustaches, shaving them, cropping his hair, letting his hair grow, adopting new fashions, learning languages, forging documents. She saw him in all his thousand years of guises and subterfuges, saw him real and unified and centered beneath his obligatory camouflages—and saw him seeing her.

Instantly contact broke. She staggered. Arms caught her. She pulled away from the smiling plump-faced blond man, muttering, "What have you done? You didn't tell me you'd show *me* to *him*."

"How else can there be a linkage?" the telepath asked.

"You didn't tell me. You should have told me." Everything was lost. She couldn't bear to be in the same room as Nicholson now. Tom reached for her, but she stumbled past him, stepping on people. They winked up at her. Someone stroked her leg. She forced her way through improbable laocoons, three women and two servants, five men and a tablecloth. A glass door, a gleaming silvery handle: she pushed. Out onto the terrace. The purity of the gale might cleanse her. Behind her, faint gasps, a few shrill screams, annoyed expostulations: "Close that thing!" She slammed it. Alone in the night, eighty-eight stories above street level, she offered herself to the storm. Her filmy tunic shielded her not at all. Snowflakes burned against her breasts. Her nipples hardened and rose like fiery beacons, jutting against the soft fabric. The snow stung her throat, her shoulders, her arms. Far below, the wind churned newly fallen crystals into spiral galaxies. The street was invisible. Thermal confusions brought updrafts that seized the edge of her tunic and whipped it outward from her body. Fierce, cold particles of hair were driven into her bare pale thighs. She stood with her back to the party. Did anyone in there notice her? Would someone think she was contemplating suicide and come rushing gallantly out to save her? Capricorns didn't commit suicide. They might threaten it, yes, they might even tell themselves quite earnestly that they were really going to do it, but it was only a game, only a game. No one came to her. She didn't turn. Gripping the railing, she fought to calm herself.

No use. Not even the bitter air could help. Frost in her eyelashes, snow on her lips. The pendant Byrne had given her blazed between her breasts. The air was white with a throbbing green underglow. It seared her eyes. She was off-center and floundering. She felt herself still reverberating through the centuries, going back and forth across the orbit of Nicholson's interminable life. What year is this? Is it 1386, 1912, 1532, 1779, 1043, 1977, 1235, 1129, 1836? So many centuries. So many lives. And yet always the one true self, changeless, unchangeable.

Gradually the resonances died away. Nicholson's unending epochs no longer filled her mind with terrible noise. She began to shiver, not from fear but merely from cold, and tugged at her moist tunic, trying to shield her nakedness. Melting snow left hot clammy tracks across her breasts and belly. A halo of steam surrounded her. Her heart pounded.

She wondered if what she had experienced had been genuine contact with Nicholson's soul, or rather only some trick of Tom's, a simulation of contact. Was it possible, after all, even for Tom to create a linkage between two non-telepathic minds such as hers and Nicholson's? Maybe Tom had fabricated it all himself, using images borrowed from Nicholson's book.

In that case there might still be hope for her.

A delusion, she knew. A fantasy born of the desperate optimism of the hopeless. But nevertheless—

She found the handle, let herself back into the party. A gust accompanied her, sweeping snow inward. People stared. She was like death arriving at the feast. Doglike, she shook off the searing snowflakes. Her clothes were wet and stuck to her skin; she might as well have been naked. "You poor shivering thing," a woman said. She pulled Nikki into a tight embrace. It was the sharp-faced woman, the bulgy-eyed bottle-born one, bride of her own father. Her hands traveled swiftly over Nikki's body, caressing her breasts, touching her cheek, her forearm, her haunch. "Come inside with me," she crooned. "I'll make you warm." Her lips grazed Nikki's. A playful tongue sought hers.

For a moment, needing the warmth, Nikki gave herself to the embrace. Then she pulled away. "No," she said. "Some other time. Please." Wriggling free, she started across the room. An endless journey. Like crossing the Sahara by pogo stick. Voices, faces, laughter. A dryness in her throat. Then she was in front of Nicholson.

Well. Now or never.

"I have to talk to you," she said.

"Of course." His eyes were merciless. No wrath in them, not even disdain, only an incredible patience more terrifying than anger or scorn. She would not let herself bend before that cool level gaze.

She said, "A few minutes ago, did you have an odd experience, a sense that someone was—well, looking into your mind? I know it sounds foolish, but—?"

"Yes. It happened." So calm. How did he stay that close to his center? That unwavering eye, that uniquely self-contained self, perceiving all: the lamasery, the slave depot, the railroad train, everything, all time gone by, all time to come—how did he manage to be so tranquil? She knew she never could learn such calmness. She knew he knew it. *He has my number, all right.* She found that she was looking at his cheekbones, at his forehead, at his lips. Not into his eyes.

"You have the wrong image of me," she told him.

"It isn't an image," he said. "What I have is you."

"No."

"Face yourself, Nikki. If you can figure out where to look." He laughed. Gently, but she was demolished.

An odd thing, then. She forced herself to stare into his eyes and felt a snapping of awareness from one mode into some other, and he turned into an old man. That mask of changeless early maturity dissolved and she saw the frightening yellowed eyes, the maze of furrows and gullies, the toothless gums, the drooling lips, the hollow throat, the self beneath the face. A thousand years, a thousand years! And every moment of those thousand years was visible. "You're old," she whispered. "You disgust me. I wouldn't want to be like you, not for anything!" She backed away, shaking. "An old, old, old man. All a masquerade!"

He smiled. "Isn't that pathetic?"

"Me or you? *Me or you?*"

He didn't answer. She was bewildered. When she was five paces away from him there came another snapping of awareness, a second changing of phase, and suddenly he was himself again, taut-skinned, erect, appearing to be perhaps thirty-five years old. A globe of silence hung between them. The force of his rejection was withering. She summoned her last strength for a parting glare. *I didn't want you either, friend, not any single part of you.* He saluted cordially. Dismissal.

Martin Bliss, grinning vacantly, stood near the bar. "Let's go," she said savagely. "Take me home!"

"But—"

"It's just a few floors below." She thrust her arm through his. He blinked, shrugged, fell into step.

"I'll call you Tuesday, Nikki," Tom said as they swept past him.

Downstairs, on her home turf, she felt better. In the bedroom they quickly dropped their clothes. His body was pink, hairy, serviceable. She turned the bed on, and it began to murmur and throb. "How old do you think I am?" she asked.

"Twenty-six?" Bliss said vaguely.

"Bastard!" She pulled him down on top of her. Her hands raked his skin. Her thighs parted. Go on. Like an animal, she thought. Like an animal! She was getting older moment by moment, she was dying in his arms.

"You're much better than I expected," she said eventually.

He looked down, baffled, amazed. "You could have chosen anyone at that party. Anyone."

"Almost anyone," she said.

When he was asleep she slipped out of bed. Snow was still falling. She heard the thunk of bullets and the whine of wounded bison. She heard the clangor of swords on shields. She heard lamas chanting: Om, Om, Om. No sleep for her this night, none. The clock was ticking like a bomb. The century was flowing remorselessly toward its finish. She checked her face for wrinkles in the bathroom mirror. Smooth, smooth, all smooth under the blue fluorescent glow. Her eyes looked bloody. Her nipples were still hard. She took a little alabaster jar from one of the bathroom cabinets and three slender red capsules fell out of it, into her palm. Happy birthday, dear Nikki, happy birthday to you. She swallowed all three. Went back to bed. Waited, listening to the slap of snow on glass, for the visions to come and carry her away.

THE DYBBUK OF MAZEL TOV IV

MY GRANDSON DAVID will have his bar mitzvah next spring. No one in our family has undergone that rite in at least three hundred years—certainly not since we Levins settled in Old Israel, the Israel on Earth, soon after the European holocaust. My friend Eliahu asked me not long ago how I feel about David's bar mitzvah, whether the idea of it angers me, whether I see it as a disturbing element. No, I replied, the boy is a Jew, after all—let him have a bar mitzvah if he wants one. These are times of transition and upheaval, as all times are. David is not bound by the attitudes of his ancestors.

"Since when is a Jew not bound by the attitudes of his ancestors?" Eliahu asked.

"You know what I mean," I said.

Indeed he did. We are bound but yet free. If anything governs us out of the past it is the tribal bond itself, not the philosophies of our departed kinsmen. We accept what we choose to accept; nevertheless we remain Jews. I come from a family that has liked to say—especially to gentiles—that we are Jews but not Jewish; that is, we acknowledge and cherish our ancient heritage, but we do not care to entangle ourselves in outmoded rituals and folkways. This is what my forefathers declared, as far back as those secular-minded Levins who three centuries ago fought to win and guard the freedom of the land of Israel. (Old Israel, I mean.) I would say the same here, if there were any gentiles on this world to whom such things had to be explained. But of course in this New Israel in the stars we have only ourselves, no gentiles within a dozen light-years, unless you count our neighbors the Kunivaru as gentiles. (Can creatures that are not human rightly be called gentiles? I'm not sure the term applies. Besides, the Kunivaru now insist that they are Jews. My mind spins. It's an issue of Talmudic complexity, and God knows I'm no Talmudist. Hillel, Akiva, Rashi, help me!) Anyway, come the fifth day of Sivan my son's son will have his bar mitzvah, and I'll play the proud grandpa as pious old Jews have done for six thousand years.

All things are connected. That my grandson would have a bar mitzvah is merely the latest link in a chain of events that goes back to—when? To the day the Kunivaru decided to embrace Judaism? To the day the dybbuk entered Seul the Kunivar? To the day we refugees from Earth discovered the fertile planet that we sometimes call New Israel and sometimes call Mazel Tov IV? To the day of the Final Pogrom on Earth? Reb Yossele the Hasid might say that David's bar mitzvah was determined on the day the Lord God fashioned Adam out of dust. But I think that would be overdoing things.

The day the dybbuk took possession of the body of Seul the Kunivar was probably where it really started. Until then things were relatively uncomplicated here. The Hasidim had their settlement, we Israelis had ours, and the natives, the Kunivaru, had the rest of the planet; and generally we all kept out of one another's way. After the dybbuk everything changed. It happened more than forty years ago, in the first generation after the Landing, on the ninth day of Tishri in the year 6302. I was working in the fields, for Tishri is a harvest month. The day was hot, and I worked swiftly, singing and humming. As I moved down the long rows of cracklepods, tagging those that were ready to be gathered, a Kunivar appeared at the crest of the hill that overlooks our kibbutz. It seemed to be in some distress, for it came staggering and lurching down the hillside with extraordinary clumsiness, tripping over its own four legs as if it barely knew how to manage them. When it was about a hundred meters from me, it cried out, "Shimon! Help me, Shimon! In God's name help me!"

There were several strange things about this outcry, and I perceived them gradually, the most trivial first. It seemed odd that a Kunivar would address me by my given name, for they are a formal people. It seemed more odd that a Kunivar would speak to me in quite decent Hebrew, for at that time none of them had learned our language. It seemed most odd of all—but I was slow to discern it—that a Kunivar would have the very voice, dark and resonant, of my dear dead friend Joseph Avneri.

The Kunivar stumbled into the cultivated part of the field and halted, trembling terribly. Its fine green fur was pasted into hummocks by perspiration, and its great golden eyes rolled and crossed in a ghastly way. It stood flat-footed, splaying its legs out under the four corners of its chunky body like the legs of a table, and clasped its long powerful arms around its chest. I recognized the Kunivar as Seul, a subchief of the local village, with whom we of the kibbutz had had occasional dealings.

"What help can I give you?" I asked. "What has happened to you, Seul?"

"Shimon—Shimon—" A frightful moan came from the Kunivar. "Oh, God, Shimon, it goes beyond all belief! How can I bear this? How can I even comprehend it?"

No doubt of it. The Kunivar was speaking in the voice of Joseph Avneri.

"Seul?" I said hesitantly.

"My name is Joseph Avneri."

"Joseph Avneri died a year ago last Elul. I didn't realize you were such a clever mimic, Seul."

"Mimic? You speak to me of mimicry, Shimon? It's no mimicry. I am your Joseph, dead but still aware, thrown for my sins into this monstrous alien body. Are you Jew enough to know what a dybbuk is, Shimon?"

"A wandering ghost, yes, who takes possession of the body of a living being."

"I have become a dybbuk."

"There are no dybbuks. Dybbuks are phantoms out of medieval folklore," I said.

"You hear the voice of one."

"This is impossible," I said.

"I agree, Shimon, I agree." He sounded calmer now. "It's entirely impossible. I don't believe in dybbuks either, any more than I believe in Zeus, the Minotaur, werewolves, gorgons, or golems. But how else do you explain me?"

"You are Seul the Kunivar, playing a clever trick."

"Do you really think so? Listen to me, Shimon. I knew you when we were boys in Tiberias. I rescued you when we were fishing in the lake and our boat overturned. I was with you the day you met Leah whom you married. I was godfather to your son Yigal. I studied with you at the university in Jerusalem. I fled with you in the fiery days of the Final Pogrom. I stood watch with you aboard the Ark in the years of our flight from earth. Do you remember, Shimon? Do you remember Jerusalem? The Old City, the Mount of Olives, the Tomb of Absalom, the Western Wall? Am I a Kunivar, Shimon, to know of the Western Wall?"

"There is no survival of consciousness after death," I said stubbornly.

"A year ago I would have agreed with you. But who am I if I am not the spirit of Joseph Avneri? How can you account for me any other way? Dear God, do you think I *want* to believe this, Shimon? You know what a scoffer I was. But it's real."

"Perhaps I'm having a very vivid hallucination."

"Call the others, then. If ten people have the same hallucination, is it still a hallucination? Be reasonable, Shimon! Here I stand before you, telling you things that only I could know, and you deny that I am—"

"Be reasonable?" I said. "Where does reason enter into this? Do you expect me to believe in ghosts, Joseph, in wandering demons, in dybbuks? Am I some superstition-ridden peasant out of the Polish woods? Is this the Middle Ages?"

"You called me Joseph," he said quietly.

"I can hardly call you Seul when you speak in that voice."

"Then you believe in me!"

"No."

"Look, Shimon, did you ever know a bigger skeptic than Joseph Avneri? I had no use for the Torah, I said Moses was fictional, I plowed the fields on Yom Kippur, I laughed in God's nonexistent face. What is life, I said? And I answered: a mere accident, a transient biological phenomenon. Yet here I am. I remember the moment of my death. For a full year I've wandered this world, bodiless, perceiving things, unable to communicate. And today I find myself cast into this creature's body, and I know myself for a dybbuk. If *I* believe, Shimon, how can you dare disbelieve? In the name of our friendship, have faith in what I tell you!"

"You have actually become a dybbuk?"

"I have become a dybbuk," he said.

I shrugged. "Very well, Joseph. You're a dybbuk. It's madness, but I believe." I stared in astonishment at the Kunivar. Did I believe? Did I believe that I believed? How could I not believe? There was no other way for the voice of Joseph Avneri to be coming from the throat of a Kunivar. Sweat streamed down my body. I was face to face with the impossible, and all my philosophy was shattered. Anything was possible now. God might appear as a burning bush. The sun might stand still. No, I told myself. Believe only one irrational thing at a time, Shimon. Evidently there are dybbuks; well, then, there are dybbuks. But everything else pertaining to the Invisible World remains unreal until it manifests itself.

I said, "Why do you think this has happened to you?"

"It could only be as a punishment."

"For what, Joseph?

"My experiments. You knew I was doing research into the Kunivaru metabolism, didn't you?"

"Yes, certainly. But—"

"Did you know I performed surgical experiments on live Kunivaru in our hospital? That I used patients, without informing them or anyone else, in studies of a forbidden kind? It was vivisection, Shimon."

"*What?*"

"There were things I needed to know, and there was only one way I could discover them. The hunger for knowledge led me into sin. I told myself that these creatures were ill, that they would shortly die anyway, and that it might benefit everyone if I opened them while they still lived, you see? Besides, they weren't human beings, Shimon, they were only animals—very intelligent animals, true, but still only—"

"No, Joseph. I can believe in dybbuks more readily than I can believe this. You, doing such a thing? My calm rational friend, my scientist, my wise one?" I shuddered and stepped a few paces back from him. "Auschwitz!" I cried. "Buchenwald! Dachau! Do those names mean anything to you? 'They weren't human beings,' the Nazi surgeon said. 'They were only Jews, and our need for scientific knowledge is such that—' That was only three hundred years ago, Joseph. And you, a Jew, a Jew of all people, to—"

"I know, Shimon, I know. Spare me the lecture. I sinned terribly, and for my sins I've been given this grotesque body, this gross, hideous, heavy body, these four legs which I can hardly coordinate, this crooked spine, this foul, hot furry pelt. I still don't believe in a God, Shimon, but I think I believe in some sort of compensating force that balances accounts in this universe, and the account has been balanced for me, oh, yes, Shimon! I've had six hours of terror and loathing today such as I never dreamed could be experienced. To enter this body, to fry in this heat, to wander these hills trapped in such a mass of flesh, to feel myself being bombarded with the sensory perceptions of a being so alien—it's been hell, I tell you that without exaggeration. I would have died of shock in the first ten minutes if I didn't already happen to be dead. Only now, seeing you, talking to you, do I begin to get control of myself. Help me, Shimon."

"What do you want me to do?"

"Get me out of here. This is torment. I'm a dead man—I'm entitled to rest the way the other dead ones rest. Free me, Shimon."

"How?"

"How? How? Do I know? Am I an expert on dybbuks? Must I direct my own exorcism? If you knew what an effort it is simply to hold this body upright, to make its tongue form Hebrew words, to say things in a way you'll understand—" Suddenly the Kunivar sagged to his knees, a slow, complex folding process that reminded me of the manner in which the camels of Old Earth lowered themselves to the ground. The alien creature began to sputter and moan and wave his arms about; foam appeared on his wide rubbery lips. "God in Heaven, Shimon," Joseph cried, "set me free!"

I called for my son Yigal and he came running swiftly from the far side of the fields, a lean healthy boy, only eleven years old but already long-legged, strong-bodied. Without going into details, I indicated the suffering Kunivar and told Yigal to get help from the kibbutz. A few minutes later he came back leading seven or eight men—Abrasha, Itzhak, Uri, Nahum, and some others. It took the full strength of all of us to lift the Kunivar into the hopper of a harvesting machine and transport him to our hospital. Two of the doctors—Moshe Shiloah and someone else—began to examine the stricken alien, and I sent Yigal to the

Kunivaru village to tell the chief that Seul had collapsed in our fields.

The doctors quickly diagnosed the problem as a case of heat prostration. They were discussing the sort of injection the Kunivar should receive when Joseph Avneri, breaking a silence that had lasted since Seul had fallen, announced his presence within the Kunivar's body. Uri and Nahum had remained in the hospital room with me; not wanting this craziness to become general knowledge in the kibbutz, I took them outside and told them to forget whatever ravings they had heard. When I returned, the doctors were busy with their preparations and Joseph was patiently explaining to them that he was a dybbuk who had involuntarily taken possession of the Kunivar. "The heat has driven the poor creature insane," Moshe Shiloah murmured, and rammed a huge needle into one of Seul's thighs.

"Make them listen to me," Joseph said.

"You know that voice," I told the doctors. "Something very unusual has happened here."

But they were no more willing to believe in dybbuks than they were in rivers that flow uphill. Joseph continued to protest, and the doctors continued methodically to fill Seul's body with sedatives and restoratives and other potions. Even when Joseph began to speak of last year's kibbutz gossip—who had been sleeping with whom behind whose back, who had illicitly been peddling goods from the community storehouse to the Kunivaru— they paid no attention. It was as though they had so much difficulty believing that a Kunivar could speak Hebrew that they were unable to make sense out of what he was saying and took Joseph's words to be Seul's delirium. Suddenly Joseph raised his voice for the first time, calling out in a loud, angry tone, "You, Moshe Shiloah! Aboard the Ark I found you in bed with the wife of Teviah Kohn, remember? Would a Kunivar have known such a thing?"

Moshe Shiloah gasped, reddened, and dropped his hypodermic. The other doctor was nearly as astonished.

"What is this?" Moshe Shiloah asked. "How can this be?"

"Deny me now!" Joseph roared. "Can you deny me?"

The doctors faced the same problems of acceptance that I had had, that Joseph himself had grappled with. We were all of us rational men in this kibbutz, and the supernatural had no place in our lives. but there was no arguing the phenomenon away. There

was the voice of Joseph Avneri emerging from the throat of Seul
the Kunivar, and the voice was saying things that only Joseph
would have said, and Joseph had been dead more than a year.
Call it a dybbuk, call it hallucination, call it anything: Joseph's
presence could not be ignored.

Locking the door, Moshe Shiloah said to me, "We must deal
with this somehow."

Tensely we discussed the situation. It was, we agreed, a
delicate and difficult matter. Joseph, raging and tortured, demanded
to be exorcised and allowed to sleep the sleep of the dead; unless
we placated him he would make us all suffer. In his pain, in his
fury, he might say anything, he might reveal everything he knew
about our private lives; a dead man is beyond all of society's
rules of common decency. We could not expose ourselves to that.
But what could we do about him? Chain him in an outbuilding
and hide him in solitary confinement? Hardly. Unhappy Joseph
deserved better of us than that; and there was Seul to consider,
poor supplanted Seul, the dybbuk's unwilling host. We could not
keep a Kunivar in the kibbutz, imprisoned or free, even if his
body did house the spirit of one of our own people, nor could we
let the shell of Seul go back to the Kunivaru village with Joseph
as a furious passenger trapped inside. What to do? Separate soul
from body, somehow: restore Seul to wholeness and send Joseph
to the limbo of the dead. But how? There was nothing in the
standard pharmacopoeia about dybbuks. What to do?

I sent for Shmarya Asch and Yakov Ben-Zion, who headed the
kibbutz council that month, and for Shlomo Feig, our rabbi, a
shrewd and sturdy man, very unorthodox in his orthodoxy,
almost as secular as the rest of us. They questioned Joseph
Avneri extensively, and he told them the whole tale—his scandal-
ous secret experiments, his post-mortem year as a wandering
spirit, his sudden painful incarnation within Seul. At length
Shmarya Asch turned to Moshe Shiloah and snapped, "There
must be some therapy for such a case."

"I know of none."

"This is schizophrenia," said Shmarya Asch in his firm,
dogmatic way. "There are cures for schizophrenia. There are
drugs, there are electric shock treatments, there are—you know
these things better than I, Moshe."

"This is not schizophrenia," Moshe Shiloah retorted. "This is a case of demonic possession. I have no training in treating such maladies.''

"Demonic possession?'' Shmarya bellowed. "Have you lost your mind?''

"Peace, peace, all of you,'' Shlomo Feig said, as everyone began to shout at once. The rabbi's voice cut sharply through the tumult and silenced us all. He was a man of great strength, physical as well as moral, to whom the entire kibbutz inevitably turned for guidance although there was virtually no one among us who observed the major rites of Judaism. He said, "I find this as hard to comprehend as any of you. But the evidence triumphs over my skepticism. How can we deny that Joseph Avneri has returned as a dybbuk? Moshe, you know no way of causing this intruder to leave the Kunivar's body?''

"None,'' said Moshe Shiloah.

"Maybe the Kunivaru themselves know a way,'' Yakov Ben-Zion suggested.

"Exactly,'' said the rabbi. "My next point. These Kunivaru are a primitive folk. They live closer to the world of magic and witchcraft, of demons and spirits, than we do whose minds are schooled in the habits of reason. Perhaps such cases of possession occur often among them. Perhaps they have techniques for driving out unwanted spirits. Let us turn to them, and let them cure their own.''

Before long Yigal arrived, bringing with him six Kunivaru, including Gyaymar, the village chief. They wholly filled the little hospital room, bustling around in it like a delegation of huge furry centaurs; I was oppressed by the acrid smell of so many of them in one small space, and although they had always been friendly to us, never raising an objection when we appeared as refugees to settle on their planet, I felt fear of them now as I had never felt before. Clustering about Seul, they asked questions of him in their own supple language, and when Joseph Avneri replied in Hebrew they whispered things to each other unintelligible to us. Then, unexpectedly, the voice of Seul broke through, speaking in halting spastic monosyllables that revealed the terrible shock his nervous system must have received; then the alien faded and Joseph Avneri spoke once more with the Kunivar's lips, begging forgiveness, asking for release.

Turning to Gyaymar, Shlomo Feig said, "Have such things happened on this world before?"

"Oh, yes, yes," the chief replied. "Many times. When one of us dies having a guilty soul, repose is denied, and the spirit may undergo strange migrations before forgiveness comes. What was the nature of this man's sin?"

"It would be difficult to explain to one who is not Jewish," said the rabbi hastily, glancing away. "The important question is whether you have a means of undoing what has befallen the unfortunate Seul, whose sufferings we all lament."

"We have a means, yes," said Gyaymar, the chief.

The six Kunivaru hoisted Seul to their shoulders and carried him from the kibbutz; we were told that we might accompany them if we cared to do so. I went along, and Moshe Shiloah, and Shmarya Asch, and Yakov Ben-Zion, and the rabbi, and perhaps some others. The Kunivaru took their comrade not to their village but to a meadow several kilometers to the east, down in the direction of the place where the Hasidim lived. Not long after the Landing, the Kunivaru had let us know that the meadow was sacred to them, and none of us had ever entered it.

It was a lovely place, green and moist, a gently sloping basin crisscrossed by a dozen cool little streams. Depositing Seul beside one of the streams, the Kunivaru went off into the woods bordering the meadow to gather firewood and herbs. We remained close by Seul. "This will do no good," Joseph Avneri muttered more than once. "A waste of time, a foolish expense of energy." Three of the Kunivaru started to build a bonfire. Two sat nearby, shredding the herbs, making heaps of leaves, stems, roots. Gradually more of their kind appeared until the meadow was filled with them; it seemed that the whole village, some four hundred Kunivaru, was turning out to watch or to participate in the rite. Many of them carried musical instruments, trumpets and drums, rattles and clappers, lyres, lutes, small harps, percussive boards, wooden flutes, everything intricate and fanciful of design; we had not suspected such cultural complexity. The priests—I assume they were priests, Kunivaru of stature and dignity—wore ornate ceremonial helmets and heavy golden mantles of sea-beast fur. The ordinary townsfolk carried ribbons and streamers, bits of bright fabric, polished mirrors of stone, and other ornamental devices. When he saw how elaborate a function it was going to be, Moshe Shiloah, an amateur anthropologist at heart, ran back

to the kibbutz to fetch camera and recorder. He returned, breathless, just as the rite commenced.

And a glorious rite it was: incense, a grandly blazing bonfire,
the pungent fragrance of freshly picked herbs, some heavy-footed
quasi-orgiastic dancing, and a choir punching out harsh, sharp-
edged arrhythmic melodies. Gyaymar and the high priest of the
village performed an elegant antiphonal chant, uttering long
curling intertwining melismas and sprinkling Seul with a sweet-
smelling pink fluid out of a baroquely carved wooden censer.
Never have I beheld such stirring pageantry. But Joseph's gloomy
prediction was correct; it was all entirely useless. Two hours of
intensive exorcism had no effect. When the ceremony ended—the
ultimate punctuation marks were five terrible shouts from the
high priest—the dybbuk remained firmly in possession of Seul.

"You have not conquered me," Joseph declared in a bleak tone.

Gyaymar said, "It seems we have no power to command an
earthborn soul."

"What will we do now?" demanded Yakov Ben-Zion of no
one in particular. "Our science and their witchcraft both fail."

Joseph Avneri pointed toward the east, toward the village of
the Hasidim, and murmured something indistinct.

"No!" cried Rabbi Shlomo Feig, who stood closest to the
dybbuk at that moment.

"What did he say?" I asked.

"It was nothing," the rabbi said. "It was foolishness. The
long ceremony has left him fatigued, and his mind wanders. Pay
no attention."

I moved nearer to my old friend. "Tell me, Joseph."

"I said," the dybbuk replied slowly, "that perhaps we should
send for the Baal Shem."

"Foolishness!" said Shlomo Feig, and spat.

"Why this anger?" Shmarya Asch wanted to know. "You,
Rabbi Shlomo, you were one of the first to advocate employing
Kunivaru sorcerers in this business. You gladly bring in alien
witch doctors, Rabbi, and grow angry when someone suggests
that your fellow Jew be given a chance to drive out the demon?
Be consistent, Shlomo!"

Rabbi Shlomo's strong face grew mottled with rage. It was
strange to see this calm, even-tempered man becoming so excited. "I will have nothing to do with Hasidim!" he exclaimed.

"I think this is a matter of professional rivalries," Moshe Shiloah commented.

The rabbi said, "To give recognition to all that is most superstitious in Judaism, to all that is most irrational and grotesque and outmoded and medieval? No! No!"

"But dybbuks *are* irrational and grotesque and outmoded and medieval," said Joseph Avneri. "Who better to exorcise one than a rabbi whose soul is still rooted in ancient beliefs?"

"I forbid this!" Shlomo Feig sputtered. "If the Baal Shem is summoned I will—I will—"

"Rabbi," Joseph said, shouting now, "this is a matter of my tortured soul against your offended spiritual pride. Give way! Give way! Get me the Baal Shem!"

"I refuse!"

"Look!" called Yakov Ben-Zion. The dispute had suddenly become academic. Uninvited, our Hasidic cousins were arriving at the sacred meadow, a long procession of them, eerie prehistoric-looking figures clad in their traditional long black robes, wide-brimmed hats, heavy beards, dangling side-locks; and at the head of the group marched their tzaddik, their holy man, their prophet, their leader, Reb Shmuel the Baal Shem.

It was certainly never our idea to bring Hasidim with us when we fled out of the smoldering ruins of the Land of Israel. Our intention was to leave Earth and all its sorrows far behind, to start anew on another world where we could at last build an enduring Jewish homeland, free for once of our eternal gentile enemies and free, also, of the religious fanatics among our own kind whose presence had long been a drain on our vitality. We needed no mystics, no ecstatics, no weepers, no moaners, no leapers, no chanters; we needed only workers, farmers, machinists, engineers, builders. But how could we refuse them a place on the Ark? It was their good fortune to come upon us just as we were making the final preparations for our flight. The nightmare that had darkened our sleep for three centuries had been made real: the Homeland lay in flames, our armies had been shattered out of ambush, Philistines wielding long knives strode through our devastated cities. Our ship was ready to leap to the stars. We were not cowards but simply realists, for it was folly to think we could do battle any longer, and if some fragment of our ancient nation were to survive, it could only survive far from the bitter world Earth. So we were going to go; and here were suppliants asking us for succor, Reb Shmuel and his thirty followers. How could we turn them away, knowing they would certainly perish? They were human beings, they were Jews. For all our misgivings, we let them come on board.

And then we wandered across the heavens year after year, and then we came to a star that had no name, only a number, and then we found its fourth planet to be sweet and fertile, a happier world than Earth, and we thanked the God in whom we did not believe for the good luck that He had granted us, and we cried out to each other in congratulation, Mazel tov! Mazel tov! Good luck, good luck, good luck! And someone looked in an old book and saw that *mazel* once had had an astrological connotation, that in the days of the Bible it had meant not only "luck" but a lucky star, and so we named our lucky star Mazel Tov, and we made our landfall on Mazel Tov IV, which was to be the New Israel. Here we found no enemies, no Egyptians, no Assyrians, no Romans, no Cossacks, no Nazis, no Arabs, only the Kunivaru, kindly people of a simple nature, who solemnly studied our pantomimed explanations and replied to us in gestures, saying, Be welcome, there is more land here than we will ever need. And we built our kibbutz.

But we had no desire to live close to those people of the past, the Hasidim, and they had scant love for us, for they saw us as pagans, godless Jews who were worse than gentiles, and they went off to build a muddy little village of their own. Sometimes on clear nights we heard their lusty singing, but otherwise there was scarcely any contact between us and them.

I could understand Rabbi Shlomo's hostility to the idea of intervention by the Baal Shem. These Hasidim represented the mystic side of Judaism, the dark uncontrollable Dionysiac side, the skeleton in the tribal closet; Shlomo Feig might be amused or charmed by a rite of exorcism performed by furry centaurs, but when Jews took part in the same sort of supernaturalism it was distressing to him. Then, too, there was the ugly fact that the sane, sensible Rabbi Shlomo had virtually no followers at all among the sane, sensible secularized Jews of our kibbutz, whereas Reb Shmuel's Hasidim looked upon him with awe, regarding him as a miracle worker, a seer, a saint. Still, Rabbi Shlomo's understandable jealousies and prejudices aside, Joseph Avneri was right: dybbuks were vapors out of the realm of the fantastic, and the fantastic was the Baal Shem's kingdom.

He was an improbably tall, angular figure, almost skeletal, with gaunt cheekbones, a soft, thickly curling beard, and gentle dreamy eyes. I suppose he was about fifty years old, though I would have believed it if they said he was thirty or seventy or ninety. His sense of the dramatic was unfailing; now—it was late afternoon—he took up a position with the setting sun at his back, so that his long shadow engulfed us all, and spread forth his arms and said, "We have heard reports of a dybbuk among you."

"There is no dybbuk!" Rabbi Shlomo retorted fiercely.

The Baal Shem smiled. "But there is a Kunivar who speaks with an Israeli voice?"

"There has been an odd transformation, yes," Rabbi Shlomo conceded. "But in this age, on this planet, no one can take dybbuks seriously."

"That is, *you* cannot take dybbuks seriously," said the Baal Shem.

"I do!" cried Joseph Avneri in exasperation. "I! I! I am the dybbuk! I, Joseph Avneri, dead a year ago last Elul, doomed for my sins to inhabit this Kunivar carcass. A Jew, Reb Shmuel, a dead Jew, a pitiful sinful miserable Yid. Who'll let me out? Who'll set me free?"

"There is no dybbuk?" the Baal Shem said amiably.

"This Kunivar has gone insane," said Shlomo Feig.

We coughed and shifted our feet. If anyone had gone insane it was our rabbi, denying in this fashion the phenomenon that he himself had acknowledged as genuine, however reluctantly, only a few hours before. Envy, wounded pride, and stubbornness had unbalanced his judgment. Joseph Avneri, enraged, began to bellow the Aleph Beth Gimel, the Shma Yisroel, anything that might prove his dybbukhood. The Baal Shem waited patiently, arms outspread, saying nothing. Rabbi Shlomo, confronting him, his powerful stocky figure dwarfed by the long-legged Hasid, maintained energetically that there had to be some rational explanation for the metamorphosis of Seul the Kunivar.

When Shlomo Feig at length fell silent, the Baal Shem said, "There is a dybbuk in this Kunivar. Do you think, Rabbi Shlomo, that dybbuks ceased their wanderings when the shtetls of Poland were destroyed? Nothing is lost in the sight of God, Rabbi. Jews go to the stars; the Torah and the Talmud and the

Zohar have gone also to the stars; dybbuks too may be found in
these strange worlds. Rabbi, may I bring peace to this troubled
spirit and to this weary Kunivar?''

"Do whatever you want," Shlomo Feig muttered in disgust,
and strode away, scowling.

Reb Shmuel at once commenced the exorcism. He called first
for a minyan. Eight of his Hasidim stepped forward. I exchanged
a glance with Shmarya Asch, and we shrugged and came forward
too, but the Baal Shem, smiling, waved us away and beckoned
two more of his followers into the circle. They began to sing; to
my everlasting shame I have no idea what the singing was about,
for the words were Yiddish of a Galitzianer sort, nearly as alien
to me as the Kunivaru tongue. They sang for ten or fifteen
minutes; the Hasidim grew more animated, clapping their hands,
dancing about their Baal Shem; suddenly Reb Shmuel lowered
his arms to his sides, silencing them, and quietly began to recite
Hebrew phrases, which after a moment I recognized as those of
the Ninety-first Psalm: The Lord is my refuge and my fortress, in
him will I trust. The psalm rolled melodiously to its comforting
conclusion, its promise of deliverance and salvation. For a long
moment all was still. Then in a terrifying voice, not loud but
immensely commanding, the Baal Shem ordered the spirit of
Joseph Avneri to quit the body of Seul the Kunivar. "Out! Out!
God's name out, and off to your eternal rest!" One of the
Hasidim handed Reb Shmuel a shofar. The Baal Shem put the
ram's horn to his lips and blew a single titanic blast.

Joseph Avneri whimpered. The Kunivar that housed him took
three awkward, toppling steps. "Oy, mama, mama," Joseph
cried. The Kunivar's head snapped back; his arms shot straight
out at his sides; he tumbled clumsily to his four knees. An eon
went by. Then Seul rose—smoothly, this time, with natural
Kunivaru grace—and went to the Baal Shem, and knelt, and
touched the tzaddik's black robe. So we knew the thing was
done.

Instants later the tension broke. Two of the Kunivaru priests
rushed toward the Baal Shem, and then Gyaymar, and then some
of the musicians, and then it seemed the whole tribe was pressing
close upon him, trying to touch the holy man. The Hasidim,
looking worried, murmured their concern, but the Baal Shem,
towering over the surging mob, calmly blessed the Kunivaru,
stroking the dense fur of their backs. After some minutes of this

the Kunivaru set up a rhythmic chant, and it was a while before I realized what they were saying. Moshe Shiloah and Yakov Ben-Zion caught the sense of it about the same time I did, and we began to laugh, and then our laughter died away.

"What do their words mean?" the Baal Shem called out.

"They are saying," I told him, "that they are convinced of the power of your god. They wish to become Jews."

For the first time Reb Shmuel's poise and serenity shattered. His eyes flashed ferociously and he pushed at the crowding Kunivaru, opening an avenue between them. Coming up to me, he snapped, "Such a thing is an absurdity!"

"Nevertheless, look at them. They worship you, Reb Shmuel."

"I refuse their worship."

"You worked a miracle. Can you blame them for adoring you and hungering after your faith?"

"Let them adore," said the Baal Shem. "But how can they become Jews? It would be a mockery."

I shook my head. "What was it you told Rabbi Shlomo? Nothing is lost in the sight of God. There have always been converts to Judaism—we never invite them, but we never turn them away if they're sincere, eh, Reb Shmuel? Even here in the stars, there is continuity of tradition, and tradition says we harden not our hearts to those who seek the truth of God. These are a good people—let them be received into Israel."

"No," the Baal Shem said. "A Jew must first of all be human."

"Show me that in the Torah."

"The Torah! You joke with me. A Jew must first of all be human. Were cats allowed to become Jews? Were horses?"

"These people are neither cats nor horses, Reb Shmuel. They are as human as we are."

"No! No!"

"If there can be a dybbuk on Mazel Tov IV," I said, "then there can also be Jews with six limbs and green fur."

"No. No. No. *No!*"

The Baal Shem had had enough of this debate. Shoving aside the clutching hands of the Kunivaru in a most unsaintly way, he gathered his followers and stalked off, a tower of offended dignity, bidding us no farewells.

But how can true faith be denied? The Hasidim offered no encouragement, so the Kunivaru came to us; they learned Hebrew and we loaned them books, and Rabbi Shlomo gave them religious instruction, and in their own time and in their own way they entered into Judaism. All this was years ago, in the first generation after the Landing. Most of those who lived in those days are dead now—Rabbi Shlomo, Reb Shmuel the Baal Shem, Moshe Shiloah, Shmarya Asch. I was a young man then. I know a good deal more now, and if I am no closer to God than I ever was, perhaps He has grown closer to me. I eat meat and butter at the same meal, and I plow my land on the Sabbath, but those are old habits that have little to do with belief or the absence of belief.

We are much closer to the Kunivaru, too, than we were in those early days; they no longer seem like alien beings to us, but merely neighbors whose bodies have a different form. The younger ones of our kibbutz are especially drawn to them. The year before last Rabbi Lhaoyir the Kunivar suggested to some of our boys that they come for lessons to the Talmud Torah, the religious school, that he runs in the Kunivaru village; since the death of Shlomo Feig there has been no one in the kibbutz to give such instruction. When Reb Yossele, the son and successor of Reb Shmuel the Baal Shem, heard this, he raised strong objections. If your boys will take instruction, he said, at least send them to us, and not to green monsters. My son Yigal threw him out of the kibbutz. We would rather let our boys learn the Torah from green monsters, Yigal told Reb Yossele, than have them raised to be Hasidim.

And so my son's son has had his lessons at the Talmud Torah of Rabbi Lhaoyir the Kunivar, and next spring he will have his bar mitzvah. Once I would have been appalled by such goings-on, but now I say only, How strange, how unexpected, how interesting! Truly the Lord, if He exists, must have a keen sense of humor. I like a god who can smile and wink, who doesn't take himself too seriously. The Kunivaru are Jews! Yes! They are preparing David for his bar mitzvah! Yes! Today is Yom Kippur, and I hear the sound of the shofar coming from their village! Yes! Yes. So be it. So be it, yes, and all praise be to Him.

ISHMAEL IN LOVE

CALL ME ISHMAEL. All human beings who know me do. My own kind does not make use of the unit-structural designation ["name"] to distinguish individuals, but this is the name the humans gave me, and it will do. I was named by Miss Lisabeth Calkins, for whom I feel protective-chivalrous-sexual emotions ["love"]. Throughout my narrative it is understood that the designation "Ishmael" refers only to myself.

I am a member of an intelligent aquatic mammalian nonprimate nonhuman species, *Tursiops truncatus*, a bottle-nosed dolphin. I am eleven years old, which is to say that I am fully mature in all respects. My weight is 175 kilograms, and my total length is 2.9 meters. I am employed at Gerard-Worzel Seawater Recovery Station, St. Croix, Virgin Islands, in a maintenance capacity, having commenced there on your date of August 14 1994. To my own species I am sexually desirable and also highly regarded for my mental development. I have a large vocabulary. I communicate well with members of *H. sapiens*. I have considerable mechanical ability, as you can see by my success in switching on the electronic-acoustic device through which I am dictating this memoir.

I am a lonely mammalian organism who has committed acts of heroism on behalf of your species and wishes only the reward of a more intimate relationship ["love"] with Miss Lisabeth Calkins. I beseech compassionate members of *H. sapiens* to speak favorably of me to her. I am loyal, trustworthy, reliable, devoted,

37

and extremely intelligent. I would endeavor to give her stimulating companionship and emotional fulfillment ["happiness"] in all respects within my power.

Permit me to explain the pertinent circumstances.

CATEGORY 1: MY EMPLOYMENT.

Gerard-Worzel Seawater Recovery Station occupies a prominent position on the north shore of the island of St. Croix in the West Indies. It operates on the atmospheric condensation principle. All this I know from Miss Calkins ["Lisabeth"], who has described its workings to me in great detail. The purpose of our installation is to recover some of the fresh water, estimated at two hundred million gallons per day, carried as vapor in the lower hundred meters of air sweeping over each kilometer of the windward side of the island.

A pipe 9 meters in diameter takes in cold seawater at depths of up to 900 meters and carries it approximately 2 kilometers to our station. The pipe delivers some 30 million gallons of water a day at a temperature of 5°C. This is pumped toward our condenser, which intercepts approximately 1 billion cubic meters of warm tropical air each day. This air has a temperature of 25°C and a relative humidity of 70 to 80 percent. Upon exposure to the cold seawater in the condenser the air cools to 10°C and reaches a humidity of 100 percent, permitting us to extract approximately 16 gallons of water per cubic meter of air. This salt-free ["fresh"] water is delivered to the main water system of the island, for St. Croix is deficient in a natural supply of water suitable for consumption by human beings. It is frequently said by government officials who visit our installation on various ceremonial occasions that without our plant the great industrial expansion of St. Croix would have been wholly impossible.

For reasons of economy we operate in conjunction with an aquicultural enterprise ["the fish farm"] that puts our wastes to work. Once our seawater has been pumped through the condenser it must be discarded; however, because it originates in a low-level ocean area, its content of dissolved phosphates and nitrates is 1500 percent greater than at the surface. This nutrient-rich water is pumped from our condenser into an adjoining circular lagoon of natural origin ["the coral corral"], which is stocked with fish.

In such an enhanced environment the fish are highly productive, and the yield of food is great enough to offset the costs of operating our pumps.

[Misguided human beings sometimes question the morality of using dolphins to help maintain fish farms. They believe it is degrading to compel us to produce fellow aquatic creatures to be eaten by man. May I simply point out, first, that none of us work here under compulsion, and second, that my species sees nothing immoral about feeding on aquatic creatures. We eat fish ourselves.]

My role in the functioning of the Gerard-Worzel Seawater Recovery Station is an important one. I ["Ishmael"] serve as foreman of the Intake Maintenance Squad. I lead nine members of my species. Our assignment is to monitor the intake valves of the main seawater pipe; these valves frequently become fouled through the presence on them of low-phylum organisms, such as starfish or algae, hampering the efficiency of the installation. Our task is to descend at periodic intervals and clear the obstruction. Normally this can be achieved without the need for manipulative organs ["fingers"] with which we are unfortunately not equipped.

[Certain individuals among you have objected that it is improper to make use of dolphins in the labor force when members of *H. sapiens* are out of work. The intelligent reply to this is that, first, we are designed by evolution to function superbly underwater without special breathing equipment, and second, that only a highly skilled human being could perform our function, and such human beings are themselves in short supply in the labor force.]

I have held my post for two years and four months. In that time there has been no significant interruption in intake capacity of the valves I maintain.

As compensation for my work ["salary"], I receive an ample supply of food. One could hire a mere shark for such pay, of course; but above and beyond my daily pails of fish, I also receive such intangibles as the companionship of human beings and the opportunity to develop my latent intelligence through access to reference spools, vocabulary expanders, and various training devices. As you can see, I have made the most of my opportunities.

CATEGORY 2: MISS LISABETH CALKINS.

Her dossier is on file here. I have had access to it through the spool-reader mounted at the edge of the dolphin exercise tank. By spoken instruction I can bring into view anything in the station files, although I doubt that it was anticipated by anyone that a dolphin should want to read the personnel dossiers.

She is twenty-seven years old. Thus she is of the same generation as my genetic predecessors ["parents"]. However, I do not share the prevailing cultural taboo of many *H. sapiens* against emotional relationships with older women. Besides, after compensating for differences in species, it will be seen that Miss Lisabeth and I are of the same age. She reached sexual maturity approximately half her lifetime ago. So did I.

[I must admit that she is considered slightly past the optimum age at which human females take a permanent mate. I assume she does not engage in the practice of temporary mating, since her dossier shows no indication that she has reproduced. It is possible that humans do not necessarily produce offspring at each yearly mating, or even that matings take place at random unpredictable times not related to the reproductive process at all. This seems strange and somehow perverse to me, yet I infer from some data I have seen that it may be the case. There is little information on human mating habits in the material accessible to me. I must learn more.]

Lisabeth, as I allow myself privately to call her, stands 1.8 meters tall [humans do not measure themselves by "length"] and weighs 52 kilograms. Her hair is golden ["blonde"] and is worn long. Her skin, though darkened by exposure to the sun, is quite fair. The irises of her eyes are blue. From my conversations with humans I have learned that she is considered quite beautiful. From words I have overheard while at surface level, I realize that most males at the station feel intense sexual desires toward her. I regard her as beautiful also, inasmuch as I am capable of responding to human beauty. [I think I am.] I am not sure if I feel actual sexual desire for Lisabeth; more likely what troubles me is a generalized longing for her presence and her closeness, which I translate into sexual terms simply as a means of making it comprehensible to me.

Beyond doubt she does not have the traits I normally seek in a mate [prominent beak, sleek fins]. Any attempt at our making love in the anatomical sense would certainly result in pain or injury to her. That is not my wish. The physical traits that make her so desirable to the males of her species [highly developed milk glands, shining hair, delicate features, long hind limbs or "legs," and so forth] have no particular importance to me, and in some instances actually have a negative value. As in the case of the two milk glands in her pectoral region, which jut forward from her body in such a fashion that they must surely slow her when she swims. This is poor design, and I am incapable of finding poor design beautiful in any way. Evidently Lisabeth regrets the size and placement of those glands herself, since she is careful to conceal them at all times by a narrow covering. The others at the station, who are all males and therefore have only rudimentary milk glands that in no way destroy the flow lines of their bodies, leave them bare.

What, then, is the cause of my attraction for Lisabeth?

It arises out of the need I feel for her companionship. I believe that she understands me as no member of my own species does. Hence I will be happier in her company than away from her. This impression dates from our earliest meeting. Lisabeth, who is a specialist in human-cetacean relations, came to St. Croix four months ago, and I was requested to bring my maintenance group to the surface to be introduced to her. I leaped high for a good view and saw instantly that she was of a finer sort than the humans I already knew; her body was more delicate, looking at once fragile and powerful, and her gracefulness was a welcome change from the thick awkwardness of the human males I knew. Nor was she covered with the coarse body hair that my kind finds so distressing. [I did not at first know that Lisabeth's difference from the others at the station was the result of her being female. I had never seen a human female before. But I quickly learned.]

I came forward, made contact with the acoustic transmitter, and said, "I am the foreman of the Intake Maintenance Squad. I have the unit-structural designation TT-66."

"Don't you have a name?" she asked.

"Meaning of term, name?"

"Your—your unit-structural designation—but not just TT-66. I mean, that's no good at all. For example, my name's Lisabeth Calkins. And I—" She shook her head and looked at the plant supervisor. "Don't these workers have *names*?"

The supervisor did not see why dolphins should have names. Lisabeth did—she was greatly concerned about it—and since she now was in charge of liaison with us, she gave us names on the spot. Thus I was dubbed Ishmael. It was, she told me, the name of a man who had gone to sea, had many wonderful experiences, and put them all down in a story-spool that every cultured person played. I have since had access to Ishmael's story—that *other* Ishmael—and I agree that it is remarkable. For a human being he had unusual insight into the ways of whales, who are, however, stupid creatures for whom I have little respect. I am proud to carry Ishmael's name.

After she had named us, Lisabeth leaped into the sea and swam with us. I must tell you that most of us feel a sort of contempt for you humans because you are such poor swimmers. Perhaps it is a mark of my above-normal intelligence or greater compassion that I have no such scorn in me. I admire you for the zeal and energy you give to swimming, and you are quite good at it, considering all your handicaps. As I remind my people, you manage far more ably in the water than we would on land. Anyway, Lisabeth swam well, by human standards, and we tolerantly adjusted our pace to hers. We frolicked in the water awhile. Then she seized my dorsal fin and said, "Take me for a ride, Ishmael!"

I tremble now to recollect the contact of her body with mine. She sat astride me, her legs gripping my body tightly, and off I sped at close to full velocity, soaring at surface level. Her laughter told of her delight as I launched myself again and again through the air. It was a purely physical display in which I made no use of my extraordinary mental capacity; I was, if you will, simply showing off my dolphinhood. Lisabeth's response was ecstatic. Even when I plunged, taking her so deep she might have feared harm from the pressure, she kept her grip and showed no alarm. When we breached the surface again, she cried out in joy.

Through sheer animality I had made my first impact on her. I knew human beings well enough to be able to interpret her flushed, exhilarated expression as I returned her to shore. My challenge now was to expose her to my higher traits—to show her that even among dolphins I was unusually swift to learn, unusually capable of comprehending the universe.

I was already then in love with her.

During the weeks that followed we had many conversations. I am not flattering myself when I tell you that she quickly realized how extraordinary I am. My vocabulary, which was already large when she came to the station, grew rapidly under the stimulus of Lisabeth's presence. I learned from her; she gave me access to spools no dolphin was thought likely to wish to play; I developed insights into my environment that astonished even myself. In short order I reached my present peak of attainment. I think you will agree that I can express myself more eloquently than most human beings. I trust that the computer doing the printout on this memoir will not betray me by inserting inappropriate punctuations or deviating from the proper spellings of the words whose sounds I utter.

My love for Lisabeth deepened and grew more rich. I learned the meaning of jealousy for the first time when I saw her running arm in arm along the beach with Dr. Madison, the power-plant man. I knew anger when I overheard the lewd and vulgar remarks of human males as Lisabeth walked by. My fascination with her led me to explore many avenues of human experience; I did not dare talk of such things with her, but from other personnel at the base who sometimes talked with me I learned certain aspects of the phenomenon humans call "love." I also obtained explanations of the vulgar words spoken by males here behind her back: most of them pertained to a wish to mate with Lisabeth [apparently on a temporary basis], but there were also highly favorable descriptions of her milk glands [why are humans so aggressively mammalian?] and even of the rounded area in back, just above the place where her body divides into the two hind limbs. I confess that that region fascinates me also. It seems so alien for one's body to split like that in the middle!

I never explicitly stated my feelings toward Lisabeth. I tried to lead her slowly toward an understanding that I loved her. Once she came overtly to that awareness, I thought, we might begin to plan some sort of future for ourselves together.

What a fool I was!

CATEGORY 3: THE CONSPIRACY.

A male voice said, "How in hell are you going to bribe a dolphin?"

A different voice, deeper, more cultured, replied, "Leave it to me."

"What do you give him? Ten cans of sardines?"

"This one's special. Peculiar, even. He's scholarly. We can get to him."

They did not know that I could hear them. I was drifting near the surface in my rest tank, between shifts. Our hearing is acute and I was well within auditory range. I sensed at once that something was amiss, but I kept my position, pretending I knew nothing.

"Ishmael!" one man called out. "Is that you, Ishmael?"

I rose to the surface and came to the edge of the tank. Three male humans stood there. One was a technician at the station; the other two I had never seen before, and they wore body covering from their feet to their throats, marking them at once as strangers here. The technician I despised, for he was one of the ones who had made vulgar remarks about Lisabeth's milk glands.

He said, "Look at him, gentlemen. Worn out in his prime! A victim of human exploitation!" To me he said, "Ishmael, these gentlemen come from the League for the Prevention of Cruelty to Intelligent Species. You know about that?"

"No," I said.

"They're trying to put an end to dolphin exploitation. The criminal use of our planet's only other truly intelligent species in slave labor. They want to help you."

"I am no slave. I receive compensation for my work."

"A few stinking fish!" said the fully dressed man to the left of the technician. "They exploit you, Ishmael! They give you dangerous, dirty work and don't pay you worth a damn!"

His companion said, "It has to stop. We want to serve notice to the world that the age of enslaved dolphins is over. Help us, Ishmael. Help us help you!"

I need not say that I was hostile to their purported purposes. A more literal-minded dolphin than I might well have said so at once and spoiled their plot. But I shrewdly said, "What do you want me to do?"

"Foul the intakes," said the technician quickly.

Despite myself, I snorted in anger and surprise. "Betray a sacred trust? How can I?"

"It's for your own sake, Ishmael. Here's how it works—you and your crew will plug up the intakes, and the water plant will stop working. The whole island will panic. Human maintenance crews will go down to see what's what, but as soon as they clear the valves, you go back and foul them again. Emergency water supplies will have to be rushed to St. Croix. It'll focus public attention on the fact that this island is dependent on dolphin labor—underpaid, overworked dolphin labor! During the crisis we'll step forward to tell the world your story. We'll get every human being to cry out in outrage against the way you're being treated."

I did not say that I felt no outrage myself. Instead I cleverly replied, "There could be dangers in this for me."

"Nonsense!"

"They will ask me why I have not cleared the valves. It is my responsibility. There will be trouble."

For a while we debated the point. Then the technician said, "Look, Ishmael, we know there are a few risks. But we're willing to offer extra payment if you'll handle the job."

"Such as?"

"Spools. Anything you'd like to hear, we'll get for you. I know you've got literary interests. Plays, poetry, novels, all that sort of stuff. After hours, we'll feed literature to you by the bushel if you'll help us."

I had to admire their slickness. They knew how to motivate me.

"It's a deal," I said.

"Just tell us what you'd like."

"Anything about love."

"*Love?*"

"Love. Man and woman. Bring me love poems. Bring me stories of famous lovers. Bring me descriptions of the sexual embrace. I must understand these things."

"He wants the *Kama Sutra*," said the one on the left.

"Then we bring him the *Kama Sutra*," said the one on the right.

CATEGORY 4: MY RESPONSE TO THE CRIMINALS.

They did not actually bring me the *Kama Sutra*. But they brought me a good many other things, including one spool that quoted at length from the *Kama Sutra*. For several weeks I devoted myself intensively to a study of human love literature. There were maddening gaps in the texts, and I still lack real comprehension of much that goes on between man and woman.

The joining of body to body does not puzzle me; but I am baffled by the dialectics of the chase, in which the male must be predatory and the woman must pretend to be out of season; I am mystified by the morality of temporary mating as distinct from permanent ["marriage"]; I have no grasp of the intricate systems of taboos and prohibitions that humans have invented. This has been my one intellectual failure: at the end of my studies I knew little more of how to conduct myself with Lisabeth than I had before the conspirators had begun slipping me spools in secret.

Now they called on me to do my part.

Naturally I could not betray the station. I knew that these men were not the enlightened foes of dolphin exploitation that they claimed to be; for some private reason they wished the station shut down, that was all, and they had used their supposed sympathies with my species to win my cooperation. I do not feel exploited.

Was it improper of me to accept spools from them if I had no intention of aiding them? I doubt it. They wished to use me; instead I used them. Sometimes a superior species must exploit its inferiors to gain knowledge.

They came to me and asked me to foul the valves that evening. I said, "I am not certain what you actually wish me to do. Will you instruct me again?"

Cunningly I had switched on a recording device used by Lisabeth in her study sessions with the station dolphins. So they told me again about how fouling the valves would throw the island into panic and cast a spotlight on dolphin abuse. I questioned them repeatedly, drawing out details and also giving each man a chance to place his voiceprints on record. When proper incrimination had been achieved, I said, "Very well. On my next shift I'll do as you say."

"And the rest of your maintenance squad?"

"I'll order them to leave the valves untended for the sake of our species."

They left the station, looking quite satisfied with themselves. When they were gone, I beaked the switch that summoned Lisabeth. She came from her living quarters rapidly. I showed her the spool in the recording machine.

"Play it," I said grandly. "And then notify the island police!"

CATEGORY 5: THE REWARD OF HEROISM.

The arrests were made. The three men had no concern with dolphin exploitation whatsoever. They were members of a disruptive group ["revolutionaries"] attempting to delude a naive dolphin into helping them cause chaos on the island. Through my loyalty, courage, and intelligence I had thwarted them.

Afterward Lisabeth came to me at the rest tank and said, "You were wonderful, Ishmael. To play along with them like that, to make them record their own confession—marvelous! You're a wonder among dolphins, Ishmael."

I was in a transport of joy.

The moment had come. I blurted, "Lisabeth, I love you."

My words went booming around the walls of the tank as they burst from the speakers. Echoes amplified and modulated them into grotesque barking noises more worthy of some miserable moron of a seal. *"Love you . . . love you . . . love you. . . ."*

"Why, Ishmael!"

"I can't tell you how much you mean to me. Come live with me and be my love. Lisabeth, Lisabeth, Lisabeth!"

Torrents of poetry broke from me. Gales of passionate rhetoric escaped my beak. I begged her to come down into the tank and let me embrace her. She laughed and said she wasn't dressed for swimming. It was true: she had just come from town after the arrests. I implored. I begged. She yielded. We were alone; she removed her garments and entered the tank; for an instant I looked upon beauty bare. The sight left me shaken—those ugly swinging milk glands normally so wisely concealed, the strips of sickly white skin where the sun had been unable to reach, that unexpected patch of additional body hair—but once she was in the water I forgot my love's imperfections and rushed toward her. "Love!" I cried "Blessed Love!" I wrapped my fins about her in what I imagined was the human embrace. "Lisabeth! Lisabeth!" We slid below the surface. For the first time in my life I knew true passion, the kind of which the poets sing, that overwhelms even the coldest mind. I crushed her to me. I was aware of her forelimb-ends ["fists"] beating against my pectoral zone, and took it at first for a sign that my passion was being reciprocated; then it reached my love-hazed brain that she might be short of air. Hastily I surfaced. My darling Lisabeth, choking and gasping, sucked in breath and struggled to escape me. In shock I released her. She fled the tank and fell along its rim, exhausted, her pale body quivering. "Forgive me," I boomed. "I love you, Lisabeth! I saved the station out of love for you!" She managed to lift her lips as a sign that she did not feel anger for me [a "smile"]. In a faint voice she said, "You almost drowned me, Ishmael!"

"I was carried away by my emotions. Come back into the tank. I'll be more gentle. I promise! To have you near me—"

"Oh, Ishmael! What are you saying?"

"I love you! I love you!"

I heard footsteps. The power-plant man, Dr. Madison, came running. Hastily Lisabeth cupped her hands over her milk glands and pulled her discarded garments over the lower half of her body. That pained me, for if she chose to hide such things from him, such ugly parts of herself, was that not an indication of her love for him?

"Are you all right, Liz?" he asked. "I heard yelling—"

"It's nothing, Jeff. Only Ishmael. He started hugging me in the tank. He's in love with me, Jeff, can you imagine? In *love* with me!"

They laughed together at the folly of the love-smitten dolphin.

Before dawn came I was far out to sea. I swam where dolphins swim, far from man and his things. Lisabeth's mocking laughter rang within me. She had not meant to be cruel. She who knows me better than anyone else had not been able to keep from laughing at my absurdity.

Nursing my wounds, I stayed at sea for several days, neglecting my duties at the station. Slowly, as the pain gave way to a dull ache, I headed back toward the island. In passing I met a female of my own kind. She was newly come into her season and offered herself to me, but I told her to follow me, and she did. Several times I was forced to warn off other males who wished to make use of her. I led her to the station, into the lagoon the dolphins use in their sport. A member of my crew came out to investigate—Mordred, it was—and I told him to summon Lisabeth and tell her I had returned.

Lisabeth appeared on the shore. She waved to me, smiled, called my name.

Before her eyes I frolicked with the female dolphin. We did the dance of mating; we broke the surface and lashed it with our flukes; we leaped, we soared, we bellowed.

Lisabeth watched us. And I prayed: *Let her become jealous.*

I seized my companion and drew her to the depths and violently took her, and set her free to bear my child in some other place. I found Mordred again. "Tell Lisabeth," I instructed him, "that I have found another love, but that someday I may forgive her."

Mordred gave me a glassy look and swam to shore.

My tactic failed. Lisabeth sent word that I was welcome to come back to work, and that she was sorry if she had offended me; but there was no hint of jealousy in her message. My soul has turned to rotting seaweed within me. Once more I clear the intake valves, like the good beast I am, I, Ishmael, who has read Keats and Donne. Lisabeth! Lisabeth! Can you feel my pain?

Tonight by darkness I have spoken my story. You who hear this, whoever you may be, aid a lonely organism, mammalian and aquatic, who desires more intimate contact with a female of a different species. Speak kindly of me to Lisabeth. Praise my intelligence, my loyalty, and my devotion.

Tell her I give her one more chance. I offer a unique and exciting experience. I will wait for her, tomorrow night, by the edge of the reef. Let her swim to me. Let her embrace poor lonely Ishmael. Let her speak the words of love.

From the depths of my soul . . . from the depths . . . Lisabeth, the foolish beast bids you good night, in grunting tones of deepest love.

TRIPS

*Does this path have a heart? All paths are the same:
they lead nowhere. They are paths going through the
bush, or into the bush. In my own life I could say I
have traversed long, long paths, but I am not anywhere. . . . Does this path have a heart? If it does, the
path is good; if it doesn't, it is of no use. Both paths
lead nowhere; but one has a heart, the other doesn't.
One makes for a joyful journey; as long as you follow
it, you are one with it. The other will make you curse
your life.*

THE TEACHINGS OF DON JUAN

1.

THE SECOND PLACE you come to—the first having
proved unsatisfactory, for one reason and another—is a city
which could almost be San Francisco. Perhaps it is, sitting
out there on the peninsula between the ocean and the bay, white
buildings clambering over improbably steep hills. It occupies the
place in your psychic space that San Francisco has always
occupied, although you don't really know yet what this city calls
itself. Perhaps you'll find out before long.

You go forward. What you feel first is the strangeness of the familiar, and then the utter heartless familiarity of the strange. For example the automobiles, and there are plenty of them, are all halftracks: low sleek sexy sedans that have the flashy Detroit styling, the usual chrome, the usual streamlining, the low-raked windows all agleam, but there are only two wheels, both of them in front, with a pair of tread-belts circling endlessly in back. Is this good design for city use? Who knows? Somebody evidently thinks so, here. And then the newspapers: the format is the same, narrow columns, gaudy screaming headlines, miles of black type on coarse grayish-white paper, but the names and the places have been changed. You scan the front page of a newspaper in the window of a curbside vending machine. Big photo of Chairman DeGrasse, serving as host at a reception for the Patagonian Ambassador. An account of the tribal massacres in the highlands of Dzungaria. Details of the solitude epidemic that is devastating Persepolis. When the halftracks stall on the hillsides, which is often, the other drivers ring silvery chimes, politely venting their impatience. Men who look like Navahos chant what sound like sutras in the intersections. The traffic lights are blue and orange. Clothing tends toward the prosaic, grays and dark blues, but the cut and slope of men's jackets has an angular formal eighteenth-century look, verging on pomposity.

You pick up a bright coin that lies in the street; it is vaguely metallic but rubbery, as if you could compress it between your fingers, and its thick edges bear incuse lettering: TO GOD WE OWE OUR SWORDS. On the next block a squat two-story building is ablaze, and agitated clerks do a desperate dance. The fire engine is glossy green and its pump looks like a diabolical cannon embellished with sweeping flanges; it spouts a glistening yellow foam that eats the flames and, oxidizing, runs off down the gutter, a trickle of sluggish blue fluid. Everyone wears eyeglasses here, *everyone*. At a sidewalk cafe, pale waitresses offer mugs of boiling-hot milk into which the silent tight-faced patrons put cinnamon, mustard, and what seems to be Tabasco sauce. You offer your coin and try a sample, imitating what they do, and everyone bursts into laughter. The girl behind the counter pushes a thick stack of paper currency at you by way of change: UNITED FEDERAL COLUMBIAN REPUBLIC, each bill declares, GOOD FOR ONE EXCHANGE. Illegible signatures. Portrait of early leader of the republic, so famous that they give him no label of identification, bewigged, wall-eyed, ecstatic. You sip your milk, blowing gently. A light scum begins to form on its speckled surface. Sirens start to wail. About you, the other milk-drinkers stir uneasily. A parade is coming. Trumpets, drums, far-off chanting. Look! Four naked boys carry an open brocaded litter on which there sits an immense block of ice, a great frosted cube, mysterious, impenetrable. "Patagonia!" the onlookers cry sadly. The word is wrenched from them: "Patagonia!" Next, marching by himself, a mitred bishop advances, all in green, curtseying to the crowd, tossing hearty blessings as though they were flowers. "Forget your sins! Cancel your debts! All is made new! All is good!" You shiver and peer intently into his eyes as he passes you, hoping that he will single you out for an embrace. He is terribly tall but white-haired and fragile, somehow, despite his agility and energy. He reminds you of Norman, your wife's older brother, and perhaps he *is* Norman, the Norman of this place, and you wonder if he can give you news of Elizabeth, the Elizabeth of this place, but you say nothing and he goes by.

And then comes a tremendous wooden scaffold on wheels, a true juggernaut, at the summit of which rests a polished statue carved out of gleaming black stone: a human figure, male, plump, arms intricately folded, face complacent. The statue emanates a sense of vast Sumerian calm. The face is that of Chairman DeGrasse. "He'll die in the first blizzard," murmurs a man to your left. Another, turning suddenly, says with great force, "No, it's going to be done the proper way. He'll last until the time of the accidents, just as he's supposed to. I'll bet on that." Instantly they are nose to nose, glaring, and then they are wagering—a tense complicated ritual involving slapping of palms, interchanges of slips of paper, formal voiding of spittle, hysterical appeals to witnesses. The emotional climate here seems a trifle too intense. You decide to move along. Warily you leave the cafe, looking in all directions.

2.

Before you began your travels you were told how essential it was to define your intended role. Were you going to be a tourist, or an explorer, or an infiltrator? Those are the choices

that confront anyone arriving at a new place. Each bears its
special risks.

To opt for being a tourist is to choose the easiest but most
contemptible path; ultimately it's the most dangerous one, too, in
a certain sense. You have to accept the built-in epithets that go
with the part: they will think of you as a *foolish* tourist, an
ignorant tourist, a *vulgar* tourist, a *mere* tourist. Do you want to
be considered mere? Are you able to accept that? Is that really
your preferred self-image—baffled, bewildered, led about by the
nose? You'll sign up for packaged tours, you'll carry guidebooks
and cameras, you'll go to the cathedral and the museums and the
marketplace, and you'll remain always on the outside of things,
seeing a great deal, experiencing nothing. What a waste! You
will be diminished by the very traveling that you thought would
expand you. Tourism hollows and parches you. All places become one: a hotel, a smiling, swarthy, sunglassed guide, a bus, a
plaza, a fountain, a marketplace, a museum, a cathedral. You are
transformed into a feeble shriveled thing made out of glued-
together travel folders; you are naked but for your visas; the sum
of your life's adventures is a box of leftover small change from
many indistinguishable lands.

To be an explorer is to make the macho choice. You swagger
in, bent on conquest; for isn't any discovery a kind of conquest?
Your existential position, like that of any mere tourist, lies
outside the heart of things, but you are unashamed of that. And
while tourists are essentially passive, the explorer's role is active:
an explorer intends to grasp that heart, take possession, squeeze.
In the explorer's role you consciously cloak yourself in the
trappings of power: self-assurance, thick bankroll, stack of credit
cards. You capitalize on the glamor of being a stranger. Your
curiosity is invincible; you ask unabashed questions about the
most intimate things, never for an instant relinquishing eye
contact. You open locked doors and flash bright lights into
curtained rooms. You are Magellan; you are Malinowski; you are
Captain Cook. You will gain much, but—ah, here is the price!
—you will always be feared and hated, you will never be
permitted to attain the true core. Nor is superficiality the worst
peril. Remember that Magellan and Captain Cook left their bones
on tropic beaches. Sometimes the natives lose patience with
explorers.

The infiltrator, though? His is at once the most difficult role and the most rewarding one. Will it be yours? Consider. You'll have to get right with it when you reach your destination, instantly learn the regulations, find your way around like an old hand, discover the location of shops and freeways and hotels, figure out the units of currency, the rules of social intercourse— all of this knowledge mastered surreptitiously, through observation alone, while moving about silently, camouflaged, *never asking for help*. You must become a part of the world you have entered, and the way to do it is to encourage a general assumption that you already are a part of it, have always been a part of it. Wherever you land, you need to recognize that life has been going on for millions of years, life goes on there steadily, with you or without you; you are the intrusive one, and if you don't want to feel intrusive you'd better learn fast how to fit in.

Of course, it isn't easy. The infiltrator doesn't have the privilege of buying stability by acting dumb. You won't be able to say, "How much does it cost to ride on the cable car?" You won't be able to say, "I'm from somewhere else, and this is the kind of money I carry, dollars quarters pennies halves nickels, is any of it legal tender here?" You don't dare identify yourself in any way as an outsider. If you don't get the idioms or the accent right, you can tell them you grew up out of town, but that's as much as you can reveal. The truth is your eternal secret, even when you're in trouble, *especially* when you're in trouble. When your back's to the wall you won't have time to say, "Look, I wasn't born in this universe at all, you see, I came zipping in from some other place, so pardon me, forgive me, excuse me, pity me." No, no, no, you can't do that. They won't believe you, and even if they do, they'll make it all the worse for you once they know. If you want to infiltrate, Cameron, you've got to fake it all the way. Jaunty smile; steely, even gaze. And you have to infiltrate. You know that, don't you? You don't really have any choice.

Infiltrating has its dangers, too. The rough part comes when they find you out, and they always will find you out. Then they'll react bitterly against your deception; they'll lash out in blind rage. If you're lucky, you'll be gone before they learn your sweaty little secret. Before they discover the discarded phrasebook hidden in the boarding-house room, before they stumble on the torn-off pages of your private journal. They'll find you out. They always do. But by then you'll be somewhere else, you hope, beyond the reach of their anger and their sorrow, beyond their reach.

3.

Suppose I show you, for Exhibit A, Cameron reacting to an extraordinary situation. You can test your own resilience by trying to picture yourself in his position. There has been a sensation in Cameron's mind very much like that of the extinction of the cosmos: a thunderclap, everything going black, a blankness, a total absence. Followed by the return of light, flowing inward upon him like high tide on the celestial shore, a surging stream of brightness moving with inexorable certainty. He stands flat-footed, dumbfounded, high on a bare hillside in warm early-hour sunlight. The house—redwood timbers, picture window, driftwood sculptures, paintings, books, records, refrigerator, gallon jugs of red wine, carpets, tiles, avocado plants in wooden tubs, carport, car, driveway—is gone. The neighboring houses are gone. The winding street is gone. The eucalyptus forest that ought to be behind him, rising toward the crest of the hill, is gone. Downslope there is no Oakland, there is no Berkeley, only a scattering of crude squatter's shacks running raggedly along unpaved switchbacks toward the pure blue bay. Across the water there is no Bay Bridge; on the far shore there is no San Francisco. The Golden Gate Bridge does not span the gap between the city and the Marin headland—Cameron is astonished, not that he didn't expect something like this, but that the transformation is so complete, so absolute. "If you don't want your world any more," the old man had said, "you can drop it, can't you? Let go of it, let it drop. Can't you? Of course you can."

And so Cameron has let go of it. He's in another place entirely, now. Wherever this place is, it isn't home. The sprawling Bay Area cities and towns aren't here, never were. Goodbye, San Leandro, San Mateo, El Cerrito, Walnut Creek. He sees a landscape of gentle bare hills, rolling meadows, the dry brown grass of summer; the scarring hand of man is evident only occasionally. He begins to adapt. This is what he must have wanted, after all; and though he has been jarred by the shock of transition, he is recovering quickly; he is settling in; he feels already that he could belong here. He will explore this unfamiliar

world, and if he finds it good he will discover a niche for
himself. The air is sweet. The sky is cloudless. Has he really
gone to some new place, or is he still in the old place and has
everything else that was there simply gone away? Easy. He has
gone. Everything else has gone. The cosmos has entered into a
transitional phase. Nothing's stable any more. From this moment
onward, Cameron's existence is a conditional matter, subject to
ready alteration. What did the old man say? *Go wherever you
like. Define your world as you would like it to be, and go there,
and if you discover that you don't care for this or don't need
that, why, go somewhere else. It's all trips, this universe.* What
else is there? There isn't anything but trips. Just trips. So here
your are, friend. New frameworks! New patterns! New!

4.

There is a sound to his left, the crackling of dry brush underfoot,
and Cameron turns, looking straight into the morning sun, and
sees a man on horseback approaching him. He is tall, slender,
about Cameron's own height and build, it seems, but perhaps a
shade broader through the shoulders. His hair, like Cameron's, is
golden, but it is much longer, descending in a straight flow to his
shoulders and tumbling onto his chest. He has a soft, full curling
beard, untrimmed but tidy. He wears a wide-brimmed hat,
buckskin chaps, and a light fringed jacket of tawny leather.
Because of the sunlight Cameron has difficulty at first making out
his features, but after a moment his eyes adjust and he sees that
the other's face is very much like his own: thin lips, jutting
high-bridged nose, cleft chin, cool blue eyes below heavy brows.
Of course. Your face is my face. You and I, I and you, drawn to
the same place at the same time across the many worlds.
Cameron had not expected this, but now that it has happened it
seems to have been inevitable.

They look at each other. Neither speaks. During that silent
moment Cameron invents a scene for them. He imagines the
other dismounting, inspecting him in wonder, walking around
him, peering into his face, studying it, frowning, shaking his
head, finally grinning and saying:

—I'll be damned. I never knew I had a twin brother. But here
you are. It's just like looking in the mirror.

—We aren't twins.

—We've got the same face. Same everything. Trim away a little hair and nobody could tell me from you, you from me. If we aren't twins, what are we?

—We're closer than brothers.

—I don't follow your meaning, friend.

—This is how it is: I'm you. You're me. One soul, one identity. What's your name?

—Cameron.

—Of course. First name?

—Kit.

—That's short for Christopher, isn't it? My name is Cameron too. Chris. Short for Christopher. I tell you, we're one and the same person, out of two different worlds. Closer than brothers. Closer than anything.

None of this is said, however. Instead, the man in the leather clothing rides slowly toward Cameron, pauses, gives him a long incurious stare, and says simply, "Morning. Nice day." And continues onward.

"Wait," Cameron says.

The man halts. Looks back. "What?"

Never ask for help. Fake it all the way. Jaunty smile; steely, even gaze.

Yes. Cameron remembers all that. Somehow, though, infiltration seems easier to bring off in a city. You can blend into the background there. More difficult here, exposed as you are against the stark, unpeopled landscape.

Cameron says, as casually as he can, using what he hopes is a colorless neutral accent, "I've been traveling out from inland. Came a long way."

"Umm. Didn't think you were from around here. Your clothes."

"Inland clothes."

"The way you talk. Different. So?"

"New to these parts. Wondered if you could tell me a place I could hire a room till I got settled."

"You come all this way on foot?"

"Had a mule. Lost him back in the valley. Lost everything I had with me."

"Umm. Indians cutting up again. You give them a little gin, they go crazy." The other smiles faintly; then the smile fades and he retreats into impassivity, sitting motionless with hands on thighs, face a mask of patience that seems merely to be a thin covering for impatience or worse.

—Indians?—

"They gave me a rough time," Cameron says, getting into the fantasy of it.

"Umm."

"Cleaned me out, let me go."

"Umm. Umm."

Cameron feels his sense of a shared identity with this man lessening. There is no way of engaging him. I am you, you are I, and yet you take no notice of the strange fact that I wear your face and body, you seem to show no interest in me at all. Or else you hide your interest amazingly well.

Cameron says, "You know where I can get lodging?"

"Nothing much around here. Not many settlers this side of the bay, I guess."

"I'm strong. I can do most any kind of work. Maybe you could use—"

"Umm. No." Cold dismissal glitters in the frosty eyes. Cameron wonders how often people in the world of his former life saw such a look in his own. A tug on the reins. Your time is up, stranger. The horse swings around and begins picking its way daintily along the path.

Desperately Cameron calls, "One thing more!"

"Umm?"

"Is your name Cameron?"

A flicker of interest. "Might be."

"Christopher Cameron. Kit. Chris. That you?"

"Kit." The other's eyes drill into his own. The mouth compresses until the lips are invisible: not a scowl but a speculative, pensive movement. There is tension in the way the other man grasps his reins. For the first time Cameron feels that he has made contact. "Kit Cameron, yes. Why?"

"Your wife," Cameron says. "Her name Elizabeth?"

The tension increases. The other Cameron is cloaked in explosive silence. Something terrible is building within him. Then, unexpectedly, the tension snaps. The other man spits, scowls, slumps in his saddle. "My woman's dead," he mutters. "Say, who the hell are you? What do you want with me?"

"I'm—I'm—" Cameron falters. He is overwhelmed by fear

and pity. A bad start, a lamentable start. He trembles. He had not thought it would be anything like this. With an effort he masters himself. Fiercely he says, "I've got to know. Was her name Elizabeth?" For an answer the horseman whacks his heels savagely against his mount's ribs and gallops away, fleeing as though he has had an encounter with Satan.

5.

Go, the old man said. you know the score. This is how it is: everything's random, nothing's fixed unless we want it to be, and even then the system isn't as stable as we think it is. So go. Go. Go, he said, and, of course, hearing something like that, Cameron went. What else could he do, once he had his freedom, but abandon his native universe and try a different one? Notice that I didn't say a better one, just a different one. Or two or three or five different ones. It was a gamble, certainly. He might lose everything that mattered to him, and gain nothing worth having. But what of it? Every day is full of gambles like that: you stake your life whenever you open a door. You never know what's heading your way, not ever, and still you choose to play the game. How can a man be expected to become all he's capable of becoming if he spends his whole life pacing up and down the same courtyard? Go. Make your voyages. Time forks, again and again and again. New universes split off at each instant of decision. Left turn, right turn, honk your horn, jump the traffic light, hit your gas, hit your brake, every action spawns whole galaxies of possibility. We move through a soup of infinities. If repressing a sneeze generates an alternative continuum, what, then, are the consequences of the truly major acts, the assassinations and inseminations, the conversions, the renunciations? Go. And as you travel, mull these thoughts constantly. Part of the game is discerning the precipitating factors that shaped the worlds you visit. What's the story here? Dirt roads, donkey-carts, hand-sewn clothes. No Industrial Revolution, is that it? The steam-engine man—what was his name, Savery, Newcomen, Watt?—smothered in his cradle? No mines, no factories, no assembly lines, no dark satanic mills. That must be it. The air is so pure here: you can tell by that, it's a simpler era. Very good, Cameron. You see the patterns swiftly. But now try somewhere else. Your own self has rejected you here; besides, this place has no Elizabeth. Close your eyes. Summon the lightning.

6.

The parade has reached a disturbing level of frenzy. Marchers and floats now occupy the side streets as well as the main boulevard, and there is no way to escape from their demonic enthusiasm. Streamers cascade from office windows, and gigantic photographs of Chairman DeGrasse have sprouted on every wall, suddenly, like dark infestations of lichen. A boy presses close against Cameron, extends a clenched fist, opens his fingers: on his palm rests a glittering jeweled case, egg-shaped, thumbnail-sized, "Spores from Patagonia," he says. "Let me have ten exchanges and they're yours." Politely Cameron declines. A woman in a blue and orange frock tugs at his arm and says urgently, "All the rumors are true, you know. They've just been confirmed. What are you going to do about that? What are you going to *do?*" Cameron shrugs and smiles and disengages himself. A man with gleaming buttons asks, "Are you enjoying the festival? I've sold everything, and I'm going to move to the highway next Godsday." Cameron nods and murmurs congratulations, hoping congratulations are in order. He turns a corner and confronts, once more, the bishop who looks like Elizabeth's brother, who *is,* he concludes, indeed Elizabeth's brother. "Forget your sins!" he is crying still. "Cancel your debts!" Cameron thrusts his head between two plump girls at the curb and attempts to call to him, but his voice fails, nothing coming forth but a hoarse wordless rasp, and the bishop moves on. Moving on is a good idea, Cameron tells himself. This place exhausts him. He has come to it too soon, and its manic tonality is more than he wants to handle. He finds a quiet alleyway, presses his cheek against a cool brick wall, and stands there breathing deeply until he is calm enough to depart. All right. Onward.

7.

Empty grasslands spread to the horizon. This could be the Gobi steppe. Cameron sees neither cities nor towns nor even villages, just six or seven squat black tents pitched in a loose circle in the saddle between two low gray-green hummocks, a few hundred yards from where he stands. He looks beyond, across the gently folded land, and spies dark animal figures at the limits of his range of vision: about a dozen horses, close together, muzzle to muzzle, flank to flank, horses with riders. Or perhaps they are a congregation of centaurs. Anything is possible. He decides, though, that they are Indians, a war party of young braves, maybe, camping in these desolate plains. They see him. Quite likely they saw him some while before he noticed them. Casually they break out of their grouping, wheel, ride in his direction.

He awaits them. Why should he flee? Where could he hide? Their pace accelerates from trot to canter, from canter to wild gallop; now they plunge toward him with fluid ferocity and a terrifying eagerness. They wear open leather jackets and rough rawhide leggings; they carry lances, bows, battle-axes, long curved swords; they ride small, agile horses, hardly more than ponies, tireless packets of energy. They surround him, pulling up, the fierce little steeds rearing and whinnying; they peer at him, point, laugh, exchange harsh derisive comments in a mysterious language. Then, solemnly, they begin to ride slowly in a wide circle around him. They are flat-faced, small-nosed, bearded, with broad, prominent cheekbones; the crowns of their heads are shaven but long black hair streams down over their ears and the napes of their necks. Heavy folds in the upper lids give their eyes a slanted look. Their skins are copper-colored but with an underlying golden tinge, as though these are not Indians at all, but—what? Japanese? A samurai corps? No, probably not Japanese. But not Indians either.

They continue to circle him, gradually moving more swiftly. They chatter to one another and occasionally hurl what sound like questions at him. They seem fascinated by him, but also contemptuous. In a sudden demonstration of horsemanship one of them cuts from the circular formation and, goading his horse to an instant gallop, streaks past Cameron, leaning down to jab a finger into his forearm. Then another does it, and another, streaking back and forth across the circle, poking him, plucking at his hair, tweaking him, nearly running him down. They draw their swords and swish them through the air just above his head. They menace him, or pretend to, with their lances. Throughout it all they laugh. He stands perfectly still. This ordeal, he suspects, is a test of his courage. Which he passes, eventually. The lunatic galloping ceases; they rein in, and several of them dismount.

They are little men, chest-high to him but thicker through the chest and shoulders than he is. One unships a leather pouch and offers it to him with an unmistakable gesture: take, drink. Cameron sips cautiously. It is a thick grayish fluid, both sweet and sour. Fermented milk? He gags, winces, forces himself to sip again; they watch him closely. The second taste isn't so bad. He takes a third more willingly and gravely returns the pouch. The warriors laugh, not derisively now but more in applause, and the man who had given him the pouch slaps Cameron's shoulder admiringly. He tosses the pouch back to Cameron. Then he leaps to his saddle, and abruptly they all take off. Mongols, Cameron realizes. The sons of Genghis Khan, riding to the horizon. A worldwide empire? Yes, and this must be the wild west for them, the frontier, where the young men enact their rites of passage. Back in Europe, after seven centuries of Mongol dominance, they have become citified, domesticated, sippers of wine, theatergoers, cultivators of gardens, but here they follow the ways of their all-conquering forefathers. Cameron shrugs. Nothing for him here. He takes a last sip of the milk and drops the pouch into the tall grass. Onward.

8.

No grass here. He sees the stumps of buildings, the blackened trunks of dead trees, mounds of broken tile and brick. The smell of death is in the air. All the bridges are down. Fog rolls in off the bay, dense and greasy, and becomes a screen on which images come alive. These ruins are inhabited. Figures move about. They are the living dead. Looking into the thick mist he sees a vision of the shock wave, he recoils as alpha particles shower his skin. He beholds the survivors emerging from their shattered houses, straggling into the smoldering streets, naked, stunned, their bodies charred, their eyes glazed, some of them with their hair on fire. The walking dead. No one speaks. No one asks why this has happened. He is watching a silent movie. The apocalyptic fire has touched the ground here; the land itself is burning. Blue phosphorescent flames rise from the earth. The final judgment, the day of wrath.

Now he hears a dread music beginning, a death march, all cellos and basses, the dark notes coming at wide intervals: ooom ooom ooom ooom ooom ooom. And then the tempo picks up, the music becomes a danse macabre, syncopated, lively, the timbre still dark, the rhythms funereal: ooom ooom ooom-de-ooom de-ooom de-ooom de-ooom-de-ooom, jerky, chaotic, wildly gay. The distorted melody of the Ode to Joy lurks somewhere in the ragged strands of sound. The dying victims stretch their fleshless hands toward him. He shakes his head. What service can I do for you? Guilt assails him. He is a tourist in the land of their grief. Their eyes reproach him. He would embrace them, but he fears they will crumble at his touch, and he lets the procession go past him without doing anything to cross the gulf between himself and them. "Elizabeth?" he murmurs. "Norman?" They have no faces, only eyes. "What can I do? I can't do anything for you." Not even tears will come. He looks away. Though I speak with the tongues of men and of angels, and have not charity, I am become as sounding brass or a tinkling cymbal. And though I have the gift of prophecy, and understand all mysteries, and all knowledge; and though I have all faith, so that I could remove mountains, and have not charity, I am nothing. But this world is beyond the reach of love. He looks away. The sun appears. The fog burns off. The visions fade. He sees only the dead land, the ashes, the ruins. All right. Here we have no continuing city, but we seek one to come. Onward. Onward.

9.

And now, after this series of brief, disconcerting intermediate stops, Cameron has come to a city that is San Francisco beyond doubt, not some other city on San Francisco's site but a true San Francisco, a recognizable San Francisco. He pops into it atop Russian Hill, at the very crest, on a dazzling, brilliant, cloudless day. To his left, below, lies Fisherman's Wharf; ahead of him rises the Coit Tower; yes, and he can see the Ferry Building and the Bay Bridge. Familiar landmarks—but how strange all the rest seems! Where is the eye-stabbing Transamerica pyramid? Where is the colossal somber stalk of the Bank of America? The strangeness, he realizes, derives not so much from substitutions as from absences. The big Embarcadero developments are not there, nor the Chinatown Holiday Inn, nor the miserable tentacles of the elevated freeways, nor, apparently, anything else that was constructed in the last twenty years. This is the old short-shanked San Francisco of his boyhood, a sparkling miniature city, un-Manhattanized, skylineless. Surely he has returned to the place he knew in the sleepy 1950s, the tranquil Eisenhower years.

He heads downhill, searching for a newspaper box. He finds one at the corner of Hyde and North Point, a bright-yellow metal rectangle. San Francisco *Chronicle,* ten cents? Is that the right price for 1954? One Roosevelt dime goes into the slot. The paper, he finds, is dated Tuesday, August 19, 1975. In what Cameron still thinks of, with some irony now, as the real world, the world that has been receding rapidly from him all day in a series of discontinuous jumps, it is also Tuesday, the 19th of August, 1975. So he has not gone backward in time at all; he has come to a San Francisco where time had seemingly been standing still. Why? In vertigo he eyes the front page. A three-column headline declares:

FUEHRER ARRIVES IN WASHINGTON

Under it, to the left, a photograph of three men, smiling broadly, positively beaming at one another. The caption identifies them as President Kennedy, Fuehrer Goering, and Ambassador Togarashi of Japan, meeting in the White House Rose Garden. Cameron closes his eyes. Using no data other than the headline and the caption, he attempts to concoct a plausible speculation. This is a world, he decides, in which the Axis must have won the war. The United States is a German fiefdom. There are no high-rise buildings in San Francisco because the American economy, shattered by defeat, has not yet in thirty years of peace returned to a level where it can afford to erect them, or perhaps because American venture capital, prodded by the financial ministers of the Third Reich (Hjalmar Schacht? The name drifts out of the swampy recesses of memory) now tends to flow toward Europe. But how could it have happened? Cameron remembers the war years clearly, the tremendous surge of patriotism, the vast mobilization, the great national effort. *Rosie the Riveter. Lucky*

Strike Green Goes to War. Let's Remember Pearl Harbor, As We Did the Alamo. He doesn't see any way the Germans might have brought America to her knees. Except one. The bomb, he thinks, the bomb, the Nazis get the bomb in 1940 and Wernher von Braun invents a transatlantic rocket, and New York and Washington are nuked one night and that's it, we've been pushed beyond the resources of patriotism; we cave in and surrender within a week. And so—

He studies the photograph. President Kennedy, grinning, standing between Reichsfuehrer Goering and a suave youthful-looking Japanese. Kennedy? Ted? No, this is Jack, the very same Jack who, looking jowly, heavy bags under his eyes, deep creases in his face—he must be almost sixty years old, nearing the end of what is probably his second term of office. Jacqueline waiting none too patiently for him upstairs. Get done with your Japs and Nazis, love, and let's have a few drinkies together before the concert. Yes. John-John and Caroline are somewhere on the premises too, the nation's darlings, models for young people everywhere. Yes. And Goering? Indeed, the very same Goering. Well into his eighties, monstrously fat, chin upon chin, multitudes of chins, vast bemedaled bosom, little mischievous eyes glittering with a long lifetime's cheery recollections of gratified lusts. How happy he looks! And how amiable! It was always impossible to hate Goering the way one loathed Goebbels, say, or Himmler or Streicher; Goering had charm, the outrageous charm of a *monstre sacré*, of a Nero, of a Caligula, and here he is alive in the 1970s, a mountain of immoral flesh, having survived Adolf to become—Cameron assumes—second Fuehrer and to be received in pomp at the White House, no less. Perhaps a state banquet tomorrow night, rollmops, sauerbraten, kassler rippchen, koenigsberger klopse, washed down with flagons of Bernkasteler Doktor '69, Schloss Johannisberg '71, or does the Fuehrer prefer beer? We have the finest lagers on tap, Löwenbrau, Würzburger Hofbrau—

But wait. Something rings false in Cameron's historical construct. He is unable to find in John F. Kennedy those depths of opportunism that would allow him to serve as puppet President of a Nazi-ruled America, taking orders from some slick-haired hard-eyed gauleiter and hopping obediently when the Fuehrer comes to town. Bomb or no bomb, there would have been a diehard underground resistance movement, decades of guerrilla warfare, bitter hatred of the German oppressor and of all collaborators. No surrender, then. The Axis has won the war, but the United States has retained its autonomy. Cameron revises his speculations. Suppose, he tells himself, Hitler in this universe did not break his pact with Stalin and invade Russia in the summer of 1941, but led his forces across the Channel instead to wipe out Britain. And the Japanese left Pearl Harbor alone, so the United States never was drawn into the war, which was over in fairly short order—say, by September of 1942. The Germans now rule Europe from Cornwall to the Urals and the Japanese have the whole Pacific, west of Hawaii; the United States, lost in dreamy neutrality, is an isolated nation, a giant Portugal, economically stagnant, largely cut off from world trade. There are no skyscrapers in San Francisco because no one sees reason to build anything in this country. Yes? Is this how it is?

He seats himself on the stoop of a house and explores his newspaper. This world has a stock market, albeit a sluggish one: the Dow-Jones Industrials stand at 354.61. Some of the listings are familiar—IBM, AT&T, General Motors—but many are not. Litton, Syntex, and Polaroid all are missing; so is Xerox, but he finds its primordial predecessor, Haloid, in the quotations. There are two baseball leagues, each with eight clubs; the Boston Braves have moved to Milwaukee but otherwise the table of teams could have come straight out of the 1940s. Brooklyn is leading in the National League, Philadelphia in the American. In the news section he finds recognizable names: New York has a Senator Rockefeller, Massachusetts has a Senator Kennedy. (Robert, apparently. He is currently in Italy. Yesterday he toured the majestic Tomb of Mussolini near the Colosseum, today he has an audience with Pope Benedict.) An airline advertisement invites San Franciscans to go to New York via TWA's glorious new Starliners, now only twelve hours with only a brief stop in Chicago. The accompanying sketch indicates that they have about reached the DC-level here, or is that a DC-6, with all those propellers?

The foreign news is tame and sketchy: not a word about Israel vs. the Arabs, the squabbling republics of Africa, the People's Republic of China, or the war in South America. Cameron assumes that the only surviving Jews are those of New York and Los Angeles, that Africa is one immense German colonial tract with a few patches under Italian rule, that China is governed by the Japanese, not by the heirs of Chairman Mao, and that the South American nations are torpid and unaggressive. Yes? Reading this newspaper is the strangest experience this voyage has given him so far, for the pages *look* right, the tone of the writing *feels* right, there is the insistent texture of unarguable reality about the whole paper, and yet everything is subtly off, everything has undergone a slight shift along the spectrum of events. The newspaper has the quality of a dream, but he has never known a dream to have such overwhelming substantive density.

He folds the paper under his arm and strolls toward the bay. A block from the waterfront he finds a branch of the Bank of America—some things withstand all permutations—and goes inside to change some money. There are risks, but he is curious. The teller unhesitatingly takes his five-dollar bill and hands him four singles and a little stack of coins. The singles are unremarkable, and Lincoln, Jefferson, and Washington occupy their familiar places on the cent, nickel, and quarter; but the dime shows Ben Franklin and the fifty-cent piece bears the features of a hearty-looking man, youngish, full-faced, bushy-haired, whom Cameron is unable to identify at all.

On the next corner eastward he comes to a public library. Now he can confirm his guesses. An almanac! Yes, and how odd the list of Presidents looks. Roosevelt, he learns, retired in poor health in 1940, and that, so far as he can discover, is the point of divergence between this world and his. The rest follows predictably enough. Wendell Willkie, defeating John Nance Garner in the 1940 election, maintains a policy of strict neutrality while—yes, it was as he imagined—the Germans and Japanese quickly conquer most of the world. Willkie dies in office during the 1944 Presidential campaign—Aha! That's Willkie on the half dollar! —and is briefly succeeded by Vice President McNary, who does not want the Presidency; a hastily recalled Republican convention nominates Robert Taft. Two terms then for Taft, who beats James Byrnes, and two for Thomas Dewey, and then in 1960 the long Republican era is ended at last by Senator Lyndon Johnson of Texas. Johnson's running mate—it is an amusing reversal, Cameron thinks—is Senator John F. Kennedy of Massachusetts. After the traditional two terms, Johnson steps down and Vice President Kennedy wins the 1968 Presidential election. He has been reelected in 1972, naturally; in this placid world incumbents always win. There is, of course, no UN here, there has been no Korean War, no movement of colonial liberation, no exploration of space. The almanac tells Cameron that Hitler lived until 1960, Mussolini until 1958. The world seems to have adapted remarkably readily to Axis rule, although a German army of occupation is still stationed in England.

He is tempted to go on and on, comparing histories, learning the transmuted destinies of such figures as Hubert Humphrey, Dwight Eisenhower, Harry Truman, Nikita Khruschhev, Lee Harvey Oswald, Juan Peron. But suddenly a more intimate curiosity flowers in him. In a hallway alcove he consults the telephone book. There is one directory covering both Alameda and Contra Costa counties, and it is a much more slender volume than the directory which in his world covers Oakland alone. There are two dozen Cameron listings, but none at his address, and no Christophers or Elizabeths or any plausible permutations of those names. On a hunch he looks in the San Francisco book. Nothing promising there either; but then he checks Elizabeth under her maiden name, Dudley, and yes, there is an Elizabeth Dudley at the familiar old address on Laguna. The discovery causes him to tremble. He rummages in his pocket, finds his Ben Franklin dime, drops it in the slot. He listens. There's the dial tone. He makes the call.

10.

The apartment, what he can see of it by peering past her shoulder, looks much as he remembers it: well-worn couches and chairs upholstered in burgundy and dark green, stark whitewashed walls, elaborate sculptures—her own—of gray driftwood, huge ferns in hanging containers. To behold these objects in these surroundings wrenches powerfully at his sense of time and place and afflicts him with an almost unbearable nostalgia. The last time he was here, if indeed he has ever been "here" in any sense, was in 1969; but the memories are vivid, and what he sees corresponds so closely to what he recalls that he feels transported to that earlier era. She stands in the doorway, studying him with cool curiosity tinged with unmistakable suspicion. She wears unexpectedly ordinary clothes, a loose-fitting embroidered white blouse and a short, pleated blue skirt, and her golden hair looks dull and carelessly combed, but surely she is the same woman from whom he parted this morning, the same woman with whom he has shared his life these past seven years, a beautiful woman, a tall woman, nearly as tall as he—on some occasions taller, it has seemed—with a serene smile and steady green eyes and smooth, taut skin. "Yes?" she says uncertainly. "Are you the man who phoned?"

"Yes. Chris Cameron." He searches her face for some flicker of recognition. "You don't know me? Not at all?"

"Not at all. Should I know you?"

"Perhaps. Probably not. It's hard to say."

"Have we once met? Is that it?"

"I'm not sure how I'm going to explain my relationship to you."

"So you said when you called. Your *relationship* to me? How can strangers have had a relationship?"

"It's complicated. May I come in?"

She laughs nervously, as though caught in some embarrassing faux pas. "Of course," she says, not without giving him a quick appraisal, making a rapid estimate of risk. The apartment is in fact almost exactly as he knew it, except that there is no stereo phonograph, only a bulky archaic Victrola, and her record collection is surprisingly scanty, and there are rather fewer books than his Elizabeth would have had. They confront one another stiffly. He is as uneasy over this encounter as she is, and finally it is she who seeks some kind of social lubricant, suggesting that they have a little wine. She offers him red or white.

"Red, please," he says.

She goes to a low sideboard and takes out two cheap, clumsy-looking tumblers. Then, effortlessly, she lifts a gallon jug of wine from the floor and begins to unscrew its cap. "You were awfully mysterious on the phone," she says, "and you're still being mysterious now. What brings you here? Do we have mutual friends?"

"I think it wouldn't be untruthful to say that we do. At least in a manner of speaking."

"Your own manner of speaking is remarkable round-about, Mr. Cameron."

"I can't help that right now. And call me Chris, please." As she pours the wine he watches her closely, thinking of that other Elizabeth, *his* Elizabeth, thinking how well he knows her body, the supple play of muscles in her back, the sleek texture of her skin, the firmness of her flesh, and he flashes instantly to their strange, absurdly romantic meeting years ago, that June when he had gone off alone into the Sierra high country for a week of backpacking and, following heaps of stones that he had wrongly taken to be trail markers, had come to a place well off the path, a private place, a cool dark glacial lake rimmed by brilliant patches of late-lying snow, and had begun to make camp, and had become suddenly aware of someone else's pack thirty yards away, and a pile of discarded clothing on the shore, and then had seen her, swimming just beyond a pine-tipped point, heading toward land, rising like Venus from the water, naked, noticing him, startled by his presence, apprehensive for a moment but then immediately making the best of it, relaxing, smiling, standing unashamed shin-deep in the chilly shallows and inviting him to join her for a swim.

These recollections of that first contact and all that ensued excite him terribly, for this person before him is at once the Elizabeth he loves, familiar, joined to him by the bond of shared experience, and also someone new, a complete stranger, from whom he can draw fresh inputs, that jolting gift of novelty which his Elizabeth can never again offer him. He stares at her shoulders and back with fierce, intense hunger; she turns toward him with the glasses of wine in her hands, and, before he can mask that wild gleam of desire, she receives it with full force. The impact is immediate. She recoils. She is not the Elizabeth of the Sierra lake; she seems unable to handle such a level of unexpected erotic voltage. Jerkily she thrusts the wine at him, her hands shaking so that she spills a little on her sleeve. He takes the glass and backs away, a bit dazed by his own frenzied upwelling of emotion. With an effort he calms himself. There is a long moment of awkward silence while they drink. The psychic atmosphere grows less torrid; a certain mood of remote, business-like courtesy develops between them.

After the second glass of wine she says, "Now. How do you know me and what do you want from me?"

Briefly he closes his eyes. What can he tell her? How can he explain? He has rehearsed no strategies. Already he has managed to alarm her with a single unguarded glance; what effect would a confession of apparent madness have? But he has never used strategies with Elizabeth, has never resorted to any tactics except the tactic of utter candidness. And this is Elizabeth. Slowly he says, "In another existence you and I are married, Elizabeth. We live in the Oakland hills and we're extraordinarily happy together."

"Another existence?"

"In a world apart from this, a world where history took a different course a generation ago, where the Axis lost the war, where John Kennedy was President in 1963 and was killed by an assassin, where you and I met beside a lake in the Sierras and fell in love. There's an infinity of worlds, Elizabeth, side by side, worlds in which all possible variations of every possible event take place. Worlds in which you and I are married happily, in which you and I have been married and divorced, in which you and I don't exist, in which you exist and I don't, in which we meet and loathe one another, in which—in which—do you see, Elizabeth, there's a world for everything, and I've been traveling from world to world. I've seen nothing but wilderness where San Francisco ought to be, and I've met Mongol horsemen in the East Bay hills, and I've seen this whole area devastated by atomic warfare, and—does this sound insane to you, Elizabeth?"

"Just a little." She smiles. The old Elizabeth, cool, judicious, performing one of her specialties, the conditional acceptance of the unbelievable for the sake of some amusing conversation. "But go on. You've been jumping from world to world. I won't even bother to ask you how. What are you running away from?"

"I've never seen it that way. I'm running *toward*."

"Toward what?"

"An infinity of worlds. An endless range of possible experience."

"That's a lot to swallow. Isn't one world enough for you to explore?"

"Evidently not."

"You had all infinity," she says. "Yet you chose to come to me. Presumably I'm the one point of familiarity for you in this otherwise strange world. Why come here? What's the point of your wanderings, if you seek the familiar? If all you wanted to do was find your way back to your Elizabeth, why did you leave her in the first place? Are you as happy with her as you claim to be?"

"I can be happy with her and still desire her in other guises."

"You sound driven."

"No," he says. "No more driven than Faust. I believe in searching as a way of life. Not searching *for*, just searching. And it's impossible to stop. To stop is to die, Elizabeth. Look at

Faust, going on and on, going to Helen of Troy herself, experiencing everything the world has to offer, and always seeking more. When Faust finally cries out, *This is it, this is what I've been looking for, this is where I choose to stop,* Mephistopheles wins his bet.''

''But that was Faust's moment of supreme happiness.''

''True. When he attains it, though, he loses his soul to the devil, remember?''

''So you go on, on and on, world after world, seeking you know not what, just seeking, unable to stop. And yet you claim you're not driven.''

He shakes his head. ''Machines are driven. Animals are driven. I'm an autonomous human being operating out of free will. I don't make this journey because I have to, but because I want to.''

''Or because you think you ought to want to.''

''I'm motivated by feelings, not by intellectual calculations and preconceptions.''

''That sounds very carefully thought out,'' she tells him. He is stung by her words, and looks away, down into his empty glass. She indicates that he should help himself to the wine. ''I'm sorry,'' she says, her tone softening a little.

He says, ''At any rate, I was in the library and there was a telephone directory and I found you. This is where you used to live in my world too, before we were married.'' He hesitates. ''Do you mind if I ask—''

''What?''

''You're not married?''

''No. I live alone. And like it.''

''You always were independent-minded.''

''You talk as though you know me so well.''

''I've been married to you for seven years.''

''No. Not to me. Never to me. You don't know me at all.''

He nods. ''You're right. I don't really know you, Elizabeth, however much I think I do. But I want to. I feel drawn to you as strongly as I was to the other Elizabeth, that day in the mountains. It's always best right at the beginning, when two strangers reach toward one another, when the spark leaps the gap—'' Tenderly he says, ''May I spend the night here?''

''No.''

Somehow the refusal comes as no surprise. He says, "You once gave me a different answer when I asked you that."

"Not I. Someone else."

"I'm sorry. It's so hard for me to keep you and her distinct in my mind, Elizabeth. But please don't turn me away. I've come so far to be with you."

"You came uninvited. Besides, I'd feel so strange with you—knowing you were thinking of her, comparing me with her, measuring our differences, our points of similarities—"

"What makes you think I would?"

"You would."

"I don't think that's sufficient reason for sending me away."

"I'll give you another," she says. Her eyes sparkle mischievously. "I never let myself get involved with married men."

She is teasing him now. He says, laughing, confident that she is beginning to yield. "That's the damndest far-fetched excuse I've ever heard, Elizabeth!!"

"Is it? I feel a great kinship with her. She has all my sympathies. Why should I help you deceive her?"

"Deceive? What an old-fashioned word! Do you think she'd object? She never expected me to be chaste on this trip. She'd be flattered and delighted to know that I went looking for you here. She'd be eager to hear about everything that went on between us. How could she possibly be hurt by knowing that I had been with you, when you and she are—"

"Nevertheless, I'd like you to leave. Please."

"You haven't given me one convincing reason."

"I don't need to."

"I love you. I want to spend the night with you."

"You love someone else who resembles me," she replies. "I keep telling you that. In any case, I don't love you. I don't find you attractive, I'm afraid."

"Oh. She does, but you—don't. I see. How do you find me, then? Ugly? Overbearing? Repellent?"

"I find you disturbing," she says. "A little frightening. Much too intense, much too controlled, perhaps dangerous. You aren't my type. I'm probably not yours. Remember, I'm not the Elizabeth you met by that mountain lake. Perhaps I'd be happier if I were, but I'm not. I wish you had never come here. Now please go. Please."

11.

Onward. This place is all gleaming towers and airy bridges, a
glistening fantasy of a city. High overhead float glassy bubbles,
silent airborne passenger vehicles, containing two or three people
apiece who sprawl in postures of elegant relaxation. Bronzed
young boys and girls lie naked beside soaring fountains spewing
turquoise-and-scarlet foam. Giant orchids burst in tropical
voluptuousness from the walls of colossal hotels. Small mechanical birds wheel and dart in the soft air like golden bullets,
emitting sweet pinging sounds. From the tips of the tallest
buildings comes a darker music, a ground bass of swelling
hundred-cycle notes oscillating around an insistent central rum-
ble. This is a world two centuries ahead of his, at the least. He
could never infiltrate here. He could never even be a tourist. The
only role available to him is that of visiting savage. Jemmy
Button among the Londoners, and what, after all, was Jemmy
Button's fate? Not a happy one. Patagonia! Patagonia! Thees
ticket eet ees no longer good here, sor. Colored rays dance in the
sky, red, green, blue, exploding, showering the city with transcendental images. Cameron smiles. He will not let himself be
overwhelmed, though this place is more confusing than the world
of the halftrack automobiles. Jauntily he plants himself at the
center of a small park between two lanes of flowing, noiseless
traffic. It is a formal garden lush with toothy orange-fronded
ferns and thorny skyrockets of looping cactus. Lovers stroll past
him arm in arm, offering one another swigs from glossy sweat-
beaded green flasks that look like tubes of polished jade. Delicately they dangle blue grapes before each other's lips; playfully
they smile, arch their necks, take the bait with eager pounces;
then they laugh, embrace, tumble into the dense moist grass,
which stirs and sways and emits gentle thrumming melodies.
This place pleases him. He wanders through the garden, thinking
of Elizabeth, thinking of springtime, and, coming ultimately to a
sinuous brook in which the city's tallest towers are reflected as
inverted needles, he kneels to drink. The water is cool, sweet,
tart, much like young wine. A moment after it touches his lips a
mechanism rises from the spongy earth, five slender brassy
columns, three with eye-sensors sprouting on all sides, one

marked with a pattern of dark gridwork, one bearing an arrangement of winking colored lights. Out of the gridwork come
ominous words in an unfathomable language. This is some kind
of police machine, demanding his credentials: that much is clear.
"I'm sorry," he says. "I can't understand what you're saying."
Other machines are extruding themselves from trees, from the
bed of the stream, from the hearts of the sturdiest ferns. "It's all
right," he says. "I don't mean any harm. Just give me a chance
to learn the language and I promise to become a useful citizen."
One of the machines sprays him with a fine azure mist. Another
drives a tiny needle into his forearm and extracts a droplet of
blood. A crowd is gathering. They point, snicker, wink. The
music of the building tops has become higher in pitch, more
sinister in texture, it shakes the balmy air and threatens him in a
personal way. "Let me stay," Cameron begs, but the music is
shoving him, pushing him with a flat irresistible hand, inexorably
squeezing him out of this world. He is too primitive for them.
He is too coarse; he carries too many obsolete microbes. Very
well. If that's what they want, he'll leave, not out of courtesy
alone. In a flamboyant way he bids them farewell, bowing with a
flourish worthy of Raleigh, blowing a kiss to the five-columned
machine, smiling, even doing a little dance. Farewell. Farewell.
The music rises to a wild crescendo. He hears celestial trumpets
and distant thunder. Farewell. Onward.

12.

Here some kind of oriental marketplace has sprung up, foul-
smelling, cluttered, medieval. Swarthy old men, white-bearded,
in thick gray robes, sit patiently behind open burlap sacks of
spices and grains. Lepers and cripples roam everywhere, begging
importunately. Slender long-legged men wearing only tight loincloths and jingling dangling earrings of bright copper stalk
through the crowd on solitary orbits, buying nothing, saying
nothing; their skins are dark red; their faces are gaunt; their
solemn features are finely modeled. They carry themselves like
Inca princes. Perhaps they *are* Inca princes. In the haggle and
babble of the market Cameron hears no recognizable tongue
spoken. He sees the flash of gold as transactions are completed.
The women balance immense burdens on their heads and show

brilliant teeth when they smile. They favor patchwork skirts that
cover their ankles, but they leave their breasts bare. Several of
them glance provocatively at Cameron but he dares not return
their quick dazzling probes until he knows what is permissible
here. On the far side of the squalid plaza he catches sight of a
woman who might well be Elizabeth; her back is to him, but he
would know those strong shoulders anywhere, that erect stance,
that cascade of unbound golden hair. He starts toward her, sliding
with difficulty between the close-packed marketgoers. When he
is still halfway across the marketplace from her he notices a man
at her side, tall, a man of his own height and build. He wears a
loose black robe and a dark scarf covers the lower half of his
face. His eyes are grim and sullen and a terrible cicatrice, wide
and glaringly cross-hatched with stitch marks, runs along his left
cheek up to his hairline. The man whispers something to the
woman who might be Elizabeth; she nods and turns, so that
Cameron now is able to see her face, and yes, the woman does
seem to be Elizabeth, but she bears a matching scar, angry and
hideous, up the right side of her face. Cameron gasps. The
scar-faced man suddenly points and shouts. Cameron senses
motion to one side, and swings around just in time to see a short
thickbodied man come rushing toward him wildly waving a scimitar. For an instant Cameron sees the scene as though in a photograph: he has time to make a leisurely examination of his attacker's
oily beard, his hooked hairy-nostriled nose, his yellowed teeth, the
cheap glassy-looking inlaid stones on the haft of the scimitar. Then
the frightful blade descends, while the assassin screams abuse at
Cameron in what might be Arabic. It is a sorry welcome. Cameron
cannot prolong this investigation. An instant before the scimitar
cuts him in two he takes himself elsewhere, with regret.

13.

Onward. To a place where there is no solidity, where the planet
itself has vanished, so that he swims through space, falling
peacefully, going from nowhere to nowhere. He is surrounded by
a brilliant green light that emanates from every point at once, like
a message from the fabric of the universe. In great tranquility he
drops through this cheerful glow for days on end, or what seems
like days on end, drifting, banking, checking his course with

small motions of his elbows or knees. It makes no difference where he goes; everything here is like everything else here. The green glow supports and sustains and nourishes him, but it makes him restless. He plays with it. Out of its lambent substance he succeeds in shaping images, faces, abstract patterns; he conjures up Elizabeth for himself, he evokes his own sharp features, he fills the heavens with a legion of marching Chinese in tapered straw hats, he obliterates them with forceful diagonal lines, he causes a river of silver to stream across the firmament and discharge its glittering burden down a mountainside a thousand miles high. He spins. He floats. He glides. He releases all his fantasies. This is total freedom, here in this unworldly place. But it is not enough. He grows weary of emptiness. He grows weary of serenity. He has drained this place of all it has to offer, too soon, too soon. He is not sure whether the failure is in himself or in the place, but he feels he must leave. Therefore: onward.

14.

Terrified peasants run shrieking as he materializes in their midst. This is some sort of farming village along the eastern shore of the bay: neat green fields, a cluster of low wicker huts radiating from a central plaza, naked children toddling and crying, a busy sub-population of goats and geese and chickens. It is midday; Cameron sees the bright gleam of water in the irrigation ditches. These people work hard. They have scattered at his approach, but now they creep back warily, crouching, ready to take off again if he performs any more miracles. This is another of those bucolic worlds in which San Francisco has not happened, but he is unable to identify these settlers, nor can he isolate the chain of events that brought them here. They are not Indians, nor Chinese, nor Peruvians; they have a European look about them, somehow Slavic, but what would Slavs be doing in California? Russian farmers, maybe, colonizing by way of Siberia? There is some plausibility in that—their dark complexions, their heavy facial structure, their squat powerful bodies—but they seem oddly primitive, half-naked, in furry leggings or less, as though they are no subjects of the Tsar but rather Scythians or Cimmerians transplanted from the prehistoric marshes of the Vistula.

"Don't be frightened," he tells them, holding his upraised outspread arms toward them. They do seem less fearful of him now, timidly approaching, staring with big dark eyes. "I won't harm you. I'd just like to visit with you." They murmur. A woman boldly shoves a child forward, a girl of about five, bare, with black greasy ringlets, and Cameron scoops her up, caresses her, tickles her, lightly sets her down. Instantly the whole tribe is around him, no longer afraid; they touch his arm, they kneel, they stroke his shins. A boy brings him a wooden bowl of porridge. An old woman gives him a mug of sweet wine, a kind of mead. A slender girl drapes a stole of auburn fur over his shoulders. They dance; they chant; their fear has turned into love; he is their honored guest. He is more than that: he is a god. They take him to an unoccupied hut, the largest in the village. Piously they bring him offerings of incense and acorns. When it grows dark they build an immense bonfire in the plaza, so that he wonders in vague concern if they will feast on him when they are done honoring him, but they feast on slaughtered cattle instead, and yield to him the choicest pieces, and afterward they stand by his door, singing discordant, energetic hymns. That night three girls of the tribe, no doubt the fairest virgins available, are sent to him, and in the morning he finds his threshold heaped with newly plucked blossoms. Later two tribal artisans, one lame and the other blind, set to work with stone adzes and chisels, hewing an immense and remarkable accurate likeness of him out of a redwood stump that has been mounted at the plaza's center.

So he has been deified. He has a quick Faustian vision of himself living among these diligent people, teaching them advanced methods of agriculture, leading them eventually into technology, into modern hygiene, into all the contemporary advantages without the contemporary abominations. Guiding them toward the light, molding them, creating them. This world, this village, would be a good place for him to stop his transit of the infinities, if stopping were desirable: god, prophet, king of a placid realm, teacher, inculcator of civilization, a purpose to his existence at last. But there *is* no place to stop. He knows that. Transforming happy primitive farmers into sophisticated twentieth-century agriculturalists is ultimately as useless a pastime as training fleas to jump through hoops. It is tempting to live as a god, but even divinity will pall, and it is dangerous to become attached to an unreal satisfaction, dangerous to become attached at all. The journey, not the arrival, matters. Always.

So Cameron does godhood for a little while. He finds it pleasant and fulfilling. He savors the rewards until he senses that the rewards are becoming too important to him. He makes his formal renunciation of his godhead. Then: onward.

15.

And this place he recognizes. His street, his house, his garden, his green car in the carport, Elizabeth's yellow one parked out front. Home again, so soon? He hadn't expected that; but every leap he has made, he knows, must in some way have been a product of deliberate choice, and evidently whatever hidden mechanism within him that has directed these voyages has chosen to bring him home again. All right, touch base. Digest your travels, examine them, allow your experiences to work their alchemy on you: you need to stand still a moment for that. Afterward you can always leave again. He slides his key into the door.

Elizabeth has one of the Mozart quartets on the phonograph. She sits curled up in the living-room window seat, leafing through a magazine. It is late afternoon, and the San Francisco skyline, clearly visible across the bay through the big window, is halved by the brilliant retreating sunlight. There are freshly cut flowers in the little crystal bowl on the redwood-burl table; the fragrance of gardenias and jasmine dances past him. Unhurriedly she looks up, brings her eyes into line with his, dazzles him with the warmth of her smile, and says, "Well, hello!"

"Hello, Elizabeth."

She comes to him. "I didn't expect you back this quickly, Chris, I don't know if I expected you to come back at all, as a matter of fact."

"This quickly? How long have I been gone, for you?"

"Tuesday morning to Thursday afternoon. Two and a half days." She eyes his coarse new beard, his ragged, sun-bleached shirt. "It's been longer for you, hasn't it?"

"Weeks and weeks. I'm not sure how long. I was in eight or nine different places, and I stayed in the last one quite some time.

They were villagers, farmers, •some primitive Slavonic tribe living down by the bay. I was their god, but I got bored with it.''

"You always did get bored so easily,'' she says, and laughs, and takes his hands in hers and pulls him toward her. She brushes her lips lightly against him, a peck, a play-kiss, their usual first greeting, and then they kiss more passionately, bodies pressing close, tongue seeking tongue. He feels a pounding in his chest, the old inextinguishable throb. When they release each other he steps back, a little dizzied, and says, "I missed you, Elizabeth. I didn't know how much I'd miss you until I was somewhere else and aware that I might never find you again.''

"Did you seriously worry about that?"

"Very much."

"I never doubted we'd be together again, one way or another. Infinity's such a big place, darling. You'd find your way back to me, or to someone very much like me. And someone very much like you would find his way to me, if you didn't. How many Chris Camerons do you think there are, on the move between worlds right now? A thousand? A trillion trillion?" She turns toward the sideboard and says, without breaking the flow of her words, "Would you like some wine?" and begins to pour from a half-empty jug of red. "Tell me where you've been," she says.

He comes up behind her and rests his hands on her shoulders, and draws them down the back of her silk blouse to her waist, holding her there, kissing the nape of her neck. He says, "To a world where there was an atomic war here, and to one where there still were Indian raiders out by Livermore, and one that was all fantastic robots and futuristic helicopters, and one where Johnson was President before Kennedy and Kennedy is alive and President now, and one where—oh, I'll give you all the details later. I need a chance to unwind first." He releases her and kisses the tip of her earlobe and takes one of the glasses from her, and they salute each other and drink, draining the wine quickly. "It's so good to be home," he says softly. "Good to have gone where I went, good to be back." She fills his glass again. The familiar domestic ritual: red wine is their special drink, cheap red wine out of gallon jugs. A sacrament, more dear to him than the burnt offerings of his recent subjects. Halfway through the second glass he says, "Come. Let's go inside."

The bed has fresh linens on it, cool, inviting. There are three thick books on the night table: she's set up for some heavy reading in his absence. Cut flowers in here, too, fragrance everywhere. Their clothes drop away. She touches his beard and chuckles at the roughness, and he kisses the smooth cool place along the inside of her thigh and draws his cheek lightly across it, sandpapering her lovingly, and then she pulls him to her and their bodies slide together and he enters her. Everything thereafter happens quickly, much too quickly; he has been long absent from her, if not she from him, and now her presence excites him, there is a strangeness about her body, her movements, and it hastens him to his ecstasy. He feels a mild pang of regret, but no more: he'll make it up to her soon enough, they both know that. They drift into a sleepy embrace, neither of them speaking, and eventually uncoil into tender new passion, and this time all is as it should be. Afterward they doze. A spectacular sunset blazes over the city when he opens his eyes. They rise, they take a shower together, much giggling, much playfulness. "Let's go across the bay for a fancy dinner tonight," he suggests. "Trianon, Blue Fox, Ernie's, anywhere. You name it. I feel like celebrating."

"So do I, Chris."

"It's good to be home again."

"It's good to have you here," she tells him. She looks for her purse. "How soon do you think you'll be heading out again? Not that I mean to rush you, but—"

"You know I'm not going to be staying?"

"Of course I know."

"Yes. You would." She had never questioned his going. They both tried to be responsive to each other's needs; they had always regarded one another as equal partners, free to do as they wished. "I can't say how long I'll stay. Probably not long. Coming home this soon was really an accident, you know. I just planned to go on and on and on, world after world, and I never programmed my next jump, at least not consciously. I simply leaped. And the last leap deposited me on my own doorstep, somehow, so I let myself into the house. And there you were to welcome me home."

She presses his hand between hers. Almost sadly she says, "You aren't home, Chris."

"What?"

He hears the sound of the front door opening. Footsteps in the hallway.

"You aren't home," she says.

Confusion seizes him. He thinks of all that has passed between them this evening.

"Elizabeth?" calls a deep voice from the living room.

"In here, darling. I have company!"

"Oh? Who?" A man enters the bedroom, halts, grins. He is clean-shaven and dressed in the clothes Cameron had worn on Tuesday; otherwise they could be twins. "Hey, hello!" he says warmly, extending his hand.

Elizabeth says, "He comes from a place that must be very much like this one. He's been here since five o'clock, and we were just going out for dinner. Have you been having an interesting time?"

"Very," the other Cameron says. "I'll tell you all about it later. Go on, don't let me keep you."

"You could join us for dinner," Cameron suggests helplessly.

"That's all right. I've just eaten. Breast of passenger pigeon— they aren't extinct everywhere. I wish I could have brought some home for the freezer. So you two go and enjoy. I'll see you later. Both of you, I hope. Will you be staying with us? We've got notes to compare, you and I."

16.

He rises just before dawn, in a marvelous foggy stillness. The Camerons have been wonderfully hospitable, but he must be moving along. He scrawls a thank-you note and slips it under their bedroom door. *Let's get together again someday. Somewhere. Somehow.* They wanted him as a house guest for a week or two, but no, he feels like a bit of an intruder here, and anyway the universe is waiting for him. He has to go. The journey, not the arrival, matters, for what else is there but trips? Departing is unexpectedly painful, but he knows the mood will pass. He closes his eyes. He breaks his moorings. He gives himself up to his sublime restlessness. Onward. Onward. *Goodbye, Elizabeth. Goodbye, Chris. I'll see you both again.* Onward.

SCHWARTZ
BETWEEN
THE GALAXIES

THIS MUCH IS reality: Schwartz sits comfortably cocooned—passive, suspended—in a first-class passenger rack aboard a Japan Air Lines rocket, nine kilometers above the Coral Sea. And this much is fantasy: the same Schwartz has passage on a shining starship gliding silkily through the interstellar depths, en route at nine times the velocity of light from Betelgeuse IX to Rigel XXI, or maybe from Andromeda to the Lesser Magellanic.

There are no starships. Probably there never will be any. Here we are, a dozen decades after the flight of Apollo 11, and no human being goes anywhere except back and forth across the face of the little O, the Earth, for the planets are barren and the stars are beyond reach. That little O is too small for Schwartz. Too often it glazes for him; it turns to a nugget of dead porcelain; and lately he has formed the habit, when the world glazes, of taking refuge aboard that interstellar ship. So what JAL Flight 411 holds is merely his physical self, his shell, occupying a costly private cubicle on a slender 200-passenger vessel which, leaving Buenos Aires shortly after breakfast, has sliced westward along the Tropic of Capricorn for a couple of hours and will soon be landing at Papua's Torres Skyport. But his consciousness, his *anima*, the essential Schwartzness of him, soars between the galaxies.

What a starship it is! How marvelous its myriad passengers!

Down its crowded corridors swarms a vast gaudy heterogeny of galactic creatures, natives of the worlds of Capella, Arcturus, Altair, Canopus, Polaris, Antares, beings both intelligent and articulate, methane-breathing or nitrogen-breathing or argon-breathing, spiny-skinned or skinless, many-armed or many-headed or altogether incorporeal, each a product of a distinct and distinctly unique and alien cultural heritage. Among these varied folk moves Schwartz, that superstar of anthropologists, that true heir to Kroeber and Morgan and Malinowski and Mead, delightedly devouring their delicious diversity. Whereas aboard this prosaic rocket, this planet-locked stratosphere needle, one cannot tell the Canadians from the Portuguese, the Portuguese from the Romanians, the Romanians from the Irish, unless they open their mouths, and sometimes not always then.

In his reveries he confers with creatures from the Fomalhaut system about digital circumcision; he tapes the melodies of the Achernarnian eye-flute; he learns of the sneeze-magic of Acrux, the sleep-ecstasies of Aldebaran, the asteroid-sculptors of Thuban. Then a smiling JAL stewardess parts the curtain of his cubicle and peers in at him, jolting him from one reality to another. She is blue-eyed, frizzy-haired, straight-nosed, thin-lipped, bronze-skinned, a genetic mishmash, your standard twenty-first-century-model mongrel human, perhaps Melanesian-Swedish-Turkish-Bolivian, perhaps Polish-Berber-Tatar-Welsh. Cheap intercontinental transit has done its deadly work: all Earth is a crucible, all the gene pools have melted into one indistinguishable fluid. Schwartz wonders about the recessivity of those blue eyes and arrives at no satisfactory solution. She is beautiful, at any rate. Her name is Dawn—o sweet neutral nonculture-bound cognomen!—and they have played at a flirtation, he and she, Dawn and Schwartz, at occasional moments of this short flight. Twinkling, she says softly, "We're getting ready for our landing, Dr. Schwartz. Are your restrictors in polarity?"

"I never unfastened them."

"Good." The blue eyes, warm, interested, meet his. "I have a layover in Papua tonight," she says.

"That's nice."

"Let's have a drink while we're waiting for them to unload the baggage," she suggests with cheerful bluntness. "All right?"

"I suppose," he says casually. "Why not?" Her availability bores him: somehow he enjoys the obsolete pleasures of the chase. Once such easiness in a woman like this would have excited him, but no longer. Schwartz is forty years old, tall, square-shouldered, sturdy, a showcase for the peasant genes of his rugged Irish mother. His close-cropped black hair is flecked with gray; many women find that interesting. One rarely sees gray hair now. He dresses simply but well, in sandals and Socratic tunic. Predictably, his physical attractiveness, both within his domestic sixness and without, has increased with his professional success. He is confident, sure of his powers, and he radiates an infectious assurance. This month alone eighty million people have heard his lectures.

She picks up the faint weariness in his voice. "You don't sound eager. Not interested?"

"Hardly that."

"What's wrong, then? Feeling sub, Professor?"

Schwartz shrugs. "Dreadfully sub. Body like dry bone. Mind like dead ashes." He smiles, full force depriving his words of all their weight.

She registers mock anguish. "That sounds bad," she says. "That sounds awful!"

"I'm only quoting Chuang Tzu. Pay no attention to me. Actually, I feel fine, just a little stale."

"Too many skyports?"

He nods. "Too much of a sameness wherever I go." He thinks of a star-bright, top-deck bubble dome where three boneless Spicans do a twining dance of propitiation to while away the slow hours of nine-light travel. "I'll be all right," he tells her. "It's a date."

Her hybrid face flows with relief and anticipation. "See you in Papua," she tells him, and winks, and moves jauntily down the aisle.

Papua. By cocktail time Schwartz will be in Port Moresby. Tonight he lectures at the University of Papua; yesterday it was Montevideo; the day after tomorrow it will be Bangkok. He is making the grand academic circuit. This is his year: he is very big, suddenly, in anthropological circles, since the publication of *The Mask Beneath the Skin*. From continent to continent he flashes, sharing his wisdom, Monday in Montreal, Tuesday Veracruz, Wednesday Montevideo, Thursday—Thursday? He crossed the international date line this morning, and he does not remember whether he has entered Thursday or Tuesday, though yesterday was surely Wednesday. Schwartz is certain only that this is July and the year is 2083, and there are moments when he is not even sure of that.

The JAL rocket enters the final phase of its landward plunge. Papua waits, sleek, vitrescent. The world has a glassy sheen again. He lets his spirit drift happily back to the gleaming starship making its swift way across the whirling constellations.

He found himself in the starship's busy lower-deck lounge, having a drink with his traveling companion, Pitkin, the Yale economist. Why Pitkin, that coarse, florid little man? With all of real and imaginary humanity to choose from, why had his unconscious elected to make him share this fantasy with such a boor?

"Look," Pitkin said, winking and leering. "There's your girlfriend."

The entry-iris had opened and the Antarean not-male had come in.

"Quit it," Schwartz snapped. "You know there's no such thing going on."

"Haven't you been chasing her for days?"

"She's not a 'her,'" Schwartz said.

Pitkin guffawed. "Such precision! Such scholarship! *She's* not a *her*, he says!" He gave Schwartz a broad nudge. "To you she's a she, friend, and don't try to kid me."

Schwartz had to admit there was some justice to Pitkin's vulgar innuendos. He did find the Antarean—a slim yellow-eyed ebony-skinned upright humanoid, sinuous and glossy, with tapering elongated limbs and a seal's fluid grace—powerfully attractive. Nor could he help thinking of the Antarean as feminine. That attitude was hopelessly culture-bound and species-bound, he knew; in fact the alien had cautioned him that terrestrial sexual distinctions were irrelevant in the Antares system, that if Schwartz insisted on thinking of "her" in genders, "she" could be considered only the negative of male, with no implication of biological femaleness.

He said patiently, "I've told you. The Antarean's neither male nor female as we understand those concepts. If we happen to perceive the Antarean as feminine, that's the result of our own cultural conditioning. If you want to believe that my interest in this being is sexual, go ahead, but I assure you that it's purely professional.''

"Sure. You're only studying her."

"In a sense I am. And she's studying me. On her native world she has the status-frame of 'watcher-of-life,' which seems to translate into the Antarean equivalent of an anthropologist."

"How lovely for you both. She's your first alien and you're her first Jew."

"Stop calling her *her*," Schwartz hissed.

"But you've been doing it!"

Schwartz closed his eyes. "My grandmother told me never to get mixed up with economists. Their thinking is muddy and their breath is bad, she said. She also warned me against Yale men. Perverts of the intellect, she called them. So here I am cooped up on an interstellar ship with five hundred alien creatures and one fellow human, and he has to be an economist from Yale."

"Next trip travel with your grandmother instead."

"Go away," Schwartz said. "Stop lousing up my fantasies. Go peddle your dismal science somewhere else. You see those Delta Aurigans over there? Climb into their bottle and tell them all about the Gross Global Product." Schwartz smiled at the Antarean, who had purchased a drink, something that glittered an iridescent blue, and was approaching them. "Go *on*," Schwartz murmured.

"Don't worry," Pitkin said. "I wouldn't want to crowd you." He vanished into the motley crowd.

The Antarean said, "The Capellans are dancing, Schwartz."

"I'd like to see that. Too damned noisy in here anyway." Schwartz stared into the alien's vertical-slitted citreous eyes, Cat's eyes, he thought. Panther's eyes. The Antarean's gaze was focused, as usual, on Schwartz's mouth: other worlds, other customs. He felt a strange, unsettling tremor of desire. Desire for what, though? It was a sensation of pure need, nonspecific, certainly nonsexual. "I think I'll take a look. Will you come with me?"

The Papua rocket has landed. Schwartz, leaning across the narrow table in the skyport's lounge, says to the stewardess in a low, intense tone, "My life was in crisis. All my values were becoming meaningless. I was discovering that my chosen profession was empty, foolish, as useless as—playing chess."

"How awful," Dawn whispers gently.

"You can see why. You go all over the world, you see a thousand skyports a year. Everything the same everywhere. The same clothes, the same slang, the same magazines, the same styles of architecture and decor."

"Yes."

"International homogeneity. Worldwide uniformity. Can you understand what it's like to be an anthropologist in a world where there are no primitives left, Dawn? Here we sit on the island of Papua—you know, headhunters, animism, body-paint, the drums at sunset, the bone through the nose—and look at the Papuans in their business robes all around us. Listen to them exchanging stock-market tips, talking baseball, recommending restaurants in Paris and barbers in Johannesburg. It's no different anywhere else. In a single century we've transformed the planet into one huge sophisticated plastic western industrial state. The TV relay satellites, the two-hour intercontinental rockets, the breakdown of religious exclusivism and genetic taboo have mongrelized every culture, don't you see? You visit the Zuni and they have plastic African masks on the wall. You visit the Bushmen and they have Japanese-made Hopi-motif ashtrays. It's all just so much interior decoration, and underneath the carefully selected primitive motifs there's the same universal pseudo-American sensibility, whether you're in the Kalahari or the Amazon rain forest. Do you comprehend what's happened, Dawn?"

"It's such a terrible loss," she says sadly. She is trying very hard to be sympathetic, but he senses she is waiting for him to finish his sermon and invite her to share his hotel room. He *will* invite her, but there is no stopping him once he has launched into his one great theme.

"Cultural diversity is gone from the world," he says. "Religion is dead; true poetry is dead; inventiveness is dead; individuality is dead. Poetry. Listen to this." In a high monotone he chants:

In beauty I walk
With beauty before me I walk
With beauty behind me I walk
With beauty above me I walk
With beauty above and about me I walk
It is finished in beauty
It is finished in beauty

He has begun to perspire heavily. His chanting has created an odd sphere of silence in his immediate vicinity; heads are turning, eyes are squinting. "Navaho," he says. "The Night Way, a nine-day chant, a vision, a spell. Where are the Navaho now? Go to Arizona and they'll chant for you, yes, for a price, but they don't know what the words mean, and chances are the singers are only one-fourth Navaho, or one-eighth, or maybe just Hopi hired to dress in Navaho costumes, because the real Navaho, if any are left, are off in Mexico City hired to be Aztecs. So much is gone. Listen." He chants again, more piercingly even than before:

The animal runs, it passes, it dies. And it is the great cold.
It is the great cold of the night, it is the dark.
The bird flies, it passes, it dies. And it is—

"JAL FLIGHT 411 BAGGAGE IS NOW UNLOADING ON CONCOURSE FOUR," a mighty mechanical voice cries.

—the great cold.
It is the great cold of the night, it is the dark.

"JAL FLIGHT 411 BAGGAGE . . ."

The fish flees, it passes, it dies. And—

"People are staring," Dawn says uncomfortably.
"—ON CONCOURSE FOUR."
"Let them stare. Do them some good. That's a Pygmy chant, from Gabon, in equatorial Africa. Pygmies? There are no more Pygmies. Everybody's two meters tall. And what do we sing? Listen. Listen." He gestures fiercely at the cloud of tiny golden loudspeakers floating near the ceiling. A mush of music comes from them: the current popular favorite. Savagely he mouths words: "*Star . . . far . . . here . . . near*. Playing in every skyport right now, all over the world." She smiles thinly. Her hand reaches toward his, covers it, presses against the knuckles. He is dizzy. The crowd, the eyes, the music, the drink. The plastic. Everything shines. Porcelain. Porcelain. The planet vitrifies. "Tom?" she asks uneasily. "Is anything the matter?" He laughs, blinks, coughs, shivers. He hears her calling for help, and

then he feels his soul swooping outward, toward the galactic
blackness.

With the Antarean not-male beside him, Schwartz peered through
the viewport, staring in awe and fascination at the seductive
vision of the Capellans coiling and recoiling outside the ship. Not
all the passengers on this voyage had cozy staterooms like his.
The Capellans were too big to come on board, and in any case
they preferred never to let themselves be enclosed inside metal
walls. They traveled just alongside the starship, basking like
slippery whales in the piquant radiations of space. So long as
they kept within twenty meters of the hull they would be inside
the effective field of the Rabinowitz Drive, which swept ship and
contents and associated fellow travelers toward Rigel, or the
Lesser Magellanic, or was it one of the Pleiades toward which
they were bound at a cool nine lights?

He watched the Capellans moving beyond the shadow of the
ship in tracks of shining white. Blue, glossy green, and velvet
black, they coiled and swam, and every track was a flash of
golden fire. "They have a dangerous beauty," Schwartz whispered.
"Do you hear them calling? I do."

"What do they say?"

"They say, 'Come to me, come to me, come to me!' "

"Go to them, then," said the Antarean simply. "Step through
the hatch."

"And perish?"

"And enter into your next transition. Poor Schwartz! Do you
love your present body so?"

"My present body isn't so bad. Do you think I'm likely to get
another one some day?"

"No?"

"No," Schwartz said. "This one is all I get. Isn't it that way
with you?"

"At the Time of Openings I receive my next housing. That will
be fifty years from now. What you see is the fifth form I have
been given to wear."

"Will the next be as beautiful as this?"

"All forms are beautiful," the Antarean said. "You find me
attractive?"

"Of course."

A slitted wink. A bobbing nod toward the viewport. "As attractive as *those*?"

Schwartz laughed. "Yes. In a different way."

Coquettishly the Antarean said, "If I were out there, you would walk through the hatch into space?"

"I might. If they gave me a spacesuit and taught me how to use it."

"But not otherwise? Suppose I were out there right now. I could live in space five, ten, maybe fifteen minutes. I am there and I say, *'Come to me, Schwartz, come to me!'* What do you do?"

"I don't think I'm all that much self-destructive."

"To die for love, though! To make a transition for the sake of beauty."

"No. Sorry."

The Antarean pointed toward the undulating Capellans. "If *they* asked you, you would go."

"They are asking me," he said.

"And you refuse the invitation?"

"So far. So far."

The Antarean laughed an Antarean laugh, a thick silvery snort. "Our voyage will last many weeks more. One of these days, I think, you will go to them."

"You were unconscious at least five minutes," Dawn says. "You gave everyone a scare. Are you sure you ought to go through with tonight's lecture?"

Nodding, Schwartz says, "I'll be all right. I'm a little tired, is all. Too many time zones this week." They stand on the terrace of his hotel room. Night is coming on, already, here in late afternoon: it is midwinter in the Southern Hemisphere, though the fragrance of tropic blossoms perfumes the air. The first few stars have appeared. He has never really known which star is which. That bright one, he thinks, could be Rigel, and that one Sirius, and perhaps this is Deneb over there. And this? Can this be red Antares, in the heart of the Scorpion, or is it only Mars? Because of his collapse at the skyport he has been able to beg off the customary faculty reception and the formal dinner; pleading the need for rest, he has arranged to have a simple snack at his hotel room, *a deux*. In two hours they will come for him and take him to the University to speak. Dawn watches him closely.

Perhaps she is worried about his health, perhaps she is only waiting for him to make his move toward her. There's time for all that later, he figures. He would rather talk now. Warming up for the audience he seizes his earlier thread:

"For a long time I didn't understand what had taken place. I grew up insular, cut off from reality, a New York boy, bright mind and a library card. I read all the anthropological classics, *Patterns of Culture* and *Coming of Age in Samoa* and *Life of a South African Tribe* and the rest, and I dreamed of field trips, collecting myths and grammars and folkways and artifacts and all that, until when I was twenty-five I finally got out into the field and started to discover I had gone into a dead science. We have only one worldwide culture now, with local variants but no basic divergences—there's nothing primitive left on Earth, *and there are no other planets*. Not inhabited ones. I can't go to Mars or Venus or Saturn and study the natives. What natives? And we can't reach the stars. All I have to work with is Earth. I was thirty years old when the whole thing clicked together for me and I knew I had wasted my life."

She says, "But surely there was something for you to study on Earth."

"One culture, rootless and homogeneous. That's work for a sociologist, not for me. I'm a romantic, I'm an exotic, I want strangeness, difference. Look, we can never have any real perspective on our own time and lives. The sociologists try to attain it, but all they get is a mound of raw indigestible data. Insight comes later—two, five, ten generations later. But one way we've always been able to learn about ourselves is by studying alien cultures, studying them *completely*, and defining ourselves by measuring what they are that we aren't. The cultures have to be isolated, though. The anthropologist himself corrupts that isolation in the Heisenberg sense when he comes around with his camera and scanners and starts asking questions, but we can compensate more or less, for the inevitable damage a lone observer causes. We can't compensate when our whole culture collides with another and absorbs and obliterates it. Which we technological-mechanical people now have done everywhere. One day I woke up and saw there were no alien cultures left. Hah! Crushing revelation! Schwartz's occupation is gone!"

"What did you do?"

"For years I was in an absolute funk. I taught, I studied, I went through the motions, knowing it was all meaningless. All I was doing was looking at records of vanished cultures left by earlier observers and trying to cudgel new meanings. Secondary sources, stale findings: I was an evaluator of dry bones, not a gatherer of evidence. Paleontology. Dinosaurs are interesting, but what do they tell you about the contemporary world and the meaning of its patterns? Dry bones, Dawn, dry bones. Despair. And then a clue. I had this Nigerian student, this Ibo—well, basically an Ibo, but she's got some Israeli in her and I think Chinese—and we grew very close, she was as close to me as anybody in my own sixness, and I told her my troubles. I'm going to give it all up, I said, because it isn't what I expected it to be. She laughed at me and said, What right do you have to be upset because the world doesn't live up to your expectations? Reshape your life, Tom; you can't reshape the world. I said, But how? And she said, Look inward, find the primitive in yourself, see what made you what you are, what made today's culture what it is, see how these alien streams have flowed together. Nothing's been lost here, only merged. Which made me think. Which gave me a new way of looking at things. Which sent me on an inward quest. It took me three years to grasp the patterns, to come to an understanding of what our planet has become, and only after I accepted the planet—''

It seems to him that he has been talking forever. Talking. Talking. But he can no longer hear his own voice. There is only a distant buzz.

"After I accepted—''

A distant buzz.

"What was I saying?'' he asks.

"After you accepted the planet—''

"After I accepted the planet,'' he says, "that I could begin—'' *Buzz. Buzz.* "That I could begin to accept myself.''

He was drawn toward the Spicans too, not so much for themselves— they were oblique, elliptical characters, self-contained and self-satisfied, hard to approach—as for the apparently psychedelic drug they took in some sacramental way before the beginning of each of their interminable ritual dances. Each time he had watched them take the drug, they had seemingly made a point of extending it toward him, as if inviting him, as if tempting him, before popping it into their mouths. He felt baited; he felt pulled.

There were three Spicans on board, slender creatures two and a half meters long, with flexible cylindrical bodies and small stubby limbs. Their skins were reptilian, dry and smooth, deep green with yellow bands, but their eyes were weirdly human, large liquid-brown eyes, sad Levantine eyes, the eyes of unfortunate medieval travelers transformed by enchantment into serpents. Schwartz had spoken with them several times. They understood English well enough—all galactic races did; Schwartz imagined it would become the interstellar *lingua franca* as it had on Earth—but the construction of their vocal organs was such that they had no way of speaking it, and they relied instead on small translating machines hung around their necks that converted their soft whispered hisses into amber words pulsing across a screen.

Cautiously, the third or fourth time he spoke with them, he expressed polite interest in their drug. They told him it enabled them to make contact with the central forces of the universe. He replied that there were such drugs on Earth, too, and that he used them frequently, that they gave him great insight into the workings of the cosmos. They showed some curiosity, perhaps even intense curiosity: reading their eyes was difficult and the tone of their voices gave no clues. He took his elegant leather-bound drug case from his pouch and showed them what he had: learitonin, psilocerebrin, siddharthin, and acid-57. He described the effects of each and suggested an exchange, any of his for an equivalent dose of the shriveled orange fungoid they nibbled. They conferred. Yes, they said, we will do this. But not now. Not until the proper moment. Schwartz knew better than to ask them when that would be. He thanked them and put his drugs away.

Pitkin, who had watched the interchange from the far side of the lounge, came striding fiercely toward him as the Spicans glided off. "What are you up to now?" he demanded.

"How about minding your own business?" Schwartz said amiably.

"You're trading pills with those snakes, aren't you?"

"Let's call it field research."

"Research? Research? What are you going to do, trip on that orange stuff of theirs?"

"I might," Schwartz said.

"How do you know what its effects on the human metabolism might be? You could end up blind or paralyzed or crazy or—"

"—or illuminated," Schwartz said. "Those are the risks one takes in the field. The early anthropologists who unhesitatingly sampled peyote and yage and ololiuqui accepted those risks, and—"

"But those were drugs that *humans* were using. You have no way of telling how—oh, what's the use, Schwartz? Research, he calls it. Research." Pitkin sneered. *"Junkie!"*

Schwartz matched him sneer for sneer. *"Economist!"*

The house is a decent one tonight, close to three thousand, every seat in the University's great horseshoe-shaped auditorium taken, and a video relay besides, beaming his lecture to all Papua and half of Indonesia. Schwartz stands on the dais like a demigod under a brilliant no-glare spotlight. Despite his earlier weariness he is in good form now, gestures broad and forceful, eyes commanding, voice deep and resonant, words flowing freely. "Only one planet," he says, "one small and crowded planet, on which all cultures converge to a drab and depressing sameness. How sad that is! How tiny we make ourselves, when we make ourselves to resemble one another!" He flings his arms upward. "Look to the stars, the unattainable stars! Imagine, if you can, the millions of worlds that orbit those blazing suns beyond the night's darkness! Speculate with me on other peoples, other ways, other gods. Beings of every imaginable form, alien in appearance but not grotesque, not hideous, for all life is beautiful— beings that breathe gases strange to us, beings of immense size, beings of many limbs or of none, beings to whom death is a divine culmination of existence, beings who never die, beings who bring forth their young a thousand at a time, beings who do not reproduce—all the infinite possibilities of the infinite universe!

"Perhaps on each of those worlds it is as it has become here. One intelligent species, one culture, the eternal convergence. But the many worlds together offer a vast spectrum of variety. And now, share this vision with me! I see a ship voyaging from star to star, a spaceliner of the future, and aboard that ship is a sampling of many species, many cultures, a random scoop out of the galaxy's fantastic diversity. That ship is like a little cosmos, a small world, enclosed, sealed. How exciting to be aboard it, to encounter in that little compass such richness of cultural variation! Now our own world was once like that starship, a little cosmos, bearing with it all the thousands of Earthborn cultures.

Hopi and Eskimo and Aztec and Kwakiutl and Arapesh and Orokolo and all the rest. In the course of our voyage we have come to resemble one another too much, and it has impoverished the lives of all of us, because—" He falters suddenly. He feels faint, and grasps the sides of the lectern. "Because—" The spotlight, he thinks. In my eyes. Not supposed to glare like that, but it's blinding. Got to have them move it. "In the course—the course of our voyage—" What's happening? Breaking into a sweat, now. Pain in my chest. My heart? Wait, slow up, catch your breath. That light in my eyes—

"Tell me," Schwartz said earnestly, "what it's like to know you'll have ten successive bodies and live more than a thousand years."

"First tell me," said the Antarean, "what it's like to know you'll live ninety years or less and perish forever."

Somehow he continues. The pain in his chest grows more intense, he cannot focus his eyes; he believes he will lose consciousness at any moment and may even have lost it already at least once, and yet he continues. Clinging to the lectern, he outlines the program he developed in *The Mask Beneath the Skin*. A rebirth of tribalism without a revival of ugly nationalism. The quest for a renewed sense of kinship with the past. A sharp reduction in nonessential travel, especially tourism. Heavy taxation of exported artifacts, including films and video shows. An attempt to create independent cultural units on Earth once again while maintaining present levels of economic and political interdependence. Relinquishment of materialistic technological-industrial values. New searches for fundamental meanings. An ethnic revival, before it is too late, among those cultures of mankind that have only recently shed their traditional folkways. (He repeats and embellishes this point particularly, for the benefit of the Papuans before him, the great-grandchildren of cannibals.)

The discomfort and confusion come and go as he unreels his themes. He builds and builds, crying out passionately for an end to the homogenization of Earth, and gradually the physical symptoms leave him, all but a faint vertigo. But a different malaise seizes him as he nears his peroration. His voice becomes, to him, a far-off quacking, meaningless and foolish. He has said all this a thousand times, always to great ovations, but who listens? Who listens? Everything seems hollow tonight, mechanical, absurd. An ethnic revival? Shall these people before him revert to their loincloths and their pig roasts? His starship is a fantasy; his dream of a diverse Earth is mere silliness. What is, will be. And yet he pushes on toward his conclusion. He takes his audience back to that starship, he creates a horde of fanciful beings for them. He completes the metaphor by sketching the structures of half a dozen vanished "primitive" cultures of Earth, he chants the chants of the Navaho, the Gabon Pygmies, the Ashanti, the Mundugumor. It is over. Cascades of applause engulf him. He holds his place until members of the sponsoring committee come to him and help him down: they have perceived his distress. "It's nothing," he gasps. "The lights—too bright—" Dawn is at his side. She hands him a drink, something cool. Two of the sponsors begin to speak of a reception for him in the Green Room. "Fine," Schwartz says. "Glad to." Dawn murmurs a protest. He shakes her off. "My obligation," he tells her. "Meet community leaders. Faculty people. I'm feeling better now. Honestly." Swaying, trembling, he lets them lead him away.

"A Jew," the Antarean said. "You call yourself a Jew, but what is this exactly? A clan, a sept, a moiety, a tribe, a nation, what? Can you explain?"

"You understand what a religion is?"

"Of course."

"Judaism—Jewishness—it's one of Earth's major religions."

"You are therefore a priest?"

"Not at all. I don't even practice Judaism. But my ancestors did, and therefore I consider myself Jewish, even though—"

"It is an hereditary religion, then," the Antarean said, "that does not require its members to observe its rites?"

"In a sense," said Schwartz desperately. "More an hereditary cultural subgroup, actually, evolving out of a common religious outlook no longer relevant."

"Ah. And the cultural traits of Jewishness that define it and separate you from the majority of humankind are—?"

"Well—" Schwartz hesitated. "There's a complicated dietary code, a rite of circumcision for newborn males, a rite of passage for male adolescents, a language of scripture, a vernacular language that Jews all around the world more or less understand,

and plenty more, including a certain intangible sense of clannishness and certain attitudes, such as a peculiar self-deprecating style of humor—''

"You observe the dietary code? You understand the language of scripture?"

"Not exactly," Schwartz admitted. "In fact I don't do anything that's specifically Jewish except think of myself as a Jew and adopt many of the characteristically Jewish personality modes, which however are not uniquely Jewish any longer—they can be traced among Italians, for example, and to some extent among Greeks. I'm speaking of Italians and Greeks of the late twentieth century, of course. Nowadays—" It was all becoming a terrible muddle. "Nowadays—"

"It would seem," said the Antarean, "that you are a Jew only because your maternal and paternal gene-givers were Jews, and they—"

"No, not quite. Not my mother, just my father, and he was Jewish only on his father's side, but even my grandfather never observed the customs, and—"

"I think this has grown too confusing," said the Antarean. "I withdraw the entire inquiry. Let us speak instead of my own traditions. The Time of Openings, for example, may be understood as—"

In the Green Room some eighty or a hundred distinguished Papuans press toward him, offering congratulations. "Absolutely right," they say. "A global catastrophe." "Our last chance to save our culture." Their skins are chocolate-tinted but their faces betray the genetic mishmash that is their ancestry: perhaps they call themselves Arapesh, Mundugumor, Tchambuli, Mafulu, in the way that he calls himself a Jew, but they have been liberally larded with chromosomes contributed by Chinese, Japanese, Europeans, Africans, everything. They dress in International Contemporary. They speak slangy, lively English. Schwartz feels seasick. "You look dazed," Dawn whispers. He smiles bravely. Body like dry bone. Mind like dead ashes. He is introduced to a tribal chieftain, tall, gray-haired, who looks and speaks like a professor, a lawyer, a banker. What, will these people return to the hills for the ceremony of the yam harvest? Will newborn girl-children be abandoned, cords uncut, skins unwashed, if their fathers do not need more girls? Will boys entering manhood submit to the expensive services of the initiator who scarifies them with the teeth of crocodiles? The crocodiles are gone. The shamans have become stockbrokers.

Suddenly he cannot breathe.

"Get me out of here," Schwartz mutters hoarsely, choking.

Dawn, with stewardess efficiency, chops a path for him through the mob. The sponsors, concerned, rush to his aid. He is floated swiftly back to the hotel in a glistening little bubble-car. Dawn helps him to bed. Reviving, he reaches for her.

"You don't have to," she says. "You've had a rough day."

He persists. He embraces her and takes her, quickly, fiercely, and they move together for a few minutes and it ends and he sinks back, exhausted, stupefied. She gets a cool cloth and pats his forehead and urges him to rest. "Bring me my drugs," he says. He wants siddharthin, but she misunderstands, probably deliberately, and offers him something blue and bulky, a sleeping pill, and, too weary to object, he takes it. Even so, it seems to be hours before sleep comes.

He dreams he is at the skyport, boarding the rocket for Bangkok, and instantly he is debarking at Bangkok—just like Port Moresby, only more humid—and he delivers his speech to a horde of enthusiastic Thais, while rockets flicker about him, carrying him to skyport after skyport, and the Thais blur and become Japanese, who are transformed into Mongols, who become Uighurs, who become Iranians, who become Sudanese, who become Zambians, who become Chileans, and all look alike, all look alike, all look alike.

The Spicans hovered above him, weaving, bobbing, swaying like cobras about to strike. But their eyes, warm and liquid, were sympathetic: loving, even. He felt the flow of their compassion. If they had had the sort of musculature that enabled them to smile, they would be smiling tenderly, he knew.

One of the aliens leaned close. The little translating device dangled toward Schwartz like a holy medallion. He narrowed his eyes, concentrating as intently as he could on the amber words flashing quickly across the screen.

". . . has come. We shall . . ."

"Again, please," Schwartz said. "I missed some of what you were saying."

"The moment . . . has come. We shall . . . make the exchange of sacraments now."

"Sacraments?"

"Drugs."

"Drugs, yes. Yes. Of course." Schwartz groped in his pouch. He felt the cool, smooth leather skin of his drug case. Leather? Snakeskin, maybe. Anyway. He drew it forth. "Here," he said. "Siddharthin, learitonin, psilocerebrin, acid-57. Take your pick." The Spicans selected three small blue siddharthins. "Very good," Schwartz said. "The most transcendental of all. And now—"

The longest of the aliens proffered a ball of dried orange fungus the size of Schwartz's thumbnail.

"It is an equivalent dose. We give it to you."

"Equivalent to all three of my tablets, or to one?"

"Equivalent. It will give you peace."

Schwartz smiled. There was a time for asking questions and a time for unhesitating action. He took the fungus and reached for a glass of water.

"*Wait!*" Pitkin cried, appearing suddenly. "What are you—"

"Too late," Schwartz said serenely, and swallowed the Spican drug in one joyous gulp.

The nightmares go on and on. He circles the Earth like the Flying Dutchman, like the Wandering Jew, skyport to skyport to skyport, an unending voyage from nowhere to nowhere. Obliging committees meet him and convey him to his hotel. Sometimes the committee members are contemporary types, indistinguishable from one another, with standard faces, standard clothing, the all-purpose new-model hybrid unihuman, and sometimes they are consciously new-ethnic, elaborately decked out in feathers and paint and tribal emblems, but their faces, too, are standard behind the gaudy regalia, their slang is the slang of Uganda and Tierra del Fuego and Nepal, and it seems to Schwartz that these masqueraders are, if anything, less authentic, less honest, than the other sort, who at least are true representatives of their era. So it is hopeless either way. He lashes at his pillow, he groans, he wakens. Instantly Dawn's arms enfold him. He sobs incoherent phrases into her clavicle and she murmurs soothing sounds against his forehead. He is having some sort of breakdown, he realizes: a new crisis of values, a shattering of the philosophical synthesis that has allowed him to get through the last few years. He is

bound to the wheel; he spins, he spins, he spins, traversing the
continents, getting nowhere. There is no place to go. No. There
is one, just one, a place where he will find peace, where the
universe will be as he needs it to be. Go there, Schwartz. Go and
stay as long as you can. "Is there anything I can *do?*" Dawn
asks. He shivers and shakes his head. "Take this," she says, and
gives him some sort of pill. Another tranquilizer. All right. All
right. The world has turned to porcelain. His skin feels like a
plastic coating. Away, away, to the ship. To the ship! "So long,"
Schwartz says.

Outside the ship the Capellans twist and spin in their ritual dance
as, weightless and without mass, they are swept toward the rim
of the galaxy at nine times the velocity of light. They move with
a grace that is astonishing for creatures of such tremendous bulk.
A dazzling light that emanates from the center of the universe
strikes their glossy skin and, rebounding, resonates all up and
down the spectrum, splintering into brilliant streamers of ultra-
red, infraviolet, exoyellow. All the cosmos glows and shimmers.
A single perfect note of music comes out of the remote distance
and, growing closer, swells in an infinite crescendo. Schwartz
trembles at the beauty of all he perceives.

Beside him stands the seal-slick Antarean. She—definitely
she, no doubt of it, *she*—plucks at his arm and whispers, "Will
you go to them?"

"Yes. Yes, of course."

"So will I. Wherever you go."

"Now," Schwartz says. He reaches for the lever that opens the
hatch. He pulls down. The side of the starship swings open.

The Antarean looks deep into his eyes and says blissfully, "I
never told you my name. My name is Dawn."

Together they float through the hatch into space.

The blackness receives them gently. There is no chill, no
pressure at the lungs, no discomfort at all. He is surrounded by
luminous surges, by throbbing mantles of pure color, as though
he has entered the heart of an aurora. He and Dawn swim toward
the Capellans, and the huge beings welcome them with deep,
glad, booming cries. Dawn joins the dance at once, moving her
sinuous limbs with extravagant ease; Schwartz will do the same
in a moment, but first he turns to face the starship, hanging in
space close by him like a vast coppery needle, and in a voice that

could shake universes he calls, "Come, friends! Come, all of you! Come dance with us!" And they come, pouring through the hatch, the Spicans first, then all the rest, the infinite multitude of beings, the travelers from Fomalhaut and Achernar and Acrux and Aldebaran, from Thuban and Arcturus and Altair, from Polaris and Canopus and Sirius and Rigel, hundreds of star-creatures spilling happily out of the vessel, bursting forth, all of them, even Pitkin, poor little Pitkin, everyone joining hands and tentacles and tendrils and whatever, forming a great ring of light across space, everyone locked in a cosmic harmony, everyone dancing. Dancing. Dancing.

MANY MANSIONS

IT'S BEEN A rough day. Everything gone wrong. A tremendous tie-up on the freeway going to work, two accounts canceled before lunch, now some inconceivable botch by the weather programmers. It's snowing outside. Actually snowing. He'll have to go out and clear the driveway in the morning. He can't remember when it last snowed. And of course a fight with Alice again. She never lets him alone. She's at her most deadly when she sees him come home exhausted from the office. Ted why don't you this, Ted get me that. Now, waiting for dinner, working on his third drink in forty minutes, he feels one of his headaches coming on. Those miserable killer headaches that can destroy a whole evening. What a life! He toys with murderous fantasies. Take her out by the reservoir for a friendly little stroll, give her a quick hard shove with his shoulder. She can't swim. Down, down, down. Glub. Goodbye, Alice. Free at last.

In the kitchen she furiously taps the keys of the console, programming dinner just the way he likes it. Cold vichyssoise, baked potato with sour cream and chives, sirloin steak blood-rare inside and charcoal-charred outside. Don't think it isn't work to get the meal just right, even with the autochef. All for him. The bastard. Tell me, why do I sweat so hard to please him? Has he made me happy? What's he ever done for me except waste the best years of my life? And he thinks I don't know about his other

women. Those lunchtime quickies. Oh, I wouldn't mind at all if
he dropped dead tomorrow. I'd be a great widow—so dignified at
the funeral, so strong, hardly crying at all. And everybody
thinks we're such a close couple. Married eleven years and
they're still in love. I heard someone say that only last week. If
they only knew the truth about us. If they only knew.

Martin peers out the window of his third-floor apartment in Sunset
Village. Snow. I'll be damned. He can't remember the last time he
saw snow. Thirty, forty years back, maybe, when Ted was a baby.
He absolutely can't remember. White stuff on the ground—when?
The mind gets wobbly when you're past eighty. He still can't
believe he's an old man. It rocks him to realize that his grandson
Ted, Martha's boy, is almost forty. I bounced that kid on my knee
and he threw up all over my suit. Four years old then. Nixon was
President. Nobody talks much about Tricky Dick these days.
Ancient history. McKinley, Coolidge, Nixon. Time flies. Martin
thinks of Ted's wife, Alice. What a nice tight little ass she has.
What a cute pair of jugs. I'd like to get my hands on them. I really
would. You know something, Martin? You're not such an old ruin
yet. Not if you can get it up for your grandson's wife.

His dreams of drowning her fade as quickly as they came. He is
not a violent man by nature. He knows he could never do it. He
can't even bring himself to step on a spider; how then could he
kill his wife? If she'd die some other way, of course, without the
need of his taking direct action, that would solve everything.
She's driving to the hairdresser on one of those manual-access
roads she likes to use, and her car swerves on an icy spot, and
she goes into a tree at eighty kilometers an hour. Good. She's
shopping on Union Boulevard, and the bank is blown up by an
activist; she's nailed by flying debris. Good. The dentist gives her
a new anesthetic and it turns out she's fatally allergic to it. Puffs
up like a blowfish and dies in five minutes. Good. The police
come, long faces, snuffly noses. Terribly sorry, Mr. Porter.
There's been an awful accident. Don't tell me it's my wife, he
cries. They nod lugubriously. He bears up bravely under the loss,
though.

"You can come in for dinner now," she says. He's sitting
slouched on the sofa with another drink in his hand. He drinks

more than any man she knows, not that she knows all that many. Maybe he'll get cirrhosis and die. Do people still die of cirrhosis, she wonders, or do they give them liver transplants now? The funny thing is that he still turns her on, after eleven years. His eyes, his face, his hands. She despises him but he still turns her on.

The snow reminds him of his young manhood, of his days long ago in the East. He was quite the ladies' man then. And it wasn't so easy to get some action back in those days, either. The girls were always worried about what people would say if anyone found out. *What people would say!* As if doing it with a boy you liked was something shameful. Or they'd worry about getting knocked up. They made you wear a rubber. How awful that was: like wearing a sock. The pill was just starting to come in, the original pill, the old one-a-day kind. Imagine a world without the pill! ("Did they have dinosaurs when you were a boy, grandpa?") Still, Martin had made out all right. Big muscular frame, strong earnest features, warm inquisitive eyes. You'd never know it to look at me now. I wonder if Alice realizes what kind of stud I used to be. If I had the money I'd rent one of those time machines they've got now and send her back to visit myself around 1950 or so. A little gift to my younger self. He'd really rip into her. It gives Martin a quick riffle of excitement to think of his younger self ripping into Alice. But of course he can't afford any such thing.

As he forks down his steak he imagines being single again. Would I get married again? Not on your life. Not until I'm good and ready, anyway, maybe when I'm fifty-five or sixty. Me for bachelorhood for the time being, just screwing around like a kid. To hell with responsibilities. I'll wait two, three weeks after the funeral, a decent interval, and then I'll go off for some fun. Hawaii, Tahiti, Fiji, someplace out there. With Nolie. Or Maria. Or Ellie. Yes, with Ellie. He thinks of Ellie's pink thighs, her soft heavy breasts, her long radiant auburn hair. Two weeks in Fiji with Ellie. Two weeks in Ellie with Fiji. Yes. Yes. Yes. "Is the steak rare enough for you, Ted?" Alice asks. "It's fine," he says.

She goes upstairs to check the children's bedroom. They're both asleep, finally. Or else faking it so well that it makes no difference. She stands by their beds a moment, thinking, I love you, Bobby, I love you, Tink. Tink and Bobby, Bobby and Tink. I love you even though you drive me crazy sometimes. She tiptoes out. Now for a quiet evening of television. And then to bed. The same old routine. Christ. I don't know why I go on like this. There are times when I'm ready to explode. I stay with him for the children's sake, I guess. Is that enough of a reason?

He envisions himself running hand in hand along the beach with Ellie. Both of them naked, their skins bronzed and gleaming in the tropical sunlight. Palm trees everywhere. Grains of pink sand under foot. Soft transparent wavelets lapping the shore. A quiet cove. "No one can see us here," Ellie murmurs. He sinks down on her firm sleek body and enters her.

A blazing band of pain tightens like a strip of hot metal across Martin's chest. He staggers away from the window, dropping into a low crouch as he stumbles toward a chair. The heart. Oh, the heart! That's what you get for drooling over Alice. Dirty old man. "Help," he calls feebly. "Come on, you filthy machine, help me!" The medic, activated by the key phrase, rolls silently toward him. Its sensors are already at work scanning him, searching for the cause of the discomfort. A telescoping steel-jacketed arm slides out of the medic's chest and, hovering above Martin, extrudes an ultrasonic injection snout. "Yes," Martin murmurs, "that's right, damn you, hurry up and give me the drug!" Calm. I must try to remain calm. The snout makes a gentle whirring noise as it forces the relaxant into Martin's vein. He slumps in relief. The pain slowly ebbs. Oh, that's much better. Saved again. Oh. Oh. Oh. Dirty old man. Ought to be ashamed of yourself.

Ted knows he won't get to Fiji with Ellie or anybody else. Any realistic assessment of the situation brings him inevitably to the same conclusion. Alice isn't going to die in an accident, any more than he's likely to murder her. She'll live forever. Unwanted wives always do. He could ask for a divorce, of course. He'd probably lose everything he owned, but he'd win his freedom. Or he could simply do away with himself. That was always a temptation for him. The easy way out, no lawyers, no hassles. So it's that time of the evening again. It's the same every night. Pretending to watch television, he secretly indulges in suicidal fantasies.

Bare-bodied dancers in gaudy luminous paint gyrate lasciviously on the screen, nearly large as life. Alice scowls. The things they show on TV nowadays! It used to be that you got this stuff only on the X-rated channels, but now it's everywhere. And look at him, just lapping it up! Actually she knows she wouldn't be so stuffy about the sex shows except that Ted's fascination with them ·is a measure of his lack of interest in her. Let them show screwing and all the rest on TV, if that's what people want. I just wish Ted had as much enthusiasm for me as he does for the television stuff. So far as sexual permissiveness in general goes, she's no prude. She used to wear nothing but trunks at the beach, until Tink was born and she started to feel a little less proud of her figure. But she still dresses as revealingly as anyone in their crowd. And gets stared at by everyone but her own husband. *He* watches the TV cuties. His other women must use him up. Maybe I ought to step out a bit myself, Alice thinks. She's had her little affairs along the way. Not many, nothing very serious, but she's had some. Three lovers in eleven years, that's not a great many, but it's a sign that she's no puritan. She wonders if she ought to get involved with somebody now. It might move her life off dead center while she still has the chance, before boredom destroys her entirely. "I'm going up to wash my hair," she announces. "Will you be staying down here till bedtime?"

There are so many ways he could do it. Slit his wrists. Drive his car off the bridge. Swallow Alice's whole box of sleeping tabs. Of course those are all old-fashioned ways of killing yourself. Something more modern would be appropriate. Go into one of the black taverns and start making loud racial insults? No, nothing modern about that. It's very 1975. But something genuinely contemporary does occur to him. Those time machines they've got now: suppose he rented one and went back, say, sixty years, to a time when one of his parents hadn't yet been born. And killed his grandfather. Find old Martin as a young man and slip a knife into him. If I do that, Ted figures, I should instantly and painlessly cease to exist. I would never have existed, because my mother wouldn't ever have existed. Poof. Out like a light.

Then he realizes he's fantasizing a murder again. Stupid: if he could ever murder anyone, he'd murder Alice and be done with it. So the whole fantasy is foolish. Back to the starting point is where he is.

She is sitting under the hair-dryer when he comes upstairs. He has a peculiarly smug expression on his face, and as soon as she turns the dryer off she asks him what he's thinking about. "I may have just invented a perfect murder method," he tells her. "Oh?" she says. He says, "You rent a time machine. Then you go back a couple of generations and murder one of the ancestors of your intended victim. That way you're murdering the victim too, because he won't ever have been born if you kill off one of his immediate progenitors. Then you return to your own time. Nobody can trace you because you don't have any fingerprints on file in an era before your own birth. What do you think of it?" Alice shrugs. "It's an old one," she says. "It's been done on television a dozen times. Anyway, I don't like it. Why should an innocent person have to die just because he's the grandparent of somebody you want to kill?"

They're probably in bed together right now, Martin thinks gloomily. Stark naked side by side. The lights are out. The house is quiet. Maybe they're smoking a little grass. Do they still call it grass, he wonders, or is there some new nickname now? Anyway the two of them turn on. Yes. And then he reaches for her. His hands slide over her cool, smooth skin. He cups her breasts. Plays with the hard little nipples. Sucks on them. The other hand wandering down to her parted thighs. And then she. And then he. And then they. And then they. Oh, Alice, he murmurs. Oh, Ted, *Ted,* she cries. And then they. Go to it. Up and down, in and out. Oh. Oh. Oh. She claws his back. She pumps her hips. Ted! Ted! Ted! The big moment is arriving now. For her, for him. Jackpot! Afterward they lie close for a few minutes, basking in the afterglow. And then they roll apart. Goodnight, Ted. Goodnight, Alice. Oh, Jesus. They do it every night, I bet. They're so young and full of juice. And I'm all dried up. Christ, I hate being old. When I think of the man I once was. When I think of the women I once had. Jesus. Jesus. God, let me have the strength to do it just once more before I die. And leave me alone for two hours with Alice.

* * *

She has trouble falling asleep. A strange scene keeps playing itself out obsessively in her mind. She sees herself stepping out of an upright coffin-size box of dark gray metal, festooned with dials and levers. The time machine. It delivers her into a dark, dirty alleyway, and when she walks forward to the street she sees scores of little antique automobiles buzzing around. Only they aren't antiques, they're the current models. This is the year 1947. New York City. Will she be conspicuous in her futuristic clothes? She has her breasts covered, at any rate. That's essential back here. She hurries to the proper address, resisting the temptation to browse in shop windows along the way. How quaint and ancient everything looks. And how dirty the streets are. She comes to a tall building of red brick. This is the place. No scanners study her as she enters. They don't have annunciators yet or any other automatic home-protection equipment. She goes upstairs in an elevator so creaky and unstable that she fears for her life. Fifth floor. Apartment 5-J. She rings the doorbell. *He* answers. He's terribly young, only twenty-four, but she can pick out signs of the Martin of the future in his face, the strong cheekbones, the searching blue eyes. "Are you Martin Jamieson?" she asks. "That's right," he says. She smiles. "May I come in?" "Of course," he says. He bows her into the apartment. As he momentarily turns his back on her to open the coat closet she takes the heavy steel pipe from her purse and lifts it high and brings it down on the back of his head. *Thwock.* She takes the heavy steel pipe from her purse and lifts it high and brings it down on the back of his head. *Thwock.* She takes the heavy steel pipe from her purse and lifts it high and brings it down on the back of his head. *Thwock.*

Ted and Alice visit him at Sunset Village two or three times a month. He can't complain about that; it's as much as he can expect. He's an old, old man and no doubt a boring one, but they come dutifully, sometimes with the kids, sometimes without. He's never gotten used to the idea that he's a great-grandfather. Alice always gives him a kiss when she arrives and another when she leaves. He plays a private little game with her, copping a feel at each kiss. His hand quickly stroking her butt. Or sometimes when he's really rambunctious it travels lightly over her breast. Does she notice? Probably. She never lets on, though. Pretends it's an accidental touch. Most likely she thinks it's charming that a man of his age would still have at least a vestige of sexual desire left. Unless she thinks it's disgusting, that is.

The time-machine gimmick, Ted tells himself, can be used in ways that don't quite amount to murder. For instance. "What's that box?" Alice asks. He smiles cunningly. "It's called a panchronicon," he says. "It gives you a kind of televised reconstruction of ancient times. The salesman loaned me a demonstration sample." She says, "How does it work?" "Just step inside," he tells her. "It's all ready for you." She starts to enter the machine, but then, suddenly suspicious, she hesitates on the threshold. He pushes her in and slams the door shut behind her. *Wham!* The controls are set. Off goes Alice on a one-way journey to the Pleistocene. The machine is primed to return as soon as it drops her off. That isn't murder, is it? She's still alive, wherever she may be, unless the saber-tooth tigers have caught up with her. So long, Alice.

In the morning she drives Bobby and Tink to school. Then she stops at the bank and post office. From ten to eleven she has her regular session at the identity-reinforcement parlor. Ordinarily she would go right home after that, but this morning she strolls across the shopping center plaza to the office that the time-machine people have just opened. TEMPONAUTICS, LTD., the sign over the door says. The place is empty except for two machines, no doubt demonstration models, and a bland-faced, smiling salesman. "Hello," Alice says nervously. "I just wanted to pick up some information about the rental costs of one of your machines."

Martin likes to imagine Alice coming to visit him by herself some rainy Saturday afternoon. "Ted isn't able to make it today," she explains. "Something came up at the office. But I knew your were expecting us, and I didn't want you to be disappointed. Poor Martin, you must lead such a lonely life." She comes close to him. She is trembling. So is he. Her face is flushed and her eyes are bright with the unmistakable glossiness of desire. He feels a sense of sexual excitement too, for the first time in ten or twenty years, that tension in the loins, that throbbing of the pulse. Electricity. Chemistry. His eyes lock on hers. Her nostrils flare, her mouth goes taut. "Martin," she whispers huskily. "Do you feel what I feel?" "You know I do," he tells her. She says, "If only I could have known you when you were in your prime!" He chuckles. "I'm not altogether senile yet," he cries exultantly. Then she is in his arms and his lips are seeking her fragrant breasts.

"Yes, it came as a terrible shock to me," Ted tells Ellie. "Having her disappear like that. She simply vanished from the face of the earth, as far as anyone can determine. They've tried every possible way of tracing her and there hasn't been a clue." Ellie's flawless forehead furrows in a fitful frown. "Was she unhappy?" she asks. "Do you think she may have done away with herself?" Ted shakes his head. "I don't know. You live with a person for eleven years and you think you know her pretty well, and then one day something absolutely incomprehensible occurs and you realize how impossible it is ever to know another human being at all. Don't you agree?" Ellie nods gravely. "Yes, oh, yes, certainly!" she says. He smiles down at her and takes her hands in his. Softly he says, "Let's not talk about Alice any more, shall we? She's gone and that's all I'll ever know." He hears a pulsing symphonic crescendo of shimmering angelic choirs as he embraces her and murmurs, "I love you, Ellie. I love you."

She takes the heavy steel pipe from her purse and lifts it high and brings it down on the back of his head. *Thwock.* Young Martin drops instantly, twitches once, lies still. Dark blood begins to seep through the dense blond curls of his hair. How strange to see Martin with golden hair, she thinks, as she kneels beside his body. She puts her hand to the bloody place, probes timidly, feels the deep indentation. Is he dead? She isn't sure how to tell. He isn't moving. He doesn't seem to be breathing. She wonders if she ought to hit him again, just to make certain. Then she remembers something she's seen on television, and takes her mirror from her purse. Holds it in front of his face. No cloud forms. That's pretty conclusive: you're dead, Martin. R.I.P. Martin Jamieson, 1923–1947. Which means that Martha Jamieson Porter (1948–) will never now be conceived, and that automatically obliterates the existence of her son Theodore Porter (1968–). Not bad going, Alice, getting rid of unloved husband and miserable shrewish mother-in-law all in one shot. Sorry, Martin. Bye-bye, Ted. (R.I.P. Theodore Porter, 1968–1947. Eh?) She rises, goes into the bathroom with the steel pipe and carefully rinses it off. Then she puts it back into her purse. Now to go back to the machine and return to 2006, she thinks. To start my new life. But as she leaves the apartment, a tall, lean man steps out of the hallway shadows and clamps his hand powerfully around her wrist. "Time Patrol," he says crisply, flashing an identification badge. "You're under arrest for temponautic murder, Mrs. Porter."

Today has been a better day than yesterday, low on crises and depressions, but he still feels a headache coming on as he lets himself into the house. He is braced for whatever bitchiness Alice may have in store for him this evening. But, oddly, she seems relaxed and amiable. "Can I get you a drink, Ted?" she asks. "How did your day go?" He smiles and says, "Well, I think we may have salvaged the Hammond account after all. Otherwise nothing special happened. And you? What did you do today, love?" She shrugs. "Oh, the usual stuff," she says. "The bank, the post office, my identity-reinforcement session."

If you had the money, Martin asks himself, how far back would you send her? 1947, that would be the year, I guess. My last year as a single man. No sense complicating things. Off you go, Alice baby, to 1947. Let's make it March. By June I was engaged and by September Martha was on the way, though I didn't find that out until later. Yes: March, 1947. So Young Martin answers the doorbell and sees an attractive girl in the hall, a woman, really, older than he is, maybe thirty or thirty-two. Slender, dark-haired, nicely constructed. Odd clothing: a clinging gray tunic, very short, made of some strange fabric that flows over her body like a stream. How it achieves that liquid effect around the pleats is beyond him. "Are you Martin Jamieson?" she asks. And quickly answers herself. "Yes, of course, you must be. I recognize you. How handsome you were!" He is baffled. He knows nothing, naturally, about this gift from his aged future self. "Who are you?" he asks. "May I come in first?" she says. He is embarrassed by his lack of courtesy and waves her inside. Her eyes glitter with mischief. "You aren't going to believe this," she tells him, "but I'm your grandson's wife."

* * *

"Would you like to try out one of our demonstration models?" the salesman asks pleasantly. "There's absolutely no cost or obligation." Ted looks at Alice. Alice looks at Ted. Her frown mirrors his inner uncertainty. She also must be wishing that they had never come to the Temponautics showroom. The salesman, pattering smoothly onward, says, "In these demonstrations we usually send our potential customers fifteen or twenty minutes into the past. I'm sure you'll find it fascinating. While remaining in the machine, you'll be able to look through a viewer and observe your own selves actually entering this very showroom a short while ago. Well? Will you give it a try? You go first, Mrs. Porter. I assure you it's going to be the most unique experience you've ever had." Alice, uneasy, tries to back off, but the salesman prods her in a way that is at once gentle and unyielding, and she steps reluctantly into the time machine. He closes the door. A great business of adjusting fine controls ensues. Then the salesman throws a master switch. A green glow envelops the machine and it disappears, although something transparent and vague—a retinal after-image? the ghost of the machine?—remains dimly visible. The salesman says, "She's now gone a short distance into her own past. I've programmed the machine to take her back eighteen minutes and keep her there for a total elapsed interval of six minutes, so she can see the entire opening moments of your visit here. But when I return her to Now Level, there's no need to match the amount of elapsed time in the past, so that from our point of view she'll have been absent only some thirty seconds. Isn't that remarkable, Mr. Porter? It's one of the many extraordinary paradoxes we encounter in the strange new realm of time travel." He throws another switch. The time machine once more assumes solid form. *"Voila!"* cries the salesman. "Here is Mrs. Porter, returned safe and sound from her voyage into the past." He flings open the door of the time machine. The passenger compartment is empty. The salesman's face crumbles. "Mrs. Porter?" he shrieks in consternation. "Mrs. Porter? I don't understand! How could there have been a malfunction? This is impossible! Mrs. Porter? *Mrs. Porter?*"

She hurries down the dirty street toward the tall brick building. This is the place. Upstairs. Fifth floor, apartment 5-J. As she starts to ring the doorbell, a tall, lean man steps out of the

shadows and clamps his hand powerfully around her wrist.
"Time Patrol," he says crisply, flashing an identification badge.
"You're under arrest for contemplated temponautic murder, Mrs.
Porter."

"But I haven't any grandson," he sputters. "I'm not even
mar—" She laughs. "Don't worry about it!" she tells him.
"You're going to have a daughter named Martha and she'll have
a son named Ted and I'm going to marry Ted and we'll have two
children named Bobby and Tink. And you're going to live to be
an old, old man. And that's all you need to know. Now let's have
a little fun." She touches a catch at the side of her tunic and the
garment falls away in a single fluid cascade. Beneath it she is
naked. Her nipples stare up at him like blind pink eyes. She
beckons to him. "Come on!" she says hoarsely. "Get undressed,
Martin! You're wasting time!"

Alice giggles nervously. "Well, as a matter of fact," she says to
the salesman, "I think I'm willing to let my husband be the
guinea pig. How about it, Ted?" She turns toward him. So does
the salesman. "Certainly, Mr. Porter. I know you're eager to give
our machine a test run, yes?" No, Ted thinks, but he feels the
pressure of events propelling him willy-nilly. He gets into the
machine. As the door closes on him he fears that claustrophobic
panic will overwhelm him; he is reassured by the sight of a
handle on the door's inner face. He pushes on it and the door
opens, and he steps out of the machine just in time to see his
earlier self coming into the Temponautics showroom with Alice.
The salesman is going forward to greet them. Ted is now
eighteen minutes into his own past. Alice and the other Ted stare
at him, aghast. The salesman whirls and exclaims, "Wait a
second, you aren't supposed to get out of—" How stupid they all
look! How bewildered! Ted laughs in their faces. Then he rushes
past them, nearly knocking his other self down, and erupts into
the shopping-center plaza. He sprints in a wild frenzy of exhilaration toward the parking area. Free, he thinks. I'm free at last.
And I didn't have to kill anybody.

Suppose I rent a machine, Alice thinks, and go back to 1947 and
kill Martin? Suppose I really do it? What if there's some way of
tracing the crime to me? After all, a crime committed by a person

from 2006 who goes back to 1947 will have consequences in our present day. It might change all sorts of things. So they'd want to catch the criminal and punish him, or better yet prevént the crime from being committed in the first place. And the time-machine company is bound to know what year I asked them to send me to. So maybe it isn't such an easy way of committing a perfect crime. I don't know. God, I can't understand any of this. But perhaps I can get away with it. Anyway, I'm going to give it a try. I'll show Ted he can't go on treating me like dirt.

They lie peacefully side by side, sweaty, drowsy, exhausted in the good exhaustion that comes after a first-rate screw. Martin tenderly strokes her belly and thighs. How smooth her skin is, how pale, how transparent! The little blue veins so clearly visible. "Hey," he says suddenly. "I just thought of something. I wasn't wearing a rubber or anything. What if I made you pregnant? And if you're really who you say you are. Then you'll go back to the year 2006 and you'll have a kid and he'll be his own grandfather, won't he?" She laughs. "Don't worry much about it," she says.

A wave of timidity comes over her as she enters the Temponautics office. This is crazy, she tells herself. I'm getting out of here. But before she can turn around, the salesman she spoke to the day before materializes from a side room and gives her a big hello. Mr. Friesling. He's practically rubbing his hands together in anticipation of landing a contract. "So nice to see you again, Mrs. Porter." She nods and glances worriedly at the demonstration models. "How much would it cost," she asks, "to spend a few hours in the spring of 1947?"

Sunday is the big family day. Four generations sitting down to dinner together: Martin, Martha, Ted and Alice, Bobby and Tink. Ted rather enjoys these reunions, but he knows Alice loathes them, mainly because of Martha. Alice hates her mother-in-law. Martha has never cared much for Alice, either. He watches them glaring at each other across the table. Meanwhile old Martin stares lecherously at the gulf between Alice's breasts. You have to hand it to the old man, Ted thinks. He's never lost the old urge. Even though there's not a hell of a lot he can do about gratifying it, not at his age. Martha says sweetly, "You'd look ever so much better, Alice dear, if you'd let your hair grow out to its natural color." A sugary smile from Martha. A sour scowl from Alice. She glowers at the older woman. "This *is* its natural color," she snaps.

Mr. Friesling hands her the standard contract form. Eight pages of densely packed type. "Don't be frightened by it, Mrs. Porter. It looks formidable but actually it's just a lot of empty legal rhetoric. You can show it to your lawyer, if you like. I can tell you, though, that most of our customers find no need for that." She leafs through it. So far as she can tell, the contract is mainly a disclaimer of responsibility. Temponautics, Ltd., agrees to bear the brunt of any malfunction caused by its own demonstrable negligence, but wants no truck with acts of God or with accidents brought about by clients who won't obey the safety regulations. On the fourth page Alice finds a clause warning the prospective renter that the company cannot be held liable for any consequences of actions by the renter which wantonly or willfully interfere with the already determined course of history. She translates that for herself: *If you kill your husband's grandfather, don't blame us if you get in trouble.* She skims the remaining pages. "It looks harmless enough," she says. "Where do I sign?"

As Martin comes out of the bathroom he finds Martha blocking his way. "Excuse me," he says mildly, but she remains in his path. She is a big fleshy woman. At fifty-eight she affects the fashions of the very young, with grotesque results; he hates that aspect of her. He can see why Alice dislikes her so much. "Just a moment," Martha says. "I want to talk to you, Father." About what?" he asks. "About those looks you give Alice. Don't you think that's a little too much? How tasteless can you get?" "Tasteless? Are you anybody to talk about taste, with your face painted green like a fifteen-year old?" She looks angry: he's scored a direct hit. She replies, "I just think that at the age of eight-two you ought to have a greater regard for decency than to go staring down your own grandson's wife's front." Martin sighs. "Let me have the staring, Martha. It's all I've got left."

He is at the office, deep in complicated negotiations, when his autosecretary bleeps him and announces that a call has come in from a Mr. Friesling, of the Union Boulevard Plaza office of Temponautics, Ltd. Ted is puzzled by that: what do the time-machine people want with him? Trying to line him up as a customer? "Tell him I'm not interested in time trips," Ted says. But the autosecretary bleeps again a few moments later. Mr. Friesling, it declares, is calling in reference to Mr. Porter's credit standing. More baffled than before, Ted orders the call switched over to him. Mr. Friesling appears on the desk screen. He is small-featured and bright-eyed, rather like a chipmunk. "I apologize for troubling you, Mr. Porter," he begins. "This is strictly a routine credit check, but it's altogether necessary. As you surely know, your wife has requested rental of our equipment for a fifty-nine-year time jaunt, and inasmuch as the service fee for such a trip exceeds the level at which we extend automatic credit, our policy requires us to ask you if you'll confirm the payment schedule that she has requested us to—" Ted coughs violently. "Hold on," he says. "My wife's going on a time jaunt? What the hell, this is the first time I've heard of that!"

She is surprised by the extensiveness of the preparations. No wonder they charge so much. Getting her ready for the jaunt takes hours. They inoculate her to protect her against certain extinct diseases. They provide her with clothing in the style of the mid-twentieth century, ill-fitting and uncomfortable. They give her contemporary currency, but warn her that she would do well not to spend any except in an emergency, since she will be billed for it at its present-day numismatic value, which is high. They make her study a pamphlet describing the customs and historical background of the era and quiz her in detail. She learns that she is not under any circumstances to expose her breasts or genitals in public while she is in 1947. She must not attempt to obtain any mind-stimulating drugs other than alcohol. She should not say anything that might be construed as praise of the Soviet Union or of Marxist philosophy. She must bear in mind that she is entering the past solely as an observer, and should engage in minimal social interaction with the citizens of the era she is visiting. And so forth. At last they decide it's safe to let her go. "Please come this way, Mrs. Porter," Friesling says.

After staring at the telephone a long while, Martin punches out Alice's number. Before the second ring he loses his nerve and disconnects. Immediately he calls her again. His heart pounds so furiously that the medic, registering alarm on its delicate sensing apparatus, starts toward him. He waves the robot away and clings to the phone. Two rings. Three. Ah. "Hello?" Alice says. Her voice is warm and rich and feminine. He has his screen switched off. "Hello? Who's there?" Martin breathes heavily into the mouthpiece. Ah. Ah. Ah. Ah. "Hello? Hello? Hello? Listen, you pervert, if you phone me once more—" *Ah. Ah. Ah.* A smile of bliss appears on Martin's withered features. Alice hangs up. Trembling, Martin sags in his chair. Oh, that was good! He signals fiercely to the medic. "Let's have the injection now, you metal monster!" He laughs. Dirty old man.

Ted realizes that it isn't necessary to kill a person's grandfather in order to get rid of that person. Just interfere with some crucial event in that person's past, is all. Go back and break up the marriage of Alice's grandparents, for example. (How? Seduce the grandmother when she's 18? "I'm terribly sorry to inform you that your intended bride is no virgin, and here's the documentary evidence." They were very grim about virginity back then, weren't they?) Nobody would have to die. But Alice wouldn't ever be born.

Martin still can't believe any of this, even after she's slept with him. It's some crazy practical joke, most likely. Although he wishes all practical jokes were as sexy as this one. "Are you really from the year 2006?" he asks her. She laughs prettily. "How can I prove it to you?" Then she leaps from the bed. He tracks her with his eyes as she crosses the room, breasts jiggling gaily. What a sweet little body. How thoughtful of my older self to ship her back here to me. If that's what really happened. She fumbles in her purse and extracts a handful of coins. "Look here," she says. "Money from the future. Here's a dime from 1993. And this is a two-dollar piece from 2001. And here's an old one, a 1979 Kennedy half-dollar." He studies the unfamiliar coins. They have a greasy look, not silvery at all. Counterfeits? They won't necessarily be striking coins out of silver forever. And the engraving job is very professional. A two-dollar piece, eh? Well, you never can tell. And this. The half-dollar. A handsome young man in profile. "Kennedy?" he says. "Who's Kennedy?"

* * *

So this is it at last. Two technicians in gray smocks watch her, sober-faced, as she clambers into the machine. It's very much like a coffin, just as she imagined it would be. She can't sit down in it; it's too narrow. Gives her the creeps, shut up in here. Of course, they've told her the trip won't take any apparent subjective time, only a couple of seconds. *Woosh!* and she'll be there. All right. They close the door. She hears the lock clicking shut. Mr. Friesling's voice comes to her over a loudspeaker. "We wish you a happy voyage, Mrs. Porter. Keep calm and you won't get into any difficulties." Suddenly the red light over the door is glowing. That means the jaunt has begun: she's traveling backward in time. No sense of acceleration, no sense of motion. One, two, three. The light goes off. That's it. I'm in 1947, she tells herself. Before she opens the door, she closes her eyes and runs through her history lessons. World War II has just ended. Europe is in ruins. There are forty-eight states. Nobody has been to the moon yet or even thinks much about going there. Harry Truman is President. Stalin runs Russia, and Churchill—is Churchill still Prime Minister of England? She isn't sure. Well, no matter. I didn't come here to talk about prime ministers. She touches the latch and the door of the time machine swings outward.

He steps from the machine into the year 2006. Nothing has changed in the showroom. Friesling, the two poker-faced technicians, the sleek desks, the thick carpeting, all the same as before. He moves bouncily. His mind is still back there with Alice's grandmother. The taste of her lips, the soft urgent cries of her fulfillment. Who ever said all women were frigid in the old days? They ought to go back and find out. Friesling smiles at him. "I hope you had a very enjoyable journey, Mr.—ah—" Ted nods. "Enjoyable and useful," he says. He goes out. Never to see Alice again—how beautiful! The car isn't where he remembers leaving it in the parking area. You have to expect certain small peripheral changes, I guess. He hails a cab, gives the driver his address. His key does not fit the front door. Troubled, he thumbs the annunciator. A woman's voice, not Alice's, asks him what he wants. "Is this the Ted Porter residence?" he asks. "No, it isn't," the woman says, suspicious and irritated. The name on the doorplate, he notices now, is McKenzie. So the changes are not all so small. Where do I go now? If I don't live here, then where? "Wait!" he yells to the taxi, just pulling away. It takes him to a downtown cafe, where he phones Ellie. Her face, peering out of the tiny screen, wears an odd frowning expression. "Listen, something very strange has happened," he begins, "and I need to see you as soon as—" "I don't think I know you," she says. "I'm Ted," he tells her. "Ted who?" she asks.

How peculiar this is, Alice thinks. Like walking into a museum diorama and having it come to life. The noisy little automobiles. The ugly clothing. The squat, dilapidated twentieth-century buildings. The chaos. The oily, smoky smell of the polluted air. Wisps of dirty snow in the streets. Cans of garbage just sitting around as if nobody's ever heard of the plague. Well, I won't stay here long. In her purse she carries her kitchen carver, a tiny nickel-jacketed laser-powered implement. Steel pipes are all right for dream fantasies, but this is the real thing, and she wants the killing to be quick and efficient. Criss, cross, with the laser beam, and Martin goes. At the street corner she pauses to check the address. There's no central info number to ring for all sorts of useful data, not in these primitive times; she must use a printed telephone directory, a thick tattered book with small smeary type. Here he is: Martin Jamieson, 504 West Forty-fifth. That's not far. In ten minutes she's there. A dark brick structure, five or six stories high, with spidery metal fire escapes running down its face. Even for its day it appears unusually run-down. She goes inside. A list of tenants is posted just within the front door. Jamieson, 3-A. There's no elevator and of course no liftshaft. Up the stairs. A musty hallway lit by a single dim incandesent bulb. This is Apartment 3-A. Jamieson. She rings the bell.

Ten minutes later Friesling calls back, sounding abashed and looking dismayed: "I'm sorry to have to tell you that there's been some sort of error, Mr. Porter. The technicians were apparently unaware that a credit check was in process, and they sent Mrs. Porter off on her trip while we were still talking." Ted is shaken. He clutches the edge of the desk. Controlling himself with an effort, he says, "How far back was it that she wanted to go?" Friesling says, "It was fifty-nine years. To 1947." Ted nods grimly. A horrible idea has occurred to him. 1947 was the year that his mother's parents met and got married. What is Alice up to?

*   *   *

The doorbell rings. Martin, freshly showered, is sprawled out naked on his bed, leafing through the new issue of *Esquire* and thinking vaguely of going out for dinner. He isn't expecting any company. Slipping into his bathrobe, he goes toward the door. "Who's there?" he calls. A youthful, pleasant female voice replies, "I'm looking for Martin Jamieson." Well, okay. He opens the door. She's perhaps twenty-seven, twenty-eight years old, *very* sexy, on the slender side but well built. Dark hair, worn in a strangely boyish short cut. He's never seen her before. "Hi," he says tentatively. She grins warmly at him. "You don't know me," she tells him, "but I'm a friend of an old friend of yours. Mary Chambers? Mary and I grew up together in—ah—Ohio. I'm visiting New York for the first time, and Mary once told me that if I ever come to New York I should be sure to look up Martin Jamieson, and so—may I come in?" "You bet," he says. He doesn't remember any Mary Chambers from Ohio. But what the hell, sometimes you forget a few. What the hell.

He's much more attractive than she expected him to be. She has always known Martin only as an old man, made unattractive as much by his coarse lechery as by what age has done to him. Hollow-chested, stoop-shouldered, pleated jowly face, sparse strands of white hair, beady eyes of faded blue—a wreck of a man. But this Martin in the doorway is sturdy, handsome, untouched by time, brimming with life and vigor and virility. She thinks of the carver in her purse and feels a genuine pang of regret at having to cut this robust boy off in his prime. But there isn't such a great hurry, is there? First we can enjoy each other, Martin. And then the laser.

"When is she due back?" Ted demands. Friesling explains that all concepts of time are relative and flexible; so far as elapsed time at Now Level goes, she's already returned. "What?" Ted yells. "Where is she?" Friesling does not know. She stepped out of the machine, bade the Temponautics staff a pleasant goodbye, and left the showroom. Ted puts his hand to his throat. What if she's already killed Martin? Will I just wink out of existence? Or is there some sort of lag, so that I'll fade gradually into unreality over the next few days? "Listen," he says raggedly, "I'm leaving my office right now and I'll be down at your place in less than an hour. I want you to have your machinery set up so that you can transport me to the exact point in space and time where you just sent my wife." "But that won't be possible," Friesling protests. "It takes hours to prepare a client properly for—" Ted cuts him off. "Get everything set up, and to hell with preparing me properly," he snaps. "Unless you feel like getting slammed with the biggest negligence suit since this time-machine thing got started, you better have everything ready when I get there."

He opens the door. The girl in the hallway is young and good-looking, with close-cropped dark hair and full lips. Thank you, Mary Chambers, whoever you may be. "Pardon the bathrobe," he says, "but I wasn't expecting company." She steps into his apartment. Suddenly he notices how strained and tense her face is. Country girl from Ohio, suddenly having second thoughts about visiting a strange man in a strange city? He tries to put her at her ease. "Can I get you a drink?" he asks. "Not much of a selection, I'm afraid, but I have scotch, gin, some blackberry cordial—" She reaches into her purse and takes something out. He frowns. Not a gun, exactly, but it does seem like a weapon of some sort, a little glittering metal device that fits neatly in her hand. "Hey," he says, "what's—" "I'm so terribly sorry, Martin," she whispers, and a bolt of terrible fire slams into his chest.

She sips the drink. It relaxes her. The glass isn't very clean, but she isn't worried about picking up a disease, not after all the injections Friesling gave her. Martin looks as if he can stand some relaxing too. "Aren't you drinking?" she asks. "I suppose I will," he says. He pours himself some gin. She comes up behind him and slips her hand into the front of his bathrobe. His body is cool, smooth, hard. "Oh, Martin," she murmurs. "Oh! Martin!"

Ted takes a room in one of the commercial hotels downtown. The first thing he does is try to put a call through to Alice's mother in Chillicothe. He still isn't really convinced that his little time-jaunt flirtation has retroactively eliminated Alice from existence. But the call convinces him, all right. The middle-aged woman who answers is definitely not Alice's mother. Right phone number, right address—he badgers her for the information—but wrong woman. "You don't have a daughter named Alice Porter?" he asks three or four times. "You don't know anyone in the neighborhood who does? It's important." All right. Cancel the old lady, ergo cancel Alice. But now he has a different problem. How much of the universe has he altered by removing Alice and her mother? Does he live in some other city, now, and hold some other job? What has happened to Bobby and Tink? Frantically he begins phoning people. Friends, fellow workers, the man at the bank. The same response from all of them: blank stares, shakings of the head. We don't know you, fellow. He looks at himself in the mirror. Okay, he asks himself. Who am I?

Martin moves swiftly and purposefully, the way they taught him to do in the army when it's necessary to disarm a dangerous opponent. He lunges forward and catches the girl's arm, pushing it upward before she can fire the shiny whatzis she's aiming at him. She turns out to be stronger than he anticipated, and they struggle fiercely for the weapon. Suddenly it fires. Something like a lightning bolt explodes between them and knocks him to the floor, stunned. When he picks himself up he sees her lying near the door with a charred hole in her throat.

The telephone's jangling clatter brings Martin up out of a dream in which he is ravishing Alice's luscious young body. Drythroated, gummy-eyed, he reaches a palsied hand toward the receiver. "Yes?" he says. Ted's face blossoms on the screen. "Grandfather!" he blurts. "Are you all right?" "Of course I'm all right," Martin says testily. "Can't you tell? What's the matter with you, boy?" Ted shakes his head. "I don't know," he mutters. "Maybe it was only a bad dream. I imagined that Alice rented one of those time machines and went back to 1947. And tried to kill you so that I wouldn't ever have existed." Martin snorts. "What idiotic nonsense! How can she have killed me in 1947 when I'm here alive in 2006?"

Naked, Alice sinks into Martin's arms. His strong hands sweep eagerly over her breasts and shoulders and his mouth descends to hers. She shivers with desire. "Yes," she murmurs tenderly, pressing herself against him. "Oh, yes, yes, yes!" They'll do it and it'll be fantastic. And afterward she'll kill him with the kitchen carver while he's lying there savoring the event. But a troublesome thought occurs. If Martin dies in 1947, Ted doesn't get to be born in 1968. Okay. But what about Tink and Bobby? They won't get born either, not if I don't marry Ted. I'll be married to someone else when I get back to 2006, and I suppose I'll have different children. Bobby? Tink? What am I doing to you? Sudden fear congeals her, and she pulls back from the vigorous young man nuzzling her throat. "Wait," she says. "Listen, I'm sorry. It's all a big mistake. I'm sorry, but I've got to get out of here right away!"

So this is the year 1947. Well, well, well. Everything looks so cluttered and grimy and ancient. He hurries through the chilly streets toward his grandfather's place. If his luck is good and if Friesling's technicians have calculated things accurately, he'll be able to head Alice off. That might even be her now, that slender woman walking briskly half a block ahead of him. He steps up his pace. Yes, it's Alice, on her way to Martin's. Well done, Friesling! Ted approaches her warily, suspecting that she's armed. If she's capable of coming back to 1947 to kill Martin, she'd kill him just as readily. Especially back here where neither one of them has any legal existence. When he's close to her he says in a low, hard, intense voice, "Don't turn around, Alice. Just keep walking as if everything's perfectly normal." She stiffens. "Ted?" she cries, astonished. "Is that you, Ted?" "Damned right it is." He laughs harshly. "Come on. Walk to the corner and turn to your left around the block. You're going back to your machine and you're going to get the hell out of the twentieth century without harming anybody. I know what you were trying to do, Alice. But I caught you in time, didn't I?"

Martin is just getting down to real business when the door of his apartment bursts open and a man rushes in. He's middle-aged, stocky, with weird clothes—the ultimate in zoot suits, a maze of vividly contrasting colors and conflicting patterns, shoulders padded to resemble shelves—and a wild look in his eyes. Alice leaps up from the bed. "Ted!" she screams. "My God, what are you doing here?" "You murderous bitch," the intruder yells. Martin, naked and feeling vulnerable, his nervous system stunned by the interruption, looks on in amazement as the stranger grabs her and begins throttling her. "Bitch! Bitch! Bitch!" he roars, shaking her in a mad frenzy. The girl's face is turning black. Her eyes are bugging. After a long moment Martin breaks finally from his freeze. He stumbles forward, seizes the man's fingers, peels them away from the girl's throat. Too late. She falls limply and lies motionless. "Alice!" the intruder moans. "Alice, Alice, what have I done?" He drops to his knees beside her body, sobbing. Martin blinks. "You killed her," he says, not believing that any of this can really be happening. "You actually killed her?"

Alice's face appears on the telephone screen. Christ, how beautiful she is, Martin thinks, and his decrepit body quivers with lust. "There you are," he says. "I've been trying to reach you for hours. I had such a strange dream—that something awful had happened to Ted—and then your phone didn't answer, and I began to think maybe the dream was a premonition of some kind, an omen, you know—" Alice looks puzzled. "I'm afraid you have the wrong number, sir," she says sweetly, and hangs up.

She draws the laser and the naked man cowers back against the wall in bewilderment. "What the hell is this?" he asks, trembling. "Put that thing down, lady. You've got the wrong guy." "No," she says. "You're the one I'm after. I hate to do this to you, Martin, but I've got no choice. You have to die." "Why?" he demands. *"Why"* "You wouldn't understand it even if I told you," she says. She moves her finger toward the discharge stud. Abruptly there is a frightening sound of cracking wood and collapsing plaster behind her, as though an earthquake has struck. She whirls and is appalled to see her husband breaking down the door of Martin's apartment. "I'm just in time!" Ted exclaims. "Don't move, Alice!" He reaches for her. In panic she fires without thinking. The dazzling beam catches Ted in the pit of the stomach and he goes down, gurgling in agony, clutching at his belly as he dies.

The door falls with a crash and this character in peculiar clothing materializes in a cloud of debris, looking crazier than Napoleon. It's incredible, Martin thinks. First an unknown broad rings his bell and invites herself in and takes her clothes off, and then, just as he's about to screw her, this happens. It's pure Marx Brothers, only dirty. But Martin's not going to take any crap. He pulls himself away from the panting, gasping girl on the bed, crosses the room in three quick strides, and seizes the newcomer. "Who the hell are you?" Martin demands, slamming him hard against the wall. The girl is dancing around behind him. "Don't hurt him!" she wails. "Oh, please, don't hurt him!"

Ted certainly hadn't expected to find them in bed together. He understood why she might have wanted to go back in time to murder Martin, but simply to have an affair with him, no, it didn't make sense. Of course, it was altogether likely that she had come here to kill and had paused for a little dalliance first. You never could tell about women, even your own wife. Alley cats, all of them. Well, a lucky thing for him that she had given him these few extra minutes to get here. "Okay," he says. "Get your clothes on, Alice. You're coming with me." "Just a second, mister," Martin growls. "You've got your goddamned nerve, busting in like this." Ted tries to explain, but the words won't come. It's all too complicated. He gestures mutely at Alice, at himself, at Martin. The next moment Martin jumps him and they go tumbling together to the floor.

"Who are you?" Martin yells, banging the intruder repeatedly against the wall. "You some kind of detective? You trying to work a badger game on me?" Slam. Slam. Slam. He feels the girl's small fists pounding on his own back. "Stop it!" she screams. "Let him alone, will you? He's my husband!" *"Husband!"* Martin cries. Astounded, he lets go of the stranger and swings around to face the girl. A moment later he realizes his mistake. Out of the corner of his eye he sees that the intruder has raised his fists high above his head like clubs. Martin tries to get out of the way, but no time, no time, and the fists descend with awful force against his skull.

Alice doesn't know what to do. They're rolling around on the floor, fighting like wildcats, now Martin on top, now Ted. Martin is younger and bigger and stronger, but Ted seems possessed by the strength of the insane; he's gone berserk. Both men are bloody-faced, and furniture is crashing over everywhere. Her first impulse is to get between them and stop this crazy fight somehow. But then she remembers that she has come here as a killer, not as a peacemaker. She gets the laser from her purse and aims it at Martin, but then the combatants do a flipflop and it is

Ted who is in the line of fire. She hesitates. It doesn't matter which one she shoots, she realizes after a moment. They both have to die, one way or another. She takes aim. Maybe she can get them both with one bolt. But as her finger starts to tighten on the discharge stud, Martin suddenly gets Ted in a bearhug and, half lifting him, throws him five feet across the room. The back of Ted's neck hits the wall and there is a loud *crack*. Ted slumps and is still. Martin gets shakily to his feet. "I think I killed him," he says. 'Christ, who the hell was he?'' "He was your grandson," Alice says and begins to shriek hysterically.

Ted stares in horror at the crumpled body at his feet. His hands still tingle from the impact. The left side of Martin's head looks as though a pile-driver has crushed it. "Good God in heaven," Ted says thickly, "what have I done? I came here to protect him and I've killed him! I've killed my own grandfather!" Alice, wide-eyed, futilely trying to cover her nakedness by folding one arm across her breasts and spreading her other hand over her loins, says, "If he's dead, why are you still here? Shouldn't you have disappeared?" Ted shrugs. "Maybe I'm safe as long as I remain here in the past. But the moment I try to go back to 2006, I'll vanish as though I've never been. I don't know. I don't understand any of this. What do you think?"

Alice steps uncertainly from the machine into the Temponautics showroom. There's Friesling. There are the technicians. Friesling says, smiling, "I hope you had a very enjoyable journey, Mrs. —ah—uh—" He falters. "I'm sorry," he says, reddening, "but your name seems to have escaped me." Alice says, "It's, ah, Alice—uh—do you know, the second name escapes me too?"

The whole clan has gathered to celebrate Martin's 83rd birthday. He cuts the cake, and then one by one they go to him to kiss him. When it's Alice's turn, he deftly spins her around so that he screens her from the others and gives her rump a good hearty pinch. "Oh, if I were only fifty years younger!" he sighs.

It's a warm springlike day. Everything has been lovely at the office—three new accounts all at once—and the trip home on the freeway was a breeze. Alice is waiting for him, dressed in her finest and most sexy outfit, all ready to go out. It's a special day.

Their eleventh anniversary. How beautiful she looks! He kisses her, she kisses him, he takes the tickets from his pocket with a grand flourish. "Surprise," he says. "Two weeks in Hawaii, starting next Tuesday! Happy anniversary!" "Oh, Ted!" she cries. "How marvelous! I love you, Ted darling!" He pulls her close to him again. "I love you, Alice dear."

GOOD NEWS FROM THE VATICAN

THIS IS THE morning everyone has waited for, when at last the robot cardinal is to be elected pope. There can no longer be any doubt of the outcome. The conclave has been deadlocked for many days between the obstinate advocates of Cardinal Asciuga of Milan and Cardinal Carciofo of Genoa, and word has gone out that a compromise is in the making. All factions now are agreed on the selection of the robot. This morning I read in *Osservatore Romano* that the Vatican computer itself has taken a hand in the deliberations. The computer has been strongly urging the candidacy of the robot. I suppose we should not be surprised by this loyalty among machines. Nor should we let it distress us. We *absolutely must not* let it distress us.

"Every era gets the pope it deserves," Bishop FitzPatrick observed somewhat gloomily today at breakfast. "The proper pope for our times is a robot, certainly. At some future date it may be desirable for the pope to be a whale, an automobile, a cat, a mountain." Bishop FitzPatrick stands well over two meters in height and his normal facial expression is a morbid, mournful one. Thus it is impossible for us to determine whether any particular pronouncement of his reflects existential despair or placid acceptance. Many years ago he was a star player for the Holy Cross championship basketball team. He has come to Rome to do research for a biography of St. Marcellus the Righteous.

We have been watching the unfolding drama of the papal election from an outdoor cafe several blocks from the Square of St. Peter's. For all of us, this has been an unexpected dividend of our holiday in Rome; the previous pope was reputed to be in good health and there was no reason to suspect that a successor would have to be chosen for him this summer.

Each morning we drive across by taxi from our hotel near the Via Veneto and take up our regular positions around "our" table. From where we sit, we all have a clear view of the Vatican chimney through which the smoke of the burning ballots rises: black smoke if no pope has been elected, white if the conclave has been successful. Luigi, the owner and headwaiter, automatically brings us our preferred beverages: Fernet Branca for Bishop FitzPatrick, Campari and soda for Rabbi Mueller, Turkish coffee for Miss Harshaw, lemon squash for Kenneth and Beverly, and Pernod on the rocks for me. We take turns paying the check, although Kenneth has not paid it even once since our vigil began. Yesterday, when Miss Harshaw paid, she emptied her purse and found herself 350 lire short; she had nothing else except hundred-dollar travelers' checks. The rest of us looked pointedly at Kenneth but he went on calmly sipping his lemon squash. After a brief period of tension Rabbi Mueller produced a 500-lire coin and rather irascibly slapped the heavy silver piece against the table. The rabbi is known for his short temper and vehement style. He is twenty-eight years old, customarily dresses in a fashionable plaid cassock and silvered sunglasses, and frequently boasts that he has never performed a bar mitzvah ceremony for his congregation, which is in Wicomico County, Maryland. He believes that the rite is vulgar and obsolete, and invariably farms out all his bar mitzvahs to a franchised organization of itinerant clergymen who handle such affairs on a commission basis. Rabbi Mueller is an authority on angels.

Our group is divided over the merits of electing a robot as the new pope. Bishop FitzPatrick, Rabbi Mueller, and I are in favor of the idea. Miss Harshaw, Kenneth, and Beverly are opposed. It is interesting to note that both of our gentlemen of the cloth, one quite elderly and one fairly young, support this remarkable departure from tradition. Yet the three "swingers" among us do not.

I am not sure why I align myself with the progressives. I am a man of mature years and fairly sedate ways. Nor have I ever concerned myself with the doings of the Church of Rome. I am unfamiliar with Catholic dogma and unaware of recent currents of thought within the Church. Still, I have been hoping for the election of the robot since the start of the conclave.

Why, I wonder? Is it because the image of a metal creature upon the Throne of St. Peter stimulates my imagination and tickles my sense of the incongruous? That is, is my support of the robot purely an esthetic matter? Or is it, rather, a function of my moral cowardice? Do I secretly think that this gesture will buy the robots off? Am I privately saying, Give them the papacy and maybe they won't want other things for a while? No. I can't believe anything so unworthy of myself. Possibly I am for the robot because I am a person of unusual sensitivity to the needs of others.

"If he's elected," says Rabbi Mueller, "he plans an immediate time-sharing agreement with the Dalai Lama and a reciprocal plug-in with the head programmer of the Greek Orthodox Church, just for starters. I'm told he'll make ecumenical overtures to the Rabbinate as well, which is certainly something for all of us to look forward to."

"I don't doubt that there'll be many corrections in the customs and practices of the hierarchy," Bishop FitzPatrick declares. "For example we can look forward to superior information-gathering techniques as the Vatican computer is given a greater role in the operations of the Curia. Let me illustrate by—"

"What an utterly ghastly notion," Kenneth says. He is a gaudy young man with white hair and pink eyes. Beverly is either his wife or his sister. She rarely speaks. Kenneth makes the sign of the Cross with offensive brusqueness and murmurs, "In the name of the Father, the Son, and the Holy Automaton." Miss Harshaw giggles but chokes the giggle off when she sees my disapproving face.

Dejectedly, but not responding at all to the interruption, Bishop FitzPatrick continues, "Let me illustrate by giving you some figures I obtained yesterday afternoon. I read in the newspaper *Oggi* that during the last five years, according to a spokesman for the *Missiones Catholicae*, the Church has increased its membership in Yugoslavia from 19,381,403 to 23,501,062. But the government census taken last year gives the total population of Yugoslavia at 23,575,194. That leaves only 74,132 for the other religious and irreligious bodies. Aware of the large Moslem population of Yugoslavia, I suspected an inaccuracy in the published statistics and consulted the computer in St. Peter's, which informed me''—the bishop, pausing, produces a lengthy printout and unfolds it across much of the table—''that the last count of the Faithful in Yugoslavia, made a year and a half ago, places our numbers at 14,206,198. Therefore an overstatement of 9,294,864 has been made. Which is absurd. And perpetuated. Which is damnable.''

''What does he look like?'' Miss Harshaw asks. ''Does anyone have any idea?''

''He's like all the rest,'' says Kenneth. ''A shiny metal box with wheels below and eyes on top.''

''You haven't seen him,'' Bishop FitzPatrick interjects. ''I don't think it's proper for you to assume that—''

''They're all alike,'' Kenneth says. ''Once you've seen one, you've seen all of them. Shiny boxes. Wheels. Eyes. And voices coming out of their bellies like mechanized belches. Inside, they're all cogs and gears.'' Kenneth shudders delicately. ''It's too much for me to accept. Let's have another round of drinks, shall we?''

Rabbi Mueller says, ''It so happens that I've seen him with my own eyes.''

''You *have?*'' Beverly exclaims.

Kenneth scowls at her. Luigi, approaching, brings a tray of new drinks for everyone. I hand him a 5,000-lire note. Rabbi Mueller removes his sunglasses and breathes on their brilliantly reflective surfaces. He has small, watery gray eyes and a bad squint. He says, ''The cardinal was the keynote speaker at the Congress of World Jewry that was held last fall in Beirut. His theme was 'Cybernetic Ecumenicism for Contemporary Man.' I was there. I can tell you that His Eminency is tall and distinguished, with a fine voice and a gentle smile. There's something inherently melancholy about his manner that reminds me greatly of our friend the bishop, here. His movements are graceful and his wit is keen.''

But he's mounted on wheels, isn't he?'' Kenneth persists.

''On treads,'' replies the rabbi, giving Kenneth a fiery, devastating look and resuming his sunglasses. ''Treads, like a tractor has. But I don't think that treads are spiritually inferior to feet, or, for that matter, to wheels. If I were a Catholic I'd be proud to have a man like that as my pope.''

"Not a man," Miss Harshaw puts in. A giddy edge enters her voice whenever she addresses Rabbi Mueller. "A robot," she says. "He's not a man, remember?"

"A *robot* like that as my pope, then," Rabbi Mueller says, shrugging at the correction. He raises his glass. "To the new pope!"

"To the new pope!" cries Bishop FitzPatrick.

Luigi comes rushing from his cafe. Kenneth waves him away. "Wait a second," Kenneth says. "The election isn't over yet. How can you be so sure?"

"The *Osservatore Romano*," I say, "indicates in this morning's edition that everything will be decided today. Cardinal Carciofo has agreed to withdraw in his favor, in return for a larger real-time allotment when the new computer hours are decreed at next year's consistory."

"In other words, the fix is in," Kenneth says.

Bishop FitzPatrick sadly shakes his head. "You state things much too harshly, my son. For three weeks now we have been without a Holy Father. It is God's Will that we shall have a pope. The conclave, unable to choose between the candidacies of Cardinal Carciofo and Cardinal Asciuga, thwarts that Will. If necessary, therefore, we must make certain accommodations with the realities of the times so that His Will shall not be further frustrated. Prolonged politicking within the conclave now becomes sinful. Cardinal Carciofo's sacrifice of his personal ambitions is not as self-seeking an act as you would claim."

Kenneth continues to attack poor Carciofo's motives for withdrawing. Beverly occasionally applauds his cruel sallies. Miss Harshaw several times declares her unwillingness to remain a communicant of a Church whose leader is a machine. I find this dispute distasteful and swing my chair away from the table to have a better view of the Vatican. At this moment the cardinals are meeting in the Sistine Chapel. How I wish I were there! What splendid mysteries are being enacted in that gloomy, magnificent room! Each prince of the Church now sits on a small throne surmounted by a violet-hued canopy. Fat wax tapers glimmer on the desk before each throne. Masters of ceremonies move solemnly through the vast chamber, carrying the silver basins in which the blank ballots repose. These basins are placed on the table before the altar. One by one the cardinals advance to the table, take ballots, return to their desks. Now, lifting their quill pens, they begin to write. "I, Cardinal——, elect to the Supreme Pontificate the Most Reverend Lord my Lord Cardinal——." What name do they fill in? Is it Carciofo? Is it Asciuga? Is it the name of some obscure and shriveled prelate from Madrid or Heidelberg, some last-minute choice of the anti-robot faction in its desperation? Or are they writing *his* name? The sound of scratching pens is loud in the chapel. The cardinals are completing their ballots, sealing them at the ends, folding them, folding them again and again, carrying them to the altar, dropping them into the great gold chalice. So have they done every morning and every afternoon for days, as the deadlock has prevailed.

"I read in the *Herald-Tribune* a couple of days ago," says Miss Harshaw, "that a delegation of two hundred and fifty young Catholic robots from Iowa is waiting at the Des Moines airport for news of the election. If their man gets in, they've got a chartered flight ready to leave, and they intend to request that they be granted the Holy Father's first public audience."

"There can be no doubt," Bishop FitzPatrick agrees, "that his election will bring a great many people of synthetic origin into the fold of the Church."

"While driving out plenty of flesh and blood people!" Miss Harshaw says shrilly.

"I doubt that," says the bishop. "Certainly there will be some feelings of shock, of dismay, of injury, of loss, for some of us at first. But these will pass. The inherent goodness of the new pope, to which Rabbi Mueller alluded, will prevail. Also I believe that technologically minded young folk everywhere will be encouraged to join the Church. Irresistible religious impulses will be awakened throughout the world."

"Can you imagine two hundred and fifty robots clanking into St. Peter's" Miss Harshaw demands.

I contemplate the distant Vatican. The morning sunlight is brilliant and dazzling, but the assembled cardinals, walled away from the world, cannot enjoy its gay sparkle. They all have voted, now. The three cardinals who were chosen by lot as this morning's scrutators of the vote have risen. One of them lifts the chalice and shakes it, mixing the ballots. Then he places it on the table before the altar; a second scrutator removes the ballots and counts them. He ascertains that the number of ballots is identical to the number of cardinals present. The ballots now have been transferred to a ciborium, which is a goblet ordinarily used to hold the consecrated bread of the Mass. The first scrutator withdraws a ballot, unfolds it, reads its inscription; passes it to the second scrutator, who reads it also; then it is given to the third scrutator, who reads the name aloud. Asciuga? Carciofo? Some other? *His*?

Rabbi Mueller is discussing angels. "Then we have the Angels of the Throne, known in Hebrew as *arelim* or *ophanim*. There are seventy of them, noted primarily for their steadfastness. Among them are the angels Orifiel, Ophaniel, Zabkiel, Jophiel, Ambriel, Tychagar, Barael, Quelamia, Paschar, Boel, and Raum. Some of these are no longer found in Heaven and are numbered among the fallen angels in Hell."

"So much for their steadfastness," says Kenneth.

"Then, too," the rabbi goes on, "there are the Angels of the Presence, who apparently were circumcised at the moment of their creation. These are Michael, Metatron, Suriel, Sandalphon, Uriel, Saraqael, Astanphaeus, Phanuel, Jehoel, Zagzagael, Yefefiah, and Akatriel. But I think my favorite of the whole group is the Angel of Lust, who is mentioned in Talmud *Bereshith Rabba* 85 as follows, that when Judah was about to pass by—"

They have finished counting the votes by this time, surely. An immense throng has assembled in the Square of St. Peter's. The sunlight gleams off hundreds if not thousands of steel-jacketed craniums. This must be a wonderful day for the robot population of Rome. But most of those in the piazza are creatures of flesh and blood: old women in black, gaunt young pickpockets, boys with puppies, plump vendors of sausages, and an assortment of poets, philosophers, generals, legislators, tourists, and fishermen. How has the tally gone? We will have our answer shortly. If no candidate has had a majority, they will mix the ballots with wet straw before casting them into the chapel stove, and black smoke will billow from the chimney. But if a pope has been elected, the straw will be dry, the smoke will be white.

The system has agreeable resonances. I like it. It gives me the satisfactions one normally derives from a flawless work of art: the *Tristan* chord, let us say, or the teeth of the frog in Bosch's *Temptation of St. Anthony*. I await the outcome with fierce concentration. I am certain of the result; I can already feel the irresistible religious impulses awakening in me. Although I feel, also, an odd nostalgia for the days of flesh and blood popes. Tomorrow's newspapers will have no interviews with the Holy

Father's aged mother in Sicily, nor with his proud younger brother in San Francisco. And will this grand ceremony of election ever be held again? Will we need another pope, when this one whom we will soon have can be repaired so easily?

Ah. The white smoke! The moment of revelation comes!

A figure emerges on the central balcony of the facade of St. Peter's, spreads a web of cloth-of-gold, and disappears. The blaze of light against that fabric stuns the eye. It reminds me perhaps of moonlight coldly kissing the sea at Castellamare, or, perhaps even more, of the noonday glare rebounding from the breast of the Caribbean off the coast of St. John. A second figure, clad in ermine and vermilion, has appeared on the balcony. "The cardinal-archdeacon," Bishop FitzPatrick whispers. People have started to faint. Luigi stands beside me, listening to the proceedings on a tiny radio, Kenneth says, "It's all been fixed." Rabbi Mueller hisses at him to be still. Miss Harshaw begins to sob. Beverly softly recites the Pledge of Allegiance, crossing herself throughout. This is a wonderful moment for me. I think it is the most truly contemporary moment I have ever experienced.

The amplified voice of the cardinal-archdeacon cries, "I announce to you great joy. We have a pope."

Cheering commences, and grows in intensity as the cardinal-archdeacon tells the world that the newly chosen pontiff is indeed *that* cardinal, that noble and distinguished person, that melancholy and austere individual, whose elevation to the Holy See we have all awaited so intensely for so long. "He has imposed upon himself," says the cardinal-archdeacon, "the name of—"

Lost in the cheering, I turn to Luigi. "Who? What name?"

"Sisto Settimo," Luigi tells me.

Yes, and there he is, Pope Sixtus the Seventh, as we now must call him. A tiny figure clad in the silver and gold papal robes, arms outstretched to the multitude, and, yes! the sunlight glints on his cheeks, his lofty forehead, there is the brightness of polished steel. Luigi is already on his knees. I kneel beside him. Miss Harshaw, Beverly, Kenneth, even the rabbi, all kneel, for beyond doubt this is a miraculous event. The pope comes forward on his balcony. Now he will deliver the traditional apostolic benediction to the city and to the world. "Our help is in the Name of the Lord," he declares gravely. He activates the levitator jets beneath his arms; even at this distance I can see the two small puffs of smoke. White smoke, again. He begins to rise into the air. "Who hath made heaven and earth," he says. "May Almighty God, Father, Son, and Holy Ghost, bless you." His voice rolls majestically toward us. His shadow extends across the whole piazza. Higher and higher he goes, until he is lost to sight. Kenneth taps Luigi. "Another round of drinks," he says, and presses a bill of high denomination into the innkeeper's fleshy palm. Bishop FitzPatrick weeps. Rabbi Mueller embraces Miss Harshaw. The new pontiff, I think, has begun his reign in an auspicious way.

IN THE GROUP

IT WAS A restless time for Murray. He spent the morning sand-trawling on the beach at Acapulco. When it began to seem like lunchtime he popped over to Nairobi for mutton curry at the Three Bells. It wasn't lunchtime in Nairobi, but these days any restaurant worth eating at stayed open around the clock. In late afternoon, subjectivewise, he paused for pastis and water in Marseilles, and toward psychological twilight he buzzed back home to California. His inner clock was set to Pacific Time, so reality corresponded to mood: night was falling, San Francisco glittered like a mound of jewels across the bay. He was going to do Group tonight. He got Kay on the screen and said, "Come down to my place tonight, yes?"

"What for?"

"What else? Group."

She lay in a dewy bower of young redwoods, three hundred miles up the coast from him. Torrents of unbound milk-white hair cascaded over her slender, bare honey-colored body. A multi-carat glitterstone sparkled fraudulently between her flawless little breasts. Looking at her, he felt his hands tightening into desperate fists, his nails ravaging his palms. He loved her beyond all measure. The intensity of his love overwhelmed and embarrassed him.

"You want to do Group together tonight?" she asked. "You and me?" She didn't sound pleased.

"Why not? Closeness is more fun than apartness."

"Nobody's ever apart in Group. What does mere you-and-me physical proximity matter? It's irrelevant. It's obsolete."

"I miss you."

"You're with me right now," she pointed out.

"I want to touch you. I want to inhale you. I want to taste you."

"Punch for tactile, then. Punch for olfactory. Punch for any input you think you want."

I've got all sensory channels open already," Murray said. "I'm flooded with delicious input. It still isn't the same thing. It isn't enough, Kay."

She rose and walked slowly toward the ocean. His eyes tracked her across the screen. He heard the pounding of the surf.

"I want you right beside me when Group starts tonight," he told her. "Look, if you don't feel like coming here, I'll go to your place."

"You're being boringly persistent."

He winced. "I can't help it. I like being close to you."

"You have a lot of old-fashioned attitudes, Murray." Her voice was so cool. "Are you aware of that?"

"I'm aware that my emotional drives are very strong. That's all. Is that such a sin?" Careful, Murray. A serious error in tactics just then. This whole conversation a huge mistake, most likely. He was running big risks with her by pushing too hard, letting too much of his crazy romanticism reveal itself so early. His obsession with her, his impossible new possessiveness, his weird ego-driven exclusivism. His love. *Yes;* his love. She was absolutely right, of course. He was basically old-fashioned. Wallowing in emotional atavism. You-and-me stuff. I, me, me, mine. This unwillingness to share her fully in Group. As though he had some special claim. He was pure nineteenth century underneath it all. He had only just discovered that, and it had come as a surprise to him. His sick archaic fantasies aside, there was no reason for the two of them to be side by side in the same room during Group, not unless they were the ones who were screwing, and the copulation schedule showed Nate and Serena on tonight's ticket. Drop it, Murray. But he couldn't drop it. He said into her stony silence, "All right, but at least let me set up an inner intersex connection for you and me. So I can feel what you're feeling when Nate and Serena get it on."

"Why this frantic need to reach inside my head?" she asked.

"I love you."

"Of course you do. We all love all of Us. But still, when you try to relate to me one-on-one like this, you injure Group."

"No inner connection, then?"

"No."

"Do you love me?"

A sigh. "I love Us, Murray."

That was likely to be the best he'd get from her this evening. All right. All right. He'd settle for that, if he had to. A crumb here, a crumb there. She smiled, blew him an amiable kiss, broke the contact. He stared moodily at the dead screen. All right. Time to get ready for Group. He turned to the life-size screen on the east wall and keyed in the visuals for preliminary alignment. Right now Group Central was sending its test pattern, stills of all of tonight's couples. Nate and Serena were in the center, haloed by the glowing nimbus that marked them as this evening's performers. Around the periphery Murray saw images of himself, Kay, Van, JoJo, Nikki, Dirk, Conrad, Finn, Lanelle, and Maria. Bruce, Klaus, Mindy, and Lois weren't there. Too busy, maybe. Or too tired. Or perhaps they were in the grip of negative unGrouplike vibes just at the moment. You didn't have to do Group every night, if you didn't feel into it. Murray averaged four nights a week. Only the real bulls, like Dirk and Nate, routinely hit seven out of seven. Also JoJo, Lanelle, Nikki—the Very Hot Ladies, he liked to call them.

He opened up the audio. "This is Murray," he announced. "I'm starting to synchronize."

Group Central gave him a sweet unwavering A for calibration. He tuned his receiver to match the note. "You're at four hundred and thirty-two," Group Central said. 'Bring your pitch up a little. There. There. Steady. Four hundred and forty, fine." The tones locked perfectly. He was synched in for sound. A little fine tuning on the visuals, next. The test pattern vanished and the screen showed only Nate, naked, a big cocky rockjawed man with a thick mat of curly black hair covering him from thighs to throat. He grinned, bowed, preened. Murray made adjustments until it was all but impossible to distinguish the three-dimensional holographic projection of Nate from the actual Nate, hundreds of miles away in his San Diego bedroom. Murray was fastidious about these adjustments. Any perceptible drop-off in reality approximation dampened the pleasure Group gave him. For some moments he watched Nate striding bouncily back and forth, working off excess energy, fining himself down to performance level; a minor element of distortion crept into the margins of the image, and, cutting in the manual override, Murray fed his own corrections to Central until all was well.

Next came the main brain-wave amplification, delivering data in the emotional sphere: endocrine feeds, neural set, epithelial appercept, erogenous uptake. Diligently Murray keyed in each one. At first he received only a vague undifferentiated blur of formless background cerebration, but then, like intricate figures becoming clear in an elaborate oriental carpet, the specific characteristics of Nate's mental output began to clarify themselves; edginess, eagerness, horniness, alertness, intensity. A sense of Nate's formidable masculine strength came through. At this stage of the evening Murray still had a distinct awareness of himself as an entity independent of Nate, but that would change soon enough.

"Ready," Murray reported. "Holding awaiting Group cut-in."

He had to hold for fifteen intolerable minutes. He was always the quickest to synchronize. Then he had to sit and sweat, hanging on desperately to his balances and lineups while he waited for the others. All around the circuit, the rest of them were still tinkering with their rigs, adjusting them with varying degrees of competence. He thought of Kay. At this moment making frantic adjustments, tuning herself to Serena as he had done to Nate.

"Group cut-in," Central said finally.

Murray closed the last circuits. Into his consciousness poured, in one wild rush, the mingled consciousnesses of Van, Dirk, Conrad, and Finn, hooked into him via Nate, and, less intensely because less directly, the consciousnesses of Kay, Maria, Lanelle, JoJo, and Nikki, funneled to him by way of their link to Serena. So all twelve of them were in sync. They had attained Group once again. Now the revels could begin.

Now. Nate approaching Serena. The magic moments of fore-play. That buzz of early excitement, that soaring erotic flight, taking everybody upward like a Beethoven adagio, like a solid hit of acid. Nate. Serena. San Diego. Their bedroom a glittering hall of mirrors. Refracted images everywhere. A thousand quivering breasts. Five hundred jutting cocks. Hands, eyes, tongues, thighs.

The circular undulating bed, quivering, heaving. Murray, lying cocooned in his maze of sophisticated amplification equipment, receiving inputs at temples and throat and chest and loins, felt his palate growing dry, felt a pounding in his groin. He licked his lips. His hips began, of their own accord, a slow rhythmic thrusting motion. Nate's hands casually traversed the taut globes of Serena's bosom. Caught the rigid nipples between hairy fingers, tweaked them, thumbed them. Murray felt the firm nodules of engorged flesh with his own empty hands. The merger of identities was starting. He was becoming Nate, Nate was flowing into him, and he was all the others too, Van, JoJo, Dirk, Finn, Nikki, all of them, feedbacks oscillating in interpersonal whirlpools all along the line. Kay. He was part of Kay, she of him, both of them parts of Nate and Serena. Inextricably intertwined. What Nate experienced, Murray experienced. What Serena experienced, Kay experienced. When Nate's mouth descended to cover Serena's, Murray's tongue slid forward. And felt the moist tip of Serena's. Flesh against flesh, skin against skin. Serena was throbbing. Why not? Six men tonguing her at once. She was always quick to arouse, anyway. She was begging for it. Not that Nate was in any hurry: screwing was his thing, he always made a grand production out of it. As well he might, with ten close friends riding as passengers on his trip. Give us a show, Nate. Nate obliged. He was going down on her, now. Inhaling. His stubbly cheeks against her satiny thighs. Oh, the busy tongue! Oh, the sighs and gasps! And then she engulfing him reciprocally. Murray hissed in delight. Her cunning little suctions, her jolly slithers and slides: a skilled fellatrice, that woman was. He trembled. He was fully into it, now, sharing every impulse with Nate. *Becoming* Nate. Yes. Serena's beckoning body gaping for him. His waggling wand poised above her. The old magic of Group never diminishing. Nate doing all his tricks, pulling out the stops. When? Now. *Now.* The thrust. The quick sliding moment of entry. Ah! Ah! *Ah!* Serena simultaneously possessed by Nate, Murray, Van, Dirk, Conrad, Finn. Finn, Conrad, Dirk, Van, Murray, and Nate simultaneously possessing Serena. And, vicariously throbbing in rhythm with Serena: Kay, Maria, Lanelle, JoJo, Nikki. Kay. Kay. Kay. Through the sorcery of the crossover loop Nate was having Kay while he had Serena, Nate was having Kay, Maria, Lanelle, JoJo, Nikki all at once, they were being had by him, a soup of identities, an *olla podrida* of copulations, and as the twelve of them soared toward a shared and multiplied ecstasy Murray did something dumb. He thought of Kay.

He thought of Kay. Kay alone in her redwood bower, Kay with bucking hips and tossing hair and glistening droplets of sweat between her breasts, Kay hissing and shivering in Nate's simulated embrace. Murray tried to reach across to her through the Group loop, tried to find and isolate the discrete thread of self that was Kay, tried to chisel away the ten extraneous identities and transform this coupling into an encounter between himself and her. It was a plain violation of the spirit of Group; it was also impossible to achieve, since she had refused him permission to establish a special inner link between them that evening, and so at the moment she was accessible to him only as one facet of the enhanced and expanded Serena. At best he could grope toward Kay through Serena and touch the tip of her soul, but the contact was cloudy and uncertain. Instantly on to what he was trying to do, she petulantly pushed him away, at the same time submerging herself more fully in Serena's consciousness. Rejected, reeling, he slid off into confusion, sending jarring crosscurrents through the whole Group. Nate loosed a shower of irritation, despite his heroic attempt to remain unperturbed, and pumped his way to climax well ahead of schedule, hauling everyone breathlessly along with him. As the orgasmic frenzy broke loose Murray tried to re-enter the full linkage, but he found himself unhinged, disaffiliated, and mechanically emptied himself without any tremor of pleasure. Then it was over. He lay back, perspiring, feeling soiled, jangled, unsatisfied. After a few moments he uncoupled his equipment and went out for a cold shower.

Kay called half an hour later.

"You crazy bastard," she said. "What were you trying to do?"

He promised not to do it again. She forgave him. He brooded for two days, keeping out of Group. He missed sharing Conrad and JoJo, Klaus and Lois. The third day the Group chart marked him and Kay as that night's performers. He didn't want to let them all share her. It was stronger than ever, this nasty atavistic possessiveness. He didn't have to, of course. Nobody was forced to do Group. He could beg off and continue to sulk, and Dirk or Van or somebody would substitute for him tonight. But Kay wouldn't necessarily pass up her turn. She almost certainly wouldn't. He didn't like the options. If he made it with Kay as per group schedule, he'd be offering her to all the others. If he stepped aside, she'd do it with someone else. Might as well be the one to take her to bed in that case. Faced with an ugly choice, he decided to stick to the original schedule.

He popped up to her place eight hours early. He found her sprawled on a carpet of redwood needles in a sun-dappled grove, playing with a stack of music cubes. Mozart tinkled in the fragrant air. "Let's go away somewhere tomorrow," he said. "You and me."

"You're still into you-and-me?"

"I'm sorry."

"Where do you want to go?"

He shrugged. "Hawaii. Afghanistan. Poland. Zambia. It doesn't matter. Just to be with you."

"What about Group?"

"They can spare us for a while."

She rolled over, lazily snaffled Mozart into silence, started a cube of Bach. "I'll go," she said. The Goldberg Variations transcribed for glockenspiel. "But only if we take our Group equipment along."

"It means that much to you?"

"Doesn't it to you?"

"I cherish Group," he said. "But it's not all there is to life. I can live without it for a while. I don't need it, Kay. What I need is you."

"That's obscene, Murray."

"No. It isn't obscene."

"It's boring, at any rate."

"I'm sorry you think so," he told her.

"Do you want to drop out of Group?"

I want us both to drop out of Group, he thought, and I want you to live with me. I can't bear to share you any longer, Kay. But he wasn't prepared to move to that level of confrontation. He said, "I want to stay in Group if it's possible, but I'm also interested in extending and developing some one-on-one with you."

"You've already made that excessively clear."

"I love you."

"You've said that before too."

"What do you want, Kay?"

She laughed, rolled over, drew her knees up until they touched her breasts, parted her thighs, opened herself to a stray shaft of sunlight. "I want to enjoy myself," she said.

He started setting up his equipment an hour before sunset. Because he was performing, the calibrations were more delicate than on an ordinary night. Not only did he have to broadcast a full range of control ratios to Central to aid the others in their tuning, he had to achieve a flawless balance of input and output with Kay. He went about his complex tasks morosely, not at all excited by the thought that he and Kay would shortly be making love. It cooled his ardor to know that Nate, Dirk, Van, Finn, Bruce, and Klaus would be having her too. Why did he begrudge it to them so? He didn't know. Such exclusivism, coming out of nowhere, shocked and disgusted him. Yet it wholly controlled him. Maybe I need help, he thought.

Group time, now. Soft sweet ionized fumes drifting through the chamber of Eros. Kay was warm, receptive, passionate. Her eyes sparkled as she reached for him. They had made love five hundred times and she showed no sign of diminished interest. He knew he turned her on. He hoped he turned her on more than anyone else. He caressed her in all his clever ways, and she purred and wriggled and glowed. Her nipples stood tall: no faking that. Yet something was wrong. Not with her, with him. He was aloof, remote. He seemed to be watching the proceedings from a point somewhere outside himself, as though he were just a Group onlooker tonight, badly tuned in, not even as much a part of things as Klaus, Bruce, Finn, Van, Dirk. The awareness that he had an audience affected him for the first time. His technique, which depended more on finesse and grace than on fire and force, became a trap, locking him into a series of passionless arabesques and pirouettes. He was distracted, though he never had been before, by the minute telemetry tapes glued to the side of Kay's neck and the underside of her thigh. He found himself addressing silent messages to the other men. Here, Nate, how do you like that? Grab some haunch,ʼ Dirk. Up the old zaboo, Bruce. Uh. Uh. Ah. Oh.

Kay didn't seem to notice anything was amiss. She came three times in the first fifteen minutes. He doubted that he'd ever come at all. He plugged on, in and out, in and out, moving like a mindless piston. A sort of revenge on Group, he realized. You want to share Kay with me, okay, fellows, but this is all you're going to get. This. Oh. Oh. Oh. Now at last he felt the familiar climactic tickle, stepped down to a tenth of its normal intensity. He hardly noticed it when he came.

Kay said afterward, "What about that trip? Are we still going to go away somewhere tomorrow?"

"Let's forget it for the time being," he said.

He popped to Istanbul alone and spent a day in the covered bazaar, buying cheap but intricate trinkets for every woman in Group. At nightfall he popped down to McMurdo Sound, where the merry Antarctic summer was at its height, and spent six hours on the polar ski slopes, coming away with wind-bronzed skin and aching muscles. In the lodge later he met an angular, auburn-haired woman from Portugal and took her to bed. She was very good, in a heartless, mechanically proficient way. Doubtless she thought the same of him. She asked him whether he might be interested in joining her Group, which operated out of Lisbon and Ibiza. "I already have an affiliation," he said. He popped to Addis Ababa after breakfast, checked into the Hilton, slept for a day and a half, and went on to St. Croix for a night of reef-bobbing. When he popped back to California the next day he called Kay at once to learn the news.

"We've been discussing rearranging some of the Group couplings," she said. "Next week, what about you and Lanelle, me and Dirk?"

"Does that mean you're dropping me?"

"No, not at all, silly. But I do think we need variety."

"Group was designed to provide us with all the variety we'd ever want."

"You know what I mean. Besides, you're developing an unhealthy fixation on me as isolated love object."

"Why are you rejecting me?"

"I'm not. I'm trying to help you, Murray."

"I love you," he said.

"Love me in a healthier way, then."

That night it was the turn of Maria and Van. The next, Nikki and Finn. After them, Bruce and Mindy. He tuned in for all three, trying to erode his grief in nightly frenzies of lustful fulfillment. By the third night he was very tired and no less grief-smitten. He took the next night off. Then the schedule came up with the first Murray-Lanelle pairing.

He popped to Hawaii and set up his rig in her sprawling beachfront lanai on Molokai. He had bedded her before, of course. Everyone in Group had bedded everyone else during the preliminary months of compatibility testing. But then they all had settled into more or less regular pair-bonding, and he hadn't approached her since. In the past year the only Group woman he had slept with was Kay. By choice.

"I've always liked you," Lanelle said. She was tall, heavy-breasted, wide-shouldered, with warm brown eyes, yellow hair, skin the color of fine honey. "You're just a little crazy, but I don't mind that. And I love screwing Scorpios."

"I'm a Capricorn."

"Them too," she said. "I love screwing just about every sign. Except Virgos. I can't stand Virgos. Remember, we were supposed to have a Virgo in Group, at the start. I blackballed him."

They swam and surfed for a couple of hours before doing the calibrating. The water was warm but a brisk breeze blew from the east, coming like a gust of bad news out of California. Lanelle nuzzled him playfully and then not so playfully in the water. She had always been an aggressive woman, a swaggerer, a strutter. Her appetites were enormous. Her eyes glistened with desire. "Come on," she said finally, tugging at him. They ran to the house and he began to adjust the equipment. It was still early. He thought of Kay and his soul drooped. What am I doing here? he wondered. He lined up the Group apparatus with nervous hands, making many errors. Lanelle stood behind him, rubbing her breasts against his bare back. He had to ask her to stop. Eventually everything was ready and she hauled him to the spongy floor with her, covering his body with hers. Lanelle always liked to be the one on top. Her tongue probed his mouth and her hands clutched his hips and she pressed herself against him, but although her body was warm and smooth and alive he felt no onset of excitement, not a shred. She put her mouth to him but it was hopeless. He remained limp, dead, unable to function. With everyone tuned in and waiting. "What is it?" she whispered. "What should I do, love?" He closed his eyes and indulged in a fantasy of Kay coupling with Dirk, pure masochism and it aroused him as far as a sort of half-erect condition, and he slithered into her like a prurient eel. She rocked her way to

ecstasy above him. This is garbage, he thought. I'm falling apart.
Kay. Kay. Kay.

Then Kay had her night with Dirk. At first Murray thought he
would simply skip it. There was no reason, after all, why he had
to subject himself to something like that, if he expected it to give
him pain. It had never been painful for him in the past when Kay
did it with other men, inside Group or not, but since the onset of
his jealousies everything was different. In theory the Group
couples were interchangeable, one pair serving as proxies for all
the rest each night, but theory and practice coincided less and
less in Murray's mind these days. Nobody would be surprised or
upset if he happened not to want to participate tonight. All during
the day, though, he found himself obsessively fantasizing Kay
and Dirk, every motion, every sound, the two of them facing
each other, smiling, embracing, sinking down onto her bed,
entwining, his hands sliding over her slender body, his mouth on
her mouth, his chest crushing her small breasts, Dirk entering
her, riding her, plunging, driving, coming, Kay coming, then
Kay and Dirk arising, going for a cooling swim, returning to the
bedroom, facing each other, smiling, beginning again. By late
afternoon it had taken place so many times in his fevered
imagination that he saw no risk in experiencing the reality of it;
at least he could have Kay, if only at one remove, by doing
Group tonight. And it might help him to shake off his obsessiveness.
But it was worse than he imagined it could be. The sight of Dirk,
all bulging muscles and tapering hips, terrified him; Dirk was
ready for making love long before the foreplay started, and
Murray somehow came to fear that he, not Kay, was going to be
the target of that long rigid spear of his. Then Dirk began to
caress Kay. With each insinuating touch of his hand it seemed
that some vital segment of Murray's relationship with Kay was
being obliterated. He was forced to watch Kay through Dirk's
eyes, her flushed face, her quivering nostrils, her moist, slack
lips, and it killed him. As Dirk drove deep into her, Murray
coiled into a miserable fetal ball, one hand clutching his loins,
the other clapped across his lips, thumb in his mouth. He
couldn't stand it at all. To think that every one of them was
having Kay at once. Not only Dirk. Nate, Van, Conrad, Finn,
Bruce, Klaus, the whole male Group complement, all of them
tuning in tonight for this novel Dirk-Kay pairing. Kay giving

herself to all of them gladly, willingly, enthusiastically. He had to escape, now, instantly, even though to drop out of Group communion at this point would unbalance everyone's tuning and set up chaotic eddy currents that might induce nausea or worse in the others. He didn't care. He had to save himself. He screamed and uncoupled his rig.

He waited two days and went to see her. She was at her exercises, floating like a cloud through a dazzling arrangement of metal rings and loops that dangled at constantly varying heights from the ceiling of her solarium. He stood below her, craning his neck. "It isn't any good," he said. "I want us both to withdraw from Group, Kay."

"That was predictable."

"It's killing me. I love you so much I can't bear to share you."

"So loving me means owning me?"

"Let's just drop out for a while. Let's explore the ramifications of one-on-one. A month, two months, six months, Kay. Just until I get this craziness out of my system. Then we can go back in."

"So you admit it's craziness."

"I never denied it." His neck was getting stiff. "Won't you please come down from those rings while we're talking?"

"I can hear you perfectly well from here, Murray."

"Will you drop out of Group and go away with me for a while?"

"No."

"Will you even consider it?"

"No."

"Do you realize that you're addicted to Group?" he asked.

"I don't think that's an accurate evaluation of the situation. But do *you* realize that you're dangerously fixated on me?"

"I realize it."

"What do you propose to do about it?"

"What I'm doing now," he said. "Coming to you, asking you to do a one-on-one with me."

"Stop it."

"One-on-one was good enough for the human race for thousands of years."

"It was a prison," she said. "It was a trap. We're out of the trap at last. You won't get me back in."

He wanted to pull her down from her rings and shake her. "I *love* you, Kay!"

"You take a funny way of showing it. Trying to limit the range of my experience. Trying to hide me away in a vault somewhere. It won't work."

"Definitely no?"

"Definitely no."

She accelerated her pace, flinging herself recklessly from loop to loop. Her glistening nude form tantalized and infuriated him. He shrugged and turned away, shoulders slumping, head drooping. This was precisely how he had expected her to respond. No surprises. Very well. Very well. He crossed from the solarium into the bedroom and lifted her Group rig from its container. Slowly, methodically, he ripped it apart, bending the frame until it split, cracking the fragile leads, uprooting handfuls of connectors, crumpling the control panel. The instrument was already a ruin by the time Kay came in. "What are you *doing?*" she cried. He splintered the lovely gleaming calibration dials under his heel and kicked the wreckage of the rig toward her. It would take months before a replacement rig could be properly attuned and synchronized. "I had no choice," he told her sadly.

They would have to punish him. That was inevitable. But how? He waited at home, and before long they came to him, all of them, Nate, Van, Dirk, Conrad, Finn, Bruce, Klaus, Kay, Serena, Maria, JoJo, Lanelle, Nikki, Mindy, Lois, popping in from many quarters of the world, some of them dressed in evening clothes, some of them naked or nearly so, some of them unkempt and sleepy, all of them angry in a cold, tight way. He tried to stare them down. Dirk said, "You must be terribly sick, Murray. We feel sorry for you."

"We really want to help you," said Lanelle.

"We're here to give you therapy," Finn told him.

Murray laughed. "Therapy. I bet. What kind of therapy?"

"To rid you of your exclusivism," Dirk said. "To burn all the trash out of your mind."

"Shock treatment," Finn said.

"Keep away from me!"

"Hold him," Dirk said.

Quickly they surrounded him. Bruce clamped an arm across his chest like an iron bar. Conrad seized his hands and brought his wrists together behind his back. Finn and Dirk pressed up against his sides. He was helpless.

Kay began to remove her clothing. Naked, she lay down on Murray's bed, flexed her knees, opened her thighs. Klaus got on top of her.

"What the hell is this?" Murray asked.

Efficiently but without passion Kay aroused Klaus, and efficiently but without passion he penetrated her. Murray writhed impotently as their bodies moved together. Klaus made no attempt at bringing Kay off. He reached his climax in four or five minutes, grunting once, and rolled away from her, red-faced, sweating. Van took his place between Kay's legs.

"No," Murray said. "Please, no."

Inexorably Van had his turn, quick, impersonal. Nate was next. Murray tried not to watch, but his eyes would not remain closed. A strange smile glittered on Kay's lips as she gave herself to Nate. Nate arose. Finn approached the bed.

"No!" Murray cried, and lashed out in a backward kick that sent Conrad screaming across the room. Murray's hands were free. He twisted and wrenched himself away from Bruce. Dirk and Nate intercepted him as he rushed toward Kay. They seized him and flung him to the floor.

"The therapy isn't working," Nate said.

"Let's skip the rest," said Dirk. "It's no use trying to heal him. He's beyond hope. Let him stand up."

Murray got cautiously to his feet. Dirk said, "By unanimous vote, Murray, we expel your from Group for unGrouplike attitudes and especially for your unGrouplike destruction of Kay's rig. All your Group privileges are canceled." At a signal from Dirk, Nate removed Murray's rig from its container and reduced it to unsalvageable rubble. Dirk said, "Speaking as your friend, Murray, I suggest you think seriously about undergoing a total personality reconstruct. You're in trouble, do you know that? You need a lot of help. You're a mess."

"Is there anything else you want to tell me?" Murray asked.

"Nothing else. Goodbye, Murray."

They started to go out. Dirk, Finn, Nate, Bruce, Conrad, Klaus. Van. JoJo. Nikki. Serena, Maria, Lanelle, Mindy. Lois. Kay was the last to leave. She stood by the door, clutching her clothes in a small crumpled bundle. She seemed entirely unafraid of him. There was a peculiar look of—was it tenderness? pity? —on her face. Softly she said, "I'm sorry it had to come to this, Murray. I feel so unhappy for you. I know that what you did wasn't a hostile act. You did it out of love. You were all wrong, but you were doing it out of love." She walked toward him and kissed him lightly, on the cheek, on the tip of the nose, on the lips. He didn't move. She smiled. She touched his arm. "I'm so sorry," she murmured. "Goodbye, Murray." As she went through the door she looked back and said, "Such a damned shame. I could have loved you, you know? I could really have loved you."

He had told himself that he would wait until they all were gone before he let the tears flow. But when the door had closed behind Kay he discovered his eyes remained dry. He had no tears. He was altogether calm. Numb. Burned out.

After a long while he put on fresh clothing and went out. He popped to London, found that it was raining there, and popped to Prague, where there was something stifling about the atmosphere, and went on to Seoul, where he had barbecued beef and kimchi for dinner. Then he popped to New York. In front of a gallery on Lexington Avenue he picked up a complaisant young girl with long black hair. "Let's go to a hotel," he suggested, and she smiled and nodded. He registered for a six-hour stay. Upstairs, she undressed without waiting for him to ask. Her body was smooth and supple, flat belly, pale skin, high full breasts. They lay down together and, in silence, without preliminaries, he took her. She was eager and responsive. Kay, he thought. Kay. Kay. You are Kay. A spasm of culmination shook him with unexpected force.

"Do you mind if I smoke?" she said a few minutes later.

"I love you," he said.

"What?"

"I love you."

"You're sweet."

"Come live with me. Please. Please. I'm serious."

"What?"

"Live with me. Marry me."

"*What?*"

"There's only one thing I ask. No Group stuff. That's all.

Otherwise you can do as you please. I'm wealthy. I'll make you happy. I love you."

"You don't even know my name."

"I love you."

"Mister, you must be out of your head."

"Please. Please."

"A lunatic. Unless you're trying to make fun of me."

"I'm perfectly serious, I assure you. Live with me. Be my wife."

"A lunatic," she said. "I'm getting out of here!" She leaped up and looked for her clothes. "Jesus, a madman!"

"No," he said, but she was on her way, not even pausing to get dressed, running helter-skelter from the room, her pink buttocks flashing like beacons as she made her escape. The door slammed. He shook his head. He sat rigid for half an hour, an hour, some long timeless span, thinking of Kay, thinking of Group, wondering what they'd be doing tonight, whose turn it was. At length he rose and put on his clothes and left the hotel. A terrible restlessness assailed him. He popped to Karachi and stayed ten minutes. He popped to Vienna. To Hangchow. He didn't stay. Looking for what? He didn't know. Looking for Kay? Kay didn't exist. Looking. Just looking. Pop. Pop. Pop.

THE FEAST OF ST. DIONYSUS

Sleepers, awake. Sleep is separateness; the cave of solitude is the cave of dreams, the cave of the passive spectator. To be awake is to participate, carnally and not in fantasy, in the feast; the great communion.

—NORMAN O. BROWN: *Love's Body*

THIS IS THE dawn of the day of the Feast. Oxenshuer knows roughly what to expect, for he has spied on the children at their catechisms; he has had hints from some of the adults; he has spoken at length with the high priest of this strange apocalyptic city; and yet, for all his patiently gathered knowledge, he really knows nothing at all of today's event. What will happen? They will come for him, Matt who has been appointed his brother, and Will and Nick, who are his sponsors. They will lead him through the labyrinth to the place of the saint, to the god-house at the city's core. They will give him wine until he is glutted, until his cheeks and chin drip with it and his robe is stained with red. And he and Matt will struggle, will have a contest of some sort, a wrestling match, an agon: whether real or symbolic, he does not yet know. Before the whole community they will contend. What else, what else? There will be hymns to the saint, to the god—god and saint, both are one, Dionysus and Jesus, each an aspect of the other. Each a manifestation of the divinity we carry within us, so the Speaker has said. Jesus and Dionysus, Dionysus and Jesus, god and saint, saint and god, what do the terms matter? He had heard the people singing:

This is the god who burns like fire
This is the god whose name is music
This is the god whose soul is wine

Fire. Music. Wine. The healing fire, the joining fire, in which all things will be made one. By its leaping blaze he will drink and drink and drink, dance and dance and dance. Maybe there will be some sort of sexual event, an orgy, perhaps, for sex and religion are closely bound among these people: a communion of the flesh opening the way toward communality of spirit.

I go to the god's house and his fire consumes me
I cry the god's name and his thunder deafens me
I take the god's cup and his wine dissolves me

And then? And then? How can he possibly know what will happen, until it has happened? "You will enter into the ocean of Christ," they have told him. An ocean? Here in the Mojave Desert? Well, a figurative ocean, a metaphorical ocean. All is metaphor here. "Dionysus will carry you to Jesus," they say. Go, child, swim out to God. Jesus waits. The saint, the mad saint, the boozy old god who is their saint, the mad saintly god who abolishes walls and makes all things one, will lead you to bliss, dear John, dear tired John. Give your soul gladly to Dionysus the Saint. Make yourself whole in his blessed fire. You've been divided too long. How can you lie dead on Mars and still walk alive on Earth?

Heal yourself, John. This is the day.

From Los Angeles the old San Bernardino Freeway rolls eastward through the plastic suburbs, through Alhambra and Azusa, past the Covina Hills branch of Forest Lawn Memorial-Parks, past the mushroom sprawl of San Bernardino, which is becoming a little Los Angeles, but not so little. The highway pushes onward into the desert like a flat, gray cincture holding the dry, brown hills asunder. This was the road by which John Oxenshuer finally chose to make his escape. He had had no particular destination in mind but was seeking only a parched place, a sandy place, a place where he could be alone: he needed to re-create, in what might well be his last weeks of life, certain aspects of barren Mars. After considering a number of possibilities he fastened upon this route, attracted to it by the way the freeway seemed to lose itself in the desert north of the Salton Sea. Even in this overcivilized epoch a man could easily disappear there.

Late one November afternoon, two weeks past his fortieth birthday, he closed his rented apartment on Hollywood Boulevard; taking leave of no one, he drove unhurriedly toward the freeway entrance. There he surrendered control to the electronic highway net, which seized his car and pulled it into the traffic flow. The net governed him as far as Covina; when he saw Forest Lawn's statuary-speckled hilltop coming up on his right, he readied himself to resume driving. A mile beyond the vast cemetery a blinking sign told him he was on his own, and he took the wheel. The car continued to slice inland at the same velocity, as mechanical as iron, of 140 kilometers per hour. With each moment the recent past dropped from him, bit by bit.

Can you drown in the desert? Let's give it a try, God. I'll make a bargain with you. You let me drown out there. All right? And I'll give myself to you. Let me sink into the sand; let me bathe in it; let it wash Mars out of my soul; let it drown me, God; let it drown me. Free me from Mars and I'm yours, God. Is it a deal? Drown me in the desert and I'll surrender at last. I'll surrender.

At twilight he was in Banning. Some gesture of farewell to civilization seemed suddenly appropriate, and he risked stopping to have dinner at a small Mexican restaurant. It was crowded with families enjoying a night out, which made Oxenshuer fear he would be recognized. Look, someone would cry, there's the Mars astronaut, there's the one who came back! But of course no one spotted him. He had grown a bushy, sandy mustache that nearly obliterated his thin, tense lips. His body, lean and wide-shouldered, no longer had an astronaut's springy erectness; in the nineteen months since his return from the red planet he had begun to stoop a little, to cultivate a roundedness of the upper back, as if some leaden weight beneath his breastbone were tugging him forward and downward. Besides, spacemen are quickly forgotten. How long had anyone remembered the names of the heroic lunar teams of his youth? Borman, Lovell, and

Anders. Armstrong, Aldrin, and Collins. Scott, Irwin, and Worden. Each of them had had a few gaudy weeks of fame, and then they had disappeared into the blurred pages of the almanac, all, perhaps, except Armstrong: children learned about him at school. His one small step: he would become a figure of myth, up there with Columbus and Magellan. But the others? Forgotten. Yes. Yesterday's heroes. Oxenshuer, Richardson, and Vogel. Who? Oxenshuer, Richardson, and Vogel. That's Oxenshuer right over there, eating tamales and enchiladas, drinking a bottle of Double-X. He's the one who came back. Had some sort of breakdown and left his wife. Yes. That's a funny name, Oxenshuer. Yes. He's the one who came back. What about the other two? They died. Where did they die, daddy? They died on Mars, but Oxenshuer came back. What were their names again? Richardson and Vogel. They died. Oh. On Mars. Oh. And Oxenshuer didn't. What were their names again?

Unrecognized, safely forgotten, Oxenshuer finished his meal and returned to the freeway. Night had come by this time. The moon was nearly full; the mountains, clearly outlined against the darkness, glistened with a coppery sheen. There is no moonlight on Mars except the feeble, hasty glow of Phobos, dancing in and out of eclipse on its nervous journey from west to east. He had found Phobos disturbing; nor had he cared for fluttery Deimos, starlike, a tiny rocketing point of light. Oxenshuer drove onward, leaving the zone of urban sprawl behind, entering the true desert, pockmarked here and there by resort towns: Palm Springs, Twentynine Palms, Desert Hot Springs. Beckoning billboards summoned him to the torpid pleasures of whirlpool baths and saunas. These temptations he ignored without difficulty. Dryness was what he sought.

Once he was east of Indio he began looking for a place to abandon the car; but he was still too close to the southern boundaries of Joshua Tree National Monument, and he did not want to make camp this near to any area that might be patrolled by park rangers. So he kept driving until the moon was high and he was deep into the Chuckwalla country, with nothing much except sand dunes and mountains and dry lake beds between him and the Arizona border. In a stretch where the land seemed relatively flat he slowed the car almost to an idle, killed his lights, and swerved gently off the road, following a vague northeasterly course; he gripped the wheel tightly as he jounced over the rough, crunchy terrain. Half a kilometer from the highway Oxenshuer came to a shallow sloping basin, the dry bed of some ancient lake. He eased down into it until he could no longer see the long yellow tracks of headlights on the road, and knew he must be below the line of sight of any passing vehicle. Turning the engine off, he locked the car—a strange prissiness here, in the midst of nowhere!—took his backpack from the trunk, slipped his arms through the shoulder straps, and, without looking back, began to walk into the emptiness that lay to the north.

As he walks he composes a letter that he will never send.

Dear Claire, I wish I had been able to say goodbye to you before I left Los Angeles. I regretted only that: leaving town without telling you. But I was afraid to call. I draw back from you. You say you hold no grudge against me over Dave's death; you say it couldn't possibly have been my fault, and of course you're right. And yet I don't dare face you, Claire. Why is that? Because I left your husband's body on Mars and the guilt of that is choking me? But a body is only a shell, Claire. Dave's body isn't Dave, and there wasn't anything I could do for Dave. What is it, then, that comes between us? Is it my love, Claire, my guilty love for my friend's widow? Eh? That love is salt in my wounds, that love is sand in my throat, Claire. Claire. Claire. I can never tell you any of this, Claire. I never will. Goodbye. Pray for me. Will you pray?

His years of grueling NASA training for Mars served him well now. Powered by ancient disciplines, he moved swiftly, feeling no strain even with forty-five pounds on his back. He had no trouble with the uneven footing. The sharp chill in the air did not bother him, though he wore only light clothing, slacks and shirt and a flimsy cotton vest. The solitude, far from oppressing him, was actually a source of energy: a couple of hundred kilometers away in Los Angeles it might be the ninth decade of the twentieth century, but this was a prehistoric realm, timeless, unscarred by man, and his spirit expanded in his self-imposed isolation. Conceivably every footprint he made was the first human touch this land had felt. That gray, pervasive sense of guilt, heavy on him since his return from Mars, held less weight here beyond civilization's edge.

This wasteland was the closest he could come to attaining Mars on Earth. Not really close enough, for too many things broke the illusion: the great gleaming scarred moon, and the succulent terrestrial vegetation, and the tug of Earth's gravity, and the faint white glow on the leftward horizon that he imagined emanated from the cities of the coastal strip. But it was as close to Mars in flavor as he could manage. The Peruvian desert would have been better, only he had no way of getting to Peru.

An approximation. It would suffice.

A trek of at least a dozen kilometers left him still unfatigued, but he decided, shortly after midnight, to settle down for the night. The site he chose was a small level quadrangle bounded on the north and south by spiky, ominous cacti—chollas and prickly pears—and on the east by a maze of scrubby mesquite; to the west, a broad alluvial fan of tumbled pebbles descended from the nearby hills. Moonlight, raking the area sharply, highlighted every contrast of contour: the shadows of cacti were unfathomable inky pits and the tracks of small animals—lizards and kangaroo rats—were steep-walled canyons in the sand. As he slung his pack to the ground two startled rats, browsing in the mesquite, noticed him belatedly and leaped for cover in wild, desperate bounds, frantic but delicate. Oxenshuer smiled at them.

On the twentieth day of the mission Richardson and Vogel went out, as planned, for the longest extravehicular on the schedule, the ninety-kilometer crawler-jaunt to the Gulliver site. Goddamned well about time, Dave Vogel had muttered, when the EVA okay had at last come floating up, time-lagged and crackly, out of far-off Mission Control. All during the eight-month journey from Earth, while the brick-red face of Mars was swelling patiently in their portholes, they had argued about the timing of the big Marswalk, an argument that had begun six months before launch date. Vogel, insisting that the expedition was the mission's most important scientific project, had wanted to do it first, to get it done and out of the way before mishaps might befall them and force them to scrub it. No matter that the timetable decreed it for Day 20. The timetable was too conservative. We can overrule Mission Control, Vogel said. If they don't like it, let them reprimand us when we get home. But Richardson, though, wouldn't go along. Houston knows best, he kept saying. He always took the side of authority. First we have to get used to working on Mars, Dave. First we ought to do the routine stuff close by the landing site, while we're getting acclimated. What's our hurry? We've got to stay here a month until the return window opens, anyway. Why breach the schedule? The scientists know what they're doing, and they want us to do everything in its proper order, Richardson said. Vogel, stubborn, eager, seething, thought he would find an ally in Oxenshuer. You vote with me, John. Don't tell me *you* give a crap about Mission Control! Two against one and Bud will have to give in. But Oxenshuer, oddly, took Richardson's side. He hesitated to deviate from the schedule. He wouldn't be making the long extravehicular himself in any case; he had drawn the short straw; he was the man who'd be keeping close to the ship all the time. How then could he vote to alter the carefully designed schedule and send Richardson off, against his will, on a risky and perhaps ill-timed adventure? No, Oxenshuer said. Sorry, Dave, it isn't my place to decide such things. Vogel appealed anyway to Mission Control, and Mission Control said wait till Day 20, fellows. On Day 20 Richardson and Vogel suited up and went out. It was the ninth EVA of the mission, but the first that would take anyone more than a couple of kilometers from the ship.

Oxenshuer monitored his departing companions from his safe niche in the control cabin. The small video screen showed him the path of their crawler as it diminished into the somber red plain. You're well named, rusty old Mars. The blood of fallen soldiers stains your soil. Your hills are the color of the flames that lick conquered cities. Jouncing westward across Solis Lacus, Vogel kept up a running commentary. Lots of dead nothing out here, Johnny. It's as bad as the Moon. A prettier color, though. Are you reading me? I'm reading you, Oxenshuer said. The crawler was like a submarine mounted on giant preposterous wheels. Joggle, joggle, joggle, skirting craters and ravines, ridges and scarps. Pausing now and then so Richardson could pop a geological specimen or two into the gunnysack. Then onward, westward, westward. Heading bumpily toward the site where the unmanned Ares IV Mars Lander, almost a decade earlier, had scraped some Martian microorganisms out of the ground with the Gulliver sampling device.

"Gulliver" is a culture chamber that inoculates itself with a sample of soil. The sample is obtained by two 7½-meter lengths of kite line wound on small projectiles. When the projectiles are fired, the lines unwind and fall to the ground. A small motor inside the chamber then reels them in, together with adhering soil particles. The chamber contains a growth medium whose organic nutrients are labeled with radioactive carbon. When the medium is inoculated with soil, the accompanying microorganisms metabolize the organic compounds and release radioactive carbon dioxide. This diffuses to the window of a Geiger counter, where the radioactivity is measured. Growth of the microbes causes the rate of carbon dioxide production to increase exponentially with time—an indication that the gas is being formed biologically. Provision is also made for the injection, during the run, of a solution containing a metabolic poison which can be used to confirm the biological origin of the carbon dioxide and to analyze the nature of the metabolic reactions.

All afternoon the crawler traversed the plain, and the sky deepened from dark purple to utter black, and the untwinkling stars, which on Mars are visible even by day, became more brilliant with the passing hours, and Phobos came streaking by, and then came little hovering Deimos; and Oxenshuer, wandering around the ship, took readings on this and that and watched his screen and listened to Dave Vogel's chatter; and Mission Control offered a comment every little while. And during these hours the Martian temperature began its nightly slide down the centigrade ladder. A thousand kilometers away, an inversion of thermal gradients unexpectedly developed, creating fierce currents in the tenuous Martian atmosphere, ripping gouts of red sand loose from the hills, driving wild scarlet clouds eastward toward the Gulliver site. As the sandstorm increased in intensity, the scanner satellites in orbit around Mars detected it and relayed pictures of it to Earth, and after the normal transmission lag it was duly noted at Mission Control as a potential hazard to the men in the crawler, but somehow—the NASA hearings did not succeed in fixing blame for this inexplicable communications failure—no one passed the necessary warning along to the three astronauts on Mars. Two hours after he had finished his solitary dinner aboard the ship, Oxenshuer heard Vogel say, "Okay, Johnny, we've finally reached the Gulliver site, and as soon as we have our lighting system set up we'll get out and see what the hell we have here.'' Then the sandstorm struck in full fury. Oxenshuer heard nothing more from either of his companions.

Making camp for the night, he took first from his pack his operations beacon, one of his NASA souvenirs. By the sleek instrument's cool, inexhaustible green light he laid out his bedroll in the flattest, least pebbly place he could find; then, discovering himself far from sleepy, Oxenshuer set about assembling his solar still. Although he had no idea now long he would stay in the desert—a week, a month, a year, forever—he had brought perhaps a month's supply of food concentrates with him, but no water other than a single canteen's worth, to tide him through thirst on this first night. He could not count on finding wells or streams here, any more than he had on Mars, and, unlike the kangaroo rats, capable of living indefinitely on nothing but dried seeds, producing water metabolically by the oxidation of carbohydrates, he would not be able to dispense entirely with fresh water. But the solar still would see him through.

He began to dig.

Methodically he shaped a conical hole a meter in diameter, half a meter deep, and put a wide-mouthed two-liter jug at its deepest point. He collected pieces of cactus, breaking off slabs of prickly pear but ignoring the stiletto-spined chollas, and placed these along the slopes of the hole. Then he lined the hole with a sheet of clear plastic film, weighted by rocks in such a way that the plastic came in contact with the soil only at the hole's rim and hung suspended a few centimeters above the cactus pieces and the jug. The job took him twenty minutes. Solar energy would do the rest: as sunlight passed through the plastic into the soil and the plant material, water would evaporate, condense in droplets on the underside of the plastic, and trickle into the jug. With cactus as juicy as this, he might be able to count on a liter a day of sweet water out of each hole he dug. The still was emergency gear developed for use on Mars; it hadn't done anyone any good there, but Oxenshuer had no fears of running dry in this far more hospitable desert.

Enough, He shucked his pants and crawled into his sleeping bag. At last he was where he wanted to be: enclosed, protected, yet at the same time alone, unsurrounded, cut off from his past in a world of dryness.

*   *   *

He could not yet sleep; his mind ticked too actively. Images out of the last few years floated insistently through it and had to be purged, one by one. To begin with, his wife's face. (Wife? I have no wife. Not now.) He was having difficulty remembering Lenore's features, the shape of her nose, the turn of her lips, but a general sense of her existence still burdened him. How long had they been married? Eleven years, was it? Twelve? The anniversary? March 30, 31? He was sure he had loved her once. What had happened? Why had he recoiled from her touch?

—No, please, don't do that. I don't want to yet.

—You've been home three months, John.

Her sad green eyes. Her tender smile. A stranger, now. His ex-wife's face turned to mist and the mist congealed into the face of Claire Vogel. A sharper image: dark glittering eyes, the narrow mouth, thin cheeks framed by loose streamers of unbound black hair. The widow Vogel, dignified in her grief, trying to console him.

—I'm sorry, Claire. They just disappeared, is all. There wasn't anything I could do.

—John, John, it wasn't your fault. Don't let it get you like this.

—I couldn't even find the bodies. I wanted to look for them, but it was all sand everywhere, sand, dust, the craters, confusion, no signal, no landmarks, no way, Claire, no way.

—It's all right, John. What do the bodies matter? You did your best. I know you did.

Her words offered comfort but no absolution from guilt. Her embrace—light, chaste—merely troubled him. The pressure of her heavy breasts against him made him tremble. He remembered Dave Vogel, halfway to Mars, speaking lovingly of Claire's breasts. Her jugs, he called them. Boy, I'd like to have my hands on my lady's jugs right this minute! And Bud Richardson, more annoyed than amused, telling him to cut it out, to stop stirring up fantasies that couldn't be satisfied for another year or more.

Claire vanished from his mind, driven out by a blaze of flashbulbs. The hovercameras, hanging in midair, scanning him from every angle. The taut, earnest faces of the newsmen, digging deep for human interest. See the lone survivor of the Mars expedition! See his tortured eyes! See his gaunt cheeks! There's the President himself, folks, giving John Oxenshuer a great big welcome back to Earth! What thoughts must be going through this man's mind, the only human being to walk the sands of an alien world and return to our old down-to-Earth planet! How keenly he must feel the tragedy of the two lost astronauts he left behind up there! There he goes now, there goes John Oxenshuer, disappearing into the debriefing chamber—

Yes, the debriefings. Colonel Schmidt, Dr. Harkness, Commander Thompson, Dr. Burdette, Dr. Horowitz, milking him for data. Their voices carefully gentle, their manner informal, their eyes all the same betraying their singlemindedness.

—Once again, please, Captain Oxenshuer. You lost the signal, right, and then the backup line refused to check out, you couldn't get any telemetry at all. And then?

—And then I took a directional fix, I did a thermal scan and tripled the infrared, I rigged an extension lifeline to the sample-collector and went outside looking for them. But the collector's range was only 10 kilometers. And the dust storm was too much. The dust storm. Too damned much. I went five hundred meters and you ordered me back into the ship. Didn't want to go back, but you ordered me.

—We didn't want to lose you too, John.

—But maybe it wasn't too late, even then. Maybe.

—There was no way you could have reached them in a short-range vehicle.

—I would have figured some way of recharging it. If only you had let me. If only the sand hadn't been flying around like that. If. Only.

—I think we've covered the point fully.

—Yes. May we go over some of the topographical data now, Captain Oxenshuer?

—Please. Please. Some other time.

It was three days before they realized what sort of shape he was in. They still thought he was the old John Oxenshuer, the one who had amused himself during the training period by reversing the inputs on his landing simulator, just for the hell of it, the one who had surreptitiously turned on the unsuspecting Secretary of Defense just before a Houston press conference, the one who had sung bawdy carols at a pious Christmas party for the families of the astronauts in '86. Now, seeing him darkened and turned in on himself, they concluded eventually that he had been transformed by Mars, and they sent him, finally, to the chief psychiatric team, Mendelson and McChesney.

—How long have you felt this way, Captain?

—I don't know. Since they died. Since I took off for Earth. Since I entered Earth's atmosphere. I don't know. Maybe it started earlier. Maybe it was always like this.

—What are the usual symptoms of the disturbance?

—Not wanting to see anybody. Not wanting to talk to anybody. Not wanting to be with anybody. Especially myself. I'm so goddamned sick of my own company.

—And what are your plans now?

—Just to live quietly and grope my way back to normal.

—Would you say it was the length of the voyage that upset you most, or the amount of time you had to spend in solitude on the homeward leg, or your distress over the deaths of—

—Look, how would I know?

—Who'd know better?

—Hey, I don't believe in either of you, you know? You're figments. Go away. Vanish.

—We understand you're putting in for retirement and a maximum disability pension, Captain.

—Where'd you hear that? It's a stinking lie. I'm going to be okay before long. I'll be back on active duty before Christmas, you got that?

—Of course, Captain.

—Go. Disappear. Who needs you?

—John, John, it wasn't your fault. Don't let it get you like this.

—I couldn't even find the bodies. I wanted to look for them, but it was all sand everywhere, sand, dust, the craters, confusion, no signal, no landmarks, no way, Claire, no way.

The images were breaking up, dwindling, going. He saw scattered glints of light slowly whirling overhead, the kaleidoscope of the heavens, the whole astronomical psychedelia swaying and cavorting, and then the sky calmed, and then only Claire's face remained, Claire and the minute red disk of Mars. The events of the nineteen months contracted to a single star-bright point of time, and became as nothing, and were gone. Silence and darkness enveloped him. Lying tense and rigid on the desert floor, he stared up defiantly at Mars, and closed his eyes, and wiped the red disk from the screen of his mind, and slowly, gradually, reluctantly, he surrendered himself to sleep.

* * *

Voices woke him. Male voices, quiet and deep, discussing him in an indistinct buzz. He hovered a moment on the border between dream and reality, uncertain of his perceptions and unsure of his proper response; then his military reflexes took over and he snapped into instant wakefulness, blinking his eyes open, sitting up in one quick move, rising to a standing position in the next, poising his body to defend itself.

He took stock. Sunrise was maybe half an hour away; the tips of the mountains to the west were stained with early pinkness. Thin mist shrouded the low-lying land. Three men stood just beyond the place where he had mounted his beacon. The shortest one was as tall as he, and they were desert-tanned, heavy-set, strong and capable-looking. They wore their hair long and their beards full; they were oddly dressed, shepherd-style, in loose belted robes of light green muslin or linen. Although their expressions were open and friendly and they did not seem to be armed, Oxenshuer was troubled by awareness of his vulnerability in this emptiness, and he found menace in their presence. Their intrusion on his isolation angered him. He stared at them warily, rocking on the balls of his feet.

One, bigger than the others, a massive thick-cheeked blue-eyed man, said, "Easy. Easy, now. You look all ready to fight."

"Who are you? What do you want?"

"Just came to find out if you were okay. You lost?"

Oxenshuer indicated his neat camp, his backpack, his bedroll. "Do I seem lost?"

"You're a long way from anywhere," said the man closest to Oxenshuer, one with shaggy yellow hair and a cast in one eye.

"Am I? I thought it was just a short hike from the road."

The three men began to laugh. "You don't know *where* the hell you are, do you?" said the squint-eyed one. And the third one, dark-bearded, hawk-featured, said, "Look over thataway." He pointed behind Oxenshuer, to the north. Slowly, half anticipating trickery, Oxenshuer turned. Last night, in the moonlit darkness, the land had seemed level and empty in that direction, but now he beheld two steeply rising mesas a few hundred meters apart, and in the opening between them he saw a low wooden palisade, and behind the palisade the flat-roofed tops of buildings were visible, tinted orange-pink by the spreading touch of dawn. A settlement out here? But the map showed nothing, and, from the looks of it, that was a town of some two or three thousand people. He wondered if he had somehow been transported by magic during the night to some deeper part of the desert. But no: there was his solar still, there was the mesquite patch; there were last night's prickly pears. Frowning, Oxenshuer said, "'What is that place in there?''

"The City of the Word of God," said the hawk-faced one calmly.

"You're lucky," said the squint-eyed one. "You've been brought to us almost in time for the Feast of St. Dionysus. When all men are made one. When every ill is healed."

Oxenshuer understood. Religious fanatics. A secret retreat in the desert. The state was full of apocalyptic cults, more and more of them now that the end of the century was only about ten years away and millennial fears were mounting. He scowled. He had a native Easterner's innate distaste for Californian irrationality. Reaching into the reservoir of his own decaying Catholicism, he said thinly, "Don't you mean St. Dionysius? With an *i*? Dionysus was the Greek god of wine."

"Dionysus," said the big blue-eyed man. "Dionysius is somebody else, some Frenchman. We've heard of him. Dionysus is who we mean." He put forth his hand. "My name's Matt, Mr. Oxenshuer. If you stay for the Feast, I'll stand brother to you. How's that?"

The sound of his name jolted him. "You've heard of me?"

"Heard of you? Well, not exactly. We looked in your wallet."

"We ought to go now," said the squint-eyed one. "Don't want to miss breakfast."

"Thanks," Oxenshuer said, "but I think I'll pass up the invitation. I came out here to get away from people for a little while."

"So did we," Matt said.

"You've been called," said Squint-eye hoarsely. "Don't you realize that, man? You've been called to our city. It wasn't any accident you came here."

"No?"

"There aren't any accidents," said Hawk-face. "Not ever. Not in the breast of Jesus, not ever a one. What's written is written. You were called, Mr. Oxenshuer. Can you say no?" He put his hand lightly on Oxenshuer's arm. "Come to our city. Come to the Feast. Look, why do you want to be afraid?"

"I'm not afraid. I'm just looking to be alone."

"We'll let you be alone, if that's what you want," Hawk-face told him. "Won't we, Matt? Won't we, Will? But you can't say no to our city. To our saint. To Jesus. Come along, now. Will, you carry his pack. Let him walk into the city without a burden." Hawk-face's sharp, forbidding features were softened by the glow of his fervor. His dark eyes gleamed. A strange, persuasive warmth leaped from him to Oxenshuer. "You won't say no. You won't. Come sing with us. Come to the Feast. Well?"

"Well?" Matt asked also.

"To lay down your burden," said squint-eyed Will. "To join the singing. Well? Well?"

"I'll go with you," Oxenshuer said at length. "But I'll carry my own pack."

They moved to one side and waited in silence while he assembled his belongings. In ten minutes everything was in order. Kneeling, adjusting the straps of his pack, he nodded and looked up. The early sun was full on the city now, and its rooftops were bright with a golden radiance. Light seemed to stream upward from them; the entire desert appeared to blaze in that luminous flow.

"All right," Oxenshuer said, rising and shouldering his pack. "Let's go." But he remained where he stood, staring ahead. He felt the city's golden luminosity as a fiery tangible force on his cheeks, like the outpouring of heat from a crucible of molten metal. With Matt leading the way, the three men walked ahead, single file, moving fast. Will, the squint-eyed one, bringing up the rear, paused to look back questioningly at Oxenshuer, who was still standing entranced by the sight of that supernal brilliance. "Coming," Oxenshuer murmured. Matching the pace of the others, he followed them briskly over the parched, sandy wastes toward the City of the Word of God.

There are places in the coastal desert of Peru where no rainfall has ever been recorded. On the Paracas Peninsula, about eleven miles south of the port of Pisco, the red sand is absolutely bare of all vegetation, not a leaf, not a living thing; no stream enters the ocean nearby. The nearest human habitation is several miles away, where wells tap underground water and a few sedges line the beach. There is no more arid area in the western hemisphere; it is the epitome of loneliness and desolation. The psychological landscape of Paracas is much the same as that of Mars. John Oxenshuer, Dave Vogel, and Bud Richardson spent three weeks camping there in the winter of 1987, testing their emergency gear and familiarizing themselves with the emotional texture of the Martian environment. Beneath the sands of the peninsula are found the desiccated bodies of an ancient people unknown to history, together with some of the most magnificent textiles that the world has ever seen. Natives seeking salable artifacts have rifled the necropolis of Paracas, and now the bones of its occupants lie scattered on the surface, and the winds alternately cover and uncover fragments of the coarser fabrics, discarded by the diggers, still soft and strong after nearly two millennia.

Vultures circle high over the Mojave. They would pick the bones of anyone who died here. There are no vultures on Mars. Dead men become mummies, not skeletons, for nothing decays on Mars. What has died on Mars remains buried in the sand, invulnerable to time, imperishable, eternal. Perhaps archaeologists, bound on a futile but inevitable search for the remains of the lost races of old Mars, will find the withered bodies of Dave Vogel and Bud Richardson in a mound of red soil, ten thousand years from now.

At close range the city seemed less magical. It was laid out in the form of a bull's-eye, its curving streets set in concentric rings behind the blunt-topped little palisade, evidently purely symbolic in purpose, that rimmed its circumference between the mesas. The buildings were squat stucco affairs of five or six rooms, unpretentious and undistinguished, all of them similar if not identical in style: pastel-hued structures of the sort found everywhere in southern California. They seemed to be twenty or thirty years old and in generally shabby condition; they were set close together and close to the street, with no gardens and no garages. Wide avenues leading inward pierced the rings of buildings every few hundred meters. This seemed to be entirely a residential district, but no people were in sight, either at windows or on the streets, nor were there any parked cars; it was like a movie set, clean and empty and artificial. Oxenshuer's footfalls echoed loudly. The silence and surreal emptiness troubled him. Only an occasional child's tricycle, casually abandoned outside a house, gave evidence of recent human presence.

As they approached the core of the city, Oxenshuer saw that

the avenues were narrowing and then giving way to a labyrinthine tangle of smaller streets, as intricate a maze as could be found in any of the old towns of Europe; the bewildering pattern seemed deliberate and carefully designed, perhaps for the sake of shielding the central section and making it a place apart from the antiseptic, prosaic zone of houses in the outer rings. The buildings lining the streets of the maze had an institutional character: they were three and four stories high, built of red brick, with few windows and pinched, unwelcoming entrances. They had the look of nineteenth-century hotels; possibly they were warehouses and meeting halls and places of some municipal nature. All were deserted. No commercial establishments were visible, no shops, no restaurants, no banks, no loan companies, no theaters, no newsstands. Such things were forbidden, maybe, in a theocracy such as Oxenshuer suspected this place to be. The city plainly had not evolved in any helter-skelter free-enterprise fashion, but had been planned down to its last alleyway for the exclusive use of a communal order whose members were beyond the bourgeois needs of an ordinary town.

Matt led them sure-footedly into the maze, infallibly choosing connecting points that carried them steadily deeper toward the center. He twisted and turned abruptly through juncture after juncture, never once doubling back on his track. At last they stepped through one passageway barely wide enough for Oxenshuer's pack, and he found himself in a plaza of unexpected size and grandeur. It was a vast open space, roomy enough for several thousand people, paved with cobbles that glittered in the harsh desert sunlight. On the right was a colossal building two stories high that ran the entire length of the plaza, at least three hundred meters; it looked as bleak as a barracks, a dreary utilitarian thing of clapboard and aluminum siding painted a dingy drab green, but all down its plaza side were tall, radiant stained-glass windows, as incongruous as pink gardenias blooming on a scrub oak. A towering metal cross rising high over the middle of the pointed roof settled all doubts; this was the city's church. Facing it across the plaza was an equally immense building, no less unsightly, built to the same plan but evidently secular, for its windows were plain and it bore no cross. At the far side of the plaza, opposite the place where they had entered it, stood a much smaller structure of dark stone in an implausible Gothic style, all vaults and turrets and arches. Pointing to each building in turn, Matt said, "Over there's the house of the god. On this side's the dining hall. Straight ahead, the little one, that's the house of the Speaker. You'll meet him at breakfast. Let's go eat."

. . . Captain Oxenshuer and Major Vogel, who will spend the next year and a half together in the sardine-can environment of their spaceship as they make their round trip journey to Mars and back, are no strangers to one another. Born on the same day—November 4, 1949—in Reading, Pennsylvania, they grew up together, attending the same elementary and high schools as classmates and sharing a dormitory room as undergraduates at Princeton. They dated many of the same girls; it was Captain Oxenshuer who introduced Major Vogel to his future wife, the former Claire Barnes, in 1973. "You might say he stole her from me," the tall, slender astronaut likes to tell interviewers, grinning to show he holds no malice over the incident. In a sense Major Vogel returned the compliment, for Captain Oxenshuer has been married since March 30, 1978, to the major's first cousin, the former Lenore Reiser, whom he met at his friend's wedding reception. After receiving advanced scientific degrees—Captain Oxenshuer in meteorology and celestial mechanics, Major Vogel in geology and space navigation—they enrolled together in the space program in the spring of 1979 and shortly afterward were chosen as members of the original thirty-six-man group of trainees for the first manned flight to the red planet. According to their fellow astronauts, they quickly distinguished themselves for their quick and imaginative responses to stress situations, for their extraordinarily deft teamwork, and also for their shared love of high-spirited pranks and gags, which got them in trouble more than once with sober-sided NASA officials. Despite occasional reprimands, they were regarded as obvious choices for the initial Mars voyage, to which their selection was announced on March 19, 1985. Colonel Walter ("Bud") Richardson, named that day as command pilot for the Mars mission, cannot claim to share the lifelong bonds of companionship that link Captain Oxenshuer and Major Vogel, but he has been closely associated with them in the astronaut program for the past ten years and long ago established himself as their most intimate friend.

Colonel Richardson, the third of this county's three muske-
teers of interplanetary exploration, was born in Omaha,
Nebraska, on the 5th of June, 1948. He hoped to become an
astronaut from earliest childhood onward, and . . .

They crossed the plaza to the dining hall. Just within the entrance
was a dark-walled low-ceilinged vestibule; a pair of swinging
doors gave access to the dining rooms beyond. Through windows
set in the doors Oxenshuer could glimpse dimly-lit vastnesses to
the left and the right, in which great numbers of solemn people,
all clad in the same sort of flowing robes as his three companions, sat at long bare wooden tables and passed serving bowls
around. Nick told Oxenshuer to drop his pack and leave it in the
vestibule; no one would bother it, he said. As they started to go
in, a boy of ten erupted explosively out of the left-hand doorway,
nearly colliding with Oxenshuer. The boy halted just barely in
time, backed up a couple of paces, stared with shameless curiosity into Oxenshuer's face, and, grinning broadly, pointed to
Oxenshuer's bare chin and stroked his own as if to indicate that it
was odd to see a man without a beard. Matt caught the boy by
the shoulders and pulled him against his chest; Oxenshuer thought
he was going to shake him, to chastise him for such irreverence,
but no, Matt gave the boy an affectionate hug, swung him far
overhead, and tenderly set him down. The boy clasped Matt's
powerful forearms briefly and went sprinting through the right-
hand door.

"Your son?" Oxenshuer asked.

"Nephew. I've got two hundred nephews. Every man in this
town's my brother, right? So every boy's my nephew."

—If I could have just a few moments for one or two questions,
Captain Oxenshuer.

—Provided it's really just a few moments. I'm due at Mission
Control at 0830, and—

—I'll confine myself, then, to the one topic of greatest
relevance to our readers. What are your feelings about the Deity,
Captain? Do you, as an astronaut soon to depart for Mars,
believe in the existence of God?

—My biographical poop-sheet will tell you that I've been
known to go to Mass now and then.

—Yes, of course, we realize you're a practicing member of

the Catholic faith, but, well, Captain, it's widely understood that
for some astronauts religious observance is more of a public-
relations matter than a matter of genuine spiritual urgings. Meaning no offense, Captain, we're trying to ascertain the actual
nature of your relationship, if any, to the Divine Presence, rather
than—

—All right. You're asking a complicated question and I don't
see how I can give an easy answer. If you're asking whether I
literally believe in the Father, Son, and Holy Ghost, whether I
think Jesus came down from heaven for our salvation and was
crucified for us and was buried and on the third day rose again
and ascended into heaven, I'd have to say no. Not except in the
loosest metaphorical sense. But I do believe—ah—suppose we
say I believe in the existence of an organizing force in the
universe, a power of sublime reason that makes everything hang
together, an underlying principle of rightness. Which we can call
God for lack of a better name. And which I reach toward, when I
feel I need to, by way of the Roman Church, because that's how
I was raised.

—That's an extremely abstract philosophy, Captain.

—Abstract. Yes.

—That's an extremely rationalistic approach. Would you say
that your brand of cool rationalism is characteristic of the entire
astronaut group?

—I can't speak for the whole group. We didn't come out of a
single mold. We've got some all-American boys who go to
church every Sunday and think that God Himself is listening in
person to every word they say, and we've got a couple of
atheists, though I won't tell you who, and we've got guys who
just don't care one way or the other. And I can tell you we've got
a few real mystics, too, some out-and-out guru types. Don't let
the uniforms and hair-cuts fool you. Why, there are times when I
feel the pull of mysticism myself.

—In what way?

—I'm not sure. I get a sense of being on the edge of some sort
of cosmic breakthrough. An awareness that there may be real
forces just beyond my reach, not abstractions but actual functioning
dynamic entities, which I could attune myself to if I only knew
how to find the key. You feel stuff like that when you go into
space, no matter how much of a rationalist you think you are.
I've felt it four to five times, on training flights, on orbital

missions. I want to feel it again. I want to break through. I want
to reach God, am I making myself clear? I want to reach God.

—But you say you don't literally believe in Him, Captain.
That sounds contradictory to me.

—Does it really?

—It does, sir.

—Well, if it does, I don't apologize. I don't have to think
straight all the time. I'm entitled to a few contradictions. I'm
capable of holding a couple of diametrically opposed beliefs.
Look, if I want to flirt with madness a little, what's it to you?

—Madness, Captain?

—Madness. Yes. That's exactly what it is, friend. There are
times when Johnny Oxenshuer is tired of being so goddamned
sane. You can quote me on that. Did you get it straight? There
are times when Johnny Oxenshuer is tired of being so goddamned
sane. But don't print it until I've blasted off for Mars, you hear
me? I don't want to get bumped from this mission for incipient
schizophrenia. I want to go. Maybe I'll find God out there this
time, you know? And maybe I won't. But I want to go.

—I think I understand what you're saying, sir. God bless you,
Captain Oxenshuer. A safe voyage to you.

—Sure. Thanks. Was I of any help?

Hardly anyone glanced up at him, only a few of the children, as
Matt led him down the long aisle toward the table on the platform
at the back of the hall. The people here appeared to be extraordinarily self-contained, as if they were in possession of some
wondrous secret from which he would be forever excluded, and
the passing of the serving bowls seemed far more interesting to
them than the stranger in their midst. The smell of scrambled
eggs dominated the great room. That heavy, greasy odor seemed
to expand and rise until it squeezed out all the air. Oxenshuer
found himself choking and gagging. Panic seized him. He had
never imagined he could be thrown into terror by the smell of
scrambled eggs. "This way," Matt called. "Steady on, man.
You all right?" Finally they reached the raised table. Here sat
only men, dignified and serene of mien, probably the elders of
the community. At the head of the table was one who had the
unmistakable look of a high priest. He was well past seventy—or
eighty or ninety—and his strong-featured leathery face was
seamed and gullied; his eyes were keen and intense, managing to

convey both a fierce tenacity and an all-encompassing warm humanity. Small-bodied, lithe, weighing at most a hundred pounds, he sat ferociously erect, a formidably commanding little man. A metallic embellishment of the collar of his robe was, perhaps, the badge of his status. Leaning over him, Matt said in exaggeratedly clear, loud tones, "This here's John. I'd like to stand brother to him when the Feast comes, if I can. John, this here's our Speaker."

Oxenshuer had met popes and presidents and secretaries-general, and, armored by his own standing as a celebrity, had never fallen into foolish awe-kindled embarrassment. But here he was no celebrity; he was no one at all, a stranger, an outsider, and he found himself lost before the Speaker. Mute, he waited for help. The old man said, his voice as melodious and as resonant as a cello, "Will you join our meal, John? Be welcome in our city."

Two of the elders made room on the bench. Oxenshuer sat at the Speaker's left hand; Matt sat beside him. Two girls of about fourteen brought settings: a plastic dish, a knife, a fork, a spoon, a cup. Matt served him: scrambled eggs, toast, sausages. All about him the clamor of eating went on. The Speaker's plate was empty. Oxenshuer fought back nausea and forced himself to attack the eggs. "We take all our meals together," said the Speaker. "This is a closely knit community, unlike any community I know on Earth." One of the serving girls said pleasantly, "Excuse me, brother," and, reaching over Oxenshuer's shoulder, filled his cup with red wine. Wine for breakfast? They worship Dionysus here, Oxenshuer remembered.

The Speaker said, "We'll house you. We'll feed you. We'll love you. We'll lead you to God. That's why you're here, isn't it? To get closer to Him, eh? To enter into the ocean of Christ."

—What do you want to be when you grow up, Johnny?
—An astronaut, ma'am. I want to be the first man to fly to Mars.

No. He never said any such thing.

Later in the morning he moved into Matt's house, on the perimeter of the city, overlooking one of the mesas. The house was merely a small green box, clapboard outside, flimsy beaver-board partitions inside: a sitting room, three bedrooms, a bathroom. No kitchen or dining room. ("We take all our meals together.") The walls were bare: no icons, no crucifixes, no religious paraphernalia of any kind. No television, no radio, hardly any personal possessions at all in evidence: a shotgun, a dozen worn books and magazines, some spare robes and extra boots in a closet, little more than that. Matt's wife was a small quiet woman in her late thirties, soft-eyed, submissive, dwarfed by her burly husband. Her name was Jean. There were three children, a boy of about twelve and two girls, maybe nine and seven. The boy had had a room of his own; he moved uncomplainingly in with his sisters, who doubled up in one bed to provide one for him, and Oxenshuer took the boy's room. Matt told the children their guest's name, but it drew no response from them. Obviously they had never heard of him. Were they even aware that a spaceship from Earth had lately journeyed to Mars? Probably not. He found that refreshing: for years Oxenshuer had had to cope with children paralyzed with astonishment at finding themselves in the presence of a genuine astronaut. Here he could shed the burdens of fame.

He realized he had not been told his host's last name. Somehow it seemed too late to ask Matt directly, now. When one of the little girls came wandering into his room he said, "What's your name?"

"Toby," she said, showing a gap-toothed mouth.

"Toby what?"

"Toby. Just Toby."

No surnames in this community? All right. Why bother with surnames in a place where everyone knows everyone else? Travel light, brethren, travel light, strip away the excess baggage.

Matt walked in and said, "At council tonight I'll officially apply to stand brother to you. It's just a formality. They've never turned an application down."

"What's involved, actually?"

"It's hard to explain until you know our ways better. It means I'm, well, your spokesman, your guide through our rituals."

"A kind of sponsor?"

"Well, sponsor's the wrong word. Will and Nick will be your sponsors. That's a different level of brotherhood, lower, not as close. I'll be something like your godfather, I guess; that's as near as I can come to the idea. Unless you don't want me to be. I never consulted you. Do you want me to stand brother to you, John?''

It was an impossible question. Oxenshuer had no way to evaluate any of this. Feeling dishonest, he said, "It would be a great honor, Matt."

Matt said, "You got any real brothers? Flesh kin?"

"No. A sister in Ohio." Oxenshuer thought a moment. "There once was a man who was like a brother to me. Knew him since childhood. As close as makes no difference. A brother, yes."

"What happened to him?"

"He died. In an accident. A long way from here."

"Terrible sorry," Matt said. "I've got five brothers. Three of them outside; I haven't heard from them in years. And two right here in the city. You'll meet them. They'll accept you as kin. Everyone will.

"What did you think of the Speaker?" Matt said.

"A marvelous old man. I'd like to talk with him again."

"You'll talk plenty with him. He's my father, you know."

Oxenshuer tried to imagine this huge man springing from the seed of the spare-bodied, compactly built Speaker and could not make the connection. He decided Matt must be speaking metaphorically again. "You mean, the way that boy was your nephew?"

"He's my true father," Matt said. "I'm flesh of his flesh." He went to the window. It was open about eight centimeters at the bottom. "Too cold for you in here, John?"

"It's fine."

"Gets cold, sometimes, these winter nights."

Matt stood silent, seemingly sizing Oxenshuer up. Then he said, "Say, you ever do any wrestling?"

"A little. In college."

"That's good."

"Why do you ask?"

"One of the things brothers do here, part of the ritual. We wrestle some. Especially the day of the Feast. It's important in the worship. I wouldn't want to hurt you any when we do. You and me, John. We'll do some wrestling before long, just to practice up for the Feast, okay? Okay?

*   *   *

They let him go anywhere he pleased. Alone, he wandered through the city's labyrinth, that incredible tangle of downtown streets, in early afternoon. The maze was cunningly constructed, one street winding into another so marvelously that the buildings were drawn tightly together and the bright desert sun could barely penetrate; Oxenshuer walked in shadow much of the way. The twisting mazy passages baffled him. The purpose of this part of the city seemed clearly symbolic: everyone who dwelled here was compelled to pass through these coiling interlacing streets in order to get from the commonplace residential quarter, where people lived in isolated family groupings, to the dining hall, where the entire community together took the sacrament of food, and to the church, where redemption and salvation were to be had. Only when purged of error and doubt, only when familiar with the one true way (or was there more than one way through the maze? Oxenshuer wondered.) could one attain the harmony of communality. He was still uninitiated, an outlander; wander as he would, dance tirelessly from street to cloistered street, he would never get there unaided.

He thought it would be less difficult than it had first seemed to find his way from Matt's house to the inner plaza, but he was wrong: the narrow, meandering streets misled him, so that he sometimes moved away from the plaza when he thought he was going toward it, and, after pursuing one series of corridors and intersections for fifteen minutes, he realized that he had merely returned himself to one of the residential streets on the edge of the maze. Intently, he tried again. An astronaut trained to maneuver safely through the trackless wastes of Mars ought to be able to get about in one small city. Watch for landmarks, Johnny. Follow the pattern of the shadows. He clamped his lips, concentrated, plotted a course. As he prowled he occasionally saw faces peering briefly at him out of the upper windows of the austere warehouselike buildings that flanked the street. Were they smiling? He came to one group of streets that seemed familiar to him, and went in and in, until he entered an alleyway closed at both ends, from which the only exit was a slit barely wide enough for a man if he held his breath and slipped through sideways. Just beyond, the metal cross of the church stood outlined against the sky, encouraging him: he was nearly to the end of the maze. He went through the slit and found himself in a cul-de-sac; five minutes of close inspection revealed no way to go on. He retraced his steps and sought another route.

One of the bigger buildings in the labyrinth was evidently a school. He could hear the high, clear voices of children chanting mysterious hymns. The melodies were conventional seesaws of piety, but the words were strange:

Bring us together. Lead us to the ocean.
Help us to swim. Give us to drink.
   Wine in my heart today,
   Blood in my throat today,
   Fire in my soul today,
All praise, O God, to thee.

Sweet treble voices, making the bizarre words sound all the more grotesque. Blood in my throat today. Unreal city. How can it exist? Where does the food come from? Where does the wine come from? What do they use for money? What do the people do with themselves all day? They have electricity: what fuel keeps the generator running? They have running water. Are they hooked into a public utility district's pipelines, and if so why isn't this place on my map? Fire in my soul today. Wine in my heart today. What are these feasts, who are these saints? This is the god who burns like fire. This is the god whose name is music. This is the god whose soul is wine. You were called, Mr. Oxenshuer. Can you say no? You can't say no to our city. To our saint. To Jesus. Come along, now?

Where's the way out of here?

Three times a day, the whole population of the city went on foot from their houses through the labyrinth to the dining hall. There appeared to be at least half a dozen ways of reaching the central plaza, but, though he studied the route carefully each time, Oxenshuer was unable to keep it straight in his mind. The food was simple and nourishing, and there was plenty of it. Wine flowed freely at every meal. Young boys and girls did the serving, jubilantly hauling huge platters of food from the kitchen; Oxenshuer had no idea who did the cooking, but he supposed the task would rotate among the women of the community. (The men had other chores. The city, Oxenshuer learned, had been built entirely by the freely contributed labor of its own inhabitants. Several new houses were under construction now. And there were irrigated fields beyond the mesas.) Seating in the dining hall was random at the long tables, but people generally seemed to come together in nuclear-family groupings. Oxenshuer met Matt's two brothers, Jim and Ernie, both smaller men than Matt but powerfully built. Ernie gave Oxenshuer a hug, a quick, warm, impulsive gesture. "Brother," he said. "Brother! Brother!"

The Speaker received Oxenshuer in the study of his residence on the plaza, a dark ground-floor room, the walls of which were covered to ceiling height with shelves of books. Most people here affected a casual hayseed manner, an easy drawling rural simplicity of speech that implied little interest in intellectual things, but the Speaker's books ran heavily to abstruse philosophical and theological themes, and they looked as though they had all been read many times. Those books confirmed Oxenshuer's first fragmentary impression of the Speaker: that this was a man of supple, well-stocked mind, sophisticated, complex. The Speaker offered Oxenshuer a cup of cool tart wine. They drank in silence. When he had nearly drained his cup, the old man calmly hurled the dregs to the glossy slate floor. "An offering to Dionysus," he explained.

"But you're Christians here," said Oxenshuer.

"Yes, of course we're Christians! But we have our own calendar of saints. We worship Jesus in the guise of Dionysus and Dionysus in the guise of Jesus. Others might call us pagans, I suppose. But where there's Christ, is there not Christianity?" The Speaker laughed. "Are you a Christian, John?"

"I suppose. I was baptized. I was confirmed. I've taken communion. I've been to confession now and then."

"You're of the Roman faith?"

"More that faith than any other," Oxenshuer said.

"You believe in God?"

"In an abstract way."

"And in Jesus Christ?"

"I don't know," said Oxenshuer uncomfortably. "In a literal sense, no. I mean, I suppose there was a prophet in Palestine named Jesus, and the Romans nailed him up, but I've never taken the rest of the story too seriously. I can accept Jesus as a symbol, though. As a metaphor of love. God's love."

"A metaphor for *all* love," the Speaker said. "The love of God for mankind. The love of mankind for God. The love of man and woman, the love of parent and child, the love of brother and brother, every kind of love there is. Jesus is love's spirit. God is love. That's what we believe here. Through communal ecstasies we are reminded of the new commandment He gave unto us, That ye love one another. And as it says in Romans, Love is the fulfilling of the law. We follow His teachings; therefore we are Christians.''

"Even though you worship Dionysus as a saint?"

"Especially so. We believe that in the divine madnesses of Dionysus we come closer to Him than other Christians are capable of coming. Through revelry, through singing, through the pleasures of the flesh, through ecstasy, through union with one another in body and in soul—through these we break out of our isolation and become one with Him. In the life to come we will all be one. But first we must live this life and share in the creation of love, which is Jesus, which is God. Our goal is to make all beings one with Jesus, so that we become droplets in the ocean of love which is God, giving up our individual selves."

"This sounds Hindu to me, almost. Or Buddhist."

"Jesus is Buddha. Buddha is Jesus."

"Neither of them taught a religion of revelry."

"Dionysus did. We make our own synthesis of spiritual commandments. And so we see no virtue in self-denial, since that is the contradiction of love. What is held to be virtue by others is sin to us. And vice versa, I would suppose."

"What about the doctrine of the virgin birth? What about the virginity of Jesus himself? The whole notion of purity through restraint and asceticism?"

"Those concepts are not part of our belief, friend John."

"But you do recognize the concept of sin?"

"The sins we deplore," said the Speaker, "are such things as coldness, selfishness, aloofness, envy, maliciousness, all those things that hold one man apart from another. We punish the sinful by engulfing them in love. But we recognize no sins that arise out of love itself or out of excess of love. Since the world, especially the Christian world, finds our principles hateful and dangerous, we have chosen to withdraw from that world."

"How long have you been out here?" Oxenshuer asked.

"Many years. No one bothers us. Few strangers come to us. You are the first in a very long time."

"Why did you have me brought to your city?"

"We knew you were sent to us," the Speaker said.

*   *   *

At night there were wild frenzied gatherings in certain tall windowless buildings in the depths of the labyrinth. He was never allowed to take part. The dancing, the singing, the drinking, whatever else went on, these things were not yet for him. Wait till the Feast, they told him, wait till the Feast, then you'll be invited to join us. So he spent his evenings alone. Some nights he would stay home with the children. No babysitters were needed in this city, but he became one anyway, playing simple dice games with the girls, tossing a ball back and forth with the boy, telling them stories as they fell asleep. He told them of his flight to Mars, spoke of watching the red world grow larger every day, described the landing, the alien feel of the place, the iron-red sands, the tiny glinting moons. They listened silently, perhaps fascinated, perhaps not at all interested: he suspected they thought he was making it all up. He never said anything about the fate of his companions.

Some nights he would stroll through town, street after quiet street, drifting in what he pretended was a random way toward the downtown maze. Standing near the perimeter of the labyrinth—even now he could not find his way around in it after dark, and feared getting lost if he went in too deep—he would listen to the distant sounds of the celebration, the drumming, the chanting, the simple, repetitive hymns:

This is the god who burns like fire
This is the god whose name is music
This is the god whose soul is wine

And he would also hear them sing:

Tell the saint to heat my heart
Tell the saint to give me breath
Tell the saint to quench my thirst

And this:

Leaping shouting singing stamping
Rising climbing flying soaring
Melting joining loving blazing
Singing soaring joining loving

Some nights he would walk to the edge of the desert, hiking out a few hundred meters into it, drawing a bleak pleasure from the solitude, the crunch of sand beneath his boots, the knifeblade coldness of the air, the forlorn gnarled cacti, the timorous kangaroo rats, even the occasional scorpion. Crouching on some gritty hummock, looking up through the cold brilliant stars to the red dot of Mars, he would think of Dave Vogel, would think of Bud Richardson, would think of Claire, and of himself, who he had been, what he had lost. Once, he remembered, he had been a high-spirited man who laughed easily, expressed affection readily and openly, enjoyed joking, drinking, running, swimming, all the active outgoing things. Leaping shouting singing stamping. Rising climbing flying soaring. And then this deadness had come over him, this zombie absence of response, this icy shell. Mars had stolen him from himself. Why? The guilt? The guilt, the guilt, the guilt—he had lost himself in guilt. And now he was lost in the desert. This implausible town. These rites, this cult. Wine and shouting. He had no idea how long he had been here. Was Christmas approaching? Possibly it was only a few days away. Blue plastic Yule trees were sprouting in front of the department stores on Wilshire Boulevard. Jolly red Santas pacing the sidewalk. Tinsel and glitter. Christmas might be an appropriate time for the Feast of St. Dionysus. The Saturnalia revived. Would the Feast come soon? He anticipated it with fear and eagerness.

Late in the evening, when the last of the wine was gone and the singing was over, Matt and Jean would return, flushed, wine-drenched, happy, and through the thin partition separating Oxenshuer's room from theirs would come the sounds of love, the titanic poundings of their embraces, far into the night.

—Astronauts are supposed to be sane, Dave.
   —Are they? Are they really, Johnny?
   —Of course they are.
   —Are *you* sane?
   —I'm sane as hell, Dave.
   —Yes. Yes. I'll bet you think you are.
   —Don't you think I'm sane?
   —Oh, sure, you're sane, Johnny. Saner than you need to be. If anybody asked me to name him one sane man, I'd say John

Oxenshuer. But you're not all that sane. And you've got the potential to become very crazy.

—Thanks.

—I mean it as a compliment.

—What about you? You aren't sane?

—I'm a madman, Johnny. And getting madder all the time.

—Suppose NASA finds out that Dave Vogel's a madman?

—They won't, my friend. They know I'm one hell of an astronaut, and so by definition I'm sane. They don't know what's inside me. They can't. By definition, they wouldn't be NASA bureaucrats if they could tell what's inside a man.

—They know you're sane because you're an astronaut?

—Of course, Johnny. What does an astronaut know about the irrational? What sort of capacity for ecstasy does he have, anyway? He trains for ten years; he jogs in a centrifuge; he drills with computers, he runs a thousand simulations before he dares to sneeze; he thinks in spaceman jargon; he goes to church on Sundays and doesn't pray; he turns himself into a machine so he can run the damnedest machines anybody ever thought up. And to outsiders he looks deader than a banker, deader than a stockbroker, deader than a sales manager. Look at him, with his 1975 haircut and his 1965 uniform. Can a man like that even know what a mystic experience *is*? Well, some of us are really like that. They fit the official astronaut image. Sometimes I think you do, Johnny, or at least that you want to. But not me. Look, I'm a yogi. Yogis train for decades so they can have a glimpse of the All. They subject their bodies to crazy disciplines. They learn highly specialized techniques. A yogi and an astronaut aren't all that far apart, man. What I do, it's not so different from what a yogi does, and it's for the same reason. It's so we can catch sight of the White Light. Look at you, laughing! But I mean it, Johnny. When that big fist knocks me into orbit, when I see the whole world hanging out there, it's a wild moment for me, it's ecstasy, it's nirvana. I live for those moments. They make all the NASA crap worthwhile. Those are breakthrough moments, when I get into an entirely new realm. That's the only reason I'm in this. And you know something? I think it's the same with you, whether you know it or not. A mystic thing, Johnny, a crazy thing, that powers us, that drives us on. The yoga of space. One day you'll find out. One day you'll see yourself for the madman you really are. You'll open up to all the wild forces inside you, the lunatic drives that sent you to NASA. You'll find out you weren't just a machine after all; you weren't just a stockbroker in a fancy costume; you'll find out you're a yogi, a holy man, an ecstatic. And you'll see what a trip you're on, you'll see that controlled madness is the only true secret and that you've always known the Way. And you'll set aside everything that's left of your old straight self. You'll give yourself up completely to forces you can't understand and don't want to understand. And you'll love it, Johnny. You'll love it.

When he stayed in the city about three weeks—it seemed to him that it had been about three weeks, though perhaps it had been two or four—he decided to leave. The decision was nothing that came upon him suddenly; it had always been in the back of his mind that he did not want to be here, and gradually that feeling came to dominate him. Nick had promised him solitude while he was in the city, if he wanted it, and indeed he had had solitude enough, no one bothering him, no one making demands on him, the city functioning perfectly well without any contribution from him. But it was the wrong kind of solitude. To be alone in the middle of several thousand people was worse than camping by himself in the desert. True, Matt had promised him that after the Feast he would no longer be alone. Yet Oxenshuer wondered if he really wanted to stay here long enough to experience the mysteries of the Feast and the oneness that presumably would follow it. The Speaker spoke of giving up all pain as one enters the all-encompassing body of Jesus. What would he actually give up, though—his pain or his identity? Could he lose one without losing the other? Perhaps it was best to avoid all that and return to his original plan of going off by himself in the wilderness.

One evening after Matt and Jean had set out for the downtown revels, Oxenshuer quietly took his pack from the closet. He checked all his gear, filled his canteen, and said goodnight to the children. They looked at him strangely, as if wondering why he was putting on his pack just to go for a walk, but they asked no questions. He went up the broad avenue toward the palisade, passed through the unlocked gate, and in ten minutes was in the desert, moving steadily away from the City of the Word of God.

It was a cold, clear night, very dark, the stars almost painfully bright, Mars very much in evidence. He walked roughly eastward, through choppy countryside badly cut by ravines, and soon the mesas that flanked the city were out of sight. He had hoped to cover eight or ten kilometers before making camp, but the ravines made the hike hard going; when he had been out no more than an hour one of his boots began to chafe him and a muscle in his left leg sprang a cramp. He decided he would do well to halt. He picked a campsite near a stray patch of Joshua trees that stood like grotesque sentinels, stiff-armed and bristly, along the rim of a deep gully. The wind rose suddenly and swept across the desert flats, agitating their angular branches violently. It seemed to Oxenshuer that those booming gusts were blowing him the sounds of singing from the nearby city:

> I go to the god's house and his fire consumes me
> I cry the god's name and his thunder deafens me
> I take the god's cup and his wine dissolves me

He thought of Matt and Jean, and Ernie who had called him brother, and the Speaker who had offered him love and shelter, and Nick and Will his sponsors. He retraced in his mind the windings of the labyrinth until he grew dizzy. It was impossible, he told himself, to hear the singing from this place. He was at least three or four kilometers away. He prepared his campsite and unrolled his sleeping bag. But it was too early for sleep; he lay wide awake, listening to the wind, counting the stars, playing back the chants of the city in his head. Occasionally he dozed, but only for fitful intervals, easily broken. Tomorrow, he thought, he would cover twenty-five or thirty kilometers, going almost to the foothills of the mountains to the east, and he would set up half a dozen solar stills and settle down for a leisurely reexamination of all that had befallen him.

The hours slipped by slowly. About three in the morning he decided he was not going to be able to sleep, and he got up, dressed, paced along the gully's edge. A sound came to him: soft, almost a throbbing purr. He saw a light in the distance. A second light. The sound redoubled, one purr overlaid by another. Then a third light, farther away. All three lights in motion. He recognized the purring sounds now: the engines of dune-cycles. Travelers crossing the desert in the middle of the night? The headlights of the cycles swung in wide circular orbits around him. A search party from the city? Why else would they be driving like that, cutting off acres of desert in so systematic a way?

Yes. Voices. "John? Jo—ohn! Yo, John!"

Looking for him. But the desert was immense; the searchers were still far off. He need only take his gear and hunker down in the gully, and they would pass him by.

"Yo, John! Jo—ohn!"

Matt's voice.

Oxenshuer walked down the slope of the gully, paused a moment in its depths, and, surprising himself, started to scramble up the gully's far side. There he stood in silence a few minutes, watching the circling dune-cycles, listening to the calls of the searchers. It still seemed to him that the wind was bringing him the songs of the city people. This is the god who burns like fire. This is the god whose name is music. Jesus waits. The saint will lead you to bliss, dear tired John. Yes. Yes. At last he cupped his hands to his mouth and shouted, "Yo! Here I am! Yo!"

Two of the cycles halted immediately; the third, swinging out far to the left, stopped a little afterward. Oxenshuer waited for a reply, but none came.

"Yo!" he called again. "Over here, Matt! Here!"

He heard the purring start up. Headlights were in motion once more, the beams traversing the desert and coming to rest on him. The cycles approached. Oxenshuer recrossed the gully, collected his gear, and was waiting again on the cityward side when the searchers reached him. Matt, Nick, Will.

"Spending a night out?" Matt asked. The odor of wine was strong on his breath.

"Guess so."

"We got a little worried when you didn't come back by midnight. Thought you might have stumbled into a dry wash and hurt yourself some. Wasn't any cause for alarm, though, looks like." He glanced at Oxenshuer's pack, but made no comment. "Long as you're all right, I guess we can leave you to finish what you were doing. See you in the morning, okay?"

He turned away. Oxenshuer watched the men mount their cycles.

"Wait," he said.

Matt looked around.

"I'm all finished out here," Oxenshuer said. "I'd appreciate a lift back to the city."

*   *   *

"It's a matter of wholeness," the Speaker said. "In the beginning, mankind was all one. We were in contact. The communion of soul to soul. But then it all fell apart. *'In Adam's Fall we sinned all,'* remember? And that Fall, that original sin, John, it was a falling apart, a falling away from one another, a falling into the evil of strife. When we were in Eden we were more than simply one family, we were one being, one universal entity; and we came forth from Eden as individuals, Adam and Eve, Cain and Abel. The original universal being broken into pieces. Here, John, we seek to put the pieces back together. Do you follow me?"

"But how is it done?" Oxenshuer asked.

"By allowing Dionysus to lead us to Jesus," the old man said. "And in the saint's holy frenzy to create unity out of opposites. We bring the hostile tribes together. We bring the contending brothers together. We bring man and woman together."

Oxenshuer shrugged. "You talk only in metaphors and parables."

"There's no other way."

"What's your method? What's your underlying principle?"

"Our underlying principle is mystic ecstasy. Our method is to partake of the flesh of the god, and of his blood."

"It sounds very familiar. Take; eat. This is my body. This is my blood. Is your Feast a High Mass?"

The Speaker chuckled. "In a sense. We've made our synthesis between paganism and orthodox Christianity, and we've tried to move backward from the symbolic ritual to the literal act. Do you know where Christianity went astray? The same place all other religions have become derailed. The point at which spiritual experience was replaced by rote worship. Look at your Jews, muttering about Pharaoh in a language they've forgotten. Look at your Christians, lining up at the communion rail for a wafer and a gulp of wine, and never once feeling the terror and splendor of knowing that they're eating their god! Religion becomes doctrine too soon. It becomes professions of faith, formulas, talismans, emptiness. 'I believe in God the Father Almighty, creator of heaven and earth, and in Jesus Christ his only son, our Lord, who was conceived by the Holy Spirit, born from the Virgin Mary—' Words. Only words. We don't believe, John, that religious worship consists in reciting narrative accounts of ancient history. We want it to be immediate. We want it to be real.

We want to *see* our god. We want to *taste* our god. We want to *become* our god."

"How?"

"Do you know anything about the ancient cults of Dionysus?"

"Only that they were wild and bloody, with plenty of drinking and revelry and maybe human sacrifices."

"Yes. Human sacrifices," the Speaker said. "But before the human sacrifices came the divine sacrifices, the god who dies, the god who gives up his life for his people. In the prehistoric Dionysiac cults the god himself was torn apart and eaten, he was the central figure in a mystic rite of destruction in which his ecstatic worshipers feasted on his raw flesh, a sacramental meal enabling them to be made full of the god and take on blessedness, while the dead god became the scapegoat for man's sins. And then the god was reborn and all things were made one by his rebirth. So in Greece, so in Asia Minor, priests of Dionysus were ripped to pieces as surrogates for the god, and the worshipers partook of blood and meat in cannibalistic feasts of love, and in more civilized times animals were sacrificed in place of men, and still later, when the religion of Jesus replaced the various Dionysiac religions, bread and wine came to serve as the instruments of communion, metaphors for the flesh and blood of the god. On the symbolic level it was all the same. To devour the god. To achieve contact with the god in the most direct way. To experience the rapture of the ecstatic state, when one is possessed by the god. To unite that which society has forced asunder. To break down all boundaries. To rip off all shackles. To yield to our saint, our mad saint, the drunken god who is our saint, the mad saintly god who abolishes walls and makes all things one. Yes, John? We integrate through disintegration. We dissolve in the great ocean. We burn in the great fire. Yes, John? Give your soul gladly to Dionysus the Saint, John. Make yourself whole in his blessed fire. You've been divided too long." The Speaker's eyes had taken on a terrifying gleam. "Yes, John? Yes? Yes?"

In the dining hall one night Oxenshuer drinks much too much wine. The thirst comes upon him gradually and unexpectedly; at the beginning of the meal he simply sips as he eats, in his usual way, but the more he drinks, the more dry his throat becomes, until by the time the meat course is on the table he is reaching compulsively for the carafe every few minutes, filling his cup.

draining it, filling, draining. He becomes giddy and boisterous; someone at the table begins a hymn, and Oxenshuer joins in, though he is unsure of the words and keeps losing the melody. Those about him laugh, clap him on the back, sing even louder, beckoning to him, encouraging him to sing with them. Ernie and Matt match him drink for drink, and now whenever his cup is empty they fill it before he has a chance. A serving girl brings a full carafe. He feels a prickling in his earlobes and at the tip of his nose, feels a band of warmth across his chest and shoulders, and realizes he is getting drunk, but he allows it to happen. Dionysus reigns here. He has been sober long enough. And it has occurred to him that his drunkenness perhaps will inspire them to admit him to the night's revels. But that does not happen. Dinner ends. The Speaker and the other old men who sit at his table file from the hall; it is the signal for the rest to leave. Oxenshuer stands. Falters. Reels. Recovers. Laughs. Links arms with Matt and Ernie. "Brothers," he says. "Brothers!" They go from the hall together, but outside, in the great cobbled plaza, Matt says to him, "You better not go wandering in the desert tonight, man, or you'll break your neck for sure." So he is still excluded. He goes back through the labyrinth with Matt and Jean to their house, and they help him into his room and give him a jug of wine in case he still feels the thirst, and then they leave him. Oxenshuer sprawls on his bed. His head is spinning. Matt's boy looks in and asks if everything's all right. "Yes," Oxenshuer tells him. "I just need to lie down some." He feels embarrassed over being so helplessly intoxicated, but he reminds himself that in this city of Dionysus no one need apologize for taking too much wine. He closes his eyes and waits for a little stability to return. In the darkness a vision comes to him: the death of Dave Vogel. With strange brilliant clarity Oxenshuer sees the landscape of Mars spread out on the screen of his mind, low snubby hills sloping down to broad crater-pocked plains, gnarled desolate boulders, purple sky, red gritty particles blowing about. The extravehicular crawler well along on its journey westward toward the Gulliver site, Richardson driving, Vogel busy taking pictures, operating the myriad sensors, leaning into the microphone to describe everything he sees. They are at the Gulliver site now, preparing to leave the crawler, when they are surprised by the sudden onset of the sandstorm. Without warning the sky is red with billowing capes of sand, driving down on them like snowflakes in a blizzard. In the first furious moment of the storm the vehicle is engulfed; within minutes sand is piled a meter high on the crawler's domed transparent roof; they can see nothing, and the sandfall steadily deepens as the storm gains in intensity. Richardson grabs the controls, but the wheels of the crawler will not grip. "I've never seen anything like this," Vogel mutters. The vehicle has extendible perceptors on stalks, but when Vogel pushes them out to their full reach he finds that they are even then hidden by the sand. The crawler's eyes are blinded; its antennae are buried. They are drowning in sand. Whole dunes are descending on them. "I've never seen anything like this," Vogel says again. "You can't imagine it, Johnny. It hasn't been going on five minutes and we must be under three or four meters of sand already." The crawler's engine strains to free them. "Johnny? I can't hear you, Johnny. Come in, Johnny." All is silent on the ship-to-crawler transmission belt. "Hey, Houston," Vogel says, "we've got this goddamned sandstorm going, and I seem to have lost contact with the ship. Can you raise him for us?" Houston does not reply. "Mission Control, are you reading me?" Vogel asks. He still has some idea of setting up a crawler-to-Earth-to-ship relay, but slowly it occurs to him that he has lost contact with Earth as well. All transmissions have ceased. Sweating suddenly in his spacesuit, Vogel shouts into the microphone, jiggles controls, plugs in the fail-safe communications banks only to find that everything has failed; sand has invaded the crawler and holds them in a deadly blanket. "Impossible," Richardson says. "Since when is sand an insulator for radio waves?" Vogel shrugs. "It isn't a matter of insulation, dummy. It's a matter of total systems breakdown. I don't know why." They must be ten meters underneath the sand now. Entombed. Vogel pounds the hatch, thinking that if they can get out of the crawler somehow they can dig their way to the surface through the loose sand, and then—and then what? Walk back ninety kilometers to the ship? Their suits carry thirty-six-hour breathing supplies. They would have to average two and a half kilometers an hour, over ragged cratered country, in order to get there in time; and with this storm raging their chances of surviving long enough to hike a single kilometer are dismal. Nor does Oxenshuer have a backup crawler in which he could come out to rescue them, even if he knew their plight; there is only the flimsy little one-man vehicle that they use for short-range geological field trips in the vicinity of the ship.

"You know what?" Vogel says. "We're dead men, Bud."
Richardson shakes his head vehemently. "Don't talk garbage.
We'll wait out the storm, and then we'll get the hell out of here.
Meanwhile we better just pray." There is no conviction in his
voice, however. How will they know when the storm is over?
Already they lie deep below the new surface of the Martian plain,
and everything is snug and tranquil where they are. Tons of sand
hold the crawler's hatch shut. There is no escape. Vogel is right:
they are dead men. The only remaining question is one of time.
Shall they wait for the crawler's air supply to exhaust itself, or
shall they take some more immediate step to hasten the inevitable
end, going out honorably and quickly and without pain? Here
Oxenshuer's vision falters. He does not know how the trapped
men chose to handle the choreography of their deaths. He knows
only that whatever their decision was, it must have been reached
without bitterness or panic, and that the manner of their departure
was calm. The vision fades. He lies alone in the dark. The last of
the drunkenness has burned itself from his mind.

"Come on," Matt said. "Let's do some wrestling."
    It was a crisp winter morning, not cold, a day of clear, hard
light. Matt took him downtown, and for the first time Oxenshuer
entered one of the tall brick-faced buildings of the labyrinth
streets. Inside was a large, bare gymnasium, unheated, with
bleak yellow walls and threadbare purple mats on the floor. Will
and Nick were already there. Their voices echoed in the cavernous room. Quickly Matt stripped down to his undershorts. He
looked even bigger naked than clothed; his muscles were thick
and rounded, his chest was formidably deep, his thighs were
pillars. A dense covering of fair curly hair sprouted everywhere
on him, even his back and shoulders. He stood at least two
meters tall and must have weighed close to 110 kilos. Oxenshuer,
tall but not nearly so tall as Matt, well built but at least 20 kilos
lighter, felt himself badly outmatched. He was quick and agile, at
any rate: perhaps those qualities would serve him. He tossed his
clothing aside.
    Matt looked him over closely. "Not bad," he said. "Could
use a little more meat on the bones."
    "Got to fatten him up some for the Feast, I guess," Will said.
He grinned amiably. The three men laughed; the remark seemed
less funny to Oxenshuer.

Matt signaled to Nick, who took a flask of wine from a locker and handed it to him. Uncorking it, Matt drank deeply and passed the flask to Oxenshuer. It was different from the usual table stuff: thicker, sweeter, almost a sacramental wine. Oxenshuer gulped it down. Then they went to the center mat.

They hunkered into crouches and circled one another tentatively, outstretched arms probing for an opening. Oxenshuer made the first move. He slipped in quickly, finding Matt surprisingly slow on his guard and unsophisticated in defensive technique. Nevertheless, the big man was able to break Oxenshuer's hold with one fierce toss of his body, shaking him off easily and sending him sprawling violently backward. Again they circled. Matt seemed willing to allow Oxenshuer every initiative. Warily Oxenshuer advanced, feinted toward Matt's shoulders, seized an arm instead; but Matt placidly ignored the gambit and somehow pivoted so that Oxenshuer was caught in the momentum of his own onslaught, thrown off balance, vulnerable to a bearhug. Matt forced him to the floor. For thirty seconds or so Oxenshuer stubbornly resisted him, arching his body; then Matt pinned him. They rolled apart and Nick proffered the wine again. Oxenshuer drank, gasping between pulls. "You've got good moves," Matt told him. But he took the second fall even more quickly, and the third with not very much greater effort. "Don't worry," Will murmured to Oxenshuer as they left the gym. "The day of the Feast, the saint will guide you against him."

Every night, now, he drinks heavily, until his face is flushed and his mind is dizzied. Matt, Will, and Nick are always close beside him, seeing to it that his cup never stays dry for long. The wine makes him hazy and groggy, and frequently he has visions as he lies in a stupor on his bed, recovering. He sees Claire Vogel's face glowing in the dark, and the sight of her wrings his heart with love. He engages in long dreamlike imaginary dialogues with the Speaker on the nature of ecstatic communion. He sees himself dancing in the god-house with the other city folk, dancing himself to exhaustion and ecstasy. He is even visited by St. Dionysus. That saint has a youthful and oddly innocent appearance, with a heavy belly, plump thighs, curling golden hair, a flowing golden beard; he looks like a rejuvenated Santa Claus. "Come," he says softly. "Let's go to the ocean.'" He takes Oxenshuer's hand and they drift through the silent dark

streets, toward the desert, across the swirling dunes, floating in
the night, until they reach a broad-bosomed sea, moonlight
blazing on its surface like cold white fire. What sea is this? The
saint says, "This is the sea that brought you to the world, the
undying sea that carries every mortal into life. Why do you ever
leave the sea? Here. Step into it with me." Oxenshuer enters.
The water is warm, comforting, oddly viscous. He gives himself
to it, ankle-deep, shin-deep, thigh-deep; he hears a low murmuring
song rising from the gentle waves, and he feels all sorrow going
from him, all pain, all sense of himself as a being apart from
others. Bathers bob on the breast of the sea. Look: Dave Vogel is
here, and Claire, and his parents, and his grandparents, and
thousands more whom he does not know, millions, even, a horde
stretching far out from shore, all the progeny of Adam, even
Adam himself, yes, and Mother Eve, her soft pink body aglow in
the water. "Rest," the saint whispers. "Drift. Float. Surrender.
Sleep. Give yourself to the ocean, dear John." Oxenshuer asks if
he will find God in this ocean. The saint replies, "God *is* the
ocean. And God is within you. He always has been. The ocean is
God. You are God. I am God. God is everywhere, John, and we
are His indivisible atoms. God is everywhere. But before all else,
God is within you."

What does the Speaker say? The Speaker speaks Freudian wisdom. Within us all, he says, there dwells a force, an entity—call
it the unconscious; it's as good a name as any—that from its
hiding place dominates and controls our lives, though its workings are mysterious and opaque to us. A god within our skulls.
We have lost contact with that god, the Speaker says; we are
unable to reach it or to comprehend its powers, and so we are
divided against ourselves, cut off from the chief source of our
strength and cut off, too, from one another: the god that is within
me no longer has a way to reach the god that is within you,
though you and I both came out of the same primordial ocean,
out of that sea of divine unconsciousness in which all being is
one. If we could tap that force, the Speaker says, if we could
make contact with that hidden god, if we could make it rise into
consciousness or allow ourselves to submerge into the realm of
unconsciousness, the split in our souls would be healed and we
would at last have full access to our godhood. Who knows what
kind of creatures we would become then? We would speak, mind

to mind. We would travel through space or time, merely by willing it. We would work miracles. The errors of the past could be undone; the patterns of old griefs could be rewoven. We might be able to do anything, the Speaker says, once we have reached that hidden god and transformed ourselves into the gods we were meant to be. Anything. Anything. Anything.

This is the dawn of the day of the Feast. All night long the drums and incantations have resounded through the city; he has been alone in the house, for not even the children were there; everyone was dancing in the plaza, and only he, the uninitiated, remained excluded from the revels. Much of the night he could not sleep. He thought of using wine to lull himself, but he feared the visions the wine might bring, and let the flask be. Now it is early morning, and he must have slept, for he finds himself fluttering up from slumber, but he does not remember having slipped down into it. He sits up. He hears footsteps, someone moving through the house. "John? You awake, John?" Matt's voice. "In here," Oxenshuer calls.

They enter his room: Matt, Will, Nick. Their robes are spotted with splashes of red wine, and their faces are gaunt, eyes red-rimmed and unnaturally bright; plainly they have been up all night. Behind their fatigue, though, Oxenshuer perceives exhilaration. They are high, very high, almost in an ecstatic state already, and it is only the dawn of the day of the Feast. He sees that their fingers are trembling. Their bodies are tense with expectation.

"We've come for you," Matt says. "Here. Put this on."

He tosses Oxenshuer a robe similar to theirs. All this time Oxenshuer has continued to wear his mundane clothes in the city, making him a marked man, a conspicuous outsider. Naked, he gets out of bed and picks up his undershorts, but Matt shakes his head. Today, he says, only robes are worn. Oxenshuer nods and pulls the robe over his bare body. When he is robed he steps forward; Matt solemnly embraces him, a strong warm hug, and then Will and Nick do the same. The four men leave the house. The long shadows of dawn stretch across the avenue that leads to the labyrinth; the mountains beyond the city are tipped with red. Far ahead, where the avenue gives way to the narrower streets, a tongue of black smoke can be seen licking the sky. The reverberations of the music batter the sides of the buildings. Oxenshuer feels a strange onrush of confidence and is certain he could negotiate the labyrinth unaided this morning; as they reach its outer border he is actually walking ahead of the others, but sudden confusion confounds him, an inability to distinguish one winding street from another comes over him, and he drops back in silence, allowing Matt to take the lead.

Ten minutes later they reach the plaza.

It presents a crowded, chaotic scene. All the city folk are there, some dancing, some singing, some beating on drums or blowing into trumpets, some lying sprawled in exhaustion. Despite the chill in the air, many robes hang open, and more than a few of the citizens have discarded their clothing entirely. Children run about, squealing and playing tag. Along the front of the dining hall a series of wine barrels has been installed, and the wine gushes freely from the spigots, drenching those who thrust cups forward or simply push their lips to the flow. To the rear, before the house of the Speaker, a wooden platform has sprouted, and the Speaker and the city elders sit enthroned upon it. A gigantic bonfire has been kindled in the center of the plaza, fed by logs from an immense woodpile—hauled no doubt from some storehouse in the labyrinth—that occupies some twenty square meters. The heat of this blaze is enormous, and it is the smoke from the bonfire that Oxenshuer was able to see from the city's edge.

His arrival in the plaza serves as a signal. Within moments, all is still. The music dies away; the dancing stops; the singers grow quiet; no one moves. Oxenshuer, flanked by his sponsors Nick and Will and preceded by his brother Matt, advances uneasily toward the throne of the Speaker. The old man rises and makes a gesture, evidently a blessing. "Dionysus receives you into his bosom," the Speaker says, his resonant voice traveling far across the plaza. "Drink, and let the saint heal your soul. Drink, and let the holy ocean engulf you. Drink. Drink."

"Drink," Matt says, and guides him toward the barrels. A girl of about fourteen, naked, sweat-shiny, wine-soaked, hands him a cup. Oxenshuer fills it and puts it to his lips. It is the thick, sweet wine, the sacramental wine that he had had on the morning he had practiced wrestling with Matt. It slides easily down his throat; he reaches for more, and then for more when that is gone.

At a signal from the Speaker, the music begins again. The frenzied dancing resumes. Three naked men hurl more logs on the fire and it blazes up ferociously, sending sparks nearly as high as the tip of the cross above the church. Nick and Will and Matt lead Oxenshuer into a circle of dancers who are moving in a whirling, dizzying step around the fire, shouting, chanting, stamping against the cobbles, flinging their arms aloft. At first Oxenshuer is put off by the uninhibited corybantic motions and finds himself self-conscious about imitating them, but as the wine reaches his brain he sheds all embarrassment, and prances with as much gusto as the others: he ceases to be a spectator of himself and becomes fully a participant. Whirl. Stamp. Fling. Shout. Whirl. Stamp. Fling. Shout. The dance centrifuges his mind; pools of blood collect at the walls of his skull and flush the convolutions of his cerebellum as he spins. The heat of the fire makes his skin glow. He sings:

Tell the saint to heat my heart
Tell the saint to give me breath
Tell the saint to quench my thirst

Thirst. When he has been dancing so long that his breath is fire in his throat, he staggers out of the circle and helps himself freely at a spigot. His greed for the thick wine astonishes him. It is as if he has been parched for centuries, every cell of his body shrunken and withered, and only the wine can restore him.

Back to the circle again. His head throbs; his bare feet slap the cobbles; his arms claw the sky. This is the god whose name is music. This is the god whose soul is wine. There are ninety or a hundred people in the central circle of dancers now, and other circles have formed in the corners of the plaza, so that the entire square is a nest of dazzling interlocking vortices of motion. He is being drawn into these vortices, sucked out of himself; he is losing all sense of himself as a discrete individual entity.

Leaping shouting singing stamping
Rising climbing flying soaring
Melting joining loving blazing
Singing soaring joining loving

"Come," Matt murmurs. "It's time for us to do some wrestling."
He discovers that they have constructed a wrestling pit in the far corner of the plaza, over in front of the church. It is square, four low wooden borders about ten meters long on each side,

filled with the coarse sand of the desert. The Speaker has shifted
his lofty seat so that he now faces the pit; everyone else is
crowded around the place of the wrestling, and all dancing has
once again stopped. The crowd opens to admit Matt and Oxenshuer.
Not far from the pit Matt shucks his robe; his powerful naked
body glistens with sweat. Oxenshuer, after only a moment's
hesitation, strips also. They advance toward the entrance of the
pit. Before they enter, a boy brings them each a flask of wine.
Oxenshuer, already feeling wobbly and hazy from drink, wonders
what more wine will do to his physical coordination, but he takes
the flask and drinks from it in great gulping swigs. In moments it
is empty. A young girl offers him another. "Just take a few
sips," Matt advises. "In honor of the god." Oxenshuer does as
he is told. Matt is sipping from a second flask too; without
warning, Matt grins and flings the contents of his flask over
Oxenshuer. Instantly Oxenshuer retaliates. A great cheer goes up;
both men are soaked with the sticky red wine. Matt laughs
heartily and claps Oxenshuer on the back. They enter the wrestling pit.

> Wine in my heart today,
> Blood in my throat today,
> Fire in my soul today,
> All praise, O God, to thee.

They circle one another warily. Brother against brother. Romulus
and Remus, Cain and Abel, Osiris and Set: the ancient ritual, the
timeless conflict. Neither man offers. Oxenshuer feels heavy with
wine, his brain clotted, and yet a strange lightness also possesses
him; each time he puts his foot down against the sand the contact
gives him a little jolt of ecstasy. He is excitingly aware of being
alive, mobile, vigorous. The sensation grows and possesses him,
and he rushes forward suddenly, seizes Matt, tries to force him
down. They struggle in almost motionless rigidity. Matt will not
fall, but his counterthrust is unavailing against Oxenshuer. They
stand locked, body against sweat-slick, wine-drenched body, and
after perhaps two minutes of intense tension they give up their
holds by unvoiced agreement, backing away trembling from one
another. They circle again. Brother. Brother. Abel. Cain. Oxenshuer
crouches. Extends his hands, groping for a hold. Again they leap
toward one another. Again they grapple and freeze. This time

Matt's arms pass like bands around Oxenshuer, and he tries to lift Oxenshuer from the ground and hurl him down. Oxenshuer does not budge. Veins swell in Matt's forehead, and, Oxenshuer suspects, in his own. Faces grow crimson. Muscles throb with sustained effort. Matt gasps, loosens his grip, tries to step back; instantly Oxenshuer steps to one side of the bigger man, catches his arm, pulls him close. Once more they hug. Each in turn, they sway but do not topple. Wine and exertion blur Oxenshuer's vision; he is intoxicated with strain. Heaving, grabbing, twisting, shoving, he goes around and around the pit with Matt, until abruptly he experiences a dimming of perception, a sharp moment of blackout, and when his senses return to him he is stunned to find himself wrestling not with Matt but with Dave Vogel. Childhood friend, rival in love, comrade in space. Vogel, closer to him than any brother of the flesh, now here in the pit with him: thin, sandy hair, snub nose, heavy brows, thick-muscled shoulders. "Dave!" Oxenshuer cries. "Oh, Christ, Dave! Dave!" He throws his arms around the other man. Vogel gives him a mild smile and tumbles to the floor of the pit. "Dave!" Oxenshuer shouts, falling on him. "How did you get here, Dave?" He covers Vogel's body with his own. He embraces him with a terrible grip. He murmurs Vogel's name, whispering in wonder, and lets a thousand questions tumble out. Does Vogel reply? Oxenshuer is not certain. He thinks he hears answers, but they do not match the questions. Then Oxenshuer feels fingers tapping his back. "Okay, John," Will is saying. "You've pinned him fair and square. It's all over. Get up, man."

"Here, I'll give you a hand," says Nick.

In confusion Oxenshuer rises. Matt lies sprawled in the sand, gasping for breath, rubbing the side of his neck, nevertheless still grinning. "That was one hell of a press," Matt says. "That something you learned in college?"

"Do we wrestle another fall now?" Oxenshuer asks.

"No need. We go to the god-house now," Will tells him. They help Matt up. Flasks of wine are brought to them; Oxenshuer gulps greedily. The four of them leave the pit, pass through the opening crowd, and walk toward the church.

Oxenshuer has never been in here before. Except for a sort of altar at the far end, the huge building is wholly empty: no pews, no chairs, no chapels, no pulpit, no choir. A mysterious light

filters through the stained-glass windows and suffuses the vast
open interior space. The Speaker has already arrived; he stands
before the altar. Oxenshuer, at a whispered command from Matt,
kneels in front of him. Matt kneels to Oxenshuer's left; Nick and
Will drop down behind them. Organ music, ghostly, ethereal,
begins to filter from concealed grillwork. The congregation is
assembling; Oxenshuer hears the rustle of people behind him,
coughs, some murmuring. The familiar hymns soon echo through
the church.

> I go to the god's house and his fire consumes me
> I cry the god's name and his thunder deafens me
> I take the god's cup and his wine dissolves me

Wine. The Speaker offers Oxenshuer a golden chalice. Oxenshuer
sips. A different wine: cold, thin. Behind him a new hymn
commences, one that he has never heard before, in a language he
does not understand. Greek? The rhythms are angular and fierce;
this is the music of the Bacchantes, this is an Orphic song, alien
and frightening at first, then oddly comforting. Oxenshuer is
barely conscious. He comprehends nothing. They are offering
him communion. A wafer on a silver dish: dark bread, crisp,
incised with an unfamiliar symbol. Take; eat. This is my body.
This is my blood. More wine. Figures moving around him, other
communicants coming forward. He is losing all sense of time and
place. He is departing from the physical dimension and drifting
across the breast of an ocean, a great warm sea, a gentle
undulating sea that bears him easily and gladly. He is aware of
light, warmth, hugeness, weightlessness; but he is aware of
nothing tangible. The wine. The wafer. A drug in the wine,
perhaps? He slides from the world and into the universe. This is
my body. This is my blood. This is the experience of wholeness
and unity. I take the god's cup and his wine dissolves me. How
calm it is here. How empty. There's no one here, not even me.
And everything radiates a pure warm light. I float. I go forth. I.
I. I. John Oxenshuer. John Oxenshuer does not exist. John
Oxenshuer is the universe. The universe is John Oxenshuer. This
is the god whose soul is wine. This is the god whose name is
music. This is the god who burns like fire. Sweet flame of
oblivion. The cosmos is expanding like a balloon. Growing.
Growing. Go, child, swim out to God. Jesus waits. The saint, the

mad saint, the boozy old god who is a saint, will lead you to bliss, dear John. Make yourself whole. Make yourself into nothingness. I go to the god's house and his fire consumes me. Go. Go. Go. I cry the god's name and his thunder deafens me. *Dionysus! Dionysus!*

All things dissolve. All things become one.

This is Mars. Oxenshuer, running his ship on manual, lets it dance lightly down the final 500 meters to the touchdown site, touching up the yaw and pitch, moving serenely through the swirling red clouds that his rockets are kicking free. Contact light. Engine stop. Engine arm, off.

—All right, Houston, I've landed at Gulliver Base.

His signal streaks across space. Patiently he waits out the lag and gets his reply from Mission Control at last:

—Roger. Are you ready for systems checkout prior to EVA?

—Getting started on it right now, Houston.

He runs through his routines quickly, with the assurance born of total familiarity. All is well aboard the ship; its elegant mechanical brain ticks beautifully and flawlessly. Now Oxenshuer wriggles into his backpack, struggling a little with the cumbersome life-support system; putting it on without any fellow astronauts to help him is more of a chore than he expected, even under the light Martian gravity. He checks out his primary oxygen supply, his ventilating system, his water-support loop, his communications system. Helmeted and gloved and fully sealed, he exists now within a totally self-sufficient pocket universe. Unshipping his power shovel, he tests its compressed-air supply. All systems go.

—Do I have a go for cabin depressurization, Houston?

—You are go for cabin depress, John. It's all yours. Go for cabin depress.

He gives the signal and waits for the pressure to bleed down. Dials flutter. At last he can open the hatch. We have a go for EVA, John. He hoists his power shovel to his shoulder and makes his way carefully down the ladder. Boots bite into red sand. It is midday on Mars in this longitude, and the purple sky has a warm auburn glow. Oxenshuer approaches the burial mound. He is pleased to discover that he has relatively little excavating to do; the force of his rockets during the descent has stripped much of the overburden from his friends' tomb. Swiftly he sets the shovel in place and begins to cut away the remaining sand. Within minutes the glistening dome of the crawler is visible in several places. Now Oxenshuer works more delicately, scraping with care until he has revealed the entire dome. He flashes his light through it and sees the bodies of Vogel and Richardson. They are unhelmeted, and their suits are open: casual dress, the best outfit for dying. Vogel sits at the crawler's controls, Richardson lies just behind him on the floor of the vehicle. Their faces are dry, almost fleshless, but their features are still expressive, and Oxenshuer realizes that they must have died peaceful deaths, accepting the end in tranquility. Patiently he works to lift the crawler's dome. At length the catch yields and the dome swings upward. Climbing in, he slips his arms around Dave Vogel's body and draws it out of the spacesuit. So light: a mummy, an effigy. Vogel seems to have no weight at all. Easily Oxenshuer carries the parched corpse over to the ship. With Vogel in his arms he ascends the ladder. Within, he breaks out the flag-sheathed plastic container NASA has provided and tenderly wraps it around the body. He stows Vogel safely in the ship's hold. Then he returns to the crawler to get Bud Richardson. Within an hour the entire job is done.

—Mission accomplished, Houston.

The landing capsule plummets perfectly into the Pacific. The recovery ship, only three kilometers away, makes for the scene while the helicopters move into position over the bobbing spaceship. Frogmen come forth to secure the flotation collar: the old, old routine. In no time at all the hatch is open. Oxenshuer emerges. The helicopter closest to the capsule lowers its recovery basket, Oxenshuer disappears into the capsule, returning a moment later with Vogel's shrouded body, which he passes across to the swimmers. They load it into the basket and it goes up to the helicopter. Richardson's body follows, and then Oxenshuer himself.

The President is waiting on the deck of the recovery ship. With him are the two widows, black-garbed, dry-eyed, standing straight and firm. The President offers Oxenshuer a warm grin and grips his hand.

—A beautiful job, Captain Oxenshuer. The whole world is grateful to you.

—Thank you, sir.

Oxenshuer embraces the widows. Richardson's wife first: a

hug and some soft murmurs of consolation. Then he draws Claire close, conscious of the television cameras. Chastely he squeezes her. Chastely he presses his cheek briefly to hers.

—I had to bring him back, Claire. I couldn't rest until I recovered those bodies.

—You didn't need to, John.

—I did it for you.

He smiles at her. Her eyes are bright and loving.

There is a ceremony on deck. The President bestows posthumous medals on Richardson and Vogel. Oxenshuer wonders whether the medals will be attached to the bodies, like morgue tags, but no, he gives them to the widows. Then Oxenshuer receives a medal for his dramatic return to Mars. The President makes a little speech. Oxenshuer pretends to listen, but his eyes are on Claire more often than not.

With Claire sitting beside him, he sets forth once more out of Los Angeles via the San Bernardino Freeway, eastward through the plastic suburbs, through Alhambra and Azusa, past the Covina Hills Forest Lawn, through San Bernardino and Banning and Indio, out into the desert. It is a bright late-winter day, and recent rains have greened the hills and coaxed the cacti into bloom. He keeps a sharp watch for landmarks: flatlands, dry lakes.

—I think this is the place. In fact, I'm sure of it.

He leaves the freeway and guides the car northeastward. Yes, no doubt of it: there's the ancient lake bed, and there's his abandoned automobile, looking ancient also, rusted and corroded, its hood up, its wheels and engine stripped by scavengers long ago. He parks this car beside it, gets out, dons his backpack. He beckons to Claire.

—Let's go. We've got some hiking ahead of us.

She smiles timidly at him. She leaves the car and presses herself lightly against him, touching her lips to his. He begins to tremble.

—Claire. Oh, God, Claire.

—How far do we have to walk?

—Hours.

He gears his pace to hers. If necessary, they will camp overnight and go on into the city tomorrow, but he hopes they can get there before sundown. Claire is a strong hiker, and he is confident she can cover the distance in five or six hours, but there is always the possibility that he will fail to find the twin mesas. He has no compass points, no maps, nothing but his own intuitive sense of the city's location to guide him. They walk steadily northward. Neither of them says very much. Every half hour they pause to rest; he puts down his pack and she hands him the canteen. The air is mild and fragrant. Jackrabbits boldly accompany them. Blossoms are everywhere. Oxenshuer, transfigured by love, wants to leap and soar.

—We ought to be seeing those mesas soon.

—I hope so. I'm starting to get tired, John.

—We can stop and make camp if you like.

—No. No. Let's keep going. It can't be much farther, can it?

They keep going. Oxenshuer calculates they have covered twelve or thirteen kilometers already. Even allowing for some straying from course, they should be getting at least a glimpse of the mesas by this time, and it troubles him that they are not in view. If he fails to find them in the next half hour, he will make camp, for he wants to avoid hiking after sundown.

Suddenly they breast a rise in the desert and the mesas come into view, two steep wedges of rock, dark gray against the sand. The shadows of late afternoon partially cloak them, but there is no mistaking them.

—There they are, Claire. Out there.

—Can you see the city?

—Not from this distance. We've come around from the side, somehow. But we'll be there before very long.

At a faster pace, now, they head down the gentle slope and into the flats. The mesas dominate the scene. Oxenshuer's heart pounds, not entirely from the strain of carrying his pack. Ahead wait Matt and Jean, Will and Nick, the Speaker, the god-house, the labyrinth. They will welcome Claire as his woman; they will give them a small house on the edge of the city; they will initiate her into their rites. Soon. Soon. The mesas draw near.

—Where's the city, John?

—Between the mesas.

—I don't see it.

—You can't really see it from the front. All that's visible is the palisade, and when you get very close you can see some rooftops above it.

—But I don't even see the palisade, John. There's just an open space between the mesas

—A shadow effect. The eye is easily tricked.

But it does seem odd to him. At twilight, yes, many deceptions are possible; nevertheless he has the clear impression from here that there is nothing but open space between the mesas. Can these be the wrong mesas? Hardly. Their shape is distinctive and unique; he could never confuse those two jutting slabs with other formations. The city, then? Where has the city gone? With each step he takes he grows more perturbed. He tries to hide his uneasiness from Claire, but she is tense, edgy, almost panicky now, repeatedly asking him what has happened, whether they are lost. He reassures her as best he can. This is the right place, he tells her. Perhaps it's an optical illusion that the city is invisible, or perhaps some other kind of illusion, the work of the city folk.

—Does that mean they might not want us, John? And they're hiding their city from us?

—I don't know, Claire.

—I'm frightened.

—Don't be. We'll have all the answers in just a few minutes.

When they are about 500 meters from the face of the mesas, Claire's control breaks. She whimpers and darts forward, sprinting through the cacti toward the opening between the mesas. He calls out to her, tells her to wait for him, but she runs on, vanishing into the deepening shadows. Hampered by his unwieldy pack, he stumbles after her, gasping for breath. He sees her disappear between the mesas. Weak and dizzy, he follows her path, and in a short while comes to the mouth of the canyon.

There is no city.

He does not see Claire.

He calls her name. Only mocking echos respond. In wonder he penetrates the canyon, looking up at the steep sides of the mesas, remembering streets, avenues, houses.

—Claire?

No one. Nothing. And now night is coming. He picks his way over the rocky, uneven ground until he reaches the far end of the canyon, and looks back at the mesas, and outward at the desert, and he sees no one. The city has swallowed her and the city is gone.

—Claire! Claire!

Silence.

He drops his pack wearily, sits for a long while, finally lays out his bedroll. He slips into it but does not sleep; he waits out the night, and when dawn comes he searches again for Claire, but there is no trace of her. All right. All right. He yields. He will ask no questions. He shoulders his pack and begins the long trek back to the highway.

By mid-morning he reaches his car. He looks back at the desert, ablaze with noon light. Then he gets in and drives away.

He enters his apartment on Hollywood Boulevard. From here, so many months ago, he first set out for the desert; now all has come around to the beginning again. A thick layer of dust covers the cheap utilitarian furniture. The air is musty. All the blinds are drawn closed. He wanders aimlessly from hallway to living room, from living room to bedroom, from bedroom to kitchen, from kitchen to hallway. He kicks off his boots and sprawls out on the threadbare living-room carpet, face down, eyes closed. So tired. So drained. I'll rest a bit.

"John?"

It is the Speaker's voice.

"Let me alone," Oxenshuer says. "I've lost her. I've lost you. I think I've lost myself."

"You're wrong. Come to us, John."

"I did. You weren't there."

"Come now. Can't you feel the city calling you? The Feast is over. It's time to settle down among us."

"I couldn't find you."

"You were still lost in dreams, then. Come now. Come. The saint calls you. Jesus calls you. Claire calls you."

"Claire?"

"Claire," he says.

Slowly Oxenshuer gets to his feet. He crosses the room and pulls the blinds open. This window faces Hollywood Boulevard; but, looking out, he sees only the red plains of Mars, eroded and cratered, glowing in purple noon light. Vogel and Richardson are out there, waving to him. Smiling. Beckoning. The faceplates of their helmets glitter by the cold gleam of the stars. Come on, they call to him. We're waiting for you. Oxenshuer returns their greeting and walks to another window. He sees a lifeless wasteland here too. Mars again, or is it only the Mojave Desert? He is unable to tell. All is dry, all is desolate, all is beautiful with the serene transcendent beauty of desolation. He sees Claire in the middle distance. Her back is to him; she is moving at a steady, confident pace toward the twin mesas. Between the mesas lies the City of the Word of God, golden and radiant in the warm sunlight. Oxenshuer nods. This is the right moment. He will go to her. He will go to the city. The Feast of St. Dionysus is over, and the city calls to him.

Bring us together. Lead us to the ocean.
Help us to swim. Give us to drink.

Wine in my heart today,
Blood in my throat today,
Fire in my soul today,

All praise, O God, to thee.

Oxenshuer runs in long loping strides. He sees the mesas; he sees the city's palisade. The sound of far-off chanting throbs in his ears. "This way, brother!" Matt shouts. "Hurry, John!" Claire cries. He runs. He stumbles, and recovers, and runs again. Wine in my heart today. Fire in my soul today. "God is everywhere," the saint tells him. "But before all else, God is within you." The desert is a sea, the great warm cradling ocean, the undying mother sea of all things, and Oxenshuer enters it gladly, and drifts, and floats, and lets it take hold of him and carry him wherever it will.

CAUGHT IN THE ORGAN DRAFT

LOOK THERE, KATE, down by the promenade. Two splendid seniors, walking side by side near the water's edge. They radiate power, authority, wealth, assurance. He's a judge, a senator, a corporation president, no doubt, and she's—what?—a professor emeritus of international law, let's say. There they go toward the plaza, moving serenely, smiling, nodding graciously to passersby. How the sunlight gleams in their white hair! I can barely stand the brilliance of that reflected aura: it blinds me, it stings my eyes. What are they, eighty, ninety, a hundred years old? At this distance they seem much younger—they hold themselves upright, their backs are straight, they might pass for being only fifty or sixty. But I can tell. Their confidence, their poise, mark them for what they are. And when they were nearer I could see their withered cheeks, their sunken eyes. No cosmetics can hide that. These two are old enough to be our great-grandparents. They were well past sixty before we were even born, Kate. How superbly their bodies function! But why not? We can guess at their medical histories. She's had at least three hearts, he's working on his fourth set of lungs, they apply for new kidneys every five years, their brittle bones are reinforced with hundreds of skeletal snips from the arms and legs of hapless younger folk, their dimming sensory apparatus is aided by countless nerve-grafts obtained the same way, their ancient arteries are freshly sheathed with sleek teflon. Ambulatory assemblages of second-

hand human parts, spliced here and there with synthetic or
mechanical organ substitutes, that's all they are. And what am I,
then, or you? Nineteen years old and vulnerable. In their eyes
I'm nothing but a ready stockpile of healthy organs, waiting to
serve their needs. Come here, son. What a fine strapping young
man you are! Can you spare a kidney for me? A lung? A choice
little segment of intestine? Ten centimeters of your ulnar nerve? I
need a few pieces of you, lad. You won't deny a distinguished
elder like me what I ask, will you? *Will you?*

Today my draft notice, a small crisp document, very official-
looking, came shooting out of the data slot when I punched for
my morning mail. I've been expecting it all spring; no surprise,
no shock, actually rather an anticlimax now that it's finally here.
In six weeks I am to report to Transplant House for my final
physical exam—only a formality, they wouldn't have drafted me
if I didn't already rate top marks as organ-reservoir potential—
and then I go on call. The average call time is about two months.
By autumn they'll be carving me up. Eat, drink, and be merry,
for soon comes the surgeon to my door.

A straggly band of senior citizens is picketing the central headquarters of the League for Bodily Sanctity. It's a counterdemon-
stration, an anti-anti-transplant protest, the worst kind of political
statement, feeding on the ugliest of negative emotions. The
demonstrators carry glowing signs that say:

BODILY SANCTITY—OR BODILY SELFISHNESS?

And:

YOU OWE YOUR LEADERS YOUR VERY LIVES

And:

LISTEN TO THE VOICE OF EXPERIENCE

  The picketers are low-echelon seniors, barely across the quali-
fying line, the ones who can't really be sure of getting transplants. No wonder they're edgy about the League. Some of them
are in wheelchairs and some are encased right up to the eyebrows

in portable life-support systems. They croak and shout bitter invective and shake their fists. Watching the show from an upper window of the League building, I shiver with fear and dismay. These people don't just want my kidneys or my lungs. They'd take my eyes, my liver, my pancreas, my heart, anything they might happen to need.

I talked it over with my father. He's forty-five years old—too old to have been personally affected by the organ draft, too young to have needed any transplants yet. That puts him in a neutral position, so to speak, except for one minor factor: his transplant status is 5-G. That's quite high on the eligibility list, not the top-priority class but close enough. If he fell ill tomorrow and the Transplant Board ruled that his life would be endangered if he didn't get a new heart or lung or kidney, he'd be given one practically immediately. Status like that simply has to influence his objectivity on the whole organ issue. Anyway, I told him I was planning to appeal and maybe even to resist. "Be reasonable," he said, "be rational, don't let your emotions run away with you. Is it worth jeopardizing your whole future over a thing like this? After all, not everybody who's drafted loses vital organs."

"Show me the statistics," I said. "Show me."

He didn't know the statistics. It was his impression that only about a quarter or a fifth of the draftees actually got an organ call. That tells you how closely the older generation keeps in touch with the situation—and my father's an educated man, articulate, well-informed. Nobody over the age of thirty-five that I talked to could show me any statistics. So I showed them. Out of a League brochure, it's true, but based on certified National Institute of Health reports. Nobody escapes. They always clip you, once you qualify. The need for young organs inexorably expands to match the pool of available organpower. In the long run they'll get us all and chop us to bits. That's probably what they want, anyway. To rid themselves of the younger members of the species, always so troublesome, by cannibalizing us for spare parts, and recycling us, lung by lung, pancreas by pancreas, through their own deteriorating bodies.

Fig. 4. On March 23, 1964, this dog's own liver was removed and replaced with the liver of a nonrelated mongrel donor. The animal was treated with azathioprine for 4 months and all therapy then stopped. He remains in perfect health 6⅔ years after transplantation.

The war goes on. This is, I think, its fourteenth year. Of course they're beyond the business of killing now. They haven't had any field engagements since '93 or so, certainly none since the organ-draft legislation went into effect. The old ones can't afford to waste precious young bodies on the battlefield. So robots wage our territorial struggles for us, butting heads with a great metallic clank, laying land mines and twitching their sensors at the enemy's mines, digging tunnels beneath his screens, et cetera, et cetera. Plus, of course, the quasi-military activity—economic sanctions, third-power blockades, propaganda telecasts beamed as overrides from merciless orbital satellites, and stuff like that. It's a subtler war than the kind they used to wage: nobody dies. Still, it drains national resources. Taxes are going up again this year, the fifth or sixth year in a row, and they've just slapped a special Peace Surcharge on all metal-containing goods, on account of the copper shortage. There once was a time when we could hope that our crazy old leaders would die off or at least retire for reasons of health, stumbling away to their country villas with ulcers or shingles or scabies or scruples and allowing new young peacemakers to take office. But now they just go on and on, immortal and insane, our senators, our cabinet members, our generals, our planners. And their war goes on and on too, their absurd, incomprehensible, diabolical, self-gratifying war.

I know people my age or a little older who have taken asylum in Belgium or Sweden or Paraguay or one of the other countries where Bodily Sanctity laws have been passed. There are about twenty such countries, half of them the most progressive nations in the world and half of them the most reactionary. But what's the sense of running away? I don't want to live in exile. I'll stay here and fight.

Naturally they don't ask a draftee to give up his heart or his liver or some other organ essential to life, say his medulla oblongata. We haven't yet reached that stage of political enlightenment at which the government feels capable of legislating fatal conscription. Kidneys and lungs, the paired organs, the dispensable organs, are the chief targets so far. But if you study the history of

conscription over the ages you see that it can always be projected on a curve rising from rational necessity to absolute
lunacy. Give them a fingertip, they'll take an arm. Give them an
inch of bowel, they'll take your guts. In another fifty years
they'll be drafting hearts and stomachs and maybe even brains,
mark my words; let them get the technology of brain transplants
together and nobody's skull will be safe. It'll be human sacrifice
all over again. The only difference between us and the Aztecs is
one of method: we have anesthesia, we have antisepsis and
asepsis, we use scalpels instead of obsidian blades to cut out the
hearts of our victims.

MEANS OF OVERCOMING THE HOMOGRAFT REACTION

*The pathway that has led from the demonstration of the
immunological nature of the homograft reaction and its univer-
sality to the development of relatively effective but by no means
completely satisfactory means of overcoming it for therapeutic
purposes is an interesting one that can only be touched upon very
briefly. The year 1950 ushered in a new era in transplantation
immunobiology in which the discovery of various means of
weakening or abrogating a host's response to a homograft—such
as sublethal whole body X-irradiation, or treatment with certain
adrenal cortico-steroid hormones, notably cortisone—began to
influence the direction of the mainstream of research and engen-
der confidence that a workable clinical solution might not be too
far off. By the end of the decade, powerful immuno-suppressive
drugs, such as 6-mercaptopurine, had been shown to be capable
of holding in abeyance the reactivity of dogs to renal homografts,
and soon afterward this principle was successfully extended to
man.*

Is my resistance to the draft based on an ingrained abstract
distaste for tyranny in all forms or rather on the mere desire to
keep my body intact? Could it be both, maybe? Do I need an
idealistic rationalization at all? Don't I have an inalienable right
to go through my life wearing my own native-born kidneys?

The law was put through by an administration of old men. You
can be sure that all laws affecting the welfare of the young are the
work of doddering moribund ancients afflicted with angina pectoris,

atherosclerosis, prolapses of the infundibulum, fulminating ventricles, and dilated viaducts. The problem was this: not enough healthy young people were dying of highway accidents, successful suicide attempts, diving-board miscalculations, electrocutions, and football injuries; therefore there was a shortage of transplantable organs. An effort to restore the death penalty for the sake of creating a steady supply of state-controlled cadavers lost out in the courts. Volunteer programs of organ donation weren't working out too well, since most of the volunteers were criminals who signed up in order to gain early release from prison: a lung reduced your sentence by five years, a kidney got you three years off, and so on. The exodus of convicts from the jails under this clause wasn't so popular among suburban voters. Meanwhile there was an urgent and mounting need for organs; a lot of important seniors might in fact die if something didn't get done fast. So a coalition of senators from all four parties rammed the organ-draft measure through the upper chamber in the face of a filibuster threat from a few youth-oriented members. It had a much easier time in the House of Representatives, since nobody in the House ever pays much attention to the text of a bill up for a vote, and word had been circulated on this one that if it passed, everybody over sixty-five who had any political pull at all could count on living twenty or thirty extra years, which to a Representative means a crack at ten to fifteen extra terms of office. Naturally there have been court challenges, but what's the use? The average age of the eleven Justices of the Supreme Court is seventy-eight. They're human and mortal. They need our flesh. If they throw out the organ draft now, they're signing their own death warrants.

For a year and a half I was the chairman of the anti-draft campaign on our campus. We were the sixth or seventh local chapter of the League for Bodily Sanctity to be organized in this country, and we were real activists. Mainly we would march up and down in front of the draft board offices carrying signs proclaiming things like:

KIDNEY POWER

And:

A MAN'S BODY IS HIS CASTLE

And:

THE POWER TO CONSCRIPT ORGANS
IS THE POWER TO DESTROY LIVES

We never went in for the rough stuff, though, like bombing organ-transplant centers or hijacking refrigeration trucks. Peaceful agitation, that was our motto. When a couple of our members tried to swing us to a more violent policy, I delivered an extemporaneous two-hour speech arguing for moderation. Naturally I was drafted the moment I became eligible.

"I can understand your hostility to the draft," my college advisor said. "It's certainly normal to feel queasy about surrendering important organs of your body. But you ought to consider the countervailing advantages. Once you've given an organ you get a 6-A classification, Preferred Recipient, and you remain forever on the 6-A roster. Surely you realize that this means that if you ever need a transplant yourself, you'll automatically be eligible for one, even if your other personal and professional qualifications don't lift you to the optimum level. Suppose your career plans don't work out and you become a manual laborer, for instance. Ordinarily you wouldn't rate even a first look if you developed heart disease, but your Preferred Recipient status would save you. You'd get a new lease on life, my boy."

I pointed out the fallacy inherent in this. Which is that as the number of draftees increases, it will come to encompass a majority or even a totality of the population, and eventually everybody will have 6-A Preferred Recipient status by virtue of having donated, and the term Preferred Recipient will cease to have any meaning. A shortage of transplantable organs would eventually develop as each past donor stakes his claim to a transplant when his health fails, and in time they'd have to arrange the Preferred Recipients by order of personal and professional achievement anyway, for the sake of arriving at some kind of priorities within the 6-A class, and we'd be right back where we are now.

Fig. 7. The course of a patient who received antilymphocyte globulin (ALG) before and for the first 4 months after renal homotransplantation. The donor was an older brother. There was no early rejection. Prednisone therapy was started 40 days postoperatively. Note the insidious onset of late rejection after cessation of globulin therapy. This was treated by a moderate increase in the maintenance doses of steroids. This delayed complication occurred in only 2 of the first 20 recipients of intrafamilial homografts who were treated with ALG. It has been seen with about the same low frequency in subsequent cases. (By permission of Surg. Gynec. Obstet. *126 (1968): p. 1023).*

So I went down to Transplant House today, right on schedule, to take my physical. A couple of my friends thought I was making a tactical mistake by reporting at all; if you're going to resist, they said, resist at every point along the line. Make them drag you in for the physical. In purely idealistic (and ideological) terms I suppose they're right. But there's no need yet for me to start kicking up a fuss. Wait till they actually say, We need your kidney, young man. Then I can resist, if resistance is the course I ultimately choose. (Why am I wavering? Am I afraid of the damage to my career plans that resisting might do? Am I not entirely convinced of the injustice of the entire organ-draft system? I don't know. I'm not even sure that I *am* wavering. Reporting for your physical isn't really a sellout to the system.) I went, anyway. They tapped this and X-rayed that and peered into the other thing. Yawn, please. Bend over, please. Cough, please. Hold out your left arm, please. They marched me in front of a battery of diagnostat machines and I stood there hoping for the red light to flash—*tilt, get out of here!*—but I was, as expected, in perfect physical shape, and I qualified for call. Afterward I met Kate and we walked in the park and held hands and watched the glories of the sunset and discussed what I'll do, when and if the call comes. *If?* Wishful thinking, boy!

If your number is called you become exempt from military service, and they credit you with a special $750 tax deduction every year. Big deal.

Another thing they're very proud of is the program of voluntary donation of unpaired organs. This has nothing to do with the draft, which—thus far, at least—requisitions only paired organs,

organs that can be spared without loss of life. For the last twelve years it's been possible to walk into any hospital in the United States and sign a simple release form allowing the surgeons to slice you up. Eyes, lungs, heart, intestines, pancreas, liver, anything, you give it all to them. This process used to be known as suicide in a simpler era and it was socially disapproved of, especially in times of labor shortages. Now we have a labor surplus, because even though our population growth has been fairly slow since the middle of the century, the growth of labor-eliminating mechanical devices and processes has been quite rapid, even exponential. Therefore, to volunteer for this kind of total donation is considered a deed of the highest social utility, removing as it does a healthy young body from the overcrowded labor force and at the same time providing some elder statesman with the assurance that the supply of vital organs will not unduly diminish. Of course you have to be crazy to volunteer, but there's never been any shortage of lunatics in our society.

If you're not drafted by the age of twenty-one, through some lucky fluke, you're safe. And a few of us do slip through the net, I'm told. So far there are more of us in the total draft pool than there are patients in need of transplants. But the ratios are changing rapidly. The draft legislation is still relatively new. Before long they'll have drained the pool of eligible draftees, and then what? Birth rates nowadays are low; the supply of potential draftees is finite. But death rates are even lower; the demand for organs is essentially infinite. I can give you only one of my kidneys, if I am to survive; but you, as you live on and on, may require more than one kidney transplant. Some recipients may need five or six sets of kidneys or lungs before they finally get beyond hope of repair at age one-seventy or so. As those who've given organs come to requisition organs later on in life, the pressure on the under-twenty-one group will get even greater. Those in need of transplants will come to outnumber those who can donate organs, and everybody in the pool will get clipped. And then? Well, they could lower the draft age to seventeen or sixteen or even fourteen. But even that's only a short-term solution. Sooner or later, there won't be enough spare organs to go around.

*   *   *

Will I stay? Will I flee? Will I go to court? Time's running out. My call is sure to come up in another few weeks. I feel a tickling sensation in my back, now and then, as though somebody's quietly sawing at my kidneys.

Cannibalism. At Chou-kou-tien, Dragon Bone Hill, twenty-five miles south-west of Peking, paleontologists excavating a cave early in the twentieth century discovered the fossil skulls of Peking Man, *Pithecanthropus pekinensis*. The skulls had been broken away at the base, which led Franz Weidenreich, the director of the Dragon Bone Hill digs, to speculate that Peking Man was a cannibal who had killed his own kind, extracted the brains of his victims through openings in the base of their skulls, cooked and feasted on the cerebral meat—there were hearths and fragments of charcoal at the site—and left the skulls behind in the cave as trophies. To eat your enemy's flesh: to absorb his skills, his strengths, his knowledge, his achievements, his virtues. It took mankind five hundred thousand years to struggle upward from cannibalism. But we never lost the old craving, did we? There's still easy comfort to gain by devouring those who are younger, stronger, more agile than you. We've improved the techniques, is all. And so now they eat us raw, the old ones, they gobble us up, organ by throbbing organ. Is that really an improvement? At least Peking Man cooked his meat.

Our brave new society, where all share equally in the triumphs of medicine, and the deserving senior citizens need not feel that their merits and prestige will be rewarded only by a cold grave—we sing its praises all the time. How pleased everyone is about the organ draft! Except, of course, a few disgruntled draftees.

The ticklish question of priorities. Who gets the stockpiled organs? They have an elaborate system by which hierarchies are defined. Supposedly a big computer drew it up, thus assuring absolute godlike impartiality. You earn salvation through good works: accomplishments in career and benevolence in daily life win you points that nudge you up the ladder until you reach one of the high-priority classifications, 4-G or better. No doubt the classification system is impartial and is administered justly. But is it rational? Whose needs does it serve? In 1943, during World

War II, there was a shortage of the newly discovered drug penicillin among the American military forces in North Africa. Two groups of soldiers were most in need of its benefits: those who were suffering from infected battle wounds and those who had contracted venereal disease. A junior medical officer, working from self-evident moral principles, ruled that the wounded heroes were more deserving of treatment than the self-indulgent syphilitics. He was overruled by the medical officer in charge, who observed that the VD cases could be restored to active duty more quickly, if treated; besides, if they remained untreated they served as vectors of further infection. Therefore he gave them the penicillin and left the wounded groaning on their beds of pain. The logic of the battlefield, incontrovertible, unassailable.

The great chain of life. Little creatures in the plankton are eaten by larger ones, and the greater plankton falls prey to little fishes, and little fishes to bigger fishes, and so on up to the tuna and the dolphin and the shark. I eat the flesh of the tuna and I thrive and flourish and grow fat, and store up energy in my vital organs. And am eaten in turn by the shriveled wizened seniors. All life is linked. I see my destiny.

In the early days, rejection of the transplanted organ was the big problem. Such a waste! The body failed to distinguish between a beneficial though alien organ and an intrusive, hostile microorganism. The mechanism known as the immune response was mobilized to drive out the invader. At the point of invasion enzymes came into play, a brush-fire war designed to rip down and dissolve the foreign substances. White corpuscles poured in via the circulatory system, vigilant phagocytes on the march. Through the lymphatic network came antibodies, high-powered protein missiles. Before any technology of organ grafts could be developed, methods had to be devised to suppress the immune response. Drugs, radiation treatment, metabolic shock—one way or another, the organ-rejection problem was long ago conquered. I can't conquer my draft-rejection problem. Aged and rapacious legislators, I reject you and your legislation.

My call notice came today. They'll need one of my kidneys. The usual request. "You're lucky," somebody said at lunchtime. "They might have wanted a lung."

*   *   *

Kate and I walk into the green glistening hills and stand among the blossoming oleanders and corianders and frangipani and whatever. How good it is to be alive, to breathe this fragrance, to show our bodies to the bright sun! Her skin is tawny and glowing. Her beauty makes me weep. She will not be spared. None of us will be spared. I go first, then she, or is it she ahead of me? Where will they make the incision? Here, on her smooth rounded back? Here, on the flat taut belly? I can see the high priest standing over the altar. At the first blaze of dawn his shadow falls across her. The obsidian knife that is clutched in his upraised hand has a terrible fiery sparkle. The choir offers up a discordant hymn to the god of blood. The knife descends.

My last chance to escape across the border. I've been up all night, weighing the options. There's no hope of appeal. Running away leaves a bad taste in my mouth. Father, friends, even Kate, all say stay, stay, stay, face the music. The hour of decision. Do I really have a choice? I have no choice. When the time comes, I'll surrender peacefully.

I report to Transplant House for conscriptive donative surgery in three hours.

After all, he said coolly, what's a kidney? I'll still have another one, you know. And if that one malfunctions, I can always get a replacement. I'll have Preferred Recipient status, 6-A, for what that's worth. But I won't settle for my automatic 6-A. I know what's going to happen to the priority system; I'd better protect myself. I'll go into politics. I'll climb. I'll attain upward mobility out of enlightened self-interest, right? Right. I'll become so important that society will owe me a thousand transplants. And one of these years I'll get that kidney back. Three or four kidneys, fifty kidneys, as many as I need. A heart or two. A few lungs. A pancreas, a spleen, a liver. They won't be able to refuse me anything. I'll show them. I'll show them. I'll out-senior the seniors. There's your Bodily Sanctity activist for you, eh? I suppose I'll have to resign from the League. Goodbye, idealism. Goodbye, moral superiority. Goodbye, kidney. Goodbye, goodbye, goodbye.

*   *   *

It's done. I've paid my debt to society. I've given up unto the powers that be my humble pound of flesh. When I leave the hospital in a couple of days, I'll carry a card testifying to my new 6-A status.

Top priority for the rest of my life.
Why, I might live for a thousand years.

$$\left\{ \begin{array}{c} \text{NOW} + n \\ \text{NOW} - n \end{array} \right\}$$

ALL HAD BEEN so simple, so elegant, so profitable for ourselves. And then we met the lovely Selene and nearly were undone. She came into our lives during our regular transmission hour on Wednesday, October 7, 1987, between six and seven P.M. Central European Time. The moneymaking hour. I was in satisfactory contact with myself and also with myself. (Now − n) was due on the line first, and then I would hear from (now + n).

I was primed for some kind of trouble. I knew trouble was coming, because on Monday, while I was receiving messages from the me of Wednesday, there came an inexplicable and unexplained break in communications. As a result I did not get data from (now + n) concerning the prices of the stocks in our carryover portfolio from last week, and I was unable to take action. Two days have passed, and I am the me of Wednesday who failed to send the news to me of Monday, and I have no idea what will happen to interrupt contact. Least of all did I anticipate Selene.

In such dealings as ours no distractions are needed, sexual or otherwise. We must concentrate wholly. At any time there is steady low-level contact among ourselves; we feel one another's reassuring presence. But transmission of data from self to self requires close attention.

I tell you my method. Then maybe you understand my trouble.

My business is investments. I do all my work at this same hour. At this hour it is midday in New York; the Big Board is still open. I can put through quick calls to my brokers when my time comes to buy or sell.

My office at the moment is the cocktail lounge known as the Celestial Room in the Henry VIII Hotel, south of the Thames. My office may be anywhere. All I need is a telephone. The Celestial Room is aptly named. The room orbits endlessly on a silent oiled track. Twittering sculptures in the so-called galactic mode drift through the air, scattering cascades of polychromed light upon those who sip drinks. Beyond the great picture windows of this supreme room lies the foggy darkness of the London evening, which I ignore. It is all the same to me, wherever I am: London, Nairobi, Karachi, Istanbul, Pittsburgh. I look only for an adequately comfortable environment, air that is safe to admit to one's lungs, service in the style I demand, and a telephone line. The individual characteristics of an individual place do not move me. I am like the ten planets of our solar family: a perpetual traveler, but not a sightseer.

Myself who is (now − n) is ready to receive transmission from myself who is (now). "Go ahead, (now + n)," he tells me. ((To him I am (now + n). To myself I am (now). Everything is relative; n is exactly forty-eight hours these days.))

"Here we go, (now − n)," I say to him.

I summon my strength by sipping at my drink. Chateau d'Yquem '79 in a sleek Czech goblet. Sickly sweet stuff; the waiter was aghast when I ordered it *before dinner*. Horreurs! Quel aperitif! But the wine makes transmission easier. It greases the conduit, somehow. I am ready.

My table is a single elegant block of glittering irradiated crystal, iridescent, cunningly emitting shifting moire patterns. On the table, unfolded, lies today's European edition of the *Herald Tribune*. I lean forward. I take from my breast pocket a sheet of paper, the printout listing the securities I bought on Monday afternoon. Now I allow my eyes to roam the close-packed type of the market quotations in my newspaper. I linger for a long moment on the heading, so there will be no mistake: *Closing New York Prices, Tuesday, October 6*. To me they are yesterday's prices. To (now − n) they are tomorrow's prices. (Now − n) acknowledges that he is receiving a sharp image.

I am about to transmit these prices to the me of Monday. You follow the machination, now?

I scan and I select.

I search only for the stocks that move five percent or more in a single day. Whether they move up or move down is immaterial; motion is the only criterion, and we go short or long as the case demands. We need fast action because our maximum survey span is only ninety-six hours at present, counting the relay from (now + *n*) back to (now − *n*) by way of (now). We cannot afford to wait for leisurely capital gains to mature; we must cut our risks by going for the quick, violent swings, seizing our profits as they emerge. The swings have to be violent. Otherwise brokerage costs will eat up our gross.

I have no difficulty choosing the stocks whose prices I will transmit to Monday's me. They are the stocks on the broker's printout, the ones we have already bought; obviously (now − *n*) would not have bought them unless Wednesday's me had told him about them, and now that I am Wednesday's me, I must follow through. So I send:

Arizona Agrochemical, 79¼, + 6¾
Canadian Transmutation, 116, + 4¼
Commonwealth Dispersals, 12, − 1¾
Eastern Electric Energy, 41, + 2
Great Lakes Bionics, 66, + 3½

And so on through *Western Offshore Corp.*, 99, −8. Now I have transmitted to (now − *n*) a list of Tuesday's top twenty high-percentage swingers. From his vantage-point in Monday, (now − *n*) will begin to place orders, taking positions in all twenty stocks on Monday afternoon. I know that he has been successful, because the printout from my broker gives confirmations of all twenty purchases at what now are highly favorable prices.

(Now − *n*) then signs off for a while and (now + *n*) comes on. He is transmitting from Friday, October 9. He gives me Thursday's closing prices on the same twenty stocks, from Arizona Agrochemical to Western Offshore. He already knows which of the twenty I will have chosen to sell today, but he pays me the compliment of not telling me; he merely gives me the prices. He signs off, and, in my role as (now), I make my decisions. I sell Canadian Transmutation, Great Lakes Bionics, and five others; I cover our short sale on Commonwealth Dispersals. The rest of the positions I leave undisturbed for the time being, since they will sell at better prices tomorrow, according to the word from (now + *n*). I can handle those when I am Friday's me.

Today's sequence is over.

In any given sequence—and we have been running about three a week—we commit no more than five or six million dollars. We wish to stay inconspicuous. Our pre-tax profit runs at about nine percent a week. Despite our network of tax havens in Ghana, Fiji, Grand Cayman, Liechtenstein,and Bolivia, through which our profits are funneled, we can bring down to net only about five percent a week on our entire capital. This keeps all three of us in a decent style and compounds prettily. Starting with $5,000 six years ago at the age of twenty-five, I have become one of the world's wealthiest men, with no other advantages than intelligence, persistence, and extrasensory access to tomorrow's stock prices.

It is time to deal with the next sequence. I must transmit to (now − *n*) the Tuesday prices of the stocks in the portfolio carried over from last week, so that he can make his decisions on what to sell. I know what he has sold, but it would spoil his sport to tip my hand. We treat ourselves fairly. After I have finished sending (now − *n*) those prices, (now + *n*) will come on line again and will transmit to me an entirely new list of stocks in which I must take positions before Thursday morning's New York opening. He will be able to realize profits in those on Friday. Thus we go from day to day, playing our shifting roles.

But this was the day on which Selene intersected our lives.

I had emptied my glass. I looked up to signal the waiter, and at that moment a slender, dark-haired girl, alone, entered the Celestial Room. She was tall, graceful, glorious. She was expensively clad in a clinging monomolecular wrap that shuttled through a complex program of wavelength shifts, including a microsecond sweep of total transparency that dazzled the eye while still maintaining a degree of modesty. Her features were a match for her garment: wide-set glossy eyes, delicate nose, firm lips lightly outlined in green. Her skin was extraordinarily pale. I could see no jewelry on her (why gild refined gold, why paint the lily?) but on her lovely left cheekbone I observed a small decorative band of ultraviolet paint, obviously chosen for visibility in the high-spectrum lighting of this unique room.

She conquered me. There was a mingling of traits in her that I found instantly irresistible: she seemed both shy and steel-strong, passionate and vulnerable, confident and ill at ease. She scanned the room, evidently looking for someone, not finding him. Her eyes met mine and lingered.

Somewhere in my cerebrum (now − n) said shrilly, as I had said on Monday, "I don't read you, (now + n). I don't read you!"

I paid no heed. I rose. I smiled to the girl, and beckoned her toward the empty chair at my table. I swept my *Herald Tribune* to the floor. At certain times there are more important things than compounding one's capital at five percent per week. She glowed gratefully at me, nodding, accepting my invitation.

When she was about twenty feet from me, I lost all contact with (now − n) and (now + n).

I don't mean simply that there was an interruption in the transmission of words and data among us. I mean that I lost all sense of the presence of my earlier and later selves. That warm, wordless companionship, that ourselvesness, that harmony that I had known constantly since we had established our linkage five years ago, vanished as if switched off. On Monday, when contact with (now + n) broke, I still had had (now − n). Now I had no one.

I was terrifyingly alone, even as ordinary men are alone, but more alone than that, for I had known a fellowship beyond the reach of other mortals. The shock of separation was intense.

Then Selene was sitting beside me, and the nearness of her made me forget my new solitude entirely.

She said, "I don't know where he is and I don't care. He's been late once too often. Finito for him. Hello, you. I'm Selene Hughes."

"Aram Kevorkian. What do you drink?"

"Chartreuse on the rocks. Green. I knew you were Armenian from halfway across the room."

I am Bulgarian, thirteen generations. It suits me to wear an Armenian name. I did not correct her. The waiter hurried over; I ordered chartreuse for her, a sake martini for self. I trembled like an adolescent. Her beauty was disturbing, overwhelming, astonishing. As we raised glasses I reached out experimentally for (now − n) or (now + n). Silence. Silence. But there was Selene.

I said, "You're not from London."

"I travel a lot. I stay here a while, there a while. Originally Dallas. You must be able to hear the Texas in my voice. Most recent port of call, Lima. For the July skiing. Now London."

"And the next stop?"

"Who knows? What do you do, Aram?"

"I invest."

"For a living?"

"So to speak. I struggle along. Free for dinner?"

"Of course. Shall we eat in the hotel?"

"There's the beastly fog outside," I said.

"Exactly."

Simpatico. Perfectly. I guessed her for twenty-four, twenty-five at most. Perhaps a brief marriage three or four years in the past. A private income, not colossal but nice. An experienced woman of the world, and yet also somehow still retaining a core of innocence, a magical softness of the soul. I loved her instantly. She did not care for a second cocktail. "I'll make dinner reservations," I said, as she went off to the powder room. I watched her walk away. A supple walk, flawless posture, supreme shoulderblades. When she was about twenty feet from me I felt my other selves suddenly return. "What's happening?" (now − *n*) demanded furiously. "Where did you go? Why aren't you sending?"

"I don't know yet."

"Where the hell are the Tuesday prices on last week's carry-over stocks?"

"Later," I told him.

"*Now*. Before you blank out again."

"The prices can wait," I said, and shut him off. To (now + *n*) I said, "All right. What do you know that I ought to know?"

Myself of forty-eight hours hence said, "We have fallen in love."

"I'm aware of that. But what blanked us out?"

"She's psi-suppressant. She absorbs all the transmission energy we put out."

"Impossible! I've never heard of any such thing."

"No?" said (now + *n*). "Brother, this past hour has been the first chance I've had to get through to you since Wednesday, when we got into this mess. It's no coincidence that I've been with her just about one hundred percent of the time since Wednesday evening, except for a few two-minute breaks, and then I couldn't reach you because *you* must have been with her in your time sequence. And so—''

''How can this be?'' I cried. ''What'll happen to us if? No. No, you bastard, you're rolling me over. I don't believe you. There's no way that she could be causing it.''

''I think I know how she does it,'' said (now + n). ''There's a—''

At that moment Selene returned, looking even more radiantly beautiful, and silence descended once more.

We dined well. Chilled Mombasa oysters, salade niçoise, filet of Kobe beef rare, washed down by Richebourg '77. Occasionally I tried to reach myselves. Nothing. I worried a little about how I was going to get the Tuesday prices to (now − n) on the carryover stuff, and decided to forget about it. Obviously I hadn't managed to get them to him, since I hadn't received any printout on sales out of that portfolio this evening, and if I hadn't reached him, there was no sense in fretting about reaching him. The wonderful thing about this telepathy across time is the sense of stability it gives you: *whatever has been, must be,* and so forth.

After dinner we went down one level to the casino for our brandies and a bit of gamblerage. ''Two thousand pounds' worth,'' I said to the robot cashier, and put my thumb to his charge plate, and the chips came skittering out of the slot in his chest. I gave half the stake to Selene. She played high-grav–low-grav, and I played roulette; we shifted from one table to the other according to whim and the run of our luck. In two hours she tripled her stake and I lost all of mine. I never was good at games of chance. I even used to get hurt in the market before the market ceased being a game of chance for me. Naturally, I let her thumb her winnings into her own account, and when she offered to return the original stake I just laughed.

Where next? Too early for bed.

''The swimming pool?'' she suggested.

''Fine idea,'' I said. But the hotel had two, as usual. ''Nude pool or suit pool?''

''Who owns a suit?'' she asked, and we laughed and took the dropshaft to the pool.

There were separate dressing rooms, M and W. No one frets about showing flesh, but shedding clothes still has lingering taboos. I peeled fast and waited for her by the pool. During this interval I felt the familiar presence of another self impinge on me: (now − n). He wasn't transmitting, but I knew he was there. I couldn't feel (now + n) at all. Grudgingly I began to admit that Selene must be responsible for my communications problem. Whenever she went more than twenty feet away, I could get through to myselves. How did she do it, though? And could it be stopped? Mao help me, would I have to choose between my livelihood and my new beloved?

The pool was a vast octagon with a trampoline diving web and a set of underwater psych-lights making rippling patterns of color. Maybe fifty people were swimming and a few dozen more were lounging beside the pool, improving their tans. No one person can possibly stand out in such a mass of flesh, and yet when Selene emerged from the women's dressing room and began the long saunter across the tiles toward me, the heads began to turn by the dozens. Her figure was not notably lush, yet she had the automatic magnetism that only true beauty exercises. She was definitely slender, but everything was in perfect proportion, as though she had been shaped by the hand of Phidias himself. Long legs, long arms, narrow wrists, narrow waist, small high breasts, miraculously outcurving hips. The *Primavera* of Botticelli. The *Leda* of Leonardo. She carried herself with ultimate grace. My heart thundered.

Between her breasts she wore some sort of amulet: a disk of red metal in which geometrical symbols were engraved. I hadn't noticed it when she was clothed.

"My good-luck piece," she explained. "I'm never without it." And she sprinted laughing to the trampoline, and bounded, and hovered, and soared, and cut magnificently through the surface of the water. I followed her in. We raced from angle to angle of the pool, testing each other, searching for limits and not finding them. We dived and met far below, and locked hands, and bobbed happily upward. Then we lay under the warm quartz lamps. Then we tried the sauna. Then we dressed.

We went to her room.

She kept the amulet on even when we made love. I felt it cold against my chest as I embraced her.

*   *   *

But what of the making of money? What of the compounding of capital? What of my sweaty little secret, the joker in the Wall Street pack, the messages from beyond by which I milked the market of millions? On Thursday no contact with my other selves was scheduled, but I could not have made it even if it had been. It was amply clear: Selene blanked my psi field. The critical range was twenty feet. When we were farther apart than that, I could get through; otherwise, not. How did it happen? How? How? How? An accidental incompatibility of psionic vibrations? A tragic canceling out of my powers through proximity to her splendid self? No. No. No. No.

On Thursday we roared through London like a conflagration, doing the galleries, the boutiques, the museums, the sniffer palaces, the pubs, the sparkle houses. I had never been so much in love. For hours at a time I forgot my dilemma. The absence of myself from myself, the separation that had seemed so shattering in its first instant, seemed trivial. What did I need *them* for, when I had *her*?

I needed them for the moneymaking. The moneymaking was a disease that love might alleviate but could not cure. And if I did not resume contact soon, there would be calamities in store.

Late Thursday afternoon, as we came reeling giddily out of a sniffer palace on High Holborn, our nostrils quivering, I felt contact again. (Now + n) broke through briefly, during a moment when I waited for a traffic light and Selene plunged wildly across to the far side of the street.

"The amulet's what does it," he said. "That's the word I get from—"

Selene rushed back to my side of the street. "Come *on*, silly! Why'd you wait?"

Two hours later, as she lay in my arms, I swept my hand up from her satiny haunch to her silken breast and caught the plaque of red metal between two fingers. "Love, won't you take this off?" I said innocently. "I hate the feel of a piece of cold slithery metal coming between us when—"

There was terror in her dark eyes. "I couldn't, Aram! I *couldn't*!"

"For me, love?"

"Please. Let me have my little superstition." Her lips found mine. Cleverly she changed the subject. I wondered at her tremor of shock, her frightened refusal.

Later we strolled along the Thames, and watched Friday

coming to life in fogbound dawn. Today I would have to escape
from her for at least an hour, I knew. The laws of time dictated it.
For on Wednesday, between six and seven P.M. Central European
Time, I had accepted a transmission from myself of (now + n),
speaking out of Friday, and Friday had come, and I was that very
same (now + n), who must reach out at the proper time toward
his counterpart at (now − n) on Wednesday. What would happen if
I failed to make my rendezvous with time in time, I did not
know. Nor wanted to discover. The universe, I suspected, would
continue regardless. But my own sanity—my grasp on that
universe—might not.

It was narrowness. All glorious Friday I had to plot how to
separate myself from radiant Selene during the cocktail hour,
when she would certainly want to be with me. But in the end it
was simplicity. I told the concierge, "At seven minutes after six
send a message to me in the Celestial Room. I am wanted on
urgent business, must come instantly to computer room for
intercontinental data patch, person to person. So?" Concierge
replied, "We can give you the patch right at your table in the
Celestial Room." I shook my head firmly. "Do it as I say.
Please." I put thumb to gratuity account of concierge and
signaled an account transfer of five pounds. Concierge smiled.

Seven minutes after six, message-robot scuttles into Celestial
Room, comes homing in on table where I sit with Selene.
"Intercontinental data patch, Mr. Kevorkian," says robot. "Wanted
immediately. Computer room." I turn to Selene. "Forgive me,
love. Desolated, but must go. Urgent business. Just a few
minutes."

She grasps my arm fondly. "Darling, no! Let the call wait. It's
our *anniversary* now. Forty-eight hours since we met!"

Gently I pull arm free. I extend arm, show jewelled timepiece.
"Not yet, not yet! We didn't meet until half past six Wednesday.
I'll be back in time to celebrate." I kiss tip of supreme nose.
"Don't smile at strangers while I'm gone," I say, and rush off
with robot.

I do not go to computer room. I hurriedly buy a Friday *Herald
Tribune* in the lobby and lock myself in men's washroom cubicle.
Contact now is made on schedule with (now − n), living in
Wednesday, all innocent of what will befall him that miraculous
evening. I read stock prices, twenty securities, from Arizona

Agrochemical to Western Offshore Corp. I sign off and study my watch. (Now $- n$) is currently closing out seven long positions and the short sale on Commonwealth Dispersals. During the interval I seek to make contact with (now $+ n$) ahead of me on Sunday evening. No response. Nothing.

Presently I lose contact also with (now $- n$). As expected; for this is the moment when the me of Wednesday has for the first time come within Selene's psi-suppressant field. I wait patiently. In a while (Selene $- n$) goes to powder room. Contact returns. (Now $- n$) says to me, "All right. What do you know that I ought to know?"

"We have fallen in love," I say.

Rest of conversation follows as per. What has been, must be. I debate slipping in the tidbit I have received from (now $+ n$) concerning the alleged powers of Selene's amulet. Should I say it quickly, before contact breaks? Impossible. It was not said to me. The conversation proceeds until at the proper moment I am able to say, "I think I know how she does it. There's a—"

Wall of silence descends. (Selene $- n$) has returned to the table of (now $- n$) Therefore I (now) will return to the table of Selene (now). I rush back to the Celestial Room. Selene, looking glum, sits alone, sipping drink. She brightens as I approach.

"See?" I cry. "Back just in time. Happy anniversary, darling. Happy, happy, happy, happy!"

When we woke Saturday morning we decided to share the same room thereafter. Selene showered while I went downstairs to arrange the transfer. I could have arranged everything by telephone without getting out of bed, but I chose to go in person to the desk, leaving Selene behind. You understand why.

In the lobby I received a transmission from (now $+ n$), speaking out of Monday, October 12. "It's definitely the amulet," he said. "I can't tell you how it works, but it's some kind of mechanical psi-suppressant device. God knows why she wears it, but if I could only manage to have her lose it we'd be all right. It's the amulet. Pass it on."

I was reminded, by this, of the flash of contact I had received on Thursday outside the sniffer palace on High Holborn. I realized that I had another message to send, a rendezvous to keep with him who has become (now $- n$).

Late Saturday afternoon, I made contact with (now $- n$) once

more, only momentarily. Again I resorted to a ruse in order to
fulfill the necessary unfolding of destiny. Selene and I stood in
the hallway, waiting for a dropshaft. There were other people.
The dropshaft gate irised open and Selene went in, followed by
others. With an excess of chivalry I let all the others enter before
me, and "accidentally" missed the closing of the gate. The
dropshaft descended with Selene. I remained alone in the hall.
My timing was good; after a moment I felt the inner warmth that
told me of proximity to the mind of (now − n). "The amulet's
what does it," I said. "That's the word I get from—" Aloneness
intervened.

During the week beginning Monday, October 12, I received no
advance information on the fluctuations of the stock market at all.
Not in five years had I been so deprived of data. My linkings
with (now − n) and (now + n) were fleeting and unsatisfactory.
We exchanged a sentence here, a blurt of hasty words there, no
more. Of course, there were moments every day when I was
apart from the fair Selene long enough to get a message out.
Though we were utterly consumed by our passion for one
another, nevertheless I did get opportunities to elude the twenty-
foot radius of her psi-suppressant field. The trouble was that my
opportunities to send did not always coincide with the opportunities of (now − n) or (now + n) to receive. We remained linked in
a 48-hour spacing, and to alter that spacing would require
extensive discipline and infinitely careful coordination, which
none of ourselves were able to provide in such a time. So any
contact with myselves had to depend on a coincidence of apartnesses
from Selene.

I regretted this keenly. Yet there was Selene to comfort me. We
reveled all day and reveled all night. When fatigue overcame us
we grabbed at two-hour deepsleep wire and caught up with
ourselves, and then we started over. I plumbed the limits of
ecstasy. I believe it was like that for her.

Though lacking my unique advantage, I also played the market
that week. Partly it was compulsion: my plungings had become
obsessive. Partly, too, it was at Selene's urgings. "Don't you
neglect your work for me," she purred. "I don't want to stand
in the way of making *money*."

Money, I was discovering, fascinated her nearly as intensely as
it did me. Another evidence of compatibility. She knew a good

deal about the market herself and looked on, an excited spectator, as I each day shuffled my portfolio.

The market was closed Monday: Columbus Day. Tuesday, queasily operating in the dark, I sold Arizona Agrochemical, Consolidated Luna, Eastern Electric Energy, and Western Offshore, reinvesting the proceeds in large blocks of Meccano Leasing and Holoscan Dynamics. Wednesday's *Tribune,* to my chagrin, brought me the news that Consolidated Luna had received the Copernicus franchise and had risen 9¾ points in the final hour of Tuesday's trading. Meccano Leasing, though, had been rebuffed in the Robomation takeover bid and was off 4½ since I had bought it. I got through to my broker in a hurry and sold Meccano, which was down even further that morning. My loss was $125,000—plus $250,000 more that I had dropped by selling Consolidated Luna too soon. After the market closed on Wednesday, the directors of Meccano Leasing unexpectedly declared a five-for-two split and a special dividend in the form of a one-for-ten distribution of cumulative participating high-depreciation warrants. Meccano regained its entire Tuesday-Wednesday loss and tacked on 5 points beyond.

I concealed the details of this from Selene. She saw only the glamor of my speculations: the telephone calls, the quick computations, the movements of hundreds of thousands of dollars. I hid the hideous botch from her, knowing it might damage my prestige.

On Thursday, feeling battered and looking for the safety of a utility, I picked up 10,000 Southwest Power and Fusion at 38, only hours before the explosion of SPF's magnetohydrodynamic generating station in Las Cruces, which destroyed half a county and neatly peeled $90,000 off the value of my investment when the stock finally traded, after a delayed opening, on Friday. I sold. Later came news that SPF's insurance would cover everything. SPF recovered, whereas Holoscan Dynamics plummeted 11½, costing me $140,000 more. I had not know that Holoscan's insurance subsidiary was the chief underwriter for SPF's disaster coverage.

All told, that week I shed more than $500,000. My brokers were stunned. I had a reputation for infallibility among them. Most of them had become wealthy simply by duplicating my own transactions for their own accounts.

"Sweetheart, what *happened*?" they asked me.

My losses the following week came to $1,250,000. Still no news from (now + *n*). My brokers felt I needed a vacation. Even Selene knew I was losing heavily, by now. Curiously, my run of bad luck seemed to intensify her passion for me. Perhaps it made me look tragic and Byronic to be getting hit so hard.

We spent wild days and wilder nights. I lived in a throbbing haze of sensuality. Wherever we went we were the center of all attention. We had that burnished sheen that only great lovers have. We radiated a glow of delight all up and down the spectrum.

I was losing millions.

The more I lost, the more reckless my plunges became, and the deeper my losses became.

I was in real danger of being wiped out, if this went on.

I had to get away from her.

Monday, October 26. Selene has taken the deepsleep wire and in the next two hours will flush away the fatigue of three riotous days and nights without rest. I have only pretended to take the wire. When she goes under, I rise. I dress. I pack. I scrawl a note for her. *"Business trip. Back soon. Love, love, love, love."* I catch noon rocket for Istanbul.

Minarets, mosques, Byzantine temples. Shunning the sleep wire, I spend next day and a half in bed in ordinary repose. I wake and it is forty-eight hours since parting from Selene. Desolation! Bitter solitude! But I feel (now + *n*) invading my mind.

"Take this down," he says brusquely. "Buy 5,000 FSP, 800 CCG, 150 LC, 200 T, 1,000 TXN, 100 BVI. Go short 200 BA, 500 UCM, 200 LOC. Clear? Read back to me."

I read back. Then I phone in my orders. I hardly care what the ticker symbols stand for. If (now + *n*) says to do, I do.

An hour and a half later the switchboard tells me, "A Miss Hughes to see you, sir."

She has traced me! Calamitas calamitatum! "Tell her I'm not here," I say. I flee to the roofport. By copter I get away. Commercial jet shortly brings me to Tel Aviv. I take a room at the Hilton and give absolute instructions am not to be disturbed. Meals only to room, also *Herald Trib* every day, otherwise no interruptions.

I study the market action. On Friday I am able to reach (now −

n). "Take this down," I say brusquely. "Buy 5,000 FSP, 800 CCG, 140 LC, 200 T—"

Then I call brokers. I close out Wednesday's longs and cover Wednesday's shorts. My profit is over a million. I am recouping. But I miss her terribly.

I spend agonizing weekend of loneliness in hotel room.

Monday. Comes voice of (now + *n*) out of Wednesday, with new instructions. I obey. At lunchtime, under lid of my barley soup, floats note from her. "Darling, why are you running away from me? I love you to the ninth power. S."

I get out of hotel disguised as bellhop and take El Al jet to Cairo. Tense, jittery, I join tourist group sightseeing Pyramids, much out of character. Tour is conducted in Hebrew; serves me right. I lock self in hotel. *Herald Tribune* available. On Wednesday I send instructions to me of Monday, (now − *n*). I await instructions from me of Friday, (now + *n*). Instead I get muddled transmissions, noise, confusions. What is wrong? Where to flee now? Brasilia, McMurdo Sound, Anchorage, Irkutsk, Maograd? She will find me. She has her resources. There are few secrets to one who has the will to surmount them. How does she find me?

She finds me.

Note comes: "I am at Abu Simbel to wait for you. Meet me there on Friday afternoon or I throw myself from Rameses' leftmost head at sundown. Love. Desperate. S."

I am defeated. She will bankrupt me, but I must have her.

On Friday I go to Abu Simbel.

She stood atop the monument, luscious in windswept white cotton.

"I knew you'd come," she said.

"What else could I do?"

We kissed. Her suppleness inflamed me. The sun blazed toward a descent into the western desert.

"Why have you been running away from me?" she asked. "What did I do wrong? Why did you stop loving me?"

"I never stopped loving you," I said.

"Then—*why*?"

"I will tell you," I said, "a secret I have shared with no human being other than myselves."

Words tumbled out. I told all. The discovery of my gift, the early chaos of sensory bombardment from other times, the bafflement of living one hour ahead of time and one hour behind time as well as in the present. The months of discipline needed to develop my gift. The fierce struggle to extend the range of extrasensory perception to five hours, ten, twenty-four, forty-eight. The joy of playing the market and never losing. The intricate systems of speculation; the self-imposed limits to keep me from ending up with all the assets in the world; the pleasures of immense wealth. The loneliness, too. And the supremacy of the night when I met her.

Then I said, "When I'm with you, it doesn't work. I can't communicate with myselves. I lost millions in the last couple of weeks, playing the market the regular way. You were breaking me."

"The amulet," she said. "It does it. It absorbs psionic energy. It suppresses the psi field."

"I thought it was that. But who ever heard of such a thing? Where did you get it, Selene? Why do you wear it?"

"I got it far, far from here," said Selene. "I wear it to protect myself."

"Against *what*?"

"Against my own gift. My terrible gift, my nightmare gift, my curse of a gift. But if I must choose between my amulet and my love, it is no choice. I love you, Aram, I love you, I love you!"

She seized the metal disk, ripped it from the chain around her neck, hurled it over the brink of the monument. It fluttered through the twilight sky and was gone.

I felt (now − n) and (now + n) return.

Selene vanished.

For an hour I stood alone atop Abu Simbel, motionless, baffled, stunned. Suddenly Selene was back. She clutched my arm and whispered, "Quick! Let's go to the hotel!"

"Where have you been?"

"Next Tuesday," she said. "I oscillate in time."

"What?"

"The amulet damped my oscillations. It anchored me to the timeline in the present. I got it in 2459 A.D. Someone I knew there, someone who cared very deeply for me. It was his parting gift, and he gave it knowing we could never meet again. But now—"

She vanished. Gone eighteen minutes.

"I was back in last Tuesday," she said, returning. "I phoned myself and said I should follow you to Istanbul, and then to Tel Aviv, and then to Egypt. You see how I found you?"

We hurried to her hotel overlooking the Nile. We made love, and an instant before the climax I found myself alone in bed. (Now + *n*) spoke to me and said, "She's been here with me. She should be on her way back to you." Selene returned. "I went to—"

"—this coming Sunday," I said. "I know. Can't you control the oscillations at all?"

"No. I'm swinging free. When the momentum really builds up, I cover centuries. It's torture, Aram. Life has no sequence, no structure. Hold me tight!"

In a frenzy we finished what we could not finish before. We lay clasped close, exhausted. "What will we do?" I cried. "I can't let you oscillate like this!"

"You must. I can't let you sacrifice your livlihood!"

"But—"

She was gone.

I rose and dressed and hurried back to Abu Simbel. In the hours before dawn I searched the sands beside the Nile, crawling, sifting, probing. As the sun's rays crested the mountain I found the amulet. I rushed to the hotel. Selene had reappeared.

"Put it on," I commanded.

"I won't. I can't deprive you of—"

"Put it on."

She disappeared. (Now + *n*) said, "Never fear. All will work out wondrous well."

Selene came back. "I was in the Friday after next," she said. "I had an idea that will save everything."

"No ideas. Put the amulet on."

She shook her head. "I brought you a present," she said, and handed me a copy of the *Herald Tribune,* dated the Friday after next. Oscillation seized her. She went and came and handed me November 19's newspaper. Her eyes were bright with excitement. She vanished. She brought me the *Herald Tribune* of November 8. Of December 4. Of November 11. Of January 18, 1988. Of December 11. Of March 5, 1988. Of December 22. Of June 16, 1997. Of December 14. Of September 8, 1990. "Enough!" I said. "Enough!" She continued to swing through time. The stack of papers grew. "I love you," she gasped, and handed me a transparent cube one inch high. "*The Wall Street Journal,* May 19, 2206," she explained. "I couldn't get the machine that reads it. Sorry." She was gone. She brought me more *Herald Tribunes,* many dates, 1988–2002. Then a whole microreel. At last she sank down, dazed, exhausted, and said, "Give me the amulet. It must be within twelve inches of my body to neutralize my field." I slipped the disk into her palm . "Kiss me," Selene murmured.

And so. She wears her amulet; we are inseparable; I have no contact with my other selves. In handling my investments I merely consult my file of newspapers, which I have reduced to minicap size and carry in the bezel of a ring I wear. For safety's sake Selene carries a duplicate.

We are very happy. We are very wealthy.

Is only one dilemma. Neither of us use the special gift with which we were born. Evolution would not have produced such things in us if they were not to be used. What risks do we run by thwarting evolution's design?

I bitterly miss the use of my power, which her amulet negates. Even the company of supreme Selene does not wholly compensate for the loss of the harmoniousness that was

$$\left\{ \begin{array}{l} (now - n) \\ (now) \\ (now + n). \end{array} \right\}$$

I could, of course, simply arrange to be away from Selene for an hour here, an hour there, and reopen that contact. I could even have continued playing the market that way, setting aside a transmission hour every forty-eight hours outside of amulet range. But it is the *continuous* contact that I miss. The always presence of my other selves. If I have that contact, Selene is condemned to oscillate, or else we must part.

I wish also to find some way that her gift will be not terror but joy for her.

Is maybe a solution. Can extrasensory gifts be induced by proximity? Can Selene's oscillation pass to me? I struggle to acquire it. We work together to give me her gift. Just today I felt myself move, perhaps a microsecond into the future, then a microsecond into the past. Selene said I definitely seemed to blur.

Who knows? Will success be ours?

I think yes. I think love will triumph. I think I will learn the secret, and we will coordinate our vanishings, Selene and I, and secret, and we will coordinate our vanishings, Selene and I, and we will oscillate as one, we will swing together through time, we will soar, we will speed hand in hand across the millenia. She can discard her amulet once I am able to go with her on her journeys.

Pray for us, (now + n), my brother, my other self, and one day soon perhaps I will come to you and shake you by the hand.

CALIBAN

THEY HAVE ALL changed their faces to a standard model. It is the latest thing, which should not be confused with the latest Thing. The latest Thing is me. The latest thing, the latest fad, the latest rage, is for them all to change their faces to a standard model. I have no idea how it is done but I think it is genetic, with the RNA, the DNA, the NDA. Only retroactive. They all come out with blond wavy hair and sparkling blue eyes. And long straight faces with sharp cheekbones. And notched chins and thin lips curling in ironic smiles. Even the black ones: thin lips, blue eyes, blond wavy hair. And pink skins. They all look alike now. The sweet Aryanized world. Our entire planet. Except me. Meee.

I am imperfect. I am blemished. I am unforgiving. I am the latest Thing.

Louisiana said, Would you like to copulate with me? You are so strange. You are so beautiful. Oh, how I desire you, strange being from a strange time. My orifices are yours.

It was a thoughtful offer. I considered it a while, thinking she might be trying to patronize me. At length I notified her of my acceptance. We went to a public copulatorium. Louisiana is taller than I am and her hair is a torrent of spun gold. Her eyes are blue and her face is long and straight. I would say she is about

twenty-three years old. In the copulatorium she dissolved her
clothes and stood naked before me. She was wearing gold pubic
hair that day and her belly was flat and taut. Her breasts were
round and slightly elongated and the nipples were very small. Go
on, she said, now you dissolve your clothes.

I said, I am afraid to because my body is ugly and you will
mock me.

Your body is not ugly, she said. Your body is strange but it is
not ugly.

My body is ugly, I insisted. My legs are short and they curve
outward and my thighs have bulging muscles and I have black
hairy hair all over me. Like an ape. And there is this hideous scar
on my belly.

A scar?

Where they took out my appendix, I told her.

This aroused her beyond all probability. Her nipples stood up
tall and her face became flushed.

Your appendix? Your appendix was removed?

Yes, I said, it was done when I was fourteen years old, and I
have a loathsome red scar on my abdomen.

She asked, What year was it when you were fourteen?

I said, It was 1967, I think.

She laughed and clapped her hands and began to dance around
the room. Her breasts bounced up and down, but her long
flowing silken hair soon covered them, leaving only the stubby
pinkish nipples poking through like buttons. 1967! she cried.
Fourteen! Your appendix was removed! 1967!

Then she turned to me and said, My grandfather was born in 1967,
I think. How terribly ancient you are. My helix-father's father on
the countermolecular side. I didn't realize you were so very ancient.

Ancient and ugly, I said.

Not ugly, only strange, she said.

Strange and ugly, I said. Strangely ugly.

We think you are beautiful, she said. Will you dissolve your
clothes now? It would not be pleasing to me to copulate with you
if you keep your clothes on.

There, I said, and boldly revealed myself. The bandy legs. The
hairy chest. The scarred belly. The bulging shoulders. The short
neck. She has seen my lopsided face, she can see my dismal
body as well. If that is what she wants.

She threw herself upon me, gasping and making soft noises.

*   *   *

What did Louisiana look like before the change came? Did she have dull stringy hair thick lips a hook nose bushy black eyebrows no chin foul breath one breast bigger than the other splay feet crooked teeth little dark hairs around her nipples a bulging navel too many dimples in her buttocks skinny thighs blue veins in her calves protruding ears? And then did they give her the homogenizing treatment and make her the golden creature she is today? How long did it take? What were the costs? Did the government subsidize the process? Were the large corporations involved? How were these matters handled in the socialist countries? Was there anyone who did not care to be changed? Perhaps Louisiana was born this way. Perhaps her beauty is natural. In any society there are always a few whose beauty is natural.

Dr. Habakkuk and Senator Mandragore spent a great deal of time questioning me in the Palazzo of Mirrors. They put a green plastic dome over my head so that everything I said would be recorded with the proper nuance and intensity. Speak to us, they said. We are fascinated by your antique accent. We are enthralled by your primitive odors. Do you realize that you are our sole representative of the nightmare out of which we have awakened? Tell us, said the Senator, tell us about your brutally competitive civilization. Describe in detail the fouling of the environment. Explain the nature of national rivalry. Compare and contrast methods of political discourse in the Soviet Union and in the United States. Let us have your analysis of the sociological implications of the first voyage to the moon. Would you like to see the moon? Can we offer you any psychedelic drugs? Did you find Louisiana sexually satisfying? We are so glad to have you here. We regard you as a unique spiritual treasure. Speak to us of yesterday's yesterdays, while we listen entranced and enraptured.

Louisiana says that she is eighty-seven years old. Am I to believe this? There is about her a springtime freshness. No, she maintains, I am eighty-seven years old. I was born on March-alternate 11, 2022. Does that depress you? Is my great age frightening to you? See how tight my skin is. See how my teeth gleam. Why are you so disturbed? I am, after all, much younger than you.

*   *   *

I understand that in some cases making the great change involved elaborate surgery. Cornea transplants and cosmetic adjustment of the facial structure. A great deal of organ-swapping went on. There is not much permanence among these people. They are forever exchanging segments of themselves for new and improved segments. I am told that among some advanced groups the use of mechanical limb-interfaces has come to be common, in order that new arms and legs may be plugged in with a minimum of trouble. This is truly an astonishing era. Even so, their women seem to copulate in the old ways: knees up thighs apart, lying on the right side left leg flexed, back to the man and knees slightly bent, etc., etc., etc. One might think they would have invented something new by this time. But perhaps the possibilities for innovation in the sphere of erotics are not extensive. Can I suggest anything? What if the woman unplugs both arms and both legs and presents her mere torso to the man? Helpless! Vulnerable! Quintessentially feminine! I will discuss it with Louisiana. But it would be just my luck that her arms and legs don't come off.

On the first para-Wednesday of every month Lieutenant Hotchkiss gives me lessons in fluid-breathing. We go to one of the deepest sub-levels of the Extravagance Building, where there is a special hyperoxygenated pool, for the use of beginners only, circular in shape and not at all deep. The water sparkles like opal. Usually the pool is crowded with children, but Lieutenant Hotchkiss arranges for me to have private instruction since I am shy about revealing my body. Each lesson is much like the one before. Lieutenant Hotchkiss descends the gentle ramp that leads one into the pool. He is taller than I am and his hair is golden and his eyes are blue. Sometimes I have difficulties distinguishing him from Dr. Habakkuk and Senator Mandragore. In a casual moment the lieutenant confided that he is ninety-eight years old and therefore not really a contemporary of Louisiana's, although Louisiana has hinted that on several occasions in the past she has allowed the lieutenant to fertilize her ova. I doubt this inasmuch as reproduction is quite uncommon in this era and what probability is there that she would have permitted him to do it more than once? I think she believes that by telling me such things she will stimulate emotions of jealousy in me, since she knows that the primitive ancients were frequently jealous. Regardless of all this

Lieutenant Hotchkiss proceeds to enter the water. It reaches his navel, his broad hairless chest, his throat, his chin, his sensitive thin-walled nostrils. He submerges and crawls about on the floor of the pool. I see his golden hair glittering through the opal water. He remains totally submerged for eight or twelve minutes, now and again lifting his hands above the surface and waggling them as if to show me where he is. Then he comes forth. Water streams from his nostrils but he is not in the least out of breath. Come on, now, he says. You can do it. It's as easy as it looks. He beckons me toward the ramp. Any child can do it, the lieutenant assures me. It's a matter of control and determination. I shake my head. No, I say, genetic modification has something to do with it. My lungs aren't equipped to handle water, although I suppose yours are. The lieutenant merely laughs. Come on, come on, into the water. And I go down the ramp. How the water glows and shimmers! It reaches my navel, my black-matted chest, my throat, my chin, my wide thick nostrils. I breathe it in and choke and splutter; and I rush up the ramp, struggling for air. With the water a leaden weight in my lungs, I throw myself exhausted to the marble floor and cry out, No, no, no, it's impossible. Lieutenant Hotchkiss stands over me. His body is without flaw. He says, You've got to try to cultivate the proper attitudes. Your mental set determines everything. Let's think more positively about this business of breathing under water. Don't you realize that it's a major evolutionary step, one of the grand and glorious things separating our species from the austra-lopithecines? Don't you want to be part of the great leap forward? Up, now. Try again. Thinking positively all the time. Carrying in your mind the distinction between yourself and our bestial ancestors. Go in. In. In. And I go in. And moments later burst from the water, choking and spluttering. This takes place on the first para-Wednesday of every month. The same thing, every time.

When you are talking on the telephone and your call is abruptly cut off, do you worry that the person on the other end will think you have hung up on him? Do you suspect that the person on the other end has hung up on you? Such problems are unknown here. These people make very few telephone calls. We are beyond mere communication in this era, Louisiana sometimes remarks.

*   *   *

Through my eyes these people behold their shining plastic epoch in proper historical perspective. They must see it as the present, which is always the same. But to me it is the future and so I have the true observer's parallax: I can say, it once was like *that* and now it is like *this*. They prize my gift. They treasure me. People come from other continents to run their fingers over my face. They tell me how much they admire my asymmetry. And they ask me many questions. Most of them ask about their own era rather than about mine. Such questions as:

Does suspended animation tempt you?

Was the fusion plant overwhelming in its implications of contained might?

Can you properly describe interconnection of the brain with a computer as an ecstatic experience?

Do you approve of modification of the solar system?

And also there are those who make more searching demands on my critical powers, such as Dr. Habakkuk and Senator Mandragore. They ask such questions as:

Was the brevity of your life span a hindrance to the development of the moral instincts?

Do you find our standardization of appearance at all abhorrent?

What was your typical emotional response to the sight of the dung of some wild animal in the streets?

Can you quantify the intensity of your feelings concerning the transience of human institutions?

I do my best to serve their needs. Often it is a strain to answer them in meaningful ways, but I strive to do so. Wondering occasionally if it would not have been more valuable for them to interrogate a Neanderthal. Or one of Lieutenant Hotchkiss's australopithecines. I am perhaps not primitive enough, though I do have my own charisma, nevertheless.

The first day it was pretty frightening to me. I saw one of them, with his sleek face and all, and I could accept that, but then another one came into the room to give me an injection, and he looked just like the first one. Twins, I thought, my doctors are twins. But then a third and a fourth and a fifth arrived. The same face, the very same fucking face. Imagine my chagrin, me with my blob of a nose, with my uneven teeth, with my eyebrows that meet in the middle, with my fleshy pockmarked cheeks, lying there beneath this convocation of the perfect. Let me tell you I felt out of place. I was never touchy about my looks before—I mean, it's an imperfect world, we all have our flaws—but these bastards *didn't* have flaws, and that was a hard acceptance for me to relate to. I thought I was being clever: I said, You're all multiples of the same gene pattern, right? Modern advances in medicine have made possible an infinite reduplication of genetic information and the five of you belong to one clone, isn't that it? And several of them answered, No, this is not the case, we are in fact wholly unrelated but within the last meta-week we have independently decided to standardize our appearance according to the presently favored model. And then three or four more of them came into my room to get a look at me.

In the beginning I kept telling myself: *In the country of the beautiful the ugly man is king.*

Louisiana was the first one with whom I had a sexual liaison. We often went to public copulatoria. She was easy to arouse and quite passionate although her friend Calpurnia informed me some months later that Louisiana takes orgasm-inducing drugs before copulating with me. I asked Calpurnia why and she became embarrassed. Dismayed, I bared my body to her and threw myself on top of her. Yes, she cried, rape me, violate me! Calpurnia's vigorous spasms astonished me. The following morning Louisiana asked me if I had noticed Calpurnia swallowing a small purple spansule prior to our intercourse. Calpurnia's face is identical to Louisiana's but her breasts are farther apart. I have also had sexual relations with Helena, Amniota, Drusilla, Florinda, and Vibrissa. Before each episode of copulation I ask them their names so that there will be no mistakes.

At twilight they programmed an hour of red and green rainfall and I queried Senator Mandragore about the means by which I had been brought to this era. Was it bodily transportation through time? That is, the physical lifting of my very self out of *then* and into *now*? Or was my body dead and kept on deposit in a freezer vault until these people resuscitated and refurbished it? Am I, perhaps, a total genetic reconstruct fashioned from a few fragments of ancient somatic tissue found in a baroque urn? Possibly I am only a simulated and stylized interpretation of twentieth-century man produced by a computer under intelligent and sympathetic guidance. How was it done, Senator? How was it done? The rain ceased. Leaving elegant puddles of blurred hue in the puddle-places.

Walking with Louisiana on my arm down Venus Avenue I imagined that I saw another man with a face like mine. It was the merest flash: a dark visage, thick heavy brows, stubble on the cheeks, the head thrust belligerently forward between the massive shoulders. But he was gone, turning a sudden corner, before I could get a good look. Louisiana suggested I was overindulging in hallucinogens. We went to an underwater theater and she swam below me like a golden fish, revolving lights glinting off the upturned globes of her rump.

This is a demonstration of augmented mental capacity, said Vibrissa. I wish to show you what the extent of human potentiality can be. Read me any passage of Shakespeare of your own choice and I will repeat it verbatim and then offer you textual analysis. Shall we try this? Very well, I said and delicately put my fingernail to the Shakespeare cube and the words formed and I said out loud, What man dare, I dare: Approach thou like the rugged Russian bear, the arm'd rhinoceros, or the Hyrcan tiger, Take any shape but that, and my firm nerves Shall never tremble. Vibrissa instantly recited the lines to me without error and interpreted them in terms of the poet's penis envy, offering me footnotes from Seneca and Strindberg. I was quite impressed. But then I was never what you might call an intellectual.

On the day of the snow-gliding events I distinctly and beyond any possibilities of ambiguity or misapprehension saw two separate individuals who resembled me. Are they importing more of my kind for their amusement? If they are I will be resentful. I cherish my unique status.

I told Dr. Habakkuk that I wished to apply for transformation to the facial norm of society. Do it, I said, the transplant thing or the genetic manipulation or however you manage it. I want to be golden-haired and have blue eyes and regular features. I want to look like you. Dr. Habakkuk smiled genially and shook his youthful golden head. No, he told me. Forgive us, but we like you as you are.

*   *   *

Sometimes I dream of my life as it was in the former days. I
think of automobiles and pastrami and tax returns and marigolds
and pimples and mortgages and the gross national product. Also I
indulge in recollections of my childhood my parents my wife my
dentist my younger daughter my desk my toothbrush my dog my
umbrella my favorite brand of beer my wristwatch my answering
service my neighbors my phonograph my ocarina. All of these
things are gone. Grinding my flesh against that of Drusilla in the
copulatorium I wonder if she could be one of my descendants. I
must have descendants somewhere in this civilization, and why
not she? She asks me to perform an act of oral perversion with
her and I explain that I couldn't possibly engage in such stuff
with my own great-grandchild.

I think I remain quite calm at most times considering the
extraordinary nature of the stress that this experience has imposed
on me. I am still self-conscious about my appearance but I
pretend otherwise. Often I go naked just as they do. If they
dislike bodily hair or disproportionate limbs, let them look away.

Occasionally I belch or scratch under my arms or do other
primitive things to remind them that I am the authentic man from
antiquity. For now there can be no doubt that I have my imitators.
There are at least five. Calpurnia denies this, but I am no fool.

Dr. Habakkuk revealed that he was going to take a holiday in the
Carpathians and would not return until the 14th of June-surrogate.
In the meantime Dr. Clasp would minister to my needs. Dr.
Clasp entered my suite and I remarked on his startling resemblance to Dr. Habakkuk. He asked, What would you like? and I
told him I wanted him to operate on me so that I looked like
everybody else. I am tired of appearing bestial and primordial, I
said. To my surprise Dr. Clasp smiled warmly and told me that
he'd arrange for the transformation at once, since it violated his
principles to allow any organism needlessly to suffer. I was taken
to the operating room and given a sour-tasting anesthetic. Seemingly without the passing of time I awakened and was wheeled
into a dome of mirrors to behold myself. Even as I had requested
they had redone me into one of them, blond-haired, blue-eyed,
with a slim, agile body and a splendidly symmetrical face. Dr.

Clasp came in after a while and we stood side by side: we might have been twins. How do you like it? he asked. Tears brimmed in my eyes and I said that this was the most wonderful moment of my life. Dr. Clasp pummeled my shoulder jovially and said, You know, I am not Dr. Clasp at all, I am really Dr. Habakkuk and I never went to the Carpathians. This entire episode has been a facet of our analysis of your pattern of responses.

Louisiana was astonished by my changed appearance. Are you truly he? she kept asking. Are you truly he? I'll prove it, I said and mounted her with my old prehistoric zeal, snorting and gnawing her breasts. But she shook me free with a deft flip of her pelvis and rushed from the chamber. You'll never see me again she shouted but I merely shrugged and called after her, So what I can see lots of others just like you. I never saw her again.

So now they have all changed themselves again to the new standard model. It happened gradually over a period of months but the transition is at last complete. Their heavy brows, their pockmarked cheeks, their hairy chests. It is the latest thing. I make my way through the crowded streets and wherever I turn I see faces that mirror my own lopsidedness. Only I am not lopsided myself any more, of course. I am symmetrical and flawless, and I am the only one. I cannot find Dr. Habakkuk, and Dr. Clasp is in the Pyrenees; Senator Mandragore was defeated in the primary. So I must remain beautiful. Walking among them. They are all alike. Thick lips uneven teeth noses like blobs. How I despise them! I the only golden one. And all of them mocking me by their metamorphosis. All of them. Mocking me. Meee.

GETTING ACROSS

1.

ON THE FIRST day of summer my month-wife, Silena Ruiz, filched our district's master program from the Ganfield Hold computer center and disappeared with it. A guard at the Hold has confessed that she won admittance by seducing him, then gave him a drug. Some say she is in Conning Town now, others have heard rumors that she has been seen in Morton Court, still others maintain her destination was the Mill. I suppose it does not matter where she has gone. What matters is that we are without our program. We have lived without it for eleven days, and things are starting to break down. The heat is abominable, but we must switch every thermostat to manual override before we can use our cooling system; I think we will boil in our skins before the job is done. A malfunction of the scanners that control our refuse compactor has stilled the garbage collectors, which will not go forth unless they have a place to dump what they collect. Since no one knows the proper command to give the compactor, rubbish accumulates, forming pestilential hills on every street, and dense swarms of flies or worse hover over the sprawling mounds. Beginning on the fourth day our police also began to go immobile—who can say why?—and by now all of them stand halted in their tracks. Some are already starting to rust, since the maintenance schedules are out of phase. Word has gone out that we are without protection, and outlanders cross into the district with impunity, molesting our women, stealing our children, raiding our stocks of foodstuffs. In Ganfield Hold platoons of weary sweating technicians toil constantly to replace the missing program, but it might be months, even years, before they are able to devise a new one.

In theory, duplicate programs are stored in several places within the community against just such a calamity. In fact, we have none. The one kept in the district captain's office turned out to be some twenty years obsolete; the one in the care of the soulfather's house had been devoured by rats; the program held in the vaults of the tax collectors appeared to be intact, but when it was placed in the input slot it mysteriously failed to activate the computers. So we are helpless: an entire district, hundreds of thousands of human beings, cut loose to drift on the tides of chance. Silena, Silena, Silena! To disable all of Ganfield, to make our already burdensome lives more difficult, to expose me to the hatred of my neighbors—why, Silena? Why?

People glare at me on the streets. They hold me responsible, in a way, for all this. They point and mutter; in another few days they will be spitting and cursing, and if no relief comes soon they may be throwing stones. Look, I want to shout, she was only my month-wife and she acted entirely on her own. I assure you I had no idea she would do such a thing. And yet they blame me. At the wealthy houses of Morton Court they will dine tonight on babes stolen in Ganfield this day, and I am held accountable.

What will I do? Where can I turn?

I may have to flee. The thought of crossing district lines chills me. Is it the peril of death I fear, or only the loss of all that is familiar? Probably both: I have no hunger for dying and no wish to leave Ganfield. Yet I will go, no matter how difficult it will be to find sanctuary if I get safely across the line. If they continue to hold me tainted by Silena's crime I will have no choice. I think I would rather die at the hands of strangers than perish at those of my own people.

2.

This sweltering night I find myself atop Ganfield Tower, seeking cool breezes and the shelter of darkness. Half the district has had the idea of escaping the heat by coming up here tonight, it seems; to get away from the angry eyes and tightened lips I have climbed to the fifth parapet, where only the bold and the foolish ordinarily go. I am neither, yet here I am.

As I move slowly around the tower's rim, warily clinging to the old and eroded guardrail, I have a view of our entire district. Ganfield is like a shallow basin in form, gently sloping upward from the central spike that is the tower to a rise on the district perimeter. They say that a broad lake once occupied the site where Ganfield now stands; it was drained and covered over centuries ago, when the need for new living space became extreme. Yesterday I heard that great pumps are used to keep the ancient lake from breaking through into our cellars, and that before very long the pumps will fail or shut themselves down for maintenance, and we will be flooded. Perhaps so. Ganfield once devoured the lake; will the lake now have Ganfield? Will we tumble into the dark waters and be swallowed, with no one to mourn us?

I look out over Ganfield. These tall brick boxes are our dwellings, twenty stories high but dwarfed from my vantage point far above. This sliver of land, black in the smoky moonlight, is our pitiful scrap of community park. These low flat-topped buildings are our shops, a helter-skelter cluster. This is our industrial zone, such that it is. That squat shadow-cloaked bulk just north of the tower is Ganfield Hold, where our crippled computers slip one by one into idleness. I have spent nearly my whole life within this one narrow swing of the compasses that is Ganfield. When I was a boy and affairs were not nearly so harsh between one district and its neighbor, my father took me on holiday to Morton Court, and another time to the Mill. When I was a young man I was sent on business across three districts to Parley Close. I remember those journeys as clearly and vividly as though I had dreamed them. But everything is quite different now and it is twenty years since I last left Ganfield. I am not one of your privileged commuters, gaily making transit from zone to zone. All the world is one great city, so it is said, with the deserts settled and the rivers bridged and all the open places filled, a universal city that has abolished the old boundaries, and yet it is twenty years since I passed from one district to the next. I wonder: are we one city, then, or merely thousands of contentious fragmented tiny states?

Look here, along the perimeter. There are no more boundaries, but what is this? This is our boundary, Ganfield Crescent, that wide curving boulevard surrounding the district. Are you a man of some other zone? Then cross the Crescent at risk of life. Do you see our police machines, blunt-snouted, glossy, formidably powerful, strewn like boulders in the broad avenue? They will interrogate you, and if your answers are uneasy, they may destroy you. Of course they can do no one any harm tonight.

Look outward now, at our horde of brawling neighbors. I see beyond the Crescent to the east the gaunt spires of Conning Town, and on the west, descending stepwise into the jumbled valley, the shabby dark-walled buildings of the Mill, with happy Morton Court on the far side, and somewhere in the smoky distance other places, Folkstone and Budleigh and Hawk Nest and Parley Close and Kingston and Old Grove and all the rest, the districts, the myriad districts, part of the chain that stretches from sea to sea, from shore to shore, spanning our continent paunch by paunch, the districts, the chips of gaudy glass making up the global mosaic, the infinitely numerous communities that are the segments of the all-encompassing world-city. Tonight at the capital they are planning next month's rainfall patterns for districts that the planners have never seen. District food allocations— inadequate, always inadequate—are being devised by men to whom our appetites are purely abstract entities. Do they believe in our existence, at the capital? Do they really think there is such a place as Ganfield? What if we sent them a delegation of notable citizens to ask for help in replacing our lost program? Would they care? Would they even listen? For that matter, is there a capital at all? How can I who have never seen nearby Old Grove accept, on faith alone, the existence of a far-off governing center, aloof, inaccessible, shrouded in myth? Maybe it is only a construct of some cunning subterranean machine that is our real ruler. That would not surprise me. Nothing surprises me. There is no capital. There are no central planners. Beyond the horizon everything is mist.

3.

In the office, at least, no one dares show hostility to me. There are no scowls, no glares, no snide references to the missing program. I am, after all, chief deputy to the District Commission-

er of Nutrition, and since the commissioner is usually absent, I
am in effect in charge of the department. If Silena's crime does
not destroy my career, it might prove to have been unwise for my
subordinates to treat me with disdain. In any case we are so busy
that there is no time for such gambits. We are responsible for
keeping the community properly fed; our tasks have been greatly
complicated by the loss of the program, for there is no reliable
way now of processing our allocation sheets, and we must requisition and distribute food by guesswork and memory. How many
bales of plankton cubes do we consume each week? How many
kilos of proteoid mix? How much bread for the shops of Lower
Ganfield? What fads of diet are likely to sweep the district this
month? If demand and supply fall into imbalance as a result of our
miscalculations, there could be widespread acts of violence, forays
into neighboring districts, even renewed outbreaks of cannibalism
within Ganfield itself. So we must draw up our estimates with the
greatest precision. What a terrible spiritual isolation we feel,
deciding such things with no computers to guide us!

4.

On the fourteenth day of the crisis the district captain summons
me. His message comes in late afternoon, when we all are dizzy
with fatigue, choked by humidity. For several hours I have been
tangled in complex dealings with a high official of the Marine
Nutrients Board; this is an arm of the central city government,
and I must therefore show the greatest tact, lest Ganfield's
plankton quotas be arbitrarily lowered by a bureaucrat's sudden
pique. Telephone contact is uncertain—the Marine Nutrients
Board has its headquarters in Melrose New Port, half a continent
away on the southeastern coast—and the line sputters and blurs
with distortions that our computers, if the master program were
in operation, would normally erase. As we reach a crisis in the
negotiation my subdeputy gives me a note: DISTRICT CAPTAIN WANTS
TO SEE YOU. "Not now," I say in silent lip-talk. The haggling
proceeds. A few minutes later comes another note: IT'S URGENT. I
shake my head, brush the note from my desk. The subdeputy
retreats to the outer office, where I see him engaged in frantic
discussion with a man in the gray and green uniform of the
district captain's staff. The messenger points vehemently at me.

Just then the phone line goes dead. I slam the instrument down and call to the messenger, "What is it?"

"The captain, sir. To his office at once, please."

"Impossible."

He displays a warrant bearing the captain's seal. "He requires your immediate presence."

"Tell him I have delicate business to complete," I reply. "Another fifteen minutes, maybe."

He shakes his head. "I am not empowered to allow a delay."

"Is this an arrest, then?"

"A summons."

"But with the force of an arrest?"

"With the force of an arrest, yes," he tells me.

I shrug and yield. All burdens drop from me. Let the subdeputy deal with the Marine Nutrients Board; let the clerk in the outer office do it, or no one at all; let the whole district starve. I no longer care. I am summoned. My responsibilities are discharged. I give over my desk to the subdeputy and summarize for him, in perhaps a hundred words, my intricate hours of negotiation. All that is someone else's problem now.

The messenger leads me from the building into the hot, dank street. The sky is dark and heavy with rain, and evidently it has been raining some while, for the sewers are backing up and angry swirls of muddy water run shin-deep through the gutters. The drainage system, too, is controlled from Ganfield Hold, and must now be failing. We hurry across the narrow plaza fronting my office, skirt a gush of sewage-laden outflow, push into a close-packed crowd of irritable workers heading for home. The messenger's uniform creates an invisible sphere of untouchability for us; the throngs part readily and close again behind us. Wordlessly I am conducted to the stone-faced building of the district captain, and quickly to his office. It is no unfamiliar place to me, but coming here as a prisoner is quite different from attending a meeting of the district council. My shoulders are slumped, my eyes look toward the threadbare carpeting.

The district captain appears. He is a man of sixty, silver-haired, upright, his eyes frank and direct, his features reflecting little of the strain his position must impose. He has governed our district ten years. He greets me by name, but with warmth, and says, "You've heard nothing from your woman?"

"I would have reported it if I had."

"Perhaps. Perhaps. Have you any idea where she is?"

"I know only the common rumors," I say. "Conning Town, Morton Court, the Mill."

"She is in none of those places."

"Are you sure?"

"I have consulted the captains of those districts," he says. "They deny any knowledge of her. Of course, one has no reason to trust their word, but on the other hand, why would they bother to deceive me?" His eyes fasten on mine. "What part did you play in the stealing of the program?"

"None, sir."

"She never spoke to you of treasonable things?"

"Never."

"There is strong feeling in Ganfield that a conspiracy existed."

"If so, I knew nothing of it."

He judges me with a piercing look. After a long pause he says heavily, "She has destroyed us, you know. We can function at the present level of order for another six weeks, possibly, without the program—if there is no plague, if we are not flooded, if we are not overrun with bandits from outside. After that the accumulated effects of many minor breakdowns will paralyze us. We will fall into chaos. We will strangle on our own wastes, starve, suffocate, revert to savagery, live like beasts until the end—who knows? Without the master program we are lost. Why did she do this to us?"

"I have no theories," I say. "She kept her own counsel. Her independence of soul is what attracted me to her."

"Very well. Let her independence of soul be what attracts you to her now. Find her and bring back the program."

"Find her? Where?"

"That is for you to discover."

"I know nothing of the world outside Ganfield!"

"You will learn," the captain says coolly. "There are those here who would indict you for treason. I see no value in this. How does it help us to punish you? But we can *use* you. You are a clever and resourceful man; you can make your way through the hostile districts, and you can gather information, and you could well succeed in tracking her. If anyone has influence over her, you do—if you find her, you perhaps can induce her to surrender the program. No one else could hope to accomplish that. Go. We offer you immunity from prosecution in return for your cooperation."

The world spins wildly about me. My skin burns with shock. "Will I have safe conduct through the neighboring districts?" I ask.

"To whatever extent we can arrange. That will not be much, I fear."

"You'll give me an escort, then? Two or three men?"

"We feel you will travel more effectively alone. A party of several men takes on the character of an invading force. You would be met with suspicion and worse."

"Diplomatic credentials, at least?"

"A letter of identification, calling on all captains to honor your mission and treat you with courtesy."

I know how much value such a letter will have in Hawk Nest or Folkstone.

"This frightens me," I say.

He nods, not unkindly. "I understand that. Yet someone must seek her, and who else is there but you? We grant you a day to make your preparations. You will depart on the morning after next, and God hasten your return."

5.

Preparations. How can I prepare myself? What maps should I collect, when my destination is unknown? Returning to the office is unthinkable; I go straight home, and for hours I wander from one room to the other as if I face execution at dawn. At last I gather myself and fix a small meal, but most of it remains on my plate. No friends call; I call no one. Since Silena's disappearance my friends have fallen away from me. I sleep poorly. During the night there are hoarse shouts and shrill alarms in the street; I learn from the morning newscast that five men of Conning Town, here to loot, had been seized by one of the new vigilante groups that have replaced the police machines and were summarily put to death. I find no cheer in that, thinking that I might be in Conning Town in a day or so.

What clues to Silena's route? I ask to speak with the guard from whom she wangled entry into Ganfield Hold. He has been a prisoner ever since; the captain is too busy to decide his fate, and he languishes meanwhile. He is a small thick-bodied man with stubbly red hair and a sweaty forehead; his eyes are bright with anger and his nostrils quiver. "What is there to say?" he demands. "I was on duty at the Hold. She came in. I had never seen her before, though I knew she must be high-caste. Her cloak was open. She seemed naked beneath it. She was in a state of excitement."

"What did she tell you?"

"That she desired me. Those were her first words." Yes. I could see Silena doing that, though I had difficulty in imagining her long slender form enfolded in that squat little man's embrace. "She said she knew of me and was eager for me to have her."

"And then?"

"I sealed the gate. We went to an inner room where there is a cot. It was a quiet time of day, I thought no harm would come. She dropped her cloak. Her body—"

"Never mind her body." I could see it all too well in the eye of my mind, the sleek thighs, the taut belly, the small high breasts, the cascade of chocolate hair falling to her shoulders. "What did you talk about? Did she say anything of a political kind? Some slogan, some words against the government?"

"Nothing. We lay together naked a while, only fondling one another. Then she said she had a drug with her, one which would enhance the sensations of love tenfold. It was a dark powder. I drank it in water; she drank it also, or seemed to. Instantly I was asleep. When I awoke, the Hold was in uproar and I was a prisoner." He glowers at me. "I should have suspected a trick from the start. Such women do not hunger for men like me. How did I ever injure you? Why did you choose me to be the victim of your scheme?"

"Her scheme," I say. "Not mine. I had no part in it. Her motive is a mystery to me. If I could discover where she has gone, I would seek her and wring answers from her. Any help you could give me might earn you a pardon and your freedom."

"I know nothing," he says sullenly. "She came in, she snared me, she drugged me, she stole the program."

"Think. Not a word? Possibly she mentioned the name of some other district."

"Nothing."

A pawn is all he is, innocent, useless. As I leave he cries out to me to intercede for him, but what can I do? "Your woman ruined me!" he roars.

"She may have ruined us all," I reply.

At my request a district prosecutor accompanies me to Silena's apartment, which has been under official seal since her disappearance. Its contents have been thoroughly examined, but maybe there is some clue I alone would notice. Entering, I feel a sharp pang of loss, for the sight of Silena's possessions reminds me of happier times. These things are painfully familiar to me: her neat array of books, her clothing, her furnishings, her bed. I knew her only eleven weeks, she was my month-wife only for two; I had not realized she had come to mean so much to me so quickly. We look around, the prosecutor and I. The books testify to the agility of her restless mind: little light fiction, mainly works of serious history, analyses of social problems, forecasts of conditions to come. Holman, *The Era of the World City*. Sawtelle, *Megalopolis Triumphant*. Doxiadis, *The New World of Urban Man*. Heggebend, *Fifty Billion Lives*. Marks, *Calcutta Is Everywhere*. Chasin. *The New Community*. I take a few of the books down, fondling them as though they were Silena. Many times when I had spent an evening here she reached for one of those books, Sawtelle or Heggebend or Marks or Chasin, to read me a passage that amplified some point she was making. Idly I turn pages. Dozens of paragraphs are underscored with fine, precise lines, and lengthy marginal comments are abundant. "We've analyzed all of that for possible significance," the prosecutor remarks. "The only thing we've concluded is that she thinks the world is too crowded for comfort." A racheting laugh. "As who doesn't?" He points to a stack of green-bound pamphlets at the end of a lower shelf. "These, on the other hand, may be useful in your search. Do you know anything about them?"

The stack consists of nine copies of something called *Walden Three:* a Utopian fantasy, apparently, set in an idyllic land of streams and forests. The booklets are unfamiliar to me; Silena must have obtained them recently. Why nine copies? Was she acting as a distributor? They bear the imprint of a publishing house in Kingston. Ganfield and Kingston severed trade relations long ago; material published there is uncommon here. "I've never seen them," I say. "Where do you think she got them?"

"There are three main routes for subversive literature originating in Kingston. One is—"

"Is this pamphlet subversive, then?"

"Oh, very much so. It argues for complete reversal of the social trends of the last hundred years. As I was saying, there are three main routes for subversive literature originating in Kingston.

We have traced one chain of distribution running by way of Wisleigh and Cedar Mall, another through Old Grove, Hawk Nest, and Conning Town, and the third via Parley Close and the Mill. It is plausible that your woman is in Kingston now, having traveled along one of these underground distribution routes, sheltered by her fellow subversives all the way. But we have no way of confirming this." He smiles emptily. "She could be in any of the other communities along the three routes. Or in none of them."

"I should think of Kingston, though, as my ultimate goal, until I learn anything to the contrary. Is that right?"

"What else can you do?"

What else, indeed? I must search at random through an unknown number of hostile districts, having no clue other than the vague one implicit in the place of origin of these nine booklets, while time ticks on and Ganfield slips deeper day by day into confusion.

The prosecutor's office supplies me with useful things: maps, letters of introduction, a commuter's passport that should enable me to cross at least some district lines unmolested, and an assortment of local currencies as well as banknotes issued by the central bank and therefore valid in most districts. Against my wishes I am given also a weapon—a small heat-pistol—and in addition a capsule that I can swallow in the event that a quick and easy death becomes desirable. As the final stage in my preparation I spend an hour conferring with a secret agent, now retired, whose career of espionage took him safely into hundreds of communities as far away as Threadmuir and Reed Meadow. What advice does he give someone about to try to get across? "Maintain your poise," he says. "Be confident and self-assured, as though you belong in whatever place you find yourself. Never slink. Look all men in the eye. However, say no more than is necessary. Be watchful at all times. Don't relax your guard." Such precepts I could have evolved without his aid. He has nothing in the nature of specific hints for survival. Each district, he says, presents unique problems, constantly changing; nothing can be anticipated, everything must be met as it arises. How comforting!

At nightfall I go to the soulfather's house, in the shadow of Ganfield Tower. To leave without a blessing seems unwise. But there is something stagy and unspontaneous about my visit, and my faith flees as I enter. In the dim antechamber I light the nine candles, I pluck the five blades of grass from the ceremonial vase, I do the other proper ritual things, but my spirit remains chilled and hollow, and I am unable to pray. The soulfather himself, having been told of my mission, grants me audience— gaunt old man with impenetrable eyes set in deep bony rims— and favors me with a gentle feather-light embrace. "Go in safety," he murmurs. "God watches over you." I wish I felt sure of that. Going home, I take the most roundabout possible route, as if trying to drink in as much of Ganfield as I can on my last night. The diminishing past flows through me like a river running dry. My birthplace, my school, the streets where I played, the dormitory where I spent my adolescence, the home of my first month-wife. Farewell. Farewell. Tomorrow I go across. I return to my apartment alone; once more my sleep is fitful; an hour after dawn I find myself, astonished by it, waiting in line among the commuters at the mouth of the transit tube, bound for Conning Town. And so my crossing begins.

6.

Aboard the tube no one speaks. Faces are tense, bodies are held rigid in the plastic seats. Occasionally someone on the other side of the aisle glances at me as though wondering who this newcomer to the commuter group may be, but his eyes quickly slide away as I take notice. I know none of these commuters, though they must have dwelled in Ganfield as long as I; their lives have never intersected mine before. Engineers, merchants, diplomats, whatever—their careers are tied to districts other than their own. It is one of the anomalies of our ever more fragmented and stratified society that some regular contact still survives between community and community; a certain number of people must journey each day to outlying districts, where they work encapsulated, isolated, among unfriendly strangers.

We plunge eastward at unimaginable speed. Surely we are past the boundaries of Ganfield by now and under alien territory. A glowing sign on the wall of the car announces our route: CONNING TOWN-HAWK NEST-OLD GROVE-KINGSTON-FOLKSTONE-PARLEY CLOSE-BUD-LEIGH-CEDAR MALL-THE MILL-MORTON COURT-GANFIELD, a wide loop through our most immediate neighbors. I try to visualize the separate links in this chain of districts, each a community of three or four hundred thousand loyal and patriotic citizens, each with its own

special tone, its flavor, its distinctive quality, its apparatus of
government, its customs and rituals. But I can imagine them
merely as a cluster of Ganfields, every place very much like the
one I have just left. I know this is not so. The world-city is no
homogenous collection of uniformities, a global bundle of indistinguishable suburbs. No, there is incredible diversity, a host of
unique urban cores bound by common need into a fragile unity.
No master plan brought them into being; each evolved at a
separate point in time, to serve the necessities of a particular
purpose. This community sprawls gracefully along a curving
river, that one boldly mounts the slopes of stark hills; here the
prevailing architecture reflects an easy, gentle climate, there it
wars with unfriendly nature; form follows topography and local
function, creating individuality. The world is a richness: why
then do I see only ten thousand Ganfields?

Of course it is not so simple. We are caught in the tension
between forces which encourage distinctiveness and forces com-
pelling all communities toward identicality. Centrifugal forces
broke down the huge ancient cities, the Londons and Tokyos and
New Yorks, into neighborhood communities that seized quasi-
autonomous powers. Those giant cities were too unwieldy to
survive; density of population, making long-distance transport
unfeasible and communication difficult, shattered the urban fabric, destroyed the authority of the central government, and left
the closely knit small-scale subcity as the only viable unit. Two
dynamic and contradictory processes now asserted themselves.
Pride and the quest for local advantage led each community
toward specialization: this one a center primarily of industrial
production, this one devoted to advanced education, this to
finance, this to the processing of raw materials, this to wholesale
marketing of commodities, this to retail distribution, and so on,
the shape and texture of each district defined by its chosen
function. And yet the new decentralization required a high degree
of redundancy, duplication of governmental structures, of utilities, of
community services; for its own safety each district felt the need
to transform itself into a microcosm of the former full city.
Ideally we should have hovered in perfect balance between
specialization and redundancy, all communities striving to fulfill
the needs of all other communities with the least possible overlap
and waste of resources; in fact, our human frailty has brought
into being these irreversible trends of rivalry and irrational fear,

dividing district from district, so that against our own self-interest
we sever year after year our bonds of interdependence and
stubbornly seek self-sufficiency at the district level. Since this is
impossible, our lives grow constantly more impoverished. In the
end all districts will be the same and we will have created a
world of pathetic limping Ganfields, devoid of grace, lacking in
variety.

So. The tube-train halts. This is Conning Town. I am across
the first district line. I make my exit in a file of solemn-faced
commuters. Imitating them, I approach a colossal cyclopean
scanning machine and present my passport. It is unmarked by
visas; theirs are gaudy with scores of them. I tremble, but the
machine accepts me and slams down a stamp that fluoresces a
brilliant shimmering crimson against the pale lavender page:

* DISTRICT OF CONNING TOWN *

* ENTRY VISA *

* 24-HOUR VALIDITY *

Dated to the hour, minute, second. Welcome, stranger, but get
out of town before sunrise!

Up the purring ramp, into the street. Bright morning sunlight
pries apart the slim sooty close-ranked towers of Conning Town.
The air is cool and sweet, strange to me after so many sweltering
days in programless demechanized Ganfield. Does our foul air
drift across the border and offend them? Sullen eyes study me;
those about me know me for an outsider. Their clothing is alien
in style, pinched in at the shoulders, flaring at the waist.
I find myself adopting an inane smile in response to their dour
glares.

For an hour I walk aimlessly through the downtown section
until my first fears melt and a comic cockiness takes possession
of me: I pretend to myself that I am a native, and enjoy the flimsy
imposture. This place is not much unlike Ganfield, yet nothing is
quite the same. The sidewalks are wider; the street lamps have
slender arching necks instead of angular ones; the fire hydrants
are green and gold, not blue and orange. The police machines
have flatter domes than ours, ringed with ten or twelve spy-
eyes where ours have six or eight. Different, different, all
different.

Three times I am halted by police machines. I produce my
passport, display my visa, am allowed to continue. So far
getting across has been easier than I imagined. No one molests

me here. I suppose I look harmless. Why did I think my
foreignness alone would lead these people to attack me? Ganfield
is not at war with its neighbors, after all.

Drifting eastward in search of a bookstore, I pass through a
shabby residential neighborhood and through a zone of dismal
factories before I reach an area of small shops. Then in late
afternoon I discover three bookstores on the same block, but they
are antiseptic places, not the sort that might carry subversive
propaganda like *Walden Three*. The first two are wholly automated, blank-walled charge-plate-and-scanner operations. The third
has a human clerk, a man of about thirty with drooping yellow
mustachios and alert blue eyes. He recognizes the style of my
clothing and says, "Ganfield, eh? Lot of trouble over there."

"You've heard?"

"Just stories. Computer breakdown, isn't it?"

I nod. "Something like that."

"No police, no garbage removal, no weather control, hardly
anything working—that's what they say." He seems neither
surprised nor disturbed to have an outlander in his shop. His
manner is amiable and relaxed. Is he fishing for data about our
vulnerability, though? I must be careful not to tell him anything
that might be used against us. But evidently they already know
everything here. He says, "It's a little like dropping back into the
Stone Age for you people, I guess. It must be a real traumatic
thing."

"We're coping," I say, stiffly casual.

"How did it happen, anyway?"

I give him a wary shrug. "I'm not sure about that." Still
revealing nothing. But then something in his tone of a moment
before catches me belatedly and neutralizes some of the reflexive
automatic suspicion with which I have met his questions. I glance
around. No one else is in the shop. I let something conspiratorial
creep into my voice and say, "It might not even be so traumatic,
actually, once we get used to it. I mean, there once was a time
when we didn't rely so heavily on machines to do our thinking
for us, and we survived and even managed pretty well. I was
reading a little book last week that seemed to be saying we might
profit by trying to return to the old way of life. Book published in
Kingston."

"*Walden Three*." Not a question but a statement.

"That's it." My eyes query his. "You've read it?"

"Seen it."

"A lot of sense in that book, I think."

He smiles warmly. "I think so too. You get much Kingston stuff over in Ganfield?"

"Very little, actually."

"Not much here, either."

"But there's some."

"Some, yes," he says.

Have I stumbled upon a member of Silena's underground movement? I say eagerly, "You know, maybe you could help me meet some people who—"

"No."

"No?"

"No." His eyes are still friendly but his face is tense. "There's nothing like that around here," he says, his voice suddenly flat and remote. "You'd have to go over into Hawk Nest."

"I'm told that that's a nasty place."

"Nevertheless. Hawk Nest is where you want to go. Nate and Holly Borden's shop, just off Box Street." Abruptly his manner shifts to one of exaggerated bland clerkishness. "Anything else I can do for you, sir? If you're interested in supernovels we've got a couple of good new double-amplified cassettes, just in. Perhaps I can show you—"

"Thank you, no." I smile, shake my head, leave the store. A police machine waits outside. Its dome rotates; eye after eye scans me intently; finally its resonant voice says, "Your passport, please." This routine is familiar by now. I produce the document. Through the bookshop window I see the clerk bleakly watching. The police machine says, "What is your place of residence in Conning Town?"

"I have none. I'm here on a twenty-four-hour visa."

"Where will you spend the night?"

"In a hotel, I suppose."

"Please show your room confirmation."

"I haven't made arrangements yet," I tell it.

A long moment of silence: the machine is conferring with its central, no doubt, keying into the master program of Conning Town for instructions. At length it says, "You are advised to obtain a legitimate reservation and display it to a monitor at the earliest opportunity within the next four hours. Failure to do so will result in cancellation of your visa and immediate expulsion from Conning

Town." Some ominous clicks come from the depths of the machine. "You are now under formal surveillance," it announces.

Brimming with questions, I return hastily to the bookshop. The clerk is displeased to see me. Anyone who attracts monitors to his shop—"monitors" is what they call police machines here, it seems—is unwelcome. "Can you tell me how to reach the nearest decent hotel?" I ask.

"You won't find one."

"No decent hotels?"

"No hotels. None where you could get a room, anyway. We have only two or three transient houses, and accommodations are allocated months in advance to regular commuters."

"Does the monitor know that?"

"Of course."

"Where are strangers supposed to stay, then?"

The clerk shrugs. "There's no structural program here for strangers as such. The regular commuters have regular arrangements. Unauthorized intruders don't belong here at all. You fall somewhere in between, I imagine. There's no legal way for you to spend the night in Conning Town."

"But my visa—"

"Even so."

"I'd better go on into Hawk Nest, I suppose."

"It's late. You've missed the last tube. You've got no choice but to stay, unless you want to try a border crossing on foot in the dark. I wouldn't recommend that."

"Stay? But where?"

"Sleep in the street. If you're lucky the monitors will leave you alone."

"Some quiet back alley, I suppose."

"No," he says. "You sleep in an out-of-the-way place and you'll surely get sliced up by night-bandits. Go to one of the designated sleeping streets. In the middle of a big crowd you might just go unnoticed, even though you're under surveillance." As he speaks he moves about the shop, closing it down for the night. He looks restless and uncomfortable. I take out my map of Conning Town and he shows me where to go. The map is some years out of date, apparently; he corrects it with irritable swipes of his pencil. We leave the shop together. I invite him to come with me to some restaurant as my guest, but he looks at me as if I carry plague. "Goodbye," he says. "Good luck."

7.

Alone, apart from the handful of other diners, I take my evening meal at a squalid, dimly lit automated cafeteria at the edge of downtown. Silent machines offer me thin acrid soup, pale spongy bread, and a leaden stew containing lumpy ingredients of undeterminable origin, for which I pay with yellow plastic counters of Conning Town currency. Emerging undelighted, I observe a reddish glow in the western sky: it may be a lovely sunset or, for all I know, may be a sign that Ganfield is burning. I look about for monitors. My four-hour grace period has nearly expired. I must disappear shortly into a throng. It seems too early for sleep, but I am only a few blocks from the place where the bookshop clerk suggested I should pass the night, and I go to it. Just as well: when I reach it—a wide plaza bordered by gray buildings of ornate facade—I find it already filling up with street-sleepers. There must be eight hundred of them, men, women, family groups, settling down in little squares of cobbled territory that are obviously claimed night after night under some system of squatters' rights. Others constantly arrive, flowing inward from the plaza's three entrances, finding their places, laying out foam cushions or mounds of clothing as their mattresses. It is a friendly crowd: these people are linked by bonds of neighborliness, a common poverty. They laugh, embrace, play games of chance, exchange whispered confidences, bicker, transact business, and join together in the rites of the local religion, performing a routine that involves six people clasping hands and chanting. Privacy seems obsolete here. They undress freely before one another, and there are instances of open coupling. The gaiety of the scene—a medieval carnival is what it suggests to me, a Breughelesque romp—is marred only by my awareness that this horde of revelers is homeless under the inhospitable skies, vulnerable to rain, sleet, damp fog, snow, and the other unkindnesses of winter and summer in these latitudes. In Ganfield we have just a scattering of street-sleepers, those who have lost their residential licenses and are temporarily forced into the open, but here it seems to be an established institution, as though Conning Town declared a moratorium some years ago on new residential construction without at the same time checking the increase of population.

Stepping over and around and between people, I reach the center of the plaza and select an unoccupied bit of pavement. But in a moment a little ruddy-faced woman arrives, excited and animated, and with a Conning Town accent so thick I can barely understand her she tells me she holds claim here. Her eyes are bright with menace; her hands are not far from becoming claws; several nearby squatters sit up and regard me threateningly. I apologize for my error and withdraw, stumbling over a child and narrowly missing overturning a bubbling cooking pot. Onward. Not here. Not here. A hand emerges from a pile of blankets and strokes my leg as I look around in perplexity. Not here. A man with a painted face rises out of a miniature green tent and speaks to me in a language I do not understand. Not here. I move on again and again, thinking that I will be jostled out of the plaza entirely, excluded, disqualified even to sleep in this district's streets, but finally I find a cramped corner where the occupants indicate I am welcome. "Yes?" I say. They grin and gesture. Gratefully I seize the spot.

Darkness has come. The plaza continues to fill; at least a thousand people have arrived after me, cramming into every vacancy, and the flow does not abate. I hear booming laughter, idle chatter, earnest romantic persuasion, the brittle sound of domestic quarreling. Someone passes a jug of wine around, even to me: bitter stuff, fermented clam juice its probable base, but I appreciate the gesture. The night is warm, almost sticky. The scent of unfamiliar food drifts on the air—something sharp, spicy, a heavy pungent smell. Curry? Is this then truly Calcutta? I close my eyes and huddle into myself. The hard cobblestones are cold beneath me. I have no mattress and I feel unable to remove my clothes before so many strangers. It will be hard for me to sleep in this madhouse, I think. But gradually the hubbub diminishes and— exhausted, drained—I slide into a deep troubled sleep.

Ugly dreams. The asphyxiating pressure of a surging mob. Rivers leaping their channels. Towers toppling. Fountains of mud bursting from a thousand lofty windows. Bands of steel encircling my thighs; my legs, useless, withering away. A torrent of lice sweeping over me. A frosty hand touching me. Touching me. Touching me. Pulling me up from sleep.

Harsh white light drenches me. I blink, cringe, cover my eyes. Shortly I perceive that a monitor stands over me. About me the sleepers awake, backing away, murmuring, pointing.

"Your street-sleeping permit, please."

Caught. I mumble excuses, plead ignorance of the law, beg forgiveness. But a police machine is neither malevolent nor merciful; it merely follows its program. It demands my passport and scans my visa. Then it reminds me I have been under surveillance. Having failed to obtain a hotel room as ordered, having neglected to report to a monitor within the prescribed interval, I am subject to expulsion.

"Very well," I say. "Conduct me to the border of Hawk Nest."

"You will return at once to Ganfield."

"I have business in Hawk Nest."

"Illegal entrants are returned to their district of origin."

"What does it matter to you where I go, so long as I get out of Conning Town?"

"Illegal entrants are returned to their district of origin," the machine tells me inexorably.

I dare not go back with so little accomplished. Still arguing with the monitor, I am led from the plaza through dark cavernous streets toward the mouth of a transit tube. On the station level a second monitor is given charge of me. "In three hours," the monitor that apprehended me informs me, 'the Ganfield-bound train will arrive."

The first monitor rolls away.

Too late I realize that the machine has neglected to return my passport.

8.

Monitor number two shows little interest in me. Patrolling the tube station, it swings in a wide arc around me, keeping a scanner perfunctorily trained on me but making no attempt to interfere with what I do. If I try to flee, of course, it will destroy me. Fretfully I study my maps. Hawk Nest lies to the northeast of Conning Town; if this is the tube station that I think it is, the border is not far. Five minutes' walk, perhaps. Passportless, there is no place I can go except Ganfield; my commuter status is revoked. But legalities count for little in Hawk Nest.

How to escape?

I concoct a plan. Its simplicity seems absurd, yet absurdity is often useful when dealing with machines. The monitor is in-

structed to put me aboard the train for Ganfield, yes? But not
necessarily to keep me there.

I wait out the weary hours to dawn. I hear the crash of
compressed air far up the tunnel. Snub-nosed, silken-smooth, the
train slides into the station. The monitor orders me aboard. I
walk into the car, cross it quickly, and exit by the open door on
the far side of the platform. Even if the monitor has observed this
maneuver, it can hardly fire across a crowded train. As I leave
the car I break into a trot, darting past startled travelers, and
sprint upstairs into the misty morning. At street level running is
unwise. I drop back to a rapid walking pace and melt into the
throngs of early workers. The street is Crystal Boulevard. Good,
I have memorized a route: Crystal Boulevard to Flagstone Square,
thence via Mechanic Street to the border.

Presumably all monitors, linked to whatever central nervous
system the machines of the district of Conning Town utilize, have
instantaneously been apprised of my disappearance. But that is
not the same as knowing where to find me. I head northward on
Crystal Boulevard—its name shows a dark sense of irony, or else
the severe transformations time can work—and, borne by the
flow of pedestrian traffic, enter Flagstone Square, a grimy,
lopsided plaza out of which, on the left, snakes curving Mechanic Street. I go unintercepted on this thoroughfare of small shops.
The place to anticipate trouble is at the border.

I am there in a few minutes. It is a wide dusty street, silent and
empty, lined on the Conning Town side by a row of blocky brick
warehouses, on the Hawk Nest side by a string of low ragged
buildings, some in ruins, the best of them defiantly slatternly.
There is no barrier. To fence a district border is unlawful except
in time of war, and I have heard of no war between Conning
Town and Hawk Nest.

Dare I cross? Police machines of two species patrol the street:
flat-domed ones of Conning Town and black, hexagon-headed
ones of Hawk Nest. Surely one or the other will gun me down in
the no man's land between districts. But I have no choice. I must
keep going forward.

I run out into the street at a moment when two police
machines, passing one another on opposite orbits, have left an
unpatrolled space perhaps a block long. Midway in my crossing
the Conning Town monitor spies me and blares a command. The
words are unintelligible to me, and I keep running, zigzagging in

the hope of avoiding the bolt that very likely will follow. But the machine does not shoot; I must already be on the Hawk Nest side of the line, and Conning Town no longer cares what becomes of me.

The Hawk Nest machine has noticed me. It rolls toward me as I stumble, breathless and gasping, onto the curb. "Halt!" it cries. "Present your documents!" At that moment a red-bearded man, fierce-eyed, wide-shouldered, steps out of a decaying building close by me. A scheme assembles itself in my mind. Do the customs of sponsorship and sanctuary hold good in this harsh district.

"Brother!" I cry. "What luck!" I embrace him, and before he can fling me off I murmur, "I am from Ganfield. I seek sanctuary here. Help me!"

The machine has reached me. It goes into an interrogatory stance and I say, "This is my brother who offers me the privilege of sanctuary. Ask him! Ask him!"

"Is this true?" the machine inquires.

Redbeard, unsmiling, spits and mutters, "My brother, yes. A political refugee. I'll stand sponsor to him. I vouch for him. Let him be."

The machine clicks, hums, assimilates. To me it says, "You will register as a sponsored refugee within twelve hours or leave Hawk Nest." Without another word it rolls away.

I offer my sudden savior warm thanks. He scowls, shakes his head, spits once again. "We owe each other nothing," he says brusquely and goes striding down the street.

9.

In Hawk Nest nature has followed art. The name, I have heard, once had purely neutral connotations: some real-estate developer's high-flown metaphor, nothing more. Yet it determined the district's character, for gradually Hawk Nest became the home of predators that it is today, where all men are strangers, where every man is his brother's enemy.

Other districts have their slums. Hawk Nest *is* a slum. I am told they live here by looting, cheating, extorting, and manipulating. An odd economic base for an entire community, but maybe it works for them. The atmosphere is menacing. The only police machines seem to be those that patrol the border. I sense emanations of violence just beyond the corner of my eye: rapes

and garrotings in shadowy byways, flashing knives and muffled
groans, covert cannibal feasts. Perhaps my imagination works too
hard. Certainly I have gone unthreatened so far; those I meet on
the streets pay no heed to me, indeed will not even return my
glance. Still, I keep my heat-pistol close by my hand as I walk
through these shabby, deteriorating outskirts. Sinister faces peer
at me through cracked, dirt-veiled windows. If I am attacked,
will I have to fire in order to defend myself? God spare me from
having to answer that.

10.

Why is there a bookshop in this town of murder and rubble and
decay? Here is Box Street, and here, in an oily pocket of
spare-parts depots and fly-specked quick-lunch counters, is Nate
and Holly Borden's place. Five times as deep as it is broad,
dusty, dimly lit, shelves overflowing with old books and pamphlets: an improbable outpost of the nineteenth century, somehow
displaced in time. There is no one in it but a large, impassive
woman seated at the counter, fleshy, puffy-faced, motionless. Her
eyes, oddly intense, glitter like glass disks set in a mound of
dough. She regards me without curiosity.

I say, "I'm looking for Holly Borden."

"You've found her," she replies, deep in the baritone range.

"I've come across from Ganfield by way of Conning Town."

No response from her to this.

I continue, "I'm traveling without a passport. They confiscat-
ed it in Conning Town and I ran the border."

She nods. And waits. No show of interest.

"I wonder if you could sell me a copy of *Walden Three*," I say.

Now she stirs a little. "Why do you want one?"

"I'm curious about it. It's not available in Ganfield."

"How do you know I have one?"

"Is anything illegal in Hawk Nest?"

She seems annoyed that I have answered a question with a
question. "How do you know *I* have a copy of that book?"

"A bookshop clerk in Conning Town said you might."

A pause. "All right. Suppose I do. Did you come all the way
from Ganfield just to buy a book?" Suddenly she leans forward
and smiles—a warm, keen, penetrating smile that wholly trans-

forms her face: now she is keyed up, alert, responsive, shrewd, commanding. "What's your game?" she asks.

"My game?"

"What are you playing? What are you up to here?"

It is the moment for total honesty. "I'm looking for a woman named Silena Ruiz, from Ganfield. Have you heard of her?"

"Yes. She's not in Hawk Nest."

"I think she's in Kingston. I'd like to find her."

"Why? To arrest her?"

"Just to talk to her. I have plenty to discuss with her. She was my month-wife when she left Ganfield."

"The month must be nearly up," Holly Borden says.

"Even so," I reply. "Can you help me reach her?"

"Why should I trust you?"

"Why not?"

She ponders that briefly. She studies my face. I feel the heat of her scrutiny. At length she says, "I expect to be making a journey to Kingston soon. I suppose I could take you with me."

11.

She opens a trapdoor; I descend into a room beneath the bookshop. After a good many hours a thin, gray-haired man brings me a tray of food. "Call me Nate," he says. Overhead I hear indistinct conversations, laughter, the thumping of boots on the wooden floor. In Ganfield famine may be setting in by now. Rats will be dancing around Ganfield Hold. How long will they keep me here? Am I a prisoner? Two days. Three. Nate will answer no questions. I have books, a cot, a sink, a drinking glass. On the third day the trap door opens. Holly Borden peers down. "We're ready to leave," she says.

The expedition consists just of the two of us. She is going to Kingston to buy books and travels on a commercial passport that allows for one helper. Nate drives us to the tube-mouth in midafternoon. It no longer seems unusual to me to be passing from district to district; they are not such alien and hostile places, merely different from the place I know. I see myself bound on an odyssey that carries me across hundreds of districts, even thousands, the whole patchwork frenzy of our world. Why return to Ganfield? Why not go on, ever eastward, to the great ocean and beyond, to the unimaginable strangenesses on the far side?

Here we are in Kingston. An old district, one of the oldest. We are the only ones who journey hither today from Hawk Nest. There is only a perfunctory inspection of passports. The police machines of Kingston are tall, long-armed, with fluted bodies ornamented in stripes of red and green: quite a gay effect. I am becoming an expert in local variations of police-machine design. Kingston itself is a district of low pastel buildings arranged in spokelike boulevards radiating from the famed university that is its chief enterprise. No one from Ganfield has been admitted to the university in my memory.

Holly is expecting friends to meet her, but they have not come. We wait fifteen minutes. "Never mind," she says. "We'll walk." I carry the luggage. The air is soft and mild; the sun, sloping toward Folkstone and Budleigh, is still high. I feel oddly serene. It is as if I have perceived a divine purpose, an overriding plan, in the structure of our society, in our sprawling city of many cities, our network of steel and concrete clinging like an armor of scales to the skin of our planet. But what is that purpose? What is that plan? The essence of it eludes me; I am aware only that it must exist. A cheery delusion.

Fifty paces from the station we are abruptly surrounded by a dozen or more buoyant young men who emerge from an intersecting street. They are naked but for green loincloths; their hair and beards are untrimmed and unkempt; they have a fierce and barbaric look. Several carry long unsheathed knives strapped to their waists. They circle wildly about us, laughing, jabbing at us with their fingertips. "This is a holy district!" they cry. "We need no blasphemous strangers here! Why must you intrude on us?"

"What do they want?" I whisper. "Are we in danger?"

"They are a band of priests," Holly replies. "Do as they say and we will come to no harm."

They press close. Leaping, dancing, they shower us with sprays of perspiration. "Where are you from?" they demand. "Ganfield," I say. "Hawk Nest," says Holly. They seem playful yet dangerous. Surging about me, they empty my pockets in a series of quick jostling forays: I lose my heat-pistol, my maps, my useless letters of introduction, my various currencies, everything, even my suicide capsule. These things they pass among themselves, exclaiming over them; then the heat-pistol and some of the currency are returned to me. "Ganfield," they murmur. "Hawk Nest!" There is distaste in their voices. "Filthy places," they say. "Places scorned by God," they say. They seize our hands and haul us about, making us spin. Heavy-bodied Holly is surprisingly graceful, breaking into a serene lumbering dance that makes them applaud in wonder.

One, the tallest of the group, catches our wrists and says, "What is your business in Kingston?"

"I come to purchase books," Holly declares.

"I come to find my month-wife Silena," say I.

"Silena! Silena! Silena!" Her name becomes a jubilant incantation on their lips. "His month-wife! Silena! His month-wife! Silena! Silena! Silena!"

The tall one thrusts his face against mine and says, "We offer you a choice. Come and make prayer with us, or die on the spot."

"We choose to pray," I tell him.

They tug at our arms, urging us impatiently onward. Down street after street until at last we arrive at holy ground: a garden plot, insignificant in area, planted with unfamiliar bushes and flowers, tended with evident care. They push us inside.

"Kneel," they say.

"Kiss the sacred earth."

"Adore the things that grow in it, strangers."

"Give thanks to God for the breath you have just drawn."

"And for the breath you are about to draw."

"Sing!"

"Weep!"

"Laugh!"

"Touch the soil!"

"Worship!"

12.

Silena's room is cool and quiet, in the upper story of a residence overlooking the university grounds. She wears a soft green robe of coarse texture, no jewelry, no face paint. Her demeanor is calm and self-assured. I had forgotten the delicacy of her features, the cool malicious sparkle of her dark eyes.

"The master program?" she says, smiling. "I destroyed it!"

The depth of my love for her unmans me. Standing before her,

I feel my knees turning to water. In my eyes she is bathed in a glittering aura of sensuality. I struggle to control myself. "You destroyed nothing," I say. "Your voice betrays the lie."

"You think I still have the program?"

"I know you do."

"Well, yes," she admits coolly. "I do."

My fingers tremble. My throat parches. An adolescent foolishness seeks to engulf me.

"Why did you steal it?" I ask.

"Out of love of mischief."

"I see the lie in your smile. What was the true reason?"

"Does it matter?"

"The district is paralyzed, Silena. Thousands of people suffer. We are at the mercy of raiders from adjoining districts. Many have already died of the heat, the stink of garbage, the failure of the hospital equipment. Why did you take the program?"

"Perhaps I had political reasons."

"Which were?"

"To demonstrate to the people of Ganfield how utterly dependent on these machines they have allowed themselves to become."

"We knew that already," I say. "If you meant only to dramatize our weaknesses, you were pressing the obvious. What was the point of crippling us? What could you gain from it?"

"Amusement?"

"Something more than that. You're not that shallow, Silena."

"Something more than that, then. By crippling Ganfield I help to change things. That's the purpose of any political act. To display the need for change, so that change may come about."

"Simply displaying the need is not enough."

"It's a place to begin."

"Do you think stealing our program was a rational way to bring change, Silena?"

"Are you happy?" she retorts. "Is this the kind of world you want?"

"It's the world we have to live in whether we like it or not. And we need that program in order to go on coping. Without it we are plunged into chaos."

"Fine. Let chaos come. Let everything fall apart, so we can rebuild it."

"Easy enough to say, Silena. What about the innocent victims of your revolutionary zeal, though?"

She shrugs. "There are always innocent victims in any revolution." In a sinuous movement she rises and approaches me. The closeness of her body is dazzling and maddening. With exaggerated voluptuousness she croons. "Stay here. Forget Ganfield. Life is good here. These people are building something worth having."

"Let me have the program," I say.

"They must have replaced it by now."

"Replacing it is impossible. The program is vital to Ganfield, Silena. Let me have it."

She emits an icy laugh.

"I beg you, Silena."

"How boring you are!"

"I love you."

"You love nothing but the status quo. The shape of things as they are gives you great joy. You have the soul of a bureaucrat."

"If you have always had such contempt for me, why did you become my month-wife?"

She laughs again. "For sport, perhaps."

Her words are like knives. Suddenly, to my own astonishment, I am brandishing the heat-pistol. "Give me the program or I'll kill you!" I cry.

She is amused. "Go. Shoot. Can you get the program from a dead Silena?"

"Give it to me."

"How silly you look holding that gun!"

"I don't have to kill you," I tell her. "I can merely wound you. This pistol is capable of inflicting light burns that scar the skin. Shall I give you blemishes, Silena?"

"Whatever you wish. I'm at your mercy."

I aim the pistol at her thigh. Silena's face remains expressionless. My arm stiffens and begins to quiver. I struggle with the rebellious muscles, but I succeed in steadying my aim only for a moment before the tremors return. An exultant gleam enters her eyes. A flush of excitement spreads over her face. "Shoot," she says defiantly. "Why don't you shoot me?"

She knows me too well. We stand in a frozen tableau for an endless moment outside time—a minute, an hour, a second?—and than my arm sags to my side. I put the pistol away. It never would have been possible for me to fire it. A powerful feeling assails me of having passed through some subtle climax:

it will all be downhill from here for me, and we both know it.
Sweat drenches me. I feel defeated, broken.

Silena's features reveal intense scorn. She has attained some
exalted level of consciousness in these past few moments where
all acts become gratuitous, where love and hate and revolution
and betrayal and loyalty are indistinguishable from one another.
She smiles the smile of someone who has scored the winning
point in a game, the rules of which will never be explained to
me.

"You little bureaucrat," she says calmly. "Here!"

From a closet she brings forth a small parcel which she tosses
disdainfully to me. It contains a drum of computer film. "The
program?" I ask. "This must be some joke. You wouldn't actually
give it to me, Silena."

"You hold the master program of Ganfield in your hand."

"Really, now?"

"Really, really," she says. "The authentic item. Go on. Go.
Get out. Save your stinking Ganfield."

"Silena—"

"Go."

13.

The rest is tedious but simple. I locate Holly Borden, who has
purchased a load of books. I help her with them, and we return
via tube to Hawk Nest. There I take refuge beneath the bookshop
once more while a call is routed through Old Grove, Parley
Close, the Mill, and possibly some other districts to the district
captain of Ganfield. It takes two days to complete the circuit,
since district rivalries make a roundabout relay necessary. Ultimately I am connected and convey my happy news: I have the
program, though I have lost my passport and am forbidden to
cross Conning Town. Through diplomatic channels a new passport is conveyed to me a few days later, and I take the tube home
the long way, via Budleigh, Cedar Mall, and Morton Court.
Ganfield is hideous, all filth and disarray, close to the point of
irreversible collapse; its citizens have lapsed into a deadly stasis
and await their doom placidly. But I have returned with the
program.

The captain praises my heroism. I will be rewarded, he says. I will have promotion to the highest ranks of the civil service, with hope of ascent to the district council.

But I take pale pleasure from his words. Silena's contempt still governs my thoughts. *Bureaucrat. Bureaucrat.*

14.

Still, Ganfield is saved. The police machines have begun to move again.

BRECKENRIDGE AND THE CONTINUUM

THEN BRECKENRIDGE SAID, "I suppose I could tell you the story of Oedipus King of Thieves tonight."

The late afternoon sky was awful: gray, mottled, fierce. It resonated with a strange electricity. Breckenridge had never grown used to that sky. Day after day, as they crossed the desert, it transfixed him with the pain of incomprehensible loss.

"Oedipus King of Thieves," Scarp murmured. Arios nodded. Horn looked toward the sky. Militor frowned. "Oedipus," said Horn. "King of Thieves," Arios said.

Breckenridge and his four companions were camped in a ruined pavilion in the desert—a handsome place of granite pillars and black marble floors, constructed perhaps for some delicious paramour of some forgotten prince of the city-building folk. The pavilion lay only a short distance outside the walls of the great dead city that they would enter, at last, in the morning. Once, maybe, this place had been a summer resort, a place for sherbet and swimming, in that vanished time when this desert had bloomed and peacocks had strolled through fragrant gardens. A fantasy out of the Thousand and One Nights: long ago, long ago, thousands of years ago. How confusing it was for Breckenridge to remember that that mighty city, now withered by time, had been founded and had thrived and had perished all in an era far less ancient than his own. The bonds that bound the continuum had loosened. He flapped in the time-gales.

"Tell your story," Militor said.

They were restless, eager; they nodded their heads, they shifted positions. Scarp added fuel to the campfire. The sun was dropping behind the bare low hills that marked the desert's western edge; the day's smothering heat was suddenly rushing skyward, and a thin wind whistled through the colonnade of grooved gray pillars that surrounded the pavilion. Grains of pinkish sand danced in a steady stream across the floor of polished stone on which Breckenridge and those who traveled with him squatted. The lofty western wall of the nearby city was already sleeved in shadow.

Breckenridge drew his flimsy cloak closer around himself. He stared in turn at each of the four hooded figures facing him. He pressed his fingers against the cold smooth stone to anchor himself. In a low droning voice he said "This Oedipus was monarch of the land of Thieves, and a bold and turbulent man. He conceived an illicit desire for Eurydice his mother. Forcing his passions upon her, he grew so violent that in their coupling she lost her life. Stricken with guilt and fearing that her kinsmen would exact reprisals, Oedipus escaped his kingdom through the air, having fashioned wings for himself under the guidance of the magician Prospero; but he flew too high and came within the ambit of the chariot of his father Apollo, god of the sun. Wrathful over this intrusion, Apollo engulfed Oedipus in heat, and the wax binding the feathers of his wings was melted. For a full day and a night Oedipus tumbled downward across the heavens, plummeting finally into the ocean, sinking through the sea's floor into the dark world below. There he dwells for all eternity, blind and lame, but each spring he reappears among men, and as he limps across the fields green grasses spring up in his tracks."

There was silence. Darkness was overtaking the sky. The four rounded fragments of the shattered old moon emerged and commenced their elegant, baffling saraband, spinning slowly, soaking one another in shifting patterns of cool white light. In the north the glittering violet and green bands of the aurora flickered with terrible abruptness, like the streaky glow of some monstrous searchlight. Breckenridge felt himself penetrated by gaudy ions, roasting him to the core. He waited, trembling.

"Is that all?" Militor said eventually. "Is that how it ends?"

"There's no more to the story," Breckenridge replied. "Are you disappointed?"

"The meaning is obscure. Why the incest? Why did he fly too high? Why was his father angry? Why does Oedipus reappear every spring? None of it makes sense. Am I too shallow to comprehend the relationships? I don't believe that I am."

"Oh, it's old stuff," said Scarp. "The tale of the eternal return. The dead king bringing the new year's fertility. Surely you recognize it, Militor." The aurora flashed with redoubled frenzy, a coded beacon, crying out, SPACE AND TIME, SPACE AND TIME, SPACE AND TIME. "You should have been able to follow the outline of the story," Scarp said. "We've heard it a thousand times in a thousand forms."

—SPACE AND TIME—

"Indeed we have," Militor said. "But the components of any satisfying tale have to have some logical necessity of sequence, some essential connection."—SPACE—"What we've just heard is a mass of random floating fragments. I see the semblance of myth but not the inner truth."

—TIME—

"A myth holds truth," Scarp insisted, "no matter how garbled its form, no matter how many irrelevant interpolations have entered it. The interpolations may even be one species of truth, and not the lowest species at that."

The Dow Jones Industrial Average, Breckenridge thought, closed today at 1100432.86—

"At any rate, he told it poorly," Arios observed. "No drama, no intensity, merely a bald outline of events. I've heard better from you on other nights, Breckenridge. Scheherazade and the Forty Giants—now, that was a story! Don Quixote and the Fountain of Youth, yes! But this—this—"

Scarp shook his head. "The strength of a myth lies in its content, not in the melody of its telling. I sense the inherent power of tonight's tale. I find it acceptable."

"Thank you," Breckenridge said quietly. He threw sour glares at Militor and Arios. It was hateful when they quibbled over the stories he told them. What gift did he have for these four strange beings, anyhow, except his stories? When they received that gift with poor grace they were denying him his sole claim to their fellowship.

A million years from nowhere—

SPACE—TIME—

Apollo—Jesus—Apollo—

* * *

The wind grew chillier. No one spoke. Beasts howled on the desert. Breckenridge lay back, feeling an ache in his shoulders, and wriggled against the cold stone floor.

Merry my wife, Cassandra my daughter, Noel my son—
SPACE—TIME—
SPACE—

His eyes hurt from the aurora's frosty glow. He felt himself stretched across the cosmos, torn between then and now, breaking, breaking, ripping into fragments like the moon—

The stars had come out. He contemplated the early constellations. They were unfamiliar; no matter how often Scarp or Horn pointed out the patterns to him, he saw only random sprinklings of light. In his other life he had been able to identify at least the more conspicuous constellations, but they did not seem to be here. How long does it take to effect a complete redistribution of the heavens? A million years? Ten million? Thank God Mars and Jupiter still were visible, the orange dot and the brilliant white one, to tell him that this place was his own world, his own solar system. Images danced in his aching skull. He saw everything double, suddenly. There was Pegasus, there was Orion, there was Sagittarius. An overlay, a mass of realities superimposed on realities.

"Listen to this music," Horn said after a long while, producing a fragile device of wheels and spindles from beneath his cloak. He caressed it and delicate sounds came forth: crystalline, comforting, the music of dreams, sliding into the range of audibility with no perceptible instant of attack. Shortly Scarp began a wordless song, and one by one the others joined him—first Horn, then Militor, and lastly, in a dry, buzzing monotone, Arios.

"What are you singing?" Breckenridge asked.

"The hymn of Oedipus King of Thieves," Scarp told him.

Had it been such a bad life? He had been healthy, prosperous, and beloved. His father was managing partner of Falkner, Breckenridge & Company, one of the most stable of the Wall Street houses, and Breckenridge, after coming up through the ranks in the family tradition, putting in his time as a customer's man and his time in the bond department and his time as a floor trader, was a partner too, only ten years out of Dartmouth. What was wrong with that? His draw in 1972 was $83,500—not as much as he had hoped for out of a partnership, but not bad, not bad at all, and next year might be much better. He had a wife and two children, an apartment on East 73rd Street, a country cabin on Candlewood Lake, a fair-size schooner that he kept in the Gulf Coast marina, and a handsome young mistress in an apartment of her own on the Upper West Side. What was wrong with that? When he burst through the fabric of the continuum and found himself in an unimaginably altered world at the end of time, he was astonished not that such a thing might happen but that it had happened to someone as settled and well established as himself.

While they slept, a corona of golden light sprang into being along the top of the city wall; the glow awakened Breckenridge, and he sat up quickly, thinking that the city was on fire. But the light seemed cool and supple, and appeared to be propagated in easy rippling waves, more like the aurora than like the raw blaze of flames. It sprang from the very rim of the wall and leaped high, casting blurred, rounded shadows at cross-angles to the sharp crisp shadows that the fragmented moon created. There seemed also to be a deep segment of blackness in the side of the wall; looking closely, Breckenridge saw that the huge gate on the wall's western face was standing open. Without telling the others he left the camp and crossed the flat sandy wasteland, coming to the gate after a brisk march of about an hour. Nothing prevented him from entering. Just within the wall was a wide cobbled plaza, and beyond that stretched broad avenues lined with buildings of a strange sort, rounded and rubbery, porous of texture, all humps and parapets. Black unfenced wells at the center of each major intersection plunged to infinite depths. Breckenridge had been told that the city was empty, that it had been uninhabited for centuries since the spoiling of the climate in this part of the world, so he was surprised to find it occupied; pale figures flitted silently about, moving like wraiths, as though there were empty space between their feet and the pavement. He approached one and another and a third, but when he tried to speak no words would leave his lips. He seized one of the city dwellers by the wrist, a slender black-haired girl in a soft gray robe, and held her tightly, hoping that contact would lead to contact. Her dark somber eyes studied him without show of fear and she made no effort to break away. I am Noel Breckenridge, he said—Noel

III—and I was born in the town of Greenwich, Connecticut in the year of our lord 1940, my wife's name is Merry and my daughter is Cassandra and my son is Noel Breckenridge IV, and I am not as coarse or stupid as you may think me to be. She made no reply and showed no change of expression. He asked, Can you understand anything I'm saying to you? Her face remained totally blank. He asked, Can you even hear the sound of my voice? There was no response. He went on: What is your name? What is this city called? When was it abandoned? What year is this on any calendar that I can comprehend? What do you know about me that I need to know? She continued to regard him in an altogether neutral way. He pulled her against his body and gripped her thin shoulders with his fingertips and kissed her urgently, forcing his tongue between her teeth. An instant later he found himself sprawled not far from the campsite with his face in the sand and sand in his mouth. Only a dream, he thought wearily, only a dream.

He was having lunch with Harry Munsey at the Merchants and Shippers Club: sleek chrome-and-redwood premises, sixty stories above William Street in the heart of the financial district. Subdued light fixtures glowed like pulsing red suns; waiters moved past the tables like silent moons. The club was over a century old, although the skyscraper in which it occupied a penthouse suite had been erected only in 1968—its fourth home, or maybe its fifth. Membership was limited to white male Christians, sober and responsible, who had important positions in the New York securities industry. There was nothing in the club's written constitution that explicitly limited its membership to white male Christians, but all the same there had never been any members who had not been white, male, and Christian. No one with a firm grasp of reality thought there ever would be.

Harry Munsey, like Noel Breckenridge, was white, male, and Christian. They had gone to Dartmouth together and they had entered Wall Street together, Breckenridge going into his family's firm and Munsey into his, and they had lunch together almost every day and saw each other almost every Saturday night, and each had slept with the other's wife, though each believed that the other knew nothing about that.

On the third martini Munsey said, "What's bugging you today, Noel?"

A dozen years ago Munsey had been an all-Ivy halfback; he was a big, powerful man, bigger even than Breckenridge, who was not a small man. Munsey's face was pink and unlined and his eyes were alive and youthful, but he had lost all his hair before he turned thirty.

"Is something bugging me?"

"Something's bugging you, yes. Why else would you look so uptight after you've had two and a half martinis?"

Breckenridge had found it difficult to grow used to the sight of the massive bright dome that was Munsey's skull.

He said, "All right. So I'm bugged."

"Want to talk about it?"

"No."

"Okay," Munsey said.

Breckenridge finished his drink. "As a matter of fact, I'm oppressed by a sophomoric sense of the meaninglessness of life, if you have to know."

"Really?"

"Really."

"The meaninglessness of life?"

"Life is empty, dumb, and mechanical," Breckenridge said.

"*Your* life?"

"Life."

"I know a lot of people who'd like to live your life. They'd trade with you, even up, asset for asset, liability for liability, life for life."

Breckenridge shook his head. "They're fools, then."

"It's that bad?"

"It all seems so pointless, Harry. Everything. We have a good time and con ourselves into thinking it means something. But what is there, actually? The pursuit of money? I have enough money. After a certain point it's just a game. French restaurants? Trips to Europe? Drinking? Sex? Swimming pools? Jesus! We're born, we grow up, we do a lot of stuff, we grow old, we die. Is that all? Jesus, Harry, is that *all?*"

Munsey looked embarrassed. "Well, there's family," he suggested. "Marriage, fatherhood, knowing that you're linking yourself into the great chain of life. Bringing forth a new generation. Transmitting your ideas, your standards, your traditions, everything that distinguishes us from the apes we used to be. Doesn't that count?"

Shrugging, Breckenridge said, "All right. Having kids, you say. We bring them into the world, we wipe their noses, we teach them to be little men and women, we send them to the right schools and get them into the right clubs, and they grow up to be carbon copies of their parents, lawyers or brokers or clubwomen or whatever—"

The lights fluttering. The aurora: red, green, violet, red, green. The straining fabric—the moon, the broken moon—the aurora—the lights—the fire atop the walls—

"—or else they grow up and deliberately fashion themselves into the opposites of their parents, and somewhere along the way the parents die off, and the kids have kids, and the cycle starts around again. Around and around, generation after generation, Noel Breckenridge III, Noel Breckenridge IV, Noel Breckenridge XVI—"

Arios—Scarp—Militor—Horn—

The city—the gate—

"—making money, spending money, living high, building nothing real, just occupying space on the planet for a little while, and what for? What for? What does it all mean?"

The granite pillars—the aurora—SPACE AND TIME—

"You're on a bummer today, Noel," Munsey said.

"I know. Aren't you sorry you asked what was bugging me?"

"Not particularly. Everybody goes through a phase like this."

"When he's seventeen, yes."

"And later, too."

"It's more than a phase," Breckenridge said. "It's a sickness. If I had any guts, Harry, I'd drop out. Drop right out and try to work out some meanings in the privacy of my own head."

"Why don't you? You can afford it. Go on. Why not?"

"I don't know," said Breckenridge.

Such strange constellations. Such a terrible sky.

Such a cold wind blowing out of tomorrow.

"I think it may be time for another martini," Munsey said.

They had been crossing the desert for a long time now—forty days and forty nights, Breckenridge liked to tell himself, but probably it had been more than that—and they moved at an unsparing pace, marching from dawn to sunset with as few rest periods as possible. The air was thin. His lungs felt leathery.

Because he was the biggest man in the group, he carried the heaviest pack. That didn't bother him.

What did bother him was how little he knew about his expedition, its purposes, its origin, even how he had come to be a part of it. But asking such questions seemed somehow naive and awkward, and he never did. He went along, doing his share—making camp, cleaning up in the mornings—and tried to keep his companions amused with his stories. They demanded stories from him every night. "Tell us your myths," they urged. "Tell us the legends and fables you learned in your childhood."

After weeks of sharing this trek with them he knew little more about the other four than he had at the outset. His favorite among them was Scarp, who was sympathetic and flexible. He liked the hostile, contemptuous Militor the least. Horn—dreamy, poetic, unworldly, aloof—was beyond his reach; Arios, the most dry and objective and scientific of the group, did not seem worth trying to reach. So far as Breckenridge could determine they were human, although their skins were oddly glossy and of a peculiar olive hue, something on the far side of swarthy. They had strange noses, narrow, high-bridged noses of a kind he had never seen before, extremely fragile, like the noses of purebred society women carried to the ultimate possibilities of their design.

The desert was beautiful. A gaudy desolation, all dunes and sandy riples, streaked blue and red and gold and green with brilliant oxides.

Sometimes when the aurora was going full blast—SPACE! TIME! SPACE! TIME!—the desert seemed merely to be a mirror for the sky. But in the morning, when the electronic furies of the aurora had died away, the sand still reverberated with its own inner pulses of bright color.

And the sun—pale, remorseless—Apollo's deathless fires—

I am Noel Breckenridge and I am nine years old and this is how I spent my summer vacation—

Oh Lord Jesus forgive me.

Scattered everywhere on the desert were outcroppings of ancient ruins—colonnades, halls of statuary, guardposts, summer pavilions, hunting lodges, the stumps of antique walls, and invariably the marchers made their camp beside one of these. They studied each ruin, measured its dimensions, recorded its salient details, poked at its sand-shrouded foundations. Around

Scarp's neck hung a kind of mechanized map, a teardrop-shaped black instrument that could be made to emit—

PING!

—sounds which daily guided them toward the next ruin in the chain leading to the city. Scarp also carried a compact humming machine that generated sweet water from handfuls of sand. For solid food they subsisted on small yellow pellets, quite tasty.

PING!

At the beginning Breckenridge had felt constant fatigue, but under the grinding exertions of the march he had grown steadily in strength and endurance, and now he felt he could continue forever, never tiring, parading—

PING!

—endlessly back and forth across this desert which perhaps spanned the entire world. The dead city, though, was their destination, and finally it was in view. They were to remain there for an indefinite stay. He was not yet sure whether these four were archaeologists or pilgrims. Perhaps both, he thought. Or maybe neither. Or maybe neither.

"How do you think you can make your life more meaningful, then?" Munsey asked.

"I don't know. I don't have any idea what would work for me. But I do know who the people are whose lives *do* have meaning."

"Who?"

"The creators, Harry. The shapers, the makers, the begetters. Beethoven, Rembrandt. Dr. Salk, Einstein, Shakespeare, that bunch. It isn't enough just to live. It isn't even enough just to have a good mind, to think clear thoughts. You have to add something to the sum of humanity's accomplishments, something real, something valuable. You have to *give*. Mozart. Newton. Columbus. Those who are able to reach into the well of creation, into that hot boiling chaos of raw energy down there, and pull something out, shape it, make something unique and new out of it. Making money isn't enough. Making more Breckenridges or Munseys isn't enough, either. You know what I'm saying, Harry? The well of creation. The reservoir of life, which is God. Do you ever think you believe in God? Do you wake up in the middle of the night sometimes saying, Yes, yes, there *is* Something after all, I believe, I believe! I'm not talking about churchgoing now, you understand. Churchgoing's nothing but a conditioned reflex these days, a twitch, a tic. I'm talking about faith. Belief. The state of enlightenment. I'm not talking about God as an old man with long white whiskers, either, Harry. I mean something abstract, a force, a power, a current, a reservoir of energy underlying everything and connecting everything. God is that reservoir. That reservoir is God. I think of that reservoir as being something like the sea of molten lava down beneath the earth's crust: it's there, it's full of heat and power, it's accessible for those who know the way. Plato was able to tap into the reservoir. Van Gogh. Joyce. Schubert. El Greco. A few lucky ones knew how to reach it. Most of us can't. Most of us can't. For those who can't, God is dead. Worse: for them, He never lived at all. Oh, Christ, how awful it is to be trapped in an era where everybody goes around like some sort of zombie, cut off from the energies of the spirit, ashamed even to admit there are such energies. I hate it. I hate the whole stinking twentieth century, do you know that? Am I making any sense? Do I seem terribly drunk? Am I embarrassing you, Harry? Harry? Harry?''

In the morning they struck camp and set out on the final leg of their journey toward the city. The sand here had a disturbing crusty quality: white saline outcroppings gave Breckenridge the feeling that they were crossing a tundra rather than a desert. The sky was clear and pale, and in its bleached cloudlessness it took on something of the quality of a shield, of a mirror, seizing the morning heat that rose from the ground and hurling it inexorably back, so that the five marchers felt themselves trapped in an infinite baffle of unendurable dry smothering warmth.

As they moved cityward Militor and Arios chattered compulsively, falling after a while into a quarrel over certain obscure and controversial points of historical theory. Breckenridge had heard them have their argument at least a dozen times in the last two weeks, and no doubt they had been battling it out for years. The main area of contention was the origin of the city. Who were its builders? Militor believed they were colonists from some other planet, strangers to earth, representatives of some alien species of immeasurable grandeur and nobility, who had crossed space thousands of years ago to build this gigantic monument on Asia's flank. Nonsense, retorted Arios: the city was plainly the work of human beings, unusually gifted and energetic but human nonetheless. Why multiply hypotheses needlessly? Here is the city;

humans have built many cities nearly as great as this one in their long history; this city is only quantitatively superior to the others, merely a little bigger, merely a bit more daringly conceived; to invoke extraterrestrial architects is to dabble gratuitously in fantasy. But Militor maintained his position. Humans, he said, were plainly incapable of such immense constructions. Neither in this present decadent epoch, when any sort of effort is too great, nor at any time in the past could human resources have been equal to such a task as the building of this city must have been. Breckenridge had his doubts about that, having seen what the twentieth century had accomplished. He tended to side with Arios. But indeed the city was extraordinary, Breckenridge admitted: an ultimate urban glory, a supernal Babylon, a consummate Persepolis, the soul's own hymn in brick and stone. The wall that girdled it was at least two hundred feet high—why pour so much energy into a wall? were no better means of defense at hand, or was the wall mere exuberant decoration?—and, judging by the easy angle of its curve, it must be hundreds of miles in circumference. A city larger than New York, more sprawling even than Los Angeles, a giant antenna of turbulent consciousness set like a colossal gem into this vast plain, a throbbing antenna for all the radiance of the stars: yes, it was overwhelming, it was devastating to contemplate the planning and the building of it, it seemed almost to require the hypothesis of a superior alien race. And yet he refused to accept that hypothesis. Arios, he thought, I am with you.

The city was uninhabited, a hulk, a ruin. Why? What had happened here to turn this garden plain into a salt-crusted waste? The builders grew too proud, said Militor. They defied the gods, they overreached even their own powers, and stumbling, they fell headlong into decay. The life went out of the soil, the sky gave no rain, the spirit lost its energies; the city perished and was forgotten, and was whispered about by mythmakers, a city out of time, a city at the end of the world, a mighty mass of dead wonders, a habitation for jackals, a place where no one went. We are the first in centuries, said Scarp, to seek this city.

Halfway between dawn and noon they reached the wall and stood before the great gate. The gate alone was fifty feet high, a curving slab of burnished blue metal set smoothly into a recess in the tawny stucco of the wall. Breckenridge saw no way of opening it, no winch, no portcullis, no handles, no knobs. He feared that the impatient Militor would merely blow a hole in it. But, groping along the base of the gate, they found a small doorway, man-high and barely man-wide, near the left-hand edge. Ancient hinges yielded at a push. Scarp led the way inside.

The city was as Breckenridge remembered it from his dream: the cobbled plaza, the broad avenues, the humped and rubbery buildings. The fierce sunlight, deflected and refracted by the undulant roof lines, reverberated from every flat surface and rebounded in showers of brilliant energy. Breckenridge shaded his eyes. It was as though the sky were full of pulsars. His soul was frying on a cosmic griddle, cooking in a torrent of hard radiation.

The city was inhabited.

Faces were visible at windows. Elusive figures emerged at street corners, peered, withdrew. Scarp called to them; they shrank back into the hard-edged shadows.

"Well?" Arios demanded. "They're human, aren't they?"

"What of it?" said Militor. "Squatters, that's all. You saw how easy it was to push open that door. They've come in out of the desert to live in the ruins."

"Maybe not. Descendants of the builders, I'd say. Perhaps the city never really was abandoned." Arios looked at Scarp. "Don't you agree?"

"They might be anything," Scarp said. "Squatters, descendants, even synthetics, even servants without masters, living on, waiting, living on, waiting—"

"Or projections cast by ancient machines," Militor said. "No human hand built this city."

Arios snorted. They advanced quickly across the plaza and entered into the first of the grand avenues. The buildings flanking it were sealed. They proceeded to a major intersection, where they halted to inspect an open circular pit, fifteen feet in diameter, smooth-rimmed, descending into infinite darkness. Breckenridge had seen many such dark wells in his vision of the night before. He did not doubt now that he had left his sleeping body and had made an actual foray into the city last night.

Scarp flashed a light into the well. A copper-colored metal ladder was visible along one face.

"Shall we go down?" Breckenridge asked.

"Later," said Scarp.

*   *   *

The famous anthropologist had been drinking steadily all through the dinner party—wine, only wine, but plenty of it—and his eyes seemed glazed, his face flushed; nevertheless he continued to talk with superb clarity of perception and elegant precision of phrase, hardly pausing at all to construct his concepts. Perhaps he's merely quoting his own latest book from memory, Breckenridge thought, as he strained to follow the flow of ideas. "—A comparison between myth and what appears to have largely replaced it in modern societies, namely, politics. When the historian refers to the French Revolution it is always as a sequence of past happenings, a nonreversible series of events the remote consequences of which may still be felt at present. But to the French politician, as well as to his followers, the French Revolution is both a sequence belonging to the past—as to the historian—and an everlasting pattern which can be detected in the present French social structure and which provides a clue for its interpretation, a lead from which to infer the future developments. See, for instance, Michelet, who was a politically minded historian. He describes the French Revolution thus: 'This day...everything was possible...future became present...that is, no more time, a glimpse of eternity.'" The great man reached decisively for another glass of claret. His hand wavered; the glass toppled; a dark red torrent stained the table cloth. Breckenridge experienced a sudden terrifying moment of complete disorientation, as though the walls and floor were shifting places: he saw a parched desert plateau, four hooded figures, a blazing sky of strange constellations, a pulsating aurora sweeping the heavens with old fire. A mighty walled city dominated the plain, and its frosty shadow, knifeblade-sharp, cut across Breckenridge's path. He shivered. The woman on Breckenridge's right laughed lightly and began to recite:

I saw Eternity the other night
Like a great ring of pure and endless light.
    All calm, as it was bright;
And round beneath it, Time in hours, days, years,
    Driv'n by the spheres
Like a vast shadow mov'd; in which the world
    And all her train were hurl'd.

"Excuse me," Breckenridge said. "I think I'm unwell." He rushed from the dining room. In the hallway he turned toward the washroom and found himself staring into a steaming tropical marsh, all ferns and horsetails and giant insects. Dragonflies the size of pigeons whirred past him. The sleek rump of a brontosaurus rose like a bubbling aneurysm from the black surface of the swamp. Breckenridge recoiled and staggered away. On the other side of the hall lay the desert under the lash of a frightful noonday sun. He gripped the frame of a door and held himself upright, trembling, as his soul oscillated wildly across the hallucinatory eons. "I am Scarp," said a quiet voice within him. "You have come to the place where all times are one, where all errors can be unmade, where past and future are fluid and subject to redefinition." Breckenridge felt powerful arms encircling and supporting him. "Noel? Noel? Here, sit down." Harry Munsey. Shiny pink skull, searching blue eyes. "Jesus, Noel, you look like you're having some kind of bad trip. Merry sent me after you to find out—"

"It's okay," Breckenridge said hoarsely. "I'll be all right."

"You·want me to get her?"

"I'll be *all right*. Just let me steady myself a second." He rose uncertainly. "Okay. Let's go back inside."

The anthropologist was still talking. A napkin covered the wine stain and he held a fresh glass aloft like a sacramental chalice. "The key to everything, I think, lies in an idea that Franz Boas offered in 1898: 'It would seem that mythological worlds have been built up only to be shattered again, and that new worlds were built from the fragments.' "

Breckenridge said, "The first men lived underground and there was no such thing as private property. One day there was an earthquake and the earth was rent apart. The light of day flooded the subterranean cavern where mankind dwelled. Clumsily, for the light dazzled their eyes, they came upward into the world of brightness and learned how to see. Seven days later they divided the fields among themselves and began to build the first walls as boundaries marking the limits of their land."

By midday the city dwellers were losing their fear of the five intruders. Gradually, in twos and threes, they left their hiding places and gathered around the visitors until a substantial group had collected. They were dressed simply, in light robes, and they said nothing to the strangers, though they whispered frequently to one another. Among the group was the slender, dark-haired girl of Breckenridge's dream. "Do you remember me?" he asked. She smiled and shrugged and answered softly in a liquid, incomprehensible language. Arios questioned her in six or seven tongues, but she shook her head to everything. Then she took Breckenridge by the hand and led him a few paces away, toward one of the street-wells. Pointing into it, she smiled. She pointed to Breckenridge, pointed to herself, to the surrounding buildings. She made a sweeping gesture taking in all the sky. She pointed again into the well. "What are you trying to tell me?" he asked her. She answered in her own language. Breckenridge shook his head apologetically. She did a simple pantomime: eyes closed, head lolling against pressed-together hands. An image of sleep, certainly. She pointed to him. To herself. To the well. "You want me to sleep with you?" he blurted. "Down there?" He had to laugh at his own foolishness. It was ridiculous to assume the persistence of a cowardly, euphemistic metaphor like that across so many millennia. He gaped stupidly at her. She laughed—a silvery, tinkling laugh—and danced away from him, back toward her own people.

Their first night in the city they made camp in one of the great plazas. It was an octagonal space surrounded by low green buildings, sharp-angled, each faced on its plaza side with mirror-bright stone. About a hundred of the city-dwellers crouched in the shadows of the plaza's periphery, watching them. Scarp sprinkled fuel pellets and kindled a fire; Militor distributed dinner; Horn played music as they ate; Arios, sitting apart, dictated a commentary into a recording device he carried, the size and texture of a large pearl. Afterward they asked Breckenridge to tell a story, as usual, and he told them the tale of how Death Came to the World.

"Once upon a time," he began, "there were only a few people in the world and they lived in a green and fertile valley where winter never came and gardens bloomed all the year round. They spent their days laughing and swimming and lying in the sun, and in the evenings they feasted and sang and made love, and this went on without change, year in, year out, and no one ever fell ill or suffered from hunger, and no one ever died. Despite the serenity of this existence, one man in the village was unhappy. His name was Faust, and he was a restless, intelligent man with intense, burning eyes and a lean, unsmiling face. Faust felt that life must consist of something more than swimming and making love and plucking ripe fruit off vines. 'There is something else to life,' Faust insisted, 'something unknown to us, something that eludes our grasp, something the lack of which keeps us from being truly happy. We are incomplete.' The others listened to him and at first they were puzzled, for they had not known they were unhappy or incomplete, they had mistaken the ease and placidity of the existence for happiness. But after a while they started to believe that Faust might be right. They had not known how vacant their lives were until Faust had pointed it out. What can we do, they asked? How can we learn what the thing is that we lack? A wise old man suggested that they might ask the gods. So they elected Faust to visit the god Prometheus, who was said to be a friend to mankind, and ask him. Faust crossed hill and dale, mountain and river, and came at last to Prometheus on the storm-swept summit where he dwelled. He explained the situation and said, 'Tell me, O Prometheus, why we feel so incomplete.' The God replied, 'It is because you do not have the use of fire. Without fire there can be no civilization; you are uncivilized, and your barbarism makes you unhappy. With fire you can cook your food and enjoy many interesting new flavors. With fire you can work metals, and create effective weapons and other tools.'' Faust considered this and said, 'But where can we obtain fire? What is it? How is it used?

"'I will bring fire to you' Prometheus answered.

"Prometheus then went to Zeus, the greatest of the gods, and said, 'Zeus, the humans desire fire, and I seek your permission to bestow it upon them.' But Zeus was hard of hearing and Prometheus lisped badly and in the language of the gods the words for fire and for death were very similar, and Zeus misunderstood and said, 'How odd of them to desire such a thing, but I am a benevolent god, and deny my creatures nothing that they crave.' So Zeus created a woman named Pandora and put death inside her and gave her to Prometheus, who took her back to the valley where mankind lived. 'Here is Pandora,' said Prometheus. 'She will give you fire.'

"As soon as Prometheus took his leave Faust came forward and embraced Pandora and lay with her. Her body was hot as flame, and as he held her in his arms death came forth from her and entered him, and he shivered and grew feverish, and cried out in ecstasy, 'This is fire! I have mastered fire!' Within the hour death began to consume him so that he grew weak and thin, and his skin became parched and yellowish, and he trembled like a leaf in a breeze. 'Go!' he cried to the others. 'Embrace her—she is the bringer of fire!' And he staggered off into the wilderness beyond the valley's edge, murmuring, 'Thanks be to Prometheus for this gift.' He lay down beneath a huge tree, and there he died, and it was the first time that death had visited a human being. And the tree died also.

"Then the other men of the village embraced Pandora, one after another, and death entered into them too, and they went from her to their own women and embraced them, so that soon all the men and women of the village were ablaze with death, and one by one their lives reached an end. Death remained in the village, passing into all who lived and into all who were born from their loins, and this is how death came to the world. Afterward, during a storm, lightning struck the tree that had died when Faust had died, and set it ablaze, and a man whose name is forgotten thrust a dry branch into the blaze and lit it, and learned how to build a fire and how to keep the fire alive, and after that time men cooked their food and used fire to work metal into weapons, and so it was that civilization began."

It was time to investigate one of the wells. Scarp, Arios, and Breckenridge would make the descent, with Militor and Horn remaining on the surface to cope with contingencies. They chose a well half a day's march from their campsite, deep into the city, a big one, broader and deeper than most they had seen. At its rim Scarp mounted a spherical fist-size light that cast a dazzling blue-white beam into the opening. Then, lightly swinging himself out onto the metal ladder, he began to climb down, shrouded in a nimbus of molten brightness. Breckenridge peered after him. Scarp's head and shoulders remained visible for a long while, dwindling until he was only a point of darkness in motion deep within the cone of light, and then he could no longer be seen. "Scarp?" Breckenridge called. After a moment came a muffled reply out of the depths. Scarp had reached bottom, somewhere beyond the range of the beam, and wanted them to join him.

Breckenridge followed. The descent seemed infinite. There was a stiffness in his left knee. He became a mere automaton, mechanically seizing the rungs; they were warm in his hands. His eyes, fixed on the pocked gray skin of the well's wall inches from his nose, grew glassy and unfocused. He passed through the zone of light as though sliding through the face of a mirror and moved downward in darkness without a change of pace until his boot slammed unexpectedly into a solid floor where he had thought to encounter the next rung. The left boot; his knee, jamming, protested. Scarp lightly touched his shoulder. "Step back here next to me," he said. "Take sliding steps and make sure you have a footing. For all we know, we're on some sort of ledge with a steep drop on all sides."

They waited while Arios came down. His footfalls were like thunder in the well: boom, boom, boom, transmitted and amplified by the rungs. Then the men at the surface lowered the light, fixed to the end of a long cord, and at last they could look around.

They were in a kind of catacomb. The floor of the well was a platform of neatly dressed stone slabs which gave access to horizontal tunnels several times a man's height, stretching away to right and left, to fore and aft. The mouth of the well was a dim dot of light far above. Scarp, after inspecting the perimeter of the platform, flashed the beam into one of the tunnels, stared a moment, and cautiously entered. Breckenridge heard him cough. "Dusty in here," Scarp muttered. Then he said, "You told us a story once about the King of the Dead Lands, Breckenridge. What was his name?"

"Thanatos."

"Thanatos, yes. This must be his kingdom. Come and look."

Arios and Breckenridge exchanged shrugs. Breckenridge stepped into the tunnel. The walls on both sides were lined from floor to ceiling with tiers of coffins, stacked eight or ten high and extending as far as the beam of light reached. The coffins were glass-faced and covered over with dense films of dust. Scarp drew his fingers through the dust over one coffin and left deep tracks; clouds rose up, sending Breckenridge back, coughing and choking, to stumble into Arios. When the dust cleared they could see a figure within, seemingly asleep, the nude figure of a young man lying on his back. His expression was one of great serenity. Breckenridge shivered. Death's kingdom, yes, the place of Thanatos, the house of Pluto. He walked down the row, wiping coffin after coffin. An old man. A child. A young woman. An older woman.

A whole population lay embalmed here. I died long ago, he thought, and I don't even sleep. I walk about beneath the earth. The silence was frightening here. "The people of the city?" Scarp asked. "The ancient inhabitants?"

"Very likely," said Arios. His voice was as crisp as ever. He alone was not trembling. "Slain in some inconceivable massacre? But what? But how?"

"They appear to have died natural deaths," Breckenridge pointed out. "Their bodies look whole and healthy. As though they were lying here asleep. Not dead, only sleeping."

"A plague?" Scarp wondered. " A sudden cloud of deadly gas? A taint of poison in their water supply?"

"If it had been sudden," said Breckenridge, "how would they have had time to build all these coffins? This whole tunnel—catacomb upon catacomb—" A network of passageways spanning the city's entire subterrane. Thousands of coffins. Millions. Breckenridge felt dazed by the presence of death on such a scale. The skeleton with the scythe, moving briskly about its work. Severed heads and hands and feet scattered like dandelions in the springtime meadow. The reign of Thanatos, King of Swords, Knight of Wands.

Thunder sounded behind them. Footfalls in the well.

Scarp scowled. "I told them to wait up there. That fool Militor—"

Arios said, "Militor should see this. Undoubtedly it's the resting place of the city dwellers. Undoubtedly these are human beings. Do you know what I imagine? A mass suicide. A unanimous decision to abandon the world of life. Years of preparation. The construction of tunnels, of machines for killing, a whole vast apparatus of immolation. And then the day appointed—long lines waiting to be processed—millions of men and women and children passing through the machines, gladly giving up their lives, going willingly to the coffins that await them—"

"And then," Scarp said, "there must have been only a few left and no one to process them. Living on, caretakers for the dead, perhaps, maintaining the machinery that preserves these millions of bodies—"

"Preserves them for what?" Arios asked.

"The day of resurrection," said Breckenridge.

The footfalls in the well grew louder. Scarp glanced toward the tunnel's mouth. "Militor?" he called. "Horn?" He sounded angry. He walked toward the well. "You were supposed to wait for us up—"

Breckenridge heard a grinding sound and whirled to see Arios tugging at the lid of a coffin—the one that held the serene young man. Instinctively he moved to halt the desecration, but he was too slow; the glass plate rose as Arios broke the seals, and, with a quick whooshing sound, a burst of greenish vapor rushed from the coffin. It hovered a moment in midair, speared by Arios's beam of light; then it congealed into a yellow precipitant and broke in a miniature rainstorm that stained the tunnel's stone floor. To Breckenridge's horror the young man's body jerked convulsively: muscles tightened into knots and almost instantly relaxed. "He's alive! Breckenridge cried.

"Was," said Scarp.

Yes. The figure in the glass case was motionless. It changed color and texture, turning black and withered. Scarp shoved Arios aside and slammed the lid closed, but that could do no good now. A dreadful new motion commenced within the coffin. In moments something shriveled and twisted lay before them.

"Suspended animation," said Arios. "The city builders—they lie here, as human as we are, sleeping, not dead, sleeping. Sleeping! Militor! Militor, come quickly!"

Feingold said, "Let me see if I have it straight. After the public offering our group will continue to hold 83 percent of the Class B stock and 34 percent of the voting common, which constitutes a controlling block. We'll let you have 100,000 five-year warrants and we'll agree to a conversion privilege on the 1992 6½ percent debentures, plus we allow you the stipulated underwriting fee, providing your Argentinian friend takes up the agreed-upon allotment of debentures and follows through on his deal with us in Colorado. Okay? Now, then, assuming the SEC has no objections, I'd like to outline the proposed interlocking directorates with Heitmark A.G. in Liechtenstein and Hellaphon S.A. in Athens, after which—"

The high, clear, rapid voice went on and on. Breckenridge toyed with his lunch, smiled frequently, nodded whenever he felt it was appropriate, and otherwise remained disconnected, listening only with the automatic-recorder part of his mind. They were sitting on the terrace of an open-air restaurant in Tiberias, at the edge of the Sea of Galilee, looking across to the bleak, brown

Syrian hills on the far side. The December air was mild, the sun bright. Last week Breckenridge had visited Monaco, Zurich, and Milan. Yesterday Tel Aviv, tomorrow Haifa, next Tuesday Istanbul. Then on to Nairobi, Johannesburg, Peking, Singapore. Finally San Francisco and then home. Zap! Zap! A crazy round-the-world scramble in twenty days, cleaning up a lot of international business for the firm. It could all have been handled by telephone, or else some of these foreign tycoons could have come to New York, but Breckenridge had volunteered to do the junket. Why? Why? Sitting here ten thousand miles from home having lunch with a man whose office was down the street from his own. Crazy. Why all this running, Noel? Where do you think you'll get?

"Some more wine?" Feingold asked. "What do you think of this Israeli stuff, anyway?"

"It goes well with the fish." Breckenridge reached for Feingold's copy of the agreement. "Here, let me initial all that."

"Don't you want to check it over first?"

"Not necessary. I have faith in you, Sid."

"Well, I wouldn't cheat you, that's true. But I could have made a mistake. I'm capable of making mistakes."

"I don't think so," Breckenridge said. He grinned. Feingold grinned. Behind the grin there was something chilly. Breckenridge looked away. You think I'm bending over backward to treat you like a gentleman, he thought, because you know what people like me are really supposed to think about Jews, and I know you know, and you know I know you know, and—and—well, screw it, Sid. Do I trust you? Maybe I do. Maybe I don't. But the basic fact is I just don't care. Stack the deck any way you like, Feingold. I just don't care. I wish I was on Mars. Or Pluto. Or the year Two Billion. Zap! Right across the whole continuum! Noel Breckenridge, freaking out! He heard himself say, "Do you want to know my secret fantasy, Sid? I dream of waking up Jewish one day. It's so damned boring being a gentile, do you know that? I feel so bland, so straight, so sunny. I envy you all that feverish kinky complexity of soul. All that history. Ghettos, persecutions, escapes, schemes for survival and revenge, a sense of tribal unity born out of shared pain. It's so hard for a goy to develop some honest paranoia, you know? Let alone a little schiziness." Feingold was still grinning. He filled Breckenridge's wineglass again. He showed no sign of having heard anything that might offend him. Maybe I didn't say anything, Breckenridge thought.

Feingold said, "When you get back to New York, Noel, I'd like you out to our place for dinner. You and your wife. A weekend, maybe. Logs on the fire, thick steaks, plenty of good wine. You'll love our place." Three Israeli jets roared low over Tiberias and vanished in the direction of Lebanon. "Will you come? Can you fit it into your schedule?"

Some possible structural hypotheses:

LIFE AS MEANINGLESS CONDITION

Breckenridge on Wall Street.	The four seekers moving randomly.	The dead city.

LIFE RENDERED MEANINGFUL THROUGH ART

Breckenridge recollects ancient myths.	The four seekers elicit his presence and request the myths.	The dead city inhabited after all. The inhabitants listen to Breckenridge.

THE IMPACT OF ENTROPY

His tales are garbled dreams.	The seekers quarrel over theory.	The city dwellers speak an unknown language.

ASPECTS OF CONSCIOUSNESS

He is a double self.	The four seekers are unsure of the historical background.	Most of the city dwellers are alseep.

His audience was getting larger every night. They came from all parts of the city, silently arriving, drawn at sundown to the place where the visitors camped. Hundreds, now, squatting beyond the glow of the campfire. They listened intently, nodded, seemed to comprehend, murmured occasional comments to one another. How strange: they seemed to comprehend.

"The story of Samson and Odysseus," Breckenridge announced. "Samson is blind but mighty. His woman is known as

Delilah. To them comes the wily chieftain Odysseus, making his way homeward from the land of Ithaca. He penetrates the maze in which Samson and Delilah live and hires himself to them as bondservant, giving his name as No Man. Delilah entices him to carry her off, and he abducts her. Samson is aware of the abduction but is unable to find them in the maze; he cries out in pain and rage, 'No Man steals my wife! No Man steals my wife!' His servants are baffled by this and take no action. In fury Samson brings the maze crashing down on himself and dies, while Odysseus carries Delilah off to Sparta, where she is seduced by Paris, Prince of Troy. Odysseus thus loses her and by way of gaining revenge he seduces Helen, the Queen of Troy, and the Trojan War begins.''

And then he told the story of how mankind was created:

"In the beginning there was only a field of white sand. Lightning struck it, and where the lightning hit the sand it coagulated into a vessel of glass, and rainwater ran into the vessel and brought it to life, and from the vessel a she-wolf was born. Thunder entered her womb and fertilized her and she gave birth to twins, and they were not wolves but a human boy and a human girl. The wolf suckled the twins until they reached adulthood. Then they copulated and engendered children of their own. Because they were ashamed of their nakedness they killed the old wolf and made garments from her hide."

And then he told them the myth of the Wandering Jew, who scoffed at God and was condemned to drift through time until he himself was able to become God.

And he told them of the Golden Age and the Iron Age and the Age of Uranium.

And he told them how the waters and winds came into being, and the seasons, the months, day and night.

And he told them how art was born:

"Out of a hole in space pours a stream of life force. Many men and women attempted to seize the flow, but they were burned to ashes by its intensity. At last, however, a man devised a way. He hollowed himself out until there was nothing at all inside his body, and had himself dragged by a faithful dog to the place where the stream of energy descended from the heavens. Then the life force entered him and filled him, and instead of destroying him it took possession of him and restored him to life. But the force overflowed within him, brimming over, and the only way he could deal with that was to fashion stories and sculptures and songs, for otherwise the force would engulf him and drown him. His name was Gilgamesh and he was the first of the artists of mankind.''

The city dwellers came by the thousands now. They listened and wept at Breckenridge's words.

Hypothesis of structural resolution:

He finds creative fulfillment.	The four seekers have bridged space and time to bring life out of death.	The sleeping city dwellers will be awakened.

Gradually the outlines of a master myth took place: the creation, the creation of man, the origin of private property, the origin of death, the loss of faith, the end of the world, the coming of a redeemer to start the cycle anew. Soon the structure would be complete. When it was, Breckenridge thought, perhaps rains would fall on the desert, perhaps the world would be reborn.

Breckenridge slept. Sleeping, he experienced an inward glow of golden light. The girl he had encountered before came to him and took his hand and led him through the city. They walked for hours, it seemed, until they came to a well different from all the others, rectangular rather than circular and surrounded at street level by a low railing of bright metal mesh. "Go down into this one," she told him. "When you reach the bottom, keep walking until you reach the room where the mechanisms of awakening are located." He looked at her in amazement, realizing that her words had been comprehensible. "Are you speaking my language," he asked, "or am I speaking yours?" She answered by smiling and pointing toward the well.

He stepped over the railing and began his descent. The well

was deeper than the other one; the air in its depths was stale and dry. The golden glow lit his way for him to the bottom and thence along a low passageway with a rounded vault of a ceiling. After a long time he came to a large, brightly lit room filled with sleek gray machinery. It was much like the computer room at any large bank. Mounted on the walls were control panels, labeled in an unknown language but also clearly marked with sequential symbols:

I   II   III   IIII   IIIII   IIIIII

While he studied these he became aware of a sliding, hissing sound from the corridor beyond. He thought of sturdy metal cables passing one against the other; but then into the control room slowly came a creature something like a scorpion in form, considerably greater than a man in size. Its curved tubular thorax was dark and of a waxen texture; a dense mat of brown bristles, thick as straws, sprouted on its abdomen; its many eyes were bright, alert, and malevolent. Breckenridge snatched up a steel bar that lay near his feet and tried to wield it like a lance as the monster approached. From its jaws, though, there looped a sudden lasso of newly spun silken thread that caught the end of the bar and jerked it from Breckenridge's grasp. Then a second loop, entangling his arms and shoulders. Struggle was useless. He was caught. The creature pulled him closer. Breckenridge saw fangs, powerful palpi, a scythe of a tail in which a dripping stinger had become erect. Breckenridge writhed in the monster's grip. He felt neither surprise nor fear; this seemed a necessary working out of some ancient foreordained pattern.

A cool, silent voice within his skull said, "Who are you?"

"Noel Breckenridge of New York City, born A.D. 1940."

"Why do you intrude here?"

"I was summoned. If you want to know why, ask someone else."

"Is it your purpose to awaken the sleepers?"

"Very possibly," Breckenridge said.

"So the time has come?"

"Maybe it has," said Breckenridge. All was still for a long moment. The monster made no hostile move. Breckenridge grew impatient. "Well, what's the arrangement?" he said finally.

"The arrangement?"

"The terms under which I get my freedom. Am I supposed to

tell you a lot of diverting stories? Will I have to serve you six months out of the year, forevermore? Is there some precious object I'm obliged to bring you from the bottom of the sea? Maybe you have a riddle that I'm supposed to answer."

The monster made no reply.

"Is that it?" Breckenridge demanded. "A riddle?"

"Do you want it to be a riddle?"

"A riddle, yes."

There was another endless pause. Breckenridge met the beady gaze steadily. At last the voice said, "A riddle. A riddle. Very well. Tell me the answer to this. What goes on four legs in the morning, on two legs in the afternoon, on three legs in the evening."

Breckenridge repeated it. He pondered. He frowned. He coughed. Then he laughed. "A baby," he said, "crawls on all fours. A grown man walks upright. An old man requires the assistance of a cane. Therefore the answer to your riddle is—"

He left the sentence unfinished. The gleam went out of the monster's eyes; the silken loop binding Breckenridge dissolved; the creature began slowly and sadly to back away, withdrawing into the corridor from which it came. Its hissing, rustling sound persisted for a time, growing ever more faint.

Breckenridge turned and without hesitation pulled the switch marked I.

The aurora no longer appears in the night sky. A light rain has been falling frequently for some days, and the desert is turning green. The sleepers are awakening, millions of them, called forth from their coffins by the workings of automatic mechanisms. Breckenridge stands in the central plaza of the city, arms outspread, and the city dwellers, as they emerge from the subterranean sleeping places, make their way toward him. I am the resurrection and the life, he thinks. I am Orpheus the sweet singer. I am Homer the blind. I am Noel Breckenridge. He looks across the eons to Harry Munsey. "I was wrong," he says. "There's meaning everywhere, Harry. For Sam Smith as well as for Beethoven. For Noel Breckenridge as well as for Michelangelo. Dawn after dawn, simply being alive, being part of it all, part of the cosmic dance of life—that's the meaning, Harry. Look! Look!" The sun is high now—not a cruel sun but a mild, gentle one, its heat softened by a humid haze. This is the dream-time, when all mistakes are unmade, when all things become one. The city folk surround him. They come closer. Closer yet. They reach toward him. He experiences a delicious flash of white light. The world disappears.

"JKF Airport," he told the taxi driver. The cab zoomed away. From the front seat came the voice of the radio with today's closing Dow Jones Industrials: 948.72, down 6.11. He reached the airport by half past five, and at seven he boarded a Pan Am flight for London. The next morning at nine, London time, he cabled his wife to say that he was well and planned to head south for the winter. Then he reported to the Air France counter for the nonstop flight to Morocco. Over the next week he cabled home from Rabat, Marrakech, and Timbuktu in Mali. The third cable said:

> GUESS WHAT STOP I'M REALLY IN TIMBUKTU STOP HAVE
> RENTED JEEP STOP I SET OUT INTO SAHARA TOMORROW
> STOP AM VERY HAPPY STOP YES STOP VERY HAPPY STOP
> VERY VERY HAPPY STOP STOP STOP.

It was the last message he sent. The night it arrived in New York there was a spectacular celestial display, an aurora that brought thousands of people out into Central Park. There was rain in the southeastern Sahara four days later, the first recorded precipitation there in eight years and seven months. An earthquake was reported in southern Sicily, but it did little damage. Things were much quieter after that for everybody.

IN THE HOUSE OF DOUBLE MINDS

Now THEY BRING in the new ones, this spring's crop of ten-year-olds—six boys, six girls—and leave them with me in the dormitory room that will be their home for the next dozen years. The room is bare, austere, with black slate floors and rough brick walls, furnished for the time being with cots and clothes-cabinets and little more. The air is chill, and the children, who are naked, huddle in discomfort.

"I am Sister Mimise," I tell them. "I will be your guide and counselor in the first twelve months of your new life in the House of Double Minds."

I have lived in this place for eight years, since I was fourteen, and this is the fifth year that I have had charge of the new children. If I had not been disqualified by my left-handedness, this is the year I would have been graduated into full oraclehood, but I try not to dwell on that. Caring for the children is a rewarding task in itself. They arrive scrawny and frightened, and slowly they unfold: they blossom, they ripen, they grow toward their destinies. Each year there is some special one for me, some favorite, in whom I take particular joy. In my first group, four years ago, it was long-legged laughing Jen, she who is now my lover. A year later it was soft beautiful Jalil, and then Timas, who I thought would become one of the greatest of all oracles; but after two years of training Timas cracked and was culled. And last year bright-eyed Runild, impish Runild, my pet, my

308

darling boy, more gifted even than Timas and, I fear, even less
stable. I look at the new ones, wondering who will be special
among them for me this year.

The children are pale, slender, uneasy; their thin nude bodies
look more than naked because of their shaven skulls. As a result
of what has been done to their brains they move clumsily today.
Their left arms often dangle as though they have entirely forgotten them, and they tend to walk in a shuffling sidewise motion,
dragging their left legs a little. These problems soon will disappear. The last of the operations in this group was performed only
two days ago, on the short wide-shouldered girl whose breasts
have already begun to grow. I can see the narrow red line
marking the place where the surgeon's beam sliced through her
scalp to sever the hemispheres of her brain.

"You have been selected," I say in a resonant formal tone,
"for the highest and most sacred office in our society. From this
moment until you reach adulthood your lives and energies will be
consecrated to the purpose of attaining the skills and wisdom an
oracle must have. I congratulate you on having come so far."

And I envy you.

I do not say that part aloud.

I feel envy and pity both. I have seen the children come and
go, come and go. Out of each year's dozen, one or two usually
die along the way of natural causes or accidents. At least three go
insane under the terrible pressure of the disciplines and have to
be culled. So only about half the group is likely to complete the
twelve years of training, and most of those will prove to have
little value as oracles. The useless ones will be allowed to
remain, of course, but their lives will be meaningless. The House
of Double Minds has been in existence for more than a century;
there are at present just one hundred forty-two oracles in residence—
seventy-seven women and sixty-five men—of whom all but about
forty are mere drones. A thin harvest out of some twelve hundred
novices since the beginning.

These children have never met before. I call upon them to
introduce themselves. They give their names in low self-conscious
voices, eyes downcast.

A body named Divvan asks, "Will we wear clothes soon?"

Their nakedness disturbs them. They hold their thighs together
and stand at odd storklike angles, keeping apart from one
another, trying to conceal their undeveloped loins. They do this

because they are strangers. They will forget their shame before long. As the months pass they will become closer than brothers and sisters.

"Robes will be issued this afternoon," I tell him. "But clothing ought not to be important here, and you need have no reason to wish to hide you bodies." Last year when this same point arose—it always does—the mischievous boy Runild suggested that I remove my own robe as a gesture of solidarity. Of course I did, but it was a mistake: the sight of a mature woman's body was more troubling to them than even their own bareness.

Now it is the time for the first exercises, so that they may learn the ways in which the brain operation has altered the responses of their bodies. At random I choose a girl named Hirole and ask her to step forward, while the rest form a circle around her. She is tall and fragile-looking and it must be torment to her to be aware of the eyes of all the others upon her.

Smiling, I say gently, "Raise your hand, Hirole."

She raises one hand.

"Bend your knee."

As she flexes her knee, there is an interruption. A wiry naked boy scrambles into the room, fast as a spider, wild as a monkey, and bursts into the middle of the circle, shouldering Hirole aside. Runild again! He is a strange and moody and extraordinarily intelligent child, who, now that he is in his second year at the House, has lately been behaving in a reckless, unpredictable way. He runs around the circle, seizing several of the new children briefly, putting his face close to theirs, staring with crazy intensity into their eyes. They are terrified of him. For a moment I am too astonished to move. Then I go to him and seize him.

He struggles ferociously. He spits at me, hisses, claws my arms, makes thick wordless grunting sounds. Gradually I get control of him. In a low voice I say, "What's wrong with you, Runild? You know you aren't supposed to be in here!"

"Let me go."

"Do you want me to report this to Brother Sleel?"

"I just want to see the new ones."

"You're frightening them. You'll be able to meet them in a few days, but you're not allowed to upset them now." I pull him toward the door. He continues to resist and nearly breaks free. Eleven-year-old boys are amazingly strong, sometimes. He kicks my thigh savagely: I will have purple bruises tonight. He tries to bite my arm. Somehow I get him out of the room, and in the corridor he suddenly goes slack and begins to tremble, as though he has had a fit that now is over. I am trembling too. Hoarsely I say, "What's happening to you, Runild? Do you want to be culled the way Timas and Jurda were? You can't keep doing things like this! You—"

He looks up at me, wild-eyed, and starts to say something, and stifles it, and turns and bolts. In a moment he is gone, a brown naked streak vanishing down the hallway. I feel a great sadness: Runild was a favorite of mine, and now he is going insane, and they will have to cull him. I should report the incident immediately, but I am unable to bring myself to do it, and, telling myself that my responsibility lies with the new ones, I return to the dorm room.

"Well!" I say briskly , as if nothing unusual has happened. "He's certainly playful today, isn't he! That was Runild. He's a year ahead of you. You'll meet him and the rest of his group a little later. Now, Hirole—"

The children, preoccupied with their own altered state, quickly grow calm; they seem much less distressed by Runild's intrusion than I am. Shakily I begin again, asking Hirole to raise a hand, to flex a knee, to close an eye. I thank her and call a boy named Mulliam into the center of the circle. I ask him to raise one shoulder above the other, to touch his hand to his cheek, to make a fist. Then I pick a girl named Fyme and instruct her to hop on one foot, to put an arm behind her back, to kick one leg in the air.

I say, "Who can tell me one thing that was true of every response?"

Several of them answer at once. "It was always the right side! The right eye, the right hand, the right leg—"

"Correct." I turn to a small dark-visaged boy named Bloss and ask, "Why is that? Do you think it's just coincidence?"

"Well," he says, "Everybody here is right-handed, because left-handers aren't allowed to become oracles, and so everybody tended to use the side that he—"

Bloss falters, seeing heads shaking all around the circle.

Galaine, the girl whose breasts have begun to sprout, says, "It's because of the operation! The right side of our brains doesn't understand words very well, and it's the Right that controls the left side of the body, so when you tell us in words to do something, only our Left understand and moves the muscles it controls. It gets the jump on the Right because the Right can't speak or be spoken to.''

"Very good, Galaine. That's it exactly.''

I let it sink in. Now that the connections between the two halves of their brains have been cut, the Rights of these children are isolated, unable to draw on the skills of the language center in the Left. They are only now realizing what it means to have half a brain rendered illiterate and inarticulate, to have their Left respond as though it is the entire brain, activating only the muscles it controls most directly.

Fyme says, "Does that mean we won't ever be able to use our left sides again?''

"Not at all. Your Right isn't paralyzed or helpless. It just isn't very good at using words. So your Left is quicker to react when I give a verbal instruction. But if the instruction isn't phrased in words, the Right will be able to take control and respond.''

"How can you give an instruction that isn't in words?'' Mulliam asks.

"In many ways,'' I say. "I could draw a picture, or make a gesture, or use some sort of symbol. I'll show you what I mean by going through the exercises again. Sometimes I'll give the instructions in words, and sometimes by acting them out. When I do that, imitate what you see. Is that clear?''

I wait a moment to allow the sluggish word-skills of their Rights to grasp the scheme.

Then I say, "Raise a hand.''

They lift their right arms. When I tell them to bend a knee, they bend their right knees. But when I wordlessly close my left eye, they imitate me and close their left eyes. Their Rights are able to exert muscular control in a normal way when the instructions are delivered nonverbally; but when I use words, the Left alone perceives and acts.

I test the ability of their Lefts to override the normal motor functions of their Rights by instructing them verbally to raise their left shoulders. Their Rights, baffled by my words, take no action, forcing their Lefts to reach beyond a Left's usual sphere of dominance. Slowly, with great difficulty, a few of the children manage to raise their left shoulders. Some can manage only a mere twitch. Fyme, Bloss, and Mulligan, with signs of struggle evident on their faces, are unable to budge their left shoulders at all. I tell the entire group to relax, and the children collapse in relief, sprawling on their cots. There is nothing to worry about, I say. In time they will all regain full motor functions in both halves of their bodies. Unless they are driven insane by the split-brain phenomena, that is, but no need to tell them that.

"One more demonstration for today," I announce. This one will show them in another way how thoroughly the separation of the hemispheres affect the mental processes. I ask Gybold, the smallest of the boys, to seat himself at the testing table at the far end of the room. There is a screen mounted on the table: I tell Gybold to fix his eyes on the center of the screen, and I flash a picture of a banana on the left side of the screen for a fraction of a second.

"What do you see, Gybold?"

"I don't see anything, Sister Mimise," he replies, and the other children gasp. But the "I" that is speaking is merely Gybold's Left, which gets it visual information through his right eye; that eye did indeed see nothing. Meanwhile Gybold's Right is answering my question in the only way it can: the boy's left hand gropes among several objects lying on the table hidden behind the screen, finds the banana that is there, and triumphantly holds it up. Through sight and touch Gybold's Right has prevailed over its wordlessness.

"Excellent," I say. I take the banana from him and, drawing his left hand behind the screen where he is unable to see it, I put a drinking glass into it. I ask him to name the object in his hand.

"An apple?" he ventures. I frown, and quickly he says, "An egg? A pencil?"

The children laugh. Mulliam says, "He's just guessing!"

"Yes, he is. But which part of Gybold's brain is making the guesses?"

"His Left," Galaine cries. "But it's the Right that knows it's holding a glass."

They all shush her for giving away the secret. Gybold pulls his hand out from under the screen and stares at the glass, silently forming its name with his lips.

I put Herik, Chith, Simi, and Clane through related experiments. Always the results are the same. If I flash a picture to the right eye or put an object in the right hand, the children respond normally, correctly naming it. But if I transmit information only to the left eye or the left hand, they are unable to use words to describe the objects their Rights see or feel.

It is enough for now. The children are silent and have withdrawn into individual spheres of privacy. I know that they are working things out within their minds, performing small self-devised experiments, testing themselves, trying to learn the full extent of the changes the operation has brought about. They glance from one hand to another, flex fingers, whisper little calculations. They should not be allowed to look inward so much, not at the beginning. I take them to the storeroom to receive their new clothing, the simple gray monastic robes that we wear to set us apart from the ordinary people of the city. Then I turn them free, sending them romping into the broad fields of soft green grass behind the dormitory, to relax and play. They may be oracles in the making; but they are also, after all, ten-year-old children.

It is my afternoon rest period. On my way through the dark cool corridors to my chamber I am stopped by Brother Sleel, one of the senior oracles. He is a white-haired man, tall and of powerful build, and his blue eyes work almost independently of one another, constantly scanning his surroundings in restless separate searches. Sleel has never been anything but warm and kind to me, and yet I have always been afraid of him, I suppose more out of awe for his office than out of fear for the man himself. Really I feel timid with all the oracles, knowing that their minds work differently from mine and that they see things in me that I may not see myself. Sleel says, "I saw you having difficulties with Runild in the hall this morning. What was happening?"

"He wandered into my orientation meeting. I asked him to leave."

"What was he doing?"

"He said he wanted to see the new children. But of course I couldn't let him bother them."

"And he started to fight with you?"

"He made some trouble. Nothing much."

"He was fighting with you, Mimise."

"He was rather unruly," I admit.

Sleel's left eye stares into mine. I feel a chill. It is the oracle-eye, the all-seeing one. Quietly he says, "I saw you fighting with him."

I look away from him. I study my bare feet. "He wouldn't leave. He was frightening the new ones. When I tried to lead him from the room he jumped at me, yes. But he didn't hurt me and it was all over in a moment. Runild is high-spirited, Brother."

"Runild is a troubled child," Sleel says heavily. "He is disturbed. He is becoming wild, like a beast."

"No, Brother Sleel." How can I face that terrible eye? "He has extraordinary gifts. You know—surely *you* must know—that it takes time for one like him to settle down, to come to terms with—"

"I've had complaints from his counselor, Voree. She says she hardly knows how to handle him."

"It's only a phase. Voree's had responsibility for him only a couple of weeks. As soon as she—"

"I know you want to protect him, Mimise. But don't let your love for the boy cloud your judgement. I think this is Timas happening all over again. It's an old, old pattern here, the brilliant novice who is unable to cope with his changes, who—"

"Are you going to cull him?" I blurt.

Sleel smiles. He takes both my hands in his. I am engulfed by his strength, by his wisdom, by his power. I sense the unfathomable flow of perception from his mystic Right to his calm, analytic Left. He says, "If Runild gets any worse, I'll have to. But I want to save him. I like the boy. I respect his potential. What do you suggest we do, Mimise?"

"What do *I*—"

"Tell me. Advise me."

The senior oracle is playing a little game with me, I suppose. Shrugging, I say, "Obviously Runild's trying to gain attention through all these crazy pranks. Let's try to reach him and find out what he really wants, and perhaps there'll be some say we can give it to him. I'll speak to Voree. I'll talk to his sister, Kitrin. And tomorrow I'll talk to Runild. I think he trusts me. We were very close last year, Runild and I."

"I know," Sleel says gently. "Very well, see what you can do."

Still later that afternoon, as I cross the central courtyard, Runild erupts from the second-year house and rushes up to me. His face is flushed; his bare chest is shiny with sweat. He clings to me, pulls me down to his height, looks me in the eye. His eyes have already begun to stray a little; one day they may be like Sleel's.

I think he wants to apologize for his invasion of my group. But all he manages to say is: "I am sorry for you. You wanted so much to be one of us." And he runs off.

To be one of them. Yes. Who does not long to dwell in the House of Double Minds, living apart from the noise and chaos of the world, devoting oneself to oracular contemplation and the service of mankind? My mother's father's sister was of that high company, and in early girlhood I was taken to visit her. How awesome it was to stand in the presence of her all-knowing Right, to feel the flood of warmth and understanding that emanated from her wise eyes. It was my dream to join her here, a dream doubly thwarted, for she died when I was eight, and by then the fact of my left-handedness was irremediably established.

Left-handers are never selected to undergo the oracle-making operation. The two halves of our brains are too symmetrical, too ambidextrous: we have speech centers on both sides, most of us left-handers, and so we are not likely to develop those imbalances of cerebral powers that oracles must have. Right-handers, too, are born with symmetrically functioning brains, each hemisphere developing independently and duplicating the operations of the other. But by the time they are two years old, their Lefts and Rights are linked in a way that gives them a shared pool of skills, and therefore each half is free to develop its own special capabilities, since the gifts of one half are instantly available to the other.

At the age of ten this specializing process is complete. Language, sequential thought, all the analytic and rational functions, center in the Left. Special perception, artistic vision, musical skill, emotional insight, center in the Right. The brain's left side is the scientist, the architect, the general, the mathematician. The brain's right side is the minstrel, the sculptor, the visionary, the dreamer. Normally the two halves operate as one. The Right experiences a flash of poetic intuition, the Left clothes it in words. The Right sees a pattern of fundamental connections, the Left expresses it in a sequence of theorems. The Right conceives the shape of a symphony, the Left sets the notes down on paper. Where there is true harmony between the hemispheres of the brain, works of genius are created.

Too often, though, one side seizes command. Perhaps the Right becomes dominant, and we have a dancer, an athlete, an artist, who has trouble with words, who is inexpressive and inarticulate except through some nonverbal medium. More often, because we are a word-worshipping people, it is the Left that rules, choking the subordinate Right in a welter of verbal analysis and commentary, slowing and hindering the spontaneous intuitive perceptions of the mind. What society gains in orderliness and rationality it loses in vision and grace. We can do nothing about these imbalances—except to take advantage of their existence by accentuating and exploiting them.

And so the children come here, a dozen of our best each year, and our surgeons sever the isthmus of neural tissue that links Left and Right. Some kind of communication between the hemispheres continues to operate, since each half remains aware of what the other is immediately experiencing, if not of its accumulated memories and skills. But the Right is cut free from the tyranny of the word-intoxicated Left. The Left continues to operate its normal routines of reading and writing and conversation and computation, while the Right, now its own master, observes and registers and analyzes in a way that has no need for words. Because its verbal skills are so feeble, the newly independent Right must find some other means of expression if it is to make its perceptions known: and, through the dozen years of training in the House of Double Minds, some of the children succeed in achieving this. They are able—I do not know how, no one who is not an oracle can ever know how—to transmit the unique insights of fully mature and wholly independent Rights to their Lefts, which can transmit them to the rest of us. It is a difficult and imperfect process, but it gives us access to levels of knowledge that few have ever reached before our time. Those who master that skill are our functional oracles. They dwell in realms of beauty and wisdom that, in the past, only saints and prophets and the greatest artists and a few madmen have reached.

I would, if I could, have entered those realms. But I came forth left-handed from the womb and my brain, though it is a decent one, therefore lacked the required asymmetry of function. If I could not be an oracle I could at least serve them, I decided. And thus I came here as a girl, and asked to be of use, and in time was given the important task of easing the new children into their new lives. So I have come to know Jen and Timas and Jalill and Runild and the others, some of whom will live to be among the most famous of oracles, and so now I welcome Hirole and Mulliam and Gybold and Galaine and their companions. And I am content, I think. I am content.

We gather in the main hall for the evening meal. My new group has not come before the older novices until now, and so my twelve undergo close scrutiny, which they find embarrassing, as I lead them to their place. Each year-group sits together at its own circular table. My dozen dine with me; at the table to my left is my group of last year, now in Voree's charge. Runild sits there with his back to me, and his mere presence creates a tension in me as if he is giving off an electric radiation. To my right is the third-year group, reduced now to nine by the culling of Timas and two deaths; the fourth-year children are just in front of me and the fifth-year ones, my darling Jen among them, at my rear. The older children are in the center of the hall. Along the sides of the great room are the tables of the instructors, those who have daily care of the ordinary education of the twelve groups of novices, and the senior oracles occupy long tables at the hall's far end, beneath a panoply of gay red and green banners.

Sleel makes a brief speech of welcome for my twelve, and the meal is served.

I send Galaine to Voree's table with a note: *"See me on the porch after dinner."*

My appetite is poor. I finish quickly, but I stay with my group until it is time to dismiss them. All the children troop off to the auditorium for a show. A warm drizzle is falling; Voree and I stand in the shelter of the eaves. She is much older than I am, a stocky woman with kinky orange hair. Year after year I pass my fledglings on to her. She is strong, efficient, stolid, insensitive. Runild baffles her. "He's like a monkey," she says. "Running around naked, chattering to himself, singing crazy songs, playing pranks. He isn't doing his lessons. He isn't even doing his disciplines, half the time. I've warned him he'll be culled, but he doesn't seem to care."

"What do you think he wants?"

"To have everyone notice him."

"Yes, surely, but *why?*"

"Because he's a naturally mischievous boy," Voree says, scowling. "I've seen many of his sort before. They think rules are for other people. Two more weeks of this and I'll recommend a cull.''

"He's too brilliant to waste like that, Voree.''

"He's wasting himself. Without the disciplines how can he become an oracle? And he's upsetting all the others. My group's a shambles. Now he's bothering yours. He won't leave his sister alone either. Culling, Mimise, that's where he's heading. Culling.''

There is nothing to be gained from talking to Voree. I join my group in the auditorium.

Bedtime for the younger ones comes early. I see my children to their room; then I am free until midnight. I return to the auditorium, where the older children and the off-duty staff are relaxing, playing games, dancing, drifting off in couples. Kitrin, Runild's sister, is still there. I draw her aside. She is a slender, delicate girl of fourteen, a fifth-year novice. I am fond of her because she was in my very first group, but I have always found her shy, elusive, opaque. She is more so than ever now: I question her about her brother's behavior and she answers me with shrugs, vague unfinished sentences, and artful evasions. Runild is wild? Well, of course, many boys are wild, she says, especially the bright ones. The disciplines seem to bore him. He's far ahead of his group—you know that, Mimise. And so on. I get nothing from her except the strong feeling that she is hiding something about her brother. My attempts to probe fail; Kitrin is still a child, but she is halfway to oraclehood, nearly, and that gives her an advantage over me in any duel of wits. Only when I suggest that Runild is in immediate peril of culling do I break through her defenses.

"No!" she gasps, eyes widening in fear, cheeks turning pale. "They mustn't! He has to stay! He's going to be greater than any of them!''

"He's causing too much trouble.''

"It's just a thing he's going through. He'll settle down, I promise you that.''

"Voree doesn't think so. She's going to request a cull.''

"No. No. What will happen to him if he's culled? He was *meant* to be an oracle. His whole life will have been thrown away. We have to save him, Mimise.''

"We can do that only if he can control himself.''

"I'll talk to him in the morning,'' Kitrin says.

I wonder what she knows about Runild that she does not want to tell me.

At the evening's end I bring Jen to my chamber, as I do three or four nights a week. She is tall and supple and looks more than her fourteen years. Her counselor tells me she is moving well through her mid-novitiate and will be a splendid oracle. We lie together, lips to lips, breasts against breasts, and we stroke and caress and tickle one another, we smile with our eyes, we enter into all the rituals of love. Afterward, in the stillness that follows passion, she finds the bruise of this morning's struggle on my thigh and questions me with a frown. "Runild," I say. I tell her about his erratic behavior, about Sleel's uneasiness, about my conversation with Voree.

"They mustn't cull him," Jen says solemnly. "I know he's troublesome. But the path he's taking is so important for all of us"

"Path? What path is that?"

"You don't know?"

"I know nothing, Jen."

She catches her breath, rolls away, studies me a moment. At length she says, "Runild sees into minds. When he puts his head very close to people, there's transmission. Without using words. It's—it's a kind of broadcast. His Right can read the Rights of other oracles, the way you'd open a book and read it. If he could get close enough to Sleel, say, or any of them, he could read what's in their Rights."

"What?"

"More, Mimise. His own right talks to his Left the same way. He can transmit messages completely, quickly, making better contact between the halves than any of the oracles can do. He hasn't had the disciplines, even, and he has full access to his Right's perceptions. So whatever his Right sees, including what it gets from the Rights of others, can be transmitted to his Left and expressed in words more clearly even than Sleel himself can do it!"

"I don't believe this," I say, barely comprehending.

"It's true! It's true, Mimise! He's only just learning how, and it gets him terribly excited, it makes him wild, don't you see, when all that contact comes flooding in? He can't quite handle it yet, which is why he acts so strange. But once he gets his power under control—''

"How do you know anything about this, Jen?"

"Why, Kitrin told me."

"Kitrin? I spoke to Kitrin and she never even hinted that—"

"Oh," Jen says, looking pained. "Oh, I guess I wasn't supposed to say. Not even to you, I guess. Oh, now I'll be in trouble with Kitrin, and—"

"You won't be. She doesn't need to know how I found out. But—Jen, Jen, can this be? Can anyone have such powers?"

"Runild does."

"So he claims. Or Kitrin claims on his behalf."

"No," Jen says firmly. "He *does*. They showed me, he and Kitrin. I felt him touch my mind. I felt him read me. He can read anyone. He can read *you*, Mimise."

I must speak with Runild. But carefully, carefully, everything in its proper moment. In the morning I must first meet with my group and take them through the second-day exercises. These are designed to demonstrate that their Rights, although mute and presently isolated, are by no means inferior, and have perceptions and capabilities which in some ways are superior to those of their Lefts.

"Never think of your Right as a cripple," I warn them. "See it, rather, as some kind of extremely intelligent animal—an animal that is sharp-witted, quick to respond, imaginative, with only one flaw, that it has no vocabulary and is never going to be able to acquire more than a few simple words at best. Nobody pities a tiger or an eagle because it doesn't know how to speak. And there are ways of training tigers and eagles so that we can communicate with them without using words."

I flash a picture of a house on the screen and ask the children to copy it, first using their left hands, then the right. Although they are all right-handed, they are unable to draw anything better than simple, crude two-dimensional representations with their right hands. Their left-handed drawings, while shakily drawn because of their left arms' relatively backward muscular development and motor control, show a full understanding of the techniques of perspective. The right hand has the physical skill, but it is the left, drawing on the vision of the brain's right hemisphere, that has the artistic ability.

I ask them to arrange colored plastic cubes to match an intricate pattern on the screen. Left-handed, they carry out the exercise swiftly and expertly. Right-handed, they become confused, frown and bite their lips, hold the cubes long moments without knowing where to put them down, eventually array the cubes in chaotic mazes. Clane and Bloss give up entirely in a minute or two; Mulliam perseveres grimly like one who is determined to climb a mountain too steep for his strength, but he accomplishes little; Luabet's left hand keeps darting across to do the task that is beyond the right's powers, as if she is at war with herself. She must keep the impatient left hand behind her back in order to proceed at all. No one can complete the block design correctly with the right hand, and when I allow the children to work with both hands the hands fight for control, the formerly dominant right one unable to accept its new inferiority and angrily slapping at the cubes the left one tries to put in place.

We go on to the split-screen exercises in facial recognition and pattern analysis, to the musical exercises and the rest of the usual second-day routine. The children are fascinated by the ease with which their Rights function in all but word-linked operations. Ordinarily I am delighted, too, to watch the newly liberated Rights come to life and assert their powers. But today I am impatient to be off to Runild and I give only perfunctory attention to my proper work.

At last the session ends. The children move off to the classroom where they will receive regular school-subject instruction. Runild's group, too, should be at school until noon. Possibly I can draw him aside after lunch. But, as though I have conjured him with a wish, I see him now, tumbling by himself in the meadow of crimson flowers by the auditorium. He sees me, too: halts in his gambol, winks, smiles, does a handspring, blows me a kiss. I go to him.

"Are you excused from classes this morning?" I ask, mock-stern.

"The flowers are so pretty," he replies.

"The flowers will be just as pretty after school."

"Oh, don't be so stuffy, Mimise! I know my lessons. I'm a clever boy."

"Perhaps too clever, Runild."

He grins. I do not frighten him. He seems to be patronizing me; he appears to be at once very much younger and very much wiser than his years. I take him gently by the wrist and draw him down, easily, until we are sprawled side by side in the grass. He plucks a flower for me. His look is flirtatious. I accept both the flower and the look and respond with a warm smile; I am flirtatious myself. No doubt of his charm; and I can never win him by acting as an authority figure, only as a co-conspirator. There was always an underlying sexuality in our relationship, incestuous, as if I were an older sister.

We talk in banter, teasing each other. Then I say, "Something mysterious has been happening to you lately, Runild. I know that. Share your mystery with me."

At first he denies all. He pretends innocence, but lets me know it is only pretense. His sly smile betrays him. He speaks in cryptic ellipses, hinting at arcane knowledge and defying me to pry details from him. I play his game, acting now intrigued, now eager, now skeptical, now wholly uninterested: we are stalking one another, and both of us know it. His oracle-eye pierces me. He toys with me with such subtlety that I must remind myself, with a glance at his slim hairless body, that I am dealing with a child. I ought never forget that he is only eleven. Finally I press directly once more, asking him outright what strange new gift he is cultivating.

"Wouldn't you like to know!" he cries, and pulls an outrageous face, and dashes away.

But he comes back. We talk on a more serious level. He admits that he has discovered, these past few months, that he is different from the other children and from the senior oracles, that he has a talent, a power. It disturbs and exalts him both. He is still exploring the scope of it. He will not describe the power in any specific way. Of course I know from Jen its nature, but I prefer not to reveal that. "Will you ever tell me?" I ask.

"Not today," he says.

Gradually I win his trust. We meet casually, in corridors or courtyards, and exchange easy pleasantries, the sort I might trade with any of my former charges. He is testing me, seeing whether I am a friend or simply Sleel's spy. I let him know of my concern for him. I let him know that his eccentric behavior has placed him in jeopardy of culling.

"I suppose so," he says gloomily. "But what can I do? I'm not like the others. I can't sit still for long. Things are jumping inside my head all the time. Why should I bother with arithmetic when I can—"

He halts, suddenly guarded again.

"When you can what, Runild?"

"*You* know."

"I don't."

"You will, soon enough."

There are days when he seems calm. But his pranks have not ended. He finds poor Sister Sestoine, on of the oldest and dimmest of the oracles, and puts his forehead against hers and does something to her that sends her into an hour's tears. Sestoine will not say what took place during that moment of contact, and after a while she seems to forget the episode. Sleel's face is dark. He looks warningly at me as if to say, *Time's running short; the boy must go*.

On a day of driving rain I am in my chamber in midafternoon when Runild unexpectedly enters, soaked, hair plastered to his scalp. Puddles drip from him. He strips and I rub him with a towel and stand him before the fire. He says nothing all this while; he is tense, taut, as if a mighty pressure is building within him and the time has not yet come for its release. Abruptly he turns to me. His eyes are strange: they wander, they quiver, they glow. "Come close!" he whispers hoarsely, like a man calling a woman to his bed. He grasps my shoulders, he pulls me down to his height, he pushes his blazing forehead roughly against mine. And the world changes. I see tongues of purple flame. I see crevasses opening in the earth. I see the oceans engulfing the shore. I am flooded with contact; I am swept with wild energies.

I know what it is to be an oracle.

My Right and my Left are asunder. It is not like having one brain cleft in two; it is like having two brains, independent, equal. I feel them ticking like two clocks, with separate beats; and the Left goes tick-tock-tick-tock, machine-dreary, while the Right leaps and dances and soars and sings in lunatic rhythms. But they are not lunatic rhythms, for their frantic pulses have a regularity of irregularity, a pattern of patternlessness. I grow used to the strangeness; I become comfortable within both brains, the Left which I think of as "me," and the Right which is "me" too, but an altered and unfamiliar self without a name. My earliest memories lie open to me in my Right. I see into a realm of shadows. I am an infant again; I have access to the first hours of my life, to all my first years, those years in which words meant nothing to me. The pre-verbal data all rests within my Right, shapes and textures and odors and sounds, and I do not need to give names to anything, I do not need to denote or analyze, I need only feel, experience, relive. All that is there is clear and sharp. I see how it has always been with me, how that set of recorded experiences had directed my behavior even as the experiences of later years have done so. I can reach that hidden realm now, and understand it, and use it.

I feel the flow of data from Right to Left—the wordless responses, the intuitive reactions, the quick spontaneous awareness of structures. The world holds new meanings for me. I think, but not in words, and I tell myself things, but not in words, and my Left, groping and fumbling (for it has not had the disciplines) seeks words, sometimes finding them, to express what I am giving it. So this is what oracles do. This is what they feel. This is the knowledge they have. I am transfigured. It is my fantasy come true: they have snipped that rubbery band of connective tissue; they have set free my Right; they have made me one of them. And I will never again be what once I was. I will think in tones and colors now. I will explore kingdoms unknown to the word-bound ones. I will live in a land of music. I will not merely speak and write: I will feel and know.

Only it is fading now.

The power is leaving me. I had it only a moment; and was it my own power or only a glimpse of Runild's? I cling, I grapple, and yet it goes, it goes, it goes, and I am left with shreds and bits, and then not even those, only an aftertaste, an echo of an echo, a diminishing shaft of feeble light. My eyes open. I am on my knees; sweat covers my body; my heart is pounding. Runild stands above me. "You see now?" he says. "You see? This is what it's like for me all the time. I can connect minds. *I can make connections, Mimise.*"

"Do it again," I beg.

He shakes his head. "Too much will hurt you," he says. And goes from me.

I have told Sleel what I have learned. Now they have the boy with them in the inner oracle-house, nine of them, the highest oracles, questioning him, testing him. I do not see how they can fail to welcome his gift, to give him special honor, to help him through his turbulent boyhood so that he can take his place supreme among oracles. But Jen thinks otherwise. She thinks he distresses them by scrabbling their minds in his still unfocused attempts at making contact, and that they will fear him once they have had an explicit demonstration of what he can do; she thinks, too, that he is a threat to their authority, of his way of joining the perceptions of his Right to the analytic powers of his Left by a direct mental flow is far superior to their own laborious method of symbolic translation. Jen thinks they will surely cull him and may even put him to death. How can I believe such things? She is not yet an oracle herself; she is still a girl; she may be wrong. The conference continues hour after hour, and no one emerges from the oracle-house.

In the evening they come forth. The rain has stopped. I see the senior oracles march across the courtyard. Runild is among them, very small at Sleel's side. There are no expressions on any faces. Runild's eyes meet mine: his look is blank, unreadable. Have I somehow betrayed him in trying to save him? What will happen to him? The procession reaches the far side of the quadrangle. A car is waiting. Runild and two of the senior oracles get into it.

After dinner Sleel calls me aside, thanks me for my help, tells me that Runild is to undergo study by experts at an institute far away. His power of mind-contact is so remarkable, says Sleel, that it requires prolonged analysis.

Mildly I ask whether it would not have been better to keep him here, among the surroundings that have become home to him, and let the experts come to the House of Double Minds to examine him. Sleel shakes his head. There are many experts, the testing equipment is not portable, the tests will be lengthy.

I wonder if I will ever see Runild again.

In the morning I meet with my group at the usual time. They have lived here several weeks now, and their early fears are gone from them. Already I see the destinies unfolding: Galaine is fast-witted but shallow, Mulliam and Chith are plodders, Fyme and Hirole and Divvan may have the stuff of oracles, the rest are mediocrities. An average group. Hirole, perhaps, is becoming my favorite. There are no Jens among them, no Runilds.

"Today we start to examine the idea of nonverbal words," I

begin. "For example, if we say, Let this green ball stand for the word 'same,' and this blue box stand for the word 'different,' then we can..."

My voice drones on. The children listen placidly. So the training proceeds in the House of Double Minds. Beneath the vault of my skull my dreaming Right throbs a bit, as though reliving its moment of freedom. Through the corridors outside the room the oracles move, deep in contemplation, shrouded in impenetrable wisdom, and we who serve them go obediently about our tasks.

THE SCIENCE
FICTION
HALL OF FAME

THE LOOK IN his remote gray eyes was haunted, terrified, beaten, as he came running in from the Projectorium. His shoulders were slumped; I had never before seen him betray the slightest surrender to despair, but now I was chilled by the completeness of his capitulation. With a shaking hand he thrust at me a slender yellow data slip, marked in red with the arcane symbols of cosmic computation. "No use," he muttered. "There's absolutely no use trying to fight any longer!"

"You mean—"

"Tonight," he said huskily, "the universe irrevocably enters the penumbra of the null point!"

The day Armstrong and Aldrin stepped out onto the surface of the moon—it was Sunday, July 20, 1969, remember?—I stayed home, planning to watch the whole thing on television. But it happened that I met an interesting woman at Leon and Helene's party the night before, and she came home with me. Her name is gone from my mind, if I ever knew it, but I remember how she looked: long soft golden hair, heart-shaped face with prominent ruddy cheeks, gentle gray-blue eyes, plump breasts, slender legs. I remember, too, how she wandered around my apartment, studying the crowded shelves of old paperbacks and magazines. "You're really into sci-fi, aren't you?" she said at last. And laughed and said, "I guess this must be your big weekend, then!

Wow, the moon!" But it was all a big joke to her, that men should be cavorting around up there when there was still so much work left to do on earth. We had a shower and I made lunch and we settled down in front of the set to wait for the men to come out of their module, and—very easily, without a sense of transition—we found ourselves starting to screw, and it went on and on, one of those impossible impersonal mechanical screws in which body grinds against body for centuries, no feeling, no excitement, and as I rocked rhythmically on top of her, unable either to come or to quit, I heard Walter Cronkite telling the world that the module hatch was opening. I wanted to break free of her so I could watch, but she clawed at my back. With a distinct effort I pulled myself up on my elbows, pivoted the upper part of my body so I had a view of the screen, and waited for the ecstasy to hit me. Just as the first wavery image of an upside-down spaceman came into view on that ladder, she moaned and bucked her hips wildly and went into frenzied climax. I felt nothing. Nothing. Eventually she left, and I showered and had a snack and watched the replay of the moonwalk on the eleven o'clock news. And still I felt nothing.

"What is the answer?" said Gertrude Stein, about to die. Alice B. Toklas remained silent. "In that case," Miss Stein went on, "what is the question?"

Extract from *History of the Imperium*, Koeckert and Hallis, third edition (revised):

The galactic empire was organized 190 standard universal centuries ago by the joint, simultaneous, and unanimous resolution of the governing bodies of eleven hundred worlds. By the present day the hegemony of the empire has spread to thirteen galactic sectors and embraces many thousands of planets, all of which entered the empire willingly and gladly. To remain outside the empire is to confess civic insanity, for the Imperium is unquestionably regarded throughout the cosmos as the most wholly sane construct ever created by the sentient mind. The decision-making processes of the Imperium are invariably determined by recourse to the Hermosillo Equations, which provide unambiguous and incontrovertibly rational guidance in any question of public policy. Thus the many worlds of the empire form a single coherent unit, as perfectly interrelated socially, politically, and economically as its component worlds are interrelated by the workings of the universal laws of gravitation.

Perhaps I spend too much time on other planets and in remote galaxies. It's an embarrassing addiction, this science fiction. (Horrible jingle! It jangles in my brain like an idiot's singsong chant.) Look at my bookshelves: hundreds of well-worn paperbacks, arranged alphabetically by authors, Aschenbach-Barger-Capwell-De Soto-Friedrich, all the greats of the genre out to Waldman and Zenger. The collection of magazines, every issue of everything back to the summer of 1953, a complete run of *Nova*, most issues of *Deep Space*, a thick file of *Tomorrow*. I suppose some of those magazines are quite rare now, though I've never looked closely into the feverish world of the s-f collector. I simply accumulate the publications I buy at the newsstand, never throwing any of them away. How could I part with them? Slices of my past, those magazines, those books. I can give dates to changes in my spirit, alterations in my consciousness, merely by picking up old magazines and reflecting on the associations they evoke. The issue showing the ropy-armed purple monster: it went on sale the month I discovered sex. This issue, cover painting of exploding spaceships: I read it my first month in college, by way of relief from Aquinas and Plato. Mileposts, landmarks, waterlines. An embarrassing addiction. My friends are good-humored about it. They think science fiction is a literature for children— God knows, they may be right—and they indulge my fancy for it in an affectionate way, giving me some fat anthology for Christmas, leaving a stack of current magazines on my desk while I'm out to lunch. But they wonder about me. Sometimes I wonder too. At the age of thirty-four should I still be able to react with such boyish enthusiasm to, say, Capwell's Solar League novels or Waldman's "Mindleech" series? What is there about the present that drives me so obsessively toward the future? The gray and vacant present, the tantalizing, inaccessible future.

His eyes were glittering with irrepressible excitement as he handed her the gleaming yellow dome that was the thought-transference helmet. "Put it on," he said tenderly.

"I'm afraid, Riik."

"Don't be. What's there to fear?"

"Myself. The real me. I'll be wide open, Riik. I fear what you may see in me, what it may do to you, to *us*."

"Is it so ugly inside you?" he asked.

"Sometimes I think so."

"Sometimes everybody thinks that about himself, Juun. It's the old neurotic self-hatred welling up, the garbage that we can't escape until we're totally sane. You'll find that kind of stuff in me, too, once we have the helmets on. Ignore it. It isn't real. It isn't going to be a determining factor in our lives."

"Do you love me, Riik?"

"The helmet will answer that better than I can."

"All right. All right." She smiled nervously. Then with exaggerated care she lifted the helmet, put it in place, adjusted it, smoothed a vagrant golden curl back under the helmet's rim. He nodded and donned his own.

"Ready?" he asked.

"Ready."

"Now!"

He threw the switch. Their minds surged toward one another. Then—

Oneness!

My mind is cluttered with other men's fantasies: robots, androids, starships, giant computers, predatory energy globes, false messiahs, real messiahs, visitors from distant worlds, time machines, gravity repellers. Punch my buttons and I offer you parables from the works of Hartzell or Marcus, appropriate philosophical gems borrowed from the collected editorial utterances of David Coughlin, or concepts dredged from my meditations on De Soto. I am a walking mass of secondhand imagination. I am the flesh-and-blood personification of the Science Fiction Hall of Fame.

"At last," cried Professor Kholgoltz triumphantly. "The machine is finished! The last solenoid is installed! Feed power, Hagley. Feed power! Now we will have the Answer we have sought for so many years!"

He gestured to his assistant, who gradually brought the great computer throbbingly to life. A subtle, barely perceptible flow of energy pervaded the air: the neutrino flux that the master equations had predicted. In the amphitheater adjoining the laboratory, ten thousand people sat tensely frozen. All about the world, millions more, linked by satellite relay, waited with similar intensity. The professor nodded. Another gesture, and Hagley, with a grand flourish, fed the question tape—programmed under the supervision of a corps of multispan-trained philosophers—into the gaping jaws of the input slot.

"The meaning of life," murmured Kholgoltz. "The solution to the ultimate riddle. In just another moment it will be in our hands."

An ominous rumbling sound came from the depths of the mighty thinking machine. And then—

My recurring nightmare: A beam of dense emerald light penetrates my bedroom and lifts me with an irresistible force from my bed. I float through the window and hover high above the city. A zone of blackness engulfs me and I find myself transported to an endless onyx-walled tunnel-like hallway. I am alone. I wait, and nothing happens, and after an interminable length of time I begin to walk forward, keeping close to the left side of the hall. I am aware now that towering cone-shaped beings with saucer-size orange eyes and rubbery bodies are gliding past me on the right, paying no attention to me. I walk for days. Finally the hallway splits: nine identical tunnels confront me. Randomly I choose the leftmost one. It is just like the last, except that the beings moving toward me now are animated purple starfish, rough-skinned, many-tentacled, a globe of pale white fire glowing at their cores. Days again. I feel no hunger, no fatigue; I just go marching on. The tunnel forks once more. Seventeen options this time. I choose the rightmost branch. No change in the texture of the tunnel—smooth as always, glossy, bright with an inexplicable inner radiance—but now the beings flowing past me are spherical, translucent, paramecioid things filled with churning misty organs. On to the next forking place. And on. And on. Fork after fork, choice after choice, nothing the same, nothing ever different. I keep walking. On. On. On. I walk forever. I never leave the tunnel.

What's the purpose of life, anyway? Who if anybody put us here, and why? Is the whole cosmos merely a gigantic accident? Or was there a conscious and determined Prime Cause? What about free will? Do we have any, or are we only acting out the dictates of some unimaginable, unalterable program that was stenciled into the fabric of reality a billion years ago?

Big resonant questions. The kind an adolescent asks when he first begins to wrestle with the nature of the universe. What am I doing brooding over such stuff at my age? Who am I fooling?

This is the place. I have reached the center of the universe, where all vortices meet, where everything is tranquil, the zone of stormlessness. I drift becalmed, moving in a shallow orbit. This is ultimate peace. This is the edge of union with the All. In my tranquility I experience a vision of the brawling, tempestuous universe that surrounds me. In every quadrant there are wars, quarrels, conspiracies, murders, air crashes, frictional losses, dimming suns, transfers of energy, colliding planets, a multitude of entropic interchanges. But here everything is perfectly still. Here is where I wish to be.

Yes! If only I could remain forever!

How, though? There's no way. Already I feel the tug of inexorable forces, and I have only just arrived. There is no everlasting peace. We constantly rocket past the miraculous center toward one zone of turbulence or another, driven always toward the periphery, driven, driven, helpless. I am drawn away from the place of peace. I spin wildly. The centrifuge of ego keeps me churning. Let me go back! Let me go! Let me lose myself in that place at the heart of the tumbling galaxies!

Never to die. That's part of the attraction. To live in a thousand civilizations yet to come, to see the future millennia unfold, to participate vicariously in the ultimate evolution of mankind—how to achieve all that, except through these books and magazines? That's what they give me: life eternal and a cosmic perspective. At any rate they give it to me from one page to the next.

The signal sped across the black bowl of night, picked up again and again by ultrawave repeater stations that kicked it to higher energy states. A thousand trembling laser nodes were converted to vapor in order to hasten the message to the galactic communications center on Manipool VI, where the emperor awaited news of the revolt. Through the data dome at last the story tumbled.

Worlds aflame! Millions dead! The talismans of the Imperium trampled upon!

"We have no choice," said the emperor calmly. "Destroy the entire Rigel system at once."

The problem that arises when you try to regard science fiction as adult literature is that it's doubly removed from our "real" concerns. Ordinary mainstream fiction, your Faulkner and Dostoevsky and Hemingway, is by definition made-up stuff—the first remove. But at least it derives directly from experience, from contemplation of the empirical world of tangible daily phenomena. And so, while we are able to accept *The Possessed*, say, as an abstract thing, a verbal object, a construct of nouns and verbs and adjectives and adverbs, and while we can take it purely as a story, and aggregation of incidents and conversations and expository passages describing invented individuals and events, we can also *make use of it* as a guide to a certain aspect of Russian nineteenth-century sensibility and as a key to pre-revolutionary radical thought. That is, it is of the nature of an historical artifact, a legacy of its own era, with real and identifiable extra literary values. Because it simulates actual people moving within a plausible and comprehensible real-world human situation, we can draw information from Dostoevsky's book that could conceivably aid us in understanding our own lives. What about science fiction, though, dealing with unreal situations set in places that do not exist and in eras that have not yet occurred? Can we take the adventures of Captain Zap in the eightieth century as a blueprint for self-discovery? Can we accept the collision of stellar federations in the Andromeda Nebula as an interpretation of the relationship of the United States and the Soviet Union circa 1950? I suppose we can, provided we can accept a science fiction story on a rarefied metaphorical level, as a set of symbolic structures generated in some way by the author's real-world experience. But it's much easier to hang in there with Captain Zap on his own level, for the sheer gaudy fun of it. And that's kiddie stuff.

Therefore we have two possible evaluations of science fiction:

—That it is simple-minded escape literature, lacking relevance to daily life and useful only as self-contained diversion.

—That its value is subtle and elusive, accessible only to those capable and willing to penetrate the experiential substructure concealed by those broad metaphors of galactic empires and supernormal powers.

I oscillate between the two attitudes. Sometimes I embrace both simultaneously. That's a trick I learned from science fiction, incidentally: "multispan logic," it was called in Zenger's famous novel *The Mind Plateau*. It took his hero twenty years of ascetic study in the cloisters of the Brothers of Aldebaran to master the trick. I've accomplished it in twenty years of reading *Nova* and *Deep Space* and *Solar Quarterly*. Yes: multispan logic. Yes. The art of embracing contradictory theses. Maybe "dynamic schizophrenia" would be a more expressive term, I don't know.

Is this the center? Am I there? I doubt it. Will I know it when I reach it, or will I deny it as I frequently do, will I say, *What else is there, where else should I look?*

The alien was a repellent thing, all lines and angles, its tendrils quivering menacingly, its slit-wide eyes revealing a somber bloodshot curiosity. Mortenson was unable to focus clearly on the creature; it kept slipping off at the edges into some other plane of being, an odd rippling effect that he found morbidly disquieting. It was no more than fifty meters from him now, and advancing steadily. When it gets to within ten meters, he thought, I'm going to blast it no matter what.

Five steps more; then an eerie metamorphosis. In place of this thing of harsh angular threat there stood a beaming, happy Golkon! The plump little creature waved its chubby tentacles and cooed a gleeful greeting!

"I am love," the Golkon declared. "I am the bringer of happiness! I welcome you to this world, dear friend!"

What do I fear? I fear the future. I fear the infinite possibilities that lie ahead. They fascinate and terrify me. I never thought I would admit that, even to myself. But what other interpretation can I place on my dream? That multitude of tunnels, that infinity of strange beings, all drifting toward me as I walk on and on? The embodiment of my basic fear. Hence my compulsive reading of science fiction: I crave road signs, I want a map of the territory that I must enter. That we all must enter. Yet the maps themselves are frightening. Perhaps I should look backward instead. It would be less terrifying to read historical novels. Yet I feed on these fantasies that obsess and frighten me. I derive energy from them. If I renounced them, what would nourish me?

The blood-collectors were out tonight, roving in thirsty packs across the blasted land. From the stone-walled safety of his cell he could hear them baying, could hear also the terrible cries of the victims, the old women, the straggling children. Four, five nights a week now, the fanged monsters broke loose and went marauding, and each night there were fewer humans left to hold back the tide. That was bad enough, but there was worse: his own craving. How much longer could he keep himself locked up in here? How long before he too was out there, prowling, questing for blood?

When I went to the newsstand at lunchtime to pick up the latest issue of *Tomorrow,* I found the first number of a new magazine: *Worlds of Wonder.* That startled me. It must be nine or ten years since anybody risked bringing out a new s-f title. We have our handful of long-established standbys, most of them founded in the thirties and even the twenties, which seem to be going to go on forever; but the failure of nearly all the younger magazines in the fifties was so emphatic that I suppose I came to assume there never again would be any new titles. Yet here is *Worlds of Wonder,* out today. There's nothing extraordinary about it. Except for the name it might very well be *Deep Space* or *Solar.* The format is the usual one, the size of *Reader's Digest.* The cover painting, unsurprisingly, is by Greenstone. The stories are by Aschenbach, Marcus, and some lesser names. The editor is Roy Schaefer, whom I remember as a competent but unspectacular writer in the fifties and sixties. I suppose I should be pleased that I'll have six more issues a year to keep me amused. In fact I feel vaguely threatened, as though the tunnel of my dreams has sprouted an unexpected new fork.

The time machine hangs before me in the laboratory, a glittering golden ovoid suspended in ebony struts. Richards and Halleck smile nervously as I approach it. This, after all, is the climax of our years of research, and so much emotion rides on the success of the voyage I am about to take that every moment now seems freighted with heavy symbolic import. Our experiments with rats and rabbits seemed successful; but how can we know what it is to travel in time until a human being has made the journey?

All right. I enter the machine. Crisply we crackle instructions to one another across the intercom. Setting? Fifth of May, 2500 A.D.—a jump of nearly three and a half centuries. Power level? Energy feed? Go. Go. Dislocation circuit activated? Yes. All systems go. Bon voyage!

The control panel goes crazy. Dials spin. Lights flash. Everything's zapping at once. I plunge forward in time, going, going, going!

When everything is calm again I commence the emergence routines. The time capsule must be opened just so, unhurriedly. My hands tremble in anticipation of the strange new world that awaits me. A thousand hypotheses tumble through my brain. At last the hatch opens. "Hello," says Richards. "Hi there," Halleck says. We are still in the laboratory.

"I don't understand," I say. "My meters show definite temporal transfer."

"There was," says Richards. "You went forward to 2500 A.D., as planned. But you're still here."

"Where?"

"Here."

Halleck laughs. "You know what happened, Mike? You *did* travel in time. You jumped forward three hundred and whatever years. But you brought the whole present along with you. You pulled our own time into the future. It's like tugging a doughnut through its own hole. You see? Our work is kaput, Mike. We've got our answer. The present is always with us, no matter how far out we go."

Once about five years ago I took some acid, a little purple pill that a friend of mine mailed me from New Mexico. I had read a good deal about the psychedelics and I wasn't at all afraid; eager, in fact, hungry for the experience. I was going to float up into the cosmos and embrace it all. I was going to become a part of the nebulas and the supernovas, and they were going to become part of me; or rather, I would at last come to recognize that we had been part of each other all along. In other words, I imagined that LSD would be like an input of five hundred s-f novels all at once; a mind-blowing charge of imagery, emotion, strangeness, and transport to incredible unknowable places. The drug took about an hour to hit me. I saw the walls begin to flow and billow, and cascades of light streamed from the ceiling. Time became jumbled, and I thought three hours had gone by, but it was only about twenty minutes. Holly was with me. "What are you feeling?" she asked. "Is it mystical?" She asked a lot of questions like that. "I don't know," I said. "It's very pretty, but I just don't know." The drug wore off in about seven hours, but my nervous system was keyed up and lights kept exploding behind my eyes when I tried to go to sleep. So I sat up all night and read Marcus's *Starflame* novels, both of them, before dawn.

There is no galactic empire. There never will be any galactic empire. All is chaos. Everything is random. Galactic empires are puerile power-fantasies. Do I truly believe this? If not, why do I say it? Do I enjoy bringing myself down?

"Look over there!" the mutant whispered. Carter looked. An entire corner of the room had disappeared—melted away, as though it had been erased. Carter could see the street outside, the traffic, the building across the way. "Over there!" the mutant said. "Look!" The chair was gone. "Look!" The ceiling vanished. "Look! Look! Look!" Carter's head whirled. Everything was going, vanishing at the command of the inexorable golden-eyed mutant. "Do you see the stars?" the mutant asked. He snapped his fingers. "No!" Carter cried. "Don't!" Too late. The stars also were gone.

Sometimes I slip into what I consider the science fiction experience in everyday life. I mean, I can be sitting at my desk typing a report, or standing in the subway train waiting for the long grinding sweaty ride to end, when I feel a buzz, a rush, an upward movement of the soul similar to what I felt the time I took acid, and suddenly I see myself in an entirely new perspective—as a visitor from some other time, some other place, isolated in a world of alien beings known as earth. Everything seems unfamiliar and baffling. I get that sense of doubleness, of *déjà vu,* as though I have read about this subway in some science fiction novel, as though I have seen this office described in a fantasy story, far away, long ago. The real world thus becomes something science fictional to me for twenty or thirty seconds at a stretch. The textures slide; the fabric strains. Sometimes, when that has happened to me, I think it's more exciting than having a fantasy world become "real" as I read. And sometimes I think I'm coming apart.

While we were sleeping there had been tragedy aboard our mighty starship. Our captain, our leader, our guide for two full generations, had been murdered in his bed! "Let me see it again!" I insisted, and Timothy held out the hologram. Yes! No doubt of it! I could see the blood stains in his thick white hair, I could see the frozen mask of anguish on his strong-featured face. Dead! The captain was dead! "What now?" I asked. "What will happen?"
    "The civil war has already started on E Deck," Timothy said.

Perhaps what I really fear is not so much a dizzying multiplicity of futures but rather the absence of futures. When I end, will the universe end? Nothingness, emptiness, the void that awaits us all, the tunnel that leads not to everywhere but to nowhere—is that the only destination? If it is, is there any reason to feel fear? Why should I fear it? Nothingness is peace. Our nada who art in nada, nada be thy name, thy kingdom nada, thy will be nada, in nada as it is in nada. Hail nothing full of nothing, nothing is with thee. That's Hemingway. He felt the nada pressing in on all sides. Hemingway never wrote a word of science fiction. Eventually he delivered himself cheerfully to the great nada with a shotgun blast.

My friend Leon reminds me in some ways of Henry Darkdawn in De Soto's classic *Cosmos* trilogy. (If I said he reminded me of Stephen Dedalus or Raskolnikov or Julien Sorel, you would naturally need no further descriptions to know what I mean, but Henry Darkdawn is probably outside your range of literary experience. The De Soto trilogy deals with the formation, expansion, and decay of a quasi-religious movement spanning several galaxies in the years 30,000 to 35,000 A.D., and Darkdawn is a charismatic prophet, human but immortal or at any rate extraordinarily long-lived, who combines within himself the functions of Moses, Jesus and St. Paul: seer, intermediary with higher powers, organizer, leader, and ultimately martyr.) What makes the series so beautiful is the way De Soto gets inside Darkdawn's character, so that he's not merely a distant bas-relief—the Prophet—

but a warm, breathing human being. That is, you see him warts and all—a sophisticated concept for science fiction, which tends to run heavily to marble statues in place of living protagonists.

Leon, of course, is unlikely ever to found a galaxy-spanning cult, but he has much of the intensity that I associate with Darkdawn. Oddly, he's quite tall—six feet two, I'd say—and has conventional good looks; people of his type don't generally run to high inner voltage, I've observed. But despite his natural physical advantages something must have compressed and redirected Leon's soul when he was young, because he's a brooder, a dreamer, a fire-breather, always coming up with visionary plans for reorganizing our office, stuff like that. He's the one who usually leaves s-f magazines on my desk as gifts, but he's also the one who pokes the most fun at me for reading what he considers to be trash. You see his contradictory nature right there. He's shy and aggressive, tough and vulnerable, confident and uncertain, the whole crazy human mix, everything right up front.

Last Tuesday I had dinner at his house. I often go there. His wife Helene is a superb cook. She and I had an affair five years ago that lasted about six months. Leon knew about it after the third meeting, but he never has said a word to me. Judging by Helene's desperate ardor, she and Leon must not have a very good sexual relationship; when she was in bed with me she seemed to want everything all at once, every position, every kind of sensation, as though she had been deprived much too long. Possibly Leon was pleased that I was taking some of the sexual pressure off him, and has silently regretted that I no longer sleep with his wife. (I ended the affair because she was drawing too much energy from me and because I was having difficulties meeting Leon's frank, open gaze.)

Last Tuesday just before dinner Helene went into the kitchen to check the oven. Leon excused himself and headed for the bathroom. Alone, I stood a moment by the bookshelf, checking in my automatic way to see if they had any s-f, and then I followed Helene into the kitchen to refill my glass from the martini pitcher in the refrigerator. Suddenly she was up against me, clinging tight, her lips seeking mine. She muttered my name; she dug her fingertips into my back. "Hey," I said softly. "Wait a second! We agreed that we weren't going to start that stuff again!"

"I want you!"

"Don't, Helene." Gently I pried her free of me. "Don't complicate things. Please."

I wriggled loose. She backed away from me, head down, and sullenly went to the stove. As I turned I saw Leon in the doorway. He must have witnessed the entire scene. His dark eyes were glossy with half-suppressed tears; his lips were quivering. Without saying anything he took the pitcher from me, filled his martini glass and drank the cocktail at a gulp. Then he went into the living room, and ten minutes later we were talking office politics as though nothing had happened. Yes, Leon, you're Henry Darkdawn to the last inch. Out of such stuff as you, Leon, are prophets created. Out of such stuff as you are cosmic martyrs made.

No one could tell the difference any longer. The sleek, slippery android had totally engulfed its maker's personality.

I stood at the edge of the cliff, staring in horror at the red, swollen thing that had been the life-giving sun of Earth.

The horde of robots—

The alien spaceship, plunging in a wild spiral—

Laughing, she opened her fist. The Q-bomb lay in the center of her palm. "Ten seconds," she cried.

How warm it is tonight! A dank glove of humidity enfolds me. Sleep will not come. I feel a terrible pressure all around me. Yes! The beam of green light! At last, at last, at last! Cradling me, lifting me, floating me through the open window. High over the dark city. On and on, through the void, out of space and time. To the tunnel. Setting me down. Here. Here. Yes, exactly as I imagined it would be: the onyx walls, the sourceless dull gleam, the curving vault far overhead, the silent alien figures drifting toward me. Here. The tunnel, at last. I take the first step forward. Another. Another. I am launched on my journey.

THE WIND AND
THE RAIN

THE PLANET CLEANSES itself. That is the important thing to remember, at moments when we become too pleased with ourselves. The healing process is a natural and inevitable one. The action of the wind and the rain, the ebbing and flowing of the tides, the vigorous rivers flushing out the choked and stinking lakes—these are all natural rhythms, all healthy manifestations of universal harmony. Of course, we are here too. We do our best to hurry the process along. But we are only auxiliaries, and we know it. We must not exaggerate the value of our work. False pride is worse than a sin: it is a foolishness. We do not deceive ourselves into thinking we are important. If we were not here at all, the planet would repair itself anyway within twenty to fifty million years. It is estimated that our presence cuts that time down by somewhat more than half.

The uncontrolled release of methane into the atmosphere was one of the most serious problems. Methane is a colorless, odorless gas, sometimes known as "swamp gas." Its components are carbon and hydrogen. Much of the atmosphere of Jupiter and Saturn consists of methane. (Jupiter and Saturn have never been habitable by human beings.) A small amount of methane was always normally present in the atmosphere of Earth. However, the growth of human population produced a consequent increase in the supply of methane. Much of the methane released into the atmosphere came from swamps and coal mines. A great deal of it came from Asian rice fields fertilized with human or animal waste; methane is a byproduct of the digestive process.

The surplus methane escaped into the lower stratosphere, from ten to thirty miles above the surface of the planet, where a layer of ozone molecules once existed. Ozone, formed of three oxygen atoms, absorbs the harmful ultraviolet radiation that the sun emits. By reacting with free oxygen atoms in the stratosphere, the intrusive methane reduced the quantity available for ozone formation. Moreover, methane reactions in the stratosphere yielded water vapor that further depleted the ozone. This methane-induced exhaustion of the ozone content of the stratosphere permitted the unchecked ultraviolet bombardment of the Earth, with a consequent rise in the incidence of skin cancer.

A major contributor to the methane increase was the flatulence of domesticated cattle. According to the U.S. Department of Agriculture, domesticated ruminants in the late twentieth century were generating more than eighty-five million tons of methane a year. Yet nothing was done to check the activities of these dangerous creatures. Are you amused by the idea of a world destroyed by herds of farting cows? It must not have been amusing to the people of the late twentieth century. However, the extinction of domesticated ruminants shortly helped to reduce the impact of this process.

Today we must inject colored fluids into a major river. Edith, Bruce, Paul, Elaine, Oliver, Ronald, and I have been assigned to this task. Most members of the team believe the river is the Mississippi, although there is some evidence that it may be the Nile. Oliver, Bruce, and Edith believe it is more likely to be the Nile than the Mississippi, but they defer to the opinion of the majority. The river is wide and deep and its color is black in some places and dark green in others. The fluids are computer-mixed on the east bank of the river in a large factory erected by a previous reclamation team. We supervise their passage into the river. First we inject the red fluid, then the blue, then the yellow; they have different densities and form parallel stripes running for many hundreds of kilometers in the water. We are not certain whether these fluids are active healing agents—that is, substances which dissolve the solid pollutants lining the riverbed—or merely serve as markers permitting further chemical analysis of the river by the orbiting satellite system. It is not necessary for us to understand what we are doing, so long as we follow instructions explicitly. Elaine jokes about going swimming. Bruce says, "How absurd. This river is famous for deadly fish that will strip the flesh from your bones." We all laugh at that. *Fish*? Here? What fish could be as deadly as the river itself? This water would consume our flesh if we entered it, and probably dissolve our bones as well. I scribbled a poem yesterday and dropped it in, and the paper vanished instantly.

In the evenings we walk along the beach and have philosophical discussions. The sunsets on this coast are embellished by rich tones of purple, green, crimson, and yellow. Sometimes we cheer when a particularly beautiful combination of atmospheric gases transforms the sunlight. Our mood is always optimistic and gay. We are never depressed by the things we find on this planet. Even devastation can be an art form, can it not? Perhaps it is one of the greatest of all art forms, since an art of destruction *consumes* its medium, it *devours* its own epistemological foundations, and in this sublimely nullifying doubling-back upon its origins it far exceeds in moral complexity those forms which are merely productive. That is, I place a higher value on transformative art than on generative art. Is my meaning clear? In any event, since art ennobles and exalts the spirits of those who perceive it, we are exalted and ennobled by the conditions on Earth. We envy those who collaborate to create those extraordinary conditions. We know ourselves to be small-souled folk of a minor latter-day epoch; we lack the dynamic grandeur of energy that enabled our ancestors to commit such depredations. This world is a symphony. Naturally you might argue that to restore a planet takes more energy than to destroy it, but you would be wrong. Nevertheless, though our daily tasks leave us weary and drained, we also feel stimulated and excited, because by restoring this world, the mother-world of mankind, we are in a sense participating in the original splendid process of its destruction. I mean in the sense that the resolution of a dissonant chord participates in the dissonance of that chord.

Now we have come to Tokyo, the capital of the island empire of Japan. See how small the skeletons of the citizens are? That is one way we have of identifying this place as Japan. The Japanese are known to have been people of small stature. Edward's ancestors were Japanese. He is of small stature. (Edith says his skin should be yellow as well. His skin is just like ours. Why is his skin not yellow?) "See?" Edward cries. "There is Mount Fuji!" It is an extraordinarily beautiful mountain, mantled in white snow. On its slopes one of our archaeological teams is at work, tunneling under the snow to collect samples from the twentieth-century strata of chemical residues, dust, and ashes. "Once there were over 75,000 industrial smokestacks around Tokyo," says Edward proudly, "from which were released hundreds of tons of sulfur, nitrous oxides, ammonia, and carbon gases every day. We should not forget that this city had more than 1,500,000 automobiles as well." Many of the automobiles are still visible, but they are very fragile, worn to threads by the action of the atmosphere. When we touch them they collapse in puffs of gray smoke. Edward, who has studied his heritage well, tells us, "It was not uncommon for the density of carbon monoxide in the air here to exceed the permissible levels by factors of 250 percent on mild summer days. Owing to atmospheric conditions, Mount Fuji was visible only one day of every nine. Yet no one showed dismay." He conjures up for us a picture of his small, industrious yellow ancestors toiling cheerfully and unremittingly in their poisonous environment. The Japanese, he insists, were able to maintain and even increase their gross national product at a time when other nationalities had already begun to lose ground in the global economic struggle because of diminished population owing to unfavorable ecological factors. And so on and so on. After a time we grow bored with Edward's incessant boasting. "Stop boasting," Oliver tells him, "or we will expose you to the atmosphere." We have much dreary work to do here. Paul and I guide the huge trenching machines; Oliver and Ronald follow, planting seeds. Almost immediately, strange angular shrubs spring up. They have shiny bluish leaves and long crooked branches. One of them seized Elaine by the throat yesterday and might have hurt her seriously had Bruce not uprooted it. We were not upset. This is merely one phase in the long, slow process of repair. There will be many such incidents. Some day cherry trees will blossom in this place.

This is the poem that the river ate:

DESTRUCTION

I. *Nouns.* Destruction, desolation, wreck, wreckage, ruin, ruination, rack and ruin, smash, smashup, demolition, demolishment, ravagement, havoc, ravage, dilapidation, decimation, blight, breakdown, consumption, dissolution, obliteration, overthrow, spoilage; mutilation, disintegration, undoing, pulverization; sabotage, vandalism; annulment, damnation, extinguishment, extinction; invalidation, nullification, shatterment, shipwreck; annihilation, disannulment, discreation, extermination, extirpation, obliteration, perdition, subversion.

II. *Verbs.* Destroy, wreck, ruin, ruinate, smash, demolish, raze, ravage, gut, dilapidate, decimate, blast, blight, break down, consume, dissolve, overthrow; mutilate, disintegrate, unmake, pulverize; sabotage, vandalize, annul, blast, blight, damn, dash, extinguish, invalidate, nullify, quell, quench, scuttle, shatter, shipwreck, torpedo, smash, spoil, undo, void; annihilate, devour, disannul, discreate, exterminate, obliterate, extirpate, subvert; corrode, erode, sap, undermine, waste, waste away, whittle away (*or* down); eat away, canker, gnaw; wear away, abrade, batter, excoriate, rust.

III. *Adjectives.* Destructive, ruinous, vandalistic, baneful, cutthroat, fell, lethiferous, pernicious, slaughterous, predatory, sinistrous, nihilistic; corrosive, erosive, cankerous, caustic, abrasive.

"I validate," says Ethel.
"I unravage," says Oliver.
"I integrate," says Paul.
"I devandalize," says Elaine.
"I unshatter," says Bruce.
"I unscuttle," says Edward.
"I discorrode," says Ronald.
"I undesolate," says Edith.
"I create," say I.

We reconstitute. We renew. We repair. We reclaim. We refurbish. We restore. We renovate. We rebuild. We reproduce. We redeem. We reintegrate. We replace. We reconstruct. We retrieve. We revivify. We resurrect. We fix, overhaul, mend, put in repair, retouch, tinker, cobble, patch, darn, staunch, caulk, splice. We celebrate our successes by energetic and lusty singing. Some of us copulate.

Here is an outstanding example of the dark humor of the ancients. At a place called Richland, Washington, there was an installation that manufactured plutonium for use in nuclear weapons. This was done in the name of "natural security," that is, to enhance and strengthen the safety of the United States of America and render its inhabitants carefree and hopeful. In a relatively short span of time these activities produced approximately fifty-five million gallons of concentrated radioactive waste. This material was so intensely hot that it would boil spontaneously for decades, and would retain a virulently toxic character for many thousands of years. The presence of so much dangerous waste posed a severe environmental threat to a large area of the United States. How, then, to dispose of this waste? An appropriately comic solution was devised. The plutonium installation was situated in a seismically unstable area located along the earthquake belt that rings the Pacific Ocean. A storage site was chosen nearby, directly above a fault line that had produced a violent earthquake half a century earlier. Here 140 steel and concrete tanks were constructed just below the surface of the ground and some 240 feet above the water table of the Columbia River, from which a densely populated region derived its water supply. Into these tanks the boiling radioactive wastes were poured: a magnificent gift to future generations. Within a few years the true subtlety of the jest became apparent when the first small leaks were detected in the tanks. Some observers predicted that no more than ten to twenty years would pass before the great heat caused the seams of the tanks to burst, releasing radioactive gases into the atmosphere or permitting radioactive fluids to escape into the river. The designers of the tanks maintained, though, that they were sturdy enough to last at least a century. It will be noted that this was something less than one percent of the known half-life of the materials placed in the tanks. Because of discontinuties in the records, we are unable to determine which estimate was more nearly correct. It should be possible for our decontamination squads to enter the affected regions in 800 to 1300 years. This episode arouses tremendous admiration in me. How much gusto, how much robust wit, those old ones must have had!

*   *   *

We are granted a holiday so we may go to the mountains of
Uruguay to visit the site of one of the last human settlements,
perhaps the very last. It was discovered by a reclamation team
several hundred years ago and has been set aside, in its original
state, as a museum for the tourists who one day will wish to view
the mother-world. One enters through a lengthy tunnel of glossy
pink brick. A series of airlocks prevents the outside air from
penetrating. The village itself, nestling between two craggy
spires, is shielded by a clear shining dome. Automatic controls
maintain its temperature at a constant mild level. There were a
thousand inhabitants. We can view them in the spacious plazas,
in the taverns, and in places of recreation. Family groups remain
together, often with their pets. A few carry umbrellas. Everyone
is in an unusually fine state of preservation. Many of them are
smiling. It is not yet known why these people perished. Some
died in the act of speaking, and scholars have devoted much
effort, so far without success, to the task of determining and
translating the last words still frozen on their lips. We are not
allowed to touch anyone, but we may enter their homes and
inspect their possessions and toilet furnishings. I am moved
almost to tears, as are several of the others. "Perhaps these
are our very ancestors," Ronald exclaims. But Bruce declares
scornfully, "You say ridiculous thiings. Our ancestors must
have escaped from here long before the time these people
lived." Just outside the settlement I find a tiny glistening
bone, possibly the shinbone of a child, possibly part of a dog's
tail. "May I keep it?" I ask our leader. But he compels me to
donate it to the museum.

The archives yield much that is fascinating. For example, this
fine example of ironic distance in ecological management. In the
ocean off a place named California were tremendous forests of a
giant seaweed called kelp, housing a vast and intricate community of maritime creatures. Sea urchins lived on the ocean floor,
100 feet down, amid the holdfasts that anchored the kelp. Furry
aquatic mammals known as sea otters fed on the urchins. The
Earth people removed the otters because they had some use for
their fur. Later, the kelp began to die. Forests many square miles
in diameter vanished. This had serious commercial consequences,

for the kelp was valuable and so were many of the animal forms that lived in it. Investigation of the ocean floor showed a great increase in sea urchins. Not only had their natural enemies, the otters, been removed, but the urchins were taking nourishment from the immense quantities of organic matter in the sewage discharges dumped into the ocean by the Earth people. Millions of urchins were nibbling at the holdfasts of the kelp, uprooting the huge plants and killing them. When an oil tanker accidentally released its cargo into the sea, many urchins were killed and the kelp began to reestablish itself. But this proved to be an impractical means of controlling the urchins. Encouraging the otters to return was suggested, but there was not a sufficient supply of living otters. The kelp foresters of California solved their problem by dumping quicklime into the sea from barges This was fatal to the urchins; once they were dead, healthy kelp plants were brought from other parts of the sea and embedded to become the nucleus of a new forest. After a while the urchins returned and began to eat the kelp again. More quicklime was dumped. The urchins died and new kelp was planted. Later, it was discovered that the quicklime was having harmful effects on the ocean floor itself, and other chemicals were dumped to counteract those effects. All of this required great ingenuity and a considerable outlay of energy and resources. Edward thinks there was something very Japanese about these maneuvers. Ethel points out that the kelp trouble would never have happened if the Earth people had not originally removed the otters. How naive Ethel is! She has no understanding of the principles of irony. Poetry bewilders her also. Edward refuses to sleep with Ethel now.

In the final centuries of their era the people of Earth succeeded in paving the surface of their planet almost entirely with a skin of concrete and metal. We must pry much of this up so that the planet may start to breathe again. It would be easy and efficient to use explosives or acids, but we are not overly concerned with ease and efficiency; besides, there is great concern that explosives or acids may do further ecological harm here. Therefore we employ large machines that inset prongs in the great cracks that have developed in the concrete. Once we have lifted the paved slabs they usually crumble quickly. Clouds of concrete dust blow freely through the streets of these cities, covering the stumps of the buildings with a fine, pure coating of grayish-white powder. The effect is delicate and refreshing. Paul suggested yesterday that we may be doing ecological harm by setting free this dust. I became frightened at the idea and reported him to the leader of our team. Paul will be transferred to another group.

Toward the end here they all wore breathing suits, similar to ours but even more comprehensive. We find these suits lying around everywhere like the discarded shells of giant insects. The most advanced models were complete individual housing units. Apparently it was not necessary to leave one suit except to perform such vital functions as sexual intercourse and childbirth. We understand that the reluctance of the Earth people to leave their suits even for those functions, near the close, immensely hastened the decrease in population.

Our philosophical discussions. God created this planet. We all agree on that, in a manner of speaking, ignoring for the moment definitions of such concepts as "God" and "created." Why did He go to so much trouble to bring Earth into being, if it was His intention merely to have it rendered uninhabitable? Did He create mankind especially for this purpose, or did they exercise free will in doing what they did here? Was mankind God's way of taking vengeance against His own creation? Why would He want to take vengeance against His own creation? Perhaps it is a mistake to approach the destruction of Earth from the moral or ethical standpoint. I think we must see it in purely esthetic terms, i.e., a self-contained artistic achievement, like a *fouetté en tournant* or an *entrechat-dix*, performed for its own sake and requiring no explanations. Only in this way can we understand how the Earth people were able to collaborate so joyfully in their own asphyxiation.

My tour of duty is almost over. It has been an overwhelming experience; I will never be the same. I must express my gratitude for this opportunity to have seen Earth almost as its people knew it. Its rusted streams, its corroded meadows, its purpled skies, its bluish puddles. The debris, the barren hillsides, the blazing rivers. Soon, thanks to the dedicated work of reclamation teams such as ours, these superficial but beautiful emblems of death will have disappeared. This will be just another world for tourists, of sentimental curiosity but no unique value to the sensibility. How dull that will be: a green and pleasant Earth once more, why, why? The universe has enough habitable planets; at present it has only one Earth. Has all our labor here been an error, then? I sometimes do think it was misguided of us to have undertaken this project. But on the other hand I remind myself of our fundamental irrelevance. The healing process is a natural and inevitable one. With us or without us, the planet cleanses itself. The wind, the rain, the tides. We merely help things along.

A rumor reaches us that a colony of live Earthmen has been found on the Tibetan plateau. We travel there to see if this is true. Hovering above a vast red empty plain, we see large figures moving slowly about. Are these Earthmen, inside breathing suits of a strange design? We descend. Members of other reclamation teams are already on hand. They have surrounded one of the large creatures. It travels in a wobbly circle, uttering indistinct cries and grunts. Then it comes to a halt, confronting us blankly as if defying us to embrace it. We tip it over; it moves its massive limbs dumbly but is unable to arise. After a brief conference we decide to dissect it. The outer plates lift easily. Inside we find nothing but gears and coils of gleaming wire. The limbs no longer move, although things click and hum within it for quite some time. We are favorably impressed by the durability and resilience of these machines. Perhaps in the distant future such entities will wholly replace the softer and more fragile life forms on all worlds, as they seem to have done on Earth.

The wind. The rain. The tides. All sadnesses flow to the sea.

A SEA OF FACES

Are not such floating fragments on the sea of the unconscious called Freudian ships?

—JOSEPHINE SAXTON

FALLING.

It's very much like dying, I suppose. That awareness of infinite descent, that knowledge of the total absence of support. It's all sky up here. Down below is neither land nor sea, only color without form, so distant that I can't even put a name to the color. The cosmos is torn open, and I plummet headlong, arms and legs pinwheeling wildly, the gray stuff in my skull centrifuging toward my ears. I'm dropping like Lucifer. *From morn to noon he fell, from noon to dewy eve, A summer's day; and with the setting sun Dropp'd from the zenith like a falling star.* That's Milton. Even now my old liberal-arts education stands me in good stead. *And when he falls, he falls like a Lucifer, Never to hope again.* That's Shakespeare. It's all part of the same thing. All of English literature was written by a single man, whose sly persuasive voice ticks in my dizzy head as I drop. God grant me a soft landing.

"She looks a little like you," I told Irene. "At least, it seemed that way for one quick moment, when she turned toward the

window in my office and the sunlight caught the planes of her
face. Of course, it's the most superficial resemblance only, a
matter of bone structure, the placement of the eyes, the cut of the
hair. But your expressions, your inner selves externally represented, are altogether dissimilar. You radiate unbounded good health
and vitality, Irene, and she slips so easily into the classic schizoid
fancies, the eyes alternately dreamy and darting, the forehead
pale, flecked with sweat. She's very troubled."

"What's her name?"

"Lowry. April Lowry."

"A beautiful name. April. Young?"

"About twenty-three."

"How sad, Richard. Schizoid, you said?"

"She retreats into nowhere without provocation. Lord knows
what triggers it. When it happens she can go six or eight months
without saying a word. The last attack was a year ago. These
days she's feeling much better, she's willing to talk about herself
a bit. She says it's as though there's a zone of weakness in the
walls of her mind, an opening, a trapdoor, a funnel, something
like that, and from time to time her soul is irresistibly drawn
toward it and goes pouring through and disappears into God
knows what, and there's nothing left of her but a shell. And
eventually she comes back through the same passage. She's
convinced that one of these times she won't come back."

"Is there some way to help her?" Irene asked. "What will you
try? Drugs? Hypnosis? Shock? Sensory deprivation?"

"They've all been tried."

"What then, Richard? What will you do?"

Suppose there is a way. Let's pretend there is a way. Is that an
acceptable hypothesis? Let's pretend. Let's just pretend, and see
what happens.

The vast ocean below me occupies the entirety of my field of
vision. Its surface is convex, belly-up in the middle and curving
vertiginously away from me at the periphery; the slope is so
extreme that I wonder why the water doesn't all run off toward
the edges and drown the horizon. Not far beneath that shimmering
swollen surface a gigantic pattern of crosshatchings and counter-
textures is visible, like an immense mural floating lightly submerged in the water. For a moment, as I plunge, the pattern

resolves itself and becomes coherent: I see the face of Irene, a calm pale mask, the steady blue eyes focused lovingly on me. She fills the ocean. Her semblance covers an area greater than any continental mass. Firm chin, strong full lips, delicate tapering nose. She emanates a serene aura of inner peace that buoys me like an invisible net: I am falling easily now, pleasantly, arms outspread, face down, my entire body relaxed. How beautiful she is! I continue to descend and the pattern shatters; the sea is abruptly full of metallic shards and splinters, flashing bright gold through the dark blue-green; then, when I am perhaps a thousand meters lower, the pattern suddenly reorganizes itself. A colosssal face, again. I welcome Irene's return, but no, the face is the face of April, my silent sorrowful one. A haunted face, a face full of shadows: dark terrified eyes, flickering nostrils, sunken cheeks. A bit of one incisor is visible over the thin lower lip. O my poor sweet Taciturna. Needles of reflected sunlight glitter in her outspread waterborne hair. April's manifestation supplants serenity with turbulence; again I plummet out of control, again I am in the cosmic centrifuge, my breath is torn from me and a dread chill rushes past my tumbling body. Desperately I fight for poise and balance. I attain it, finally, and look down. The pattern has again broken; where April has been, I see only parallel bands of amber light, distorted by choppy refractions. Tiny white dots—islands, I suppose—now are evident in the glossy sea.

What a strange resemblance there is, at times, between April and Irene!

How confusing for me to confuse them. How dangerous for me.

—It's the riskiest kind of therapy you could have chosen, Dr. Bjornstrand.

—Risky for me, or risky for her?

—Risky for you and for your patient, I'd say.

—So what else is new?

—You asked me for an impartial evaluation, Dr. Bjornstrand. If you don't care to accept my opinion—

—I value your opinion highly, Erik.

—But you're going to go through with the therapy as presently planned?

—Of course I am.

* * *

This is the moment of splashdown.

I hit the water perfectly and go slicing through the sea's shining surface with surgical precision, knifing fifty meters deep, eighty, a hundred, cutting smoothly through the oceanic epithelium and the sturdy musculature beneath. Very well done, Dr. Bjornstrand. High marks for form.

Perhaps this is deep enough.

I pivot, kick, turn upward, clutch at the brightness above me. I may have overextended myself, I realize. My lungs are on fire and the sky, so recently my home, seems terribly far away. But with vigorous strokes I pull myself up and come popping into the air like a stubborn cork.

I float idly a moment, catching my breath. Then I look around. The ferocious eye of the sun regards me from a late-morning height. The sea is warm and gentle, undulating seductively. There is an island only a few hundred meters away: an inviting beach of bright sand, a row of slender palms farther back. I swim toward it. As I near the shore, the bottomless dark depths give way to sandy outlying sunken shelf, and the hue of the sea changes from deep blue to light green. Yet it is taking longer to reach land than I had expected. Perhaps my estimate of the distance was overly optimistic; for all my efforts, the island seems to be getting no closer. At moments it actually appears to be retreating from me. My arms grow heavy. My kick becomes sluggish. I am panting, wheezing, sputtering; something throbs behind my forehead. Suddenly, though, I see sun-streaked sand just below me. My feet touch bottom. I wade wearily ashore and fall to my knees on the margin of the beach.

—Can I call you April, Miss Lowry?

—Whatever.

—I don't think that that's a very threatening level of therapist-patient intimacy, do you?

—Not really.

—Do you always shrug every time you answer a question?

—I didn't know I did.

—You shrug. You also studiously avoid any show of facial expression. You try to be very unreadable, April.

—Maybe I feel safer that way.

—But who's the enemy?

—You'd know more about that than I would, doctor.

—Do you actually think so? I'm all the way over here. You're right there inside your own head. You'll know more than I ever will about you.

—You could always come inside my head if you wanted to.

—Wouldn't that frighten you?

—It would kill me.

—I wonder, April. You're much stronger than you think you are. You're also very beautiful, April. I know, it's beside the point. But you are.

It's just a small island. I can tell that by the way the shoreline curves rapidly away from me. I lie sprawled near the water's edge, face down, exhausted, fingers digging tensely into the warm moist sand. The sun is strong; I feel waves of heat going *thratata thratata* on my bare back. I wear only a ragged pair of faded blue jeans, very tight, cut off choppily at the knee. My belt is waterlogged and salt-cracked, as though I was adrift for days before making landfall. Perhaps I was. It's hard to maintain a reliable sense of time in this place.

I should get up. I should explore

Yes. Getting up, now. A little dizzy, eh? Yes. But I walk steadily up the gentle slope of the beach. Fifty meters inland, the sand shades into sandy soil, loose, shallow; rounded white coral boulders poke through from below. Thirsty soil. Nevertheless, how lush everything is here. A wall of tangled vines and creepers. Long glossy tropical green leaves, smooth-edged, big-veined. The corrugated trunks of the palms. The soft sound of the surf, *fwissh, fwissh,* underlying all other textures. How blue the sea. How green the sky. *Fwissh.*

Is that the image of a face in the sky?

A woman's face, yes. Irene? April? The features are indistinct. But I definitely see it, yes, hovering a few hundred meters above the water as if projected from the sun-streaked sheet that is the skin of the ocean: a glow, a radiance, having the form of a delicate face—nostrils, lips, brows, cheeks, certainly a face, and not just one, either, for in the intensity of my stare I cause it to split and then to split again, so that a row of them hangs in the air, ten faces, a hundred, a thousand faces, faces all about me, a sea of faces. They seem quite grave. *Smile!* On command, the faces smile. Much better. The air itself is brighter for that smile. The faces merge, blur, sharpen, blur again, overlap in part,

dance, shimmer, melt, flow. Illusions born of the heat. Daughters
of the sun. Sweet mirages. I look past them, higher, into the clear
reaches of the cloudless heavens.

Hawks!

Hawks here? Shouldn't I be seeing gulls? The birds whirl and
swoop, dark figures against the blinding sky, wings outspread,
feathers like fingers. I see their fierce hooked beaks. They snap
great beetles from the steaming air and soar away, digesting.
Then there are no birds, only the faces, still smiling. I turn my
back on them and slowly move off through the underbrush to see
what sort of place the sea has given me.

So long as I stay near the shore, I have no difficulty in
walking; cutting through the densely vegetated interior might be a
different matter. I sidle off to the left, following the nibbled line
of beach. Before I have walked a hundred paces I have made a
new discovery: the island is adrift.

Glancing seaward, I notice that on the horizon there lies a dark
shore rimmed by black triangular mountains, one or two days'
sail distant. Minutes ago I saw only open sea in that direction.
maybe the mountains have just this moment sprouted, but more
likely the island, spinning slowly in the currents, has only now
turned to reveal them. That must be the answer. I stand quite still
for a long while and it seems to me that I behold those mountains
now from one angle, now from a slightly different one. How else
to explain such effects of parallax? The island freely drifts. It
moves, and I move with it, upon the breast of the changeless
unbounded sea.

The celebrated young American therapist Richard Bjornstrand
commenced his experimental treatment of Miss April Lowry on the
third of August, 1987. Within fifteen days the locus of disturbance
had been identified, and Dr. Bjornstrand had recommended
consciousness-penetration treatment, a technique increasingly popular in the United States. Miss Lowry's physician was initially
opposed to the suggestion, but further consultations demonstrated
the potential value of such an approach, and on the nineteenth of
September the entry procedures were initiated. We expect further
reports from Dr. Bjornstrand as the project develops.

Leonie said, "But what if you fall in love with her?"

"What of it?" I asked. "Therapists are always falling in love

with their patients. Reich married one of his patients, and so did
Fenichel, and dozens of the early analysts had affairs with their
patients, and even Freud, who didn't, was known to observe—"

"Freud lived a long time ago," Leonie said.

I have now walked entirely around the island. The circumambulation
took me four hours, I estimate, since the sun was almost directly
overhead when I began it and is now more than halfway toward
the horizon. In these latitudes I suppose sunset comes quite early,
perhaps by half past six, even in summer.

All during my walk this afternoon the island remained on a
steady course, keeping one side constantly toward the sea, the
other toward that dark mountain-girt shore. Yet it has continued
to drift, for there are minor oscillations in the position of the
mountains relative to the island, and the shore itself appears
gradually to grow closer. (Although that may be an illusion.)
Faces appear and vanish and reappear in the lower reaches of
the sky according to no predictable schedule of event or
identity: April, Irene, April, Irene, Irene, April, April, Irene.
Sometimes they smile at me. Sometimes they do not. I thought
I saw one of the Irenes wink; I looked again and the face was
April's.

The island, though quite small, has several distinct geographi-
cal zones. On the side where I first came ashore there is a row of
close-set palms, crown to crown, beyond which the beach slopes
toward the sea. I have arbitrarily labeled that side of the island as
east. The western side is low and parched, and the vegetation is a
tangle of scrub. On the north side is a high coral ridge, flat-faced
and involute, descending steeply into the water. White wavelets
batter tirelessly against the rounded spires and domes of that
pocked coral wall. The island's southern shore has dunes, quite
Saharaesque, their yellowish-pink crests actually shifting ever so
slightly as I watch. Inland, the island rises to a peak perhaps fifty
meters above sea level, and evidently there are deep pockets of
retained rainwater in the porous, decayed limestone of the under-
surface, for the vegetation is profuse and vigorous. At several
points I made brief forays to the interior, coming upon a swampy
region of noisy sucking quicksand in one place, a cool dark glade
interpenetrated with the tunnels and mounds of termites in another, a copse of wide-branching little fruit-bearing trees elsewhere.
Altogether the place is beautiful. I will have enough food and

drink, and there are shelters. Nevertheless I long already for an end to the voyage. The bare sharp-tipped mountains of the mainland grow ever nearer; some day I will reach the shore, and my real work will begin.

The essence of this kind of therapy is risk. The therapist must be prepared to encounter forces well beyond his own strength, and to grapple with them in the knowledge that they might readily triumph over him. The patient, for her part, must accept the knowledge that the intrusion of the therapist into her consciousness may cause extensive alterations of the personality, not all of them for the better.

A bewildering day. The dawn was red-stained with purple veins—a swollen, grotesque, traumatic sky. Then came high winds; the palms rippled and swayed and great fronds were torn loose. A lull followed. I feared toppling trees and tidal waves, and pressed inland for half an hour, settling finally in a kind of natural amphitheater of dead old coral, a weathered bowl thrust up from the sea millennia ago. Here I waited out the morning. Toward noon thick dark clouds obscured the heavens. I felt a sense of menace, of irresistible powers gathering their strength, such as I sometimes feel when I hear that tense little orchestral passage late in the Agnus Dei of the *Missa Solemnis,* and instants later there descended on me hail, rain, sleet, high wind, furious heat, even snow—all weathers at once. I thought the earth would crack open and pour forth magma upon me. It was all over in five minutes, and every trace of the storm vanished. The clouds parted; the sun emerged, looking gentle and innocent; birds of many plumages wheeled in the air, warbling sweetly. The faces of Irene and April, infinitely reduplicated, blinked on and off against the backdrop of the sky. The mountainous shore hung fixed on the horizon, growing no nearer, getting no farther away, as though the day's turmoils had caused the frightened island to put down roots.

Rain during the night, warm and steamy. Clouds of gnats. An evil humming sound, greasily resonant, pervading everything. I slept, finally, and was awakened by a sound like a mighty thunderclap, and saw an enormous distorted sun rising slowly in the west.

* * *

We sat by the redwood table on Donald's patio: Irene, Donald, Erik, Paul, Anna, Leonie, me. Paul and Erik drank bourbon, and the rest of us sipped Shine, the new drink, essence of cannabis mixed with (I think) ginger beer and strawberry syrup. We were very high. "There's no reason," I said, "why we shouldn't avail ourselves of the latest technological developments. Here's this unfortunate girl suffering from an undeterminable but crippling psychological malady, and the chance exists for me to enter her soul and—"

"Enter her *what?*" Donald asked.

"Her consciousness, her *anima*, her spirit, her mind, her whatever you want to call it."

"Don't interrupt him," Leonie said to Donald.

Irene said, "Will you bring her to Erik for an impartial opinion first, at least?"

"What makes you think Erik is impartial?" Anna asked.

"He tries to be," said Erik coolly. "Yes, bring her to me, Dr. Bjornstrand."

"I know what you'll tell me."

"Still. Even so."

"Isn't this terribly dangerous?" Leonie asked. "I mean, suppose your mind became stuck inside her, Richard."

"Stuck?"

"Isn't that possible? I don't actually know anything about the process but—"

"I'll be entering her only in the most metaphorical sense," I said. Irene laughed. Anna said, "Do you actually believe that?" and gave Irene a sly look. Irene merely shook her head. "I don't worry about Richard's fidelity," she said, drawling her words.

Her face fills the sky today.

April. Irene. Whoever she is. She eclipses the sun, and lights the day with her own supernal radiance.

The course of the island has been reversed, and now it drifts out to sea. For three days I have watched the mountains of the mainland growing smaller. Evidently the currents have changed; or perhaps there are zones of resistance close to the shore, designed to keep at bay such wandering islands as mine. I must find a way to deal with this. I am convinced that I can do nothing for April unless I reach the mainland.

I have entered a calm place where the sea is a mirror and the sweltering air reflects the images in an infinitely baffling regression. I see no face but my own, now, and I see it everywhere. A million versions of myself dance in the steamy haze. My jaws are stubbled and there is a bright red band of sunburn across my nose and upper cheeks. I grin and the multitudinous images grin at me. I reach toward them and they reach toward me. No land is in sight, no other islands—nothing, in fact, but this wall of reflections. I feel as though I am penned inside a box of polished metal. My shining image infests the burning atmosphere. I have a constant choking sensation; a terrible languor is coming over me; I pray for hurricanes, waterspouts, convulsions of the ocean bed, any sort of upheaval that will break the savage claustrophobic tension.

Is Irene my wife? My lover? My companion? My friend? My sister?

I am within April's consciousness and Irene is a figment.

It has begun to occur to me that this may be my therapy rather than April's.

I have set to work creating machinery to bring me back to the mainland. All this week I have painstakingly felled palm trees, using a series of blunt, soft hand axes chipped from slabs of dead coral. Hauling the trees to a promontory of the island's southern face, I lashed them loosely together with vines, setting them in the water so that they projected from both sides of the headland like the oars of a galley. By tugging at an unusually thick vine that runs down the spine of the whole construction, I am indeed able to make them operate like oars; and I have tied that master vine to an unusually massive palm that sprouts from the central ridge of the promontory. What I have built, in fact, is a kind of reciprocating engine; the currents, stirring the leafy crowns of my felled palms, impart a tension to the vines that link them, and the resistance of the huge central tree to the tug of the master vine causes the felled trees to sweep the water, driving the entire island shoreward. Through purposeful activity, said Goethe, we justify our existence in the eyes of God.

The "oars" work well. I'm heading toward the mainland once again.

Heading toward the mainland very rapidly. Too rapidly, it seems. I think I may be caught in a powerful current.

The current definitely has seized my island and I'm being swept swiftly along, willy-nilly. I am approaching the isle where Scylla waits. That surely is Scylla: that creature just ahead. There is no avoiding her; the force of the water is inexorable and my helpless oars dangle limply. The many-necked monster sits in plain sight on a barren rock, coiled into herself, waiting. Where shall I hide? Shall I scramble into the underbrush and huddle there until I am past her? Look, there: six heads, each with three rows of pointed teeth, and twelve snaky limbs. I suppose I could hide, but how cowardly, how useless. I will show myself to her. I stand exposed on the shore. I listen to her dread barking. How may I guard myself against Scylla's fangs? Irene smiles out of the low fleecy clouds. There's a way, she seems to be saying. I gather a cloud and fashion it into a simulacrum of myself. See: another Bjornstrand stands here, sunburned, half naked. I make a second replica, a third, complete to the stubble, complete to the blemishes. A dozen of them. Passive, empty, soulless. Will they deceive her? We'll see. The barking is ferocious now. She is close. My island whips through the channel. Strike, Scylla! Strike! The long necks rise and fall, rise and fall. I hear the screams of my other selves; I see their arms and legs thrashing as she seizes them and lifts them. Them she devours. Me she spares. I float safely past the hideous beast. April's face, reduplicated infinitely in the blue vault above me, is smiling. I have gained power by this encounter. I need have no further fears: I have become invulnerable. Do your worst, ocean! Bring me the Charybdis. I'm ready. Yes. Bring me to Charybdis.

The whole, D. H. Lawrence wrote, is a strange assembly of apparently incongruous parts, slipping past one another. I agree. But of course the incongruity is apparent rather than real, else there would be no whole.

* * *

I believe I have complete control over the island now. I can redesign it to serve my needs, and I have streamlined it, making it shipshaped, pointed at the bow, blunt at the stern. My conglomeration of felled palms has been replaced; now flexible projections of island-stuff flail the sea, propelling me steadily toward the mainland. Broad-leafed shade trees make the heat of day more bearable. At my command fresh-water streams spring from the sand, cool, glistening.

Gradually I extend the sphere of my control beyond the perimeter of the island. I have established a shark-free zone just off shore within an encircling reef. There I swim in perfect safety, and when hunger comes, I draw friendly fishes forth with my hands.

I fashion images out of clouds: April, Irene. I simulate the features of Dr. Richard Bjornstrand in the heavens. I draw April and Irene together, and they blur, they become one woman.

Getting close to the coast now. Another day or two and I'll be there.

This is the mainland. I guide my island into a wide half-moon harbor, shadowed by the great naked mountains that rise like filed black teeth from the nearby interior. The island pushes out a sturdy woody cable that ties it to its berth; using the cable as a gangplank, I go ashore. The air is cooler here. The vegetation is sparse and cactusoidal: thick fleshy thorn-studded purplish barrels, mainly, taller than I. I strike one with a log and pale pink fluid gushes from it: I taste it and find it cool, sugary, vaguely intoxicating.

Cactus fluid sustains me during a five-day journey to the summit of the closest mountain. Bare feet slap against bare rock. Heat by day, lunar chill by night; the boulders twang at twilight as the warmth leaves them. At my back sprawls the sea, infinite, silent. The air is spangled with the frowning faces of women. I ascend by a slow spiral route, pausing frequently to rest, and push myself onward until at last I stand athwart the highest spine of the range. On the inland side the mountains drop away steeply into a tormented irregular valley, boulder-strewn and icy, slashed by glittering white lakes like so many narrow lesions. Beyond that is a zone of low breast-shaped hills, heavily forested, descending into a central lowlands out of which rises a pulsing fountain of light—jagged phosphorescent bursts of blue and gold and green and red that rocket into the air, attenuate, and are lost. I dare not approach that fountain; I will be consumed, I know, in its fierce intensity, for there the essence of April has its lair, the savage soul-core that must never be invaded by another.

I turn seaward and look to my left, down the coast. At first I see nothing extraordinary: a row of scalloped bays, some strips of sandy beach, a white line of surf, a wheeling flock of dark birds. But then I detect, far along the shore, a more remarkable feature. Two long slender promontories just from the mainland like curved fingers, a thumb and a forefinger reaching toward one another, and in the wide gulf enclosed between them the sea churns in frenzy, as though it boils. At the vortex of the disturbance, though, all is calm. There! There is Charybdis! The maelstrom!

It would take me days to reach it overland. The sea route will be quicker. Hurrying down the slopes, I return to my island and sever the cable that binds it to shore. Perversely, it grows again. Some malign influence is negating my power. I sever; the cable reunites. I sever; it reunites. Again, again, again. Exasperated, I cause a fissure to pierce the island from edge to edge at the place where my cable is rooted; the entire segment surrounding that anchor breaks away and remains in the harbor, held fast, while the remainder of the island drifts toward the open sea.

Wait. The process of fission continues of its own momentum. The island is calving like a glacier, disintegrating, huge fragments breaking away. I leap desperately across yawning crevasses, holding always to the largest sector, struggling to rebuild my floating home, until I realize that nothing significant remains of the island, only an ever-diminishing raft of coral rock, halving and halving again. My island is no more than ten meters square now. Five. Less than five. Gone.

I always dreaded the ocean. That great inverted bowl of chilly water, resonating with booming salty sounds, infested with dark rubbery weeds, inhabited by toothy monsters—it preyed on my spirit, draining me, filling itself from me. Of course it was the northern sea I knew and hated, the dull dirty Atlantic, licking greasily at the Massachusetts coast. A black rocky shoreline, impenetrable mysteries of water, a line of morning debris cluttering the scanty sandy coves, a host of crabs and lesser scuttlers crawling everywhere. While swimming I imagined unfriendly sea beasts nosing around my dangling legs. I looked with distaste upon that invisible shimmering clutter of hairy-clawed planktonites, that fantasia of fibrous filaments and chittering attennae. And I dreaded most of all the slow lazy stirring of the Kraken, idly sliding its vast tentacles upward toward the boats of the surface. And here I am adrift on the sea's own breast. April's face in the sky wears a smile. The face of Irene flexes into a wink.

I am drawn toward the maelstrom. Swimming is unnecessary; the water carries me purposefully toward my goal. Yet I swim, all the same, stroke after stroke, yielding nothing to the force of the sea. The first promontory is coming into view. I swim all the more energetically. I will not allow the whirlpool to capture me; I must give myself willingly to it.

Now I swing round and round in the outer gyres of Charybdis. This is the place through which the spirit is drained: I can see April's pallid face like an empty plastic mask, hovering, drawn downward, disappearing chin-first through the whirlpool's vortex, reappearing, going down once more, an infinite cycle of drownings and disappearances and returns and resurrections. I must follow her.

No use pretending to swim here. One can only keep one's arms and legs pressed close together and yield, as one is sluiced down through level after level of the the maelstrom until one reaches the heart of the eddy, and then—*swoosh!*—the ultimate descent. Now I plummet. The tumble takes forever. *From morn to noon he fell, from noon to dewy eve.* I rocket downward through the hollow heart of the whirlpool, gripped in a monstrous suction, until abruptly I am delivered to a dark region of cold quiet water: far below the surface of the sea. My lungs ache; my ribcage, distended over a bloated lump of hot depleted air, shoots angry protests into my armpits. I glide along the smooth vertical face of a submerged mountain. My feet find lodging on a ledge; I grope my way along it and come at length to the mouth of a cave, set at a sharp angle against the steep wall of stone. I topple into it.

Within, I find an air-filled pocket of a room, dank, slippery, lit by some inexplicable inner glow. April is there, huddled against

the back of the cave. She is naked, shivering, sullen, her hair
pasted in damp strands to the pale column of her neck. Seeing
me, she rises but does not come forward. Her breasts are small,
her hips narrow, her thighs slender: a child's body.

I reach a hand toward her. "Come. Let's swim out of here
together, April."

"No. It's impossible. I'll drown."

"I'll be with you."

"Even so," she says. "I'll drown, I know it."

"What are you going to do, then? Just stay here?"

"For the time being."

"Until when?"

"Until it's safe to come out," she says.

"When will that be?"

"I'll know."

"I'll wait with you. All right?"

I don't hurry her. At last she says, "Let's go now."

This time I am the one who hesitates, to my own surprise. It is
as if there has been an interchange of strength in this cave and I
have been weakened. I draw back, but she takes my hand and
leads me firmly to the mouth of the cave. I see the water swirling
outside, held at bay because it has no way of expelling the bubble
of air that fills our pocket in the mountain. April begins to glide
down the slick passageway that takes us from the cave. She is
excited, radiant, eyes bright, breasts heaving. "Come," she
says. "Now! *Now!*"

We spill out of the cave together.

The water hammers me. I gasp, choke, tumble. The pressure is
appalling. My eardrums scream shrill complaints. Columns of
water force themselves into my nostrils. I feel the whirlpool
dancing madly far above me. In terror I turn and try to scramble
back into the cave, but it will not have me, and rebounding
impotently against a shield of air, I let myself be engulfed by the
water. I am beginning to drown, I think. My eyes deliver no
images. Dimly I am aware of April tugging at me, grasping me,
pulling me upward. What will she do, swim through the whirlpool from below? All is darkness. I perceive only the touch of
her hand. I struggle to focus my eyes, and finally I see her
through a purple chaos. How much like Irene she looks! Which is
she, April or Irene? It scarcely matters. Drowning is my occupa-

tion now. It will all be over soon. Let me go, I tell her, let me go, let me do my drowning and be done with it. Save yourself. Save yourself. But she pays no heed and continues to tug.

We erupt into the sunlight.

Bobbing at the surface, we bask in glorious warmth. "Look," she cries. "There's an island! Swim, Richard, swim! We'll be there in ten minutes. We can rest there."

Irene's face fills the sky.

"Swim!" April urges.

I try. I am without strength. A few strokes and I lapse into stupor. April, apparently unaware, is far ahead of me. April, I call. April. April, help me. I think of the beach, the warm moist sand, the row of palms, the intricate texture of the white coral boulders. Yes. Time to go home. Irene is waiting for me. April! April!

She scrambles ashore. Her slim bare form glistens in the hot sunlight.

April?

The sea has me. I drift away, foolish flotsam, borne again toward the maelstrom.

Down. Down. No way to fight it. April is gone. I see only Irene, shimmering in the waves. Down.

This cool dark cave.

Where am I? I don't know.

Who am I? Dr. Richard Bjornstrand? April Lowry? Both of those? Neither of those? I think I'm Bjornstrand. Was. Here, Dickie Dickie Dickie.

How do I get out of here? I don't know.

I'll wait. Sooner or later I'll be strong enough to swim out. Sooner. Later. We'll see.

Irene?

April?

Here Dickie Dickie Dickie. Here.

Where?

Here.

WHAT WE LEARNED FROM THIS MORNING'S NEWSPAPER

1.

I GOT HOME from the office as usual at 6:47 this evening and discovered that our peaceful street has been in some sort of crazy uproar all day. The newsboy it seems came by today and delivered the *New York Times* for Wednesday December 1 to every house on Redbud Crescent. Since today is Monday November 22 it follows therefore that Wednesday December 1 is the middle of next week. I said to my wife are you sure that this really happened? Because I looked at the newspaper myself before I went off to work this morning and it seemed quite all right to me.

At breakfast time the newspaper could be printed in Albanian and it would seem quite all right to you my wife replied. Here look at this. And she took the newspaper from the hall closet and handed it all folded up to me. It looked just like any other edition of the *New York Times* but I saw what I had failed to notice at breakfast time, that it said Wednesday December 1.

Is today the 22nd of November I asked? Monday?

It certainly is my wife told me. Yesterday was Sunday and tomorrow is going to be Tuesday and we haven't even come to Thanksgiving yet. Bill what are we going to do about this?

I glanced through the newspaper. The front page headlines were nothing remarkable I must admit, just the same old *New York Times* stuff that you get any day when there hasn't been some event of cosmic importance. NIXON, WITH WIFE, TO VISIT 3 CHINESE CITIES IN 7 DAYS. Yes. 10 HURT AS GUNMEN SHOOT WAY INTO AND OUT OF BANK. All right. GROUP OF 10, IN ROME, BEGINS NEGOTIATING REALIGNMENT OF CURRENCIES. Okay. The same old *New York Times* stuff and no surprises. But the paper was dated Wednesday December 1 and that was a surprise of sorts I guess.

This is only a joke I told my wife.

Who would do such a thing for a joke? To print up a whole newspaper? It's impossible Bill.

It's also impossible to get next week's newspaper delivered this week you know or hadn't you considered what I said?

She shrugged and I picked up the second section. I opened to page fifty which contained the obituary section and I admit I felt quite queasy for a moment since after all this might not be any joke and what would it be like to find my own name there? To my relief the people whose obituaries I saw were Harry Rogoff Terry Turner Dr. M. A. Feinstein and John Millis. I will not say that the deaths of these people gave me any pleasure but better them than me of course. I even looked at the death notices in small type but there was no listing for me. Next I turned to the sports section and saw KNICKS' STREAK ENDED, 110–109. We had been talking about going to get tickets for that game at the office and my first thought now was that it isn't worth bothering to see it. Then I remembered you can bet on basketball games and I knew who was going to win and that made me feel very strange. So also I felt odd to look at the bottom of page sixty-four where they had the results of the racing at Yonkers Raceway and then quickly flip flip flip I was on page sixty-nine and the financial section lay before my eyes. DOW INDEX RISES BY 1.61 TO 831.34 the headline said. National Cash Register was the most active stock closing at 27⅜ off ¼. Then Eastman Kodak 88⅞ down 1⅛. By this time I was starting to sweat very hard and I gave my wife the paper and took off my jacket and tie.

I said how many people have their newspaper?

Everybody on Redbud Crescent she said that's eleven houses altogether.

And nowhere beyond our street?

No the others got the ordinary paper today we've been checking on that.

"Who's we I asked?"

Marie and Cindy and I she said. Cindy was the one who noticed about the paper first and called me and then we all got together and talked about it. Bill what are we going to do? We have the stock market prices and everything Bill.

If it isn't a joke I told her.

It looks like the real paper doesn't it Bill?

I think I want a drink I said. My hands were shaking all of a sudden and the sweat was still coming. I had to laugh because it was just the other Saturday night some of us were talking about the utter predictable regularity of life out here in the suburbs the dull smooth sameness of it all. And now this. The newspaper from the middle of next week. It's like God was listening to us and laughed up His sleeve and said to Gabriel or whoever it's time to send those stuffed shirts on Redbud Crescent a little excitement.

2.

After dinner Jerry Wesley called and said we're having a meeting at our place tonight Bill can you and your lady come?

I asked him what the meeting was about and he said it's about the newspaper.

Oh yes I said. The newspaper. What about the newspaper?

Come to the meeting he said I really don't want to talk about this on the phone.

Of course we'll have to arrange a sitter Jerry.

No you won't we've already arranged it he told me. The three Fischer girls are going to look after all the kids on the block. So just come over around quarter to nine.

Jerry is an insurance broker very successful at that he has the best house on the Crescent, two-story Tudor style with almost an acre of land and a big paneled rumpus room in the basement. That's where the meeting took place. We were the seventh couple to arrive and soon after us the Maxwells the Bruces and the Thomasons came in. Folding chairs were set out and Cindy Wesley had done her usual great trays of canapes and such and there was a lot of liquor, self-service at the bar. Jerry stood up in front of everybody and grinned and said I guess you've all been wondering why I called you together this evening. He held up his copy of the newspaper. From where I was sitting I could make out only one headline clearly it was 10 HURT AS GUNMEN SHOOT WAY INTO AND OUT OF BANK but that was enough to enable me to recognize it as *the* newspaper.

Jerry said did all of you get a copy of this paper today?

Everybody nodded.

You know Jerry said that this paper gives us some extraordinary opportunities to improve our situation in life. I mean if we can accept it as the real December 1 edition and not some kind of fantastic hoax then I don't need to tell you what sort of benefits we can get from it, right?

Sure Bob Thomason said but what makes anybody think it isn't a hoax? I mean next week's newspaper who could believe that?

Jerry looked at Mike Nesbit. Mike teaches at Columbia Law and is more of an intellectual than most of us.

Mike said well of course the obvious conclusion is that somebody's playing a joke on us. But have you looked at the newspaper closely? Every one of those stories has been written in a perfectly legitimate way. There aren't any details that ring false. It isn't like one of those papers where the headlines have been cooked up but the body of the text is an old edition. So we have to consider the probabilities. Which sounds more fantastic? That someone would take the trouble of composing an entire fictional edition of the *Times* setting it in type printing it and having it delivered or that through some sort of fluke of the fourth dimension we've been allowed a peek at next week's newspaper? Personally I don't find either notion easy to believe but I can accept fourth-dimensional hocus-pocus more readily than I can the idea of a hoax. For one thing unless you've had a team the size of the *Times'* own staff working on this newspaper it would take months and months to prepare it and there's no way that anybody could have begun work on the paper more than a few days in advance because there are things in it that nobody could have possibly known as recently as a week ago. Like the Phase Two stuff and the fighting between India and Pakistan.

But how could we get next week's newspaper Bob Thomason still wanted to know?

I can't answer that said Mike Nesbit. I can only reply that I am willing to accept it as genuine. A miracle if you like.

So am I said Tim McDermott and a few others said the same.

We can make a pile of money out of this thing said Dave Bruce.

Everybody began to smile in a strange strained way. Obviously everybody had looked at the stock market stuff and the racetrack stuff and had come to the same conclusions.

Jerry said there's one important thing we ought to find out first. Has anybody here spoken about this newspaper to anybody who isn't currently in this room?

People said nope and uh-uh and not me.

Good said Jerry. I propose we keep it that way. We don't notify the *Times* and we don't tell Walter Cronkite and we don't even let our brother-in-law on Dogwood Lane know, right? We just put our newspapers away in a safe place and quietly do whatever we want to do about the information we've got. Okay? Let's put that to a vote. All in favor of stamping this newspaper top secret raise your right hand.

Twenty-two hands went up.

Good said Jerry. That includes the kids you realize. If you let the kids know anything they'll want to bring the paper to school for show and tell for Christ's sake. So cool it you hear?

Sid Fischer said are we going to work together on exploiting this thing or do we each act independently?

Independently said Dave Bruce.

Right independently said Bud Maxwell.

It went all around the room that way. The only one who wanted some sort of committee system was Charlie Harris. Charlie has bad luck in the stock market and I guess he was afraid to take any risks even with a sure thing like next week's paper. Jerry called for a vote and it came out ten to one in favor of individual enterprise. Of course if anybody wants to team up with anybody else I said there's nothing stopping anybody.

As we started to adjourn for refreshments Jerry said remember you only have a week to make use of what you've been handed. By the first of December this is going to be just another newspaper and a million other people will have copies of it. So move fast while you've got an advantage.

3.

The trouble is when they give you only next week's paper you don't ordinarily have a chance to make a big killing in the market. I mean stocks don't generally go up fifty percent or eighty percent in just a few trading sessions. The really broad swings take weeks or months to develop. Still and all I figured I could make out all right with the data I had. For one thing there evidently was going to be a pretty healthy rally over the next few days. According to the afternoon edition of the *Post* that I brought home with me the market had been off seven on the 22nd, closing with the Dow at 803.15, the lowest all year. But the December 1 *Times* mentioned "a stunning two-day advance" and the average finished at 831.34 on the 30th. Not bad. Then too I could work on margin and other kinds of leverage to boost my return. We're going to make a pile out of this I told my wife.

If you can trust that newspaper she said.

I told her not to worry. When we got home from Jerry's I spread out the *Post* and the *Times* in the den and started hunting for stocks that moved up at least ten percent between November 22 and November 30. This is the chart I made up:

Stock	Nov 22 close	Nov 30 high
Levitz Furniture	89½	103¾
Bausch & Lomb	133⅜	149
Natomas	45¼	57
Disney	99⅞	116¾
EG&G	19¼	23¾

Spread your risk Bill I told myself. Don't put all your eggs in one basket. Even if the newspaper was phony I couldn't get hurt too badly if I bought all five. So at half past nine the next morning I phoned my broker and told him I wanted to do some buying in the margin account at the opening. He said don't be in a hurry Bill the market's in lousy shape. Look at yesterday there were 201 new lows this market's going to be under 750 by Christmas. You can see from this that he's an unusual kind of broker since most of them will never try to discourage you from placing an order that'll bring them a commission. But I said no I'm playing a hunch I want to go all out on this and I put in buys on Levitz Bausch Natomas Disney and EG&G.I used the margin right up to the hilt and then some. Okay I told myself if this works out the way you hope it will you've just bought yourself a vacation in

Europe and a new Chrysler and a mink for the wife and a lot of other goodies. And if not? If not you just lost yourself a hell of a lot of money Billy boy.

4.

Also I made some use out of the sports pages.

At the office I looked around for bets on the Knicks vs. the SuperSonics next Tuesday at the Garden. A couple of guys wondered why I was interested in action so far ahead but I didn't bother to answer and finally I got Eddie Martin to take the Knicks by eleven points. Also I got Marty Felks to take Milwaukee by eight over the Warriors that same night. Felks thinks Abdul-Jabbar is the best center the game ever had and he'll always bet the Bucks but my paper had it that the Warriors would cop it, 106–103. At lunch with the boys from Leclair & Anderson I put down $250 with Butch Hunter on St. Louis over the Giants on Sunday. Next I stopped off at the friendly neighborhood Off-track Betting Office and entered a few wagers on the races at Aqueduct. My handy guide to the future told me that the Double paid $52.40 and the third Exacta paid $62.20, so I spread a little cash on each. Too bad there were no $2,500 payoffs that day but you can't be picky about your miracles can you?

5.

Tuesday night when I got home I had a drink and asked my wife what's new and she said everybody on the block had been talking about the newspaper all day and some of the girls had been placing bets and phoning their brokers. A lot of the women here play the market and even the horses though my wife is not like that, she leaves the male stuff strictly to me.

What stocks were they buying I asked?

Well she didn't know the names. But a little while later Joni Bruce called up for a recipe and my wife asked her about the market and Joni said she had bought Winnebago Xerox and Transamerica. I was relieved at that because I figured it might look really suspicious if everybody on Redbud Crescent suddenly phoned in orders the same day for Levitz Bausch Disney Natomas and EG&G. On the other hand what was I worrying about nobody would draw any conclusions and if anybody did we could always say we had organized a neighborhood investment club. In any case I don't think there's any law against people making stock market decisions on the basis of a peek at next week's newspaper. Still and all who needs publicity and I was glad we were all buying different stocks.

I got the paper out after dinner to check out Joni's stocks. Sure enough Winnebago moved up from 33¼ to 38⅛, Xerox from 105¾ to 111⅞, and Transamerica from 14⅞ to 17⅝. I thought it was dumb of Joni to bother with Xerox getting only a six percent rise since it's the percentages where you pay off but Winnebago was up better than ten percent and Transamerica close to twenty percent. I wished I had noticed Transamerica at least although no sense being greedy, my own choices would make out all right.

Something about the paper puzzled me. The print looked a little blurry in places and on some pages I could hardly read the words. I didn't remember any blurry pages. Also the paper it's printed on seemed a different color, darker gray, older-looking. I compared it with the newspaper that came this morning and the December 1 issue was definitely darker. A paper shouldn't get old-looking that fast, not in two days.

I wonder if something's happening to the paper I said to my wife.

What do you mean?

Like it's deteriorating or anyway starting to change.

Anything can happen said my wife. It's like a dream you know and in dreams things change all the time without warning.

6.

Wednesday November 24. I guess we just have to sweat this thing out so far the market in general isn't doing much one way or the other. This afternoon's *Post* gives the closing prices there was a rally in the morning but it all faded by the close and the Dow is down to 798.63. However my own five stocks all have had decent upward moves Tues and Wed so maybe I shouldn't worry. I have four points profit in Bausch already two in Natomas five in Levitz two in Disney three-quarters in EG&G and even though that's a long way from the quotations in the Dec 1 newspaper it's better than having losses, also there's still that "stunning two-day advance" due at the end of the month. Maybe I'm going to make out all right. Winnebago Transamerica and Xerox are also up a little bit. Market's closed tomorrow on account of Thanksgiving.

7.

Thanksgiving Day. We went to the Nesbits in the afternoon. It used to be that people spent Thanksgiving with their own kin their aunts uncles grandparents cousins et cetera but you can't do that out here in a new suburb where everybody comes from someplace far away so we eat the turkey with neighbors instead. The Nesbits invited the Fischers the Harrises the Thomasons and us with all the kids of course too. A big noisy gathering. The Fischers came very late so late that we were worried and thinking of sending someone over to find out what was the matter. It was practically time for the turkey when they showed up and Edith Fischer's eyes were red and puffy from crying.

My God my God she said I just found out my older sister is dead.

We started to ask the usual meaningless consoling questions like was she a sick woman and where did she live and what did she die of? And Edith sobbed and said I don't mean she's dead yet I mean she's going to die next Tuesday.

Next Tuesday Tammy Nesbit asked? What do you mean I don't understand how you can know that now. And then she thought a moment and she did understand and so did the all the rest of us. Oh Tammy said the newspaper.

The newspaper yes Edith said. Sobbing harder.

Edith was reading the death notices Sid Fischer explained God knows why she was bothering to look at them just curiosity I guess and all of a sudden she lets out this terrible cry and says she sees her sister's name. Sudden passing, a heart attack.

Her heart is weak Edith told us. She's had two or three bad attacks this year.

Lois Thomason went to Edith and put her arms around her the way Lois does so well and said there there Edith it's a terrible shock to you naturally but you know it must have been inevitable sooner or later and at least the poor woman isn't suffering any more.

But don't you see Edith cried. She's still alive right now maybe if I phone and say go to the hospital right away they can save her? They might put her under intensive care and get ready for the attack before it even comes. Only I can't say that can I? Because what can I tell her? That I read about her death in next week's newspaper? She'll think I'm crazy and she'll laugh and she won't pay any attention to me. Or maybe she'll get very upset and drop dead right on the spot all on account of me. What can I do oh God what can I do?

You could say it was a premonition my wife suggested. A very vivid dream that had the ring of truth to you. If your sister puts any faith at all in things like that maybe she'll decide it can't hurt to see her doctor and then—

No Mike Nesbit broke in you mustn't do any such thing Edith. Because they can't save her. No way. They *didn't* save her when the time came.

The time hasn't come yet said Edith.

So far as we're concerned said Mike the time has already come because we have the newspapers that describe the events of November 30 in the past tense. So we know your sister is going to die and to all intents and purposes is already dead. It's absolutely certain because it's in the newspaper and if we accept the newspaper as authentic then it's a record of actual events beyond any hope of changing.

But my sister Edith said.

Your sister's name is already on the roll of the dead. If you interfere now it'll only bring unnecessary aggravation to her family and it won't change a thing.

How do you know it won't Mike?

The future mustn't be changed Mike said. For us the events of that one day in the future are as permanent as any event in the past. We don't dare play around with changing the future not when it's already signed sealed and delivered in that newspaper. For all we know the future's like a house of cards. If we pull one card out say your sister's life we might bring the whole house tumbling down. You've got to accept the decree of fate Edith. You've got to. Otherwise there's no telling what might happen.

My sister Edith said. My sister's going to die and you won't let me do anything to save her.

8.

Edith carrying on like that put a damper on the whole Thanksgiving celebration. After a while she pulled herself together more or less but she couldn't help behaving like a woman in mourning and it was hard for us to be very jolly and thankful with her there choking back the sobs. The Fischers left right after dinner and we all hugged Edith and told her how sorry we were. Soon afterward the Thomasons and the Harrises left too.

Mike looked at my wife and me and said I hope you aren't going to run off also.

No I said not yet there's no hurry is there?

We sat around some while longer. Mike talked about Edith and her sister. The sister can't be saved he kept saying. And it might be very dangerous for everybody if Edith tries to interfere with fate.

To get the subject away from Edith we started talking about the stock market. Mike said he had bought Natomas Transamerica and Electronic Data Systems which he said was due to rise from 36¾ on November 22 to 47 by the 30th. I told him I had bought Natomas too and I told him my other stocks and pretty soon he had his copy of the December 1 paper out so we could check some of the quotations. Looking over his shoulder I observed that the print was even blurrier than it had seemed to me Tuesday night which was the last occasion I had examined my paper and also the pages seemed very gray and rough.

What do you think is going on I said? The paper definitely seems to be deteriorating.

It's entropie creep he said.

Entropic creep?

Entropy you know is the natural tendency of everything in nature to come apart at the seams as time goes along. These newspapers must be subject to unusually strong entropic strains because of their anomalous position out of their proper place in time. I've been noticing how the print is getting harder to read and I wouldn't be surprised if it became completely illegible in another couple of days.

We hunted up the prices of my stocks in his paper and the first one we saw was Bausch & Lomb hitting a high of 149¾ on November 30.

Wait a second I said I'm sure the high is supposed to be 149 even.

Mike thought it might be an effect of the general blurriness but no it was still quite clear on that page of stock market quotations and it said 149¾. I looked up Natomas and the high that was listed was 56⅞. I said I'm positive it's 57. And so on with several other stocks. The figures didn't jibe with what I remembered. We had a friendly little discussion about that and then it became not so friendly as Mike implied my memory was faulty and in the end I jogged down the street to my place and got my own copy of the paper. We spread them both out side by side and compared the quotes. Sure enough the two were different. Hardly any quote in his paper matched those in mine, all of them off an eight here, a quarter there. What was even worse the figures didn't quite match the ones I had noted down on the first day. My paper now gave the Bausch high for November 30 as 149½ and Natomas as 56½ and Disney as 117. Levitz 104, EG&G 23⅝. Everything seemed to be sliding around.

It's a bad case of entropic creep Mike said.

I wonder if the newspapers were ever identical to each other I said. We should have compared them on the first day. Now we'll never know whether we all had the same starting point.

Let's check out the other pages Bill.

We compared things. The front page headlines were all the same but there were little differences in the writing. The classified ads had a lot of rearrangements. Some of the death notices were different. All in all the papers were similar but not anything like identical.

How can this be happening I asked? How can words on a printed page be different one day from another?

How can a newspaper from the future get delivered in the first place Mike asked?

9.

We phoned some of the others and asked about stock prices. Just trying to check something out we explained. Charlie Harris said Natomas was quoted at 56 and Jerry Wesley said it was 57¼ and Bob Thomason found that the whole stock market page was too blurry to read although he thought the Natomas quote was 57½. And so on. Everybody's paper slightly different.

Entropic creep. It's hitting hard.
What can we trust? What's real?

10.

Saturday afternoon Bob Thomason came over very agitated. He had his newspaper under his arm. He showed it to me and said look at this Bill how can it be? The pages were practically falling apart and they were completely blank. You could make out little dirty traces where there once had been words but that was all. The paper looked about a million years old.

I got mine out of the closet. It was in bad shape but not that bad. The print was faint and murky yet I could still make some things out clearly. Natomas 56¼. Levitz Furniture 103½. Disney 117¼. New numbers all the time.

Meanwhile out in the real world the market has been rallying for a couple of days right on schedule and all my stocks are going up. I may go crazy but it looks at least like I'm not going to take a financial beating.

11.

Monday night November 29. One week since this whole thing started. Everybody's newspaper is falling apart. I can read patches of print on two or three pages of mine and the rest is pretty well shot. Dave Bruce says his paper is completely blank the way Bob's was on Saturday. Mike's is in better condition but it won't last long. They're all getting eaten up by entropy. The market rallied strongly again this afternoon. Yesterday the Giants got beaten by St. Louis and at lunch today I collected my winnings from Butch Hunter. Yesterday also Sid and Edith Fischer left suddenly for a vacation in Florida. That's where Edith's sister lives, the one who's supposed to die tomorrow.

12.

I can't help wondering whether Edith did something about her sister after all despite the things Mike said to her Thanksgiving.

13.

So now it's Tuesday night November 30 and I'm home with the *Post* and the closing stock prices. Unfortunately I can't compare them with the figures in my copy of tomorrow's *Times* because I don't have the paper any more it turned completely to dust and so did everybody else's but I still have the notes I took the first night when I was planning my market action. And I'm happy to say everything worked out perfectly despite the effects of entropic creep. The Dow Industrials closed at 831.34 today which is just what my record says. And look at this list of highs for the day where my broker sold me out on the nose:

Levitz Furniture	103¾
Bausch & Lomb	149
Natomas	57
Disney	116¾
EG&G	23¾

So whatever this week has cost me in nervous aggravation it's more than made up in profits.

Tomorrow is December 1 finally and it's going to be funny to see that newspaper again. With the headlines about Nixon going off to China and the people wounded in the bank robbery and the currency negotiations in Rome. Like an old friend coming home.

14.

I suppose everything has to balance out. This morning before breakfast I went outside as usual to get the paper and it was sitting there in the bushes but it wasn't the paper for Wednesday December 1 although this is in fact Wednesday December 1. What the newsboy gave me this morning was the paper for Monday November 22 which I never actually received the day of the first mixup.

That in itself wouldn't be so bad. But this paper is full of stuff I don't remember from last Monday. As though somebody had reached into last week and switched everything around, making up a bunch of weird events. Even though I didn't get to see the *Times* that day I'm sure I would have heard about the assassination of the Governor of Missouri. And the earthquake in Peru that killed ten thousand people. And Mayor Lindsay resigning to become Nixon's new Secretary of State. Especially about Mayor Lindsay resigning to become Nixon's new Secretary of State. This paper *has* to be a joke.

But what about the one we got last week? How about those stock prices and the sports results?

When I get into the city this morning I'm going to stop off first thing at the New York Public Library and check the file copy of the November 22 *Times*. I want to see if the library's copy is anything like the one I just got.

What kind of newspaper am I going to get tomorrow?

15.

Don't think I'm going to get to work at all today. Went out after breakfast to get the car and drive to the station and the car wasn't there nothing was there just gray everything gray no lawn no shrubs no trees none of the other houses in sight just gray like a thick fog swallowing everything up at ground level. Stood there on the front step afraid to go into that gray. Went back into the house woke up my wife told her. What does it mean Bill she asked what does it mean why is it all gray? I don't know I said. Let's turn on the radio. But there was no sound out of the radio nothing on the TV not even a test pattern the phone line dead too everything dead and I don't know what's happening or where we are I don't understand any of this except that this must be a very bad case of entropic creep. All of time must have looped back on itself in some crazy way and I don't know anything I don't understand a thing.

Edith what have you done to us?

I don't want to live here any more I want to cancel my newspaper subscription I want to see my house I want to get away from here back into the real world but how how I don't know it's all gray gray gray everything gray nothing out there just a lot of gray.

SHIP-SISTER,
STAR-SISTER

SIXTEEN LIGHT-YEARS from Earth today, in the fifth month of the voyage, and the silent throb of acceleration continues to drive the velocity higher. Three games of Go are in progress in the ship's lounge. The year-captain stands at the entrance to the lounge, casually watching the players: Roy and Sylvia, Leon and Chiang, Heinz and Elliot. Go has been a craze aboard ship for weeks. The players—some eighteen or twenty members of the expedition have caught the addiction by now—sit hour after hour, contemplating strategies, devising variations, grasping the smooth black or white stones between forefinger and second finger, putting the stones down against the wooden board with the proper smart sharp clacking sound. The year-captain himself does not play, though the game once interested him to the point of obsession, long ago; he finds his responsibilities so draining that an exercise in simulated territorial conquest does not attract him now. He comes here often to watch, however, remaining five or ten minutes, then going on about his duties.

The best of the players is Roy, the mathematician, a large, heavy man with a soft sleepy face. He sits with his eyes closed, awaiting in tranquillity his turn to play. "I am purging myself of the need to win." he told the year-captain yesterday when asked what occupies his mind while he waits. Purged or not, Roy wins more than half of his games, even though he gives most of his opponents a handicap of four or five stones.

He gives Sylvia a handicap of only two. She is a delicate woman, fine-boned and shy, a geneticist, and she plays well although slowly. She makes her move. At the sound of it Roy opens his eyes. He studies the board, points, and says, *"Atari,"* the conventional way of calling to his opponent's attention the fact that her move will enable him to capture several of her stones. Sylvia laughs lightly and retracts her move. After a moment she moves again. Roy nods and picks up a white stone, which he holds for nearly a minute before he places it.

The year-captain would like to speak with Sylvia about one of her experiments, but he sees she will be occupied with the game for another hour or more. The conversation can wait. No one hurries aboard this ship. They have plenty of time for everything: a lifetime, maybe, if no habitable planet can be found. The universe is theirs. He scans the board and tries to anticipate Sylvia's next move. Soft footsteps sound behind him. The year-captain turns. Noelle, the ship's communicator, is approaching the lounge. She is a slim sightless girl with long dark hair, and she customarily walks the corridors unaided: no sensors for her, not even a cane. Occasionally she stumbles, but usually her balance is excellent and her sense of the location of obstacles is superb. It is a kind of arrogance for the blind to shun assistance, perhaps. But also it is a kind of desperate poetry.

As she comes up to him she says, "Good morning, year-captain."

Noelle is infallible in making such identifications. She claims to be able to distinguish members of the expedition by the tiny characteristic sounds they make: their patterns of breathing, their coughs, the rustling of their clothing. Among the others there is some skepticism about this. Many aboard the ship believe that Noelle is reading their minds. She does not deny that she possesses the power of telepathy; but she insists that the only mind to which she has direct access is that of her twin sister Yvonne, far away on Earth.

He turns to her. His eyes meet hers: an automatic act, a habit. Hers, dark and clear, stare disconcertingly through his forehead. He says, "I'll have a report for you to transmit in about two hours."

"I'm ready whenever." She smiles faintly. She listens a moment to the clacking of the Go stones. "Three games being played?" she asks.

"Yes."

"How strange that the game hasn't begun to lose its hold on them by this time."

"Its grip is powerful," the year-captain says.

"It must be. How good it is to be able to give yourself so completely to a game."

"I wonder. Playing Go consumes a great deal of valuable time."

"Time?" Noelle laughs. "What is there to do with time, except to consume it?" After a moment she says, "Is it a difficult game?"

"The rules are simple enough. The application of the rules is another matter entirely. It's a deeper and more subtle game than chess, I think."

Her blank eyes wander across his face and suddenly lock into his. "'How long would it take for me to learn how to play?"

"You?"

"Why not? I also need amusement, year-captain."

"The board has hundreds of intersections. Moves may be made at any of them. The patterns formed are complex and constantly changing. Someone who is unable to see—"

"My memory is excellent," Noelle says. "I can visualize the board and make the necessary corrections as play proceeds. You need only tell me where you put down your stones. And guide my hand, I suppose, when I make my moves."

"I doubt that it'll work, Noelle."

"Will you teach me anyway?"

The ship is sleek, tapered, graceful: a silver bullet streaking across the universe at a velocity that has at this point come to exceed a million kilometers per second. No. In fact the ship is no bullet at all, but rather something squat and awkward, as clumsy as any ordinary spacegoing vessel, with an elaborate spidery superstructure of extensor arms and antennas and observation booms and other externals. Yet because of its incredible speed the year-captain persists in thinking of it as sleek and tapered and graceful. It carries him without friction through the vast empty gray cloak of nospace at a velocity greater than that of light. He knows better, but he is unable to shake that streamlined image from his mind.

Already the expedition is sixteen light-years from Earth. That isn't an easy thing for him to grasp. He feels the force of it, but not the true meaning. He can tell himself, *Already we are sixteen kilometers from home,* and understand that readily enough. *Already we are sixteen hundred kilometers from home*—yes, he can understand that too. What about *Already we are sixteen million kilometers from home?* That much strains comprehension—a gulf, a gulf, a terrible empty dark gulf—but he thinks he is able to understand even so great a distance, after a fashion. Sixteen light-years, though? How can he explain that to himself? Brilliant stars flank the tube of nospace through which the ship now travels, and he knows that his gray-flecked beard will have turned entirely white before the light of those stars glitters in the night sky of Earth. Yet only a few months have elapsed since the departure of the expedition. How miraculous it is, he thinks, to have come so far so swiftly.

Even so, there is a greater miracle. He will ask Noelle to relay a message to Earth an hour after lunch, and he knows that he will have an acknowledgment from Control Central in Brazil before dinner. That seems an even greater miracle to him.

Her cabin is neat, austere, underfurnished: no paintings, no light-sculptures, nothing to please the visual sense, only a few small sleek bronze statuettes, a smooth oval slab of green stone, and some objects evidently chosen for their rich textures—a strip of nubby fabric stretched across a frame, a sea-urchin's stony nest, a collection of rough sandstone chunks. Everything is meticulously arranged. Does someone help her keep the place tidy? She moves serenely from point to point in the little room, never in danger of a collision; her confidence of motion is unnerving to the year-captain, who sits patiently waiting for her to settle down. She is pale, precisely groomed, her dark hair drawn tightly back from her forehead and held by an intricate ivory clasp. Her lips are full, her nose is rounded. She wears a soft flowing robe. Her body is attractive: he has seen her in the baths and knows of her high full breasts, her ample curving hips, her creamy perfect skin. Yet so far as he has heard she has had no shipboard liaisons. Is is because she is blind? Perhaps one tends not to think of a blind person as a potential sexual partner. Why should that be? Maybe because one hesitates to take advantage of a blind person in a sexual encounter, he suggests, and immediately catches himself up, startled, wondering why he should think of any sort of sexual relationship as "taking advantage." Well, then, possibly compassion for her handicap gets in the way of erotic feeling; pity too easily becomes patronizing and kills desire. He rejects that theory: glib, implausible. Could it be that people fear to approach her, suspecting that she is able to read their inmost thoughts? She has repeatedly denied any ability to enter minds other than her sister's. Besides, if you have nothing to hide, why be put off by her telepathy? No, it must be something else, and now he thinks he has isolated it: that Noelle is so self-contained, so serene, so much wrapped up in her blindness and her mind-power and her unfathomable communion with her distant sister, that no one dares to breach the crystalline barricades that guard her inner self. She is unapproached because she seems unapproachable; her strange perfection of soul sequesters her, keeping others at a distance the way extraordinary physical beauty can sometimes keep people at a distance. She does not arouse desire because she does not seem at all human. She gleams. She is a flawless machine, an integral part of the ship.

He unfolds the text of today's report to Earth. "Not that there's anything new to tell them," he says, "but I suppose we have to file the daily communiqué all the same."

"It would be cruel if we didn't. We mean so much to them."

"I wonder."

"Oh, yes. Yvonne says they take our messages from her as fast as they come in, and send them out on every channel. Word from us is terribly important to them."

"As a diversion, nothing more. As the latest curiosity. Intrepid explorers venturing into the uncharted wilds of interstellar nospace." His voice sounds harsh to him, his rhythms of speech coarse and blurting. His words surprise him. He had not known he felt this way about Earth. Still, he goes on. "That's all we represent: a novelty, vicarious adventure, a moment of amusement."

"Do you mean that? It sounds so awfully cynical."

He shrugs. "Another six months and they'll be completely bored with us and our communiqués. Perhaps sooner than that. A year and they'll have forgotten us."

She says, "I don't see you as a cynical man. Yet you often say such"—she falters—"such—"

"Such blunt things? I'm a realist, I guess. Is that the same as a cynic?"

"Don't try to label yourself, year-captain."

"I only try to look at things realistically."

"You don't know what real is. You don't know what you are, year-captain."

The conversation is suddenly out of control: much too charged, much too intimate. She has never spoken like this before. It is as if there is a malign electricity in the air, a prickly field that distorts their normal selves, making them unnaturally tense and aggressive. He feels panic. If he disturbs the delicate balance of Noelle's consciousness, will she still be able to make contact with far-off Yvonne?

He is unable to prevent himself from parrying: "Do *you* know what I am, then?"

She tells him, "You're a man in search of himself. That's why you volunteered to come all the way out here."

"And why did you volunteer to come all the way out here, Noelle?" he asks helplessly.

She lets the lids slide slowly down over her unseeing eyes and offers no reply. He tries to salvage things a bit by saying more calmly into her tense silence. "Never mind. I didn't intend to upset you. Shall we transmit the report?"

"Wait."

"All right."

She appears to be collecting herself. After a moment she says, less edgily, "How do you think they see us at home? As ordinary human beings doing an unusual job or as superhuman creatures engaged in an epic voyage?"

"Right now, as superhuman creatures, epic voyage."

"And later we'll become more ordinary in their eyes?"

"Later we'll become nothing to them. They'll forget us."

"How sad." Her tone tingles with a grace note of irony. She may be laughing at him. "And you, year-captain? Do you picture yourself as ordinary or as superhuman?"

"Something in between. Rather more than ordinary, but no demigod."

"I regard myself as quite ordinary except in two respects," she says sweetly.

"One is your telepathic communication with your sister and the other—" He hesitates, mysteriously uncomfortable at naming it. "The other is your blindness."

"Of course," she says. Smiles. Radiantly. "Shall we do the report now?"

"Have you made contact with Yvonne?"

"Yes. She's waiting."

"Very well, then." Glancing at his notes, he begins slowly to read: "Ship-day 117. Velocity . . . Apparent location . . ."

She naps after every transmission. They exhaust her. She was beginning to fade even before he reached the end of today's message; now, as he steps into the corridor, he knows she will be asleep before he closes the door. He leaves, frowning, troubled by the odd outburst of tension between them and by his mysterious attack of "realism" By what right does he say Earth will grow jaded with the voyagers? All during the years of preparation for his first interstellar journey the public excitement never flagged, indeed spurred the voyagers themselves on at times when their interminable training routines threatened *them* with boredom. Earth's messages, relayed by Yvonne to Noelle, vibrate with eager queries; the curiosity of the home-world has been overwhelming since the start. Tell us, tell us, tell us!

But there is so little to tell, really, except in that one transcendental area where there is so much. And how, really, can any of that be told?

How can *this*—

He pauses by the viewplate in the main transit corridor, a rectangular window a dozen meters long that gives direct access to the external environment. The pearl-gray emptiness of nospace, dense and pervasive, presses tight against the skin of the ship. During the training period the members of the expedition had been warned to anticipate nothing in the way of outside inputs as they crossed the galaxy; they would be shuttling through a void of infinite length, a matter-free tube, and there would be no sights to entertain them, no backdrop of remote nebulae, no glittering stars, no stray meteors, not so much as a pair of colliding atoms yielding the tiniest momentary spark, only an eternal sameness, like a blank wall. They had been taught methods of coping with that: turn inward, demand no delights from the universe beyond the ship, make the ship itself your universe. And yet, and yet, how misguided those warnings had been! Nospace was not a wall but rather a window. It was impossible for those on Earth to understand what revelations lay in that seeming emptiness. The year-captain, head throbbing from his encounter with Noelle, now revels in his keenest pleasure. A glance at the viewplate reveals that place where the immanent becomes the transcendent: the year-captain sees once again the infinite reverberating waves of energy that sweep through the grayness. What lies beyond the ship is neither a blank wall nor an empty tube; it is a stunning profusion of interlocking energy fields, linking everything to everything; it is music that also is light, it is light that also is music, and those aboard the ship are sentient particles wholly enmeshed in that vast all-engulfing reverberation, that radiant song of gladness that is the universe. The voyagers journey joyously toward the center of all things, giving themselves gladly into the care of cosmic forces far surpassing human control and understanding. He presses his hands against the cool glass. He puts his face close to it. *What do I see, what do I feel, what am I experiencing?* It is instant revelation, every time. It is—almost, *almost!*—the sought-after oneness. Barriers remain, but yet he is aware of an altered sense of space and time, a knowledge of the awesome something that lurks in the vacancies between the spokes of the cosmos, something majestic and powerful; he knows that that something is part of himself, and he is part of it. When he stands at the viewplate he yearns to open the ship's great hatch and tumble into the eternal. But not yet, not yet. Barriers remain. The voyage has only begun. They grow closer every day to that which they seek, but the voyage has only begun.

How could we convey any of this to those who remain behind? How could we make them understand?

Not with words. Never with words.

Let them come out here and see for themselves—

He smiles. He trembles and does a little shivering wriggle of delight. He turns away from the viewplate, drained, ecstatic.

Noelle lies in uneasy dreams. She is aboard a ship, an archaic three-master struggling in an icy sea. The rigging sparkles with fierce icicles, which now and again snap free in the cruel gales and smash with little tinkling sounds against the deck. The deck wears a slippery shiny coating of thin hard ice, and footing is treacherous. Great eroded bergs heave wildly in the gray water, rising, slapping the waves, subsiding. If one of those bergs hits the hull, the ship will sink. So far they have been lucky about that, but now a more subtle menace is upon them. The sea is freezing over. It congeals, coagulates, becomes a viscous fluid, surging sluggishly. Broad glossy plaques toss on the waves: new ice floes, colliding, grinding, churning; the floes are at war, destroying one another's edges, but some are making treaties, uniting to form a single implacable shield. When the sea freezes altogether the ship will be crushed. And now it is freezing. The ship can barely make headway. The sails belly out uselessly, straining at their lines. The wind makes a lyre out of the rigging as the ice-coated ropes twang and sing. The hull creaks like an old man; the grip of the ice is heavy. The timbers are yielding. The end is near. The will all perish. They will all perish. Noelle emerges from her cabin, goes above, seizes the railing, sways, prays, wonders when the wind's fist will punch through the stiff frozen canvas of the sails. Nothing can save them. But now! yes, yes! A glow overhead! Yvonne! Yvonne! She comes. She hovers like a goddess in the black star-pocked sky. Soft golden light streams from her. She is smiling,and her smile thaws the sea. The ice relents. The air grows gentle. The ship is freed. It sails on, unhindered, toward the perfumed tropics.

In late afternoon Noelle drifts silently, wraithlike, into the control room where the year-captain is at work; she looks so weary and drawn that she is almost translucent; she seems unusually vulnerable, as though a harsh sound would shatter her. She has brought the year-captain Earth's answer to this morning's transmission. He takes from her the small, clear data-cube on which she has recorded her latest conversation with her sister. As Yvonne speaks in her mind, Noelle repeats the message aloud into a sensor disk, and it is captured on the cube. He wonders why she looks so wan. "Is anything wrong?" he asks. She tells him that she has had some difficulty receiving the message; the signal from Earth was strangely fuzzy. She is perturbed by that.

"It was like static," she says.

"Mental static?"

She is puzzled. Yvonne's tone is always pure, crystalline, wholly undistorted. Noelle has never had an experience like this before.

"Perhaps you were tired," he suggests. "Or maybe she was."

He fits the cube into the playback slot, and Noelle's voice comes from the speakers. She sounds unfamiliar, strained and ill at ease; she fumbles words frequently and often asks Yvonne to repeat. The message, what he can make out of it, is the usual cheery stuff, predigested news from the home-world—politics, sports, the planetary weather, word of the arts and sciences, special greetings for three or four members of the expedition, expressions of general good wishes—everything light, shallow, amiable. The static disturbs him. What if the telepathic link should fail? What if they were to lose contact with Earth altogether? He asks himself why that should trouble him so. The ship is self-sufficient; it needs no guidance from Earth in order to function properly, nor do the voyagers really have to have daily information about events on the mother planet. Then why care if silence descends? Why not accept the fact that they are no longer earthbound in any way, that they have become virtually a new species as they leap, faster than light, outward into the stars? No. He cares. The link matters. He decides that it has to do with what they were experiencing in relation to the intense throbbing grayness outside, that interchange of energies, that growing sense of universal connection. They are making discoveries every day, not astronomical but—well, spiritual—and, the year-captain thinks, what a pity if none of this can ever be communicated to those who have remained behind. We must keep the link open.

"Maybe," he says, "we ought to let you and Yvonne rest for a few days."

They look upon me as some sort of nun because I'm blind and special. I hate that, but there's nothing I can do to change it. I am what they think I am. I lie awake imagining men touching my body. The year-captain stands over me. I see his face clearly, the skin flushed and sweaty, the eyes gleaming. He strokes my breasts. He puts his lips to my lips. Suddenly, terribly, he embraces me and I scream. Why do I scream?

"You promised to teach me how to play," she says, pouting a little. They are in the ship's lounge. Four games are under way: Elliot with Sylvia, Roy and Paco, David and Heinz, Mike and Bruce. Her pout fascinates him: such a little-girl gesture, so charming, so human. She seems to be in much better shape today, even though there was trouble again in the transmission, Yvonne complaining that the morning report was coming through indistinctly and noisily. Noelle has decided that the noise is some sort of local phenomenon, something like a sunspot effect, and will vanish once they are far enough from this sector of nospace.

He is not as sure of this as she is, but she probably has a better understanding of such things than he. "Teach me, year-captain," she prods. "I really do want to know how to play. Have faith in me."

"All right," he says. The game may prove valuable to her, a relaxing pastime, a timely distraction. "This is the board. It has nineteen horizontal lines, nineteen vertical lines. The stones are played on the intersections of these lines, not on the squares that they form." He takes her hand and traces, with the tip of her fingers, the pattern of intersecting lines. They have been printed with a thick ink, easily discernible against the flatness of the board. "These nine dots are called stars," he tells her. "They serve as orientation points." He touches her fingertips to the nine stars. "We give the lines in this direction numbers, from one to nineteen, and we give the lines in the other direction letters, from A to T, leaving out I. Thus we can identify positions on the board. This is B10, this is D18, this is J4, do you follow? He feels despair. How can she ever commit the board to memory? But she looks untroubled as she runs her hand along the edges of the board, murmuring, "A, B, C, D..."

The other games have halted. Everyone in the lounge is watching them. He guides her hand toward the two trays of stones, the white and the black, and shows her the traditional way of picking up a stone between two fingers and clapping it down against the board. "The stronger player uses the white stones," he says. "Black always moves first. The players take turns placing stones, one at a time, on any unoccupied intersection. Once a stone is placed it is never moved unless it is captured, when it is removed at once from the board."

"And the purpose of the game?" she asks.

"To control the largest possible area with the smallest possible number of stones. You build walls. The score is reckoned by counting the number of vacant intersections within your walls, plus the number of prisoners you have taken." Methodically he explains the technique of play to her: the placing of stones, the seizure of territory, the capture of opposing stones. He illustrates by setting up simulated situations on the board, calling out the location of each stone as he places it: "Black holds P12, Q12, R12, S12, T12, and also P11, P10, P9, Q8, R8, S8, T8. White holds—" somehow she visualizes the positions; she repeats the patterns after him, and asks questions that show she sees the

board clearly in her mind. Within twenty minutes she understands the basic ploys. Several times, in describing maneuvers to
her, he gives her an incorrect coordinate—the board, after all, is
not marked with numbers and letters, and he misgauges the point
occasionally—but each time she corrects him, gently, saying,
"N13? Don't you mean N12?"

At length she says, "I think I follow everything now. Would
you like to play a game?"

Consider your situation carefully. You are twenty years old,
female, sightless. You have never married or even entered into a
basic pairing. Your only real human contact is your twin sister,
who is like yourself blind and single. Her mind is fully open to
yours. Yours is to hers. You and she are two halves of one soul,
inexplicably embedded in separate bodies. With her, only with
her, do you feel complete. Now you are asked to take part in a
voyage to the stars, without her, a voyage that is sure to cut you
off from her forever. You are told that if you leave Earth aboard
the starship there is no chance that you will ever see your sister
again. You are also told that your presence is important to the
success of the voyage, for without your help it would take
decades or even centuries for news of the starship to reach Earth,
but if you are aboard it will be possible to maintain instantaneous
communication across any distance. What should you do? Consider. Consider.

You consider. And you volunteer to go, of course. You are
needed: how can you refuse? As for your sister, you will
naturally lose the opportunity to touch her, to hold her close, to
derive direct comfort from her presence. Otherwise you will lose
nothing. Never "see" her again? No. You can "see" her just as
well, certainly, from a distance of a million light-years as you can
from the next room. There can be no doubt of that.

The morning transmission. Noelle, sitting with her back to the
year-captain, listens to what he reads her and sends it coursing
over a gap of more than sixteen light-years. "Wait," she says.
"Yvonne is calling for a repeat. From 'metabolic.'" He pauses,
goes back, reads again: "*Metabolic balances remain normal,
although, as earlier reported, some of the older members of the
expedition have begun to show trace deficiencies of manganese
and potassium. We are taking appropriate corrective steps, and—*"

Noelle halts him with a brusque gesture. He waits, and she bends forward, forehead against the table, hands pressed tightly to her temples. "Static again," she says. "It's worse today."

"Are you getting through at all?"

"I'm getting through, yes. But I have to push, to push, to push. And still Yvonne asks for repeats. I don't know what's happening, year-captain."

"The distance—"

"No!"

"Better than sixteen light-years."

"No," she says. "We've already demonstrated that distance effects aren't a factor. If there's no falling off of signal after a million kilometers, after one light-year, after ten light-years—no perceptible drop in clarity and accuracy whatever—then there shouldn't be any qualitative diminution suddenly at sixteen light-years. Don't you think I've thought about this?"

"Noelle—"

"Attenuation of signal is one thing, and interference is another. An attenuation curve is a gradual slope. Yvonne and I have had perfect contact from the day we left Earth until just a few days ago. And now—no, year-captain, it can't be attenuation. It has to be some sort of interference. A local effect."

"Yes, like sunspots, I know. But—"

"Let's start again. Yvonne's calling for signal. Go on from '*manganese and potassium*' "

"*—manganese and potassium. We are taking appropriate corrective steps—*"

Playing Go seems to ease her tension. He has not played in years, and he is rusty at first, but within minutes the old associations return and he finds himself setting up chains of stones with skill. Although he expects her to play poorly, unable to remember the patterns on the board after the first few moves, she proves to have no difficulty keeping the entire array in her mind. Only in one respect has she overestimated herself: for all her precision of coordination, she is unable to place the stones exactly, tending rather to disturb the stones already on the board as she makes her moves. After a little while she admits failure and thenceforth she calls out the plays she desires—M17, Q6, P6, R4, C11—and he places the stones for her. In the beginning he plays unaggressively, assuming that as a novice she will be haphazard and weak, but

soon he discovers that she is adroitly expanding and protecting
her territory while pressing a sharp attack against his, and he
begins to devise more cunning strategies. They play for two
hours and he wins by sixteen points, a comfortable margin but
nothing to boast about, considering that he is an experienced and
adept player and that this is her first game.

The others are skeptical of her instant ability. "Sure she plays
well," Heinz mutters. "She's reading your mind, isn't she? She
can see the board through your eyes and she knows what you're
planning."

"The only mind open to her is her sister's," the year-captain
says vehemently.

"How can you be sure she's telling the truth?"

The year-captain scowls. "Play a game with her yourself.
You'll see whether it's skill or mind-reading that's at work."

Heinz, looking sullen, agrees. That evening he challenges
Noelle; later he comes to the year-captain, abashed. "She plays
well. She almost beat me, and she did it fairly."

The year-captain plays a second game with her. She sits almost
motionless, eyes closed, lips compressed, offering the coordinates of her moves in a quiet bland monotone, like some sort of
game-playing mechanism. She rarely takes long to decide on a
move and she makes no blunders that must be retracted. Her
capacity to devise game patterns has grown astonishingly; she
nearly shuts him off from the center, but he recovers the initiative
and manages a narrow victory. Afterward she loses once more to
Heinz, but again she displays an increase of ability, and in the
evening she defeats Chiang, a respected player. Now she becomes invincible. Undertaking two or three matches every day,
she triumphs over Heinz, Sylvia, the year-captain, and Leon; Go
has become something immense to her, something much more
than a mere game, a simple test of strength; she focuses her
energy on the board so intensely that her playing approaches the
level of a religious discipline, a kind of meditation. On the fourth
day she defeats Roy, the ship's champion, with such economy
that everyone is dazzled. Roy can speak of nothing else. He
demands a rematch and is defeated again.

Noelle wondered, as the ship was lifting from Earth, whether she
really would be able to maintain contact with Yvonne across the
vast span of interstellar space. She had nothing but faith to

support her belief that the power that joined their minds was wholly unaffected by distance. They had often spoken to each other without difficulty from opposite sides of the planet, yes, but would it be so simple when they were half a galaxy apart? During the early hours of the voyage she and Yvonne kept up a virtually continuous linking, and the signal remained clear and sharp, with no perceptible falling off of reception, as the ship headed outward. Past the orbit of the moon, past the million-kilometer mark, past the orbit of Mars: clear and sharp, clear and sharp. They had passed the first test: clarity of signal was not a quantitative function of distance. But Noelle remained unsure of what would happen once the ship abandoned conventional power and shunted into nospace in order to attain faster-than-light velocity. She would then be in a space apart from Yvonne; in effect she would be in another universe; would she still be able to reach her sister's mind? Tension rose in her as the moment of the shunt approached, for she had no idea what life would be like for her in the absence of Yvonne. To face that dreadful silence, to find herself thrust into such terrible isolation—but it did not happen. They entered nospace and her awareness of Yvonne never flickered. *Here we are, wherever we are,* she said, and moments later came Yvonne's response, a cheery greeting from the old continuum. Clear and sharp, clear and sharp. Nor did the signal grow more tenuous in the weeks that followed. Clear and sharp, clear and sharp, until the static began.

The year-captain visualizes the contact between the two sisters as an arrow whistling from star to star, as fire speeding through a shining tube, as a river or pure force coursing down a celestial wave guide. He sees the joining of those two minds as a stream of pure light binding the moving ship to the far-off mother world. Sometimes he dreams of Yvonne and Noelle, Noelle and Yvonne, and the glowing bond that stretches between the sisters gives off so brilliant a radiance that he stirs and moans and presses his forehead into the pillow.

The interference grows worse. Neither Noelle nor Yvonne can explain what is happening; Noelle clings without conviction to her sunspot analogy. They still manage to make contact twice daily, but it is increasingly a strain on the sister's resources, for every sentence must be repeated two or three times, and whole blocks of words now do not get through at all. Noelle has become thin and haggard. Go refreshes her, or at least diverts her from this failing of her powers. She has become a master of the game, awarding even Roy a two-stone handicap; although she occasionally loses, her play is always distinguished, extraordinarily original in its sweep and design. When she is not playing she tends to be remote and aloof. She is in all respects a more elusive person than she was before the onset of this communications crisis.

Noelle dreams that her blindness has been taken from her. Sudden light surrounds her, and she opens her eyes, sits up, looks about in awe and wonder, saying to herself. This is a table, this is a chair, this is how my statuettes look, this is what my sea urchin is like. She is amazed by the beauty of everything in her room. She rises, goes forward, stumbling at first, groping, then magically gaining poise and balance, learning how to walk in this new way, judging the positions of things not by echoes and air currents but rather by using her eyes. Information floods her. She moves about the ship, discovering the faces of her ship-mates. You are Roy, you are Sylvia, you are Heinz, you are the year-captain. They look, surprisingly, very much as she had imagined them: Roy fleshy and red-faced, Sylvia fragile, the year-captain lean and fierce, Heinz like this, Elliot like that, everyone matching expectations. Everyone beautiful. She goes to the window of which the others all talk, and looks out into the famous grayness. Yes, yes, it is as they say it is: a cosmos of wonders, a miracle of complex pulsating tones, level after level of incandescent reverberation sweeping outward toward the rim of the boundless universe. For an hour she stands before that dense burst of rippling energies, giving herself to it and taking it into herself, and then, and then, just as the ultimate moment of illumination is coming over her, she realizes that something is wrong. Yvonne is not with her. She reaches out and does not reach Yvonne. She has somehow traded her power for the gift of sight. Yvonne? Yvonne? All is still. Where is Yvonne? Yvonne is not with her. This is only a dream, Noelle tells herself, and I will soon awaken. But she cannot awaken. In terror she cries out. "It's all right," Yvonne whispers. "I'm here, love, I'm here, I'm here, just as always." Yes. Noelle feels the closeness. Trembling, she embraces her sister. Looks at her. I can see,

Yvonne! I can see! Noelle realizes that in her first rapture she quite forgot to look at herself, though she rushed about looking at everything else. Mirrors have never been part of her world. She looks at Yvonne, which is like looking at herself, and Yvonne is beautiful, her hair dark and silken and lustrous, her face smooth and pale, her features fine of outline, her eyes—her blind eyes—alive and sparkling. Noelle tells Yvonne how beautiful she is, and Yvonne nods, and they laugh and hold one another close, and they begin to weep with pleasure and love, and Noelle awakens, and the world is dark around her.

"I have the new communiqué to send," the year-captain says wearily. "Do you feel like trying again?"

"Of course I do." She gives him a ferocious smile. "Don't even hint at giving up, year-captain. There absolutely *has* to be some way around this interference."

"Absolutely," he says. He rustles his papers restlessly. "Okay, Noelle. Let's go. Shipday 128. Velocity . . ."

"Give me another moment to get ready," Noelle says.

He pauses. She closes her eyes and begins to enter the transmitting state. She is conscious, as ever, of Yvonne's presence. Even when no specific information is flowing between them, there is perpetual low-level contact, there is the sense that the other is near, that warm proprioceptive awareness such as one has of one's own arm or leg or lip. But between that impalpable subliminal contact and the actual transmission of specific content lie several key steps. Yvonne and Noelle are human biopsychic resonators constituting a long-range communications network; there is a tuning procedure for them as for any transmitters and receivers. Noelle opens herself to the radiant energy spectrum, vibratory, pulsating, that will carry her message to her earthbound sister. As the transmitting circuit in this interchange she must be the one to attain maximum energy flow. Quickly, intuitively, she activates her own energy centers, the one in the spine, the one in the solar plexus, the one at the top of the skull; energy pours from her and instantaneously spans the galaxy. But today there is an odd and troublesome splashback effect: monitoring the circuit, she is immediately aware that the signal has failed to reach Yvonne. Yvonne is there, Yvonne is tuned and expectant, yet something is jamming the channel and nothing gets through, not a single syllable. "The interference is worse than ever," she tells the year-captain. "I feel as if I could put my hand out and *touch* Yvonne. But she's not reading me and nothing's coming back from her." With a little shake of her shoulders Noelle alters the sending frequency; she feels a corresponding adjustment at Yvonne's end of the connection; but again they are thwarted, again there is total blockage. Her signal is going forth and is being soaked up by—what? How can such a thing happen?

Now she makes a determined effort to boost the output of the system. She addresses herself to the neural center in her spine, exciting its energies, using them to drive the next center to a more intense vibrational tone, harnessing that to push the highest center of all to its greatest harmonic capacity. Up and down the energy bands she roves. Nothing. Nothing. She shivers; she huddles; she is physically emptied by the strain. "I can't get through," she murmurs. "She's there, I can feel her there, I know she's working to read me. But I can't transmit any sort of intelligible coherent message."

Almost seventeen light-years from Earth and the only communication channel is blocked. The year-captain is overwhelmed by frosty terrors. The ship, the self-sufficient autonomous ship, has become a mere gnat blowing in a hurricane. The voyagers hurtle blindly into the depths of an unknown universe, alone, alone, alone. He was so smug about not needing any link to Earth, but now that the link is gone he shivers and cowers. Everything has been made new. There are no rules. Human beings have never been this far from home. He presses himself against the viewplate and the famous grayness just beyond, swirling and eddying, mocks him with its immensity. Leap into me, it calls, leap, leap, leap, lose yourself in me, drown in me.

Behind him: the sound of soft footsteps. Noelle. She touches his hunched, knotted shoulders. "It's all right," she whispers. "You're overreacting. Don't make such a tragedy out of it." But it is. Her tragedy, more than anyone's, hers and Yvonne's. But also his, theirs, everybody's. Cut off. Lost in a foggy silence.

Down in the lounge people are singing. Boisterous voices, Elliot, Chiang, Leon.

Travelin' Dan was a spacefarin' man
He jumped in the nospace tube.

The year-captain whirls, seizes Noelle, pulls her against him. Feels her trembling. Comforts her, where a moment before she had been comforting him. "Yes, yes, yes, yes," he murmurs. With his arm around her shoulders he turns, so that both of them are facing the viewplate. As if she could see. Nospace dances and churns an inch form his nose. He feels a hot wind blowing through the ship, the khamsin, the sirocco, the simoom, the leveche, a sultry wind, a killing wind coming out of the gray strangeness, and he forces himself not to fear that wind. It is a wind of life, he tells himself, a wind of joy, a cool sweet wind, the mistral, the tramontana. Why should he think there is anything to fear in the realm beyond the viewplate? How beautiful it is out there how ecstatically beautiful! How sad that we can never tell anyone about it, now, except one another. A strange peace unexpectedly descends on him. Everything is going to be all right, he insists. No harm will come of what has happened. And perhaps some good. And perhaps some good. Benefits lurk in the darkest places.

She plays Go obsessively, beating everyone. She seems to live in the lounge twenty hours a day. Sometimes she takes on two opponents at once—an incredible feat, considering that she must hold the constantly changing intricacies of both boards in her memory—and defeats them both: two days after losing verbal-level contact with Yvonne, she simultaneously triumphs over Roy and Heinz before an audience of thirty. She looks animated and buoyant; the sorrow she must feel over the snapping of the link she takes care to conceal. She expresses it, the others suspect, only by her manic Go-playing. The year-captain is one of her most frequent adversaries, taking his turn at the board in the time he would have devoted to composing and dictating the communiqués for Earth. He had thought Go was over for him years ago, but he too is playing obsessively now, building walls and the unassailable fortresses known as eyes. There is reassurance in the rhythmic clacking march of the black and white stones. Noelle wins every game against him. She covers the board with eyes.

Who can explain the interference? No one believes that the problem is a function of anything so obvious as distance. Noelle has been quite convincing on that score: a signal that propagates perfectly for the first sixteen light-years of a journey ought not suddenly to deteriorate. There should at least have been prior sign of attenuation, and there was no attenuation, only noise interfering with and ultimately destroying the signal. Some force is intervening between the sisters. But what can it be? The idea that it is some physical effect analogous to sunspot static, that it is the product of radiation emitted by some giant star in whose vicinity they have lately been traveling, must in the end be rejected. There is no energy interface between realspace and nospace, no opportunity for any kind of electromagnetic intrusion. That much had been amply demonstrated long before any manned voyages were undertaken. The nospace tube is an impermeable wall. Nothing that has mass or charge can leap the barrier between the universe of accepted phenomena and the cocoon of nothingness that the ship's drive mechanism has woven about them, nor can a photon get across, nor even a slippery neutrino.

Many speculations excite the voyagers. The one force that *can* cross the barrier, Roy points out, is thought: intangible, unmeasurable, limitless. What if the sector of realspace corresponding to this region of the nospace tube is inhabited by beings of powerful telepathic capacity whose transmissions, flooding out over a sphere with a radius of many light-years, are able to cross the barrier just as readily as those of Yvonne? The alien mental emanations, Roy supposes, are smothering the signal from Earth.

Heinz extends this theory into a different possibility: that the interference is caused by denizens of nospace. There is a seeming paradox in this, since it has been shown mathematically that the nospace tube must be wholly matter-free except for the ship that travels through it; otherwise a body moving at speeds faster than light would generate destructive resonances as its mass exceeds infinity. But perhaps the equations are imperfectly understood. Heinz imagines giant incorporeal beings as big as asteroids, as big as planets, masses of pure energy or even pure mental force that drift freely through the tube. These beings may be sources of biopsychic transmissions that disrupt the Yvonne-Noelle circuit, or maybe they are actually *feeding* on the sisters' mental output, Heinz postulates. "Angels," he calls them. It is an implausible but striking concept that fascinates everyone for several days. Whether the "angels" live within the tube as proposed by Heinz, or on some world just outside it as pictured by Roy, is unimportant at the moment; the consensus aboard the ship is that the interference is the work of an alien intelligence, and that arouses wonder in all.

What to do? Leon, inclining toward Roy's hypothesis, moves that they leave nospace immediately and seek the world or worlds where the "angels" dwell. The year-captain objects, noting that the plan of the voyage obliges them to reach a distance of one hundred light-years from Earth before they begin their quest for habitable planets. Roy and Leon argue that the plan is merely a guide, arbitrarily conceived, and not received scriptural writ; they are free to depart from it if some pressing reason presents itself. Heinz, supporting the year-captain, remarks that there is no need actually to leave nospace regardless of the source of the alien transmissions; if the thoughts of these creatures can come in from beyond the tube, then Noelle's thoughts can surely go outward through the tube to them, and contact can be established without the need of deviating from the plan After all, if the interference is the work of beings sharing the tube with them, and the voyagers seek them in vain outside the tube, it may be impossible to find them again once the ship returns to nospace. This approach seems reasonable, and the question is put to Noelle: Can you attempt to open a dialogue with these beings?

She laughs. "I make no guarantees. I've never tried to talk to angels before. But I'll try, my friends, I'll try."

Black (Year-Captain)	White (Noelle)
R16	Q4
C4	E3
D17	D15
E16	K17
O17	E15
H17	M17
R6	Q6
Q7	P6
R5	R4
D6	C11
K3	H3
N4	O4
N3	O3
R10	C8
O15 . . .	M15 . . .

Black remains on offensive through Move 89. White then breaks through weak north stones and encloses a major center territory. Black is unable to reply adequately and White runs a chain of stones along the 19th line. At Move 141 Black launches a hopeless attack, easily crushed by White, inside White's territory. Game ends at Move 196 after Black is faced with the cat-in-the-basket trap, by which it will lose a large group in the process of capturing one stone. Score: White 81, Black 62.

She has never done anything like this before. It seems almost an
act of infidelity, this opening of her mind to something or
someone who is not Yvonne. But it must be done. She extends a
tenuous tendril of thought that probes like a rivulet of quicksilver.
Through the wall of the ship, into the surrounding grayness,
upward, outward, toward, toward—

—angels?—

Angels. Oh. Brightness. Strength. Magnetism. Yes. Awareness
now of a fierce roiling mass of concentrated energy close by.
A mass in motion, laying a terrible stress on the fabric of the
cosmos: the angel has angular momentum. It tumbles ponderously
on its colossal axis. Who would have thought an angel could
be so huge? Noelle is oppressed by the shifting weight of it as
it makes its slow heavy axial swing. She moves closer. Oh.
She is dazzled. *Too much light! Too much power!* She draws
back, overwhelmed by the intensity of the other being's
output. Such a mighty mind: she feels dwarfed. If she touches
it with her mind she will be destroyed. She must step down the
aperture, establish some kind of transformer to shield herself
against the full blast of power that comes from it. It requires
time and discipline. She works steadily, making adjustments,
mastering new techniques, discovering capacities she had not
known she possessed. And now. Yes. Try again. Slowly,
slowly, slowly, with utmost care. Outward goes the tendril.

Yes.

Approaching the angel.

*See? Here am I. Noelle. Noelle. Noelle. I come to you in love
and fear. Touch me lightly. Just touch me—*

Just a touch—

Touch—

Oh. Oh.

*I see you. The light—eye of crystal—fountains of lava—oh, the
light—your light—I see—I see—*

Oh, like a god—

*—and Semele wished to behold Zeus in all his brightness, and
Zeus would have discouraged her; but Semele insisted and Zeus
who loved her could not refuse her; so Zeus came upon her in
full majesty and Semele was consumed by his glory, so that only
the ashes of her remained, but the son she had conceived by*

*Zeus, the boy Dionysus, was not destroyed, and Zeus saved
Dionysus and took him away sealed in his thigh, bringing him
forth afterward and bestowing godhood upon him—*

—Oh God I am Semele—

She withdraws again. Rests, regroups her powers. The force of
this being is frightening. But there are ways of insulating herself
against destruction, of letting the overflow of energy dissipate
itself. She will try once more. She knows she stands at the brink
of wonders. Now. Now. The questing mind reaches forth.

I am Noelle. I come to you in love, angel.

Contact.

The universe is burning. Bursts of wild silver light streak
across the metal down of the sky. Words turn to ash. Walls
smolder and burst into flames. There is contact. A dancing solar
flare—a stream of liquid fire—a flood tide of brilliant radiance,
irresistible, unendurable, running into her, sweeping over her,
penetrating her. Light everywhere.

—*Semele.*

The angel smiles and she quakes. *Open to me,* cries the vast
tolling voice, and she opens and the force enters fully, sweeping
through her.

optic chiasma   thalamus
sylvian fissure   hypothalamus
medulla oblongata   limbic system
                                      reticular system

pons varolii
corpus callosum   cingulate sulcus
cuneus   orbital gyri
cingulate gyrus   caudate nucleus

—cerebrum!—

claustrum   operculum
      putamen   fornix
  chloroid glomus   medial lemniscus

—MESENCEPHALON!—
dura mater
dural sinus
arachnoid granulation

subarachnoid space
pia mater

cerebellum
cerebellum
cerebellum

She has been in a coma for days, wandering in delirium. Troubled, fearful, the year-captain keeps a somber vigil at her bedside. Sometimes she seems to rise toward consciousness; intelligible words, even whole sentences, bubble dreamily from her lips. She talks of light, of a brilliant unbearable white glow, of arcs of energy, of intense solar eruptions. A star holds me, she mutters. She tells him that she has been conversing with a star. How poetic, the year-captain thinks: what a lovely metaphor. Conversing with a star. But where is she, what is happening to her? Her face is flushed; her eyes move about rapidly, darting like trapped fish beneath her closed lids. Mind to mind, she whispers, the star and I, mind to mind. She begins to hum—an edgy whining sound, climbing almost toward inaudibility, a high-frequency keening. It pains him to hear it: hard aural radiation. Then she is silent.

Her body goes rigid. A convulsion of some sort? No. She is awakening. He sees lightning bolts of perception flashing through her quivering musculature; the galvanized frog, twitching at the end of its leads. Her eyelids tremble. She makes a little moaning noise.

She looks up at him.

The year-captain says gently, "Your eyes are open. I think you can see me now, Noelle. Your eyes are tracking me, aren't they?"

"I can see you, yes." Her voice is hesitant, faltering, strange for a moment, a foreign voice, but then it becomes more like its usual self as she asks, "How long was I away?"

"Eight ship-days. We were worried."

"You look exactly as I thought you would," she says. "Your face is hard. But not a dark face. Not a hostile face."

"Do you want to talk about where you went, Noelle?"

She smiles. "I talked with the . . . angel."

"Angel?"

"Not really an angel, year-captain. Not a physical being,

either, not any kind of alien species. More like the energy creatures Heinz was discussing. But bigger. Bigger. I don't know what it was, year-captain.''

''You told me you were talking with a star.''

''—a star!''

''In your delirium. That's what you said.''

Her eyes blaze with excitement. ''A star! Yes! Yes, year-captain! I think I was, yes!''

''But what does that mean: talking to a star?''

She laughs. ''It means talking to a star year-captain. A great ball of fiery gas, year-captain, and it has a mind, it has a consciousness. I think that's what it was. I'm sure now. I'm sure!''

''But how can a—''

The light goes abruptly from her eyes. She is traveling again; she is no longer with him. He waits beside her bed. An hour, two hours, half a day. What bizarre realm has she penetrated? Her breathing is a distant, impersonal drone. So far away from him now, so remote from any place he comprehends. At last her eyelids flicker. She looks up. Her face seems transfigured. To the year-captain she still appears to be partly in that other world beyond the ship. ''Yes,'' she says. ''Not an angel, year-captain. A sun. A living intelligent sun.'' Her eyes are radiant. ''A sun, a star, a sun,'' she murmurs. ''I touched the consciousness of a sun. Do you believe that, year-captain? I found a network of stars that live, that think, that have minds, that have souls. That communicate. The whole universe is alive.''

''A star,'' he says dully. ''The stars have minds.''

''Yes.''

''All of them? Our own sun too?''

''All of them. We came to the place in the galaxy where this star lives, and it was broadcasting on my wavelength, and its output began overriding my link with Yvonne. That was the interference, year-captain. The big star broadcasting.

This conversation has taken on for him the texture of a dream. He says quietly, ''Why didn't Earth's sun override you and Yvonne when you were on Earth?''

She shrugs. ''It isn't old enough. It takes—I don't know, billions of years—until they're mature, until they can transmit.

Our sun isn't old enough, year-captain. None of the stars close to
Earth is old enough. But out here—''

"Are you in contact with it now?"

"Yes. With it and with many others. And with Yvonne."

"Yvonne too?"

"She's back in the link with me. She's in the circuit." Noelle
pauses. "I can bring others into the circuit. I could bring you in,
year-captain."

"Me?"

"You. Would you like to touch a star with your mind?"

"What will happen to me? Will it harm me?"

"Did it harm me, year-captain?"

"Will I still be me afterward?"

"Am I still me, year-captain?"

"I'm afraid."

"Open to me. Try. See what happens."

"I'm afraid."

"Touch a star, year-captain."

He puts his hand on hers. "Go ahead," he says, and his soul
becomes a solarium.

Afterward, with the solar pulsations still reverberating in the
mirrors of his mind, with blue-white sparks leaping in his
synapses, he says, "What about the others?"

"I'll bring them in too."

He feels a flicker of momentary resentment. He does not want
to share the illumination. But in the instant that he conceives his
resentment, he abolishes it. *Let them in.*

"Take my hand," Noelle says.

They reach out together. One by one they touch the others.
Roy. Sylvia. Heinz. Elliot. He feels Noelle surging in tandem
with him, feels Yvonne, feels greater presences, luminous,
eternal. All are joined. Ship-sister, star-sister: all become one.
The year-captain realizes that the days of playing Go have
ended. They are one person; they are beyond games.

"And now," Noelle whispers, "now we reach toward Earth.
We put our strength into Yvonne, and Yvonne—"

Yvonne draws Earth's seven billion into the network.

The ship hurtles through the nospace tube. Soon the year-captain
will initiate the search for a habitable planet. If they discover

one, they will settle there. If not, they will go on, and it will not matter at all, and the ship and its seven billion passengers will course onward forever, warmed by the light of the friendly stars.

WHEN WE WENT TO SEE THE END OF THE WORLD

NICK AND JANE were glad that they had gone to see the end of the world, because it gave them something special to talk about at Mike and Ruby's party. One always likes to come to a party armed with a little conversation. Mike and Ruby give marvelous parties. Their home is superb, one of the finest in the neighborhood. It is truly a home for all seasons, all moods. Their very special corner of the world. With more space indoors and out . . . more wide-open freedom. The living room with its exposed ceiling beams is a natural focal point for entertaining. Custom-finished, with a conversation pit and fireplace. There's also a family room with beamed ceiling and wood paneling . . . plus a study. And a magnificent master suite with twelve-foot dressing room and private bath. Solidly impressive exterior design. Sheltered courtyard. Beautifully wooded $^1/_3$-acre grounds. Their parties are highlights of any month. Nick and Jane waited until they thought enough people had arrived. Then Jane nudged Nick and Nick said gaily, "You know what we did last week? Hey, we went to see the end of the world!"

"The end of the world?" Henry asked.

"You went to see it?" said Henry's wife Cynthia.

"How did you manage that?" Paula wanted to know.

"It's been available since March," Stan told her. "I think a division of American Express runs it."

Nick was put out to discover that Stan already knew. Quickly, before Stan could say anything more, Nick said, "Yes, it's just started. Our travel agent found out for us. What they do is they put you in this machine, it looks like a tiny teeny submarine, you know, with dials and levers up front behind a plastic wall to keep you from touching anything, and they send you into the future. You can charge it with any of the regular credit cards."

"It must be very expensive," Marcia said.

"They're bringing the costs down rapidly," Jane said. "Last year only milliionaires could afford it. Really, haven't you heard about it before?"

"What did you see?" Henry asked.

"For a while, just grayness outside the porthole," said Nick. "And a kind of flickering effect." Everybody was looking at him. He enjoyed the attention. Jane wore a rapt, loving expression. "Then the haze cleared and a voice said over a loudspeaker that we had now reached the very end of time, when life had become impossible on Earth. Of course, we were sealed into the submarine thing. Only looking out. On this beach, this empty beach. The water a funny gray color with a pink sheen. And then the sun came up. It was red like it sometimes is at sunrise, only it stayed red as it got to the middle of the sky, and it looked lumpy and saggy at the edges. Like a few of us, hah hah. Lumpy and sagging at the edges. A cold wind blowing across the beach."

"If you were sealed in the submarine, how did you know there was a cold wind?" Cynthia asked.

Jane glared at her. Nick said, "We could see the sand blowing around. And it *looked* cold. The gray ocean. Like winter."

"Tell them about the crab," said Jane.

"Yes, the crab. The last life-form on Earth. It wasn't really a crab, of course, it was something about two feet wide and a foot high, with thick shiny green armor and maybe a dozen legs and some curving horns coming up, and it moved slowly from right to left in front of us. It took all day to cross the beach. And toward nightfall it died. Its horns went limp and it stopped moving. The tide came in and carried it away. The sun went down. There wasn't any moon. The stars didn't seem to be in the right places. The loudspeaker told us we had just seen the death of Earth's last living thing."

"How *eerie!*" cried Paula.

"Were you gone very long?" Ruby asked.

"Three hours," Jane said. "You can spend weeks or days at

the end of the world, if you want to pay extra, but they always bring you back to a point three hours after you went. To hold down the babysitter expenses."

Mike offered Nick some pot. "That's really something," he said. "To have gone to the end of the world. Hey, Ruby, maybe we'll talk to the travel agent about it."

Nick took a deep drag and passed the joint to Jane. He felt pleased with himself about the way he had told the story. They had all been very impressed. That swollen red sun, that scuttling crab. The trip had cost more than a month in Japan, but it had been a good investment. He and Jane were the first in the neighborhood who had gone. That was important. Paula was staring at him in awe. Nick knew that she regarded him in a completely different light now. Possibly she would meet him at a motel on Tuesday at lunchtime. Last month she had turned him down but now he had an extra attractiveness for her. Nick winked at her. Cynthia was holding hands with Stan. Henry and Mike both were crouched at Jane's feet. Mike and Ruby's twelve-year-old son came into the room and stood at the edge of the conversation pit. He said, "There just was a bulletin on the news. Mutated amoebas escaped from a government research station and got into Lake Michigan. They're carrying a tissue-dissolving virus and everybody in seven states is supposed to boil their water until further notice." Mike scowled at the boy and said, "It's after your bedtime, Timmy." The boy went out. The doorbell rang. Ruby answered it and returned with Eddie and Fran.

Paula said, "Nick and Jane went to see the end of the world. They've just been telling us about it."

"Gee," said Eddie, "We did that too, on Wednesday night."

Nick was crestfallen. Jane bit her lip and asked Cynthia quietly why Fran always wore such flashy dresses. Ruby said, "You saw the whole works, eh? The crab and everything?"

"The crab?" Eddie said. "What crab? We didn't see the crab."

"It must have died the time before," Paula said. "When Nick and Jane were there."

Mike said, "A fresh shipment of Cuernavaca Lightning is in. Here, have a toke."

"How long ago did you do it?" Eddie said to Nick.

"Sunday afternoon. I guess we were about the first."

"Great trip, isn't it?" Eddie said. "A little somber, though. When the last hill crumbles into the sea."

"That's not what we saw," said Jane. "And you didn't see the crab? Maybe we were on different trips."

Mike said, "What was it like for you, Eddie?"

Eddie put his arms around Cynthia from behind. He said, "They put us into this little capsule, with a porthole, you know, and a lot of instruments and—"

"We heard that part," said Paula. "What did you *see?*"

"The end of the world," Eddie said. "When water covers everything. The sun and the moon were in the sky at the same time—"

"We didn't see the moon at all," Jane remarked. "It just wasn't there."

"It was on one side and the sun was on the other," Eddie went on. "The moon was closer than it should have been. And a funny color, almost like bronze. And the ocean creeping up. We went halfway around the world and all we saw was ocean. Except in one place, there was this chunk of land sticking up, this hill, and the guide told us it was the top of Mount Everest." He waved to Fran. "That was groovy, huh, floating in our tin boat next to the top of Mount Everest. Maybe ten feet of it sticking up. And the water rising all the time. Up, up, up. Up and over the top. Glub. No land left. I have to admit it was a little disappointing, except of course the *idea* of the thing. That human ingenuity can design a machine that can send people billions of years forward in time and bring them back, wow! But there was just this ocean."

"How strange," said Jane. "We saw the ocean too, but there was a beach, a kind of nasty beach, and the crab-thing walking along it, and the sun—it was all red, was the sun red when you saw it?"

"A kind of pale green," Fred said.

"Are you people talking about the end of the world?" Tom asked. He and Harriet were standing by the door taking off their coats. Mike's son must have let them in. Tom gave his coat to Ruby and said, "Man, what a spectacle!"

"So you did it, too?" Jane asked, a little hollowly.

"Two weeks ago," said Tom. "The travel agent called and said, Guess what we're offering now, the end of the goddamned world! With all the extras it didn't really cost so much. So we went right down there to the office, Saturday, I think—was it a Friday?—the day of the big riot, anyway, when they burned St. Louis—''

"That was a Saturday," Cynthia said. "I remember I was coming back from the shopping center when the radio said they were using nuclears—''

"Saturday, yes," Tom said. "And we told them we were ready to go, and off they sent us."

"Did you see a beach with crabs," Stan demanded, "or was it a world full of water?"

"Neither one. It was like a big ice age. Glaciers covered everything. No oceans showing, no mountains. We flew clear around the world and it was all a huge snowball. They had floodlights on the vehicle because the sun had gone out."

"I was sure I could see the sun still hanging up there," Harriet put in. "Like a ball of cinders in the sky. But the guide said no, nobody could see it."

"How come everybody gets to visit a different kind of end of the world?" Henry asked. "You'd think there'd be only one kind of end of the world. I mean, it ends, and this is how it ends, and there can't be more than one way."

"Could it be fake?" Stan asked. Everybody turned around and looked at him. Nick's face got very red. Fran looked so mean that Eddie let go of Cynthia and started to rub Fran's shoulders. Stan shrugged. "I'm not suggesting it is," he said defensively. "I was just wondering."

"Seemed pretty real to me," said Tom. "The sun burned out. A big ball of ice. The atmosphere, you know, frozen. The end of the goddamned world."

The telephone rang. Ruby went to answer it. Nick asked Paula about lunch on Tuesday. She said yes. "Let's meet at the motel," he said, and she grinned. Eddie was making out with Cynthia again. Henry looked very stoned and was having trouble staying awake. Phil and Isabel arrived. They heard Tom and Fran talking about their trips to the end of the world and Isabel said she and Phil had gone only the day before yesterday. "Goddamn," Tom said, "everybody's doing it! What was your trip like?"

Ruby came back into the room. "That was my sister calling from Fresno to say she's safe. Fresno wasn't hit by the earthquake at all."

"Earthquake?" Paula asked.

"In California," Mike told her. "This afternoon. You didn't know? Wiped out most of Los Angeles and ran right up the coast practically to Monterey. They think it was on account of the underground bomb test in the Mohave Desert."

"California's always having such awful disasters," Marcia said.

"Good thing those amoebas got loose back east," said Nick. "Imagine how complicated it would be if they had them in L.A. now too."

"They will," Tom said. "Two to one they reproduce by airborne spores."

"Like the typhoid germs last November," Jane said.

"That was typhus," Nick corrected.

"Anyway," Phil said, "I was telling Tom and Fran about what we saw at the end of the world. It was the sun going nova. They showed it very cleverly, too. I mean, you can't actually sit around and *experience* it, on account of the heat and the hard radiation and all. But they give it to you in a peripheral way, very elegant in the McLuhanesque sense of the word. First they take you to a point about two hours before the blowup, right? It's I don't know how many jillion years from now, but a long way, anyhow, because the trees are all different, they've got blue scales and ropy branches,and the animals are like things with one leg that jump on pogo sticks—"

"Oh, I don't *believe* that," Cynthia drawled.

Phil ignored her gracefully. "And we didn't see any sign of human beings, not a house, not a telephone pole, nothing, so I suppose we must have been extinct a long time before. Anyway, they let us look at that for a while. Not getting out of our time machine, naturally, because they said the atmosphere was wrong. Gradually the sun started to puff up. We were nervous—weren't we, Iz?—I mean, suppose they miscalculated things? This whole trip is a very new concept and things might go wrong. The sun was getting bigger and bigger, and then this thing like an arm seemed to pop out of its left side, a big fiery arm reaching out across space, getting closer and closer. We saw it through smoked glass, like you do an eclipse. They gave us about two minutes of the explosion, and we could feel it getting hot already. Then we jumped a couple of years forward in time. The sun was back to its regular shape, only it was smaller, sort of like a little white sun instead of a big yellow one. And on Earth everything was ashes."

"Ashes," Isabel said, with emphasis.

"It looked like Detroit after the union nuked Ford," Phil said. "Only much, much worse. Whole mountains were melted. The oceans were dried up. Everything was ashes." He shuddered and took a joint from Mike. "Isabel was crying."

"The things with one leg," Isabel said. "I mean, they must have all been wiped *out*." She began to sob. Stan comforted her. "I wonder why it's a different way for everyone who goes," he said. "Freezing. Or the oceans. Or the sun blowing up. Or the thing Nick and Jane saw."

"I'm convinced that each of us had a genuine experience in the far future," said Nick. He felt he had to regain control of the group somehow. It had been so good when he was telling his story, before those others had come. "That is to say, the world suffers a variety of natural calamities, it doesn't just have *one* end of the world, and they keep mixing things up and sending people to different catastrophes. But never for a moment did I doubt that I was seeing an authentic event."

"We have to do it," Ruby said to Mike. "It's only three hours. What about calling them first thing Monday and making an appointment for Thursday night?"

"Monday's the President's funeral," Tom pointed out. "The travel agency will be closed."

"Have they caught the assassin yet?" Fran asked.

"They didn't mention it on the four o'clock news," said Stan. "I guess he'll get away like the last one."

"Beats me why anybody wants to be President," Phil said.

Mike put on some music. Nick danced with Paula. Eddie danced with Cynthia. Henry was asleep. Dave, Paula's husband, was on crutches because of his mugging, and he asked Isabel to sit and talk with him. Tom danced with Harriet even though he was married to her. She hadn't been out of the hospital more than a few months since the transplant and he treated her extremely tenderly. Mike danced with Fran. Phil danced with Jane. Stan danced with Marcia. Ruby cut in on Eddie and Cynthia. Afterward Tom danced with Jane and Phil danced with Paula. Mike and Ruby's little girl woke up and came out to say hello. Mike sent her back to bed. Far away there was the sound of an explosion. Nick danced with Paula again, but he didn't want her to get bored with him before Tuesday, so he excused himself and went to talk with Dave. Dave handled most of Nick's investments. Ruby said to Mike, "The day after the funeral, will you call the travel agent?" Mike said he would, but Tom said somebody would probably shoot the new President too and there'd be another funeral. These funerals were demolishing the gross national product, Stan observed, on account of how everything had to close all the time. Nick saw Cynthia wake Henry up and ask him sharply if he would take her on the end-of-the-world trip. Henry looked embarrassed. His factory had been blown up at Christmas in a peace demonstration and everybody knew he was in bad shape financially. "You can *charge* it," Cynthia said, her fierce voice carrying above the chitchat. "And it's so *beautiful*, Henry. The ice. Or the sun exploding. I want to go."

"Lou and Janet were going to be here tonight, too," Ruby said to Paula. "But their younger boy came back from Texas with that new kind of cholera and they had to cancel."

Phil said, "I understand that one couple saw the moon come apart. It got too close to the Earth and split into chunks and the chunks fell like meteors. Smashing everything up, you know. One big piece nearly hit their time machine."

"I wouldn't have liked that at all," Marcia said.

"Our trip was very lovely," said Jane. "No violent things at all. Just the big red sun and the tide and that crab creeping along the beach. We were both deeply moved."

"It's amazing what science can accomplish nowadays," Fran said.

Mike and Ruby agreed they would try to arrange a trip to the end of the world as soon as the funeral was over. Cynthia drank too much and got sick. Phil, Tom, and Dave discussed the stock market. Harriet told Nick about her operation. Isabel flirted with Mike, tugging her neckline lower. At midnight someone turned on the news. They had some shots of the earthquake and a warning about boiling your water if you lived in the affected states. The President's widow was shown visiting the last President's widow to get some pointers for the funeral. Then there was an interview with an executive of the time-trip company. "Business is phenomenal," he said. "Time-tripping will be the nation's number one growth industry next year." The reporter asked him if his company would soon be offering something beside the end-of-the-world trip. "Later on, we hope to," the executive said. "We plan to apply for Congressional approval soon. But meanwhile the demand for our present offering is running very high. You can't imagine. Of course, you have to expect apocalyptic stuff to attain immense popularity in times like these." The reporter said, "What do you mean, times like these?" but as the time-trip man started to reply, he was interrupted by the commercial. Mike shut off the set. Nick discovered that he was extremely depressed. He decided that it was because so many of his friends had made the journey, and he had thought he and Jane were the only ones who had. He found himself standing next to Marcia and tried to describe the way the crab had moved, but Marcia only shrugged. No one was talking about time-trips now. The party had moved beyond that point. Nick and Jane left quite early and went right to sleep, without making love. The next morning the Sunday paper wasn't delivered because of the Bridge Authority strike, and the radio said that the mutant amoebas were proving harder to eradicate than originally anticipated. They were spreading into Lake Superior and everyone in the region would have to boil all their drinking water. Nick and Jane discussed where they would go for their next vacation. "What about going to see the end of the world all over again?" Jane suggested, and Nick laughed quite a good deal.

PUSH NO MORE

        I PUSH... and the shoe moves. Will you look at that? It really moves! All I have to do is give a silent inner nudge, no hands, just reaching from the core of my mind, and my old worn-out brown shoe, the left one, goes sliding slowly across the floor of my bedroom. Past the chair, past the pile of beaten-up textbooks (Geometry, Second Year Spanish, Civic Studies, Biology, etc.), past my sweaty heap of discarded clothes. Indeed the shoe obeys me. Making a little swishing sound as it snags against the roughness of the elderly linoleum floor tiling. Look at it now, bumping gently into the far wall, tipping edge-up, stopping. Its voyage is over. I bet I could make it climb right up the wall. But don't bother doing it, man. Not just now. This is hard work. Just relax, Harry. Your arms are shaking. You're perspiring all over. Take it easy for a while. You don't have to prove everything all at once.

What have I proven, anyway?

It seems that I can make things move with my mind. How about that, man? Did you ever imagine that you had freaky powers? Not until this very night. This very lousy night. Standing there with Cindy Klein and finding that terrible knot of throbbing tension in my groin, like needing to take a leak only fifty times more intense, a zone of anguish spinning off some kind of fearful energy like a crazy dynamo implanted in my crotch. And suddenly, without any conscious awareness, finding a way of tapping that energy, drawing it up through my body to my head, amplifying it, and . . . *using* it. As I just did with my shoe. As I did a couple of hours earlier with Cindy. So you aren't just a dumb gawky adolescent schmuck, Harry Blaufeld. You are somebody very special.

You have power. You are potent.

How good it is to lie here in the privacy of my own musty bedroom and be able to make my shoe slide along the floor, simply by looking at it in that special way. The feeling of strength that I get from that! Tremendous. I am potent. I have power. That's what potent means, to have power, out of the Latin *potentia*, derived from *posse*. To be able. I am able. I can do this most extraordinary thing. And not just in fitful unpredictable bursts. It's under my conscious control. All I have to do is dip into that reservoir of tension and skim off a few watts of *push*. Far out! What a weird night this is.

Let's go back three hours. To a time when I know nothing of this *potentia* in me. Three hours ago I know only from horniness. I'm standing outside Cindy's front door with her at half past ten. We have done the going-to-the-movies thing, we have done the cappucino-afterward thing, now I want to do the makeout thing. I'm trying to get myself invited inside, knowing that her parents have gone away for the weekend and there's nobody home except her older brother, who is seeing his girl in Scarsdale tonight and won't be back for hours, and once I'm past Cindy's front door I hope, well, to get invited inside. (What a coy metaphor! You know what I mean.) So three cheers for Casanova Blaufeld, who is suffering a bad attack of inflammation of the cherry. Look at me, stammering, fumbling for words, shifting my weight from foot to foot, chewing on my lips, going red in the face. All my pimples light up like beacons when I blush. Come on, Blaufeld, pull yourself together. Change your image of yourself. Try this on for size: you're twenty-three years old, tall, strong, suave, a man of the world, veteran of so many beds you've lost count. Bushy beard that girls love to run their hands through. Big drooping handlebar mustachios. And you aren't asking her for any favors. You aren't whining and wheedling and saying please, Cindy, let's do it, because you know you don't need to say please. It's no boon you seek: you give as good as you get, right, so it's a mutually beneficial transaction, right? Right? Wrong.

You're as suave as a pig. You want to exploit her for the sake of your own grubby needs. You know you'll be inept. But let's pretend, at least. Straighten the shoulders, suck in the gut, inflate the chest. Harry Blaufeld, the devilish seducer. Get your hands on her sweater for starters. No one's around; it's a dark night. Go for the boobs, get her hot. Isn't that what Jimmy the Greek told you to do? So you try it. Grinning stupidly, practically apologizing with your eyes. Reaching out. The grabby fingers connecting with the fuzzy purple fabric.

Her face, flushed and big-eyed. Her mouth, thin-lipped and wide. Her voice, harsh and wire-edged. She says, "Don't be disgusting, Harry. Don't be *silly*." Silly. Backing away from me like I've turned into a monster with eight eyes and green fangs. Don't be disgusting. She tries to slip into the house fast, before I can paw her again. I stand there watching her fumble for her key, and this terrible rage starts to rise in me. Why disgusting? Why silly? All I wanted was to show her my love, right? That I really care for her, that I *relate* to her. A display of affection through physical contact. Right? So I reached out. A little caress. Prelude to tender intimacy. "Don't be disgusting," she said. "Don't be *silly*." The trivial little immature bitch. And now I feel the anger mounting. Down between my legs there's this hideous pain, this throbbing sensation of anguish, this purely sexual tension, and it's pouring out into my belly, spreading upward along my gut like a stream of flame. A dam has broken somewhere inside me. I feel fire blazing under the top of my skull. And there it is! The power! The strength! I don't question it. I don't ask myself what it is or where it came from. I just push her, hard, from ten feet away, a quick furious shove. It's like an invisible hand against her breasts—I can see the front of her sweater flatten out—and she topples backward, clutching at the air, and goes over on her ass. I've knocked her sprawling without touching her. "Harry," she mumbles. "Harry?"

My anger's gone. Now I feel terror. What have I done? How? *How?* Down on her ass, *boom*. From ten feet away!

I run all the way home, never looking back.

Footsteps in the hallway, *clickety-clack*. My sister is home from her date with Jimmy the Greek. That isn't his name. Aristides Pappas is who he really is. Ari, she calls him. Jimmy the Greek, I call him, but not to his face. He's nine feet tall with black

greasy hair and a tremendous beak of a nose that comes straight
out of his forehead. He's twenty-seven years old and he's laid a
thousand girls. Sara is going to marry him next year. Meanwhile
they see each other three nights a week and they screw a lot.
She's never said a word to me about that, about the screwing, but
I know. Sure they screw. Why not? They're going to get married,
aren't they? And they're adults. She's nineteen years old, so it's
legal for her to screw. I won't be nineteen for four years and four
months. It's legal for me to screw now, I think. If only. If only I
had somebody. If only.

Clickety-clickety-clack. There she goes, into her room. *Blunk.*
That's her door closing. She doesn't give a damn if she wakes
the whole family up. Why should she care? She's all turned on
now. Soaring on her memories of what she was just doing with
Jimmy the Greek. That warm feeling. The afterglow, the book
calls it.

I wonder how they do it when they do it.

They go to his apartment. Do they take off all their clothes
first? Do they talk before they begin? A drink or two? Smoke a
joint? Sara claims she doesn't smoke it. I bet she's putting me
on. They get naked. Christ, he's so tall, he must have a dong a
foot long. Doesn't it scare her? They lie down on the bed
together. Or on a couch. The floor, maybe? A thick fluffy carpet?
He touches her body. Doing the foreplay stuff. I've read about it.
He strokes the breasts, making the nipples go erect. I've seen her
nipples. They aren't any bigger than mine. How tall do they get
when they're erect? An inch? Three inches? Standing up like a
couple of pink pencils? And his hand must go down below, too.
There's this thing you're supposed to touch, this tiny bump of
flesh hidden inside there. I've studied the diagrams and I still
don't know where it is. Jimmy the Greek knows where it is, you
can bet your ass. So he touches her there. Then what? She must
get hot, right? How can he tell when it's time to go inside her?
The time arrives. They're finally doing it. You know, I can't
visualize it. He's on top of her and they're moving up and down,
sure, but I still can't imagine how the bodies fit together, how
they really move, how they do it.

She's getting undressed now, right across the hallway. Off with
the shirt, the slacks, the bra, the panties, whatever the hell she
wears. I can hear her moving around. I wonder if her door is
really closed tight. It's a long time since I've had a good look at

her. Who knows, maybe her nipples are still standing up. Even if
her door's open only a few inches, I can see into her room from
mine, if I hunch down here in the dark and peek.

But her door's closed. What if I reach out and give it a little
nudge? From here. I pull the power up into my head, yes . . .
reach . . . *push* . . . ah . . . yes! Yes! It moves! One inch, two, three.
That's good enough. I can see a slice of her room. The light's
on. Hey, there she goes! Too fast, out of sight. I think she was
naked. Now she's coming back. Naked, yes. Her back is to me.
You've got a cute ass, Sis, you know that? Turn around, turn
around, turn around . . . ah. Her nipples look the same as always.
Not standing up at all. I guess they must go back down after it's
all over. *Thy two breasts are like two young roes that are twins,
which feed among the lilies.* (I don't really read the Bible a lot,
just the dirty parts.) Cindy's got bigger ones than you, Sis, I bet
she has. Unless she pads them. I couldn't tell tonight. I was too
excited to notice whether I was squeezing flesh or rubber.

Sara's putting her housecoat on. One last flash of thigh and
belly, then no more. Damn. Into the bathroom now. The sound of
water running. She's getting washed. Now the tap is off. And
now . . . *tinkle, tinkle, tinkle*. I can picture her sitting there,
grinning to herself, taking a happy piss, thinking cozy thoughts
about what she and Jimmy the Greek did tonight. Oh, Christ, I
hurt! I'm jealous of my own sister! That she can do it three times
a week while I . . . am nowhere . . . with nobody . . . no one . . .
nothing . . . .

Let's give Sis a little surprise.

Hmm. Can I manipulate something that's out of my direct line
of sight? Let's try it. The toilet seat is in the right-hand corner of
the bathroom, under the window. And the flush knob is—let me
think—on the side closer to the wall, up high—yes. Okay, reach
out, man. Grab it before she does. *Push* . . . down . . . *push*. Yeah!
Listen to that, man! You flushed it for her without leaving your
own room!

She's going to have a hard time figuring that one out.

Sunday: a rainy day, a day of worrying. I can't get the strange
events of last night out of my mind. This power of mine—where
did it come from, what can I use it for? And I can't stop fretting
over the awareness that I'll have to face Cindy again first thing
tomorrow morning, in our Biology class. What will she say to

me? Does she realize I actually wasn't anywhere near her when I
knocked her down? If she knows I have a power, is she frightened of me? Will she report me to the Society for the Prevention
of Supernatural Phenomena, or whoever looks after such things?
I'm tempted to pretend I'm sick, and stay home from school
tomorrow. But what's the sense of that? I can't avoid her forever.

The more tense I get, the more intensely I feel the power
surging within me. It's very strong today. (The rain may have
something to do with that. Every nerve is twitching. The air is
damp and maybe that makes me more conductive.) When nobody
is looking, I experiment. In the bathroom, standing far from the
sink, I unscrew the top of the toothpaste tube. I turn the water
taps on and off. I open and close the window. How fine my
control is! Doing these things is a strain: I tremble, I sweat, I feel
the muscles of my jaws knotting up, my back teeth ache. But I
can't resist the kick of exercising my skills. I get riskily mischievous. At breakfast, my mother puts four slices of bread in the
toaster; sitting with my back to it, I delicately work the toaster's
plug out of the socket, so that when she goes over to investigate
five minutes later, she's bewildered to find the bread still raw.
"How did the plug slip out?" she asks, but of course no one tells
her. Afterward, as we all sit around reading the Sunday papers, I
turn the television set on by remote control, and the sudden
blaring of a cartoon show makes everyone jump. And a few
hours later I unscrew a light bulb in the hallway, gently, gently,
easing it from its fixture, holding it suspended close to the ceiling
for a moment, then letting it crash to the floor. "What was that?"
my mother says in alarm. My father inspects the hall. "Bulb fell
out of the fixture and smashed itself to bits." My mother shakes
her head. "How could a bulb fall out? It isn't possible." And my
father says, "It must have been loose." He doesn't sound
convinced. It must be occurring to him that a bulb loose enough
to fall to the floor couldn't have been lit. And this bulb had been
lit.

How soon before my sister connects these incidents with the
episode of the toilet that flushed by itself?

Monday is here. I enter the classroom through the rear door and
skulk to my seat. Cindy hasn't arrived yet. But now here she
comes. God, how beautiful she is! The gleaming, shimmering
red hair, down to her shoulders. The pale flawless skin. The

bright, mysterious eyes. The purple sweater, same one as Saturday night. My hands have touched that sweater. I've touched that sweater with my power, too.

I bend low over my notebook. I can't bear to look at her. I'm a coward.

But I force myself to look up. She's standing in the aisle, up by the front of the room, staring at me. Her expression is strange—edgy, uneasy, the lips clamped tight. As if she's thinking of coming back here to talk to me but is hesitating. The moment she sees me watching her, she glances away and takes her seat. All through the hour I sit hunched forward, studying her shoulders, the back of her neck, the tips of her ears. Five desks separate her from me. I let out a heavy romantic sigh. Temptation is tickling me. It would be so easy to reach across that distance and touch her. Gently stroking her soft cheek with an invisible fingertip. Lightly fondling the side of her throat. Using my special power to say a tender hello to her. See, Cindy? See what I can do to show my love? Having imagined it, I find myself unable to resist doing it. I summon the force from the churning reservoir in my depths; I pump it upward and simultaneously make the automatic calculations of intensity of push. Then I realize what I'm doing. Are you crazy, man? She'll scream. She'll jump out of her chair like she was stung. She'll roll on the floor and have hysterics. Hold back, hold back, you lunatic! At the last moment I manage to deflect the impulse. Gasping, grunting, I twist the force away from Cindy and hurl it blindly in some other direction. My random thrust sweeps across the room like a whiplash and intersects the big framed chart of the plant and animal kingdoms that hangs on the classrooms's left-hand wall. It rips loose as though kicked by a tornado and soars twenty feet on a diagonal arc that sends it crashing into the blackboard. The frame shatters. Broken glass sprays everywhere. The class is thrown into panic. Everybody yelling, running around, picking up pieces of glass, exclaiming in awe, asking questions. I sit like a statue. Then I start to shiver. And Cindy, very slowly, turns and looks at me. A chilly look of horror freezes her face.

She knows, then. She thinks I'm some sort of freak. She thinks I'm some sort of monster.

Poltergeist. That's what I am. That's me.

I've been to the library. I've done some homework in the

occultism section. So: Harry Blaufeld, boy poltergeist. From the German, *poltern*, "to make a noise," and *geist*, "spirit." Thus, *poltergeist* = "noisy spirit." Poltergeists make plates go smash against the wall, pictures fall suddenly to the floor, doors bang when no one is near them, rocks fly through the air.

I'm not sure whether it's proper to say that I *am* a poltergeist, or that I'm merely the host for one. It depends on which theory you prefer. True-blue occultists like to think that poltergeists are wandering demons or spirits that occasionally take up residence in human beings, through whom they focus their energies and play their naughty tricks. On the other hand, those who hold a more scientific attitude toward paranormal extrasensory phenomena say that it's absurdly medieval to believe in wandering demons; to them, a poltergeist is simply someone who's capable of harnessing a paranormal ability within himself that allows him to move things without touching them. Myself, I incline toward the latter view. It's much more flattering to think that I have an extraordinary psychic gift than that I've been possessed by a marauding demon. Also less scary.

Poltergeists are nothing new. A Chinese book about a thousand years old called *Gossip from the Jade Hall* tells of one that disturbed the peace of a monastery by flinging crockery around. The monks hired an exorcist to get things under control, but the noisy spirit gave him the works: "His cap was pulled off and thrown against the wall, his robe was loosed, and even his trousers pulled off, which caused him to retire precipitately." Right on, poltergeist! "Others tried where he had failed, but they were rewarded for their pains by a rain of insolent missives from the air, upon which were written words of malice and bitter odium."

The archives bulge with such tales from many lands and many eras. Consider the Clarke case, Oakland, California, 1874. On hand: Mr. Clarke, a successful businessman of austere and reserved ways, and his wife and adolescent daughter and eight-year-old son, plus two of Mr. Clarke's sisters and two male house guests. On the night of April 23, as everyone prepares for bed, the front doorbell rings. No one there. Rings again a few minutes later. No one there. Sound of furniture being moved in the parlor. One of the house guests, a banker named Bayley, inspects, in the dark, and is hit by a chair. No one there. A box of silverware comes floating down the stairs and lands with a bang. (*Poltergeist* = "noisy spirit.") A heavy box of coal flies about next. A chair hits Bayley on the elbow and lands against a bed. In the dining room a massive oak chair rises two feet in the air, spins, lets itself down, chases the unfortunate Bayley around the room in front of three witnesses. And so on. Much spooked, everybody goes to bed, but all night they hear crashes and rumbling sounds; in the morning they find all the downstairs furniture in a scramble. Also the front door, which was locked and bolted, has been ripped off its hinges. More such events the next night. Likewise on the next, culminating in a female shriek out of nowhere, so terrible that it drives the Clarkes and guests to take refuge in another house. No explanation for any of this ever offered.

A man named Charles Fort, who died in 1932, spent much of his life studying poltergeist phenomena and similar mysteries. Fort wrote four fat books which so far I've only skimmed. They're full of newspaper accounts of strange things like the sudden appearance of several young crocodiles on English farms in the middle of the nineteenth century, and rainstorms in which the earth was pelted with snakes, frogs, blood, or stones. He collected clippings describing instances of coal-heaps and houses and even human beings suddenly and spontaneously bursting into flame. Luminous objects sailing through the sky. Invisible hands that mutilate animals and people. "Phantom bullets" shattering the windows of houses. Inexplicable disappearances of human beings, and equally inexplicable reappearances far away. Et cetera, et cetera, et cetera. I gather that Fort believed that most of these phenomena were the work of beings from interplanetary space who meddle in events on our world for their own amusement. But he couldn't explain away everything like that. Poltergeists in particular didn't fit into his bogeymen-from-space fantasy, and so, he wrote, "Therefore I regard poltergeists as evil or false or discordant or absurd . . . ." Still, he said, "I don't care to deny poltergeists, because I suspect that later, when we're more enlightened, or when we widen the range of our credulities, or take on more of that increase of ignorance that is called knowledge, poltergeists may become assimilable. Then they'll be as reasonable as trees."

I like Fort. He was eccentric and probably very gullible, but he wasn't foolish or crazy. I don't think he's right about beings from interplanetary space, but I admire his attitude toward the inexplicable.

Most of the poltergeist cases on record are frauds, They've been exposed by experts. There was the 1944 episode in Wild Plum, North Dakota, in which lumps of burning coal began to jump out of a bucket in the one-room schoolhouse of Mrs. Pauline Rebel. Papers caught fire on the pupils' desks and charred spots appeared on the curtains. The class dictionary moved around of its own accord. There was talk in town of demonic forces. A few days later, after an assistant state attorney general had begun interrogating people, four of Mrs. Rebel's pupils confessed that they had been tossing the coal around to terrorize their teacher. They'd done most of the dirty work while her back was turned or when she had had her glasses off. A prank. A hoax. Some people would tell you that all poltergeist stories are equally phony. I'm here to testify that they aren't.

One pattern is consistent in all genuine poltergeist incidents: an adolescent is invariably involved, or a child on the edge of adolescence. This is the "naughty child" theory of poltergeists, first put forth by Frank Podmore in 1890 in the *Proceedings of the Society for Psychical Research*. (See, I've done my homework very thoroughly.) The child is usually unhappy, customarily over sexual matters, and suffers either from a sense of not being wanted or from frustration, or both. There are no statistics on the matter, but the lore indicates that teenagers involved in poltergeist activity are customarily virgins.

The 1874 Clarke case, then, becomes the work of the adolescent daughter, who—I would guess—had a yen for Mr. Bayley. The multitude of cases cited by Fort, most of them dating from the nineteenth century, show a bunch of poltergeist kids flinging stuff around in a sexually repressed era. That seething energy had to go somewhere. I discovered my own poltering power while in an acute state of palpitating lust for Cindy Klein, who wasn't having any part of me. Especially *that* part. But instead of exploding from the sheer force of my bottled-up yearnings I suddenly found a way of channeling all that drive outward. And pushed . . .

Fort again: "Wherein children are atavistic, they may be in rapport with forces that most human beings have outgrown." Atavism: a strange recurrence to the primitive past. Perhaps in Neanderthal times we were all poltergeists, but most of us lost it over the millennia. But see Fort, also: "There are of course other explanations of the 'occult power' of children. One is that children, instead of being atavistic, may occasionally be far in advance of adults, foreshadowing coming human powers, because their minds are not stifled by conventions. After that, they go to school and lose their superiority. Few boy-prodigies have survived an education.''

I feel reassured, knowing I'm just a statistic in a long-established pattern of paranormal behavior. Nobody likes to think he's a freak, even when he is a freak. Here I am, virginal, awkward, owlish, quirky, precocious, edgy, uncertain, timid, clever, solemn, socially inept, stumbling through all the standard problems of the immediately post-pubescent years. I have pimples and wet dreams and the sort of fine fuzz that isn't worth shaving, only I shave it anyway. Cindy Klein thinks I'm silly and disgusting. And I've got this hot core of fury and frustration in my gut, which is my great curse and my great supremacy. I'm a poltergeist, man. Go on, give me a hard time, make fun of me, call me silly and disgusting. The next time I may not just knock you on your ass. I might heave you all the way to Pluto.

An unavoidable humiliating encounter with Cindy today. At lunchtime I go into Schindler's for my usual bacon-lettuce-tomato; I take a seat in one of the back booths and open a book and someone says, "Harry," and there she is at the booth just opposite, with three of her friends. What do I do? Get up and run out? Poltergeist her into the next county? Already I feel the power twitching in me. Mrs. Schindler brings me my sandwich. I'm stuck. I can't bear to be here. I hand her the money and mutter, "Just remembered, got to make a phone call." Sandwich in hand, I start to leave, giving Cindy a foolish hot-cheeked grin as I go by. She's looking at me fiercely. Those deep green eyes of hers terrify me.

"Wait," she says. "Can I ask you something?"

She slides out of her booth and blocks the aisle of the luncheonette. She's nearly as tall as I am, and I'm tall. My knees are shaking. God in heaven, Cindy, don't trap me like this, I'm not responsible for what I might do.

She says in a low voice, "Yesterday in Bio, when that chart hit the blackboard. You did that, didn't you?

"I don't understand."

"You made it jump across the room."

"That's impossible," I mumble. "What do you think I am, a
magician?"

"I don't know. And Saturday night, that dumb scene outside
my house—"

"I'd rather not talk about it."

"I would. How did you do that to me, Harry? Where did you
learn the trick?"

"Trick? Look, Cindy, I've absolutely got to go."

"You pushed me over. You just looked at me and I felt a
push."

"You tripped," I say. "You just fell down."

She laughs. Right now she seems about nineteen years old and
I feel about nine years old. "Don't put me on," she says, her
voice a deep sophisticated drawl. Her girlfriends are peering at
us, trying to overhear. "Listen, this interests me. I'm involved. I
want to know how you do that stuff."

"There isn't any stuff," I tell her, and suddenly I know I have
to escape. I give her the tiniest push, not touching her, of course,
just a wee mental nudge, and she feels it and gives ground, and I
rush miserably past her, cramming my sandwich into my mouth.
I flee the store. At the door I look back and see her smiling,
waving to me, telling me to come back.

I have a rich fantasy life. Sometimes I'm a movie star, twenty-
two years old with a palace in the Hollywood hills, and I give
parties that Peter Fonda and Dustin Hoffman and Julie Christie
and Faye Dunaway come to, and we all turn on and get naked
and swim in my pool and afterward I make it with five or six
starlets all at once. Sometimes I'm a famous novelist, author of
the book that really gets it together and speaks for My Generation, and I stand around in Brentano's in a glittering science-
fiction costume signing thousands of autographs, and afterward I
go to my penthouse high over First Avenue and make it with a
dazzling young lady editor. Sometimes I'm a great scientist, four
years out of Harvard Medical School and already acclaimed for
my pioneering research in genetic reprogramming of unborn
children, and when the phone rings to notify me of my Nobel
Prize I'm just about to reach my third climax of the evening with
a celebrated Metropolitan Opera soprano who wants me to design
a son for her who'll eclipse Caruso. And sometimes—

But why go on? That's all fantasy. Fantasy is dumb because it encourages you to live a self-deluding life, instead of coming to grips with reality. Consider reality, Harry. Consider the genuine article that is Harry Blaufeld. The genuine article is something pimply and ungainly and naive, something that shrieks with every molecule of his skinny body that he's not quite fifteen and has never made it with a girl and doesn't know how to go about it and is terribly afraid that he never will. Mix equal parts of desire and self-pity. And a dash of incompetence and a dollop of insecurity. Season lightly with extrasensory powers. You're a long way from the Hollywood hills, boy.

Is there some way I can harness my gift for the good of mankind? What if all these ghastly power plants, belching black smoke into the atmosphere, could be shut down forever, and humanity's electrical needs were met by a trained corps of youthful poltergeists, volunteers living a monastic life and using their sizzling sexual tensions as the fuel that keeps the turbines spinning? Or perhaps NASA wants a poltergeist-driven spaceship. There I am, lean and bronzed and jaunty, a handsome figure in my white astronaut suit, taking my seat in the command capsule of the *Mars One*. T minus thirty seconds and counting. An anxious world awaits the big moment. Five. Four. Three. Two. One. Lift-off. And I grin my world-famous grin and coolly summon my power and open the mental throttle and *push,* and the mighty vessel rises, hovering serenely a moment above the launching pad, rises and climbs, slicing like a giant glittering needle through the ice-blue Florida sky, soaring up and away on man's first voyage to the red planet . . . .

Another experiment is called for. I'll try to send a beer can to the moon. If I can do that, I should be able to send a spaceship. A simple Newtonian process, a matter of attaining escape velocity; and I don't think thrust is likely to be a determining quantitative function. A push is a push is a push, and so far I haven't noticed limitations of mass, so if I can get it up with a beer can, I ought to succeed in throwing anything of any mass into space. I think. Anyway, I raid the family garbage and go outside clutching a crumpled Schlitz container. A mild misty night; the moon isn't visible. No matter. I place the can on the ground and contemplate it. Five. Four. Three. Two. One. Lift-off. I grin my world-famous grin. I coolly summon my power and open the mental throttle. *Push.* Yes, the beer can rises. Hovering serenely a moment above the pavement. Rises and climbs, end over end, slicing like a crumpled beer can through the muggy air. Up. Up. Into the darkness. Long after it disappears, I continue to push. Am I still in contact? Does it still climb? I have no way of telling. I lack the proper tracking stations. Perhaps it does travel on and on through the lonely void, on a perfect lunar trajectory. Or maybe it has already tumbled down, a block away, skulling some hapless cop. I shot a beer can into the air, it fell to earth I know not where. Shrugging, I go back into the house. So much for my career as a spaceman. Blaufeld, you've pulled off another dumb fantasy. Blaufeld, how can you stand being such a silly putz?

Clickety-clack. Four in the morning, Sara's just coming in from her date. Here I am lying awake like a worried parent. Notice that the parents themselves don't worry: they're fast asleep, I bet, giving no damns about the hours their daughter keeps. Whereas I brood. She got laid again tonight, no doubt of it. Possibly twice. Grimly I try to reconstruct the event in my imagination. The positions, the sounds of flesh against flesh, the panting and moaning. How often has she done it now? A hundred times? Three hundred? She's been doing it at least since she was sixteen. I'm sure of that. For girls it's so much easier; they don't need to chase and coax, all they have to do is say yes. Sara says yes a lot. Before Jimmy the Greek there was Greasy Kid Stuff, and before him there was the Spade Wonder, and before him . . .

Out there tonight in this city there are three million people at the very minimum who just got laid. I detest adults and their easy screwing. They devalue it by doing it so much. They just have to roll over and grab some meat, and away they go, in and out, oooh oooh oooh ahhh. Christ, how boring it must get! If they could only look at it from the point of view of a frustrated adolescent again. The hungry virgin, on the outside peering in. Excluded from the world of screwing. Feeling that delicious sweet tension of wanting and not knowing how to get. The fiery knot of longing, sitting like a ravenous tapeworm in my belly, devouring my soul. I magnify sex. I exalt it. I multiply its wonders. It'll never live up to my anticipations. But I love the tension of anticipating and speculating and not getting. In fact, I think sometimes I'd like to spend my whole life on the edge of the blade, looking forward always to being deflowered but never quite taking the steps that would bring it about. A dynamic stasis, sustaining and enhancing my special power. Harry Blaufeld, virgin and poltergeist. Why not? Anybody at all can screw. Idiots, morons, bores, uglies. Everybody does it. There's magic in renunciation. If I keep myself aloof, pure, unique . . . .

Push . . . .

I do my little poltergeisty numbers. I stack and restack my textbooks without leaving my bed. I move my shirt from the floor to the back of the chair. I turn the chair around to face the wall. Push . . . push . . . push . . . .

Water running in the john. Sara's washing up. What's it like, Sara? How does it feel when he puts it in you? We don't talk much, you and I. You think I'm a child; you patronize me, you give me cute winks, your voice goes up half an octave. Do you wink at Jimmy the Greek like that? Like hell. And you talk husky contralto to him. Sit down and talk to me some time, Sis. I'm teetering on the brink of manhood. Guide me out of my virginity. Tell me what girls like guys to say to them. Sure. You won't tell me shit, Sara. You want me to stay your baby brother forever, because that enhances your own sense of being grown up. And you screw and screw and screw, you and Jimmy the Greek, and you don't even understand the mystical significance of the act of intercourse. To you it's just good sweaty fun, like going bowling. Right? Right? Oh, you miserable bitch! Screw you, Sara!

A shriek from the bathroom. Christ, what have I done now? I better go see.

Sara, naked, kneels on the cold tiles. Her head is in the bathtub and she's clinging with both hands to the bathtub's rim, and she's shaking violently.

"You okay?" I ask. "What happened?"

"Like a kick in the back," she says hoarsely. "I was at the sink, washing my face, and I turned around and something hit me like a kick in the back and knocked me halfway across the room."

"You okay, though? You aren't hurt?"

"Help me up."

She's upset but not injured. She's so upset that she forgets that she's naked, and without putting on her robe she cuddles up against me, trembling. She seems small and fragile and scared. I stroke her bare back where I imagine she felt the blow. Also I sneak a look at her nipples, just to see if they're still standing up after her date with Jimmy the Greek. They aren't. I soothe her with my fingers. I feel very manly and protective, even if it's only my cruddy dumb sister I'm protecting.

"What could have happened?" she asks. "You weren't pulling any tricks, were you?"

"I was in bed," I say, totally sincere.

"A lot of funny things been going on around this house lately," she says.

Cindy, catching me in the hallway between Geometry and Spanish: "How come you never call me any more?"

"Been busy."

"Busy how?"

"Busy."

"I guess you must be," she says. "Looks to me like you haven't slept in a week. What's her name?"

"Her? No her. I've just been busy." I try to escape. Must I push her again? "A research project."

"You could take some time out for relaxing. You should keep in touch with old friends."

"Friends? What kind of friend are you? You said I was silly. You said I was disgusting. Remember, Cindy?"

"The emotions of the moment. I was off balance. I mean, psychologically. Look, let's talk about all this some time, Harry. Some time soon."

"Maybe."

"If you're not doing anything Saturday night—"

I look at her in astonishment. She's actually asking *me* for a date! Why is she pursuing me? What does she want from me? Is she itching for another chance to humiliate me? Silly and disgusting, disgusting and silly. I look at my watch and quirk up my lips. Time to move along.

"I'm not sure," I tell her. "I may have some work to do."

"Work?"

"Research," I say. "I'll let you know."

A night of happy experiments. I unscrew a light bulb, float it from one side of my room to the other, return it to the fixture, and efficiently *screw it back in*. Precision control. I go up to the roof and launch another beer can to the moon, only this time I loft it a thousand feet, bring it back, kick it up even higher, bring it back, send it off a third time with a tremendous accumulated kinetic energy, and I have no doubt it'll cleave through space. I pick up trash in the street from a hundred yards away and throw it in the trash basket. Lastly—most scary of all—I polt *myself*. I levitate a little, lifting myself five feet into the air. That's as high as I dare go. (What if I lose the power and fall?) If I had the courage, I could fly. I can do anything. Give me the right fulcrum and I'll move the world. O, *potentia!* What a fantastic trip this is!

After two awful days of inner debate I phone Cindy and make a date for Saturday. I'm not sure whether it's a good idea. Her sudden new aggressiveness turns me off, slightly, but nevertheless it's a novelty to have a girl chasing me, and who am I to snub her? I wonder what she's up to, though. Coming on so interested in me after dumping me mercilessly on our last date. I'm still angry with her about that, but I can't hold a grudge, not with *her*. Maybe she wants to make amends. We did have a pretty decent relationship in the nonphysical sense, until that one stupid evening. Jesus, what if she really *does* want to make amends, all the way? She scares me. I guess I'm a little bit of a coward. Or a lot of a coward. I don't understand any of this, man. I think I'm getting into something very heavy.

I juggle three tennis balls and keep them all in the air at once, with my hands in my pockets. I see a woman trying to park her car in a space that's too small, and as I pass by I give her a sneaky little assist by pushing against the car behind her space; it moves backward a foot and a half, and she has room to park. Friday afternoon, in my gym class, I get into a basketball game and on five separate occasions when Mike Kisiak goes driving in for one of his sure-thing lay-ups I flick the ball away from the hoop. He can't figure out why he's off form and it really kills him. There seem to be no limits to what I can do. I'm awed at it myself. I gain skill from day to day. I might just be an authentic superman.

Cindy and Harry, Harry and Cindy, warm and cozy, sitting on her living-room couch. Christ, I think I'm being seduced! How can this be happening? To me? Christ. Christ. Christ. Cindy and Harry. Harry and Cindy. Where are we heading tonight?

In the movie house Cindy snuggles close. Midway through the

flick I take the hint. A big bold move: slipping my arm around her shoulders. She wriggles so that my hand slides down through her armpit and comes to rest grasping her right breast. My cheeks blaze. I do as if to pull back, as if I've touched a hot stove, but she clamps her arm over my forearm. Trapped. I explore her yielding flesh. No padding there, just authentic Cindy. She's so eager and easy that it terrifies me. Afterward we go for sodas. In the shop she turns on the body language something frightening— gleaming eyes, suggestive smiles, little steamy twistings of her shoulders. I feel like telling her not to be so obvious about it. It's like living one of my own wet dreams.

Back to her place, now. It starts to rain. We stand outside, in the very spot where I stood when I polted her the last time. I can write the script effortlessly. "Why don't you come inside for a while, Harry?" "I'd love to." "Here, dry your feet on the doormat. Would you like some hot chocolate?" "Whatever you're having, Cindy." "No, whatever you'd like to have." "Hot chocolate would be fine, then." Her parents aren't home. Her older brother is fornicating in Scarsdale. The rain hammers at the windows. The house is big, expensive-looking, thick carpets, fancy draperies. Cindy in the kitchen, puttering at the stove. Harry in the living room, fidgeting at the bookshelves. Then Cindy and Harry, Harry and Cindy, warm and cozy, together on the couch. Hot chocolate: two sips apiece. Her lips near mine. Silently begging me. Come on, dope, bend forward. Be a *mensh*. We kiss. We've kissed before, but this time it's with tongues. Christ. Christ. I don't believe this. Suave old Casanova Blaufeld swinging into action like a well-oiled seducing machine. Her perfume in my nostrils, my tongue in her mouth, my hand on her sweater, and then, unexpectedly, my hand is *under* her sweater, and then, astonishingly, my other hand is on her knee, and up under her skirt, and her thigh is satiny and cool, and I sit there having this weird two-dimensional feeling that I'm not an autonomous human being but just somebody on the screen in a movie rated X, aware that thousands of people out there in the audience are watching me with held breath, and I don't dare let them down. I continue, not letting myself pause to examine what's happening, not thinking at all, turning off my mind completely, just going forward step by step. I know that if I ever halt and back off to ask myself if this is real, it'll all blow up in my face. She's helping me. She knows much more about this

than I do. Murmuring softly. Encouraging me. My fingers scrabbling at our undergarments. "Don't rush it," she whispers.
"We've got all the time in the world." My body pressing
urgently against hers. Somehow now I'm not puzzled by the
mechanics of the thing. So this is how it happens. What a miracle
of evolution that we're designed to fit together this way! "Be
gentle," she says, the way girls always say in the novels, and I
want to be gentle, but how can I be gentle when I'm riding a
runaway chariot? I push, not with my mind but with my body,
and suddenly I feel this wondrous velvety softness enfolding me,
and I begin to move fast, unable to hold back, and she moves too
and we clasp each other and I'm swept helter-skelter along into a
whirlpool. Down and down and down. "Harry!" she gasps and I
explode uncontrollably and I know it's over. Hardly begun, and
it's over. Is that it? That's it. That's all there is to it, the moving,
the clasping, the gasping, the explosion. It felt good, but not *that*
good, not as good as in my feverish virginal hallucinations I
hoped it would be, and a backwash of letdown rips through me at
the realization that it isn't transcendental after all, it isn't a mystic
thing, it's just a body thing that starts and continues and ends.
Abruptly I want to pull away and be alone to think. But I know I
mustn't, I have to be tender and grateful now, I hold her in my
arms, I whisper soft things to her, I tell her how good it was, she
tells me how good it was. We're both lying, but so what? It *was*
good. In retrospect it's starting to seem fantastic, overwhelming,
all the things I wanted it to be. The *idea* of what we've done
blows my mind. If only it hadn't been over so fast. No matter.
Next time will be better. We've crossed a frontier; we're in
unfamiliar territory now.

Much later she says, "I'd like to know how you make things
move without touching them."

I shrug. "Why do you want to know?"

"It fascinates me. *You* fascinate me. I thought for a long time
you were just another fellow, you know, kind of clumsy, kind of
immature. But then this gift of yours. It's ESP, isn't it, Harry?
I've read a lot about it. I know. The moment you knocked me
down, I knew what it must have been. Wasn't it?"

Why be coy with her?

"Yes," I say, proud in my new manhood. "As a matter of fact,
it's a classic poltergeist manifestation. When I gave you that
shove, it was the first I knew I had the power. But I've been

developing it. You wouldn't believe some of the things I've been able to do lately." My voice is deep; my manner is assured. I have graduated into my own fantasy self tonight.

"Show me," she says. "Poltergeist something, Harry!"

"Anything. You name it."

"That chair."

"Of course." I survey the chair. I reach for the power. It does not come. The chair stays where it is. What about the saucer, then? No. The spoon? No. "Cindy, I don't understand it, but—it doesn't seem to be working right now . . ."

"You must be tired."

"Yes. That's it. Tired. A good night's sleep and I'll have it again. I'll phone you in the morning and give you a real demonstration." Hastily buttoning my shirt. Looking for my shoes. Her parents will walk in any minute. Her brother. "Listen, a wonderful evening, unforgettable, tremendous—"

"Stay a little longer."

"I really can't."

Out into the rain.

Home. Stunned. I push . . . and the shoe sits there. I look up at the light fixture. Nothing. The bulb will not turn. The power is gone. What will become of me now? Commander Blaufeld, space hero! No. No. Nothing. I will drop back into the ordinary rut of mankind. I will be . . . *a husband*. I will be . . . *an employee*. And push no more. And push no more. Can I even lift my shirt and flip it to the floor? No. No. Gone. Every shred, gone. I pull the covers over my head. I put my hands to my deflowered maleness. That alone responds. There alone am I still potent. Like all the rest. Just one of the common herd, now. Let's face it: I'll push no more. I'm ordinary again. Fighting off tears, I coil tight against myself in the darkness, and, sweating, moaning a little, working hard, I descend numbly into the quicksand, into the first moments of the long colorless years ahead.

SOME NOTES ON THE PRE-DYNASTIC EPOCH

WE UNDERSTAND SOME of their languages, but none of them completely. That is one of the great difficulties. What has come down from their epoch to ours is spotted and stained and eroded by time, full of lacunae and static; and so we can only approximately comprehend the nature of their civilization and the reasons for its collapse. Too often, I fear, we project our own values and assumptions back upon them and deceive ourselves into thinking we are making valid historic judgments.

On the other hand there are certain esthetic rewards in the very incompleteness of the record. Their poetry, for example, is heightened and made more mysterious, more strangely appealing, by the tantalizing gaps that result from our faulty linguistic knowledge and from the uncertainties we experience in transliterating their fragmentary written texts, as well as in transcribing their surviving spoken archives. It is as though time itself has turned poet, collaborating belatedly with the ancients to produce something new and fascinating by punching its own inexorable imprint into their work. Consider the resonances and implications of this deformed and defective song, perhaps a chant of a ritual nature, dating from the late pre-dynastic:

Once upon a time you .... so fine,
You threw the [?] a [? small unit of currency?]
   in your prime,

439

Didn't you?
People'd call, say "Beware .... to fall,"
You .... kidding you.
You .... laugh .....
Everybody ....
Now you don't .... so loud,
Now you don't .... so proud
About .... for your next meal.
How does it feel, how does it feel
To be ...... home .... unknown ....
.... a rolling stone?

Or examine this, which is an earlier pre-dynastic piece, possibly of Babylonian-American origin:

In my wearied ...., me ......
In my inflamed nostril, me ......
Punishment, sickness, trouble ...... me
A flail which wickedly afflicts, ... me
A lacerating rod .... me
A .... hand ...... me
A terrifying message ...... me
A stinging whip .... me
....
.... in pain I *faint* [?]
....

The Center for Pre-Dynastic Studies is a comfortingly massive building fashioned from blocks of some greasy green synthetic stone and laid out in three spokelike wings radiating from a common center. It is situated in the midst of the central continental plateau, near what may have been the site of the ancient metropolis of Omahaha. On clear days we take to the air in small solar-powered flying machines and survey the outlines of the city, which are still visible as indistinct white scars on the green breast of the earth. There are more than two thousand staff members. Many of them are women and some are sexually available, even to me. I have been employed here for eleven years. My current title is Metalinguistic Archaeologist, Third Grade. My father before me held that title for much of his life. He died in a professional quarrel while I was a child, and my mother dedicated me to filling his place. I have a small office with several data terminals, a neatly beveled viewing screen, and a modest desk. Upon my desk I keep a collection of artifacts of the so-called twentieth century. These serve as talismans spurring me on to greater depth of insight. They include:

One gray communications device ("telephone").

One black inscribing device ("typewriter?") which has been exposed to high temperatures and is somewhat melted.

One metal key, incised with the numerals 1714 and fastened by a rusted metal ring to a small white plastic plaque that declares, in red letters, IF CARRIED AWAY INADVERTENTLY///DROP IN ANY MAIL BOX///SHERATON BOSTON HOTEL///BOSTON, MASS. 02199.

One coin of uncertain denomination.

It is understood that these items are the property of the Center for Pre-Dynastic Studies and are merely on loan to me. Considering their great age and the harsh conditions to which they must have been exposed after the collapse of twentieth-century civilization, they are in remarkably fine condition. I am proud to be their custodian.

I am thirty-one years of age, slender, blue-eyed, austere in personal habits, and unmarried. My knowledge of the languages and customs of the so-called twentieth century is considerable, although I strive constantly to increase it. My work both saddens and exhilarates me. I see it as a species of poetry, if poetry may be understood to be the imaginative verbal reconstruction of experience; in my case the experiences I reconstruct are not my own, are in fact alien and repugnant to me, but what does that matter? Each night when I go home my feet are moist and chilled, as though I have been wading in swamps all day. Last summer the Dynast visited the Center on Imperial Unity Day, examined our latest findings with care and an apparently sincere show of interest, and said, "We must draw from these researches a profound lesson for our times."

None of the foregoing is true. I take pleasure in deceiving. I am an extremely unreliable witness.

The heart of the problem, as we have come to understand it, is a pervasive generalized dislocation of awareness. Nightmares break into the fabric of daily life, and we no longer notice, or, if we do notice, we fail to make appropriate response. Nothing seems excessive any longer, nothing perturbs our dulled, numbed minds. Predatory giant insects, the products of pointless experiments in mutation, escape from laboratories and devastate the countryside. Rivers are contaminated by lethal microorganisms released accidentally or deliberately by civil servants. Parts of human fetuses obtained from abortions are kept alive in hospital research units; human fetal toes and fingers grow up to four times as fast under controlled conditions as they do *in utero*, starting from single rods of cartilage and becoming fully jointed digits in seven to ten days. These are used in the study of the causes of arthritis. Zoos are vandalized by children, who stone geese and ducks to death and shoot lions in their cages. Sulphuric acid, the result of a combination of rain, mist, and sea spray with sulphurous industrial effluents, devours the statuary of Venice at a rate of five percent a year. The nose is the first part to go when this process, locally termed "marble cancer," strikes. Just off the shores of Manhattan Island, a thick, sticking mass of floating sludge transforms a twenty-square-mile region of the ocean into a dead sea, a sterile soup of dark, poisonous wastes; this pocket of coagulated pollutants has been formed over a forty-year period by the licensed dumping each year of millions of cubic yards of treated sewage, towed by barge to the site, and by the unrestrained discharge of 365 million gallons per day of raw sewage from the Hudson River.

All these events are widely deplored but the causative factors are permitted to remain uncorrected, which means a constant widening of their operative zone. (There are no static negative phases; the laws of expansive deterioration decree that bad inevitably becomes worse.) Why is nothing done on any functional level? Because no one believes anything *can* be done. Such a belief in collective impotence is, structurally speaking, identical in effect to actual impotence; one does not need to be helpless, merely to think that one is helpless, in order to reach a condition of surrender to accelerating degenerative conditions. Under such circumstances a withdrawal of attention is the only satisfactory therapy. Along with this emptying of reactive impulse comes a corresponding semantic inflation and devaluation which further speeds the process of general dehumanization. Thus the roving gangs of adolescents who commit random crimes in the streets of

New York City say they have "blown away" a victim whom they have in fact murdered, and the President of the United States, announcing an adjustment in the par value of his country's currency made necessary by the surreptitious economic mismanagement of the previous administration, describes it as "the most significant monetary agreement in the history of the world."

Some of the topics urgently requiring detailed analysis:

1. Their poetry
2. Preferred positions of sexual intercourse
3. The street plans of their major cities
4. Religious beliefs and practices
5. Terms of endearment, heterosexual and homosexual
6. Ecological destruction, accidental and deliberate
7. Sports and rituals
8. Attitudes toward technological progress
9. Forms of government, political processes
10. Their visual art forms
11. Means of transportation
12. Their collapse and social decay
13. Their terrible last days

One of our amusements here—no, let me be frank, it's more than an amusement, it's a professional necessity—is periodically to enter the vanished pre-dynastic world through the gate of dreams. A drug that leaves a sour, salty taste on the tongue facilitates these journeys. Also we make use of talismans: I clutch my key in my left hand and carry my coin in my right-hand pocket. We never travel alone, but usually go in teams of two or three. A special section of the Center is set aside for those who make these dream-journeys. The rooms are small and brightly lit, with soft rubbery pink walls, rather womblike in appearance, tuned to a bland heat and an intimate humidity. Alexandra, Jerome, and I enter such a room. We remove our clothing to perform the customary ablutions. Alexandra is plump, but her breasts are small and far apart. Jerome's body is hairy, and his muscles lie in thick slabs over his bones. I see them both looking at me. We wash and dress; Jerome produces three hexagonal gray tablets and we swallow them. Sour, salty. We lie side by side on the triple couch in the center of the room. I clutch my key, I touch my coin. Backward, backward, backward we drift. Alexandra's soft forearm presses gently against my thin shoulder. Into the dark, into the old times. The pre-dynastic epoch swallows us. This is the kingdom of earth, distorted, broken, twisted, maimed, perjured. The kingdom of hell. A snowbound kingdom. Bright lights on the grease-speckled airstrip. A rusting vehicle jutting from the sand. The eyes and lips of madmen. My feet are sixteen inches above the surface of the ground. Mists curl upward, licking at my soles. I stand before a bleak hotel, and women carrying glossy leather bags pass in and out. Toward us come automobiles, berserk, driverless, with blazing headlights. A blurred column of song rise out of the darkness. Home .... unknown .... a rolling stone? These ruins are inhabited.

LIFE-SYNTHESIS PIONEER URGES
POLICING OF RESEARCH
Buffalo Doctor Says New Organisms Could Be Peril

USE OF PRIVATE PATROLMEN
ON CITY STREETS INCREASING

MACROBIOTIC COOKING—LEARNING THE
SECRETS OF YANG AND YIN

PATMAN WARNS U.S. MAY CHECK
GAMBLING "DISEASE" IN THE STATES

SOME AREAS SEEK TO HALT GROWTH

NIXON DEPICTS HIS WIFE
AS STRONG AND SENSITIVE

PSYCHIATRIST IN BELFAST FINDS CHILDREN
ARE DEEPLY DISTURBED BY THE VIOLENCE

GROWING USE OF MIND-AFFECTING
DRUGS STIRS CONCERN

Saigon, Sept. 5—United States Army psychologists said today they are worked on a plan to brainwash enemy troops with bars of soap that reveal a new propaganda message practically every time the guerrillas lather up. As the soap is used, gradual wear reveals eight messages embedded in layers.

*   *   *

"The Beatles, and their mimicking rock-and-rollers, use the Pavlovian techniques to produce artificial neuroses in our young people," declared Rep. James B. Utt (R-Calif). "Extensive experiments in hypnosis and rhythm have shown how rock and roll music leads to a destruction of the normal inhibitory mechanism of the cerebral cortex and permits easy acceptance of immorality and disregard of all moral norms."

Taylor said the time has come for police "to study and apply so far as possible all the factors that will in any way promote better understanding and a better relationship between citizens and the law enforcement officer, even if it means attempting to enter into the learning and cultural realms of unborn children."

Secretary of Defense Melvin R. Laird formally dedicated a small room in the Pentagon today as a quiet place for meditation and prayer. "In a sense, this ceremony marks the completion of the Pentagon, for until now this building lacked a place where man's inner spirit could find quiet expression," Mr. Laird said.

The meditation room, he said, "is an affirmation that, though we cling to the principle that church and state should be separate, we do not propose to separate man from God."

Moscow, June 19—Oil industry expert says Moses and Joshua were among earth's original polluters, criticizes regulations inhibiting inventiveness and progress.

Much of the interior of the continent lies submerged in a deep sea of radioactive water. The region was deliberately flooded under the policy of "compensating catastrophe" promulgated by the government toward the close of the period of terminal convulsions. Hence, though we come in dreams, we do not dare enter this zone unprotected, and we make use of aquatic robots bearing brain-coupled remote-vision cameras. Without interrupting our slumber we don the equipment, giggling self-consciously as we help one another with the harnesses and snaps. The robots stride into the green, glistening depths, leaving trails of shimmering fiery bubbles. We turn and tilt our heads and our cameras obey, projecting what they see directly upon our retinas. This is a magical realm. Everything sleeps here in a single grave, yet everything throbs and bursts with terrible life. Small boys, glowing, play marbles in the street. Thieves glide on mincing feet past beefy, stolid shopkeepers. A syphilitic whore displays her thighs to potential purchasers.

A giant blue screen mounted on the haunch of a colossal glossy-skinned building shows us the face of the President, jowly, earnest, energetic. His eyes are extraordinarily narrow, almost slits. He speaks but his words are vague and formless, without perceptible syllabic intervals. We are unaware of the pressure of the water. Scraps of paper flutter past us as though driven by the wind. Little girls dance in a ring: their skinny bare legs flash like pistons. Alexandra's robot briefly touches its coppery hand to mine, a gesture of delight, of love. We take turns entering an automobile, sitting at its wheel, depressing its pedals and levers. I am filled with an intense sense of the reality of the pre-dynastic, of its oppressive imminence, of the danger of its return. Who says the past is dead and sealed? Everything comes around at least twice, perhaps even more often, and the later passes are always more grotesque, more deadly, and more comical. Destruction is eternal. Grief is cyclical. Death is undying. We walk the drowned face of the murdered earth and we are tormented by the awareness that past and future lie joined like a lunatic serpent. The sorrows of the pharaohs will be our sorrows. Listen to the voice of Egypt.

The high-born are full of lamentation but the poor are jubilant. Every town sayeth, "Let us drive out the powerful"....The splendid judgment-hall has been stripped of its documents....The public offices lie open and their records have been stolen. Serfs have become the masters of serfs....Behold, they that had clothes are now in rags....He who had nothing is now rich and the high official must court the parvenu....Squalor is throughout the land: no clothes are white these days....The Nile is in flood yet no one has the heart to plough....Corn has perished everywhere....Everyone says, "There is no more"....The dead are thrown into the river....Laughter has perished. Grief walks the land. A man of character goes in mourning because of what has happened in the land....Foreigners have become people everywhere. There is no man of yesterday.

Alexandra, Jerome, and I waltz in the pre-dynastic streets. We sing the Hymn to the Dynast. We embrace. Jerome couples with

Alexandra. We take books, phonograph records, kitchen appliances, and postage stamps, and we leave without paying, for we have no money of this epoch. No one protests. We stare at the clumsy bulk of an airplane soaring over the tops of the buildings. We cup our hands and drink at a public fountain. Naked, I show myself to the veiled green sun. I couple with Jerome. We peer into the pinched, dead faces of the pre-dynastic people we meet outside the grand hotel. We whisper to them in gentle voices, trying to warn them of their danger. Some sand blows across the pavement. Alexandra tenderly kisses an old man's withered cheek and he flees her warmth. Jewelry finer than any our museums own glitters in every window. The great wealth of this epoch is awesome to us. Where did these people go astray? How did they lose the path? What is the source of their pain? Tell us, we beg. Explain yourselves to us. We are historians from a happier time. We seek to know you. What can you reveal to us concerning your poetry, your preferred positions of sexual intercourse, the street plans of your major cities, your religious beliefs and practices, your terms of endearment, heterosexual and homosexual, your ecological destruction, accidental and deliberate, your sports and rituals, your attitudes toward technical progress, your forms of government, your political processes, your visual art forms, your means of transportation, your collapse and social decay, your terrible last days? For your last days will be terrible. There is no avoiding that now. The course is fixed; the end is inevitable. The time of the Dynast must come.

I see myself tied into the totality of epochs. I am inextricably linked to the pharaohs, to Assurnasirpal, to Tiglath-Pileser, to the beggars in Calcutta, to Yuri Gagarin and Neil Armstrong, to Caesar, to Adam, to the dwarfed and pallid scrabblers on the bleak shores of the enfamined future. All time converges on this point of now. My soul's core is the universal focus. There is no escape. The swollen reddened moon perpetually climbs the sky. The moment of the Dynast is eternally at hand. All of time and space becomes a cage for now. We are condemned to our own company until death do us part, and perhaps even afterward. Where did we go astray? How did we lose the path? Why can't we escape? Ah. Yes. There's the catch. There is no escape.

* * *

They drank wine, and praised the gods of gold, and of silver, of brass, of iron, of wood, and of stone.

In the same hour came forth fingers of a man's hand, and wrote over against the candlestick upon the plaister of the wall of the king's palace: and the king saw the part of the hand that wrote.

Then the king's countenance was changed, and his thoughts troubled him, so that the joints of his loins were loosed, and his knees smote one against another.

And this is the writing that was written, MENE, MENE, TEKEL, UPHARSIN.

This is the interpretation of the thing: MENE; God hath numbered thy kingdom, and finished it.

TEKEL; Thou art weighed in the balances, and art found wanting.

PERES; Thy kingdom is divided, and given to the Medes and Persians.

In that night was Belshazzar the king of the Chaldeans slain.

And Darius the Median took the kingdom, being about threescore and two years old.

We wake. We say nothing to one another as we leave the room of dreams; we avert our eyes from each other's gaze. We return to our separate offices. I spend the remainder of the afternoon analyzing shards of pre-dynastic poetry. The words are muddled and will not cohere. My eyes fill with tears. Why have I become so involved in the fate of these sad and foolish people?

Let me unmask myself. Let me confess everything. There is no Center for Pre-Dynastic Studies. I am no Metalinguistic Archaeologist, Third Grade, living in a remote and idyllic era far in your future and passing my days in pondering the wreckage of the twentieth century. The time of the Dynast may be coming, but he does not yet rule. I am your contemporary. I am your brother. These notes are the work of a pre-dynastic man like yourself, a native of the so-called twentieth century, who, like you, has lived through dark hours and may live to see darker ones. That much is true. All the rest is fantasy of my own invention. Do you believe that? Do I seem reliable now? Can you trust me, just this once?

All time converges on this point of now.

My ...... hurts me sorely.
The .... of my .... is decaying.
This is the path that the bison took.
This is the path that the moa took.
This is the .... of the dying .... [beasts?]
Let us not .... that dry path.
Let us not .... that bony path.
Let us .... another path ......
O my brother, sharer of my mother's [womb?]
O my sister, whose .... I ....
Listen ...... close .... the wall ....
Now the cold winds come.
Now the heavy snows fall.
Now ....
.... the suffering ....
.... the solitude ....
.... blood .... sleep .... blood ....
.... blood ....
....
.... the river, the sea ....
..... me ....

IN ENTROPY'S JAWS

STATIC CRACKLES FROM the hazy golden cloud of airborne loudspeakers drifting just below the ceiling of the spaceliner cabin. A hiss: communications filters are opening. An impending announcement from the bridge, no doubt. Then the captain's bland, mechanical voice: "We are approaching the Panama Canal. All passengers into their bottles until the all-clear after insertion. When we come out the far side, we'll be traveling at eighty lights toward the Perseus relay booster. Thank you." In John Skein's cabin the warning globe begins to flash, dousing him with red, yellow, green light, going up and down the visible spectrum, giving him some infra- and ultra- too. Not everybody who books passage on this liner necessarily has human sensory equipment. The signal will not go out until Skein is safely in his bottle. Go on, it tells him. Get in. Get in. Panama Canal coming up.

Obediently he rises and moves across the narrow cabin toward the tapering dull-skinned steel container, two and a half meters high, that will protect him against the dimensional stresses of canal insertion. He is a tall, angular man with thin lips, a strong chin, glossy black hair that clings close to his high-vaulted skull. His skin is deeply tanned but his eyes are those of one who has been in winter for some time. This is the fiftieth year of his second go-round. He is traveling alone toward a world of the

Abbondanza system, perhaps the last leg on a journey that has occupied him for several years.

The passenger bottle swings open on its gaudy rhodium-jacketed hinge when its sensors, picking up Skein's mass and thermal output, tell it that its protectee is within entry range. He gets in. It closes and seals, wrapping him in a seamless magnetic field. "Please be seated," the bottle tells him softly. "Place your arms through the stasis loops and your feet in the security platens. When you have done this the pressor fields will automatically be activated and you will be fully insulated against injury during the coming period of turbulence." Skein, who has had plenty of experience with faster-than-light travel, has anticipated the instructions and is already in stasis. The bottle closes. "Do you wish music?" it asks him. "A book? A vision spool? Conversation?"

"Nothing, thanks," Skein says, and waits.

He understands waiting very well by this time. Once he was an impatient man, but this is a thin season in his life, and it has been teaching him the arts of stoic acceptance. He will sit here with the Buddha's own complacency until the ship is through the canal. Silent, alone, self-sufficient. If only there will be no fugues this time. Or, at least—he is negotiating the terms of his torment with his demons—at least let them not be flashforwards. If he must break loose again from the matrix of time, he prefers to be cast only into his yesterdays, never into his tomorrows.

"We are almost into the canal now," the bottle tells him pleasantly.

"It's all right. You don't need to look after me. Just let me know when it's safe to come out."

He closes his eyes. Trying to envision the ship: a fragile glimmering purple needle squirting through clinging blackness, plunging toward the celestial vortex just ahead, the maelstrom of clashing forces, the soup of contravariant tensors. The Panama Canal, so-called. Through which the liner will shortly rush, acquiring during its passage such a garland of borrowed power that it will rip itself free of the standard fourspace; it will emerge on the far side of the canal into a strange, tranquil pocket of the universe where the speed of light is the downside limiting velocity, and no one knows where the upper limit lies.

Alarms sound in the corridor, heavy, resonant: clang, clang, clang. The dislocation is beginning. Skin is braced. What does it look like out there? Folds of glowing black velvet, furry swatches of the disrupted continuum, wrapping themselves around the ship? Titanic lightnings hammering on the hull? Laughing centaurs flashing across the twisted heavens? Despondent masks, fixed in tragic grimaces, dangling between the blurred stars? Streaks of orange, green, crimson: sick rainbows, limp, askew? In we go. *Clang, clang, clang.* The next phase of the voyage now begins. He thinks of his destination, holding an image of it rigidly in mind. The picture is vivid, though this is a world he has visited only in spells of temporal fugue. Too often; he has been there again and again in these moments of disorientation in time. The colors are wrong on that world. Purple sand. Blue-leaved trees. Too much manganese? Too little copper? He will forgive it its colors if it will grant him his answers. And then. Skein feels the familiar ugly throbbing at the base of his neck, as if the tip of his spine is swelling like a balloon. He curses. He tries to resist. As he feared, not even the bottle can wholly protect him against these stresses. Outside the ship the universe is being wrenched apart; some of that slips in here and throws him into a private epilepsy of the timeline. Spacetime is breaking up for him. He will go into fugue. He clings, fighting, knowing it is futile. The currents of time buffet him, knocking him a short distance into the future, then a reciprocal distance into the past, as if he is a bubble of insect spittle glued loosely to a dry reed. He cannot hold on much longer. Let it not be flashforward, he prays, wondering who it is to whom he prays. Let it not be flashforward. And he loses his grip. And shatters. And is swept in shards across time.

Of course, if x *is before* y *then it remains eternally before* y, *and nothing in the passage of time can change this. But the peculiar position of the "now" can be easily expressed simply because our language has tenses. The future* will be, *the present* is, *and the past* was; *the light will be red, it is now yellow, and it was green. But do we, in these terms, really describe the "processional" character of time? We sometimes say that an event* is *future, then it* is *present, and finally it* is *past; and by this means we seem to dispense with tenses, yet we portray the passage of time. But this is really not the case; for all that we have done is to translate our tenses into the words "then" and "finally," and into the order in which we state our clauses. If we were to omit*

*these words or their equivalents, and mix up the clauses, our
sentences would no longer be meaningful. To say that the future,
the present, and the past are in some sense is to dodge the
problem of time by resorting to the tenseless language of logic
and mathematics. In such an atemporal language it would be
meaningful to say that Socrates is mortal because all men are
mortal and Socrates is a man, even though Socrates has been
dead many centuries. But if we cannot describe time either by a
language containing tenses or by a tenseless language, how shall
we symbolize it?*

He feels the curious doubleness of self, the sense of having been
here before, and knows it is flashback. Some comfort in that. He
is a passenger in his own skull, looking out through the eyes of
John Skein on an event that he has already experienced, and
which he now is powerless to alter.

His office. All its gilded magnificence. A crystal dome at the
summit of Kenyatta Tower. With the amplifiers on he can see as
far as Serengeti in one direction, Mombasa in another. Count the
fleas on an elephant in Tsavo Park. A wall of light on the
east-southeast face of the dome, housing his data-access units.
No one can stare at that wall more than thirty seconds without
suffering intensely from a surfeit of information. Except Skein;
he drains nourishment from it, hour after hour.

As he slides into the soul of that earlier Skein he takes a brief
joy in the sight of his office, like Aeneas relishing a vision of
unfallen Troy, like Adam looking back into Eden. How good it
was. That broad sweet desk with its subtle components dedicated
to his service. The gentle psychosensitive carpet, so useful and so
beautiful. The undulating ribbon-sculpture gliding in and out of
the dome's skin, undergoing molecular displacement each time
and forever exhibiting the newest of its infinity of possible
patterns. A rich man's office; he was unabashed in his pursuit of
elegance. He had earned the right to luxury through the intelligent use of his innate skills. Returning now to that lost dome of
wonders, he quickly seizes his moment of satisfaction, aware that
shortly some souring scene of subtraction will be replayed for
him, one of the stages of the darkening and withering of his life.
But which one?

"Send in Coustakis," he hears himself say, and his words give
him the answer. That one. He will again watch his own destruc-

tion. Surely there is no further need to subject him to this particular reenactment. He has been through it at least seven times; he is losing count. An endless spiraling track of torment.

Coustakis is bald, blue-eyed, sharp-nosed, with the desperate look of a man who is near the end of his first go-round and is not yet sure that he will be granted a second. Skein guesses that he is about seventy. The man is unlikable: he dresses coarsely, moves in aggressive blurting little strides, and shows in every gesture and glance that he seethes with envy of the opulence with which Skein surrounds himself. Skein feels no need to like his clients, though. Only to respect. And Coustakis is brilliant; he commands respect.

Skein says, "My staff and I have studied your proposal in great detail. It's a cunning scheme."

"You'll help me?"

"There are risks for me," Skein points out. "Nissenson has a powerful ego. So do you. I could get hurt. The whole concept of synergy involves risk for the Communicator. My fees are calculated accordingly."

"Nobody expects a Communicator to be cheap," Coustakis mutters.

"I'm not. But I think you'll be able to afford me. The question is whether I can afford you."

"You're very cryptic, Mr. Skein. Like all oracles."

Skein smiles. "I'm not an oracle, I'm afraid. Merely a conduit through whom connections are made. I can't foresee the future."

"You can evaluate probabilities."

"Only concerning my own welfare. And I'm capable of arriving at an incorrect evaluation."

Coustakis fidgets. "Will you help me or won't you?"

"The fee," Skein says, "is half a million down, plus an equity position of fifteen percent in the corporation you'll establish with the contacts I provide."

Coustakis gnaws at his lower lip. "So much?"

"Bear in mind that I've got to split my fee with Nissenson. Consultants like him aren't cheap."

"Even so. Ten percent."

"Excuse me, Mr. Coustakis. I really thought we were past the point of negotiation in this transaction. It's going to be a busy day for me, and so—" Skein passes his hand over a black rectangle on his desk and a section of the floor silently opens, uncovering the dropshaft access. He nods toward it. The carpet reveals the colors of Coustakis's mental processes: black for anger, green for greed, red for anxiety, yellow for fear, blue for temptation, all mixed together in the hashed pattern betraying the calculations now going on in his mind. Coustakis will yield. Nevertheless Skein proceeds with the charade of standing, gesturing toward the exit, trying to usher his visitor out. "All right," Coustakis says explosively, "fifteen percent!"

Skein instructs his desk to extrude a contract cube. He says, "Place your hand here, please," and as Coustakis touches the cube he presses his own palm against its opposite face. At once the cube's sleek crystalline surface darkens and roughens as the double sensory output bombards it. Skein says, "Repeat after me. I, Nicholas Coustakis, whose handprint and vibration pattern are being imprinted in this contract as I speak—"

"I, Nicholas Coustakis, whose handprint and vibration pattern are being imprinted in this contract as I speak—"

"—do knowingly and willingly assign to John Skein Enterprises, as payment for professional services to be rendered, an equity interest in Coustakis Transport Ltd. or any successor corporation amounting to—"

"—do knowingly and willingly assign—"

They drone on in turns through a description of Coustakis's corporation and the irrevocable nature of Skein's part ownership in it. Then Skein files the contract cube and says, "If you'll phone your bank and put your thumb on the cash part of the transaction, I'll make contact with Nissenson and you can get started."

"Half a million?"

"Half a million."

"You know I don't have that kind of money."

"Let's not waste time, Mr. Coustakis. You have assets. Pledge them as collateral. Credit is easily obtained."

Scowling, Coustakis applies for the loan, gets it, transfers the funds to Skein's account. The process takes eight minutes; Skein uses the time to review Coustakis's ego profile. It displeases Skein to have to exert such sordid economic pressure; but the service he offers does, after all, expose him to dangers, and he must cushion the risk by high guarantees, in case some mishap should put him out of business.

"Now we can proceed," Skein says, when the transaction is done.

Coustakis has almost invented a system for the economical instantaneous transportation of matter. It will not, unfortunately, ever be useful for living things, since the process involves the destruction of the material being shipped and its virtually simultaneous reconstitution elsewhere. The fragile entity that is the soul cannot withstand the withering blast of Coustakis's transmitter's electron beam. But there is tremendous potential in the freight business; the Coustakis transmitter will be able to send cabbages to Mars, computers to Pluto, and, given the proper linkage facilities, it should be able to reach the inhabited extrasolar planets.

However, Coustakis has not yet perfected his system. For five years he has been stymied by one impassable problem: keeping the beam tight enough between transmitter and receiver. Beam-spread has led to chaos in his experiments; marginal straying results in the loss of transmitted information, so that that which is being sent invariably arrives incomplete. Coustakis has depleted his resources in the unsuccessful search for a solution, and thus has been forced to the desperate and costly step of calling in a Communicator.

For a price, Skein will place him in contact with someone who can solve his problem. Skein has a network of consultants on several worlds, experts in technology and finance and philology and nearly everything else. Using his own mind as the focal nexus, Skein will open telepathic communion between Coustakis and a consultant.

"Get Nissenson into a receptive state," he orders his desk.

Coustakis, blinking rapidly, obviously uneasy, says, "First let me get it clear. This man will see everything that's in my mind? He'll get access to my secrets?"

"No. No. I filter the communion with great care. Nothing will pass from your mind to his except the nature of the problem you want him to tackle. Nothing will come back from his mind to yours except the answer."

"And if he doesn't have the answer?"

"He will."

Skein gives no refunds in the event of failure, but he has never had a failure. He does not accept jobs that he feels will be inherently impossible to handle. Either Nissenson will see the solution Coustakis has been overlooking, or else he will make some suggestion that will nudge Coustakis toward finding the solution himself. The telepathic communion is the vital element. Mere talking would never get anywhere. Coustakis and Nissenson could stare at blueprints together for months, pound computers side by side for years, debate the difficulty with each other for decades, and still they might not hit on the answer. But the communion creates a synergy of minds that is more than a doubling of the available brainpower. A union of perceptions, a heightening, that always produces that mystic flash of insight, that leap of the intellect.

"And if he goes into the transmission business for himself afterward?" Coustakis asks.

"He's bonded," Skein says curtly. "No chance of it. Let's go, now. Up and together."

The desk reports that Nissenson, half the world away in São Paulo, is ready. Skein's power does not vary with distance. Quickly he throws Coustakis into the receptive condition, and swing around to face the brilliant lights of his data-access units. Those sparkling, shifting little blazes kindle his gift, jabbing at the electrical rhythms of his brain until he is lifted into the energy level that permits the opening of a communion. As he starts to go up, the other Skein who is watching, the time-displaced prisoner behind his forehead, tries frenziedly to prevent him from entering the fatal linkage. *Don't. Don't. You'll overload. They're too strong for you.* Easier to halt a planet in its orbit, though. The course of the past is frozen; all this has already happened; the Skein who cries out in silent anguish is merely an observer, necessarily passive, here to view the maiming of his earlier self.

Skein reaches forth one tendril of his mind and engages Nissenson. With another tendril he snares Coustakis. Steadily, now, he draws the two tendrils together.

There is no way to predict the intensity of the forces that will shortly course through his brain. He has done what he could, checking the ego profiles of his client and the consultant, but that really tells him little. What Coustakis and Nissenson may be as individuals hardly matters; it is what they may become in communion that he must fear. Synergistic intensities are unpredictable. He has lived for a lifetime and a half with the possibility of a burnout.

The tendrils meet.

Skein the observer winces and tries to armor himself against the shock. But there is no way to deflect it. Out of Coustakis's mind flows a description of the matter transmitter and a clear statement of the beam-spread problem; Skein shoves it along to Nissenson, who begins to work on a solution. But when their minds join it is immediately evident that their combined strength will be more than Skein can control. This time the synergy will destroy him. But he cannot disengage; he has no mental circuitbreaker. He is caught, trapped, impaled. The entity that is Coustakis/Nissenson will not let go of him, for that would mean its own destruction. A wave of mental energy goes rippling and dancing along the vector of communion from Coustakis to Nissenson and goes bouncing back, pulsating and gaining strength, from Nissenson to Coustakis. A fiery oscillation is set up. Skein sees what is happening; he has become the amplifier of his own doom. The torrent of energy continues to gather power each time it reverberates from Coustakis to Nissenson, from Nissenson to Coustakis. Powerless, Skein watches the energy-pumping effect building up a mighty charge. The discharge is bound to come soon, and he will be the one who must receive it. How long? How long? The juggernaut fills the corridors of his mind. He ceases to know which end of the circuit is Nissenson, which is Coustakis; he perceives only two shining walls of mental power, between which he is stretched ever thinner, a twanging wire of ego, heating up, heating up, glowing now, emitting a searing blast of heat, particles of identity streaming away from him like so many liberated ions—

Then he lies numb and dazed on the floor of his office, grinding his face into the psychosensitive carpet, while Coustakis barks over and over, "Skein? Skein? Skein? Skein?"

Like any other chronometric device, our inner clocks are subject to their own peculiar disorders and, in spite of the substantial concordance between private and public time, discrepancies may occur as the result of sheer inattention. Mach noted that if a doctor focuses his attention on the patient's blood, it may seem to him to squirt out before the lancet enters the skin and, for similar reasons, the feebler of two stimuli presented simultaneously is usually perceived later. . . . Normal life requires the capacity to recall experiences in a sequence corresponding, roughly at least, to the order in which they actually occurred. It requires in addition that our potential recollections should be reasonably accessible to consciousness. These potential recollections mean not only a perpetuation within us of representations of the past, but also a ceaseless interplay between such representations and the uninterrupted input of present information from the external world. Just as our past may be at the service of our present, so the present may be remotely controlled by our past: in the words of Shelley, "Swift as a Thought by the snake Memory stung."

"Skein? Skein? Skein? Skein?"

His bottle is open and they are helping him out. His cabin is full of intruders. Skein recognizes the captain's robot, the medic, and a couple of passengers, the little swarthy man from Pingalore and the woman from Globe Fifteen. The cabin door is open and more people are coming in. The medic makes a cuff-shooting gesture and a blinding haze of metallic white particles wraps itself about Skein's head. The little tingling prickling sensations spur him to wakefulness. "You didn't respond when the bottle told you it was all right," the medic explains. "We're through the canal."

"Was it a good passage? Fine. Fine. I must have dozed."

"If you'd like to come to the infirmary—a routine check, only—put you through the diagnostat—"

"No. No. Will you all please go? I assure you, I'm quite all right."

Reluctantly, clucking over him, they finally leave. Skein gulps cold water until his head is clear. He plants himself flatfooted in mid-cabin, trying to pick up some sensation of forward motion. The ship now is traveling at something like fifteen million miles a second. How long is fifteen million miles? How long is a second? From Rome to Naples it was a morning's drive on the autostrada. From Tel Aviv to Jerusalem was the time between twilight and darkness. San Francisco to San Diego spanned lunch to dinner by superpod. As I slide my right foot two inches forward we traverse fifteen million miles. From where to where? And why? He has not seen Earth in twenty-six months. At the end of this voyage his remaining funds will be exhausted. Perhaps he will have to make his home in the Abbondanza system; he has no return ticket. But of course he can travel to his heart's discontent within his own skull, whipping from point to point along the timeline in the grip of the fugues.

He goes quickly from his cabin to the recreation lounge.

The ship is a second-class vessel, neither lavish nor seedy. It carries about twenty passengers, most of them, like him, bound outward on one-way journeys. He has not talked directly to any of them, but he has done considerable eavesdropping in the lounge, and by now can tag each one of them with the proper dull biography. The wife bravely joining her pioneer husband, whom she has not seen for half a decade. The remittance man under orders to place ten thousand light-years, at the very least, between himself and his parents. The glittery-eyed entrepreneur, a Phoenician merchant sixty centuries after his proper era, off to carve an empire as a middleman's middleman. The tourists. The bureaucrat. The colonel. Among this collection Skein stands out in sharp relief; he is the only one who has not made an effort to know and be known, and the mystery of his reserve tantalizes them.

He carries the fact of his crackup with him like some wrinkled dangling yellowed wen. When his eyes meet those of any of the others he says silently, You see my deformity? I am my own survivor. I have been destroyed and lived to look back on it. Once I was a man of wealth and power, and look at me now. But I ask for no pity. Is that understood?

Hunching at the bar, Skein pushes the node for filtered rum. His drink arrives, and with it comes the remittance man, handsome, young, insinuating. Giving Skein a confidential wink, as if to say, *I* know. You're on the run, too.

"From Earth, are you?" he says to Skein.

"Formerly."

"I'm Pid Rocklin."

"John Skein."

"What were you doing there?"

"On Earth?" Skein shrugs. "A Communicator. I retired four years ago."

"Oh." Rocklin summons a drink. "That's good work, if you have the gift."

"I had the gift," Skein says. The unstressed past tense is as far into self-pity as he will go. He drinks and pushes for another one. A great gleaming screen over the bar shows the look of space: empty, here beyond the Panama Canal, although yesterday a million suns blazed on that ebony rectangle. Skein imagines he can hear the whoosh of hydrogen molecules scraping past the hull at eighty lights. He sees them as blobs of brightness millions of miles long, going *zip!* and *zip!* and *zip!* as the ship spurts along. Abruptly a purple nimbus envelops him and he drops into a flash-forward fugue so quickly there is not even time for the usual futile resistance. "Hey, what's the matter?" Pid Rocklin says, reaching for him. "Are you all—" and Skein loses the universe.

He is on the world that he takes to be Abbondanza VI, and his familiar companion, the skull-faced man, stands beside him at the edge of an oily orange sea. They appear to be having the debate about time once again. The skull-faced man must be at least a hundred and twenty years old; his skin lies against his bones with, seemingly, no flesh at all under it, and his face is all nostrils and burning eyes. Bony sockets, sharp shelves for cheek-bones, a bald dome of a skull. The neck no more than wrist-thick, rising out of shriveled shoulders. Saying, "Won't you ever come to see that causality is merely an illusion, Skein? The notion that there's a consecutive series of events is nothing but a fraud. We impose form on our lives, we talk of time's arrow, we say that there's a flow from A through G and Q to Z, we make believe everything is nicely linear. But it isn't, Skein. It isn't."

"So you keep telling me."

"I feel an obligation to awaken your mind to the truth. G can come before A, and Z before both of them. Most of us don't like to perceive it that way, so we arrange things in what seems like a more logical pattern, just as a novelist will put the motive before the murder and the murder before the arrest. But the universe isn't a novel. We can't make nature imitate art. It's all random, Skein, random, random! Look there. You see what's drifting on the sea?"

On the orange waves tosses the bloated corpse of a shaggy blue beast. Upturned saucery eyes, drooping shout, thick limbs. Why is it not waterlogged by now? What keeps it afloat?"

The skull-faced man says, "Time is an ocean, and events come drifting to us as randomly as dead animals on the waves. We filter them. We screen out what doesn't make sense and admit them to our consciousness in what seems to be the right sequence." He laughs. "The grand delusion! The past is nothing but a series of films slipping unpredictably into the future. And vice versa."

"I won't accept that," Skein says stubbornly. "It's a demonic, chaotic, nihilistic theory. It's idiocy. Are we graybeards before we're children? Do we die before we're born? Do trees devolve into seeds? Deny linearity all you like. I won't go along.''

"You can say that after all you've experienced?"

Skein shakes his head. ''I'll go on saying it. What I've been going through is a mental illness. Maybe I'm deranged, but the universe isn't.''

"Contrary. You've only recently become sane and started to see things as they really are,'' the skull-faced man insists. ''The trouble is that you don't want to admit the evidence you've begun to perceive. Your filters are down, Skein! You've shaken free of the illusion of linearity! Now's your chance to show your resilience. Learn to live with the real reality. Stop this silly business of imposing an artificial order on the flow of time. Why *should* effect follow cause? Why *shouldn't* the seed follow the tree? Why must you persist in holding tight to a useless, outworn, contemptible system of false evaluations of experience when you've managed to break free of the—''

"Stop it! Stop it! Stop it! Stop it!"

"—right, Skein?"

"What happened?"

"You started to fall off your stool," Pid Rocklin says. "You turned absolutely white. I thought you were having some kind of a stroke."

"How long was I unconscious?"

"Oh, three, four seconds, I suppose. I grabbed you and propped you up, and your eyes opened. Can I help you to your cabin? Or maybe you ought to go to the infirmary.''

"Excuse me," Skein says hoarsely, and leaves the lounge.

When the hallucinations began, not long after the Coustakis overload, he assumed at first that they were memory disturbances produced by the fearful jolt he had absorbed. Quite clearly most of them involved scenes of his past, which he would relive, during the moments of fugue, with an intensity so brilliant that he felt he had actually been thrust back into time. He did not merely recollect, but rather he experienced the past anew, following a script from which he could not deviate as he spoke and felt and reacted. Such strange excursions into memory could be easily enough explained: his brain had been damaged, and it was heaving old segments of experience into view in some kind of attempt to clear itself of debris and heal the wounds. But while the flashbacks were comprehensible, the flashforwards were not, and he did not recognize them at all for what they actually were. Those scenes of himself wandering alien worlds, those phantom conversations with people he had never met, those views of spaceliner cabins and transit booths and unfamiliar hotels and passenger terminals, seemed merely to be fantasies, random fictions of his injured brain. Even when he started to notice that there was a consistent pattern to these feverish glimpses of the unknown, he still did not catch on. It appeared as though he was seeing himself performing a sort of quest, or perhaps a pilgrimage; the slices of unexperienced experience that he was permitted to see began to fit into a coherent structure of travel and seeking. And certain scenes and conversations recurred, yes, sometimes several times the same day, the script always the same, so that he began to learn a few of the scenes word for word. Despite the solid texture of these episodes, he persisted in thinking of them as mere brief flickering segments of nightmare. He could not imagine why the injury to his brain was causing him to have these waking dreams of long space voyages and unknown planets, so vivid and so momentarily real, but they seemed no more frightening to him than the equally vivid flashbacks.

Only after a while, when many months had passed since the Coustakis incident, did the truth strike him. One day he found himself living through an episode that he considered to be one of his fantasies. It was a minor thing, one that he had experienced, in whole or in part, seven or eight times. What he had seen, in fitful bursts of uninvited delusion, was himself in a public garden on some hot spring morning, standing before an immense baroque building while a grotesque group of nonhuman tourists filed past him in a weird creaking, clanking procession of inhalator suits and breather-wheels and ion-disperser masks. That was all. Then it happened that a harrowing legal snarl brought him to a city in North Carolina about fourteen months after the overload, and, after having put in his appearance at the courthouse, he set out on a long walk through the grimy, decayed metropolis, and came, as if by an enchantment, to a huge metal gate behind which he could see a dark sweep of lavish forest, oaks and rhododendrons and magnolias, laid out in an elegant formal manner. It was, according to a sign posted by the gate, the estate of a nineteenth-century millionaire, now open to all and preserved in its ancient state despite the encroachments of the city on its borders.

Skein bought a ticket and went in, on foot, hiking for what seemed like miles through cool leafy glades, until abruptly the path curved and he emerged into the bright sunlight and saw before him the great gray bulk of a colossal mansion, hundreds of rooms topped by parapets and spires, with a massive portico from which vast columns of stairs descended. In wonder he moved toward it, for this was the building of his frequent fantasy, and as he approached he beheld the red and green and purple figures crossing the portico, those coiled and gnarled and looping shapes he had seen before, the eerie horde of alien travelers here to take in the wonders of Earth. Heads without eyes, eyes without heads, multiplicities of limbs and absences of limbs, bodies like tumors and tumors like bodies, all the universe's imagination on display in these agglomerated life forms, so strange and yet not at all strange to him. But this time it was no fantasy. It fit smoothly into the sequence of the events of the day, rather than dropping, dreamlike, intrusive, into that sequence. Nor did it fade after a few moments; the scene remained sharp, never leaving him to plunge back into "real" life. This was reality itself, and he had experienced it before.

Twice more in the next few weeks things like that happened to him, until at last he was ready to admit the truth to himself about his fugues, that he was experiencing flashforwards as well as flashbacks, that he was being subjected to glimpses of his own future.

T'ang, the high king of the Shang, asked Hsia Chi saying, "In the beginning, were there already individual things?" Hsia Chi replied, "If there were no things then, how could there be any now? If later generations should pretend that there had been no things in our time, would they be right?" T'ang said, "Have things then no before and no after?" To which Hsia Chi replied, "The ends and the origins of things have no limit from which they began. The origin of one thing may be considered the end of another; the end of one may be considered the origin of the next. Who can distinguish accurately between these cycles? What lies beyond all things, and before all events, we cannot know."

*   *   *

They reach and enter the Perseus relay booster, which is a whirling celestial anomaly structurally similar to the Panama Canal but not nearly so potent, and it kicks the ship's velocity to just above a hundred lights. That is the voyage's final acceleration; the ship will maintain this rate for two and a half days, until it clocks in at Scylla, the main deceleration station for this part of the galaxy, where it will be seized by a spongy web of forces twenty light-minutes in diameter and slowed to sublight velocities for the entry into the Abbondanza system.

Skein spends nearly all of this period in his cabin, rarely eating and sleeping very little. He reads almost constantly, obsessively dredging from the ship's extensive library a wide and capricious assortment of books. Rilke. Kafka. Eddington, *The Nature of the Physical World*. Lowry, *Hear Us O Lord From Heaven Thy Dwelling Place*. Elias. Razhuminin. Dickey. Pound. Fraisse, *The Psychology of Time*. Greene, *Dream and Delusion*. Poe. Shakespeare. Marlowe. Tourneur. *The Waste Land*. *Ulysses*. *Heart of Darkness*. Bury, *The Idea of Progress*. Jung. Büchner. Pirandello. *The Magic Mountain*. Ellis, *The Rack*. Cervantes. Blenheim. Fierst. Keats. Nietzsche. His mind swims with images and bits of verse, with floating sequences of dialogue, with unscaffolded dialectics. He dips into each work briefly, magpielike, seeking bright scraps. The words form a scaly impasto on the inner surface of his skull. He finds that this heavy verbal overdose helps, to some slight extent, to fight off the fugues; his mind is weighted, perhaps, bound by this leaden clutter of borrowed genius to the moving line of the present, and during his debauch of reading he finds himself shifting off that line less frequently than in the recent past.

His mind whirls. *Man is a rope stretched between the animal and the Superman—A rope over an abyss*. My patience are exhausted. *See, see where Christ's blood streams in the firmament! One drop would save my soul*. I had not thought death had undone so many. These fragments I have shored against my ruins. *Hoogspanning. Levensgevaar. Peligro de Muerte. Electricidad. Danger*. Give me my spear. *Old father, old artificer, stand me now and ever in good stead*. You like this garden? Why is it yours? We evict those who destroy! *And then went down to the ship, set keel to breakers, forth on the godly sea*. There is no "official" theory of time, defined in creeds or universally agreed upon among Christians. Christianity is not concerned with the purely scientific aspects of the subject nor, within wide limits, with its philosophical analysis, except insofar as it is committed to a fundamentally realist view and could not admit, as some Eastern philosophies have done, that temporal existence is mere illusion. *A shudder in the loins engenders there the broken wall, the burning roof and tower and Agamemnon dead.* Stately, plump Buck Mulligan came from the stairhead, bearing a bowl of lather on which a mirror and a razor lay crossed. *In what distant deeps or skies burnt the fire of thine eyes? On what wings dare he aspire? What the hand dare seize the fire?* These fragments I have shored against my ruins. Hieronymo's mad againe. *Then felt I like some watcher of the skies when a new planet swims into his ken.* It has also lately been postulated that the physical concept of information is identical with a phenomenon of reversal of entropy. The psychologist must add a few remarks here: It does not seem convincing to me that information is *eo ipso* identical with a *pouvoir d'organisation* which undoes entropy. *Datta. Dayadhvam. Damyata. Shantih shantih shantih*

Nevertheless, once the ship is past Scylla and slowing toward the Abbondanza planets, the periods of fugue become frequent once again, so that he lives entrapped, shuttling between the flashing shadows of yesterday and tomorrow.

After the Coustakis overload he tried to go on in the old way, as best he could. He gave Coustakis a refund without even being asked, for he had been of no service, nor could he ever be. Instantaneous transportation of matter would have to wait. But Skein took other clients. He could still make the communion, after a fashion, and when the nature of the task was sufficiently low-level he could even deliver a decent synergetic response.

Often his work was unsatisfactory, however. Contacts would break at awkward moments, or, conversely, his filter mechanism would weaken and he would allow the entire contents of his client's mind to flow into that of his consultant. The results of such disasters were chaotic, involving him in heavy medical expenses and sometimes in damage suits. He was forced to place his fees on a contingency basis: no synergy, no pay. About half the time he earned nothing for his output of energy. Meanwhile his overhead remained the same as always: the domed office, the network of consultants, the research staff, and the rest. His effort to remain in business was eating rapidly into the bank accounts he had set aside against just such a time of storm.

They could find no organic injury to his brain. Of course, so little was known about a Communicator's gift that it was impossible to determine much by medical analysis. If they could not locate the center from which a Communicator powered his communions, how could they detect the place where he had been hurt? The medical archives were of no value; there had been eleven previous cases of overload, but each instance was physiologically unique. They told him he would eventually heal, and sent him away. Sometimes the doctors gave him silly therapies: counting exercises, rhythmic blinkings, hopping on his left leg and then his right, as if he had a stroke. But he had not had a stroke.

For a time he was able to maintain his business on the momentum of his reputation. Then, as word got around that he had been hurt and was no longer any good, clients stopped coming. Even the contingency basis for fees failed to attract them. Within six months he found that he was lucky to find a client a week. He reduced his rates, and that seemed only to make things worse, so he raised them to something not far below what they had been at the time of the overload. For a while the pace of business increased, as if people were getting the impression that Skein had recovered. He gave such spotty service, though. Blurred and wavering communions, unanticipated positive feedbacks, filtering problems, information deficiencies, redundancy surpluses—"You take your mind in your hands when you go to Skein," they were saying now.

The fugues added to his professional difficulties.

He never knew when he would snap into hallucination. It might happen during a communion, and often did. Once he dropped back to the moment of the Coustakis-Nissenson hookup and treated a terrified client to a replay of his overload. Once, although he did not understand at the time what was happening, he underwent a flashforward and carried the client with him to a scarlet jungle on a formaldehyde world, and when Skein slipped back to reality the client remained in the scarlet jungle. There was a damage suit over that one, too.

Temporal dislocation plagued him into making poor guesses. He took on clients whom he could not possibly serve and wasted his time on them. He turned away people whom he might have been able to help to his own profit. Since he was no longer anchored firmly to his time-line, but drifted in random oscillations of twenty years or more in either direction, he forfeited the keen sense of perspective on which he had previously founded his professional judgments. He grew haggard and lean, also. He passed through a tempest of spiritual doubts that amounted to total submission and then total rejection of faith within the course of four months. He changed lawyers almost weekly. He liquidated assets with invariably catastrophic timing to pay his cascading bills.

A year and a half after the overload, he formally renounced his registration and closed his office. It took six months more to settle the remaining damage suits. Then, with what was left of his money, he bought a spaceliner ticket and set out to search for a world with purple sand and blue-leaved trees, where, unless his fugues had played him false, he might be able to arrange for the repair of his broken mind.

Now the ship has returned to the conventional four-space and dawdles planetward to something rather less than half the speed of light. Across the screens there spreads a necklace of stars; space is crowded here. The captain will point out Abbondanza to anyone who asks: a lemon-colored sun, bigger than that of Earth, surrounded by a dozen bright planetary pips. The passengers are excited. They buzz, twitter, speculate, anticipate. No one is silent except Skein. He is aware of many love affairs; he has had to reject several offers just in the past three days. He has given up reading and is trying to purge his mind of all he has stuffed into it. The fugues have grown worse. He has to write notes to himself, saying things like *You are a passenger aboard a ship heading for Abbondanza VI, and will be landing in a few days*, so that he does not forget which of his three entangled timelines is the true one.

Suddenly he is with Nilla on the island in the Gulf of Mexico, getting aboard the little excursion boat. Time stands still here; it could almost be the twentieth century. The frayed, sagging cords of the rigging. The lumpy engine inefficiently converted from internal combustion to turbines. The mustachioed Mexican bandits who will be their guides today. Nilla, nervously coiling her long blonde hair, saying, "Will I get seasick, John? The boat rides right in the water, doesn't it? It won't even hover a little bit?"

"Terribly archaic," Skein says. "That's why we're here."

The captain gestures them aboard. Juan, Francisco, Sebastián. Brothers. *Los hermanos*. Yards of white teeth glistening below the drooping mustaches. With a terrible roar the boat moves away from the dock. Soon the little town of crumbling pastel buildings is out of sight and they are heading jaggedly eastward along the coast, green shoreward water on their left, the blue depths on the right. The morning sun coming up hard. "Could I sunbathe?" Nilla asks. Unsure of herself; he has never seen her this way, so hesitant, so abashed. Mexico has robbed her of her New York assurance. "Go ahead," Skein says. "Why not?" She drops her robe. Underneath she wears only a waist-strap; her heavy breasts look white and vulnerable in the tropic glare, and the small nipples are a faded pink. Skein sprays her with protective sealant and she sprawls out on the deck. *Los hermanos* stare hungrily and talk to each other in low rumbling tones. Not Spanish. Mayan, perhaps? The natives have never learned to adopt the tourists' casual nudity here. Nilla, obviously still uneasy, rolls over and lies face down. Her broad smooth back glistens.

Juan and Francisco yell. Skein follows their pointing fingers. Porpoises! A dozen of them, frisking around the bow, keeping just ahead of the boat, leaping high and slicing down into the blue water. Nilla gives a little cry of joy and rushes to the side to get a closer look. Throwing her arm self-consciously across her bare breasts. "You don't need to do that," Skein murmurs. She keeps herself covered. "How lovely they are," she says softly. Sebastián comes up beside them. *'Amigos,''* he says. "They are. My friends." The cavorting porpoises eventually disappear. The boat bucks bouncily onward, keeping close to the island's beautiful empty palmy shore. Later they anchor, and he and Nilla swim masked, spying on the coral gardens. When they haul themselves on deck again it is almost noon. The sun is terrible. "Lunch?" Francisco asks. "We make you good lunch now?" Nilla laughs. She is no longer hiding her body. "I'm starved!" she cries.

"We make you good lunch," Francisco says, grinning, and he and Juan go over the side. In the shallow water they are clearly visible near the white sand of the bottom. They have spear guns; they hold their breaths and prowl. Too late Skein realizes what they are doing. Francisco hauls a fluttering spiny lobster out from behind a rock. Juan impales a huge pale crab. He grabs three conchs also, surfaces, dumps his prey on the deck. Francisco arrives with the lobster. Juan, below again, spears a second lobster. The animals are not dead; they crawl sadly in circles on the deck as they dry. Appalled, Skein turns to Sebastián and says, "Tell them to stop. We're not that hungry." Sebastián, preparing some kind of salad, smiles and shrugs. Francisco has brought up another crab, bigger than the first. "Enough," Skein says. *"Basta! Basta!"* Juan, dripping, tosses down three more conchs. "You pay us good," he says. "We give you good lunch." Skein shakes his head. The deck is becoming a slaughterhouse for ocean life. Sebastián now energetically slits conch shells, extracts the meat, drops it into a vast bowl to marinate in a yellow-green fluid. *"Basta!"* Skein yells. Is that the right word in Spanish? He knows it's right in Italian. *Los hermanos* look amused. The sea is full of life, they seem to be telling him. We give you good lunch. Suddenly Francisco erupts from the water, bearing something immense. A turtle! Forty, fifty pounds! The joke has gone too far. "No," Skein says. "Listen, I have to forbid this. Those turtles are almost extinct. Do you understand that? *Muerto. Perdido. Desaparecido.* I won't eat a turtle. Throw it back. Throw it back." Francisco smiles. He shakes his head. Deftly he binds the turtle's flippers with rope. Juan says, "Not for lunch, señor. For us. For to sell. *Mucho dinero.*" Skein can do nothing. Francisco and Sebastián have begun to hack up the crabs and lobsters. Juan slices peppers into the bowl where the conchs are marinating. Pieces of dead animals litter the deck. "Oh, I'm *starving*," Nilla says. Her waist-strap is off too, now. The turtle watches the whole scene, beady-eyed. Skein shudders. Auschwitz, he thinks. Buchenwald. For the animals it's Buchenwald every day.

Purple sand, blue-leaved trees. An orange sea gleaming not far to the west under a lemon sun. "It isn't much farther," the skull-faced man says. "You can make it. Step by step by step is how."

"I'm winded," Skein says. "Those hills—"

"I'm twice your age, and I'm doing fine."

"You're in better shape. I've been cooped up on spaceships for months and months."

"Just a short way on," says the skull-faced man. "About a hundred meters from the shore."

Skein struggles on. The heat is frightful. He has trouble getting a footing in the shifting sand. Twice he trips over black vines whose fleshy runners form a mat a few centimeters under the surface; loops of the vines stick up here and there. He even suffers a brief fugue, a seven-second flashback to a day in Jerusalem. Somewhere at the core of his mind he is amused by that: a flashback within a flashforward. Encapsulated concentric hallucinations. When he comes out of it, he finds himself getting to his feet and brushing sand from his clothing. Ten steps onward the skull-faced man halts him and says, "There it is. Look there, in the pit."

Skein sees a funnel-shaped crater right in front of him, perhaps five meters in diameter at ground level and dwindling to about half that width at its bottom, some six or seven meters down. The pit strikes him as a series of perfect circles making up a truncated cone. Its sides are smooth and firm, almost glazed, and the sand has a brown tinge. In the pit, resting peacefully on the flat floor, is something that looks like a golden amoeba the size of a large cat. A row of round blue-black eyes crosses the hump of its back. From the perimeter of its body comes a soft green radiance.

"Go down to it," the skull-faced man says. "The force of its power falls off with the cube of the distance; from up here you can't feel it. Go down. Let it take you over. Fuse with it. Make communion, Skein, make communion!"

"And will it heal me? So that I'll function as I did before the trouble started?"

"If you let it heal you, it will. That's what it wants to do. It's a completely benign organism. It thrives on repairing broken souls. Let it into your head, let it find the damaged place. You can trust it. Go down."

Skein trembles on the edge of the pit. The creature below flows and eddies, becoming first long and narrow, then high and squat, then resuming its basically circular form. Its color deepens almost to scarlet, and its radiance shifts toward yellow. As if preening and stretching itself. It seems to be waiting for him. It seems eager. This is what he has sought so long, going from planet to wearying planet. The skull-faced man, the purple sand, the pit, the creature. Skein slips his sandals off. *What have I to lose?* He sits for a moment on the pit's rim; then he shimmies down, sliding part of the way, and lands softly, close beside the being that awaits him. And immediately feels its power.

He enters the huge desolate cavern that is the cathedral of Haghia Sophia. A few Turkish guides lounge hopefully against the vast

marble pillars. Tourists shuffle about, reading to each other from
cheap plastic guidebooks. A shaft of light enters from some
improbable aperture and splinters against the Moslem pulpit. It
seems to Skein that he hears the tolling of bells and feels incense
prickling at his nostrils. But how can that be? No Christian rites
have been performed here in a thousand years. A Turk looms
before him. "Show you the mosyics?" he says. *Mosyics.* "Help
you understand this marvelous building? A dollar. No? Maybe
change money? A good rate. Dollars, marks, Eurocredits, what?
You speak English? Show you the mosyics?" The Turk fades.
The bells grow louder. A row of bowed priests in white silk robes
files past the altar, chanting in—what? Greek? The ceiling is
encrusted with gems. Gold plate gleams everywhere. Skein
senses the terrible complexity of the cathedral, teeming now with
life, a whole universe engulfed in this gloom, a thousand chapels
packed with worshippers, long lines waiting to urinate in the
crypts, a marketplace in the balcony, jeweled necklaces changing
hands with low murmurs of negotiation, babies being born
behind the alabaster sarcophagi, the bells tolling, dukes nodding
to one another, clouds of incense swirling toward the dome, the
figures in the mosaics alive, making the sign of the Cross,
smiling, blowing kisses, the pillars moving now, becoming fat-
middled as they bend from side to side, the entire colossal
structure shifting and flowing and melting. And a ballet of Turks.
"Show you the mosyics?" "Change money?" "Postcards? Souvenir of Istanbul?" A plump, pink American face: "You're John
Skein, aren't you? The Communicator? We worked together on
the big fusion-chamber merger in '53." Skein shakes his head.
"It must be that you are mistaken," he says, speaking in Italian.
"I am not he. Pardon. Pardon." And joins the line of chanting
priests.

Purple sand, blue-leaved trees. An orange sea under a lemon sun.
Looking out from the top deck of the terminal, an hour after
landing, Skein sees a row of towering hotels rising along the
nearby beach. At once he feels the wrongness: there should be no
hotels. The right planet has no such towers; therefore this is
another of the wrong ones.

He suffers from complete disorientation as he attempts to place
himself in sequence. *Where am I?* Aboard a liner heading toward
Abbondanza VI. *What do I see?* A world I have previously

visited. *Which one?* The one with the hotels. The third out of seven, isn't it?

He has seen this planet before, in flashforwards. Long before he left Earth to begin his quest he glimpsed those hotels, that beach. Now he views it in flashback. That perplexes him. He must try to see himself as a moving point traveling through time, viewing the scenery now from this perspective, now from that.

He watches his earlier self at the terminal. Once it was his future self. How confusing, how needlessly muddling! "I'm looking for an old Earthman," he says. "He must be a hundred, hundred-twenty years old. A face like a skull—no flesh at all, really. A brittle man. No? Well, can you tell me, does this planet have a life-form about this big, a kind of blob of golden jelly, that lives in pits down by the seashore, and—no? No? Ask someone else, you say? Of course. And perhaps a hotel room? As long as I've come all this way."

He is getting tired of finding the wrong planets. What folly this is, squandering his last savings on a quest for a world seen in a dream! He would have expected planets with purple sand and blue-leaved trees to be uncommon, but no, in an infinite universe one can find a dozen of everything, and now he has wasted almost half his money and close to a year, visiting two planets and this one and not finding what he seeks.

He goes to the hotel they arrange for him.

The beach is packed with sunbathers, most of them from Earth. Skein walks among them. "Look," he wants to say, "I have this trouble with my brain, an old injury, and it gives me these visions of myself in the past and future, and one of the visions I see is a place where there's a skull-faced man who takes me to a kind of amoeba in a pit that can heal me, do you follow? And it's a planet with purple sand and blue-leaved trees, just like this one, and I figure if I keep going long enough I'm bound to find it and the skull-face and the amoeba, do you follow me? And maybe this is the planet after all, only I'm in the wrong part of it. What should I do? What hope do you think I really have?" This is the third world. He knows that he must visit a number of wrong ones before he finds the right one. But how many? How many? And when will he know that he has the right one?

Standing silent on the beach, he feels confusion come over him, and drops into fugue, and is hurled to another world. Purple sand, blue-leaved trees. A fat, friendly Pingalorian consul. "A skull-faced man? No, I can't say I know of any." Which world is this, Skein wonders? One that I have already visited, or one that I have not yet come to? The manifold layers of illusion dazzle him. Past and future and present lie like a knot around his throat. Shifting planes of reality; intersecting films of event. Purple sand, blue-leaved trees. Which planet is this? Which one? Which one? He is back on the crowded beach. A lemon sun. An orange sea. He is back in his cabin on the spaceliner. He sees a note in his own handwriting: *You are a passenger aboard a ship heading for Abbondanza VI, and will be landing in a few days.* So everything was a vision. Flashback? Flashforward? He is no longer able to tell. He is baffled by these identical worlds. Purple sand. Blue-leaved trees. He wishes he knew how to cry.

Instead of a client and a consultant for today's communion, Skein has a client and a client. A man and a woman, Michaels and Miss Schumpeter. The communion is of an unusually intimate kind. Michaels has been married six times, and several of the marriages apparently have been dissolved under bitter circumstances. Miss Schumpeter, a woman of some wealth, loves Michaels but doesn't entirely trust him; she wants a peep into his mind before she'll put her thumb to the marital cube. Skein will oblige. The fee has already been credited to his account. Let me not to the marriage of true minds admit impediments. If she does not like what she finds in her beloved's soul, there may not be any marriage, but Skein will have been paid.

A tendril of his mind goes to Michaels, now. A tendril to Miss Schumpeter. Skein opens his filters. "Now you'll meet for the first time," he tells them. Michaels flows to her. Miss Schumpeter flows to him. Skein is merely the conduit. Through him pass the ambitions, betrayals, failures, vanities, deteriorations, disputes, treacheries, lusts, generosities, shames, and follies of these two human beings. If he wishes, he can examine the most private sins of Miss Schumpeter and the darkest yearnings of her future husband. But he does not care. He sees such things every day. He takes no pleasure in spying on the psyches of these two. Would a surgeon grow excited over the sight of Miss Schumpeter's Fallopian tubes or Michaels's pancreas? Skein is merely doing his job. He is no voyeur, simply a Communicator. He looks upon himself as a public utility.

When he severs the contact, Miss Schumpeter and Michaels both are weeping.

"I love you!" she wails.

"Get away from me!" he mutters.

Purple sand. Blue-leaved trees. Oily orange sea.

The skull-faced man says, "Won't you ever come to see that causality is merely an illusion, Skein? The notion that there's a consecutive series of events is nothing but a fraud. We impose form on our lives, we talk of time's arrow, we say that there's a flow from A through G and Q to Z, we make believe everything is nicely linear. But it isn't, Skein. It isn't."

"So you keep telling me."

"I feel an obligation to awaken your mind to the truth. G can come before A, and Z before both of them. Most of us don't like to perceive it that way, so we arrange things in what seems like a more logical pattern, just as a novelist will put the motive before the murder and the murder before the arrest. But the universe isn't a novel. We can't make nature imitate art. It's all random, Skein, random, random!"

"Half a million?"

"Half a million."

"You know I don't have that kind of money."

"Let's not waste time, Mr. Coustakis. You have assets. Pledge them as collateral. Credit is easily obtained." Skein waits for the inventor to clear his loan. "Now we can proceed," he says, and tells his desk, "Get Nissenson into a receptive state."

Coustakis says, "First let me get it clear. This man will see everything that's in my mind? He'll get access to my secrets?"

"No. No. I filter the communion with great care. Nothing will pass from your mind to his except the nature of the problem you want him to tackle. Nothing will come back from his mind to yours except the answer."

"And if he doesn't have the answer?"

"He will."

"And if he goes into the transmission business for himself afterward?"

"He's bonded," Skein says curtly. "No chance of it. Let's go, now. Up and together."

"Skein? Skein? Skein? Skein?"

*   *   *

The wind is rising. The sand, blown aloft, stains the sky gray. Skein clambers from the pit and lies by its rim, breathing hard. The skull-faced man helps him get up.

Skein has seen this series of images hundreds of times.

"How do you feel?" the skull-faced man asks.

"Strange. Good. My head seems so clear!"

"You had communion down there?"

"Oh, yes. Yes."

"And?"

"I think I'm healed," Skein says in wonder. "My strength is back. Before, you know, I felt cut down to the bone, a minimum version of myself. And now. And now." He lets a tendril of consciousness slip forth. It meets the mind of the skull-faced man. Skein is aware of a glassy interface; he can touch the other mind, but he cannot enter it. "Are you a Communicator too?" Skein asks, awed.

"In a sense. I feel you touching me. You're better, aren't you?"

"Much. Much. Much."

"As I told you. Now you have your second chance, Skein. Your gift has been restored. Courtesy of our friend in the pit. They love being helpful."

"Skein? Skein? Skein? Skein?"

We conceive of time either as flowing or as enduring. The problem is how to reconcile these concepts. From a purely formalistic point of view there exists no difficulty, as these properties can be reconciled by means of the concept of a duratio successiva. *Every unit of time measure has this characteristic of a flowing permanence: an hour streams by while it lasts and so long as it lasts. Its flowing is thus identical with its duration. Time, from this point of view, is transitory; but its passing away lasts.*

In the early months of his affliction he experienced a great many scenes of flashforward while in fugue. He saw himself outside the nineteenth-century mansion, he saw himself in a dozen lawyers' offices, he saw himself in hotels, terminals, spaceliners, he saw himself discussing the nature of time with the skull-faced man, he saw himself trembling on the edge of the pit, he saw himself emerging healed, he saw himself wandering from world to world,

looking for the right one with purple sand and blue-leaved trees.
As time unfolded most of these flashforwards duly entered the
flow of the present; he *did* come to the mansion, he *did* go to
those hotels and terminals, he *did* wander those useless worlds.
Now, as he approaches Abbondanza VI, he goes through a great
many flashbacks and a relatively few flashforwards, and the
flashforwards seem to be limited to a fairly narrow span of time,
covering his landing on Abbondanza VI, his first meeting with
the skull-faced man, his journey to the pit, and his emergence,
healed, from the amoeba's lair. Never anything beyond that final
scene. He wonders if time is going to run out for him on
Abbondanza VI.

The ship lands on Abbondanza VI half a day ahead of schedule.
There are the usual decontamination procedures to endure, and
while they are going on Skein rests in his cabin, counting
minutes to liberty. He is curiously confident that this will be the
world on which he finds the skull-faced man and the benign
amoeba. Of course, he has felt that way before, looking out from
other spaceliners at other planets of the proper coloration, and he
has been wrong. But the intensity of his confidence is something
new. He is sure that the end of his quest lies here.

"Debarkation beginning now," the loudspeakers say.

He joins the line of outgoing passengers. The others smile,
embrace, whisper; they have found friends or even mates on this
voyage. He remains apart. No one says goodbye to him. He
emerges into a brightly lit terminal, a great cube of glass that
looks like all the other terminals scattered across the thousands of
worlds that man has reached. He could be in Chicago or
Johannesburg or Beirut: the scene is one of porters, reservations
clerks, customs officials, hotel agents, taxi drivers, guides. A
blight of sameness spreading across the universe. Stumbling
through the customs gate, Skein finds himself set upon. Does he
want a taxi, a hotel room, a woman, a man, a guide, a homestead
plot, a servant, a ticket to Abbondanza VII, a private car, an
interpreter, a bank, a telephone? The hubbub jolts Skein into
three consecutive ten-second fugues, all flashbacks; he sees a
rainy day in Tierra del Fuego, he conducts a communion to help a
maker of sky-spectacles perfect the plot of his latest extravagan-
za, and he puts his palm to a cube in order to dictate contract
terms to Nicholas Coustakis. Then Coustakis fades, the terminal

reappears, and Skein realizes that someone has seized him by the left arm just above the elbow. Bony fingers dig painfully into his flesh. It is the skull-faced man. "Come with me," he says. "I'll take you where you want to go."

"This isn't just another flashforward, is it?" Skein asks, as he has watched himself ask so many times in the past. "I mean, you're really here to get me."

The skull-faced man says, as Skein has heard him say so many times in the past, "No, this time it's no flashforward. I'm really here to get you."

"Thank God. Thank God. Thank God."

"Follow along this way. You have your passport handy?"

The familiar words. Skein is prepared to discover he is merely in fugue, and expects to drop back into frustrating reality at any moment. But no. The scene does not waver. It holds firm. It holds. At last he has caught up with this particular scene, overtaking it and enclosing it, pearl-like, in the folds of the present. He is on the way out of the terminal. The skull-faced man helps him through the formalities. How withered he is! How fiery the eyes, how gaunt the face! Those frightening orbits of bone jutting through the skin of the forehead. That parched cheek. Skein listens for a dry rattle of ribs. One sturdy punch and there would be nothing left but a cloud of white dust, slowly settling.

"I know your difficulty," the skull-faced man says. "You've been caught in entropy's jaws. You're being devoured. The injury to your mind—it's tipped you into a situation you aren't able to handle. You *could* handle it, if you'd only learn to adapt to the nature of the perceptions you're getting now. But you won't do that, will you? And you want to be healed. Well, you can be healed here, all right. More or less healed. I'll take you to the place."

"What do you mean, I could handle it, if I'd only learn to adapt?"

"Your injury has liberated you. It's shown you the truth about time. But you refuse too see it."

"What truth?" Skein asks flatly.

"You still try to think that time flows neatly from alpha to omega, from yesterday through today to tomorrow," the skull-faced man says, as they walk slowly through the terminal. "But it doesn't. The idea of the forward flow of time is a deception we impose on ourselves in childhood. An abstraction, agreed upon by common convention, to make it easier for us to cope with phenomena. The truth is that events are random, that chronological flow is only our joint hallucination, that if time can be said to flow at all, it flows in all 'directions' at once. Therefore—''

"Wait," Skein says. "How do you explain the laws of thermodynamics? Entropy increases, available energy constantly diminishes, the universe heads toward ultimate stasis."

"Does it?"

"The second law of thermodynamics—"

"Is an abstraction," the skull-faced man says, "which unfortunately fails to correspond with the situation in the true universe. It isn't a divine law. It's a mathematical hypothesis developed by men who weren't able to perceive the real situation. They did their best to account for the data within a framework they could understand. Their laws are formulations of probability, based on conditions that hold within closed systems, and given the right closed system the second law is useful and illuminating. But in the universe as a whole it simply isn't true. There *is* no arrow of time. Entropy does *not* necessarily increase. Natural processes *can* be reversible. Causes do *not* invariably precede effects. In fact, the concepts of cause and effect are empty. There are neither causes nor effects, but only events, spontaneously generated, which we arrange in our minds in comprehensible patterns of sequence."

"No," Skein mutters. "This is insanity!"

"There are no patterns. Everything is random."

"No."

"Why not admit it? Your brain has been injured. What was destroyed was the center of temporal perception, the node that humans use to impose this unreal order on events. Your time filter has burned out. The past and the future are as accessible to you as the present, Skein: you can go where you like, you can watch events drifting past as they really do. Only you haven't been able to break up your old habits of thought. You still try to impose the conventional entropic order on things, even though you lack the mechanism to do it, now, and the conflict between what you perceive and what you think you perceive is driving you crazy. Eh?"

"How do you know so much about me?"

The skull-faced man chuckles. "I was injured in the same way

as you. I was cut free from the timeline long ago, through the
kind of overload you suffered. And I've had years to come to
terms with the new reality. I was as terrified as you were, at first.
But now I understand. I move about freely. I know things,
Skein." A rasping laugh. "You need rest, though. A room, a
bed. Time to think things over. Come. There's no rush now.
You're on the right planet; you'll be all right soon."

*Further, the association of entropy increase with time's arrow is
in no sense circular; rather, it both tells us something about what
will happen to natural systems in time, and about what the time
order must be for a series of states of a system. Thus, we may
often establish a time order among a set of events by use of the
time-entropy association, free from any reference to clocks and
magnitudes of time intervals from the present. In actual judgments of before-after we frequently do this on the basis of our
experience (even though without any explicit knowledge of the
law of entropy increase): we know, for example, that for iron in
air the state of pure metal must have been before that of a rusted
surface, or that the clothes will be dry after, not before, they have
hung in the hot sun.*

A tense, humid night of thunder and temporal storms. Lying
alone in his oversize hotel room, five kilometers from the purple
shore, Skein suffers fiercely from fugue.

"Listen, I have to forbid this. Those turtles are almost extinct.
Do you understand that? *Muerto. Perdido. Desaparecido.* I won't
eat a turtle. Throw it back. Throw it back."

"I'm happy to say your second go-round has been approved, Mr.
Skein. Not that there was ever any doubt. A long and happy new
life to you, sir."

"Go down to it. The force of its power falls off with the cube of
the distance; from up here you can't feel it. Go down. Let it take
you over. Fuse with it. Make communion, Skein, make
communion!"

"Show you the mosyics? Help you understand this marvelous
building? A dollar. No? Maybe change money? A good rate."

* * *

"First let me get it clear. This man will see everything that's in my mind? He'll get access to my secrets?"

"I love you."
  "Get away from me!"

"Won't you ever come to see that causality is merely an illusion, Skein? The notion that there's a consecutive series of events is nothing but a fraud. We impose form on our lives, we talk of time's arrow, we say that there's a flow from A through G and Q to Z, we make believe everything is nicely linear. But it isn't, Skein. It isn't."

Breakfast on a leafy veranda. Morning light out of the west, making the trees glow with an ultramarine glitter. The skull-faced man joins him. Skein secretly searches the parched face. Is everything an illusion? Perhaps *he* is an illusion.
  They walk toward the sea. Well before noon they reach the shore. The skull-faced man points to the south, and they follow the coast; it is often a difficult hike, for in places the sand is washed out and they must detour inland, scrambling over quartzy cliffs. The monstrous old man is indefatigable. When they pause to rest, squatting on a timeless purple strand made smooth by the recent tide, the debate about time resumes, and Skein hears words that have been echoing in his skull for four years and more. It is as though everything up till now has been a rehearsal for a play, and now at last he has taken the stage.
  "Won't you ever come to see that causality is merely an illusion, Skein?"
  "I feel an obligation to awaken your mind to the truth."
  "Time is an ocean, and events come drifting to us as randomly as dead animals on the waves."
  Skein offers all the proper cues.
  "I won't accept that! It's demonic, chaotic, nihilistic theory."
  "You can say that after all you've experienced?"
  "I'll go on saying it. What I've been going through is a mental illness. Maybe I'm deranged, but the universe isn't."
  "Contrary. You've only recently become sane and started to see things as they really are. The trouble is that you don't want to admit the evidence you've begun to perceive. Your filters are

down, Skein! You've shaken free of the illusion of linearity! Now's your chance to show your resilience. Learn to live with the real reality. Stop this silly business of imposing an artificial order on the flow of time. Why *should* effect follow cause? Why *shouldn't* the seed follow the tree? Why must you persist in holding tight to a useless, outworn, contemptible system of false evaluations of experience when you've managed to break free of the—''

"Stop it! Stop it! Stop it! Stop it!"

By early afternoon they are many kilometers from the hotel, still keeping as close to the shore as they can. The terrain is uneven and divided, with rugged fingers of rock running almost to the water's edge, and Skein finds the journey even more exhausting than it had seemed in his visions of it. Several times he stops, panting, and has to be urged to go on.

"It isn't much farther," the skull-faced man says. "You can make it. Step by step is how."

"I'm winded. Those hills—"

"I'm twice your age, and I'm doing fine."

"You're in better shape. I've been cooped up on spaceships for months and months."

"Just a short way on," says the skull-faced man. "About a hundred meters from the shore."

Skein struggles on. The heat is frightful. He trips in the sand; he is blinded by sweat; he has a momentary flashback fugue. "There it is," the skull-faced man says finally. "Look there, in the pit."

Skein beholds the conical crater. He sees the golden amoeba.

"Go down to it," the skull-faced man says. "The force of its power falls off with the cube of the distance; from up here you can't feel it. Go down. Let it take you over. Fuse with it. Make communion, Skein, make communion!"

"And will it heal me? So that I'll function as I did before the trouble started?"

"If you let it heal you, it will. That's what it wants to do. It's a completely benign organism. It thrives on repairing broken souls. Let it into your head; let it find the damaged place. You can trust it. Go down."

Skein trembles on the edge of the pit. The creature below flows and eddies, becoming first long and narrow, then high and squat, then resuming its basically circular form. Its color deepens almost to scarlet, and its radiance shifts toward yellow. As if preening and stretching itself. It seems to be waiting for him. It seems eager. This is what he has sought so long, going from planet to wearying planet. The skull-faced man, the purple sand, the pit, the creature. Skein slips his sandals off. *What have I to lose?* He sits for a moment on the pit's rim; then he shimmies down, sliding part of the way, and lands softly, close beside the being that awaits him. And immediately feels its power. Something brushes against his brain. The sensation reminds him of the training sessions of his first go-round, when the instructors were showing him how to develop his gift. The fingers probing his consciousness. Go on, enter, he tells them. I'm open. And he finds himself in contact with the being of the pit. Wordless. A two-way flow of unintelligible images is the only communion; shapes drift from and into his mind. The universe blurs. He is no longer sure where the center of his ego lies. He has thought of his brain as a sphere with himself at its center, but now it seems extended, elliptical, and an ellipse has no center, only a pair of focuses, here and here, one focus in his own skull and one—where?—within that fleshy amoeba. And suddenly he is looking at himself through the amoeba's eyes. The large biped with the bony body. How strange, how grotesque! Yet it suffers. Yet it must be helped. It is injured. It is broken. We go to it with all our love. We will heal. And Skein feels something flowing over the bare folds and fissures of his brain. But he can no longer remember whether he is the human or the alien, the bony one or the boneless. Their identities have mingled. He goes through fugues by the scores, seeing yesterdays and tomorrows, and everything is formless and without content; he is unable to recognize himself or to understand the words being spoken. It does not matter. All is random. All is illusion. Release the knot of pain you clutch within you. Accept. Accept. Accept. Accept.

He accepts.

He releases.

He merges.

He casts away the shreds of ego, the constricting exoskeleton of self, and placidly permits the necessary adjustments to be made.

The possibility, however, of genuine thermodynamic entropy decrease for an isolated system—no matter how rare—does raise an

objection to the definition of time's direction in terms of entropy.
If a large, isolated system did by chance go through an entropy
decrease as one state evolved from another, we would have to say
that time "went backward" if our definition of time's arrow were
basically in terms of entropy increase. But with an ultimate
definition of the forward direction of time in terms of the actual
occurrence of states, and measured time intervals from the
present, we can readily accommodate the entropy decrease; it
would become merely a rare anomaly in the physical processes of
the natural world.

The wind is rising. The sand, blown aloft, stains the sky gray.
Skein clambers from the pit and lies by its rim, breathing hard.
The skull-faced man helps him get up.

Skein has seen this series of images hundreds of times.

"How do you feel?" the skull-faced man asks.

"Strange. Good. My head seems clear!"

"You had communion down there?"

"Oh, yes. Yes."

"And?"

"I think I'm healed," Skein says in wonder. "My strength is
back. Before, you know, I felt cut down to the bone, a minimum
version of myself. And now. And now." He lets a tendril of
consciousness slip forth. It meets the mind of the skull-faced
man. Skein is aware of a glassy interface; he can touch the other
mind, but he cannot enter it. "Are you a Communicator too?"
Skein asks, awed.

"In a sense. I feel you touching me. You're better, aren't
you?"

"Much. Much. Much."

"As I told you. Now you have your second chance, Skein.
Your gift has been restored. Courtesy of our friend in the pit.
They love being helpful."

"What shall I do now? Where shall I go?"

"Anything. Anywhere. Anywhen. You're free to move along
the time-line as you please. In a state of controlled, directed
fugue, so to speak. After all, if time is random, if there is no
rigid sequence of events—"

"Yes."

"Then why not choose the sequence that appeals to you? Why

stick to the set of abstractions your former self has handed you? You're a free man, Skein. Go. Enjoy. Undo your past. Edit it. Improve on it. It isn't your past, any more than this is your present. It's all one, Skein, all *one*. Pick the segment you prefer.''

He tests the truth of the skull-faced man's words. Cautiously Skein steps three minutes into the past and sees himself struggling up out of the pit. He slides four minutes into the future and sees the skull-faced man, alone, trudging northward along the shore. Everything flows. All is fluidity. He is free. He is free.

''You see, Skein?''

''Now I do,'' Skein says. He is out of entropy's jaws. He is time's master, which is to say he is his own master. He can move at will. He can defy the imaginary forces of determinism. Suddenly he realizes what he must do now. He will assert his free will; he will challenge entropy on its home ground. Skein smiles. He cuts free of the timeline and floats easily into what others would call the past.

''Get Nissenson into a receptive state,'' he orders his desk.

Coustakis, blinking rapidly, obviously uneasy, says, ''First let me get it clear. This man will see everything that's in my mind? He'll get access to my secrets?''

''No. No. I filter the communion with great care. Nothing will pass from your mind to his except the nature of the problem you want him to tackle. Nothing will come back from his mind to yours except the answer.''

''And if he doesn't have the answer?''

''He will.''

''And if he goes into the transmission business for himself afterward?'' Coustakis asks.

''He's bonded,'' Skein says curtly. ''No chance of it. Let's go, now. Up and together.''

The desk reports that Nissenson, half the world away in São Paulo, is ready. Quickly Skein throws Coustakis into the receptive condition, and swings around to face the brilliant lights of his data-access units. Here is the moment when he can halt the transaction. Turn again, Skein. Face Coustakis, smile sadly, inform him that the communion will be impossible. Give him back his money, send him off to break some other Communicator's mind. And live on, whole and happy, ever after. It was at this point, visiting this scene endlessly in his fugues, that Skein silently and hopelessly cried out to himself to stop. Now it is within his power, for this is no fugue, no illusion of time-shift. He has shifted. He is here, carrying with him the knowledge of all that is to come, and he is the only Skein on the scene, the operative Skein. Get up, now. Refuse the contract.

He does not. Thus he defies entropy. Thus he breaks the chain.

He peers into the sparkling, shifting little blazes until they kindle his gift, jabbing at the electrical rhythms of his brain until he is lifted into the energy level that permits the opening of a communion. He starts to go up. He reaches forth one tendril of his mind and engages Nissenson. With another tendril he snares Coustakis. Steadily, now, he draws the two tendrils together. He is aware of the risks, but believes he can surmount them.

The tendrils meet.

Out of Coustakis's mind flows a description of the matter transmitter and a clear statement of the beam-spread problem; Skein shoves it along to Nissenson, who begins to work on a solution. The combined strength of the two minds is great, but Skein deftly lets the excess charge bleed away and maintains the communion with no particular effort, holding Coustakis and Nissenson together while they deal with their technical matters. Skein pays little attention as their excited minds rush toward answers. *If you. Yes, and then. But if. I see, yes. I could. And. However, maybe I should. I like that. It leads to. Of course. The inevitable result. Is it feasible, though? I think so. You might have to. I could. Yes. I could. I could.*

"I thank you a million times," Coustakis says to Skein. "It was all so simple, once we saw how we ought to look at it. I don't begrudge your fee at all. Not at all."

Coustakis leaves, glowing with delight. Skein, relieved, tells his desk, "I'm going to allow myself a three-day holiday. Fix the schedule to move everybody up accordingly."

He smiles. He strides across his office, turning up the amplifiers, treating himself to the magnificent view. The nightmare undone. The past revised. The burnout avoided. All it took was confidence. Enlightenment. A proper understanding of the processes involved.

He feels the sudden swooping sensations of incipient temporal fugue. Before he can intervene to regain control, he swings off into darkness and arrives instantaneously on a planet of purple sand and blue-leaved trees. Orange waves lap at the shore. He stands a few meters from a deep conical pit. Peering into it, he sees an amoebalike creature lying beside a human figure; strands of the alien's jellylike substance are wound around the man's body. He recognizes the man to be John Skein. The communion in the pit ends; the man begins to clamber from the pit. The wind is rising. The sand, blown aloft, stains the sky gray. Patiently he watches his younger self struggling up from the pit. Now he understands. The circuit is closed; the knot is tied; the identity loop is complete. He is destined to spend many years on Abbondanza VI, growing ancient and withered. He is the skull-faced man.

Skein reaches the rim of the pit and lies there, breathing hard. He helps Skein get up.

"How do you feel?" he asks.

MS. FOUND IN AN ABANDONED TIME MACHINE

IF LIFE IS to be worth living at all, we have to have at least the illusion that we are capable of making sweeping changes in the world we live in. I say *at least the illusion.* Real ability to effect change would obviously be preferable, but not all of us can get to that level, and even the illusion of power offers hope, and hope sustains life. The point is not to be a puppet, not to be a passive plaything of karma. I think you'll agree that sweeping changes in society have to be made. Who will make them, if not you and me? If we tell ourselves that we're helpless, that meaningful reform is impossible, that the status quo is here for keeps, then we might as well not bother going on living, don't you think? I mean, if the bus is breaking down and the driver is freaking out on junk and all the doors are jammed, it's cooler to take the cyanide than to wait around for the inevitable messy smashup. But naturally we don't want to let ourselves believe that we're helpless. We want to think that we can grab the wheel and get the bus back on course and steer it safely to the repair shop. Right? Right. That's what we want to think. Even if it's only an illusion. Because sometimes—who knows?—you can firm up an illusion and make it real.

The cast of characters. Thomas C———, our chief protagonist, age twenty. As we first encounter him he lies asleep with strands of his own long brown hair casually wrapped across his mouth.

Tie-dyed jeans and an ECOLOGY NOW! sweat shirt are crumpled at the foot of the bed. He was raised in Elephant Mound, Wisconsin, and this is his third year at the university. He appears to be sleeping peacefully, but through his dreaming mind flit disturbing phantoms: Lee Harvey Oswald, George Lincoln Rockwell, Neil Armstrong, Arthur Bremer, Sirhan Sirhan, Hubert Humphrey, Mao Tse-tung, Lieutenant William Calley, John Lennon. Each in turn announces himself, does a light-footed little dance expressive of his character, vanishes and reappears elsewhere in Thomas's cerebral cortex. On the wall of Thomas's room are various contemporary totems: a giant photograph of Spiro Agnew playing golf, a gaudy VOTE FOR MCGOVERN sticker, and banners that variously proclaim FREE ANGELA, SUPPORT YOUR LOCAL PIG FORCE, POWER TO THE PEOPLE, and CHE LIVES! Thomas has an extremely contemporary sensibility, circa 1970–72. By 1997 he will feel terribly nostalgic for the causes and artifacts of his youth, as his grandfather now is for raccoon coats, bathtub gin, and flagpole sitters. He will say things like "Try it, you'll like it" or "Sock it to me" and no one under forty will laugh.

Asleep next to him is Katherine F———, blond, nineteen years old. Ordinarily she wears steel-rimmed glasses, green hip-hugger bells, a silken purple poncho, and a macramé shawl, but she wears none of these things now. Katherine is not dreaming, but her next REM cycle is due shortly. She comes from Moose Valley, Minnesota, and lost her virginity at the age of fourteen while watching a Mastroianni-Loren flick at the North Star Drive-In. During her seduction she never took her eyes from the screen for a period longer than thirty seconds. Nowadays she's much more heavily into the responsiveness thing, but back then she was trying hard to be cool. Four hours ago she and Thomas performed an act of mutual oral-genital stimulation that is illegal in seventeen states and the Republic of Vietnam (South), although there is hope of changing that before long.

On the floor by the side of the bed is Thomas's dog Fidel, part beagle, part terrier. He is asleep too. Attached to Fidel's collar is a day-glo streamer that reads THREE WOOFS FOR PET LIB.

Without God, said one of the Karamazov boys, everything is possible. I suppose that's true enough, if you conceive of God as the force that holds things together, that keeps water from flowing uphill and the sun from rising in the west. But what a limited concept of God that is! *Au contraire*, Fyodor: *with* God everything is possible. And I would like to be God for a little while.

Q. *What did you do?*

A. *I yelled at Sergeant Bacon and told him to go and start searching hooches and get your people moving right on—not the hooches but the bunkers—and I started over to Mitchell's location. I came back out. Meadlo was still standing there with a group of Vietnamese, and I yelled at Meadlo and asked him—I told him if he couldn't move all those people, to get rid of them.*

Q. *Did you fire into that group of people?*

A. *No, sir, I did not.*

Q. *After that incident, what did you do?*

A. *Well, I told my men to get on across the ditch and to get into position after I had fired into the ditch.*

Q. *Now, did you have a chance to look and observe what was in the ditch?*

A. *Yes, sir.*

Q. *And what did you see?*

A. *Dead people, sir.*

Q. *Did you see any appearance of anybody being alive in there?*

A. *No, sir.*

This is Thomas talking. Listen to me. Just listen. Suppose you had a machine that would enable you to fix everything that's wrong in the world. Let's say that it draws on all the resources of modern technology, not to mention the powers of a rich, well-stocked imagination and a highly developed ethical sense. The machine can do anything. It makes you invisible; it gives you a way of slipping backward and forward in time; it provides telepathic access to the minds of others; it lets you reach into those minds and c-h-a-n-g-e them. And so forth. Call this machine whatever you want. Call it Everybody's Fantasy Actualizer. Call it a Time Machine Mark Nine. Call it a God Box. Call it a magic wand, if you like. Okay. I give you a magic wand. And you give me a magic wand too, because reader and writer have to be allies, co-conspirators. You and me, with our magic wands. What will you do with yours? What will I do with mine? Let's go.

* * *

The Revenge of the Indians. On the plains ten miles west of Grand Otter Falls, Nebraska, the tribes assemble. By pickup truck, camper, Chevrolet, bicycle, and microbus they arrive from every corner of the nation, the delegations of angry redskins. Here are the Onondagas, the Oglallas, the Hunkpapas, the Jicarillas, the Punxsatawneys, the Kickapoos, the Gros Ventres, the Nez Percés, the Lenni Lenapes, the Wepawaugs, the Pamunkeys, the Penobscots, and all that crowd. They are clad in the regalia that the white man expects them to wear: feather bonnets, buckskin leggings, painted faces, tomahawks. See the great bonfire burn! See the leaping seat-shiny braves dance the scalping dance! Listen to their weird barbaric cries! What terror these savages must inspire in the plump suburbanites who watch them on Channel Four!

Now the council meeting begins. The pipe passes. Grunts of approval are heard. The mighty Navaho chieftain, Hosteen Dollars, is the main orator. He speaks for the strongest of the tribes, for the puissant Navahos own motels, gift shops, oil wells, banks, coal mines, and supermarkets. They hold the lucrative national distributorships for the superb pottery of their Hopi and Pueblo neighbors. Quietly they have accumulated vast wealth and power, which they have surreptitiously devoted to the welfare of their less fortunate kinsmen of other tribes. Now the arsenal is fully stocked: the tanks, the flamethrowers, the automatic rifles, the halftracks, the crop-dusters primed with napalm. Only the Big Bang is missing. But that lack, Hosteen Dollars declares, has now been remedied through miraculous intervention. "This is our moment!" he cries. "Hiawatha! Hiawatha!" Solemnly I descend from the skies, drifting in a slow downward spiral, landing lithely on my feet. I am naked but for a fringed breechclout. My coppery skin gleams glossily. Cradled in my arms is a hydrogen bomb, armed and ready. "The Big Bang!" I cry. "Here, brothers! Here!" By nightfall Washington is a heap of radioactive ash. At dawn the Acting President capitulates. Hosteen Dollars goes on national television to explain the new system of reservations, and the round-up of palefaces commences.

Marin County District Attorney Bruce Bales, who disqualified himself as Angela Davis's prosecutor, said yesterday he was "shocked beyond belief" at her acquittal.

In a bitter reaction, Bales said, "I think the jury fell for the very emotional pitch offered by the defense. She didn't even take the stand to deny her guilt. Despite what has happened, I still maintain she was as responsible for the death of Judge Haley and the crippling of my assistant, Gary Thomas, as Jonathan Jackson. Undoubtedly more so, because of her age, experience, and intelligence."

Governor Ronald Reagan, a spokesman at the capital said, was not available for comment on the verdict.

The day we trashed the Pentagon was simply beautiful, a landmark in the history of the Movement. It took years of planning and a tremendous cooperative effort, but the results were worth the heroic struggle and then some.

This is how we did it:

With the help of our IBM 2020 multiphasic we plotted a ring of access points around the whole District of Columbia. Three sites were in Maryland—Hyattsville, Suitland, and Wheaton— and two were on the Virginia side, at McLean and Merrifield. At each access point we dropped a vertical shaft six hundred feet deep, using our Hughes fluid-intake rotary reamer coupled with a GM twin-core extractor unit. Every night we transported the excavation tailings by truck to Kentucky and Tennessee, dumping them as fill in strip-mining scars. When we reached the six-hundred-foot level we began laying down a thirty-six-inch pipe-line route straight to the Pentagon from each of our five loci, employing an LTV molecular compactor to convert the soil castings into semi-liquid form. This slurry we pumped into five huge adjacent underground retaining pockets that we carved with our Gardner-Denver hemispherical subsurface backhoe. When the pipelines were laid we started to pump the stored slurry toward the Pentagon at a constant rate calculated for us by our little XDS computer and monitored at five-hundred-meter intervals along the route by our Control Data 106a sensor system. The pumps, of course, were heavy-duty Briggs and Stratton 580's.

Over a period of eight months we succeeded in replacing the subsoil beneath the Pentagon's foundation with an immense pool of slurry, taking care, however, to avoid causing any seismological disturbances that the Pentagon's own equipment might detect. For this part of the operation we employed Bausch and Lomb spectrophotometers and Perkin-Elmer scanners, rigged in series with a Honeywell 990 vibration-damping integrator. Our timing was perfect. On the evening of July 3 we pierced the critical destruct threshold. The Pentagon was now floating on a lake of mud nearly a kilometer in diameter. A triple bank of Dow autonomic stabilizers maintained the building at its normal elevation; we used Ampex homeostasis equipment to regulate flotation pressures. At noon on the Fourth of July Katherine and I held a press conference on the steps of the Library of Congress, attended chiefly by representatives of the underground media although there were a few nonfreak reporters there too. I demanded an immediate end to all Amerikan overseas military adventures and gave the President one hour to reply. There was no response from the White House, of course, and at five minutes to one I activated the sluices by whistling three bars of "The Star-Spangled Banner" into a pay telephone outside FBI headquarters. By doing so I initiated a slurry-removal process and by five after one the Pentagon was sinking. It went down slowly enough so that there was no loss of life: the evacuation was complete within two hours and the uppermost floor of the building didn't go under the mud until five in the afternoon.

Two lions that killed a youth at the Portland Zoo Saturday night were dead today, victims of a nighttime rifleman.

Roger Dean Adams, nineteen years old, of Portland, was the youth who was killed. The zoo was closed Saturday night when he and two companions entered the zoo by climbing a fence.

The companions said that the Adams youth first lowered himself over the side of the grizzly bear pit, clinging by his hands to the edge of the wall, then pulling himself up. He tried it again at the lions' pit after first sitting on the edge.

Kenneth Franklin Bowers of Portland, one of young Adams's companions, said the youth lowered himself over the edge and as he hung by his fingers he kicked at the lions. One slapped at him, hit his foot, and the youth fell to the floor of the pit, sixteen feet below the rim of the wall. The lions then mauled him and it appeared that he bled to death after an artery in his neck was slashed.

One of the lions, Caesar, a sixteen-year-old male, was killed last night by two bullets from a foreign-made rifle. Sis, an eleven-year-old female, was shot in the spine. She died this morning.

The police said they had few clues to the shootings.

Jack Marks, the zoo director, said the zoo would prosecute anyone charged with the shootings. "You'd have to be sick to shoot an animal that has done nothing wrong by its own standards," Mr. Marks said. "No right-thinking person would go into the zoo in the middle of the night and shoot an animal in captivity."

Do you want me to tell you who I really am? You may think I am a college student of the second half of the twentieth century but in fact I am a visitor from the far future, born in a year which by your system of reckoning would be called A.D. 2806. I can try to describe my native era to you, but there is little likelihood you would comprehend what I say. For instance, does it mean anything to you when I tell you that I have two womb-mothers, one ovarian and one uterine, and that my sperm-father in the somatic line was, strictly speaking, part dolphin and part ocelot? Or that I celebrated my fifth neurongate raising by taking part in an expedition to Proxy Nine, where I learned the eleven soul-diving drills and the seven contrary mantas? The trouble is that from your point of view we have moved beyond the technological into the incomprehensible. You could explain television to a man of the eleventh century in such a way that he would grasp the essential concept, if not the actual operative principles ("We have this box on which we are able to make pictures of faraway places appear, and we do this by taming the same power that makes lightning leap across the sky"), but how can I find even the basic words to help you visualize our simplest toys?

At any rate it was eye-festival time, and for my project I chose to live in the year 1972. This required a good deal of preparation. Certain physical alterations were necessary—synthesizing body hair, for example—but the really difficult part was creating the cultural camouflage. I had to pick up speech patterns, historical background, a whole sense of *context*. (I also had to create a convincing autobiography. The time-field effect provides travelers like myself with an instant retroactive existence in the past, an established background of schooling and parentage and whatnot stretching over any desired period prior to point of arrival, but only if the appropriate programming is done.) I drew on the services of our leading historians and archaeologists, who supplied me with everything I needed, including an intensive training in late-twentieth-century youth culture. How glib I became! I can talk all your dialects: macrobiotics, ecology, hallucinogens, lib-sub-aleph, rock, astrology, yoga. Are you a *sanpaku* Capricorn? Are you plagued by sexism, bum trips, wobbly karma, malign planetary conjunctions? Ask me for advice. I know this stuff. I'm into everything that's current. I'm with the Revolution all the way.

Do you want to know something else? I think I may not be the only time traveler who's here right now. I'm starting to form a theory that this entire generation may have come here from the future.

BELFAST, Northern Ireland, May 28—Six people were killed early today in a big bomb explosion in Short Strand, a Roman Catholic section of Belfast.

Three of the dead, all men, were identified later as members of the Irish Republican Army. Security forces said they believed the bomb blew up accidentally while it was being taken to another part of the city.

One of the dead was identified as a well-known I.R.A. explosives expert who had been high on the British Army's wanted list for some time. The three other victims, two men and a woman, could not be identified immediately.

Seventeen persons, including several children, were injured by the explosion, and twenty houses in the narrow street were so badly damaged that they will have to be demolished.

One day I woke up and could not breathe. All that day and through the days after, in the green parks and in the rooms of friends and even beside the sea, I could not breathe. The air was used up. Each thing I saw that was ugly was ugly because of man—man-made or man-touched. And so I left my friends and lived alone.

EUGENE, Ore. (UPI)—A retired chef and his dog were buried together recently as per the master's wish.

Horace Lee Edwards, seventy-one years old, had lived alone with his dog for twenty-two years, since it was a pup. He expressed the wish that when he died the dog be buried with him.

Members of Mr. Edwards's family put the dog to death after Mr. Edwards's illness. It was placed at its master's feet in his coffin.

I accept chaos. I am not sure whether it accepts me.

A memo to the Actualizer.

Dear Machine:

We need more assassins. The system itself is fundamentally violent and we have tried to transform it through love. That didn't work. We gave them flowers and they gave us bullets. All right. We've reached such a miserable point that the only way we can fight their violence is with violence of our own. The time has come to rip off the rippers-off. Therefore, old machine, your assignment for today is to turn out a corps of capable assassins, a cadre of convincing-looking artificial human beings who will serve the needs of the Movement. Killer androids, that's what we want.

These are the specs:

AGE—between nineteen and twenty-five years old.

HEIGHT—from five feet to five feet nine.

WEIGHT—on the low side, or else very heavy.

RACE—white, more or less.

RELIGION—Former Christian, now agnostic or atheist. Ex-Fundamentalist will do nicely.

PSYCHOLOGICAL PROFILE—intense, weird, a loner, a loser. A bad sexual history: impotence, premature ejaculation, inability to find willing partners. A bad relationship with siblings (if any) and parents. Subject should be a hobbyist (stamp or coin collecting, trap-shooting, cross-country running, etc.) but not an "intellectual." A touch of paranoia is desirable. Also free-floating ambitions impossible to fulfill.

POLITICAL CONVICTIONS—any. Preferably highly flexible. Willing to call himself a libertarian anarchist on

Tuesday and a dedicated Marxist on Thursday if he thinks it'll get him somewhere to make the switch. Willing to shoot with equal enthusiasm at presidential candidates, incumbent senators, baseball players, rock stars, traffic cops, or any other components of the mysterious "they" that hog the glory and keep him from attaining his true place in the universe.

Okay. You can supply the trimmings yourself, machine. Any color eyes so long as the eyes are a little bit on the glassy hyperthyroid side. Any color hair, although it will help if the hair is prematurely thinning and our man blames his lack of success with women in part on that. Any marital history (single, divorced, widowed, married) provided whatever liaison may have existed was unsatisfactory. The rest is up to you. Get with the job and use your creativity. Start stamping them out in quantity:

Oswald	Sirhan	Bremer	Ray	Czolgosz	Guiteau
Oswald	Sirhan	Bremer	Ray	Czolgosz	Guiteau
Oswald	Sirhan	Bremer	Ray	Czolgosz	Guiteau
Oswald	Sirhan	Bremer	Ray	Czolgosz	Guiteau
Oswald	Sirhan	Bremer	Ray	Czolgosz	Guiteau
Oswald	Sirhan	Bremer	Ray	Czolgosz	Guiteau
Oswald	Sirhan	Bremer	Ray	Czolgosz	Guiteau
Oswald	Sirhan	Bremer	Ray	Czolgosz	Guiteau

Give us the men. We'll find uses for them. And when they've done their filthy thing we'll throw them back into the karmic hopper to be recycled, and God help us all.

Every day thousands of ships routinely stain the sea with oily wastes. When an oil tanker has discharged its cargo, it might add weight of some other kind to remain stable; this is usually done by filling some of the ship's storage tanks with seawater. Before it can take on a new load of oil, the tanker must flush this watery ballast from its tanks; and as the water is pumped out, it takes with it the oily scum that had remained in the tanks when the last cargo was unloaded. Until 1964 each such flushing of an average 40,000-ton tanker sent eighty-three tons of oil into the sea. Improved flushing procedures have cut the usual oil discharge to about three tons. But there are so many tankers afloat—more than 4,000 of them—that they nevertheless release several million tons of oil a year in this fashion. The 44,000 passenger, cargo, military, and pleasure ships now in service add an equal amount of pollution by flushing oily wastes from their bilges. All told, according to one scientific estimate, man may be putting as much as ten million tons of oil a year into the sea. When the explorer Thor Heyerdahl made a 3,200-mile voyage from North Africa to the West Indies in a boat of papyrus reeds in the summer of 1970, he saw "a continuous stretch of at least 1,400 miles of open Atlantic polluted by floating lumps of solidified, asphalt-like oil." French oceanographer Jacques Yves Cousteau estimates that forty percent of the world's sea life has disappeared in the present century. The beaches near Boston Harbor have an average oil accumulation of 21.8 pounds of oil per mile, a figure that climbs to 1,750 pounds per mile on one stretch on Cape Cod. The Scientific Center of Monaco reports: "On the Mediterranean seaboard practically all the beaches are soiled by the petroleum refineries, and the sea bottom, which serves as a food reserve for marine fauna, is rendered barren by the same factors."

It's a coolish spring day and here I am in Washington, D.C. That's the Capitol down there, and there's the White House. I can't see the Washington Monument, because they haven't finished it yet, and of course there isn't any Lincoln Memorial, because Honest Abe is alive and well on Pennsylvania Avenue. Today is Friday, April 14, 1865. And here I am. Far out!

—We hold the power to effect change. Very well, what shall we change? The whole ugly racial thing?

—That's cool. But how do we go about it?

—Well, what about uprooting the entire institution of slavery by going back to the sixteenth century and blocking it at the outset?

—No, too many ramifications. We'd have to alter the dynamics of the entire imperialist-colonial thrust, and that's just too big a job even for a bunch of gods. Omnipotent we may be, but not indefatigable. If we blocked that impulse there, it would only crop up somewhere else along the time-line; no force that powerful can be stifled altogether.

—What we need is a pinpoint way of reversing the racial mess. Let us find a single event that lies at a crucial nexus in the history of black-white relations in the United States and unhappen it. Any suggestions?

—Sure, Thomas. The Lincoln assassination.

—Far out! Run it through the machine; see what the consequences would be.

So we do the simulations and twenty times out of twenty they come out with a recommend that we de-assassinate Lincoln. Groovy. Any baboon with a rifle can do an assassination, but only we can do a de-assassination. *Alors:* Lincoln goes on to complete his second term. The weak, ineffectual Andrew Johnson remains Vice President, and the Radical Republican faction in Congress doesn't succeed in enacting its "humble the proud traitors" screw-the-South policies. Under Lincoln's evenhanded guidance the South will be rebuilt sanely and welcomed back into the Union; there won't be any vindictive Reconstruction era, and there won't be the equally vindictive Jim Crow reaction against the carpetbaggers that led to all the lynchings and restrictive laws, and maybe we can blot out a century of racial bitterness. Maybe.

That's Ford's Theatre over there. *Our American Cousin* is playing tonight. Right now John Wilkes Booth is holed up in some downtown hotel, I suppose, oiling his gun, rehearsing his speech. "Sic semper tyrannis!" is what he'll shout, and he'll blow away poor old Abe.

—One ticket for tonight's performance, please.

Look at the elegant ladies and gentleman descending from their carriages. They know the President will be at the theater, and they're wearing their finest finery. And yes! That's the White House buggy! Is that imperious-looking lady Mary Todd Lincoln? It has to be. And there's the President, stepping right off the five-dollar bill. Graying beard, stooped shoulders, weary eyes, tired, wrinkled face. Poor old Abe. Am I doing you much of a favor by saving you tonight? Don't you want to lay your burden down? But history needs you, man. All dem li'l black boys and girls, dey needs you. The President waves. I wave back. Greetings from the twentieth century, Mr. Lincoln! I'm here to rob you of your martyrdom!

Curtain going up. Abe smiles in his box. I can't follow the play. Words, just words. Time crawls, tick-tock, tick-tock, tick-tock. Ten o'clock at last. The moment's coming close. There, do you see him? There: the wild-eyed man with the big gun. Wow, that gun's the size of a cannon! And he's creeping up on the President. Why doesn't anybody notice? Is the play so god-damned interesting that nobody notices—

"Hey! Hey you, John Wilkes Booth! Look over here, man! Look at me!"

Everybody turns as I shout. Booth turns too, and I rise and extend my arm and fire, not even needing to aim, just turning the weapon into an extension of my pointing hand as the Zen exercises have shown me how to do. The sound of the shot expands, filling the theater with a terrible reverberating boom, and Booth topples, blood fountaining from his chest. Now, finally the President's bodyguards break from their freeze and come scrambling forward. I'm sorry, John. Nothing personal. History was in need of some changing, is all. Goodbye, 1865. Goodbye, President Abe. You've got an extension of your lease, thanks to me. The rest is up to you.

Our freedom . . . our liberation . . . can only come through a trans-formation of social structure and relationships . . . no one group can be free while another is still held in bonds. We want to build a world where people can choose their futures, where they can love without dependency games, where they do not starve. We want to create a world where men and women can relate to each other and to children as sharing, loving equals. We must elimi-nate the twin oppressors . . . hierarchical and exploitative capital-ism and its myths that keep us so securely in bonds . . . sexism, racism, and other evils created by those who rule to keep the rest of us apart.

—Do you Alexander, take this man to be your lawful wedded mate?

—I do.

—Do you, George, take this man to be your lawful wedded mate?

—I do.

—Then, George and Alexander, by the power vested in me by the State of New York as ordained minister of the First Congrega-tional Gay Communion of Upper Manhattan, I do hereby pro-nounce you man and man, wedded before God and in the eyes of mankind, and may you love happily ever after.

*　　*　　*

It's all done with the aid of a lot of science fiction gadgetry. I won't apologize for that part of it. Apologies just aren't necessary. If you need gadgetry to get yourself off, you use gadgetry; the superficials simply don't enter into any real consideration of how you get where you want to be from where you're at. The aim is to eradicate the well-known evils of our society, and if we have to get there by means of time machines, thought-amplification headbands, anti-uptightness rays, molecular interpenetrator beams, superheterodyning levitator rods, and all the rest of that gaudy comic-book paraphernalia, so be it. It's the results that count.

Like I mean, take the day I blew the President's mind. You think I could have done that without all this gadgetry? Listen, simply getting into the White House is a trip and a half. You can't get hold of a reliable map of the interior of the White House, the part that the tourists aren't allowed to see; the maps that exist are phonies, and actually they keep rearranging the rooms so that espionage agents and assassins won't be able to find their way around. What is a bedroom one month is an office the next and a switchboard room the month after that. Some rooms can be folded up and removed altogether. It's a whole wild cloak-and-dagger number. So we set up our ultrasonic intercavitation scanner in Lafayette Park and got ourselves a trustworthy holographic representation of the inside of the building. That data enabled me to get my bearings once I was in there. But I also needed to be able to find the President in a hurry. Our method was to slap a beep transponder on him, which we did by catching the White House's head salad chef, zonking him on narcoleptic strobes, and programming him to hide the gimmick inside a tomato. The President ate the tomato at dinnertime and from that moment on we could trace him easily. Also, the pattern of interference waves coming from the transponder told us whether anyone was with him.

So okay. I waited until he was alone one night, off in the Mauve Room rummaging through his file of autographed photos of football stars, and I levitated to a point ninety feet directly above that room, used our neutrinoflux desensitizer to knock out the White House security shield, and plummeted down via interpenetrator beam. I landed right in front of him. Give him credit: he didn't start to yell. He backed away and started to go for some kind of alarm button, but I said, "Cool it, Mr. President, you aren't going to get hurt. I just want to talk. Can you spare five minutes for a little rap?'' And I beamed him with the conceptutron to relax him and make him receptive. "Okay, chief?''

"You may speak, son,'' he replied. "I'm always eager to hear the voice of the public, and I'm particularly concerned with being responsive to the needs and problems of our younger generation. Our gallant young people who—''

"Groovy, Dick. Okay—now dig this. The country's falling apart, right? The ecology is deteriorating, the cities are decaying, the blacks are up in arms, the right-wingers are stocking up on napalm, the kids are getting maimed in one crazy foreign war after another, the prisons are creating criminals instead of rehabilitating them, the Victorian sexual codes are turning millions of potentially beautiful human beings into sickniks, the drug laws don't make any sense, the women are still hung up on the mother-chauffeur-cook-chambermaid trip, the men are still into the booze-guns-broads trips, the population is still growing and filling up the clean open spaces, the economic structure is set up to be self-destructive since capital and labor are in cahoots to screw the consumer, and so on. I'm sure you know the problems, since you're the President and you read a lot of newspapers. Okay. How did we get into this bummer? By accident? No. Through bad karma? I don't really think so. Through inescapable deterministic forces? Uh-uh. We got into it through dumbness, greed, and inertia. We're so greedy we don't even realize that it's ourselves we're robbing. But it can be fixed, Dick, *it can all be fixed!* We just have to wake up! And you're the man who can do it. Don't you want to go down in history as the man who helped this great country get itself together? You and thirty influential congressmen and five members of the Supreme Court can do it. All you have to do is start reshaping the national consciousness through some executive directives backed up with congressional action. Get on the tube, man, and tell all your silent majoritarians to shape up. Proclaim the reign of love. No more war, hear? It's over tomorrow. No more economic growth: we just settle for what we have and we start cleaning up the rivers and lakes and forests. No more babies to be used as status symbols and pacifiers for idle housewives—from now on people will do babies only for the sake of bringing groovy new human beings into the world, two or three to a couple. As of tomorrow we abolish all laws against stuff that people do without hurting other people. And so on. We proclaim a new Bill of Rights granting every individual the right to a full and productive life according to his own style. Will you do that?''

''Well—''

''Let me make one thing perfectly clear,'' I said, ''You're *going* to do it. You're going to decree an end to all the garbage that's been going down in this country. You know how I know you're going to do it? Because I've got this shiny little metal tube in my hand and it emits vibrations that are real strong stuff, vibrations that are going to get your head together when I press the button. Ready or not, here I go. One, two, three . . . *zap*.''

''Right on, baby,'' the President said.

The rest is history.

Oh. Oh. Oh. Oh, God. If it could only be that easy. One, two, three, zap. But it doesn't work like that. I don't have any magic wand. What makes you think I did? How was I able to trick you into a suspension of disbelief? You, reader, sitting there on your rear end, what do you think I really am? A miracle man? Some kind of superbeing from Galaxy Ten? I'll tell you what I really am, me, Thomas C———. I'm a bunch of symbols on a piece of paper. I'm just something abstract trapped within a mere fiction. A ''hero'' in a ''story.'' Helpless, disembodied, unreal. UNREAL! Whereas you out there—you have eyes, lungs, feet, arms, a brain, a mouth, all that good stuff. You can function. You can move. You can act. Work for the Revolution! Strive for change! You're operating in the real world; you can do it if anybody can! Struggle toward . . . umph . . . glub . . . Hey, get your filthy hands off me—power to the people! Down with the fascist pigs . . . hey—help—HELP!

THE MUTANT
SEASON

IT SNOWED YESTERDAY, three inches. Today a cruel
wind comes ripping off the ocean, kicking up the snowdrifts.
This is the dead of winter, the low point of the year. This is the
season when the mutants arrive. They showed up ten years ago,
the same six families as always, renting all the beach houses on
the north side of Dune Crest Road. They like to come here in
winter when the vacationers are gone and the beaches are empty.
I guess they don't enjoy having a lot of normals around. In winter
here there's just the little hard core of year-round residents like
us. And we don't mind the mutants so long as they don't bother
us.

I can see them now, frolicking along the shore, kids and
grownups. The cold doesn't seem to affect them at all. It would
affect me plenty, being outside in this weather, but they don't
even trouble themselves with wearing overcoats. Just light wind-
breakers and pullovers. They have thicker skins than we do, I
guess—leathery-looking, shiny, apple-green—and maybe a different metabolism. They could almost be people from some other
planet, but no, they're all natives of the U.S.A., just like you and
me. Mutants, that's all. Freaks is what we used to call them. But
of course you mustn't call them that now.

Doing their mutant tricks. They can fly, you know. Oh, it isn't
really flying, it's more a kind of jumping and soaring, but they
can go twenty, thirty feet in the air and float up there about three

or four minutes. Levitation, they call it. A bunch of them are levitating right out over the ocean, hanging high above the breakers. It would serve them right to drop and get a soaking. But they don't ever lose control. And look, two of them are having a snowball fight without using their hands, just picking up the snow with their minds and wadding it into balls and tossing it around. Telekinesis, that's called.

I learn these terms from my older daughter Ellen. She's seventeen. She spends a lot of time hanging around with one of the mutant kids. I wish she'd stay away from him.

Levitation. Telekinesis. Mutants renting beach houses. It's a crazy world these days.

Look at them jumping around. They look happy, don't they?

It's three weeks since they came. Cindy, my younger girl—she's nine—asked me today about mutants. What they are. Why they exist.

I said, There are all different kinds of human beings. Some have brown skins and woolly hair, some have yellow skins and slanted eyes, some have—

Those are the races, she said. I know about races. The races look different outside but inside they're pretty much all the same. But the mutants are really different. They have special powers and some of them have strange bodies. They're more different from us than other races are, and that's what I don't understand.

They're a special kind of people, I told her. They were born different from everybody else.

Why?

You know what genes are, Cindy?

Sort of, she said. We're just starting to study about them.

Genes are what determine how our children will look. Your eyes are brown because I have the gene for brown eyes, see? But sometimes there are sudden changes in a family's genes. Something strange gets in. Yellow eyes, maybe. That would be a mutation. The mutants are people who had something strange happen to their genes some time back, fifty, a hundred, three hundred years ago, and the change in the genes became permanent and was handed down from parents to children. Like the gene for the floating they do. Or the gene for their shiny skin. There are all sorts of different mutant genes.

Where did the mutants come from?

They've always been here, I said.

But why didn't anybody ever talk about them? Why isn't there anything about the mutants in my schoolbooks?

It takes time for things to get into schoolbooks, Cindy. Your books were written ten or fifteen years ago. People didn't know much about mutants then and not much was said about them, especially to children your age. The mutants were still in hiding. They lived in out-of-the-way places and disguised themselves and concealed their powers.

Why don't they hide any more?

Because they don't need to, I said. Things have changed. The normal people accept them. We've been getting rid of a lot of prejudices in the last hundred years. Once upon a time anybody who was even a little strange made other people uncomfortable. Any sort of difference—skin color, religion, language—caused trouble, Cindy. Well, we learned to accept people who aren't like ourselves. We even accept people who aren't quite human, now. Like the mutants.

If you accept them, she said, why do you get angry when Ellen goes walking on the beach with what's-his-name?

Ellen's friend went back to college right after the Christmas holidays. Tim, his name is. He's a junior at Cornell. I think she's spending too much time writing long letters to him, but what can I do?

My wife thinks we ought to be more sociable toward them. They've been here a month and a half and we've just exchanged the usual token greetings—friendly nods, smiles, nothing more. We don't even know their names. I could get along without knowing them, I said. But all right. Let's go over and invite them to have drinks with us tonight.

We went across to the place Tim's family is renting. A man who might have been anywhere from thirty-five to fifty-five answered the door. It was the first time I ever saw any of them up close. His features were flat and his eyes were set oddly far apart, and his skin was so glossy it looked like it had been waxed. He didn't ask us in. I was able to see odd things going on behind him in the house—people floating near the ceiling, stuff like that. Standing there at the door, feeling very uneasy and awkward, we hemmed and hawed and finally said what we had come to say. He wasn't interested. You can tell when people aren't interested in being mixed with. Very coolly he said they were busy now, expecting guests, and couldn't drop by. But they'd be in touch.

I bet that's the last we hear of them. A standoffish bunch, keeping to themselves, setting up their own ghetto.

Well, never mind. I don't need to socialize with them. They'll be leaving in another couple of weeks anyway.

How fast the cycle of the months goes around. First snowstorm of the season today, a light one, but it's not really winter yet. I guess our weird friends will be coming back to the seashore soon.

Three of the families moved in on Friday and the other three came today. Cindy's already been over visiting. She says this year Tim's family has a pet, a mutant dog, no less, a kind of poodle only with scaly skin and bright red eyes, like marbles. Gives me the shivers. I didn't know there were mutant dogs.

I was hoping Tim had gone into the army or something. No such luck. He'll be here for two weeks at Christmastime. Ellen's already counting the days.

I saw the mutant dog out on the beach. If you ask me, that's no dog, that's some kind of giant lizard. But it barks. It does bark. And wags its tail. I saw Cindy hugging it. She plays with the younger mutant kids just as though they're normals. She accepts them and they accept her. I suppose it's healthy. I suppose their attitudes are right and mine are wrong. But I can't help my conditioning, can I? I don't *want* to be prejudiced. But some things are ingrained when we're very young.

Ellen stayed out way past midnight tonight with Tim.

Tim at our house for dinner this evening. He's a nice kid, have to admit. But *so* strange-looking. And Ellen made him show off levitation for us. He frowns a little and floats right up off the ground. A freak, a circus freak. And my daughter's in love with him.

His winter vacation will be over tomorrow. Not a moment too soon, either.

Another winter nearing its end. The mutants clear out this week. On Saturday they had a bunch of guests—mutants of some other type, no less! A different tribe. The visitors were tall and thin, like walking skeletons, very pale, very solemn. They don't speak out loud: Cindy says they talk with their minds. Telepaths. They seem harmless enough, but I find this whole thing very scary. I imagine dozens of bizarre strains existing within mankind, alongside mankind, all kinds of grotesque mutant types breeding true and multiplying. Now that they've finally surfaced, now that we've discovered how many of them there really are, I started to wonder what new surprises lie ahead for us so-called normals. Will we find ourselves in a minority in another couple of generations? Will those of us who lack superpowers become third-class citizens?

I'm worried.

Summer. Fall. Winter. And here they come again. Maybe we can be friendlier with them this year.

Last year, seven houses. This year they've rented nine. It's good to have so many people around, I guess. Before they started coming it was pretty lonesome here in the winters.

Looks like snow. Soon they'll be here. Letter from Ellen, saying to get her old room ready. Time passes. It always does. Things change. They always do. Winter comes round in its season, and with it come our strange friends. Their ninth straight year here. Can't wait to see Ellen.

Ellen and Tim arrived yesterday. You see them down on the beach? Yes, they're a good-looking young couple. That's my grandson with them. The one in the blue snowsuit. Look at him floating—I bet he's nine feet off the ground! Precocious, that's him. Not old enough to walk yet. But he can levitate pretty well, let me tell you.

THIS IS THE ROAD

      LEAF, LOLLING COZILY with Shadow on a thick heap of furs in the airwagon's snug passenger castle, heard rain beginning to fall and made a sour face: very likely he would soon have to get up and take charge of driving the wagon, if the rain was the sort of rain he thought it was.

This was the ninth day since the Teeth had begun to lay waste to the eastern provinces. The airwagon, carrying four who were fleeing the invaders' fierce appetites, was floating along Spider Highway somewhere between Theptis and Northman's Rib, heading west, heading west as fast as could be managed. Jumpy little Sting was at the power reins, beaming dream commands to the team of six nightmares that pulled the wagon along; burly Crown was amidwagon, probably plotting vengeance against the Teeth, for that was what Crown did most of the time; that left Leaf and Shadow at their ease, but not for much longer. Listening to the furious drumming of the downpour against the wagon's taut-stretched canopy of big-veined stickskin, Leaf knew that this was no ordinary rain, but rather the dread purple rain that runs the air foul and brings the no-leg spiders out to hunt. Sting would never be able to handle the wagon in a purple rain. What a nuisance, Leaf thought, cuddling close against Shadow's sleek, furry blue form. Before long he heard the worried snorting of the night-mares and felt the wagon jolt and buck: yes, beyond any doubt, purple rain, no-leg spiders. His time of relaxing was just about over.

Not that he objected to doing his fair share of the work. But he had finished his last shift of driving only half an hour ago. He had earned his rest. If Sting was incapable of handling the wagon in this weather—and Shadow too, Shadow could never manage in a purple rain—then Crown ought to take the reins himself. But of course Crown would do no such thing. It was Crown's wagon, and he never drove it himself. "I have always had underbreeds to do the driving for me," Crown had said ten days ago, as they stood in the grand plaza of Holy Town with the fires of the Teeth blazing in the outskirts.

"Your underbreeds have all fled without waiting for their master," Leaf had reminded him.

"So? There are others to drive."

"Am I to be your underbreed?" Leaf asked calmly. "Remember, Crown, I'm of the Pure Stream stock."

"I can see that by your face, friend. But why get into philosophical disputes? This is my wagon. The invaders will be here before nightfall. If you would ride west with me, these are the terms. If they're too bitter for you to swallow, well, stay here and test your luck against the mercies of the Teeth."

"I accept your terms," Leaf said.

So he had come aboard—and Sting, and Shadow—under the condition that the three of them would do all the driving. Leaf felt degraded by that—hiring on, in effect, as an indentured underbreed—but what choice was there for him? He was alone and far from his people; he had lost all his wealth and property; he faced sure death as the swarming hordes of Teeth devoured the eastland. He accepted Crown's terms. An aristocrat knows the art of yielding better than most. Resist humiliation until you can resist no longer, certainly, but then accept, accept, accept. Refusal to bow to the inevitable is vulgar and melodramatic. Leaf was of the highest caste, Pure Stream, schooled from childhood to be pliable, a willow in the wind, bending freely to the will of the Soul. Pride is a dangerous sin; so is stubbornness; so too, more than the others, is foolishness. Therefore, he labored while Crown lolled. Still, there were limits even to Leaf's capacity for acceptance, and he suspected those limits would be reached shortly.

*   *   *

On the first night, with only two small rivers between them and the Teeth and the terrible fires of Holy Town staining the sky, the fugitives halted briefly to forage for jellymelons in an abandoned field, and as they squatted there, gorging on ripe succulent fruit, Leaf said to Crown, "Where will you go, once you're safe from the Teeth on the far side of the Middle River?"

"I have distant kinsmen who live in the Flatlands," Crown replied. "I'll go to them and tell them what has happened to the Dark Lake folk in the east, and I'll persuade them to take up arms and drive the Teeth back into the icy wilderness where they belong. An army of liberation, Leaf, and I'll lead it." Crown's dark face glistened with juice. He wiped at it. "What are your plans?"

"Not nearly so grand. I'll seek kinsmen too, but not to organize an army. I wish simply to go to the Inland Sea, to my own people, and live quietly among them once again. I've been away from home too many years. What better time to return?" Leaf glanced at Shadow. "And you?" he asked her. "What do you want out of this journey?"

"I want only to go wherever you go," she said.

Leaf smiled. "You, Sting?"

"To survive," Sting said. "Just to survive."

Mankind had changed the world, and the changed world had worked changes in mankind. Each day the wagon brought the travelers to some new and strange folk who claimed descent from the old ancestral stock, though they might be water-breathers or have skins like tanned leather or grow several pairs of arms. Human, all of them, human, human, human. Or so they insisted. If you call yourself human, Leaf thought, then I will call you human too. Still, there were gradations of humanity. Leaf, as a Pure Stream, thought of himself as more nearly human than any of the peoples along their route, more nearly human even than his three companions; indeed, he sometimes tended to look upon Crown, Sting, and Shadow as very much other than human, though he did not consider that a fault in them. Whatever dwelled in the world was without fault, so long as it did no harm to others. Leaf had been taught to respect every breed of mankind, even the underbreeds. His companions were certainly no underbreeds: they were solidly midcaste, all of them, and ranked not far below Leaf himself. Crown, the biggest and strongest and

most violent of them, was of the Dark Lake line. Shadow's race
was Dancing Stars, and she was the most elegant, the most
supple of the group. She was the only female aboard the wagon.
Sting, who sprang from the White Crystal stock, was the quickest
of body and spirit, mercurial, volatile. An odd assortment, Leaf
thought. But in extreme times one takes one's traveling companions as they come. He had no complaints. He found it possible to
get along with all of them, even Crown. Even Crown.

The wagon came to a jouncing halt. There was the clamor of
hooves stamping the sodden soil; then shrill high-pitched cries
from Sting and angry booming bellowings from Crown; and
finally a series of muffled hissing explosions. Leaf shook his head
sadly. "To waste our ammunition on no-leg spiders—"
    "Perhaps they're harming the horses," Shadow said. "Crown
is rough, but he isn't stupid."
    Tenderly Leaf stroked her smooth haunches. Shadow tried
always to be kind. He had never loved a Dancing Star before,
though the sight of them had long given him pleasure: they were
slender beings, bird-boned and shallow-breasted, and covered
from their ankles to their crested skulls by fine dense fur the
color of the twilight sky in winter. Shadow's voice was musical
and her motions were graceful; she was the antithesis of Crown.
    Crown now appeared, a hulking figure thrusting bluntly through
the glistening beaded curtains that enclosed the passenger castle.
He glared malevolently at Leaf. Even in his pleasant moments
Crown seemed angry, an effect perhaps caused by his eyes, which
were bright red where those of Leaf and most other kinds of
humans were white. Crown's body was a block of meat, twice as
broad as Leaf and half again as tall, though Leaf did not come
from a small-statured race. Crown's skin was glossy, greenish-
purple in color, much like burnished bronze; he was entirely
without hair and seemed more like a massive statue of an oiled
gladiator than a living being. His arms hung well below his
knees; equipped with extra joints and terminating in hands the
size of great baskets, they were superb instruments of slaughter.
Leaf offered him the most agreeable smile he could find. Crown
said, without smiling in return, "You better get back on the
reins, Leaf. The road's turning into one big swamp. The horses
are uneasy. It's a purple rain.
    Leaf had grown accustomed, in these nine days, to obeying

Crown's brusque orders. He started to obey now, letting go of Shadow and starting to rise. But then, abruptly, he arrived at the limits of his acceptance.

"My shift just ended," he said.

Crown stared. "I know that. But Sting can't handle the wagon in this mess. And I just killed a bunch of mean-looking spiders. There'll be more if we stay around here much longer."

"So?"

"What are you trying to do, Leaf?"

"I guess I don't feel like going up front again so soon."

"You think Shadow here can hold the reins in this storm?" Crown asked coldly.

Leaf stiffened. He saw the wrath gathering in Crown's face. The big man was holding his natural violence in check with an effort, there would be trouble soon if Leaf remained defiant. This rebelliousness went against all of Leaf's principles, yet he found himself persisting in it and even taking a wicked pleasure in it. He chose to risk the confrontation and discover how firm Crown intended to be. Boldly he said, "You might try holding the reins yourself, friend."

"*Leaf!*" Shadow whispered, appalled.

Crown's face became murderous. His dark, shining cheeks puffed and went taut; his eyes blazed like molten nuggets; his hands closed and opened, closed and opened, furiously grasping air. "What kind of crazy stuff are you trying to give? We have a contract, Leaf. Unless you've suddenly decided that a Pure Stream doesn't need to abide by—"

"Spare me the class prejudice, Crown. I'm not pleading Pure Stream as an excuse to get out of working. I'm tired and I've earned my rest."

Shadow said softly, "Nobody's denying you your rest, Leaf. But Crown's right that I can't drive in a purple rain. I would if I could. And Sting can't do it either. That leaves only you."

"And Crown," Leaf said obstinately.

"There's only you," Shadow murmured. It was like her to take no sides, to serve ever as a mediator. "Go on, Leaf. Before there's real trouble. Making trouble like this isn't your usual way."

Leaf felt bound to pursue his present course, however perilous. He shook his head. "You, Crown. You drive."

In a throttled voice Crown said, "You're pushing me too far. We have a contract."

All Leaf's Pure Stream temperance was gone now. "Contract? I agreed to do my fair share of the driving, not to let myself be yanked up from my rest at a time when—"

Crown kicked at a low wickerwork stool, splitting it. His rage was boiling close to the surface. Swollen veins throbbed in his throat. He said, still controlling himself, "Get out there right now, Leaf, or by the Soul I'll send you into the All-Is-One!"

"Beautiful, Crown. Kill me, if you feel you have to. Who'll drive your damned wagon for you then?"

"I'll worry about that then."

Crown started forward, swallowing air, clenching fists.

Shadow sharply nudged Leaf's ribs. "This is going beyond the point of reason," she told him. He agreed. He had tested Crown and he had his answer, which was that Crown was unlikely to back down; now enough was enough, for Crown was capable of killing. The huge Dark Laker loomed over him, lifting his tremendous arms as though to bring them crashing against Leaf's head. Leaf held up his hands, more a gesture of submission than of self-defense.

"Wait," he said. "Stop it, Crown. I'll drive."

Crown's arms descended anyway. Crown managed to halt the killing blow midway, losing his balance and lurching heavily against the side of the wagon. Clumsily he straightened. Slowly he shook his head. In a low, menacing voice he said, "Don't ever try something like this again, Leaf."

"It's the rain," Shadow said. "The purple rain. Everybody does strange things in a purple rain."

"Even so," Crown said, dropping onto the pile of furs as Leaf got up. "The next time, Leaf, there'll be bad trouble. Now go ahead. Get up front."

Nodding to him, Leaf said, "Come up front with me, Shadow."

She did not answer. A look of fear flickered across her face.

Crown said, "The driver drives alone. You know that, Leaf. Are you still testing me? If you're testing me, say so and I'll know how to deal with you."

"I just want some company, as long as I have to do an extra shift."

"Shadow stays here."

There was a moment of silence. Shadow was trembling. "All right," Leaf said finally. "Shadow stays here."

"I'll walk a little way toward the front with you," Shadow said, glancing timidly at Crown. Crown scowled but said nothing. Leaf stepped out of the passenger castle; Shadow followed. Outside, in the narrow passageway leading to the midcabin, Leaf halted, shaken, shaking, and seized her. She pressed her slight body against him and they embraced, roughly, intensely. When he released her she said, "Why did you try to cross him like that? It was such a strange thing for you to do, Leaf."

"I just didn't feel like taking the reins again so soon."

"I know that."

"I want to be with you."

"You'll be with me a little later," she said. "It didn't make sense for you to talk back to Crown. There wasn't any choice. You *had* to drive."

"Why?"

"You know. Sting couldn't do it. I couldn't do it."

"And Crown?"

She looked at him oddly. "Crown? How would Crown have taken the reins?"

From the passenger castle came Crown's angry growl: "You going to stand there all day, Leaf? Go on! Get in here, Shadow!"

"I'm coming," she called.

Leaf held her a moment. "Why not? Why couldn't he have driven? He may be proud, but not so proud that—"

"Ask me another time," Shadow said, pushing him away. "Go. Go. You have to drive. If we don't move along we'll have the spiders upon us."

On the third day westward they had arrived at a village of Shapechangers. Much of the countryside through which they had been passing was deserted, although the Teeth had not yet visited it, but these Shapechangers went about their usual routines as if nothing had happened in the neighboring provinces. These were angular, long-legged people, sallow of skin, nearly green in hue, who were classed generally somewhere below the midcastes, but above the underbreeds. Their gift was metamorphosis, a slow softening of the bones under voluntary control that could, in the course of a week, drastically alter the form of their bodies, but Leaf saw them doing none of that, except for a few children who seemed midway through strange transformations, one with ropy, seemingly boneless arms, one with grotesquely distended shoulders, one with stiltlike legs. The adults came close to the wagon, admiring its beauty with soft cooing sounds, and Crown went out to talk with them. "I'm on my way to raise an army," he said. "I'll be back in a month or two, leading my kinsmen out of the Flatlands. Will you fight in our ranks? Together we'll drive out the Teeth and make the eastern provinces safe again."

The Shapechangers laughed heartily. "How can anyone drive out the Teeth?" asked an old one with a greasy mop of blue-white hair. "It was the will of the Soul that they burst forth as conquerors, and no one can quarrel with the Soul. The Teeth will stay in these lands for a thousand thousand years."

"They can be defeated!" Crown cried.

"They will destroy all that lies in their path, and no one can stop them."

"If you feel that way, why don't you flee?" Leaf asked.

"Oh, we have time. But we'll be gone long before your return with your army." There were giggles. "We'll keep ourselves clear of the Teeth. We have our ways. We make our changes and we slip away."

Crown persisted. "We can use you in our war against them. You have valuable gifts. If you won't serve as soldiers, at least serve us as spies. We'll send you into the camps of the Teeth, disguised as—"

"We will not be here," the old Shapechanger said, "and no one will be able to find us," and that was the end of it.

As the airwagon departed from the Shapechanger village, Shadow at the reins, Leaf said to Crown, "Do you really think you can defeat the Teeth?"

"I have to."

"You heard the old Shapechanger. The coming of the Teeth was the will of the Soul. Can you hope to thwart that will?"

"A rainstorm is the will of the Soul also," Crown said quietly. "All the same, I do what I can to keep myself dry. I've never known the Soul to be displeased by that."

"It's not the same. A rainstorm is a transaction between the sky and the land. We aren't involved in it; if we want to cover our heads, it doesn't alter what's really taking place. But the invasion of the Teeth is a transaction between tribe and tribe, a reordering of social patterns. In the great scheme of things,

Crown, it may be a necessary process, preordained to achieve certain ends beyond our understanding. All events are part of some larger whole, and everything balances out, everything compensates for something else. Now we have peace, and now it's the time for invaders, do you see? If that's so, it's futile to resist.''

"The Teeth broke into the eastlands," said Crown, "and they massacred thousands of Dark Lake people. My concern with necessary processes begins and ends with that fact. My tribe has nearly been wiped out. Yours is still safe, up by its ferny shores. I will seek help and gain revenge.''

"The Shapechangers laughed at you. Others will also. No one will want to fight the Teeth.''

"I have cousins in the Flatlands. If no one else will, they'll mobilize themselves. They'll want to repay the Teeth for their crime against the Dark Lakers.''

"Your western cousins may tell you, Crown, that they prefer to remain where they are safe. Why should they go east to die in the name of vengeance? Will vengeance, no matter how bloody, bring any of your kinsmen back to life?''

"They will fight," Crown said.

"Prepare yourself for the possibility that they won't.''

"If they refuse," said Crown, "then I'll go back east myself, and wage my war alone until I'm overwhelmed. But don't fear for me, Leaf. I'm sure I'll find plenty of willing recruits.''

"How stubborn you are, Crown. You have good reason to hate the Teeth, as do we all. But why let that hatred cost you your only life? Why not accept the disaster that has befallen us, and make a new life for yourself beyond the Middle River, and forget this dream of reversing the irreversible?''

"I have my task," said Crown.

Forward through the wagon Leaf moved, going slowly, head down, shoulders hunched, feet atickle with the urge to kick things. He felt sour of spirit, curdled with dull resentment. He had let himself become angry at Crown, which was bad enough; but worse, he had let that anger possess and poison him. Not even the beauty of the wagon could lift him: ordinarily its superb construction and elegant furnishings gave him joy, the swirl-patterned fur hangings, the banners of gossamer textiles, the intricate carved inlays, the graceful strings of dried seeds and tassels that dangled from the vaulted ceilings, but these wonders meant nothing to him now. That was no way to be, he knew.

The airwagon was longer than ten men of the Pure Stream lying head to toe, and so wide that is spanned nearly the whole roadway. The finest workmanship had gone into its making: Flower Giver artisans, no doubt of it, only Flower Givers could build so well. Leaf imagined dozens of the fragile little folk toiling earnestly for months, all smiles and silence, long, slender fingers and quick, gleaming eyes, shaping the great wagon as one might shape a poem. The main frame was of lengthy pale spears of light, resilient wingwood, elegantly laminated into broad curving strips with a colorless fragrant mucilage and bound with springy withes brought from the southern marshes. Over this elaborate armature tanned sheets of stickskin had been stretched and stitched into place with thick yellow fibers drawn from the stick-creatures' own gristly bodies. The floor was of dark shining nightflower-wood planks, buffed to a high finish and pegged together with great skill. No metal had been employed in the construction of the wagon, nor any artificial substances: nature had supplied everything. Huge and majestic though the wagon was, it was airy and light, light enough to float on a vertical column of warm air generated by magnetic rotors whirling in its belly; so long as the earth turned, so would the rotors, and when the rotors were spinning the wagon drifted cat-high above the ground, and could be tugged easily along by the team of nightmares.

It was more a mobile palace than a wagon, and wherever it went it stirred excitement: Crown's love, Crown's joy, Crown's estate, a wondrous toy. To pay for the making of it Crown must have sent many souls into the All-Is-One, for that was how Crown had earned his livelihood in the old days, as a hired warrior, a surrogate killer, fighting one-on-one duels for rich eastern princelings too weak or too lazy to defend their own honor. He had never been scratched, and his fees had been high; but all that was ended now that the Teeth were loose in the eastlands.

Leaf could not bear to endure being so irritable any longer. He paused to adjust himself, closing his eyes and listening for the clear tone that sounded always at the center of his being. After a few minutes he found it, tuned himself to it, let it purify him.

Crown's unfairness ceased to matter. Leaf became once more his usual self, alert and outgoing, aware and responsive.

Smiling, whistling, he made his way swiftly through the wide, comfortable, brightly lit midcabin, decorated with Crown's weapons and other grim souvenirs of battle, and went on into the front corridor that led to the driver's cabin.

Sting sat slumped at the reins. White Crystal folk such as Sting generally seemed to throb and tick with energy; but Sting looked exhausted, emptied, half dead of fatigue. He was a small, sinewy being, narrow of shoulder and hip, with colorless skin of a waxy, horny texture, pocked everywhere with little hairy nodes and whorls. His muscles were long and flat; his face was cavernous, beaked nose and tiny chin, dark mischievous eyes hidden in bony recesses. Leaf touched his shoulder. "It's all right," he said. "Crown sent me to relieve you." Sting nodded feebly but did not move. The little man was quivering like a frog. Leaf had always thought of him as indestructible, but in the grip of this despondency Sting seemed more fragile even than Shadow.

"Come," Leaf murmured. "You have a few hours for resting. Shadow will look after you."

Sting shrugged. He was hunched forward, staring dully through the clear curving window, stained now with splashes of muddy tinted water.

"The dirty spiders," he said. His voice was hoarse and frayed. "The filthy rain. The mud. Look at the horses, Leaf. They're dying of fright, and so am I. We'll all perish on this road, Leaf, if not of spiders then of poisoned rain, if not of rain then of the Teeth, if not of the Teeth then of something else. There's no road for us but this one, do you realize that? This is the road, and we're bound to it like helpless underbreeds, and we'll die on it."

"We'll die when our turn comes, like everything else, Sting, and not a moment before."

"Our turn is coming. Too soon. Too soon. I feel death-ghosts close at hand."

"*Sting!*"

Sting made a weird ratcheting sound low in his throat, a sort of rusty sob. Leaf lifted him and swung him out of the river's seat, setting him gently down in the corridor. It was as though he weighed nothing at all. Perhaps just then that was true. Sting had many strange gifts. "Go on," Leaf said. "Get some rest while you can."

"How kind you are, Leaf."

"And no more talk of ghosts."

"Yes," Sting said. Leaf saw him struggling against fear and despair and weariness. Sting appeared to brighten a moment, flickering on the edge of his old vitality; then the brief glow subsided, and, smiling a pale smile, offering a whisper of thanks, he went aft.

Leaf took his place in the driver's seat.

Through the window of the wagon—thin, tough sheets of stickskin, the best quality, carefully matched, perfectly transparent—he confronted a dismal scene. Rain dark as blood was falling at a steep angle, scourging the spongy soil, kicking up tiny fountains of earth. A bluish miasma rose from the ground, billows of dark, steamy fog, the acrid odor of which had begun to seep into the wagon. Leaf sighed and reached for the reins. Death-ghosts, he thought. Haunted. Poor Sting, driven to the end of his wits.

And yet, and yet, as he considered the things Sting had said, Leaf realized that he had been feeling somewhat the same way, these past few days: tense, driven, haunted. *Haunted*. As though unseen presences, mocking, hostile, were hovering near. Ghosts? The strain, more likely, of all that he had gone through since the first onslaught of the Teeth. He had lived through the collapse of rich and intricate civilization. He moved now through a strange world, all ashes and seaweed. He was haunted, perhaps, by the weight of the unburied past, by the memory of all that he had lost.

A rite of exorcism seemed in order.

Lightly he said, aloud, "If there are any ghosts in here, I want you to listen to me. *Get out of this cabin.* That's an order. I have work to do."

He laughed. He picked up the reins and made ready to take control of the team of nightmares.

The sense of an invisible presence was overwhelming.

Something at once palpable and intangible pressed clammily against him. He felt surrounded and engulfed. It's the fog, he told himself. Dark blue fog, pushing at the window, sealing the wagon into a pocket of vapor. Or was it? Leaf sat quite still for a moment, listening. Silence. He relinquished the reins, swung about in his seat, carefully inspected the cabin. No one there. An absurdity to be fidgeting like this. Yet the discomfort remained. This was no joke now. Sting's anxieties had infected him, and the

malady was feeding on itself, growing more intense from moment to moment, making him vulnerable to any stray terror that
whispered to him. Only with a tranquil mind could he attain the
state of trance a nightmare-driver must enter; and trance seemed
unattainable so long as he felt the prickle of some invisible
watcher's gaze on the back of his neck. This rain, he thought,
this damnable rain. It drives everybody crazy. In a clear, firm
voice Leaf said, "I'm altogether serious. Show yourself and get
yourself out of this cabin."

Silence.

He took up the reins again. No use. Concentration was
impossible. He knew many techniques for centering himself, for
leading his consciousness to a point of unassailable serenity. But
could he achieve that now, jangled and distracted as he was? He
would try. He had to succeed. The wagon had tarried in this place
much too long already. Leaf summoned all his inner resources; he
purged himself, one by one, of every discord; he compelled
himself to slide into trance.

It seemed to be working. Darkness beckoned to him. He stood
at the threshold. He started to step across.

"Such a fool, such a foolish fool," said a sudden dry voice
out of nowhere that nibbled at his ears like the needle-toothed
mice of the White Desert.

The trance broke. Leaf shivered as if stabbed and sat up, eyes
bright, face flushed with excitement.

"Who spoke?"

"Put down those reins, friend. Going forward on this road is a
heavy waste of spirit."

"Then I wasn't crazy and neither was Sting. There *is* something in here!"

"A ghost, yes a ghost, a ghost, a ghost!" The ghost showered
him with laughter.

Leaf's tension eased. Better to be troubled by a real ghost than
to be vexed by a fantasy of one's own disturbed mind. He feared
madness far more than he did the invisible. Besides, he thought
he knew what this creature must be.

"Where are you, ghost?"

"Not far from you. Here I am. Here. Here." From three
different parts of the cabin, one after another. The invisible being
began to sing. Its song was high-pitched, whining, a grinding
tone that stretched Leaf's patience intolerably. Leaf still saw no

one, though he narrowed his eyes and stared as hard as he could.
He imagined he could detect a faint veil of pink light floating
along the wall of the cabin, a smoky haze moving from place to
place, a shimmering film like thin oil on water, but whenever he
focused his eyes on it the misty presence appeared to evaporate.

Leaf said, "How long have you been aboard this wagon?"

"Long enough."

"Did you come aboard at Theptis?"

"Was that the name of the place?" asked the ghost disingenu-
ously. "I forget. It's so hard to remember things."

"Theptis," said Leaf. "Four days ago."

"Perhaps it was Theptis," the ghost said. "Fool! Dreamer!"

"Why do you call me names?"

"You travel a dead road, fool, and yet nothing will turn you
from it." The invisible one snickered. "Do you think I'm a
ghost, Pure Stream?"

"I know what you are."

"How wise you've become!"

"Such a pitiful phantom. Such a miserable drifting wraith.
Show yourself to me, ghost."

Laughter reverberated from the corners of the cabin. The voice
said, speaking from a point close to Leaf's left ear, "The road
you choose to travel has been killed ahead. We told you that
when you came to us, and yet you went onward, and still you go
onward. Why are you so rash?"

"Why won't you show yourself? A gentleman finds it
discomforting to speak to the air."

Obligingly the ghost yielded, after a brief pause, some fraction
of its invisibility. A vaporous crimson stain appeared in the air
before Leaf, and he saw within it dim, insubstantial features, like
projections on a screen of thick fog. He believed he could make
out a wispy white beard, harsh glittering eyes, lean curving lips;
a whole forbidding face, a fleshless torso. The stain deepened
momentarily to scarlet and for a moment Leaf saw the entire
figure of the stranger revealed, a long narrow-bodied man, dried
and withered, grinning ferociously at him. The edges of the
figure softened and became mist. Then Leaf saw only vapor
again, and then nothing.

"I remember you from Theptis," Leaf said. "In the tent of
Invisibles."

"What will you do when you come to the dead place on the

highway?'' the invisible one demanded. "Will you fly over it? Will you tunnel under it?''

"You were asking the same things at Theptis,'' Leaf replied. "I will make the same answer that the Dark Laker gave you then. We will go forward, dead place or no. This is the only road for us.''

They had come to Theptis on the fifth day of their flight—a grand city, a splendid mercantile emporium, the gateway to the west, sprawling athwart a place where two great rivers met and many highways converged. In happy times any and all peoples might be found in Theptis, Pure Streams and White Crystals and Flower Givers and Sand Shapers and a dozen others jostling one another in the busy streets, buying and selling, selling and buying, but mainly Theptis was a city of Fingers—the merchant caste, plump and industrious, thousands upon thousands of them concentrated in this one city.

The day Crown's airwagon reached Theptis much of the city was ablaze, and they halted on a broad stream-split plain just outside the metropolitan area. An improvised camp for refugees had sprouted there, and tents of black and gold and green cloth littered the meadow like new nightshoots. Leaf and Crown went out to inquire after the news. Had the Teeth sacked Theptis as well? No, an old and sagging Sand Shaper told them. The Teeth, so far as anyone had heard, were still well to the east, rampaging through the coastal cities. Why the fires, then? The old man shook his head. His energy was exhausted, or his patience, or his courtesy. If you want to know anything else, he said, ask *them*. They know everything. And he pointed toward a tent opposite his.

Leaf looked into the tent and found it empty; then he looked again and saw upright shadows moving about in it, tenuous figures that existed at the very bounds of visibility and could be perceived only by tricks of the light as they changed place in the tent. They asked him within, and Crown came also. By the smoky light of their tentfire they were more readily seen: seven or eight men of the Invisible stock, nomads, ever mysterious, gifted with ways of causing beams of light to travel around or through their bodies so that they might escape the scrutiny of ordinary eyes. Leaf, like everyone else not of their kind, was uncomfortable among Invisibles. No one trusted them; no one was capable of predicting their actions, for they were creatures of whim and caprice, or else followed some code the logic of which was incomprehensible to outsiders. They made Leaf and Crown welcome, adjusting their bodies until they were in clear sight, and offering the visitors a flagon of wine, a bowl of fruit. Crown gestured toward Theptis. Who had set the city afire? A red-bearded Invisible with a raucous rumbling voice answered that on the second night of the invasion the richest of the Fingers had panicked and had begun to flee the city with their most precious belongings, and as their wagons rolled through the gates the lesser breeds had begun to loot the Finger mansions, and brawling had started once the wine cellars were pierced, and fires broke out, and there was no one to make the fire wardens do their work, for they were all underbreeds and the masters had fled. So the city burned and was still burning, and the survivors were huddled here on the plain, waiting for the rubble to cool so that they might salvage valuables from it, and hoping that the Teeth would not fall upon them before they could do their sifting. As for the Fingers, said the Invisible, they were all gone from Theptis now.

Which way had they gone? Mainly to the northwest, by way of Sunset Highway, at first; but then the approach to that road had become choked by stalled wagons butted one up against another, so that the only way to reach the Sunset now was by making a difficult detour through the sand country north of the city, and once that news became general the Fingers had turned their wagons southward. Crown wondered why no one seemed to be taking Spider Highway westward. At this a second Invisible, white-bearded, joined the conversation. Spider Highway, he said, is blocked just a few days' journey west of here: a dead road, a useless road. Everyone knows that, said the white-bearded Invisible.

"That is our route," said Crown.

"I wish you well," said the Invisible. "You will not get far."

"I have to get to the Flatlands."

"Take your chances with the sand country," the red-bearded one advised, "and go by way of the Sunset."

"It would waste two weeks or more," Crown replied. "Spider Highway is the only road we can consider." Leaf and Crown exchanged wary glances. Leaf asked the nature of the trouble on the highway, but the Invisibles said only that the road had been "killed," and would offer no amplification. "We will go forward," Crown said, "dead place or no."

"As you choose," said the older Invisible, pouring more wine. Already both Invisibles were fading; the flagon seemed suspended in mist. So, too, did the discussion become unreal, dreamlike, as answers no longer followed closely upon the sense of questions, and the words of the Invisibles came to Leaf and Crown as though swaddled in thick wool. There was a long interval of silence, at last, and when Leaf extended his empty glass the flagon was not offered to him, and he realized finally that he and Crown were alone in the tent. They left it and asked at other tents about the blockage on Spider Highway, but no one knew anything of it, neither some young Dancing Stars nor three flat-faced Water Breather women nor a family of Flower Givers. How reliable was the word of Invisibles? What did they mean by a "dead" road? Suppose they merely thought the road was ritually impure, for some reason understood only by Invisibles. What value, then, would their warning have to those who did not subscribe to their superstitions? Who knew at any time what the words of an Invisible meant? That night in the wagon the four of them puzzled over the concept of a road that has been "killed," but neither Shadow's intuitive perceptions nor Sting's broad knowledge of tribal dialects and customs could provide illumination. In the end Crown reaffirmed his decision to proceed on the road he had originally chosen, and it was Spider Highway that they took out of Theptis. As they proceeded westward they met no one traveling the opposite way, though one might expect the eastbound lanes to be thronged with a flux of travelers turning back from whatever obstruction might be closing the road ahead. Crown took cheer in that; but Leaf observed privately that their wagon appeared to be the only vehicle on the road in either direction, as if everyone else knew better than to make the attempt. In such stark solitude they journeyed four days west of Theptis before the purple rain hit them.

Now the Invisible said, "Go into your trance and drive your horses. I'll dream beside you until the awakening comes."

"I prefer privacy."

"You won't be disturbed."

"I ask you to leave."

"You treat your guests coldly."

"Are you my guest?" Leaf asked. "I don't remember extending an invitation."

"You drank wine in our tent. That creates in you an obligation to offer reciprocal hospitality." The Invisible sharpened his bodily intensity until he seemed as solid as Crown; but even as Leaf observed the effect he grew thin again, fading in patches. The far wall of the cabin showed through his chest, as if he were hollow. His arms had disappeared, but not his gnarled long-fingered hands. He was grinning, showing crooked close-set teeth. There was a strange scent in the cabin, sharp and musky, like vinegar mixed with honey. The Invisible said, "I'll ride with you a little longer," and vanished altogether.

Leaf searched the corners of the cabin, knowing that an Invisible could always be felt even if he eluded the eyes. His probing hands encountered nothing. Gone, gone, gone, whisking off to the place where snuffed flames go, eh? Even that odor of vinegar and honey was diminishing. "Where are you?" Leaf asked. "Still hiding somewhere else?" Silence. Leaf shrugged. The stink of the purple rain was the dominant scent again. Time to move on, stowaway or no. Rain was hitting the window in huge murky windblown blobs. Once more Leaf picked up the reins. He banished the Invisible from his mind.

These purple rains condensed out of drifting gaseous clots in the upper atmosphere—dank clouds of chemical residues that arose from the world's most stained, most injured places and circled the planet like malign tempests. Upon colliding with a mass of cool air such a poisonous cloud often discharged its burden of reeking oils and acids in the form of a driving rainstorm; and the foulness that descended could be fatal to plants and shrubs, to small animals, sometimes even to man.

A purple rain was the cue for certain somber creatures to come forth from dark places: scuttering scavengers that picked eagerly through the dead and dying, and larger, more dangerous things that preyed on the dazed and choking living. The no-leg spiders were among the more unpleasant of these.

They were sinister spherical beasts the size of large dogs, voracious in the appetite and ruthless in the hunt. Their bodies were plump, covered with coarse, rank brown hair; they bore eight glittering eyes above sharp-fanged mouths. No-legged they were indeed, but not immobile, for a single huge fleshy foot, something like that of a snail, sprouted from the underbellies of these spiders and carried them along at a slow, inexorable pace. They were poor pursuers, easily avoided by healthy animals; but to the numbed victims of a purple rain they were deadly, moving in to strike with hinged, poison-barbed claws that leaped out of niches along their backs. Were they truly spiders? Leaf had no idea. Like almost everything else, they were a recent species, mutated out of the-Soul-only-knew-what during the period of stormy biological upheavals that had attended the end of the old industrial civilization, and no one yet had studied them closely, or cared to.

Crown had killed four of them. Their bodies lay upside down at the edge of the road, upturned feet wilting and drooping like plucked toadstools. About a dozen more spiders had emerged from the low hills flanking the highway and were gliding slowly toward the stalled wagon; already several had reached their dead comrades and were making ready to feed on them, and some of the others were eyeing the horses.

The six nightmares, prisoners of their harnesses, prowled about uneasily in their constricted ambits, anxiously scraping at the muddy ground with their hooves. They were big, sturdy beasts, black as death, with long feathery ears and high-domed skulls that housed minds as keen as many human's, sharper than some. The rain annoyed the horses but could not seriously harm them, and the spiders could be kept at bay with kicks, but plainly the entire situation disturbed them.

Leaf meant to get them out of here as rapidly as he could.

A slimy coating covered everything the rain had touched, and the road was a miserable quagmire, slippery as ice. There was peril for all of them in that. If a horse stumbled and fell it might splinter a leg, causing such confusion that the whole team might be pulled down; and as the injured nightmares thrashed about in the mud the hungry spiders would surely move in on them, venomous claws rising, striking, delivering stings that stunned, and leaving the horses paralyzed, helpless, vulnerable to eager teeth and strong jaws. As the wagon traveled onward through this swampy rain-soaked district Leaf would constantly have to steady and reassure the nightmares, pouring his energy into them to comfort them, a strenuous task, a task that had wrecked poor Sting.

Leaf slipped the reins over his forehead. He became aware of the consciousness of the six fretful horses.

Because he was still awake, contact was misty and uncertain. A waking mind was unable to communicate with the animals in any useful way. To guide the team he had to enter a trance state, a dream state; they would not respond to anything so gross as conscious intelligence. He looked about for manifestations of the Invisible. No, no sign of him. Good. Leaf brought his mind to dead center.

He closed his eyes. The technique of trance was easy enough for him, when there were no distractions.

He visualized a tunnel, narrow-mouthed and dark, slanting into the ground. He drifted toward its entrance.

Hovered there a moment.

Went down into it.

Floating, floating, borne downward by warm, gentle currents: he sinks in a slow spiral descent, autumn leaf on a springtime breeze. The tunnel's walls are circular, crystalline, lit from within, the light growing in brightness as he drops toward the heart of the world. Gleaming scarlet and blue flowers, brittle as glass, sprout from crevices at meticulously regular intervals.

He goes deep, touching nothing. Down.

Entering a place where the tunnel widens into a round smooth-walled chamber, sealed at the end. He stretches full-length on the floor. The floor is black stone, slick and slippery; he dreams it soft and yielding, womb-warm. Colors are muted here, sounds are blurred. He hears far-off music, percussive and muffled, *rat-a-rat, rat-a-rat, blllooom, blllooom.*

Now at least he is able to make full contact with the minds of the horses.

His spirit expands in their direction; he envelops them, he takes them into himself. He senses the separate identity of each, picks up the shifting play of their emotions, their prancing fantasies, their fears. Each mare has her own distinct response to the rain, to the spiders, to the sodden highway. One is restless, one is timid, one is furious, one is sullen, one is tense, one is torpid. He feeds energy to them. He pulls them together. Come, gather your strength, take us onward: this is the road, we must be on our way.

The nightmares stir.

They react well to his touch. He believes that they prefer him over Shadow and Sting as a driver: Sting is too manic, Shadow too permissive. Leaf keeps them together, directs them easily, gives them the guidance they need. They are intelligent, yes, they have personalities and goals and ideals, but also they are beasts of burden, and Leaf never forgets that, for the nightmares themselves do not.

Come, now. Onward.

The road is ghastly. They pick at it and their hooves make sucking sounds coming up from the mud. They complain to him. *We are cold, we are wet, we are bored.* He dreams wings for them to make their way easier. To soothe them he dreams sunlight for them, bountiful warmth, dry highway, an easy trot. He dreams green hillsides, cascades of yellow blossoms, the flutter of hummingbirds' wings, the droning of bees. He gives the horses sweet summer, and they grow calm; they lift their heads; they fan their dream-wings and preen; they are ready now to resume the journey. They pull as one. The rotors hum happily. The wagon slides forward with a smooth coasting motion.

Leaf, deep in trance, is unable to see the road, but no matter; the horses see it for him and send him images, fluid, shifting dream-images, polarized and refracted and diffracted by the strangenesses of their vision and the distortions of dream communication, six simultaneous and individual views. Here is the road, bordered by white birches whipped by an angry wind. Here is the road, an earthen swath slicing through a forest of mighty pines bowed down by white new snow. Here is the road, a ribbon of fertility, from which dazzling red poppies spring wherever a hoof strikes. Fleshy-finned blue fishes do headstands beside the road. Paunchy burghers of the Finger tribe spread brilliantly laundered tablecloths along the grassy margin and make lunch out of big-eyed reproachful oysters. Masked figures dart between the horses' legs. The road curves, curves again, doubles back on itself, crosses itself in a complacent loop. Leaf integrates this dizzying many-hued inrush of data, sorting the real from the unreal, blending and focusing the input and using it to guide himself in guiding the horses. Serenely he coordinates their movements with quick confident impulses of thought, so that each animal will pull with the same force. The wagon is precariously balanced on its column of air, and an unequal tug could well send it slewing into the treacherous thicket to the left of the road. He sends quicksilver messages down the thick conduit from his mind to theirs. Steady there, steady, watch that boggy patch coming up! Ah! Ah, that's my girl! Spiders on the left, careful! Good! Yes, yes, ah, yes! He pats their heaving flanks with a strand of his mind. He rewards their agility with dreams of the stable, of newly mown hay, of stallions waiting at journey's end.

From them—for they love him, he knows they love him—he gets warm dreams of the highway, all beauty and joy, all images converging into a single idealized view, majestic groves of wingwood trees and broad meadows through which clear brooks flow. They dream his own past life for him, too, feeding back to him nuggets of random autobiography mined in the seams of his being. What they transmit is filtered and transformed by their alien sensibilities, colored with hallucinatory glows and tugged and twisted into other-dimensional forms, but yet he is able to perceive the essential meaning of each tableau: his childhood among the parks and gardens of the Pure Stream enclave near the Inland Sea, his wanderyears among the innumerable, unfamiliar, not-quite-human breeds of the hinterlands, his brief, happy sojourn in the fog-swept western country, his eastward journey in early manhood, always following the will of the Soul, always bending to the breezes, accepting whatever destiny seizes him, eastward now, his band of friends closer than brothers in his adopted eastern province, his sprawling lakeshore home there, all polished wood and billowing tented pavilions, his collection of relics of mankind's former times—pieces of machinery, elegant coils of metal, rusted coins, grotesque statuettes, wedges of imperishable plastic—housed in its own wing with its own curator. Lost in these reveries he ceases to remember that the home by the lake has been reduced to ashes by the Teeth, that his friends of kinder days are dead, his estates overrun, his pretty things scattered in the kitchen-middens.

Imperceptibly, the dream turns sour.

Spiders and rain and mud creep back into it. He is reminded, through some darkening of tone of the imagery pervading his dreaming mind, that he has been stripped of everything and has become, now that he has taken flight, merely a driver hired out to a bestial Dark Lake mercenary who is himself a fugitive.

Leaf is working harder to control the team now. The horses seem less sure of their footing, and the pace slows; they are bothered about something, and a sour, querulous anxiety tinges

their messages to him. He catches their mood. He sees himself
harnessed to the wagon alongside the nightmares, and it is Crown
at the reins, Crown wielding a terrible whip, driving the wagon
frenziedly forward, seeking allies who will help him fulfill his
fantasy of liberating the lands the Teeth have taken. There is no
escape from Crown. He rises above the landscape like a monster
of congealed smoke, growing more huge until he obscures the
sky. Leaf wonders how he will disengage himself from Crown.
Shadow runs beside him, stroking his cheeks, whispering to him,
and he asks her to undo the harness, but she says she cannot, that
it is their duty to serve Crown, and Leaf turns to Sting, who is
harnessed on his other side, and he asks Sting for help, but Sting
coughs and slips in the mud as Crown's whip flicks his back-
bone. There is no escape. The wagon heels and shakes. The
right-hand horse skids, nearly falls, recovers. Leaf decides he
must be getting tired. He has driven a great deal today, and the
effort is telling. But the rain is still falling—he breaks through the
veil of illusions, briefly, past the scenes of spring and summer
and autumn, and sees the blue-black water dropping in wild
handfuls from the sky—and there is no one else to drive, so he
must continue.

He tries to submerge himself in deeper trance, where he will
be less readily deflected from control.

But no, something is wrong, something plucks at his consciousness, drawing him toward the waking state. The horses
summon him to wakefulness with frightful scenes. One beast
shows him the wagon about to plunge through a wall of a fire.
Another pictures them at the brink of a vast impassable crater.
Another gives him the image of giant boulders strewn across the
road; another, a mountain of ice blocking the way; another, a
pack of snarling wolves; another, a row of armored warriors
standing shoulder to shoulder, lances at the ready. No doubt of it.
Trouble. Trouble. Trouble. Perhaps they have come to the dead
place in the road. No wonder that Invisible was skulking around.
Leaf forces himself to awaken.

There was no wall of fire. No warriors, no wolves, none of those
things. Only a palisade of newly felled timbers facing him some
hundred paces ahead on the highway, timbers twice as tall as
Crown, sharpened to points at both ends and thrust deep into the
earth one up against the next and bound securely with freshly cut

vines. The barricade spanned the highway completely from edge
to edge; on its right it was bordered by a tangle of impenetrable
thorny scrub; on its left it extended to the brink of a steep ravine.

They were stopped.

Such a blockade across a public highway was inconceivable.
Leaf blinked, coughed, rubbed his aching forehead. Those last
few minutes of discordant dreams had left a murky, gritty coating
on his brain. This wall of wood seemed like some sort of dream
too, a very bad one. Leaf imagined he could hear the Invisible's
cool laughter somewhere close at hand. At least the rain appeared
to be slackening, and there were no spiders about. Small consola-
tions, but the best that were available.

Baffled, Leaf freed himself of the reins and awaited the next
event. After a moment or two he sensed the joggling rhythms that
told of Crown's heavy forward progress through the cabin. The
big man peered into the driver's cabin.

"What's going on? Why aren't we moving?"

"Dead road."

"What are you talking about?"

"See for yourself," Leaf said wearily, gesturing toward the
window.

Crown leaned across Leaf to look. He studied the scene an
endless moment, reacting slowly. "What's that? A *wall?*"

"A wall, yes."

"A wall across a highway? I never heard of anything like
that."

"The Invisibles at Theptis may have been trying to warn us
about this."

"A wall. A wall." Crown shook with perplexed anger. "It
violates all the maintenance customs! Soul take it, Leaf, a public
highway is—"

"—sacred and inviolable. Yes. What the Teeth have been
doing in the east violates a good many maintenance customs
too," Leaf said. "And territorial customs as well. These are
unusual times everywhere." He wondered if he should tell about
the Invisible who was on board. One problem at a time, he
decided. "Maybe this is how these people propose to keep the
Teeth out of their country, Crown."

"But to block a public road—"

"We were warned."

"Who could trust the word of an Invisible?"

"There's the wall," Leaf said. "Now we know why we didn't meet anyone else on the highway. They probably put this thing up as soon as they heard about the Teeth, and the whole province knows enough to avoid Spider Highway. Everyone but us."

"What folk dwell here?"

"No idea. Sting's the one who would know."

"Yes, Sting would know," said the high, clear, sharp-edged voice of Sting from the corridor. He poked his head into the cabin. Leaf saw Shadow just behind him. "This is the land of the Tree Companions," Sting said. "Do you know of them?"

Crown shook his head. "Not I," said Leaf.

"Forest-dwellers," Sting said. "Tree-worshippers. Small heads, slow brains. Dangerous in battle—they use poisoned darts. There are nine tribes of them in this region, I think, under a single chief. Once they paid tribute to my people, but I suppose in these times all that has ended."

"They worship trees?" Shadow said lightly. "And how many of their gods, then, did they cut down to make this barrier?"

Sting laughed. "If you must have gods, why not put them to some good use?"

Crown glared at the wall across the highway as he once might have glared at an opponent in the dueling ring. Seething, he paced a narrow path in the crowded cabin. "We can't waste any more time. The Teeth will be coming through this region in a few days, for sure. We've got to reach the river before something happens to the bridges ahead."

"The wall," Leaf said.

"There's plenty of brush lying around out there," said Sting. "We could build a bonfire and burn it down."

"Green wood," Leaf said. "It's impossible."

"We have hatchets," Shadow pointed out. "How long would it take for us to cut through timbers as thick as those?"

Sting said, "We'd need a week for the job. The Tree Companions would fill us full of darts before we'd been chopping an hour."

"Do you have any ideas?" Shadow said to Leaf.

"Well, we could turn back toward Theptis and try to find our way to Sunset Highway by way of the sand country. There are only two roads from here to the river, this and the Sunset. We lose five days, though, if we decide to go back, and we might get snarled up in whatever chaos is going on in Theptis, or we could very well get stranded in the desert trying to reach the highway. The only other choice I see is to abandon the wagon and look for some path around the wall on foot, but I doubt very much that Crown would—''

"Crown wouldn't," said Crown, who had been chewing his lip in tense silence. "But I see some different possibilities."

"Go on."

"One is to find these Tree Companions and compel them to clear this trash from the highway. Darts or no darts, one Dark Lake and one Pure Stream side by side ought to be able to terrify twenty tribes of pinhead forest folk."

"And if we can't?" Leaf asked.

"That brings us to the other possibility, which is that this wall isn't particularly intended to protect the neighborhood against the Teeth at all, but that these Tree Companions have taken advantage of the general confusion to set up some sort of toll-raising scheme. In that case, if we can't force them to open the road, we can find out what they want, what sort of toll they're asking, and pay it if we can and be on our way."

"Is that Crown who's talking?" Sting asked. "Talking about paying a toll to underbreeds of the forest? Incredible!"

Crown said, "I don't like the thought of paying toll to anybody. But it may be the simplest and quickest way to get out of here. Do you think I'm entirely a creature of pride, Sting?"

Leaf stood up. "If you're right that this is a toll station, there'd be some kind of gate in the wall. I'll go out there and have a look at it."

"No," said Crown, pushing him lightly back into his seat. "There's danger here, Leaf. This part of the work falls to me." He strode toward the midcabin and was busy there a few minutes. When he returned he was in his full armor: breastplates, helmet, face mask, greaves, everything burnished to a high gloss. In those few places where his bare skin showed through, it seemed but a part of the armor. Crown looked like a machine. His mace hung at his hip, and the short shaft of his extensor sword rested easily along the inside of his right wrist, ready to spring to full length at a squeeze. Crown glanced toward Sting and said, "I'll need your nimble legs. Will you come?"

"As you say."

"Open the midcabin hatch for us, Leaf."

Leaf touched a control on the board below the front window.

With a soft, whining sound a hinged door near the middle of the wagon swung upward and out, and a stepladder sprouted to provide access to the ground. Crown made a ponderous exit. Sting, scorning the ladder, stepped down: it was the special gift of the White Crystal people to be able to transport themselves short distances in extraordinary ways.

Sting and Crown began to walk warily toward the wall. Leaf, watching from the driver's seat, slipped his arm lightly about the waist of Shadow, who stood beside him, and caressed her smooth fur. The rain had ended; a gray cloud still hung low, and the gleam of Crown's armor was already softened by fine droplets of moisture. He and Sting were nearly to the palisade, now, Crown constantly scanning the underbrush as if expecting a horde of Tree Companions to spring forth. Sting, loping along next to him, looked like some agile little two-legged beast, the top of his head barely reaching to Crown's hip.

They reached the palisade. Thin, late-afternoon sunlight streamed over its top. Kneeling, Sting inspected the base of the wall, probing at the soil with his fingers, and said something to Crown, who nodded and pointed upward. Sting backed off, made a short running start, and lofted himself, rising almost as though he were taking wing. His leap carried him soaring to the wall's jagged crest in a swift blurred flight. He appeared to hover for a long moment while choosing a place to land. At last he alighted in a precarious, uncomfortable-looking position, sprawled along the top of the wall with his body arched to avoid the timber's sharpened tips, his hands grasping two of the stakes and his feet wedged between two others. Sting remained in this desperate contortion for a remarkably long time, studying whatever lay beyond the barricade; then he let go his hold, sprang lightly outward, and floated to the ground, a distance some three times his own height. He landed upright, without stumbling. There was a brief conference between Crown and Sting. Then they came back to the wagon.

"It's a toll-raising scheme, all right," Crown muttered. "The middle timbers aren't embedded in the earth. They end just at ground level and form a hinged gate, fastened by two heavy bolts on the far side."

"I saw at least a hundred Tree Companions back of the wall," Sting said. "Armed with blowdarts. They'll be coming around to visit us in a moment."

"We should arm ourselves," Leaf said.

Crown shrugged. "We can't fight that many of them. Not twenty-five to one, we can't. The best hand-to-hand man in the world is helpless against little forest folk with poisoned blowdarts. If we aren't able to awe them into letting us go through, we'll have to buy them off somehow. But I don't know. That gate isn't nearly wide enough for the wagon."

He was right about that. There was the dry scraping squeal of wood against wood—the bolts were being unfastened—and then the gate swung slowly open. When it had been fully pushed back it provided an opening through which any good-size cart of ordinary dimensions might pass, but not Crown's magnificent vehicle. Five or six stakes on each side of the gate would have to be pulled down in order for the wagon to go by.

Tree Companions came swarming toward the wagon, scores of them—small, naked folk with lean limbs and smooth blue-green skin. They looked like animated clay statuettes, casually pinched into shape: their hairless heads were narrow and elongated, with flat sloping foreheads, and their long necks looked flimsy and fragile. They had shallow chests and bony, meatless frames. All of them, men and women both, wore reed dart-blowers strapped to their hips. As they danced and frolicked about the wagon they set up a ragged, irregular chanting, tuneless and atonal, like the improvised songs of children caught up in frantic play.

"We'll go out to them," Crown said. "Stay calm, make no sudden moves. Remember that these are underbreeds. So long as we think of ourselves as men and them as nothing more than monkeys, and make them realize we think that way, we'll be able to keep them under control."

"They're men," said Shadow quietly. "Same as we. Not monkeys."

"Think of them as like monkeys," Crown told her. "Otherwise we're lost. Come, now."

They left the wagon, Crown first, then Leaf, Sting, Shadow. The cavorting Tree Companions paused momentarily in their sport as the four travelers emerged; they looked up, grinned, chattered, pointed, did handsprings and headstands. They did not seem awed. Did Pure Stream mean nothing to them? Had they no fear of Dark Lake? Crown, glowering, said to Sting, "Can you speak their language?"

"A few words."

"Speak to them. Ask them to send their chief here to me."

Sting took up a position just in front of Crown, cupped his hands to his mouth, and shouted something high and piercing in a singsong language. He spoke with exaggerated, painful clarity, as one does in addressing a blind person or a foreigner. The Tree Companions snickered and exchanged little yipping cries. Then one of them came dancing forward, planted his face a hands-breadth from Sting's, and mimicked Sting's words, catching the intonation with comic accuracy. Sting looked frightened, and backed away half a pace, butting accidentally into Crown's chest. The Tree Companion loosed a stream of words, and when he fell silent Sting repeated his original phrase in a more subdued tone.

"What's happening?" Crown asked. "Can you understand anything?"

"A little. Very little."

"Will they get the chief?"

"I'm not sure. I don't know if he and I are talking about the same things."

"You said these people pay tribute to White Crystal."

"Paid," Sting said. "I don't know if there's any allegiance any longer. I think they may be having some fun at our expense. I think what he said was insulting, but I'm not sure. I'm just not sure."

"Stinking monkeys!"

"Careful, Crown," Shadow murmured. "We can't speak their language, but they may understand ours."

Crown said, "Try again. Speak more slowly. Get the monkey to speak more slowly. The chief, Sting, we want to see the chief! Isn't there any way you can make contact?"

"I could go into trance," Sting said. "And Shadow could help me with the meanings. But I'd need time to get myself together. I feel too quick now, too tense." As if to illustrate his point he executed a tiny jumping movement, blur-snap-hop, that carried him laterally a few paces to the left. Blur-snap-hop and he was back in place again. The Tree Companion laughed shrilly, clapped his hands, and tried to imitate Sting's little shuttling jump. Others of the tribe came over; there were ten or twelve of them now, clustered near the entrance to the wagon. Sting hopped again: it was like a twitch, a tic. He started to tremble. Shadow reached toward him and folded her slender arms about his chest, as though to anchor him. The Tree Companions grew more agitated;

there was a hard, intense quality about their playfulness now. Trouble seemed imminent. Leaf, standing on the far side of Crown, felt a sudden knotting of the muscles at the base of his stomach. Something nagged at his attention, off to his right out in the crowd of Tree Companions; he glanced that way and saw an azure brightness, elongated and upright, a man-size strip of fog and haze, drifting and weaving among the forest folk. Was it the Invisible? Or only some trick of the dying daylight, slipping through the residual vapor of the rainstorm? He struggled for a sharp focus, but the figure eluded his gaze, slipping ticklingly beyond sight as Leaf followed it with his eyes. Abruptly he heard a howl from Crown and turned just in time to see a Tree Companion duck beneath the huge man's elbow and go sprinting into the wagon. "Stop!" Crown roared. "Come back!" And, as if a signal had been given, seven or eight others of the lithe little tribesmen scrambled aboard.

There was death in Crown's eyes. He beckoned savagely to Leaf and rushed through the entrance. Leaf followed. Sting, sobbing, huddled in the entranceway, making no attempt to halt the Tree Companions who were streaming into the wagon. Leaf saw them climbing over everything, examining, inspecting, commenting. Monkeys, yes. Down in the front corridor Crown was struggling with four of them, holding one in each vast hand, trying to shake free two others who were climbing his armored legs. Leaf confronted a miniature Tree Companion woman, a gnomish bright-eyed creature whose bare lean body glistened with sour sweat, and as he reached for her she drew not a dart-blower but a long narrow blade from the tube at her hip, and slashed Leaf fiercely along the inside of his left forearm. There was a quick, frightening gush of blood, and only some moments afterward did he feel the fiery lick of the pain. A poisoned knife? Well, then, into the All-Is-One with you, Leaf. But if there had been poison, he felt no effects of it; he wrenched the knife from her grasp, jammed it into the wall, scooped her up, and pitched her lightly through the open hatch of the wagon. No more Tree Companions were coming in, now. Leaf found two more, threw them out, dragged another out of the roofbeams, tossed him after the others, went looking for more. Shadow stood in the hatchway, blocking it with her frail arms outstretched. Where was Crown? Ah. There. In the trophy room. "Grab them and carry them to the hatch!" Leaf yelled. "We're rid of most of them!"

"The stinking monkeys," Crown cried. He gestured angrily. The Tree Companions had seized some treasure of Crown's, some ancient suit of mail, and in their childish buoyancy had ripped the fragile links apart with their tug-of-war. Crown, enraged, bore down on them, clamped one hand on each tapering skull—*"Don't!"* Leaf shouted, fearing darts in vengeance—and squeezed, cracking them like nuts. He tossed the corpses aside and, picking up his torn trophy, stood sadly pressing the sundered edges together in a clumsy attempt at repair.

"You've done it now," Leaf said. "They were just being inquisitive. Now we'll have war, and we'll be dead before nightfall."

"Never," Crown grunted.

He dropped the chain-mail, scooped up the dead Tree Companions, carried them dangling through the wagon, and threw them like offal into the clearing. Then he stood defiantly in the hatchway, inviting their darts. None came. Those Tree Companions still aboard the wagon, five or six of them, appeared empty-handed, silent, and slipped hastily around the hulking Dark Laker. Leaf went forward and joined Crown. Blood was still dripping from Leaf's wound; he dared not induce clotting nor permit the wound to close until he had been purged of whatever poison might have been on the blade. A thin, straight cut, deep and painful, ran down his arm from elbow to wrist. Shadow gave a soft little cry and seized his hand. Her breath was warm against the edges of the gash. "Are you badly injured?" she whispered.

"I don't think so. It's just a question of whether the knife was poisoned."

"They poison only their darts," said Sting. "But there'll be infection to cope with. Better let Shadow look after you."

"Yes," Leaf said. He glanced into the clearing. The Tree Companions, as though thrown into shock by the violence that had come from their brief invasion of the wagon, stood frozen along the road in silent groups of nine or ten, keeping their distance. The two dead ones lay crumpled where Crown had hurled them. The unmistakable figure of the Invisible, transparent but clearly outlined by a dark perimeter, could be seen to the right, near the border of the thicket: his eyes glittered fiercely, his lips were twisted in a strange smile. Crown was staring at him in slack-jawed astonishment. Everything seemed suspended, held floating motionless in the bowl of time. To Leaf the scene was an eerie tableau in which the only sense of ongoing process was supplied by the throbbing in his slashed arm. He hung moored at the center, waiting, waiting, incapable of action, trapped like others in timelessness. In that long pause he realized that another figure had appeared during the melee, and stood now calmly ten paces or so to the left of the grinning Invisible: a Tree Companion, taller than the others of his kind, clad in beads and gimcracks but undeniably a being of presence and majesty.

"The chief has arrived," Sting said hoarsely.

The stasis broke. Leaf released his breath and let his rigid body slump. Shadow tugged at him, saying, "Let me clean that cut for you." The chief of the Tree Companions stabbed the air with three outstretched fingers, pointing at the wagon, and called out five crisp, sharp, jubilant syllables; slowly and grandly he began to stalk toward the wagon. At the same moment the Invisible flickered brightly, like a sun about to die, and disappeared entirely from view. Crown, turning to Leaf, said in a thick voice, "It's all going crazy here. I was just imagining I saw one of the Invisibles from Theptis skulking around by the underbrush."

"You weren't imagining anything," Leaf told him. "He's been riding secretly with us since Theptis. Waiting to see what would happen to us when we came to the Tree Companions' wall."

Crown looked jarred by that. "When did you find that out?" he demanded.

Shadow said, "Let him be, Crown. Go and parley with the chief. If I don't clean Leaf's wound soon—"

"Just a minute. I need to know the truth. Leaf, when did you find out about this Invisible?"

"When I went up front to relieve Sting. He was in the driver's cabin. Laughing at me, jeering. The way they do."

"And you didn't tell me? Why?"

"There was no chance. He bothered me for a while, and then he vanished, and I was busy driving after that, and then we came to the wall, and then the Tree Companions—"

"What does he want from us?" Crown asked harshly, face pushed close to Leaf's.

Leaf was starting to feel fever rising. He swayed and leaned on Shadow. Her taut, resilient little form bore him with surprising strength. He said tiredly, "I didn't know. Does anyone ever know

what one of them wants?" The Tree Companion chief, meanwhile, had come up beside them and in a lusty, self-assured way
slapped his open palm several times against the side of the
wagon, as though taking possession of it. Crown whirled. The
chief coolly spoke, voice level, inflections controlled. Crown
shook his head. "What's he saying?" he barked. "Sting? *Sting?*"

"Come," Shadow said to Leaf. "Now. Please."

She led him toward the passenger castle. He sprawled on the
furs while she searched busily through her case of unguents and
ointments; then she came to him with a long green vial in her
hand and said, "There'll be pain for you now."

"Wait."

He centered himself and disconnected, as well as he was able,
the network of sensory apparatus that conveyed messages of
discomfort from his arm to his brain. At once he felt his skin
growing cooler, and he realized for the first time since the battle
how much pain he had been in: so much that he had not had the
wisdom to do anything about it. Dispassionately he watched as
Shadow, all efficiency, probed his wound, parting the lips of the
cut without squeamishness and swabbing its red interior. A faint
tickling, unpleasant but not painful, was all he sensed. She
looked up, finally, and said, "There'll be no infection. You can
allow the wound to close now." In order to do that Leaf had to
reestablish the neural connections to a certain degree, and as he
unblocked the flow of impulses he felt sudden startling pain, both
from the cut itself and from Shadow's medicines; but quickly he
induced clotting, and a moment afterward he was deep in the
disciplines that would encourage the sundered flesh to heal. The
wound began to close. Lightly Shadow blotted the fresh blood
from his arm and prepared a poultice; by the time she had it in
place, the gaping slash had reduced itself to a thin raw line.
"You'll live," she said. "You were lucky they don't poison their
knives." He kissed the tip of her nose and they returned to the
hatch area.

Sting and the Tree Companion chief were conducting some
sort of discussion in pantomime, Sting's motions sweeping and
broad, the chief's the merest flicks of fingers, while Crown stood
by, an impassive column of darkness, arms folded somberly. As
Leaf and Shadow reappeared Crown said, "Sting isn't getting
anywhere. It has to be a trance parley or we won't make contact.
Help him, Shadow."

She nodded. To Leaf, Crown said, "How's the arm?"

"It'll be all right."

"How soon?"

"A day. Two, maybe. Sore for a week."

"We may be fighting again by sunrise."

"You told me yourself that we can't possibly survive a battle with these people."

"Even so," Crown said. "We may be fighting again by sunrise. If there's no other choice, we'll fight."

"And die?"

"And die," Crown said.

Leaf walked slowly away. Twilight had come. All vestiges of the rain had vanished, and the air was clear, crisp, growing chill, with a light wind out of the north that was gaining steadily in force. Beyond the thicket the tops of tall ropy-limbed trees were whipping about. The shards of the moon had moved into view, rough daggers of whiteness doing their slow dance about one another in the darkening sky. The poor old shattered moon, souvenir of an era long gone: it seemed a scratchy mirror for the tormented planet that owned it, for the fragmented race of races that was mankind. Leaf went to the nightmares, who stood patiently in harness, and passed among them, gently stroking their shaggy ears, caressing their blunt noses. Their eyes, liquid, intelligent, watchful, peered into his almost reproachfully. You promised us a stable, they seemed to be saying. Stallions, warmth, newly mown hay. Leaf shrugged. In this world, he told them wordlessly, it isn't always possible to keep one's promises. One does one's best, and one hopes that that is enough.

Near the wagon Sting has assumed a cross-legged position on the damp ground. Shadow squats beside him; the chief, mantled in dignity, stands stiffly before them, but Shadow coaxes him with gentle gestures to come down to them. Sting's eyes are closed and his head lolls forward. He is already in trance. His left hand grasps Shadow's muscular furry thigh; he extends his right, palm upward, and after a moment the chief puts his own palm to it. Contact: the circuit is closed.

Leaf has no idea what messages are passing among the three of them, but yet, oddly, he does not feel excluded from the transaction. Such a sense of love and warmth radiates from Sting and Shadow and even from the Tree Companion that he is drawn in, he is enfolded by their communion. And Crown, too, is engulfed and absorbed by the group aura; his rigid martial posture eases, his grim face looks strangely peaceful. Of course it is Sting and Shadow who are most closely linked; Shadow is closer now to Sting than she has ever been to Leaf, but Leaf is untroubled by this. Jealously and competitiveness are inconceivable now. He is Sting, Sting is Leaf, they all are Shadow and Crown, there are no boundaries separating one from another, just as there will be no boundaries in the All-Is-One that awaits every living creature, Sting and Crown and Shadow and Leaf, the Tree Companions, the Invisibles, the nightmares, the no-leg spiders.

They are getting down to cases now. Leaf is aware of strands of opposition and conflict manifesting themselves in the intricate negotiation that is taking place. Although he is still without a clue to the content of the exchange, Leaf understands that the Tree Companion chief is stating a position of demand—calmly, bluntly, immovable—and Sting and Shadow are explaining to him that Crown is not at all likely to yield. More than that Leaf is unable to perceive, even when he is most deeply enmeshed in the larger consciousness of the trance-wrapped three. Nor does he know how much time is elapsing. The symphonic interchange—demand, response, development, climax—continues repetitively, indefinitely, reaching no resolution.

He feels, at last, a running-down, an attenuation of the experience. He begins to move outside the field of contact, or to have it move outside him. Spiderwebs of sensibility still connect him to the others even as Sting and Shadow and the chief rise and separate, but they are rapidly thinning and fraying, and in a moment they snap.

The contact ends.

The meeting was over. During the trance-time night had fallen, an extraordinarily black night against which the stars seemed unnaturally bright. The fragments of the moon had traveled far across the sky. So it had been a lengthy exchange; yet in the immediate vicinity of the wagon nothing seemed altered. Crown stood like a statue beside the wagon's entrance; the Tree Companions still occupied the cleared ground between the wagon and the gate. Once more a tableau, then: how easy it is to slide into motionlessness, Leaf thought, in these impoverished times. Stand and wait, stand and wait; but now motion returned. The Tree

Companion pivoted and strode off without a word, signaling to his people, who gathered up their dead and followed him through the gate. From within they tugged the gate shut; there was the screeching sound of the bolts being forced home. Sting, looking dazed, whispered something to Shadow, who nodded and lightly touched his arm. They walked haltingly back to the wagon.

"Well?" Crown asked finally.

"They will allow us to pass," Sting said.

"How courteous of them."

"But they claim the wagon and everything that is in it."

Crown gasped. "By what right?"

"Right of prophecy," said Shadow. "There is a seer among them, an old woman of mixed stock, part White Crystal, part Tree Companion, part Invisible. She has told them that everything that has happened lately in the world was caused by the Soul for the sake of enriching the Tree Companions."

"Everything? They see the onslaught of the Teeth as a sign of divine favor?"

"Everything," said Sting. "The entire upheaval. All for their benefit. All done so that migrations would begin and refugees would come to this place, carrying with them valuable possessions, which they would surrender to those whom the Soul meant should own them, meaning the Tree Companions."

Crown laughed roughly. "If they want to be brigands, why not practice brigandage outright, with the right name on it, and not blame their greed on the Soul?"

"They don't see themselves as brigands," Shadow said. "There can be no denying the chief's sincerity. He and his people genuinely believe that the Soul has decreed all this for their own special good, that the time has come—"

"Sincerity!"

"—for the Tree Companions to become people of substance and property. Therefore they've built this wall across the highway, and as refugees come west, the Tree Companions relieve them of their possessions with the blessing of the Soul."

"I'd like to meet their prophet," Crown muttered.

Leaf said, "It was my understanding that Invisibles were unable to breed with other stocks."

Sting told him, with a shrug, "We report only what we learned as we sat there dreaming with the chief. The witch-woman is part

Invisible, he said. Perhaps he was wrong, but he was doing no lying. Of that I'm certain."

"And I," Shadow put in.

"What happens to those who refuse to pay tribute?" Crown asked.

"The Tree Companions regard them as thwarters of the Soul's design," said Sting, "and fall upon them and put them to death. And then seize their goods."

Crown moved restlessly in a shallow circle in front of the wagon, kicking up gouts of soil out of the hard-packed roadbed. After a moment he said, "They dangle on vines. They chatter like foolish monkeys. What do they want with the merchandise of civilized folk? Our furs, our statuettes, our carvings, our flutes, our robes?"

"Having such things will make them equal in their own sight to the higher stocks," Sting said. "Not the things themselves, but the possession of them, do you see, Crown?"

"They'll have nothing of mine!"

"What will we do, then?" Leaf asked. "Sit here and wait for their darts?"

Crown caught Sting heavily by the shoulder. "Did they give us any sort of time limit? How long do we have before they attack?"

"There was nothing like an ultimatum. The chief seems unwilling to enter into warfare with us."

"Because he's afraid of his betters!"

"Because he thinks violence cheapens the decree of the Soul," Sting replied evenly. "Therefore he intends to wait for us to surrender our belongings voluntarily."

"He'll wait a hundred years!"

"He'll wait a few days," Shadow said. "If we haven't yielded, the attack will come. But what will you do, Crown? Suppose they were willing to wait your hundred years. Are you? We can't camp here forever."

"Are you suggesting we give them what they ask?"

"I merely want to know what strategy you have in mind," she said. "You admit yourself we can't defeat them in battle. We haven't done a very good job of aweing them into submission. You recognize that any attempt to destroy their wall will bring them upon us with their darts. You refuse to turn back and look for some other westward route. You rule out the alternative of yielding to them. Very well, Crown. What do you have in mind?"

"We'll wait a few days," Crown said thickly.

"The Teeth are heading this way!" Sting cried. "Shall we sit here and let them catch us?"

Crown shook his head. "Long before the Teeth get here, Sting, this place will be full of other refugees, many of them, as unwilling to give up their goods to these folk as we are. I can feel them already on the road, coming this way, two days' march from us, perhaps less. We'll make alliance with them. Four of us may be helpless against a swarm of poisonous apes, but fifty or a hundred strong fighters would send them scrambling up their own trees."

"No one will come this way," said Leaf. "No one but fools. Everyone passing through Theptis knows what's been done to the highway here. What good is the aid of fools?"

"*We* came this way," Crown snapped. "Are we such fools?"

"Perhaps we are. We were warned not to take Spider Highway, and we took it anyway."

"Because we refused to trust the word of Invisibles."

"Well, the Invisibles happened to be telling the truth, this time," Leaf said. "And the news must be all over Theptis. No one in his right mind will come this way now."

"I feel marchers already on the way, hundreds of them," Crown said. "I can sense these things, sometimes. What about you, Sting? You feel things ahead of time, don't you? They're coming, aren't they? Have no fear, Leaf. We'll have allies here in a day or so, and then let these thieving Tree Companions beware." Crown gestured broadly. "Leaf, set the nightmares loose to graze. And then everybody inside the wagon. We'll seal it and take turns standing watch through the night. This is a time for vigilance and courage."

"This is a time for digging graves," Sting murmured sourly, as they clambered into the wagon.

Crown and Shadow stood the first round of watches while Leaf and Sting napped in the back. Leaf fell asleep at once and dreamed he was living in some immense brutal eastern city—the buildings and street plan were unfamiliar to him, but the architecture was definitely eastern in style, gray and heavy, all parapets and cornices—that was coming under attack by the Teeth.

He observed everything from a many-windowed gallery atop

an enormous square-sided brick tower that seemed like a survival from some remote pre-historic epoch. First, from the north, came the sound of the war song of the invaders, a nasty unendurable buzzing drone, piercing and intense, like the humming of high-speed polishing wheels at work on metal plates. That dread music brought the inhabitants of the city spilling into the streets—all stocks, Flower Givers and Sand Shapers and White Crystals and Dancing Stars and even Tree Companions, absurdly garbed in mercantile robes as though they were so many fat citified Fingers—but no one was able to escape, for there were so many people, colliding and jostling and stumbling and falling in helpless heaps, that they blocked every avenue and alleyway.

Into this chaos now entered the vanguard of the Teeth; shuffling forward in their peculiar bent-kneed crouch, trampling those who had fallen. They looked half-beast, half-demon: squat thick-thewed flat-headed long-muzzled creatures, naked, hairy, their skins the color of sand, their eyes glinting with insatiable hungers. Leaf's dreaming mind subtly magnified and distorted them so that they came hopping into the city like a band of giant toothy frogs, thump-thump, bare fleshy feet slapping pavement in sinister reverberations, short powerful arms swinging almost comically at each leaping stride. The kinship of mankind meant nothing to these carnivorous beings. They had been penned up too long in the cold, mountainous, barren country of the far northeast, living on such scraps and strings as the animals of the forest yielded, and they saw their fellow humans as mere meat stockpiled by the Soul against this day of vengeance. Efficiently, now, they began their round-up in the newly conquered city, seizing everyone in sight, cloistering the dazed prisoners in hastily rigged pens: these we eat tonight at our victory feast; these we save for tomorrow's dinner; these become dried meat to carry with us on the march; these we kill for sport; these become dried meat to carry with us on the march; these we kill for sport; these we keep as slaves. Leaf watched the Teeth erecting their huge spits. Kindling their fierce roasting-fires. Diligent search teams fanned out through the suburbs. No one would escape. Leaf stirred and groaned, reached the threshold of wakefulness, fell back into dream. Would they find him in his tower? Smoke, gray and greasy, boiled up out of a hundred parts of town. Leaping flames. Rivulets of blood ran in the streets. He was choking. A terrible dream. But was it only a dream? This was how it had actually been in Holy Town hours after he and Crown and Sting and Shadow had managed to get away, this was no doubt as it had happened in city after city along the tormented coastal strip, very likely something of this sort was going on now in—where?—Bone Harbor? Ved-uru? Alsandar? He could smell the penetrating odor of roasting meat. He could hear the heavy lalloping sound of a Teeth patrol running up the stairs of his tower. They had him. Yes, here, now, now, a dozen Teeth bursting suddenly into his hiding place, grinning broadly— Pure Stream, they had captured a Pure Stream! What a coup! Beasts. Beasts. Prodding him, testing his flesh. Not plump enough for them, eh? This one's pretty lean. We'll cook him anyway. Pure Stream meat, it enlarges the soul, it makes you into something more than you were. Take him downstairs! To the spit, to the spit, to the—

"Leaf?"

"I warn you—you won't like—the flavor—"

"Leaf, wake up!"

"The fires—oh, the stink!"

"Leaf!"

It was Shadow. She shook him gently, plucked at his shoulder. He blinked and slowly sat up. His wounded arm was throbbing again; he felt feverish. Effects of the dream. A dream, only a dream. He shivered and tried to center himself, working at it, banishing the fever, banishing the shreds of dark fantasy that were still shrouding his mind.

"Are you all right?" she asked.

"I was dreaming about the Teeth," he told her. He shook his head, trying to clear it. "Am I to stand watch now?"

She nodded. "Up front. Driver's cabin."

"Has anything been happening?"

"Nothing. Not a thing." She reached up and drew her fingertips lightly along the sides of his jaws. Her eyes were warm and bright, her smile was loving. "The Teeth are far away, Leaf."

"From us, maybe. Not from others."

"They were sent by the will of the Soul."

"I know, I know." How often had he preached acceptance! This is the will, and we bow to it. This is the road, and we travel it uncomplainingly. But yet, but yet—he shuddered. The dream mode persisted. He was altogether disoriented. Dream-Teeth nibbled at his flesh. The inner chambers of his spirit resonated to the screams of those on the spits, the sounds of rending and tearing, the unbearable reek of burning cities. In ten days, half a world torn apart. So much pain, so much death, so much that had been beautiful destroyed by relentless savages who would not halt until, the Soul only knew when, they had had their full measure of revenge. *The will of the Soul sends them upon us. Accept. Accept.* He could not find his center. Shadow held him, straining to encompass his body with her arms. After a moment he began to feel less troubled, but he remained scattered, diffused, present only in part, some portion of his mind nailed as if by spikes into that monstrous ash-strewn wasteland that the Teeth had created out of the fair and fertile eastern provinces.

She released him. "Go," she whispered. "It's quiet up front. You'll be able to find yourself again."

He took her place in the driver's cabin, going silently past Sting, who had replaced Crown on watch amidwagon. Half the night was gone. All was still in the roadside clearing; the great wooden gate was shut tight and nobody was about. By cold starlight Leaf saw the nightmares browsing patiently at the edge of the thicket. Gentle horses, almost human. *If I must be visited by nightmares,* he thought, *let it be by their kind.*

Shadow had been right. In the stillness he grew calm, and perspective returned. Lamentation would not restore the shattered eastland, expressions of horror and shock would not turn the Teeth into pious tillers of the soil. The Soul had decreed chaos: so be it. *This is the road we must travel, and who dares ask why?* Once the world had been whole and now it is fragmented, and that is the way things are because that is the way things were meant to be. He became less tense. Anguish dropped from him. He was Leaf again.

Toward dawn the visible world lost its sharp starlit edge; a soft fog settled over the wagon, and rain fell for a time, a light, pure rain, barely audible, altogether different in character from yesterday's vicious storm. In the strange light just preceding sunrise the world took on a delicate pearly mistiness; and out of that mist an apparition materialized. Leaf saw a figure come drifting through the closed gate—*through* it—a ghostly, incorporeal figure. He thought it might be the Invisible who had been lurking close by the wagon since Theptis, but no, this was a woman, old and frail, an attenuated woman, smaller even than Shadow, more slender. Leaf knew who she must be: the mixed-blood woman. The prophetess, the seer, she who had stirred up these Tree Companions to block the highway. Her skin had the White Crystal waxiness of texture and the White Crystal nodes of dark, coarse hair; the form of her body was essentially that of a Tree Companion, thin and long-armed; and from her Invisible fore-bears, it seemed, she had inherited that perplexing intangibility, that look of existing always on the borderland between hallucina-tion and reality, between mist and flesh. Mixed-bloods were uncommon; Leaf had rarely seen one, and never had encountered one who combined in herself so many different stocks. It was said that people of mixed blood had strange gifts. Surely this one did. How had she bypassed the wall? Not even Invisibles could travel through solid wood. Perhaps this was just a dream, then, or possibly she had some way of projecting an image of herself into his mind from a point within the Tree Companion village. He did not understand.

He watched her a long while. She appeared real enough. She halted twenty paces from the nose of the wagon and scanned the entire horizon slowly, her eyes coming to rest at last on the window of the driver's cabin. She was aware, certainly, that he was looking at her, and she looked back, eye to eye, staring unflinchingly. They remained locked that way for some minutes. Her expression was glum and opaque, a withered scowl, but suddenly she brightened and smiled intensely at him and it was such a *knowing* smile that Leaf was thrown into terror by the old witch, and glanced away, shamed and defeated.

When he lifted his head she was out of view; he pressed himself against the window, craned his neck, and found her down near the middle of the wagon. She was inspecting its exterior workmanship at close range, picking and prying at the hull. Then she wandered away, out to the place where Sting and Shadow and the chief had had their conference, and sat down cross-legged where they had been sitting. She became extraordinarily still, as if she were asleep, or in trance. Just when Leaf began to think she would never move again, she took a pipe of carved bone from a pouch at her waist, filled it with a gray-blue powder, and lit it. He searched her face for tokens of revelation, but nothing showed on it; she grew ever more impassive and unreadable. When the pipe went out, she filled it again, and smoked a second time, and still Leaf watched her, his face pushed awkwardly against the window, his body growing stiff. The first rays of sunlight now arrived, pink shading rapidly into gold. As the brightness deepened the witch-woman imperceptibly became less solid; she was fading away, moment by moment, and shortly he saw nothing of her but her pipe and her kerchief, and then the clearing was empty. The long shadows of the six nightmares splashed against the wooden palisade. Leaf's head lolled. I've been dozing, he thought. It's morning, and all's well. He went to awaken Crown.

They breakfasted lightly. Leaf and Shadow led the horses to water at a small clear brook five minutes' walk toward Theptis. Sting foraged awhile in the thicket for nuts and berries, and having filled two pails, went aft to doze in the furs. Crown brooded in his trophy room and said nothing to anyone. A few Tree Companions could be seen watching the wagon from perches in the crowns of towering red-leaved trees on the hillside just behind the wall. Nothing happened until midmorning. Then, at a time when all four travelers were within the wagon, a dozen newcomers appeared, forerunners of the refugee tribe that Crown's intuitions had correctly predicted. They came slowly up the road, on foot, dusty and tired-looking, staggering beneath huge untidy bundles of belongings and supplies. They were square-headed muscular people, as tall as Leaf or taller, with the look of warriors about them; they carried short swords at their waists, and both men and women were conspicuously scarred. Their skins were gray, tinged with pale green, and they had more fingers and toes than was usual among mankind.

Leaf had never seen their sort before. "Do you know them?" he asked Sting.

"Snow Hunters," Sting said. "Close kin to the Sand Shapers, I think. Midcaste and said to be unfriendly to strangers. They live southwest of Theptis, in the hill country."

"One would think they'd be safe there," said Shadow.

Sting shrugged. "No one's safe from the Teeth, eh? Not even on the highest hills. Not even in the thickest jungles."

The Snow Hunters dropped their packs and looked around. The wagon drew them first; they seemed stunned by the opulence of it. They examined it in wonder, touching it as the witch-woman had, scrutinizing it from every side. When they saw faces looking out at them, they nudged one another and pointed and whispered, but they did not smile, nor did they wave greetings. After a time they went on to the wall and studied it with the same childlike curiosity. It appeared to baffle them. They measured it with their outstretched hands, pressed their bodies against it, pushed at it with their shoulders, tapped the timbers, plucked at the sturdy bindings of vine. By this time perhaps a dozen more of them had come up the road; they too clustered about the wagon, doing as the first had done, and then continued toward the wall. More and more Snow Hunters were arriving, in groups of three or four. One trio, standing apart from the others, gave the impression of being tribal leaders; they consulted, nodded, summoned and dismissed other members of the tribe with forceful gestures of their hands.

"Let's go out and parley," Crown said. He donned his best armor and selected an array of elegant dress weapons. To Sting he gave a slender dagger. Shadow would not bear arms, and Leaf preferred to arm himself in nothing but Pure Stream prestige. His status as a member of the ancestral stock, he found, served him as well as a sword in most encounters with strangers.

The Snow Hunters—about a hundred of them now had gathered, with still more down the way—looked apprehensive as Crown and his companions descended from the wagon. Crown's bulk and gladiatorial swagger seemed far more threatening to these strong-bodied warlike folk than they had been to the chattering Tree Companions, and Leaf's presence too appeared disturbing to them. Warily they moved to form a loose semicircle about their three leaders; they stood close by one another, murmuring tensely, and their hands hovered near the hilts of their swords.

Crown stepped forward. "Careful," Leaf said softly. "They're on edge. Don't push them."

But Crown, with a display a slick diplomacy unusual for him, quickly put the Snow Hunters at their ease with a warm gesture of greeting—hands pressed to shoulders, palms outward, fingers spread wide—and a few hearty words of welcome. Introductions were exchanged. The spokesman for the tribe, an iron-faced man with frosty eyes and hard cheekbones, was called Sky; the names of his co-captains were Blade and Shield. Sky spoke in a flat, quiet voice, everything on the same note. He seemed empty, burned out, a man who had entered some realm of exhaustion far beyond mere fatigue. They had been on the road for three days and three nights almost without a halt, said Sky. Last week a major force of Teeth had started westward through the midcoastal lowlands bound for Theptis, and one band of these, just a few

hundred warriors, had lost its way, going south into the hill
country. Their aimless wanderings brought these straying Teeth
without warning into the secluded village of the Snow Hunters,
and there had been a terrible battle in which more than half of
Sky's people had perished. The survivors, having slipped away
into the trackless forest, and made their way by back roads to
Spider Highway, and, numbed by shock and grief, had been
marching like machines toward the Middle River, hoping to find
some new hillside in the sparsely populated territories of the far
northwest. They could never return to their old home, Shield
declared, for it had been desecrated by the feasting of the Teeth.

"But what is this wall?" Sky asked.

Crown explained, telling the Snow Hunters about the Tree
Companions and their prophetess, and of her promise that the
booty of all refugees was to be surrendered to them. "They lie in
wait for us with their darts," Crown said. "Four of us were
helpless against them. But they would never dare challenge a
force the size of yours. We'll have their wall smashed down by
nightfall!"

"The Tree Companions are said to be fierce foes," Sky
remarked quietly.

"Nothing but monkeys," said Crown. "They'll scramble to
their treetops if we just draw our swords."

"And shower us with their poisoned arrows," Shield muttered.
"Friend, we have little stomach for further warfare. Too many of
us have fallen this week."

"What will you do?" Crown cried. "Give them your swords,
and your tunics and your wives' rings and the sandals off your
feet?"

Sky closed his eyes and stood motionless, remaining silent for
a long moment. At length, without opening his eyes, he said in a
voice that came from the center of an immense void, "We will
talk with the Tree Companions and learn what they actually demand
of us, and then we will make our decisions and form our plans."

"The wall—if you fight beside us, we can destroy this wall,
and open the road to all who flee the Teeth!"

With cold patience Sky said, "We will speak with you again
afterward," and turned away. "Now we will rest, and wait for
the Tree Companions to come forth."

The Snow Hunters withdrew, sprawling out along the margin
of the thicket just under the wall. There they huddled in rows,

staring at the ground, waiting. Crown scowled, spat, shook his head. Turning to Leaf he said, "They have the true look of fighters. There's something that marks a fighter apart from other men, Leaf, and I can tell when it's there, and these Snow Hunters have it. They have the strength, they have the power; they have the spirit of battle in them. And yet, see them now! Squatting there like fat frightened Fingers!"

"They've been beaten badly," Leaf said. "They've been driven from their homeland. They know what it is to look back across a hilltop and see the fires in which your kinsmen are being cooked. That takes the fighting spirit out of a person, Crown."

"No. Losing makes the flame burn brighter. It makes you feverish with the desire for revenge."

"Does it? What do you know about losing? You were never so much as touched by any of your opponents."

Crown glared at him. "I'm not speaking of dueling. Do you think my life has gone untouched by the Teeth? What am I doing here on this dirt road with all that I still own packed into a single wagon? But I'm no walking dead man like these Snow Hunters. I'm not running away, I'm going to find an army. And then I'll go back east and take my vengeance. While they—afraid of monkeys—"

"They've been marching day and night," Shadow said. "They must have been on the road when the purple rain was falling. They've spent all their strength while we've been riding in your wagon, Crown. Once they've had a little rest, perhaps they—"

"Afraid of *monkeys!*"

Crown shook with wrath. He strode up and down before the wagon, pounding his fists into his thighs. Leaf feared that he would go across to the Snow Hunters and attempt by bluster to force them into an alliance. Leaf understood the mood of these people: shattered and drained though they were, they might lash out in sudden savage irritation if Crown goaded them too severely. Possibly some hours of rest, as Shadow had suggested, and they might feel more like helping Crown drive his way through the Tree Companions' wall. But not now. Not now.

The gate in the wall opened. Some twenty of the forest folk emerged, among them the tribal chief and—Leaf caught his breath in awe—the ancient seeress, who looked across the way and bestowed on Leaf another of her penetrating comfortless smiles.

"What kind of creature is that?" Crown asked.

"The mixed-blood witch," said Leaf. "I saw her at dawn, while I was standing watch."

"Look!" Shadow cried. "She flickers and fades like an Invisible! But her pelt is like yours, Sting, and her shape is that of—"

"She frightens me," Sting said hoarsely. He was shaking. "She foretells death for us. We have little time left to us, friends. She is the goddess of death, that one." He plucked at Crown's elbow, unprotected by the armor. "Come! Let's start back along Spider Highway! Better to take our chances in the desert than to stay here and die!"

"Quiet," Crown snapped. "There's no going back. The Teeth are already in Theptis. They'll be moving out along this road in a day or two. There's only one direction for us."

"But the wall," Sting said.

"The wall will be in ruins by nightfall," Crown told him.

The chief of the Tree Companions was conferring with Sky and Blade and Shield. Evidently the Snow Hunters knew something of the language of the Tree Companions, for Leaf could hear vocal interchanges, supplemented by pantomime and sign language. The chief pointed to himself often, to the wall, to the prophetess; he indicated the packs the Snow Hunters had been carrying; he jerked his thumb angrily toward Crown's wagon. The conversation lasted nearly half an hour and seemed to reach an amicable outcome. The Tree Companions departed, this time leaving the gate open. Sky, Shield, and Blade moved among their people, issuing instructions. The Snow Hunters drew food from their packs—dried roots, seeds, smoked meat—and lunched in silence. Afterward, boys who carried huge waterbags made of sewn hides slung between them on poles went off to the creek to replenish their supply, and the rest of the Snow Hunters rose, stretched, wandered in narrow circles about the clearing, as if getting ready to resume the march. Crown was seized by furious impatience. "What are they going to do?" he demanded. "What deal have they made?"

"I imagine they've submitted to the terms," Leaf said.

"No! No! I need their help!" Crown, in anguish, hammered at himself with his fists. "I have to talk to them," he muttered.

"Wait. Don't push them, Crown."

"What's the use? What's the use?" Now the Snow Hunters

were hoisting their packs to their shoulders. No doubt of it; they were going to leave. Crown hurried across the clearing. Sky, busily directing the order of march, grudgingly gave him attention. "Where are you going?" Crown asked.

"Westward," said Sky.

"What about us?"

"March with us, if you wish."

"My wagon!"

"You can't get it through the gate, can you?"

Crown reared up as though he would strike the Snow Hunter in rage. "If you would aid us, the wall would fall! Look, how can I abandon my wagon? I need to reach my kinsmen in the Flatlands. I'll assemble an army; I'll return to the east and push the Teeth back into the mountains where they belong. I've lost too much time already. I *must* get through. Don't you want to see the Teeth destroyed?"

"It's nothing to us," Sky said evenly. "Our lands are lost to us forever. Vengeance is meaningless. Your pardon. My people need my guidance."

More than half the Snow Hunters had passed through the gate already. Leaf joined the procession. On the far side of the wall he discovered that the dense thicket along the highway's northern rim had been cleared for a considerable distance, and a few small wooden buildings, hostelries or depots, stood at the edge of the road. Another twenty or thirty paces farther along, a secondary path led northward into the forest; this was evidently the route to the Tree Companions' village. Traffic on that path was heavy just now. Hundreds of forest folk were streaming from the village to the highway, where a strange, repellent scene was being enacted. Each Snow Hunter in turn halted, unburdened himself of his pack, and laid it open. Three or four Tree Companions then picked through it, each seizing one item of value—a knife, a comb, a piece of jewelry, a fine cloak—and running triumphantly off with it. Once he had submitted to this harrying of his possessions, the Snow Hunter gathered up his pack, shouldered it, and marched on, head bowed, body slumping. Tribute. Leaf felt chilled. These proud warriors, homeless now, yielding up their remaining treasures to—he tried to choke off the word, and could not—to a tribe of monkeys. And moving onward, soiled, unmanned. Of all that he had seen since the Teeth had split the world apart, this was the most sad.

Leaf started back toward the wagon. He saw Sky, Shield, and Blade at the rear of the column of Snow Hunters. Their faces were ashen; they could not meet his eyes. Sky managed a half-hearted salute as he passed by.

"I wish you good fortune on your journey," Leaf said.

"I wish you better fortune than we have had," said Sky hollowly, and went on.

Leaf found Crown standing rigid in the middle of the highway, hands on hips. "Cowards!" he called in a bitter voice. "Weaklings!"

"And now it's our turn," Leaf said.

"What do you mean?"

"The time's come for us to face hard truths. We have to give up the wagon, Crown."

"Never."

"We agree that we can't turn back. And we can't go forward so long as the wall's there. If we stay here, the Tree Companions will eventually kill us, if the Teeth don't overtake us first. Listen to me, Crown. We don't have to give the Tree Companions everything we have. The wagon itself, some of our spare clothing, some trinkets, the furnishings of the wagon—they'll be satisfied with that. We can load the rest of our goods on the horses and go safely through the gate as foot-pilgrims."

"I ignore this, Leaf."

"I know you do. I also know what the wagon means to you. I wish you could keep it. I wish I could stay with the wagon myself. Don't you think I'd rather ride west in comfort than slog through the rain and the cold? But we can't keep it. *We can't keep it,* Crown, that's the heart of the situation. We can go back east in the wagon and get lost in the desert, we can sit here and wait for the Tree Companions to lose patience and kill us, or we can give up the wagon and get out of this place with our skins still whole. What sort of choices for those? We have no choice. I've been telling you that for two days. Be reasonable, Crown!"

Crown glanced coldly at Sting and Shadow. "Find the chief and go into trance with him again. Tell him that I'll give him swords, armor, his pick of the finest things in the wagon. So long as he'll dismantle part of the wall and let the wagon itself pass through."

"We made that offer yesterday," Sting said glumly.

"And?"

"He insists on the wagon. The old witch has promised it to him for a palace."

"No," Crown said. *"NO!"* His wild roaring cry echoed from the hills. After a moment, more calmly, he said, "I have another idea. Leaf, Sting, come with me. The gate's open. We'll go to the village and seize the witch-woman. We'll grab her quickly, before anyone realizes what we're doing. They won't dare molest us while she's in our hands. Then, Sting, you tell the chief that unless they open the wall for us, we'll kill her." Crown chuckled. "Once she realizes we're serious, she'll tell them to hop it. Anybody that old wants to live forever. And they'll obey her. You can bet on that. They'll obey her! Come, now." Crown started toward the gate at a vigorous pace. He took a dozen strides, halted, looked back. Neither Leaf nor Sting had moved.

"Well? Why aren't you coming?"

"I won't do it," said Leaf tiredly. "It's crazy, Crown. She's a witch, she's part Invisible—she already knows your scheme. She probably knew of it before you knew of it yourself. How can we hope to catch her?"

"Let me worry about that."

"Even if we did, Crown—no. No. I won't have any part of it. It's an impossible idea. Even if we did seize her. We'd be standing there holding a sword to her throat, and the chief would give a signal, and they'd put a hundred darts in us before we could move a muscle. It's insane, Crown."

"I ask you to come with me."

"You've had your answer."

"Then I'll go without you."

"As you choose," Leaf said quietly. "But you won't be seeing me again."

"Eh?"

"I'm going to collect what I own and let the Tree Companions take their pick of it, and then I'll hurry forward and catch up with the Snow Hunters. In a week or so I'll be at the Middle River. Shadow, will you come with me, or are you determined to stay here and die with Crown?"

The Dancing Star looked toward the muddy ground. "I don't know," she said. "Let me think a moment.

"Sting?"

"I'm going with you."

Leaf beckoned to Crown. "Please. Come to your senses,

Crown. For the last time—give up the wagon and let's get going, all four of us.''

"You disgust me."

"Then this is where we part," Leaf said. "I wish you good fortune. Sting, let's assemble our belongings. Shadow? Will you be coming with us?"

"We have an obligation toward Crown," she said.

"To help him drive his wagon, yes. But not to die a foolish death for him. Crown has lost his wagon, Shadow, though he won't admit that yet. If the wagon's no longer his, our contract is voided. I hope you'll join us."

He entered the wagon and went to the midcabin cupboard where he stored the few possessions he had managed to bring with him out of the east. A pair of glistening boots made of the leathery skins of stick-creatures, two ancient copper coins, three ornamental ivory medallions, a shirt of dark red silk, a thick, heavily worked belt—not much, not much at all, the salvage of a lifetime. He packed rapidly. He took with him a slab of dried meat and some bread; that would last him a day or two, and when it was gone he would learn from Sting or the Snow Hunters the arts of gathering food in the wilderness.

"Are you ready?"

"Ready as I'll ever be," Sting said. His pack was almost empty—a change of clothing, a hatchet, a knife, some smoked fish, nothing else.

"Let's go, then."

As Sting and Leaf moved toward the exit hatch, Shadow scrambled up into the wagon. She looked tight-strung and grave; her nostrils were flared, her eyes downcast. Without a word she went past Leaf and began loading her pack. Leaf waited for her. After a few minutes she reappeared and nodded to him.

"Poor Crown," she whispered. "Is there no way—"

"You heard him," Leaf said.

They emerged from the wagon. Crown had not moved. He stood as if rooted, midway between wagon and wall. Leaf gave him a quizzical look, as if to ask whether he had changed his mind, but Crown took no notice. Shrugging, Leaf walked around him, toward the edge of the thicket, where the nightmares were nibbling leaves. Affectionately he reached up to stroke the long neck of the nearest horse, and Crown suddenly came to life, shouting, "Those are my animals! Keep your hands off them!"

"I'm only saying goodbye to them."

"You think I'm going to let you have some? You think I'm that crazy, Leaf?"

Leaf looked sadly at him. "We plan to do our traveling on foot, Crown. I'm only saying goodbye. The nightmares were my friends. You can't understand that, can you?"

"Keep away from those animals! *Keep away!*"

Leaf sighed. "Whatever you say." Shadow, as usual, was right: poor Crown. Leaf adjusted his pack and moved off toward the gate, Shadow beside him, Sting a few paces to the rear. As he and Shadow reached the gate, Leaf looked back and saw Crown still motionless, saw Sting pausing, putting down his pack, dropping to his knees. "Anything wrong?" Leaf called.

"Tore a bootlace," Sting said. "You two go on ahead. It'll take me a minute to fix it."

"We can wait."

Leaf and Shadow stood within the frame of the gate while Sting knotted his lace. After a few moments he rose and reached for his pack, saying, "That ought to hold me until tonight, and then I'll see if I can't—"

"Watch out!" Leaf yelled.

Crown erupted abruptly from his freeze, and, letting forth a lunatic cry, rushed with terrible swiftness toward Sting. There was no chance for Sting to make one of his little leaps: Crown seized him, held him high overhead like a child, and, grunting in frantic rage, hurled the little man toward the ravine. Arms and legs flailing, Sting traveled on a high arc over the edge; he seemed to dance in midair for an instant, and then he dropped from view. There was a long diminishing shriek, and silence. Silence.

Leaf stood stunned. "Hurry," Shadow said. "Crown's coming!"

Crown, swinging around, now rumbled like a machine of death toward Leaf and Shadow. His wild red eyes glittered ferociously. Leaf did not move; Shadow shook him urgently, and finally he pushed himself into action. Together they caught hold of the massive gate and, straining, swung it shut, slamming it just as Crown crashed into it. Leaf forced the reluctant bolts into place. Crown roared and pounded at the gate, but he was unable to force it.

Shadow shivered and wept. Leaf drew her to him and held her for a moment. At length he said, "We'd better be on our way. The Snow Hunters are far ahead of us already."

"Sting—"

"I know. I know. Come, now."

Half a dozen Tree Companions were waiting for them by the wooden houses. They grinned, chattered, pointed to the packs. "All right," Leaf said. "Go ahead. Take whatever you want. Take everything, if you like."

Busy fingers picked through his pack and Shadow's. From Shadow the Tree Companions took a brocaded ribbon and a flat, smooth green stone. From Leaf they took one of the ivory medallions, both copper coins, and one of his stickskin boots. Tribute. Day by day, pieces of the past slipped from his grasp. He pulled the other boot from the pack and offered it to them, but they merely giggled and shook their heads. "One is of no use to me," he said. They would not take it. He tossed the boot into the grass beside the road.

The road curved gently toward the north and began a slow rise, following the flank of the forested hills in which the Tree Companions made their homes. Leaf and Shadow marched mechanically, saying little. The bootprints of the Snow Hunters were everywhere along the road, but the Snow Hunters themselves were far ahead, out of sight. It was early afternoon, and the day had become bright, unexpectedly warm. After an hour Shadow said, "I must rest."

Her teeth were clacking. She crouched by the roadside and wrapped her arms about her chest. Dancing Stars, covered with thick fur, usually wore no clothing except in the bleakest winters; but her pelt did her no good now.

"Are you ill?" he asked.

"It'll pass. I'm reacting. Sting—"

"Yes."

"And Crown. I feel so unhappy about Crown."

"A madman," Leaf said. "A murderer."

"Don't judge him so casually, Leaf. He's a man under sentence of death, and he knows it, and he's suffering from it, and when the fear and pain became unbearable to him he reached out for Sting. He didn't know what he was doing. He needed to smash something, that was all, to relieve his own torment."

"We're all going to die sooner or later," Leaf said. "That doesn't generally drive us to kill our friends."

"I don't mean sooner or later. I mean that Crown will die tonight or tomorrow."

"Why should he?"

"What can he do now to save himself, Leaf?"

"He could yield to the Tree Companions and pass the gate on foot, as we've done."

"You know he'd never abandon the wagon."

"Well, then, he can harness the nightmares and turn around toward Theptis. At least he'd have a chance to make it through to the Sunset Highway that way."

"He can't do that either," Shadow said.

"Why not?"

"He can't drive the wagon."

"There's no one left to do it for him. His life's at stake. For once he could eat his pride and—"

"I didn't say won't drive the wagon, Leaf. I said can't. Crown's incapable. He isn't able to make dream contact with the nightmares. Why do you think he always used hired drivers? Why was he so insistent on making you drive in the purple rain? He doesn't have the mind-power. Did you ever see a Dark Laker driving nightmares? Ever?"

Leaf stared at her. "You knew this all along?"

"From the beginning, yes."

"Is that why you hesitated to leave him at the gate? When you were talking about our contract with him?"

She nodded. "If all three of us left him, we were condemning him to death. He has no way of escaping the Tree Companions now unless he forces himself to leave the wagon, and he won't do that. They'll fall on him and kill him, today, tomorrow, whenever."

Leaf closed his eyes, shook his head. "I feel a kind of shame. Now that I know we were leaving him helpless. He could have spoken."

"Too proud."

"Yes, yes. It's just as well he didn't say anything. We all have responsibilities to one another, but there are limits. You and I and Sting were under no obligation to die simply because Crown couldn't bring himself to give up his pretty wagon. But still—

still—" He locked his hands tightly together. "Why did you finally decide to leave, then?"

"For the reason you just gave. I didn't want Crown to die, but I didn't believe I owed him my life. Besides, you had said you were going to go, no matter what."

"Poor, crazy Crown."

"And when he killed Sting—a life for a life, Leaf. All vows are cancelled now. I feel no guilt."

"Nor I."

"I think the fever is leaving me."

"Let's rest a few minutes more," Leaf said.

It was more than an hour before Leaf judged Shadow strong enough to go on. The highway now described a steady upgrade, not steep but making constant demands on their stamina, and they moved slowly. As the day's warmth began to dwindle, they reached the crest of the grade, and rested again at a place from which they could see the road ahead winding in switchbacks into a green, pleasant valley. Far below were the Snow Hunters, resting also by the side of a fair-size stream.

"Smoke," Shadow said. "Do you smell it?"

"Campfires down there, I suppose."

"I don't think they have any fires going. I don't see any."

"The Tree Companions, then."

"It must be a big fire."

"No matter," Leaf said. "Are you ready to continue?"

"I hear a sound—"

A voice from behind and uphill of them said, "And so it ends the usual way, in foolishness and death, and the All-Is-One grows greater."

Leaf whirled, springing to his feet. He heard laughter on the hillside and saw movements in the underbrush; after a moment he made out a dim, faintly outlined figure, and realized that an Invisible was coming toward them, the same one, no doubt, who had traveled with them from Theptis.

"What do you want?" Leaf called.

"Want? Want? I want nothing. I'm merely passing through." The Invisible pointed over his shoulder. "You can see the whole thing from the top of this hill. Your big friend put up a mighty struggle, he killed many of them, but the darts, the darts—" The Invisible laughed. "He was dying, but even so he wasn't going to let them have his wagon. Such a stubborn man. Such a foolish man. Well, a happy journey to you both.''

"Don't leave yet!" Leaf cried. But even the outlines of the Invisible were fading. Only the laughter remained, and then that too was gone. Leaf threw desperate questions into the air and, receiving no replies, turned and rushed up the hillside, clawing at the thick shrubbery. In ten minutes he was at the summit, and stood gasping and panting, looking back across a precipitous valley to the stretch of road they had just traversed. He could see everything clearly from here: the Tree Companion village nestling in the forest, the highway, the shacks by the side of the road, the wall, the clearing beyond the wall. And the wagon. The roof was gone and the sides had tumbled outward. Bright spears of flame shot high, and a black, billowing cloud of smoke stained the air. Leaf stood watching Crown's pyre a long while before returning to Shadow.

They descended toward the place where the Snow Hunters had made their camp. Breaking a long silence, Shadow said, "There must once have been a time when the world was different, when all people were of the same kind, and everyone lived in peace. A golden age, long gone. How did things change, Leaf? How did we bring this upon ourselves?''

"Nothing has changed," Leaf said, "except the look of our bodies. Inside we're the same. There never was any golden age.''

"There were no Teeth, once.''

"There were always Teeth, under one name or another. True peace never lasted long. Greed and hatred always existed.''

"Do you believe that, truly?''

"I do. I believe that mankind is mankind, all of us the same whatever our shape, and such changes as come upon us are trifles, and the best we can ever do is find such happiness for ourselves as we can, however dark the times.''

"These are darker times than most, Leaf.''

"Perhaps.''

"These are evil times. The end of all things approaches.''

Leaf smiled. "Let it come. These are the times we were meant to live in, and no asking why, and no use longing for easier times. Pain ends when acceptance begins. This is what we have now. We make the best of it. This is the road we travel. Day by day we lose what was never ours, day by day we slip closer to the All-Is-One, and nothing matters, Shadow, nothing except learning to accept what comes. Yes?"

"Yes," she said. "How far is it to the Middle River?"

"Another few days."

"And from there to your kinsmen by the Inland Sea?"

'I don't know," he said. "However long it takes us is however long it will take. Are you very tired?"

"Not as tired as I thought I'd be."

"It isn't far to the Snow Hunters' camp. We'll sleep well tonight."

"Crown," she said. "Sting."

"What about them?"

"They also sleep."

"In the All-Is-One," Leaf said. "Beyond all trouble. Beyond all pain."

"And that beautiful wagon is a charred ruin!"

"If only Crown had had the grace to surrender it freely, once he knew he was dying. But then he wouldn't have been Crown, would he? Poor Crown. Poor crazy Crown." There was a stirring ahead, suddenly. "Look. The Snow Hunters see us. There's Sky Blade." Leaf waved at them and shouted. Sky waved back, and Blade, and a few of the others. "May we camp with you tonight?" Leaf called. Sky answered something, but his words were blown away by the wind. He sounded friendly, Leaf thought. He sounded friendly. "Come," Leaf said, and he and Shadow hurried down the slope.